THE SPARROW UNSUNG

Sovereign Wings: Book I

Ian Gilbraith

ISBN-13: 979-8-9923962-2-5
Cover design by: Vashneochsosed - mads.aleks@gmail.com

Printed in the United States of America

Contents

Prologue

All the earth had been laid bare before him as an ocean of sand he had no measure of strength left in his body to swim across, boiling as the grainy tides were under the crimson robes of the emperor sun ruling from above. He broke the surface of the very world with his heavy footfalls, the weight of the blistering air pushing him down towards an assured grave amongst that sand with every step he took like the hand of a fire demon palming him into submission. His skin was as crispy as any roast bird over the fire, his sweat pulling the very plasma of his body from his corroded pores, his feet dead and black from the salt and fire kissing at his soles. The traveler walked, a corpse of conflicted state, pulled endlessly into the searing day that turned his flesh to carbon. The traveler's desert had no beginning and no end, yet he carved his path through the sands directly in its middle, each nonexistent shore behind and before him a perfectly immeasurable distance away no matter how many steps he took. It had possessed him, this desert, this waste, and in so doing he possessed it: as the sun rules the sky, this traveler ruled his kingdom of sand, surveying his domain, walking its scorched gardens to behold his reward of endless nothing.

The Csar had cast Oded and his vanity into exile, not just from his rightful seat on the high chair above his anointed people, but from death itself. A holy writ had been sewn in blessed ink across his face: he was rendered half man, half scroll, given his visage, a tattoo of markings reciting one of the most holy of life-giving spells ever borne from a shaman's tongue. Only it was not for his own life this blessing was written.

He felt it even now, as his blisters popped and his scars oozed and his knees creaked, he felt it still, the life he carried in him. Malignancy. A tumorous thing, neither parasite nor child yet as hungry as either, feeding off the very magic pressed into his face. The cancerous Exdeath; the anti-death, a living creature no more complex in design than a fruit plucked from an orchard, deposited just between his kidneys by the Csar's holy men. Whomsoever bore the Exdeath within them experienced a life prolonged entirely by the appetites of this tumor, forbidden to die until it had feasted on a hundred or more years of their torment and sickness, allowing them to pass away as desiccated mummies drained dry of animus—then, just before they passed into the next life, they would be recalled back into their cursed body. A rotten thing, pursuant to the end of all life, barred from the heavens and underworlds of all faiths. This was the curse Oded carried with him, terrible purpose matched only by the cruelty of the Csar that had planted it inside him.

The Csar had given the Exdeath within his body a holy gift of interminable life. The scripture marking his face spoke the name of the Exdead root, not the name of Oded. His soul turned ouroboros upon itself was his curse, his living body kept alive by the very thing killing him slowly from within, itself permitted to deny its own death as it guaranteed its host a torturously long life to feed off of.

Oded was barred from death, and tossed into the desert of the world to wander lost, a mockery of his sentence: he could live a thousand years and finally be granted the collapse of his body a single step away from a river's verdant edge, only to rise again as a soulless vessel of decay. Only the evilest hearts of men could devise such a curse.

Oded had taken a hundred thousand steps. Ten million steps. A world away he had traveled, step by damning step. Days stretched into longer days into blinked nights that offered little respite from the heat, the Exdeath burning him from within as the sun did from without. And yet never deterred and never wavering before this moment, he simply...stopped.

The air sizzled around him. Oded could feel the sand stir, as if it were indeed water receding from the shore. The earth was alive, and even the seared nerve endings in his feet could sense the disturbance.

And he saw it.

Before the setting sun dipping into the horizon, a spire. A rising black shadow of continental importance, larger than the grandest river, stretching higher than the grandest tower. A world eater, a serpent of the apocalypse, a colossus casting a shadow across the desert from miles and miles away. The black silhouette cut out of the rust sky simply appearing from naught in a moment of quietly deafening terror, the neck of the beast surely rooted into the core of the earth itself.

When the Godhead spoke, it wasn't aloud. It wasn't towards Oded. It was from within him, rushing up his spine and along his nervous system, echoing within his very living essence as an electrical current, the accursed man's body receiving transmission as a conduit to the voice of an everlasting dragon.

It began with a single syllable.

"I."

The announcement of the presence of the Godhead, a formal greeting, a statement of courtesy, and a warning rolled into one word that rolled through the flesh of Oded and spiraled his senses into bedlam. A moment of nausea, his vision tunneling, his skin tingling and the light behind his eyes blossoming with psilocybin colors and waves.

Oded fell to his knees, spine stiffened, fingers clutching the air before his hips as if seeking the railing of a bridge to keep him from falling over the side. The desert swam in rainbows, washing over and around and through him, and squeezed his mind through a vise before—

"BREATHE."

And Oded sighed, and the color rushed from his vision, a hypoxia evacuation of strangled consciousness given sudden relief in the lungful of hot air he sucked in. Just like that he was back to himself, only now attuned to the frequency of the voice speaking from within his body. He wiped the sweat from his eyes and blinked away the fog from the corners of his sight, and beheld the speaker across the desert sea.

The Godhead swayed above the horizon as a great tree would in the breeze. The eyes of a dragon that had seen the creation of the world itself were fixed to Oded's own, impassive and unconcerned yet forbidding even the briefest notion of contempt. The Godhead spoke to Oded as a birdkeeper would a sparrow, His purpose in this moment to purvey great singular interest in a creature so tiny and frail that the intent could only be to nurture.

The voice returned, and Oded shuddered, but did not seize again.

"YOU DREDGE THE SANDS WITH WEIGHT OF ACCURSED SPITE. A DETESTABLE ANCHOR ON YOUR SOUL AFFIXED BY CREATURES OF FAITHLESSNESS."

Oded coughed, then swallowed, sucking the spit from the corners of his mouth to speak. He hadn't spoken in weeks, months maybe, the desert turning his tongue to wool.

"Priests of the Csar in my homeland. He bade them cast me out. I walk with the Exdeath inside me." He pressed fingers to the scripture on his face. "This blessing keeps it alive, and denies my death."

The Godhead said nothing for a moment. Oded was naked before him, inside and out. His explanation of his damnation was surely not new information to a creature of omniscience, but faintly, he recalled the statement of greeting that brokered this conversation: respect was offered, and owed in return.

He took this notion into him, and continued. "I was punished for my ambition. My vanity. I was—I felt...I was owed my chance to take rule. To be Csar myself."

"APOCRYPHAL, YOUR PENITENCE. I CARE NOT."

The reply was as gentle as silk and yet Oded's shame at having said something to disappoint the Godhead turned his stomach.

"DENY COWARDS ALL APOLOGIES. OWED TO YOU SUPREMACY; IN ITS PLACE, THE GREED OF LICENTIOUS MEN FILLED YOU WITH THEIR BLASPHEMY. A DEBT IS OWED TO THIS RULER."

Oded spread his palms. "This...is business of humans. Are we not petty in your eyes? What could a God care for a single man's hardship?"

"I AM A SHEPHERD TO THE EARTH THAT HAS BORNE YOU, CRADLED YOU. I HAVE CARVED MY PATH THROUGH THIS LITHOS ENDLESSLY, AND SHALL SWIM EVERLONG, MY HOME ONE OF STONE AND MAGMA. EVERY GRAIN OF SAND

ON THIS GLOBE HAS KNOWN THE TOUCH OF MY SCALES, AND WILL AGAIN AND AGAIN ERE COME THE END OF TIME."

Oded sensed the faintest ribbon of melancholy whisked away into the dust before he could grasp at it. While the words the Godhead spoke may be translated so his body could contain them, the breadth of the great dragon's emotions surely would be shielded from Oded lest his tiny human heart burst.

"EVERY LIFE SEEDED ON THIS PLANE WE SHARE HAS BLESSED MY JOURNEY. I SIFT THE MOUNTAINS THAT THEY MAY FLOURISH, I PLOW THE MOLTEN FIELDS THAT HISTORY MAY CONTINUE TO BE SOWN. EACH MOTE OF DUST SHED FROM YOUR SKIN IS HONORBOUND TO ME, AND IN RETURN SHALL FOSTER THE RESTORATION OF YOUR GLORY."

Oded shook his head. "I'm sorry, I don't understand...you're going to undo this curse for me? Drive out the usurpers and make me the Csar?"

"YOUR DOOM IS FINAL."

This was said with as much sympathy behind it as frustration, and Oded slumped. If an immortal dragon couldn't cure him then he surely would know no end to his suffering.

"THE DEBT OF LORDSHIP TO YOU IS RESCINDED TODAY. REVENGE WILL NOT BE DEALT BY YOU, BUT IN THE MILLENIA AHEAD. MY FANGS WILL TILL THE BLASPHEMERS' REMAINS AMONG THE SALT AND ASH OF DEAD SEAS. THEIR ANIMUS SHALL BE STERILIZED, NEVER TO GROW NEW LIFE. THEIR FALSE FAITH HAS GUARANTEED THEM OBLIVION."

Oded dared not let this goodwill go ignored, bowing his head in thanks. "You are gracious, Ser." He stood, knees shaky, but he held firm, drawing himself up to full height.

"My culture sees every gift met with another, but I have no gifts to bring to bear for such a Lord. What must I do to pay tithes?"

The Godhead gave the slightest of nods. Embedded deep in his own memories as if it had been there his whole life suddenly was a single image, a frame of recollection Oded now knew, a moment returned to him from another life. Standing in a jungle, wet and verdant and resplendent with bulbs of capsicum fruit, he beheld a feldspar statue carved in the likeness of a great jungle cat. A totem of a long-forgotten religion standing undisturbed in a rainforest far, far away from the eyes of sentient man, its worshippers long removed from their home among the rubber trees.

The Godhead gave now for the first time a command, single and perfunctory.

"RAZE THIS FALSE IDOL. STRIKE ITS IMAGE FROM HISTORY. ITS WORSHIPPERS HAVE BEEN ADJUDICATED, AND ITS STAY OF EXECUTION LIFTED. DO THIS AND YOU WILL REIGN ETERNAL IN DESERVED SPLENDOR."

A single small statue lost in a fruitful bed of growth and life stretching miles wide and deep. A biome that would see permanence, a natural shield surrounding it from the Godhead who dared not harm a single flower or crush a single ant to see it returned to the earth. Oded was tasked to be not so much as demolitionist, but as a surgeon.

He bowed again, face tight—if he'd any water left in his body, he would be weeping.

"A humble price to ask of your servant. I will see it done."

Oded wobbled, taking a knee. For a moment, he thought his nausea had returned, or maybe the parasite in him had stolen his breath, but neither proved to be the case as the sands around him swirled. The dune before him parted as if a giant unseen hand cut it away, and rising from the valley, he beheld a circle of statues. Oded regained his balance and stepped forward as bidden: the Godhead had revealed to him long buried relics of an ancient history that had been just beneath his feet, awaiting excavation and rediscovery. Oded came to the center of this circle, amidst the carvings, all standing roughly his own height save for the pedestals elevating them from a mineral dais. He rotated in place, surveying each in turn, admiring their hewn brutalist form. Lifelike they were not, but radiating power and verve, their sculptor evoking the strength of their being through a steady hand and precise geometry.

A slender gentleman, his stance militant, head bowed from a lifetime of labor.

A horseman, imposing but warm, fists raised in a pugilist's invitation.

A stern woman, autocannon across her shoulders, a true vanguard.

A priest of unusual garb, his book of scripture held in bandaged hands.

A manwolf hunched low, one paw gripping spear.

A corsair of impressive regality, pistol and saber raised high.

An automaton, with features almost insectoid in nature, twirling two pistols.

A shifty looking raven, her featureless face nonetheless tilted at a mischievous angle.

Oded came to a stop, the circle broken by a gap in the statues. He leaned low, brushing away the sand hiding a ninth pedestal, smooth and empty. There was no trace of damage or erosion—there simply never was a statue here, yet the deliberate inclusion of this space couldn't be ignored.

"There's one missing."

The Godhead rumbled in acknowledgment.

"THE UNSUNG ONE."

Oded revisited each statue in turn, puzzling this site out for himself as much he could, admiring the history of this small little oasis in the sand as he was surely its first visitor in eons. "Who were they? What did they do to be worthy of this?"

"DEATH IS CERTAIN, REMEMBRANCE IS NOT. YOU SPEAK TRUE. THOSE HONORED IN THE COURTS OF DRAGONS ARE IMPRINTED UPON THE PASSAGE OF HISTORY ITSELF, REMOVED FROM THE WILTED MEMORY OF

HUMANKIND."

Oded paced the circle, not even minding his flayed feet upon the craggy stone dais. "But dragons don't write their history the same way men do. Great deeds aren't enough to earn an idol carved in your image."

"ABOVE ALL ELSE, ETERNITY VALUES SUBMISSION TO PATHOS. REJECTING VAINGLOURIOUS SELF IDOLATRY AND CHOOSING, UNBIDDEN, THE PATH OF SACRIFICE."

Oded arrived back at the empty plinth, staring at its base. "And in so being forgotten, paradoxically, becoming unforgettable.

He paused. "You said this was the 'Unsung One'. But, if their deeds hadn't been worth remembering…"

"A NINTH PEDESTAL, INDEED, WOULD NOT HAVE BEEN CARVED."

The Godhead wasn't obfuscating the truth, Oded knew for certain, there was a lesson here he was meant to receive. A blessing for his own journey ahead, to be allowed retrospective on this curiosity. So why the mystery?

And then it was clear.

Oded turned to face the horizon, looking back at the ancient deity. "I'm to receive this story from you today—the tale of this 'unsung' one."

"MEANINGLESS, THE HOARDING OF KNOWLEDGE WITH NO AUDIENCE TO FEED. THE HELD TONGUE IS THE ENEMY OF MEMORY."

Oded put his hand to his heart, feeling its weak rhythm. One step removed from being undead, he feared greatly the idea of his memory being lost to those who knew him before he himself expired. Truly a fate worse than death itself. But if he was being given a chance to chart a new course for himself into the future, then surely, he could afford a moment of humility to honor the ones here who came before him.

This Unsung One in particular.

If the Godhead deemed this story worthy of being told, and he its worthy audience, then even in his half-dead state Oded would not deny such an invitation. With great effort, Oded lowered himself to sit cross legged before the empty pedestal. An apostle receiving the sermon of his new savior, the first to hear a story untold before this very moment.

"Alright then. Who was he?"

ACT I

RUN BOY RUN

1. The Assay

He always killed one.

Rumors of all brands were passed through the ranks of the academy, young men with frustrated minds casually slipping whatever inspired thought they had pondered that morning into the ear of the recruit next to them in the mess hall; ideas grew and warped into colorful stories the further they spiraled away from their source. Some of these rumors died early on the vine, lacking the interest or vigor of the more popular school myths, while others had at least a few weeks of tantalizing the gullible before expiration. While these young recruits could always be counted on to bring these new tall tales into life to pass the time, there was always the one that awaited them at the end of their training like a bouncer barring their exit to graduation and service:

He always killed one.

Four simple words of unwavering certainty and dread, a cloak of gut-tightening apprehension descending on the dozens of graduates currently gathered beneath the ceremonial courtyard of the palace. Every man weighed in about the same, diet was a steep restriction among the ranks of the military; every age within a narrow range of numbers, the recruits almost always left home immediately following primary schooling and emerged from training just at the age of intelligent thought. They all sat on warped benches in the dark tunnel leading up behind the staging area, all wearing their newly modified infantry armor redressed to reflect the signature pine green and platinum colors of the Geihan flag.

Among the ranks of no portent, one particularly ill-faced young man sat doubled over between the other recruits sharing his bench, his combat visor between his knees and head in his hands. Brann's stomach was sticky with the sickly repetition of those four words, a fear he couldn't shake that he might be the one chosen as the example made for the rest of his peers—why not him? It made no difference to the Marshal which recruit was offered forth as the sacrificial lamb and Brann certainly hadn't accrued any reliable stock of friends in his time in training to take his place should his name be called. Marshal Tark's overwrought reputation spoke for itself, a ledger filled with indecipherable warrior codes and ethics etched with a pen inked with centuries of war-shed blood. If the promise of at least one certain death at the selection ceremony wasn't enough to make even the ballsier recruits hesitate, none turned a deaf ear to the stories of how Tark and his Uhlen squads had sacked every House on the fringes of the Wild. Barrier City stood alone and proud as the last sovereign bastion of civil society left in the known world, all thanks to the uncompromising vision of the Marshal and his stone-cut military ideals—if he didn't kill at least one recruit simply for show, it was almost universally believed he would make an example of the first one who broke rank during the Assay.

Brann himself hailed from the fallen House Lachlan, the lake people hailing from the deep west, far beyond the boundary of what was now considered Wild. He had left home long before the sacking of course, being witness to none of the horrors, but even still he felt little sadness over having his Housename stripped. The families were a quarrelsome sort and stubborn beyond belief, their fate being an almost comical example of what happened to a House that didn't comply with Geiha's reclamation: if the Uhlen didn't burn down the town, then the Wild Raiders certainly would. Lachlan was beyond the reach of a quick and decisive attack from Barrier City, but there was no shortage of raider camps in the region, and when news finally reached Brann that Lachlan was taken back into the Wild it only came as a surprise in that it hadn't happened sooner. Joining the academy was, at least at first, his idea of a vacation from a life of fishing and farming: carry a gun, look handsome in shiny green armor on the city battlements during semi-weekly patrols, and spend a few months at a time seeing the Wild in expeditionary campaigns. What wasn't attractive about all that to a young man with no Housename? It was practically an honor for a wandering vagrant to be treated so well and command such admiration from the citizens. Hell, the free meals were worth the negligible risk of being taken by Wild monsters during those uncommon expeditions.

Everything about the station he sought to occupy was nothing short of a treat in Brann's mind. He swallowed down a nasty swell, the cold anxiety washing through him again as he looked around the nearly silent room packed with sweaty young men. A treat on the other side of fear, was the problem. Fear that he might not survive the Assay, or somehow almost worse: the fear that he might actually be chosen for the Uhlen. Every recruit's education and House background was personally investigated by the Marshal, their records lay bare for him. Physical prowess mattered, but not much more than the potential social or political connections their House might hold that could distract from a life in the Uhlen. Being an elite soldier with the exclusive mission of warfighting and peacekeeping and answering directly to the Marshal was not a savory lifestyle to those who might like to return to a life after their service, and such undesirables held little interest for him during the selection ceremony. The Assay was a method of handpicking those he felt were malleable enough that he could train them to almost subhuman levels of obedience, and Tark always showed favor to those with less tying them down to their old lives.

Especially those who no longer had a House.

The tunnel was flooded with sunlight as the iron door atop the stairs screeched open, the heavy footfalls of the Division Captain heard before the man himself was seen. He strode confidently between the benches, visor tucked under one arm, his other brandishing a ceremonial baton that he used to direct the recruits' attention to the newly unlocked portal to the outside.

"Recruits, ears! Time to pull chocks, kids. You will all file out through that doorway in the order mirroring your entry and form up immediately above in the staging area. You will submit yourselves for final inspection, you will equip your visors at the command given to march into the courtyard, and you will do this all in complete silence. You miss a step, you drop your visor, you will be disciplined. If any man needs to cough, sneeze, or otherwise emit any unflattering sounds that could identify you in a crowd, do so now, as it will be your last chance before the Assay is underway."

The room was silent, save for a few uncomfortable shifting of breastplates. The captain spun to face the doorway. "Outstanding. Recruits, feet!"

From this point on, most of what Brann saw and heard went by in a blur. Reflexively he stood with the rest of the division and moved in step with the queue filing out of the tunnel—he was acutely aware of his boots clicking against the steps in perfect unison with the set of boots directly ahead of him—before he was momentarily blinded by the emergence into the first piercing light of the waking day. The staging area they now stood in was filled with already waiting divisions having emerged from their own tunnels. The captains of each unit stood astride their ranks, the inspections already underway: the Quartermasters garbed in white suits moved up and down each column of recruits, taking brief measurements of their blousings and slipping a hand under each breastplate to ensure a properly tightened fit. Brann's division formed up in the open space in the staging area at the end of the line, and he vaguely wondered if this meant their division would be the very first or very last to enter the courtyard. The moment his marching stopped the nearest Quartermaster descended on his row, making his inspection of this last division with the speed and apathy of someone who knew their job was about done for the day.

Brann clenched his rear in anticipation as the inspector neared closer, and as the white glove was removed from the chest of the recruit ahead of him Brann suddenly felt a cold shock as he realized he could feel air moving across his back—the pistol had caused enough friction to untuck his undershirt, and surely would be discovered. His vision blurred as he felt the inspector's hand swipe under his breastplate, the intrusion causing Brann to wobble briefly—and, screaming internally as the Quartermaster stopped moving entirely, he closed his eyes in surrender as that same hand gripped the back of his shirt.

"Untucked. Demerit."

The undershirt was swiftly jammed back down into his waistband, and the inspector moved on, taking a note of the number designation stitched to Brann's shoulder as he went.

Just like that, he was in the clear. The beads of sweat that dared not break the skin finally spilled over the bridge of his nose, and Brann choked back a shudder of breath. The Quartermaster may have his number today, but apparently so did Lady Luck: he'd be scrubbing the common area tonight and whistling a carefree tune the whole time.

The captain assumed his position just astride the recruit ahead of Brann, nodding to the other captains before clicking his heels together authoritatively. This was the command, and down the line it was passed wordlessly, each recruit bringing up their visors and snapping them into place on their heads swiftly. Brann followed suit, the magnetic clasp on the back of his bevor catching the visor and locking it in place around his neck, and his vision again temporarily left him as the opaque screen in front of his face scanned his surroundings. Once the image was rendered, the visor hummed to life and he could see through the screen again, albeit with slightly sharper detail and drained of almost all blue light to enhance visible skin tones and highlight movement. It always took a few minutes for his eyes to adjust to viewing the world coated in hues of red and sepia, but Brann definitely understood the benefits as the rippling sea of green and platinum around him positively popped with radiance; it would be a fair bet to assume identifying friendlies in the heat of battle would be no issue for anyone wearing their visor.

The division stood motionless, and in the next passing moments Brann's suspicions were confirmed; they weren't moving as they would be the last division into the courtyard. Likely, this meant they would be furthest from the center of the arrangement, and therefore less of a target for the Marshal, should he be standing in a fixed position facing them.

Another stroke of luck. Brann tallied it mentally, and the recruits in his rank began marching forward. He fell into stride seamlessly, his fears all but completely abated at this point.

Maybe it was all in his head. The Assay may not even be worth the stress, just another brief formality tacked onto the graduation ceremonies with a reputation played up by all the rumors spawned from nervous recruits like himself.

Likely, Brann would have nothing to worry about at all.

*

There had been a serious flaw in Brann's calculations.

The divisions stood in perfectly measured groupings, a grid of tightly squared formations with enough room for a single person to walk between them. They occupied the south half of the courtyard, facing north and the entrance to the Grand Foyer, gateway exits leading out of the inner grounds on the three remaining sides. The silence was deafening, the stony recruits taking care not to even let their armor click against itself, standing at attention with elbows angled outward. No breeze disturbed the grass, no boots scraping the stone pavers. All eyes were fixed ahead to the north, staring into nothingness; the unfortunate recruits who had fallen in center formation at the front of their respective columns got a straightaway view into the foyer entrance, wherefrom Marshal Tark was expected to emerge at any moment. Unfortunate recruits like Brann, whose division had indeed been the last into the courtyard, but instead of being shifted to the back of the grid as he'd previously hoped had instead made their landing perfectly in the middle column.

And Brann stood right in the front row.

It was an especially muggy day; he had to admit. A sticky trail of sweat, like warm honey, oozed down the length of his spine. The earmuffs built into the visor were feeling slippery from the moisture. In fact, the heat was unbearable; it wasn't just a warm day, it was...he checked himself mentally. It was all in his head, nerves getting to him and pumping his blood hot. Brann swallowed an imaginary dry lump and blinked away the fuzz in his eyes, focusing his stare dead ahead. The only thing that could help him or any of the other recruits now was a composed demeanor and a straight back. The Marshal wouldn't be impressed by—

They moved swiftly, uniformly, a line of them streaming from the foyer entrance and parting evenly to form up in a crescent row facing the divisions. The Uhlen wasted no time with pomp and circumstance, every step they took deliberately casual and with no absence of swagger, their positions in the courtyard known to them before ever stepping foot outside the palace. The first thing Brann noticed about them was their strange armor—or rather, the lack of it. They all sported the same breastplates, boots, helmets...but most of their uniforms were anything but. Comprised largely of an almost gladiatorial garb, asymmetrical dashings of scarves and cloth wrappings adorning their simple tunics and culottes. Personal touches were given to each in turn; this soldat had two hefty looking pauldrons cresting his shoulders, almost as high as his helmet, with his wrists wrapped in what looked like chains; that soldat bore a single, smoothly rounded pauldron and wore his saber slung horizontally across his back rather than affixed to his hip with his wrist resting on the hilt and gloved fingers tapping the air as if to a musical beat. They all bore the colors of Geiha, their helmets all alike in their shiny platinum finish with green accents, but nothing about their overall appearances indicated to Brann that aside from the identifying articles of Uhlen armor were there any restrictions on how they could present themselves. The Uhlen were a sovereign force, operating outside of the time-honored traditions and restrictions of the military, and the only unit under the Marshal's command allowed to operate outside the walls of Barrier City with no expeditionary force attached. They could come and go as they pleased.

For a moment that almost sounded tempting.

The strangely dressed superior force assembled fully, what looked to be about thirty of them. Brann didn't know if that number meant anything, if these soldaten were hand-picked by Tark for presentation at the ceremony today...or if they were, indeed, the Uhlen entire. Their postures were all similarly hostile: if they were ordered to be here, they certainly didn't look happy about it. Some swung their arms, pacing like chained animals; some stood stony like they had been planted there along with the grass, the glow of their visors focused on the recruits like neon green spotlights. Brann dared not turn his head, but from the corner of his vision, he could swear he saw one crouching like a gargoyle. None of them spoke, a few chuckled to themselves. One whistled an ominous tune, the sound being distorted eerily by his electronic communicator.

The Division Captain directly to Brann's left stiffened, and a loud crackle above his head as an unseen loudspeaker whined to life made Brann wince. The centermost Uhlen took a few steps forward, addressing the divisions through a hand radio wired into his chestplate, his voice harshly apathetic through the layers of electric distortion.

"Recruits. Your attention goes now to the Marshal Tark, your commander and benefactor. Conduct yourselves accordingly, or the fine boys of the Geihan Uhlen you see behind me will remove you from the palace grounds with no small amount of satisfaction."

He paused, his faceless gaze scanning the crowd, his posture languid yet derisive, like a dissatisfied customer awaiting an explanation for why his time was being wasted. He keyed the hand radio again. "That is all. The Assay is now in full effect."

It came like a silent sawblade spinning inversely to its own arc, the massive weight of the colossal object suspending it briefly in the air before losing all forward momentum and slicing smoothly into the concrete with a deafening thunderclap that made the entire assembly of recruits flinch. Not a single member among the Uhlen was fazed, least of all the Speaker, who would have been split down the middle had the object fallen even a meter short of where he stood. Brann couldn't help it, his neck clicking from its stiff position just enough to let him turn his head and see what it was: the single most intimidating weapon he'd ever seen in his short life, a single bladed axe that very surely stood taller embedded in the ground as it were than any soldat in the courtyard. The sheer size promised an owner of inhuman strength and stature, and a lance of cold dread pierced Brann's bowels and glued itself to his innards in sticky webs making him very suddenly feel ill.

The Speaker clicked off his radio dramatically with a dismissive thumb, stepping to the side of the foyer entrance just as the doorway was occupied by an enormous creature. Brann had never seen a kuaneach in person before, and there was no pictorial that could do them justice; while he knew members of their race were altogether alien in their appearance, he was not prepared for the commanding presence that now strode across the courtyard. The Marshal Tark stood a head above even the most impressive Uhlen soldat, and was certainly twice as wide around as any armored human: wearing no visible combat armor save for a plated brigandine with loose-fitted sleeves sewn into the vest, his muscled arms bulged through the cloth visibly with every swing of those arms. His clawed feet thudded dully, punctuated by the report of his wicked talons clicking in rapid succession against the stone with each step, sounding like the most frightening game of dice ever played. A tail almost as long as Brann was tall swirled in the air behind the Marshal, held aloft by the sheer density of the packed muscle at its base, while a pair of what Brann surmised to be folded wings were kept securely fastened to his wide back with a complicated-looking leather harness. Tark's saurian visage was augmented with a platinum mask forming around his snout in tight fashion, so detailed in its craft it even reflected the loreal pits behind his nostrils. A pentad of bony horns flared out from all sides of his skull, the ones that appeared to emerge from his ridged brow stabbing skyward and at least double the size of the others, they themselves stained with a metallic sheen of greenish platinum. There were no adornments to the Marshal's body that lacked a utilitarian feel, even the almost pithy shoulder capelet pinned to his chest by a fibula hanging high and tight enough on his bicep as to avoid obstructing his movement or being tossed about by the wind. Everything about his appearance was a tactical choice, much like the Uhlen who took apparent inspiration from his presentation, this being that heavy armors and flashy baubles merely encumbered one rather than protected, and flexibility was key. A philosophy behind the appearance of the Marshal Tark and by extension the Uhlen was made perfectly clear without a word bespoke: defending his body was unnecessary as he simply would have killed his opponent before harm to himself was even a risk.

The castanet clacking of his talons came to a stop as the Marshal stood astride the great weapon, and Brann could see at his feet now the textured concrete slab was not textured at all, but a series of segmented gashes where the axe had previously fallen in Assays past, the even parallel cracks indicating a frightening level of surgical precision. The Marshal swung his arm upwards and swiped at the axe grip with an underhanded impact, the momentum spinning the huge polearm around in a great loop with a lethal sounding swoosh of wind before he caught it on the prograde, now grasping the weapon properly as if it were merely a light carpenter's hammer. Raising it with no more effort than if it were just that, the Marshal leveled the armament at the recruits and spoke with a voice that shocked Brann almost as much as the saurian's entrance itself.

"I represent the vaunted heroes of House Geiha that stepped forward in time to where I stand now from armies past, and through me, speak to you all now to give you purpose in the time-honored ceremony we call The Assay. It is on this day you will all have an opportunity as soldaten to follow their footsteps into history—beginning with two candidates handpicked by me to give a demonstration to the rest of what you can expect from your individual examinations. Only the most skilled and deserving of recruits will advance to the next stage of consideration, and the chance to join the ranks of the prestigious Uhlen: free agents operating proactively to ensure a safe future for the citizens of Geiha against any potential foreign threat."

Smokey, sophisticated, and disproportionately baritone given his barreled chest, Brann had expected as anyone would that the Marshal have a great booming roar when he spoke; as it were the kuaneach simply let his words waft through the air as if he'd never had to shout once in his life. If Tark had been a performing voice on one of the audioplays Brann and the other recruits had listened to for entertainment during their scarce holiday recesses he'd have been none the wiser.

The dragonman deftly twirled the axe and let it clink gently on the ground with his clawed hand hooked on the butt end as if it were a gentleman's cane. He raised his other hand and motioned through his speech with coolly flicking fingers that had the soldat recruits following his motions with their eyes like frightened pigeons. "Make no mistake young warfighters: you are here to defend history itself, and warfighters are what you are. In times of peace, the enemies of Geiha scrabble and scheme with aim to bring harm to the denizens behind these walls as they always have, and it is in these times of peace the history of this great House is under the greatest threat."

Another surprise that struck Brann: in all the classes the recruits took during training, they were disciplined with the utmost severity to never refer to the Geihan Empire as a "House". It seemed the closer he drew towards the surface of the real world and away from the claustrophobic channels of military tutelage, the more contradictory the seemingly rigid life of a soldat became. Or was Tark simply screwing around with their heads and daring someone to slip up when their time to speak came?

The Marshal twirled his axe back up and began stomping a path astride the faces of the front row of recruits, looking directly at none of them but addressing all of them, speaking as if to himself were it not for the thousands of ears pinned to catch every word he spoke. "They will tell you that you have graduated, that you have become fully fledged soldat ready to see the world through new eyes. Do not believe this for a second. A soldat does not stop his education until his ability to learn is cleaved from his shoulders or blown out of his skull by a well-placed shot from a sniper. A well-educated soldier is one who can stave off this inevitable final lesson as soon as possible. You have not graduated from my teachings until you have earned your very own funeral procession carried on the shoulders of your compatriots."

The Marshal was drawing closer to where Brann stood in the ranks now, a wave of palpable tension approaching him like an electrical wave passing through the bodies of the recruits. Standing at attention was becoming less difficult by the second.

"I know what some of you are thinking, seeing your Marshal for the first time in person, the truth your DC's kept from you during training, why there are no pictures of the man in charge of telling you where and how you will die decorating the mess hall where you enjoyed the generous servings of mostly edible victuals heaped on your trays by our veteran cooks."

He cocked his head back a bit and slung the axe over a shoulder, examining a claw with feigned interest. "You're thinking how much the Marshal looks exactly like what you imagined he would when you finally met him."

A sharp hooting laugh from a recruit shot up from one of the back rows before quickly being cut short, likely by the swift backhand of a terrified DC. Marshal Tark continued unabated.

"Though my family tree hails from altogether different soils than those the rest of you sprouted from, I want to make one thing exceptionally clear to this fine batch of 'rickeys' today. Your Marshal is as devoted a servant to House Geiha and the hardworking citizens within the walls of Barrier City as any man standing beside you. I am not only your leader and educator, I am—as of this moment onward—family."

He finally came to a stop with a final click of his footclaws. Directly in front of Brann.

The Marshal turned his head, but Brann didn't dare raise his eyes to see if the towering dragon was looking directly at him or not.

"For all intents and purposes, I am your new father."

Brann wanted to fucking puke.

The air hung silent for far too long after this statement, as if the Marshal was scanning the crowd for any kind of reaction. In this suspended moment, Brann had a clear view straight ahead of him of the Marshal's arm—the nearly imperceptible glint of pearlescent indigo capping his otherwise inky black scales and the way those same scales shrunk and yielded to smoother, lighter skin just beneath his wrist, likely his entire underbelly matching the softer flesh while his scaled hide protected his head, back and shoulders. Brann could also see up close the strange and bulky design of the battleaxe Tark wielded: a pole of chordated metal segmented by stippled grips, the bladed head fat and segmented into four distinctly separate edges that were nonetheless fixed closely together by a mechanical looking lug cylinder that jointed the blades to the throat of the weapon. The formidable tool wouldn't just cut a man down, it would dig his grave for him in the same stroke.

Satisfied that his words had the intended effect, the Marshal spun on his clawed heel and drew away from the ranks of young men with the huge axe once again trailing alongside. Brann was given a much more comprehensive look at the profile of his commanding officer now, at the slick and steely scales running up over the hem of his scarf and terminating just beneath his horns, as well as that thick tail kept aloft and rigid behind him with the merest of swaying motions to match his militant gait. No doubt even that fifth limb was a weapon unto itself, and Brann imagined a well-placed whip-strike skinning a tree bare—or a person.

"Recruit Caleb, of House Saintmarie. Step forward."

Tark was speaking to the recruit immediately to Brann's left, their shoulders practically touching.

Caleb DID fucking puke.

Tark almost pretended not to notice as the Assay's first potential selection keeled over and let fly from beneath his hastily raised visor, the recruits in his immediate radius (including Brann) doing their best to lean out of the way without breaking rank entirely. Brann was quick on the draw and surreptitiously keyed the mute button on his comm set, saving him from having to listen to the sound of retching. Once everyone seemed to drift back into position, he unmuted, catching only the shaky breathing of the unfortunate Caleb.

"A promising start, no doubt," Tark commented dryly, glancing back at the giggling Uhlen behind him. "Compose yourself and come to attention here next to me.

Once Caleb was no longer dying, he spat the dregs of sick out and exhaled roughly, the pneumatic click of his visor being slid back down. Restoring himself to a mostly presentable appearance, the young recruit marched with deceptive confidence towards the Marshal. With a moment of hesitation, he brought his heel down into an uncertain about face, now standing at attention before the rest of the masses like a pawn that had been moved forward in the first turn of a match and was wordlessly saying goodbye to his waiting comrades.

The Marshal held his axe perpendicular to his body, and silently two of the Uhlen slinked forward to shoulder it and carry it off between the two of them, the two soldat sagging beneath its weight even with their own respectably noticeable musculature. The Speaker slipped in like a wraith to replace the weapon with a much more diplomatic looking instrument, a rubbery looking baton ill-fitted for causing any permanent damage but likely the perfect tool for knocking about frightened recruits in a display of force. Tark kept his eyes on the ranks, still not looking directly at Recruit Caleb, but spoke in a manner clearly addressing him.

"House Saintmarie submitted you among their last season's batch of conscripts, yet here you are, your second time attending The Assay. Explain to the other recruits surely as curious as I am as to why you did not attend last season's graduation ceremony, Recruit Caleb."

Caleb wavered before speaking, and though he did so quickly, Brann caught him locking his knees to keep them from shaking. "Sir, uh, M-Marshal Tark, sir—"

"Just Marshal, recruit, I know my own name," Tark said kindly, prompting another round of laughs from the Uhlen.

"Yes, Marshal—I, last season, I had spoken to—been spoken to my DC, uh, Color Sergeant Laek, who informed me my academics had been slipping up to the time—"

"You pissed away your study periods trying to be a showoff in the Color Guard and got yourself bumped back down to an underclass division," Tark finished for him. "Perhaps your talent for ineffectuality would be better suited to a career in the Nightwatch? They could certainly use another cowardly slacker to bolster their ample ranks."

"...Yes, Marshal." Caleb's voice could barely be heard as a whisper above the light breeze.

"Color Guard is an elective, not a responsibility, and certainly not a substitute for paying attention in Military History," Tark continued, twirling the baton around to align it with his forearm like a tonfa. As he spoke, the Speaker had sidled up to Caleb and offered up a matching baton with all the candor of a disgusted grandmother holding up a dead rat, and when Caleb accepted, rolled his shoulders and head back in a silent scoff before returning to stand with the other Uhlen. "I believe I've made myself clear on the importance I place in the history of this great ruling House, and Color Sergeant Laek if anything showed leniency by not tossing you in the brig for a month before allowing you back as a new conscript to begin your training again from the very start. Since memory seems to be a gap in your skillset, I'll do you the unearned courtesy of refreshing your memory on this first demonstration.

"You have been given a simple, defensive weapon. Your goal, should it prove none-too-complex for your simple-minded self, is to land what would be a fatal blow on me while defending yourself in an accordant manner against my own attacks." Tark paused. "If indeed you paid attention in Combat Anatomy as well as you did Military History, you will remember that, yes, I do indeed have a heart, a liver, a brain, and a set of lungs in the same places you do. Just one of these will do, son, you don't have to hit them all."

The Uhlen laughed harder as Caleb deflated from Tark's taunts, and though Brann never personally liked him, he felt oddly defensive of his fellow recruit. The humiliation must be unbearable for him—thankfully, no one else among the ranks facing him seemed to be joining in laughing.

Marshal Tark's luminescent eyes narrowed over the gleaming edge of his mask's eye sockets. Brann let his visor's sights focus in slightly on the saurian's face, and for the briefest of moments, he could swear Tark's eyes flitted ever so slightly towards him.

"You have three attempts, Recruit. Now, attack me."

Caleb stood stock still for a second, steeling himself, before drawing himself back up and snapping the baton across his own chest as he would have if he were still a color guard with a ceremonial saber. He shifted into the most basic offensive stance of a Geihan combatant, left arm drawn up before him with elbow cocked at a right angle as if holding an invisible shield, right arm drawn low by his hip with the baton's business end pointed outward towards his mark, knees bent to give him more solid support and bring him closer to the ground. Brann immediately knew why the Marshal had labelled Caleb a showoff; while there was nothing immediately incorrect about the stance itself, the amount of time he spent in that position locked in on Tark without moving was an obvious attempt to show everyone how well he had studied the stance and how long he could hold it for. Tark, as ever, still did not look directly at Caleb, proving the display in vain.

Caleb's back foot swiveled with his boot scraping the concrete, and he kicked off the ground, lancing the baton forward in a smooth lunge directly ahead and at the Marshal, admittedly much quicker and more aggressively than Brann had expected a moment ago. The weapon was aimed directly at the Marshal's heart, and without even turning his head, Tark wafted the lunge away with the air of a cat swatting away an offending feather. Caleb spun in midair and landed facing the reverse direction of where he'd started, bouncing a moment before his momentum put him directly onto his ass, the young man sprawling end over end with his legs kicking out in either direction before slamming back down on his front with a pained wheeze.

"That's one, Recruit," Tark said, finally turning to look directly at his prey, showing no indication of making this an easy job for Caleb.

Caleb pushed himself back up, his polished visor now bearing an angry looking scrape across its once-pristine surface. He steadied himself, no doubt taking extra time to regain his breath after the wind was knocked out of him, and this time assumed a more reserved stance. Brann recognized it as one used in more impromptu close-counter scenarios, as if one had been disarmed by a surprise attack from behind. Caleb may not have paid attention in class his first go-round, but he was definitely learning his lesson now.

"Sloppy, very sloppy," Tark said, his tail curling around the back of his legs in a semi-circle as his knees ever so gently crooked forward, his stance still entirely relaxed but now more balanced. "Again. Try to make contact this time."

Caleb bounced up onto his toes, his baton in both hands turned low to ready for an upward swing, and again he leapt forward directly at the Marshal. Apparently, Brann was wrong about him learning his lesson; Caleb again was counting on being quick and aggressive to slip past the dragon's defenses. No thought or strategy, just changing his stance before charging forward.

Tark's second punishment was far less gentle. He dipped back to avoid the upward arc of Caleb's baton, the slow arc swinging wide of its target, and he let Caleb know exactly how impressed he was by this by an open-palmed slap. The force of the stinging blow split the air with a crack and sent Caleb's visor spinning away like a hunk of debris, and the boy's face was exposed to the crowd. Pale face flushed with impotent anger, his eyes popped wide from the sudden evacuation of his augmented vision and the disbelief that he'd just been the subject of such a humiliating display.

"That's two." Tark was losing patience now, his slitted pupils shrinking as he dipped lower, hackles rising—for the first time since the fight started, he looked as if he was actually in combat.

Caleb wiped sweat away from his ruddy cheek which, though the helmet had protected him from a direct blow, surely must still burn from the shame of the slap. His lip curled and nostrils flared as he snorted, surely upset that his careful recreation of proper combat stances was getting him no recognition. He was going nowhere until he landed a hit, and Brann knew Caleb was thinking he couldn't afford to fail a third time if it meant being kicked back to the first week of training again.

Brann could see the wheels turning in Caleb's head. *Don't do it,*

Brann thought to himself, suspecting the worst was yet to come.

He was, unfortunately, all too right. Caleb dropped all pomp and ceremony in favor of the time-tested strategy of "going feral", gripping the baton in both hands like a claymore and giving a stilted shriek as his pitiful attempt at a battle cry. He sprinted full bore at the Marshal for the third...and final time, not making it more than a step or two in his stride. With almost preternatural speed the flash of a small blade spun up from Tark's beltline and, with a deft flick of the dragon's wrist, shrieked through the air like a bullet and directly into Caleb's upper thigh, sending the hapless young man cartwheeling face first into the ground.

Marshal Tark had already turned away as if bored by the time Caleb began screaming, and once more his gaze was cast over the ranks of conscripts as two DCs hurried forward from the front row to collect Caleb. The speed and absolute contempt of that skirmish-ending knife throw had Brann's heart pounding in his ears—the Marshal was unbelievably fast and clearly without mercy, a warfighter through and through with no regard to artifice for the sake of ceremony. The leader of the Geihan military was truly a symbol to brutality and Caleb's blood trailing away behind his elevated body as he was scuttled off was more than enough proof of that. And yet, despite everything, Brann was strangely comforted by the slow and opaque realization of a simple truth that brought relief to his insides: in all mathematical certainty, because the Marshal had selected his first victim to be the recruit standing directly beside him, Brann was surely safe from being selected to be a part of the next demonstration of the officer's viciousness. That, coupled with the knowledge that all throughout training Brann had largely sidestepped any real kind of incendiary situations and had kept on top of his studies (albeit with moments of shaky results now and then), he had nothing on his record to draw the ire of the kuaneach down on his head.

Thanks to Caleb's card being pulled, Brann was safe. He was in the clear.

He hoped his DC didn't hear his heavy exhale as he finally stopped holding his breath.

"What you just witnessed was the end of the illustrious military career of Color Guard Recruit Caleb of Saintmarie," Tark called out over the fading cries of Caleb's agony, twirling the baton and strolling almost casually back to the center of the dais. "He will be shipped back to his House without honors and without pay, and House Saintmarie will foot the bill of his failure. You can imagine how pleased they will be to see him return home with a Notice of Service Forfeiture stapled to his chest, along with the understanding that they will be subject to far greater scrutiny in the future in regards to their standards of proffered conscripts they submit to Geiha's military training center. I don't need to tell you all, I'm sure, that this shame will follow young Master Caleb for the rest of his life." He took a beat. "As will that new limp in his step."

The Speaker had retrieved the fallen baton and stood at ease, tapping it impatiently against his knee. An air of bloodthirsty expectation hung about his silhouette, as Brann suspected all the Uhlen shared in a similar desire to see more recruits fall under the Assay's dismissal. Thankfully, with only one selection left for The Marshal to make, the rest of the recruits would be dismissed in a short time to be individually challenged out in the training grounds by their own respective Division Commanders. Still, the question hung about the air—who would be next to bleed under Tark's claws?

The Marshal waved over The Speaker, and leaned in to hear the inaudible whispers the Uhlen relayed to his superior officer. Brann took Marshal Tark as someone who rarely, if ever, laughed, yet he detected the faintest curl of amusement at the corners of his scaly lips when The Speaker pulled back. A private joke between the two, perhaps.

Tark spoke again. His words took a full turn of the sun to reach Brann's ears, the cruel irony occupying this singular second in time worthy of study by scholars in the years to come.

"Recruit Brann, of House Lachlan. Step forward."

2. The Unlucky

All the recruits in the division were gathered around their bunks in the dark, using the natural light of the moon and the streetlamps outside filtering through their windows to illuminate their after dark activities. The Assay was a mere twelve hours from now and they were spending their final night in the division barracks enjoying themselves and sharing a sense of accomplishment together over games of cards and carousels. Some of the loner types wrote in their journals, others bickered over trivial bullshit rivalries they'd endured in their time together, but most just took it easy and wasted the energy leftover from the day's trainings to play stupid children's games and chat. Brann wasn't playing himself but was watching his two bunkmates duel in a game of Four Card Choke, sitting against the wall beneath the window across from their tiered beds with his chin on his knees.

"There's always one man, I'm telling you. Caleb from Bunk 12 said he saw it himself when he went through his first Assay."

"Caleb is a fuckin' quail." Jefette was from House Falco in the Central Steppes, and could win arguments with his dark and bushy eyebrows alone, before he ever opened his mouth to let loose his most creative obscenities. "I once saw him yanking his cock in the laundry cabinets."

"Stupid, just because he's a pervert doesn't mean he's a liar, he's been through all this shit before," retorted Groose. House Papoli was famously protective of its verdant farmlands in a literal sense as they also boasted the highest number of veteran combatants who were conscripted into Geiha's rank to return home with honors—not to mention alive. His vitiligo was a sight to behold and often drew taunts from the more pigheaded recruits, only because they hadn't learned where Groose was born and raised until his elbow introduced itself to their windpipes.

"And everyone knows it's the job of the upperclassmen to scare the younger recruits to motivate them into not fuckin' off during the ceremony," Jefette said, throwing down a card derisively. "Penisboy Caleb wants to scare

us into thinkin' we're gonna get murdered in front of a crowd, but how's the biggest fightin' force on the planet gonna get any kind of reputation for being, and I repeat, the biggest, if they're killin' off half their recruits? Draw me two."

Groose pulled two cards from the deck and slid them across the dirty tile ground to Jefette, rubbing his eye as he looked at the added totals of the cards with Jefette's newest play. "They don't kill half, they kill one, everyone knows it, and Penisboy Caleb didn't invent the stories himself, they were running around the recruitment boards before any of us even signed up. Draw me three."

Jefette watched Groose put down his card and spat on the ground next to himself, clearly unhappy with the way his luck had just turned in the game. "Penisboy Caleb didn't have to invent them, Penisboy Caleb just likes to run his fuckin' mouth about how great being a fuckin' Color Guard is so we all think Penisboy Caleb is the next fuckin' war hero to come out of this fuckin' place before any of us have even fuckin' graduated."

"Stop saying 'Penisboy'," Brann chimed in dully, not taking his eyes off the cards.

"Yeah Groose, watch your fuckin' mouth." Jefette slapped down another card. "Draw me one. And anyway, how's a guy like Tark gonna waste time wastin' recruits instead of ridin' out onto some fuckin' battlefield with a flag to lead the troops? He's got better shit to do than make us fuckin' twerp rickeys afraid we're gonna get smeared all over the courtyard."

"It's not about us, it's about tradition, we're just living what everyone else who graduated lived. They gotta make a statement somehow that we're all gonna probably die in battle at some point, so, hey, why not smoke a dumb rickey who probably couldn't even pass Weapons Safety to do it?" Groose dropped a card decisively, pointing at it in a sign of victory. "Choke."

"Fuck you." Jefette's accented drawl delivered his defeated curse in a way that made Brann snicker, and the loser tossed the rest of his hand down before sitting back on his palms. "You fuckin' farmers and your cards."

Groose dutifully began stacking together and shuffling the scattered cards, nodding to himself in quiet pride. Jefette leaned in closer to Brann, dropping his already hushed voice even lower so as to avoid the interested eavesdroppers who could be huddled on their nearby bunks. "So, what's up guy, you made up your mind yet?"

Brann's eyebrows arched as he made eye contact. "You still on that dumb shit?"

Jefette scooted his butt closer, wiping his palms on his dark green sleeping shorts. "I'm serious guy, I got a line on it as we speak, I can be back in two seconds. Just say the fuckin' word."

Brann wiped his hand across his face, suddenly feeling very tired, despite his anxiety being further stoked by having to face this decision yet again after already turning his bunkmate down before. "You don't believe the stories, you're gonna see it happen for yourself if I show up to the Assay tomorrow with something like that in my pants."

Groose cleared his throat in warning, and Jefette shot him a dirty look before turning back to Brann. "Guy, you're like the nicest fuckin' person on this side of the hall, nobody is gonna suspect it. Shit, if anythin' Tark would probably be impressed by the balls on you by drawin' down on him like that in front of anyone, and that's even if'n you get picked to begin with, which you fuckin' ain't gonna be."

Brann frowned, shaking his head, disliking how conflicted he was by this whole thing. "Nah, I can't. I'll get killed out there."

Jefette shook his head in a mirror to Brann's movements. "You're not combat material, guy. Yeah, okay, you pretty fuckin' okay on the range, but you ain't a killer, and they want killers in the Uhlen. So, do me this favor. Take the fuckin' thing. You're gonna killed if you don't—trust me. I ain't tryin' to see you get hurt before you can land that cushy hospital gig out on some beach outpost. You got bigger things meant for you than all this dumb shit."

Brann looked to Groose as if for support in invalidating Jefette's arguments, but Groose didn't meet his eyes in return, keeping his attention on *pretending like the cards really needed a good and thorough shuffling.*

He sighed, squeezing his eyes shut and rubbing his temples in resignation. "Fine. Go get it. Don't get caught, either."

Jefette clapped his hands together and leapt up, looking around to make sure they weren't being spied on before whispering, "Two seconds," and darting off between the darkened bunks. Lights out meant the DCs were back in their own barracks for the night, but there would still be patrolling recruit watchmen, so he'd have to be quick.

The two bunkmates sat in silence in the darkness as the minutes ticked by, Groose stacking the cards back neatly in his footlocker. He withdrew a tin of polish along with his boots, setting to work with a boarhair brush while still avoiding looking Brann in the face. "You made the right decision, you know," he finally said, smearing the pasty polish all over his boot's outsole. "He's stupid, but he's right."

"No, he's not right. I'm just even more stupid than he is." Brann pulled himself up to a crouch, tiptoeing over to lift the lid on his own footlocker, not wanting to risk being unprepared when Jefette returned. "With my luck I'm definitely gonna be picked tomorrow."

Groose paused, looking up and cocking his head thoughtfully. "Yeah, probably."

They shared a beat before suppressing snorts of laughter, and as if on cue Jefette sprung forward from the darkness silently with a greasy looking bundle in his hands. "Here, fuckin' take it, quick," he hissed while shoving it into Brann's arms, leaping up like a frightened rodent back up into his top bunk.

Brann fumbled for a moment before stuffing the object down into a gap between his books and rolled socks. He lowered his locker's lid as low as he could while still allowing a single beam of light to filter into the gap before lifting the rags away.

There, illuminated as if in a spotlight at a crime scene, a compact autopistol peeked its barrel out from between the oily cloth rags, the bulb of its attached laser sight glinting back at Brann like an accusatory red eye. He felt a chill run up him and spread through the veins of his arms, and he closed the lid quietly before snapping the padlock shut.

*

That same pistol was snugly fixed against his hip, cutting off circulation to his leg which was starting to tingle from how long he'd been standing still without adjusting it. Brann hadn't dared make any unbidden moves lest anyone catch him and ask why he couldn't stand still, and he was sure he'd have the shape of the pistol tattooed on his flesh for the rest of his life with how uncomfortable it had become. That worldly pain fell away in an instant, however, once Marshal Tark spoke Brann's name out louder than he think anyone ever had said it before.

The weight of his boots was unforgiving as he marched forward without a second thought besides how deeply and terribly screwed he was. Seeing how roughly Caleb had been tossed about, it was only a matter of seconds before the autopistol would be sent clattering against the ground for everyone to see, and the order for his execution would be handed down before Marshal Tark sat down to lunch.

Assuming the warlord wouldn't want to just carry out the sentence himself.

It felt like an eternity had elapsed between when Tark spoke and when Brann took his first step, but it felt like an instant between his first and his last step, coming to an unsteady halt beside the Marshal. He planted his toe against his heel and pivoted in what must have been the worst example of an about face anyone had ever performed, needing to rotate himself further to make sure he was facing straight back at the rest of the recruits. Thousands of faceless visors reflecting the peachy orange light of the morning sun back at him, bathing him like a heat-lamp. There was no way out of this, and anyone who was about to leave this courtyard today thinking that Caleb's humiliation was the worst thing they could have witnessed was in for the surprise of a lifetime.

The predatory clicks of Tark's talons on the concrete punctured Brann's perception, his vision growing slightly blurred as the superior combatant positioned himself to stand opposite the doomed recruit. On his other side, the Speaker had sidled up to Brann like a ninja, smacking the baton against Brann's chest so suddenly he couldn't help but startle. Brann reached up to wrap a gloved hand around the grip.

He pulled, but the weapon didn't budge. The Speaker was holding it tightly, baiting him to react.

Brann fell for it. He turned his head and, with as much mock bluster as he could summon, issued a quiet challenge to his superior. "You wanna test me? Thought that was your boss's job."

The mouthpiece of the Uhlen's visor crackled in distorted amusement, the returned laugh more devastating to Brann's ego than any verbal reply he could have given. The Speaker released the baton and clapped Brann on the shoulder, the gesture speaking for itself:

Enjoy what's coming to you, you mouthy fuck.

"Recruit, I'm curious." Tark's voice snapped Brann's attention back to him, and he corrected his posture accordingly, spine straightening itself so quickly he felt it pop. "You were conscripted from the streets of Barrier City, your papers claiming heritage from House Lachlan. How much do you know of your background, really, and the House you hail from?"

Brann hesitated to answer. Not out of impudence, but because he couldn't swallow enough saliva to moisten his suddenly parched throat. "Nothing, s—Marshal," he finally said, his voice hoarse and annoying even to his own ears.

The Marshal hummed thoughtfully in reply, examining the baton he held. "Would you say your parentage is unimportant to you, then?"

Another swallow. "I would, Marshal."

"Disappointing." Tark rotated to face Brann, and as if under telepathic control, Brann found himself mimicking the facing movement until he was staring directly across at the draconian officer. Like a child expecting to be smacked, Brann felt every word punctuate the air as a delay of his sentence, designed for the sole purpose of drawing out his punishment as long as possible.

The next question threw Brann for a loop, and immediately he knew something was wrong.

"Have you ever killed anyone, recruit?"

The air shifted with this, and Brann's unease was peaking to the point of becoming unbearable. Something was very, very wrong. With a prick against the small of his back, he realized he didn't recall seeing Jefette getting dressed beside him this morning during reveille.

"No, Marshal."

The great beastman's gaze punched directly through Brann's breastplate, and no amount of decor or armor could keep Brann from feeling more naked than he did at this point. He couldn't be sure, but he almost felt like his boot was sticking to the concrete—as if he'd accidentally stepped in a puddle of Caleb's blood. He laughed nervously; not quietly, but out loud, and he knew everyone heard him, especially the Marshal. For some reason, he couldn't help but think of the night before, his bunkmate repeating the word 'Penisboy' over and over. Like that was the final, appropriately fucking stupid thought Brann was doomed to have echoing in his brain as he died.

Tark knew. Brann knew he knew. And now Tark was telling Brann he knew.

"Would you like to kill me, recruit?"

There was a shocked gasp that washed over Brann like a wave, the entire body of his fellow recruits stunned at what they were seeing, and Brann could even see some of the Uhlen leap up in his peripheral vision. The autopistol had been drawn from his beltline without hesitation, and though Brann had brought the sights up directly in front of him, the only thing he could see was the dangerous glare of Tark's unblinking eyes. He'd toed the edge of the cliff and decided to take the plunge, and now Brann was just waiting for the sudden stop at the end—but until then, he was going to make like he had secretly packed a parachute for himself.

The Marshal was shaking his head curtly, and Brann knew it was meant for the Speaker, who had no doubt drawn his weapon behind him. Whatever happened next, it was going to be because the Marshal decided it to happen.

"The recruit before you was an ideal choice because of his stupidity, of his inability to adhere to what was expected of him at even the baseline of military tradition," Tark said, not raising his voice one bit. "I know every detail about every conscript that has stood before me in this place, and you are no exception, Brann of House Lachlan. The absent House, Lachlan the disappeared. Rubbed away from the pages of history by the crimes of raiders and conquerors. Dare I say, you and I are the sole living stewards of the knowledge it ever even existed. You are not standing before me because you were an excellent choice for selection, you are not standing before me because you were a terrible choice for selection. You are standing before me because, for you, recruit, there is no choice. Without you, House Lachlan does not exist; without me, you do not exist. You continue to live under the supervision of House Geiha as an adoptee because I have allowed you to do so. For that, you owe me your life."

The Marshal's arm was a blur as he threw down the baton so powerfully it snapped in two, a thundercrack splitting the quiet between them.

"I expect you to pay what is owed."

Brann didn't know if it was fear, if it was bravery, or if it was simply sweat in his glove making him do it, but the moment Tark stepped towards him to engage, he squeezed the pistol in his hand and felt the snap of the trigger as a shot was fired off. The initial pop was muffled by his visor's ear protection, but nothing was more deafening than the following silence: a bright shower of sparks, and Tark stopped still, a puff of blue smoke disappearing into the air above his shoulder. A scorch mark where the bullet had struck his mask and ricocheted off was streaked across his snout just below the orbital ridge, his head cocked to the side, and for a moment Brann thought he must have been genuinely surprised he'd actually been shot. The bright sclera of the dragon's eyes reappeared as he opened them, looking back at Brann with no small amount of distaste for what he'd just done.

"You intend to run."

Brann took a step backwards, then another. Though the pistol rattled, his hand shaking uncontrollably, his aim never wavered from where he held the firearm, never lowering for a second. "I'm leaving. I'm just—gonna go. Don't stop me. Don't any of you stop me. I'm done, and I'm leaving. I'm not a soldat, you can't make me be here." Another step. "I'm just...leaving."

Someone was speaking through him, someone he hadn't known since before his time in training, someone who said he'd run if they ever tried to conscript him, someone who was perfectly happy living off the streets and the generosity of the city's work placement programs. Brann hadn't wanted this, ever, and he was materializing it now, speaking it into truth, and who better to make it known clearly what he wanted with his life than the very leader of his captors to begin with. He hated wearing these uniforms. He hated being taught the quickest way to kill another person, being told that was his purpose. He hated learning how to cut someone open to pull out a bullet or a spearhead, and how to stitch them back together without them dying under his care. He hated all of this, and until now, he'd never had a chance to say it out loud.

"I'm just leaving," Brann said again, louder, as if the lack of a response meant Tark hadn't heard him the first time.

Marshal Tark looked over his shoulder at the waiting Uhlen, all of them poised and ready for a chance to spring into action. None of them showed alarm—if anything, they were excited. This was it, the day these sociopathic killers had dreamed of, examining and listening to these pathetic, whiny young recruits at countless bygone Assays. The moment where a rickey finally snapped and did the absolute, most gloriously dumb thing possible by smuggling a lethal weapon into the demonstrations. The day had finally come where the Uhlen would be able to tear this young man limb from limb. Not because of any real threat...but because he'd fucked up *just* that badly.

Other plans had formed in the Marshal's mind, it seemed, however, and in a similarly contradictory manner to everything that he'd been expected to say to the recruits today, he raised a hand to wave the Uhlen back.

"Then run, little boy. Run away. No one will stop you. The front gates are open just past the foyer. You can go."

He clasped the snout of his mask between two fingers and, recognizing the Assay had come to an end and it was time to do away with ceremony, Tark lifted away the platinum adornment to reveal his full visage. The unflinching gaze he held was no less intimidating without the mask, though his scarred and battle-weary facial scales bore a lifetime of experience, the wordless expression of his utter lack of interest in being cowed by such a small creature as Brann of House Lachlan.

"But I will follow. I will catch you. And I will collect what you owe."

Brann said nothing. The cool air of the city was blowing in against his back from beyond the foyer's entrance. The Uhlen drew themselves to surround their Marshal Tark, all of them staring at Brann, expressionless yet terrifying in their obvious hunger for him.

He turned, and he ran.

3. The Escape

For all the time spent in training, learning his facing movements and marching from the division hall to studies to the commissary, Brann hadn't yet learned how to run in his combat boots yet. He was made painfully aware of this by how sluggish every wide swing of his legs felt, his sprint in friction with gravity, the steel toes of the boots keeping him from ever reaching what felt like full speed. Still, he ran without stopping, without caring, moving at the pace of fear with no regard to where he was headed. Vaulted hallways, tall decorative windows, all moving at a blur with no clear defining path leading him free. The common areas of the palace beyond the foyer were mercifully empty in the early morning hours, no dignitaries or public officials thronging about as they often did during the day, so Brann's path to freedom was clear, albeit unknown.

One hallway opened up to a broad flight of stairs, wide enough for a dozen people to traverse simultaneously—this must have been the way to the main entrance. Even in his panic Brann wasn't stupid enough to make for the front gates; no guardsmen or member of the Nightwatch that may be milling about in their right mind would let a recruit with no rank or command patches who was so obviously being chased go without making efforts to intercede, let alone raise the alarm. He'd need to find a side entrance, some kind of maintenance or sentry path, where even if he were to run into a guard he could dip into a shadowy spot. Hell, even a broom closet would do.

There—an arched hallway he recognized from when he'd first been escorted through the palace grounds as a first day conscript, a pair of sentries were trading watch just beside it. Brann leapt down the stairs four at a time, making for the dark little portal. The walls narrowed so tightly he felt he had to duck low as he ran, a tunnel that curved around away from the main grounds and towards the gate. He dared not look back, the mental image of Marshal Tark clawing at the walls just behind him spurring his flight, convinced there was a pursuing party even in spite of the officer's threat at Brann's departure. There was no chance that even if he didn't chase

Brann himself, Tark hadn't sent one of those freak Uhlen after him—

—Sparks alit behind Brann's eyes, and he found himself on the ground, his hand burning in pain and his chest heaving. He'd run headlong into a wall where the tunnel made a sharp turn, failing to give his visor's augmented vision time to adjust to account for the sudden disappearance of daylight. The sound of his armor smashing against brick was loud enough to echo all throughout the tunnel and, gritting his teeth as he cradled his arm in the crook of his elbow (his other hand still gripping the pistol) while standing back up, Brann knew he'd made enough noise to alert anyone within passing distance of either exit. Stumbling forward into the dark as his visor's sights pitched up the illumination, bathing the walls in a phosphorous lime coat of illusory paint, he flexed the hand that had been crushed between the wall and his own body when he'd collided with the bricks: a finger failed to respond with movement but stung with shards of pain digging into his wrist. A broken finger, maybe even one of the metacarpals. His sprint was reduced forcefully to a brisk jog, the impact and time spent recovering from it proving he was not being immediately pursued...still, he needed to make for the exit quick.

The visor's sights adjusted again, and the green light faded with the reintroduction of a more natural source of illumination, where ahead the tunnel curved back in the opposite direction. The gate leading outside was almost in sight. Brann upped his pace again, the clop of his bootsoles against the paved ground raising in volume as well. He was nearly there, almost outside, then he'd just need to find a road and hail for a taxi leading to the city walls. He'd figure out where he'd land later, he just needed to get away from Barrier City and disappear into the Wilds, find some small fringe town to hide away in and find some labor work to provide for his food and board at some inn somewhere...

The gate appeared before him, opening wide automatically on his approach as if tripped by a sensor. It very likely was, given that any sentries passing in and out would likely be wearing the same permission chip he had in his breastplate that allowed Geihan units to travel freely in restricted palace spaces.

It wasn't until the light was suddenly blotted out by a dark figure that this notion was dispelled, the gate having been opened by the last thing Brann had wanted to see so near to freedom: a guard coming off morning watch, heading back in to be relieved.

His visor flashed a brief wall of green to indicate the figure was friendly. A useful tool in combat scenarios, surely, to avoid friendly fire. Brann didn't care. He didn't think. He just knew he couldn't risk being caught so near to his escape.

The words leaving the sentry's mouthpiece didn't even register over the sound of the shot, the whole tunnel splashed in a microsecond of white light, the crack of the autopistol again muffled in Brann's earpiece. The sentry stumbled back out of the gate, crumpling to the ground. Brann hop-skipped over the prone man's leg to avoid tripping, not paying the body a second glance before his visor's illuminating sights flicked off entirely as he met with the open air.

The tunnel exited at the crest of a grassy hill. Beyond it, a copse of trees, their leaves a ruddy brown. The small park that separated the industrial district from the palace grounds; Brann recognized the small moat leading into a manmade river he'd often glimpsed from the other side of the park when he worked at the warehouses hidden just from view. He was in familiar territory once more, and nothing was stopping him now, the grassy knoll and the park alike both empty of any onlookers.

Brann made it about halfway down the hill before stopping. He was frozen in place, confused as to why he wasn't making for those trees.

Then it finally connected. The buzz in his fingertip, hand still gripping the pistol. He turned, slowly, gaze drawn back up the hill, at the palace wall and the tunnel he'd just exited. There, still holding onto one of the gate's bars from his resting place flat on the ground, the sentry twitched and coughed with a hand clutching the air just above his chest. He looked as if he were trying to pull an arrow free from himself, which of course was impossible, as the bullet had lodged itself between his ribs beyond his reach.

The green garb he wore was soaking through in dark pitch, the fade of blood washing through his ceremonial colors like a ghostly black waterfall towards the grass beneath him.

Brann had just shot someone.

The thought of leaving the man there to bleed out didn't evaporate quickly enough to leave him feeling without a filthy knob of shame in his guts, and Brann ripped the corpsman pouch from his left shoulder while scrambling back up the hill almost on all fours. His knees slid through the dewy grass as he dropped beside the sentry, already tearing open a packet of antiseptic between his gloved fingers.

"Hang on man, just hang on, I got you," he breathed through his comms in his best effort to sound reassuring, cringing from the idea of how it must feel to be comforted by the same person who had just shot you. His free hand looped around a horseshoe shaped razor, the surgical tool designed to cut through clothing making short work of the sentry's jacket, a quick jerk away tearing the front of his blouse off with it to expose the man's torso. The violent red oil slick of his blood smeared down his side branched off as the flow of liquid was now unimpeded, and Brann immediately spotted the gaping source of the flow. He wiped away the worst of the obstructing crimson bog with the wadded blouse and tossed the dripping cloth away, shaking out a healthy stream of powdery blue crystals around and into the gunshot wound.

The magic infused silica absorbed the blood in seconds, quickly expanding in volume and congealing into a neon purple jelly that leeched out any possible infectants while packing into any severed vasculature or torn organ tissues. Brann counted backwards from five under his breath and watched the bright purple mass blacken and shrivel until the surface turned orange, cracking like an old scab. Now that the disinfectant had done its job, he pressed a tiny lancet of numbing fluid directly into the hard surface of the candied silica and depressed the plunger, the thin solvent similarly turning gooey as it was introduced to the man's bloodstream, ensuring any nerve endings that were close to the wound were annulled of any feeling of what was coming next. As an afterthought, his broken finger still throbbing, Brann pressed the needle behind his own swollen knuckle, using the last droplet to ease his own nagging pain.

"This can't be sanitary..."

Brann flung away the empty sachet and lancet, pulling the final tool from his pouch: a small, thin roll of paper, twisted together and capped at one end by what looked like the head of a flare. Brann fanned out the thin, crispy paper and flattened it as best he could against the crackling surface of the silica until it turned sticky and melded into it. One had supporting just under the wound and the other grabbing at the plastic cap, Brann steadied himself.

"Sharp twist till it clicks, pull away in one smooth motion," he recited to himself, repeating the words of his Division Captain in the Field Dressing training course. "One smooth motion, one smooth..."

He twisted his wrist, the cap clicking as the seal snapped, and pulled it away before tossing it in one smooth motion just as he'd been taught. The flame leapt up bright, colorful sparks hissing as the sodium coating was vaporized, and the fire bored straight down into the wound and cauterized it in an instant, leaving behind only the ashy orange paste of the silica around the radius that hadn't absorbed enough blood to fully harden. What was left of the gory hole had been filled in with a milky white inorganic polymer that resembled molding clay, a smooth-surfaced crater wide and deep enough that Brann could probably fit his thumb in, the edges of the repaired wound lined with tiny branches of excess that had fused directly into the man's flesh. It wasn't any substitute for proper surgery, but it would keep the man alive far longer than it would take for him to be discovered, and a real doctor could finish the job Brann had started.

The man's convulsing limbs settled as the anesthetic took over, radiating outwards from the site of the partially healed wound. His distorted electronic breathing quieted, and he went limp, passing out gently. If it weren't for the scattered bloody rags and gouged grass surrounding him, he'd easily look as if he'd simply laid down for an early morning nap after a long night of watch.

Brann steadied himself on his palms, looking over his handiwork one last time before standing. He'd almost killed, then subsequently saved this man, and all the time it took he easily could have been discovered and recaptured by Tark's Uhlen or the oncoming watch. He wiped a rogue spray of blood from his visor—and a small flash in his vision drew his eyes away from the unconscious sentry.

An emerald and platinum rifle patterned to match the sentry's Nightwatch garb lay in a patch of flattened grass where it had fallen. If he was going to fool anyone into thinking he was a free agent, this was the perfect way for Brann to complete his disguise as he made for the city walls. He squatted to scoop up the rifle, tossing it over his shoulder with his arm looped into the carrying strap, and just for good measure he also ripped free the plastic badge magnetically affixed to the sentry's pauldron that indicated his rank of Specialist.

Brann clasped the identifying badge to his own armor then, satisfied he'd done everything he could to make a clean break, reached into the sentry's scarf and felt around till he wrapped his fingers around a small tube. He pulled away the object and snapped the plastic cable keeping it connected to the man's collar: a distress beacon, one end glowing green. Brann clicked the small stiff switch at the other end and waited till the tiny device chirped, the light flashing red rapidly. Then, taking a step backwards, he lobbed it as high and as hard as he could away from him towards the road leading alongside the palace wall before turning and running for the trees. By the time another patrol found the fallen sentry, Brann would have already made it through the park and out the other side, maybe even over the fence that encircled the warehouses of the industrial district.

Come to think of it, there was a shipyard not far from those warehouses—it was in the other direction from the main roads, but given that Brann now had to keep his hands clenched in fists to keep his blood-soaked palms from being visible, he'd say it was probably better for his chances of survival to try to catch a commercial airship out of the city rather than ride around in the backseat of some nervous civilian's taxi for the afternoon.

*

At a point when the various scattered warehouses and other industrial buildings had become sparse the river rejoined the main road which ran elevated above the water, a concrete walking path winding snugly between the two. It was on this path Brann had crossed half the length of the shipyard, nearly a three-mile trek that put the sun nearly centered in the teal sky above him. Counting it as a miracle he hadn't already been caught yet, he'd resolved that his next objective be to simply find a passing trade ship, assert himself as a mandated escort meant to travel with them to the nearest merchant authority hub outside of Barrier City, and split off to take his chances on foot once there. The way he figured, no civilian was going to challenge a Geihan soldat under orders, and if they showed any sort of suspicion, he just needed to put up an intimidating display of authority with the help of his new rank badge. The important thing was that he simply pretended he was doing exactly what he was supposed to and anyone who didn't go along with it was the real problem.

Above his head he could hear the mostly distant sounds of thumping rotors and propulsion engines whining up to prepare for liftoff, punctuated by the odd warning alarm of a reversing tuglift. The early morning flights had mostly been waved off by now, nervous diplomats or merchants eager to get to their destinations on their tight schedules, with the easier traffic of the day being composed of prime candidates for hitchhiking. The trick was finding a ship that wasn't so big like a freighter that would never believably be escorted by only a single soldat, but also not so small that the need for an escort wouldn't be required at all.

The concrete embankment above him broke off at a sharp right angle, and rounding this corner, Brann slowed his pace to a more deliberate gait—he saw his mark, and luckier he couldn't be. Moored in the concrete lagoon where the river tapered off towards the inner walls of the city, a single vessel was berthed of a uniquely sightly nature: amphibious floats nearly as big around as the abdomen of the ship itself kept it buoyed on the surface of the river, the flow of water appearing not to disturb the steadiness of the ship due to its sheer size and balance. Mounted atop these floats by thick, riveted cowlings was the beaklike cockpit bent slightly downward away from the main fuselage, a smoothly beveled torso separating the bow from the stern which swept upwards in a wide fanning ducktail that split in a 'V' shape and ended with two sets of powerful looking twin engines. Overall, the mid-sized airship resembled a great noble lobster at rest on the seafloor, gently rocking in place undisturbed, the comparison given even more credence by the most striking feature of all.

This ship was *shiny*.

Easily the most vibrant looking and gaudy craft Brann had ever seen docked at the spaceyard, likely its amphibious nature was meant to keep it safe in ports away from the average landlocked bands of roaming raiders who would otherwise leap at the chance to commandeer such a showy vessel. Despite this, there was no doubt whoever owned the craft intended everyone with working eyes to see this ship from miles off; the paintjob was a painstakingly cultivated series of pearlescent nimbus patterns of poison purple and aquamarine streaking backwards from the bow that broke over a rose gold foundation of metallic paint, separated only by the panelings and brake flaps; an eye-popping triadic display that nevertheless had a professional and harmonious intent. This was someone's baby, no doubt.

Shaking away his amazement, Brann reminded himself he didn't have time to stand about and made a beeline directly for the descended cargo bay, the ramp spilling out directly onto the concrete platform with its flexible lip fixed in place by a pair of drill-chocks burrowed into two of the evenly arranged plugholes that ran all along the river wall to allow ships of all bay-sizes to dock. A tuglift was already wheeling away in the opposite direction with a completely empty bed and its grasping forks locked facing up, meaning its delivery of cargo was complete—the lack of personnel standing about the barren dockspace likely meant the ship was on its final stage of preparing to depart, and Brann had to hurry if he wanted to stow away before the ramp lifted. Breaking into a swift run, boots yet again clopping in an awkwardly loud tattoo against the pavement like a graceless foal learning to trot for the first time, he did his best to keep the rifle shouldered while his hands worked to slot the magnetic ranking badge in place on his armor, flecks of pink water splashing against the polished surface after having quickly washed away most of the sentry's blood in the muddy bankwater of the river on his way. A Geihan soldat running late to a post wasn't suspicious, but a soldat out of uniform was, no matter how many times they'd hit the snooze on their morning alarm: no ranked soldat would have removed their ranking badges for any reason until their next ranking ceremony.

He drew down to stop directly at the lip of the ramp, having a clear view directly into the cargo bay now—a single stack of handcrates stacked in a pyramid sat waiting for stow, and atop them in the coolest and most unbothered posture sat an older engineer in his grease-stained jumpsuit. The man held a manifest holoscreen at arm's length, his other hand twirling an e-pen between his fingers deftly, his lips pursed around a crumpled beige cigarillo that wreathed his sweat-glistened face in blue smoke curls. If he noticed Brann running up to the ship, he made no indication of it, keeping his eyes fixed on his work.

Brann paused to catch his breath, steadying himself for his act, his nerves mingling with his cardio exercise to keep his heart pounding at a healthy machine-gun rate. Swallowing down the dry in his throat, he stood to his full height and stomped in place, slapping his balled fist against his opposite shoulder across his chest in the manner a soldat would acknowledge a civilian respectfully without giving them a ranking salute.

"YOU there—" he gasped, coughing and swallowing again, his voice cracking like a boy in puberty as he began speaking. He started over. "You there, civvy, I respectfully request permission to board. I'm on orders as your escort today."

The dark-skinned man flicked his ashes and slipped his pen behind an ear, still not looking up from his screen. "Huh. Usually, I gotta pay for that."

Brann blinked beneath his impassive visor. "...What?"

"Nothing." The engineer thumbed off his screen and uncurled his gangly body over the crates to stand, his gangly limbs popping as he did so, indicating stiffness after a hard night's work, his screen being slipped casually into his front zippered pocket. He surveyed Brann from his place above him on the ramp, squinting down at the nervous mock soldat, puffing away at his tight roll of burning yamgrass and planting his hands behind his back to pop it. Giving a satisfied grunt, he plucked the cigarillo away to ash it again. "You're pretty young for a Specialist. One of those fast-track programs I guess?"

Brann did his best not to show signs of faltering, pushing out his chest a bit, just enough so that the rifle on his back made a rattling noise as it shifted against his armor. "Respectfully—requesting permission to board," he reasserted, trying his best to sound less nervous and more impatient. He didn't know if it was working or not.

"Right, right," the civilian worker chuckled knowingly, the smoke wafting out in bursts from between his lips as he did. "Specialist Escort will be able to board momentarily, though, I'll tell you what—I didn't see an escort assigned today on the flight schedule, so you mind just confirming for me some details?"

Brann shifted in pretend annoyance. "Yeah, sure, go ahead I guess, but make it quick."

"Outstanding." Another puff, then the cigarillo was flicked away in a spiral of blue sparks. The engineer wiped his hands together. "Actually, just one detail. Easy one." His grin widened mischievously. "What's the name of this ship?"

Fuck.

Brann was silent. His finger was beginning to ache again. One second, three seconds. Too long. He scrambled for an answer, not expecting this at all. He was caught, his bluff was called with no trouble at all.

"The name of this ship," he repeated, as if confirming he'd heard the question clearly.

"Yes dear," the man taunted, hands on his hips. "If you'll oblige an old fool his litigious ways. What's the ship called you've been assigned to?"

The sweat once again ran cold along Brann's back, having wrongly assumed the Marshal Tark would be his only challenge he'd have to face down today. His mind splintered towards a solution to this unsolvable riddle and finally his mouth intervened where his wits sputtered out.

"The name of this ship...is 'Welcome aboard,' which is the only thing I should be hearing in reply from you, civvy, as I've requested twice now to do so."

Brann mentally patted himself on the shoulder for that one. He threw in a chaser for good measure.

"I won't do so a third time."

If this wasn't the answer he was expecting, it definitely amused the aged workhand to no end, as he gave a hearty belly laugh to that reply. He bowed overly respectfully and held up his hands in surrender. "No sir, my apologies, no offense intended Mister Specialist. Of course, welcome aboard the *AKC Myrmidon*, though as any of us regulars all know, well...we just call her 'Donnie'." He looked up and down the river wall as if checking for onlookers, then gestured to the crates behind him. "Tell you what, boss, I'll even show you to your private quarters myself if you lend this old dog a hand getting these last few supplies stowed. Lifting heavy cargo all night long, well...it just ain't as fun as it used to be for a younger me."

Brann was fist pumping inwardly, but shrugged outwardly, relieved to just be over this last hurdle. "Yeah, fine, just show me where they go."

Another cigarillo had appeared in between the man's lips. "Outstanding," he said again, as Brann clambered loudly up the ramp. Now that they were close enough that Brann's visor adjusted to account for the contrast of the dark cargo bay obscured from the daylight, he could finally make out the name sewn onto the greasy jumpsuit in big block letters:

'NESTOR'.

"Right this way, boss," Nestor motioned, hands stuffed in his rear pockets as he walked just alongside Brann towards a mostly full cargo locker. "Should stack up nicely right in, I counted out the crates perfectly."

Brann held the crate at chest height, noting sourly how light it actually was but saying nothing, keeping up appearances. "So, 'Nestor,' you'll be letting me off at your first trade authority stop. As I recall the route isn't taking us that far out of B.C."

"Well, we ain't exactly a trade ship but, yeah, there's a trade authority at our first landing," Nestor said with some thoughtfulness behind his voice. "Wouldn't be too out of our way to dock closer to it than originally intended, it's upriver in an old fishing town but we can always float down to our stop once we've let you off. Hell, I'm such a nice guy I'll even help you get checked in for your flight back; least I can do for a helpful young soldat."

"That won't be necessary," Brann said quickly, slotting the first crate into place in the locker (Nestor wasn't kidding, it was perfectly aligned with the other crates already stacked inside.) "Just drop me off and I'll find my way back. So long as we don't run into any trouble," he added, nearly forgetting he was meant to be playing guard duty.

"Whatever you say boss," Nestor conceded, his new cig now freshly lit at the end. "In fact, I'm feeling much better, so let's get you stowed yourself up above and I'll finish up down here. Don't wanna have to split my paycheck with you, no offense."

He led Brann back from the lockers to a slender open hatchway, a dimly lit ladderwell visible just inside. "Oh, and 'Nes' will work just fine, boss, we ain't all that formal on the Donnie." He held out an arm towards the ladder. "After you."

Climbing up into the passageway above, the mechanical and complicated looking utility cabinets and piped bulkheads gave way to an altogether different interior on the main passenger deck: Brann stood on velvety, burgundy carpeting that ran partly up the slightly curved walls before joining with stitched bronze leather decorative cushioning that separated it from the ochre wallpaper. If he hadn't just climbed up a ladder, Brann would have thought he'd woken up in a fancy hotel he'd never be able to afford to stay in. The crystalline sconces bouncing their soft radial glows off the ceiling gave it all a relaxing ambience, providing the only source of light to the passageway in the absence of any portholes or windscreens.

Nes joined Brann moments later, the slender man straightening as he dusted off his knees. "Just down here, the living quarters are midship so they don't have all the noise of the engines bouncing people off the walls." He strolled down the passage with silent footsteps on the soft carpeting, Brann keeping just behind out of Nestor's immediate peripheral vision so he could look around at the rest of the luxury ship. "Yessir, you sure got yourself a snug assignment on the Donnie. You won the lottery in guard duty as far as civilian clients go."

Nes open a stiffly fastened handle on a light hatch door into a nearly identical passageway beyond, though this one honeycombed off into various recesses opposite each other, where Brann could see numbered doors on them all. Shit, this really was like a hotel.

"In fact, I'd be bold enough to say you'd be hard pressed to get a post this good on even The Good Marshal's ship," Nes said while turning one such corner to stand beside a door marked '2'. "Your stop, Mister Specialist. Room 2, second only to the big man himself, reserved only for esteemed guests. None more esteemed than the finest the Geihan military has to offer our humble ship, if you ask me," he said sweetly, and at this point Brann couldn't tell if he was being sincere or if this was the biggest lip service con he'd ever been subject to in his life. Either way, he wasn't going to rock the boat too much on his luck.

"Appreciated. What kind of ETA we looking at before landing?"

"Belljar is about a day's flight, low altitude, we won't be going too high on account of that big lightning storm tracking to move over the Coral

Wastes, so our flightpath takes us around all that noise. Scenic, cozy flights are the name of the game with this ship, so I hope you ain't in any rush to get back to your itchy cot in soldat housing."

"Not at all," Brann said with a small laugh that surprised himself because it wasn't faked. He opened the hatch with another soft click and stepped inside. While the space was relatively small, the most glorious, softest, most plush looking bed draped in a warm comforter that matched the ochre of the walls sat alongside the far wall. The baseboard rested against a small cooler unit, atop which was a small lamp for reading and a neatly arranged sleepwear kit including a tightly plastic-wrapped eyemask and set of longbottoms. A writing desk stood in the corner with a small holoscreen suspended on a flexible arm, which likely could bend out to face the bed for nighttime viewing. Sitting on the desk was a thick leatherbound journal and fountain pen set both in the matching burgundy and golden ochre colors of the rest of the ship, with the word 'MYRMIDON' emblazoned across them both in wreathlike lettering.

"...I don't mind sleeping away from home now and then," Brann finished, concealing his absolute delight.

He turned face, seeing a familiar set of hooks on the wall and recognizing it as a place to rest his rifle, which he did so with an assurance that convinced even himself that he expected it to be there before even entering. He hesitated, then remembered that even if he wanted to keep up his act, he couldn't stay concealed in his visor forever. So, with some reluctance, Brann reached up to unfasten the hydraulic clamp at his neck with a small squeaking hiss, then lifted up with both thumbs to remove the electronic helm and uncover himself. A soldat wouldn't keep his visor on while in his living quarters or in social spaces, after all, so neither should he.

Nes nodded with another grin as he saw Brann's face for the first time, as disheveled and sweat-slicked as it was, his features running flushed from his run. Referring to his joke earlier about Brann's apparent age, Nes snapped and pointed like he'd won a bet. "Like I said, Specialist..." He held with a pregnant pause, leaning in expectantly.

Brann stiffened, then realized what Nes meant. "Oh, right. B..." He hesitated yet again, knowing all these lapses and pauses in his speech were bound to get him caught if he couldn't keep his reactions timely. Thinking this, he opted not to lie this one time, knowing it wouldn't matter in the long-term anyway. "Brann. Specialist Brann. Corpsman Specialist, actually. Hospital Division."

"Oh, perfect," Nes said, nodding energetically. "The big guy is gonna like you for sure, he needs good keepers around who can stitch him up. You wouldn't believe how many times he's been dragged aboard losing blood all over the damn place and we couldn't find our fuckin' Doc to put him back together." He gave another wry smile on seeing Brann's face going pale so suddenly, deciding to leave him in suspense at this. "Well, anyway, welcome aboard again, Mister Corpsman Specialist. Enjoy the flight." And with a wink, Nestor slipped away behind the hatch as it closed with a soft click.

Brann took a step back, letting the visor clatter onto the desk as his arms went slack, the accumulated body heat trapped within the helm making small waves of condensation appear on the polished wood. As ominous as Nestor's last parting statement was, for the time being, he wasn't going to concern himself with that particular mystery just yet. For now, there was only one final objective on his mind.

He stripped away one glove. Then the other. Both smacked against the far wall. The one, two, three, four sharp clicks of his breastplate being unbuckled, falling to the carpeted floor with a muted clang. His damp blouse was torn open at the collar, his tight utility harness and belt ripped off, taking only the briefest of moments to kneel and swipe open the release clips on his boots before kicking them away against the door loud enough to surely echo in the passageway outside. And, finally, with a shaky and almost orgasmic sigh of relief of both physical and emotional exertion, Brann's pants were discarded in a wild fashion, draping over the headboard before he yielded his stripped form to gravity and fell into the waiting bed behind him. Lying there, seeing the steam of his body's elevated temperature introduce itself to the purified cold air of a bedroom fit for a nobleman, he felt at last the fear and exhilaration begin to drain from him. Brann wasn't quite free yet, but with that being a mere technicality in his mercifully uninhibited escape, he wondered why he'd ever been afraid to desert the service before.

Swaddled in luxury comfort, Brann spun around to bring his legs up onto the bed as well, peeling away his socks as he did and rubbing at the pocked red grooves in his newly exposed ankles. He wasn't tired or relaxed enough to fall asleep, but he allowed himself the small respite of allowing his eyes to close and a smile to tug at the corners of his panting mouth. He didn't even mind the pain in his hand—he'd tie a splint after he'd had himself a victory nap.

"Jefette, you're my goddamn hero," Brann whispered as he heard a rumble, then a whine that started pitching up from somewhere barely audible through many padded walls and compartments.

The engines were starting.

4. The Fighter

The *Myrmidon* had given Brann the comfort of a few hours' sleep, his anxiety giving way only once he was completely sure the ship had travelled long and far enough to be out of danger to a new pressing matter: that he was incredibly hungry. He'd considered just steeling himself and waiting patiently until someone came to notify him of any room services, then felt ridiculous when he reminded himself this was a private vessel.

Wary of who he might bump into that befit the description Nestor had given him of the ship's captain—that of a "frequently bloodied" individual, suggesting he was a violent and well-trained combatant—Brann didn't want to wander aimlessly about the ship and run afoul of the one person who could pose a serious threat to his entire escape plan. After pacing about for a bit, he had gotten curious and cracked open the cooler by his headboard—sure enough, it had been filled with all sorts of miniature bottles and cans decorated with labels and logos he had never seen before, though tragically it lacked any manner of available food, save for a small tray of brightfruit he assumed was meant for garnishing the beverages with. All in all, his cautiousness was wearing down in the face of a young man's gnawing metabolism, and eventually he caved.

After stabilizing his finger in a flexible knuckle brace, he'd redressed in everything but the visor, washing his face and hair in the water closet he'd discovered the hatch to in his room opposite his desk. Giving a more professional and presentable look than the sweaty, bedraggled mess Nestor had seen, Brann also opted to shoulder his rifle on his patrol through the ship—considering leaving it behind briefly he reasoned an assigned escort would need to be ready at a moment's notice, not to mention he'd want any excuse for civilian crew or passengers to avoid interacting with him. Despite the relatively slim profile of the *Myrmidon* as he'd observed it—at least compared to other, larger transport ships he was more familiar with—the inside of the ship was deceptively sprawling in its square footage. Travelling from midship to stern took only a minute or two when following the series of segmented passageways that led to the living quarters, but once he moved inwards towards the main deck spaces, he found himself maneuvering around several sealed passageways that he dared not enter lest he wander into some sensitive private area or, worse, the occupied crew spaces. The passages leading between these compartments were much more cramped than the main hallway, assuring that the illusion of a ship that was much bigger on the inside than on the outside was a result of very careful interior planning; Brann wagered to himself that if he were to enter a workspace to investigate, he'd find it to be exactly as big as it needed to be for whatever purpose it served and not an inch more. He kept this bet to himself though as he avoided opening any other side hatchways until he finally met with one that very obviously invited public access.

Clicking it open and stepping through, he recognized the somewhat ellipsis shaped chamber he was in from the outside of the ship, putting him somewhere about the thorax of the *Myrmidon*. His head nearly touched the ceiling in this space, but just before his feet was an angled set of carpeted stairs leading into a much wider space below, and sure enough, he could hear the sounds of low voices and the clinking of dining ware—he was right where he hoped to end up. Fixing his breastplate and taking a few deep breaths to steady himself, Brann gripped the stair railing and stepped on down with the confidence and noise any self-preening soldat would when accompanying civilians.

Once his head cleared the lower ceiling of the stairwell, he immediately knew this was the main common area of the entire ship: the stairs he'd just descended were centered directly in the middle of a wide equilateral compartment, before him even more velvet carpeting cascading into the recessed flooring of what could only be described as a manorly den. Pillows adorned every armrest of a semicircle of doublewide loveseats placed around a huge folding table that sprouted from a circular pit directly in the middle of them all, looking like a small flattop tree growing out of the floor, likely a game or conference table of some sort. Holoscreens bigger than any he'd seen, as wide as Brann was tall even, were stacked on atop the other on the far wall, most of them translucent and motionless save for on in a lower quadrant near a corner where a tired looking pair of flight crew were lounging together watching a holofilm together with a shared set of earjacks. The first people he'd seen other than Nes since he'd been aboard, he figured most of the crew were likely on a set work schedule and only used the common areas outside of their shifts.

When Brann turned away from the sprawling lounge area, the back half of the large compartment was more immediately interesting to his needs. The carpeted floor terminated just at the stairs where it gave way to clean, polished amber glasswood, and evenly arranged tables suitable for three or four diners were bolted into the floor. This was obviously the galley, provably so as just beyond the tables a waist high bar lined with stools spanned almost the width of the compartment, save for a strategically placed gap where personnel and food carts could pass through. A swinging door with no latch aligned with this gap on the wall behind the bar. The kitchen entrance, and the source of the sounds of cookware clinking and scraping that wafted out of the door. His lucky streak continued as no crew sat at any of the tables, and only one at the bar: Brann recognized the temple faded haircut as Nestor's immediately, the older contract worker's tight and low afro sparsely peppered with flecks of grey. He wasn't ancient by any means, but given his behavior at the cargo bay area and his posture slumped over the bar nursing a tall glass garnished with another one of his cigarillos, Brann suspected he was nearing the final years of what was probably an arduous career in the labor force. This softened Brann's annoyance at the older man a bit, realizing Nestor likely meant no ill will and was just having some fun teasing what was probably the ten thousandth young upstart soldat who he'd crossed paths with in his life.

Still, Brann was in no rush to strike up another conversation with him, and instead turned his eyes to the opposite end of the bar. Running perpendicular with it along the concaved wall was a brightly illuminated set of transparent cooler cabinets, each one stacked floor to ceiling with enough convenient foods, snacks and drinks to satisfy a hundred passengers. A few small pockets where someone had reached in to pull out a fruit or a sandwich could be seen dotting each cabinet, otherwise it seemed they were kept filled at all times by a dutiful staff that ensured no one would ever go without easy access to food even outside of kitchen hours. Brann took care not to make too much noise with his boots against the glasswood as he crossed the galley to the cabinets, eyes darting about so quickly his brain was spinning in the pan of his skull—such a broad display of readily available treats was unheard of to him, having graduated from street urchin to disciplined conscript before he'd ever even had his first real chance at proper balanced civilian life. Sneaking a glance to and fro—to Nestor, who didn't notice him, fro the pair of air crew, who didn't notice him—Brann gleefully set to work swiping one of every edible that looked appetizing to him and stuffing it all in his pockets.

When his pants were full of candied fruits, he worked on his blouse; when his blouse was filled with stacks of meaty wedge sandwiches, he wiggled ropes of braided cheesebreads into the space between the blouse and his breastplate. Soon he was using one arm to cradle a heap of assorted junk food bags he didn't even know he'd like the taste of, but wasn't about to deny himself this chance at the good life, even if it only lasted him the day. Eventually satisfied he couldn't carry anymore without posing a great risk to his own safety trying to navigate back up the stars and through the ship to his quarters, he settled on a humble single item to occupy his one free hand: an enormously tall bottle of what looked like fizzy, syrupy tonic, the bright radioactive pink beverage radiating so much artificial color from the glass container it cast a mauve glow across his front as he held it close to his body.

A gnoll pup skipping back to its lair with the juicy leg of its first kill held aloft in its jaws wouldn't make as proud a sight as Brann as he swaggered back towards the stairs, his whole body crinkling and clinking with the added twenty pounds of shrink-wrapped foods he'd swindled, not knowing and not caring what the *Myrmidon*'s policy on food in personal rooms were, only knowing tonight he was about to either break every rule there was on the matter or make such a mess of that immaculate compartment that after he left the ship they'd surely enact such rules after he'd gone. No sooner had he congratulated himself on such a successful heist of vittles than the sound of a hatch swinging open loudly overhead sparked the instant return of his fear, this time more out of a sense of childlike guilt than out of the threat of capture by the military.

It was a small entourage that had entered the stairwell, led by one particularly heavy body—and no doubt the voice he heard ringing about the echoing space above belonged to this person, the coarse baritone loud enough even on a higher deck that it could draw the attention of anyone in the common area below.

"—Didn't HAVE the reach, is what I'm sayin' to you. What he HAD was an overextended jab which, if you were payin' attention in that first couple'a rounds he was dumb enough to use it, lost all power on the connect because his snapback was so weak his arm went as flaccid as my dick in an icebath."

The voice drew even louder as the first footsteps reached the stairs...and for all the weight in Brann's boots, each one of this man's steps outclassed the noise Brann himself had made coming down the stairs by several decibels. A sort of hollow, reverberating clap, like the person was walking in shoes made of sheetrock. Brann was frozen in place just behind the stairs, looking directly between the narrow gaps in the steps. The dark shape of a set of legs blocked the gaps, and the voice broke out into the common area from under the low ceiling.

A smaller, much more subservient voice made a reply. "You can't depend on the other guy making the mistake every time to win, is my point, Champ, you gotta start assuming a more aggressive attitude out there so no one notices that soft knee—"

"Well, they're GONNA notice if'n you keep blabbin' to everyone about it, shit!" The final step now, those loud feet finally meeting solid ground...wearing the strangest shoes Brann had ever seen, like rounded geodes that had been split open down the middle. Carefully sneaking around the other side of the stairs than the direction those feet turned in, Brann moved like an assassin evading detection to remain behind the entourage, what looked like about three more sets of legs trailing along behind the leader's—their shoes looking far more normal. Brann waited until he just saw the passing blur of the larger man from behind the broadside of the stairwell before hurriedly rounding them to ascend, trying with no small effort to hold the railing with the same hand that held the (in hindsight, quite unnecessarily ridiculous) bottle of fizzy drink. The conversation popped through in loud disconnected spurts from the gaps in the stairs as he climbed, sure of himself that no one had seen him abscond with half the ship's food stuffed in his uniform.

That is, until a rogue cheesebread slipped free of his breastplate.

A foolish effort to save it before it hit the stair was rewarded with a fool's punishment: Brann's grip on the glass bottle was lost entirely in his wide swing to grab the falling snack, and the heavy beverage bounced like a pinwheel down the stairs, each impact on each step it connected with paired with the deafening crack of reinforced glass on lightly cushioned metal. Brann crouched in horror watching the drink miraculously survive every wild bounce until, quite inevitably, the broadside of the bottle smacked into the floor below in a glimmering explosion of pink tonic and glass shards.

The moment of terror passed, Brann remained still, hearing the conversation below had ground to a total halt. Knowing he wasn't getting out of this one, he had but one choice: to face the music, and likely the anger of what was probably the captain of the ship himself down in the galley. Brann's thoughts flashed back to how Nestor described him as 'The Big Guy'. Well, it was a fun flight while it lasted.

Gingerly setting down his armfuls of wrapped treats, Brann tucked them away from the edge of the step to ensure they too wouldn't tumble down before standing and clenching his fists, marching down like he was headed to the firing squad.

The ground beneath his boots crunched with sugary wet glass that clung to the rubber, and with his face starkly painted in an expression of abject remorse, Brann turned the corner to greet his waiting punishment.

"My apologies, I'm...I was, I had just come down for a late lunch, and...uh."

Brann stopped in his tracks. He hadn't trailed off out of guilt for the accident—it was who he saw once he came down the steps that rendered him mute. Or rather, *what* he saw.

The captain of the ship certainly merited the description of a big guy, but where Brann's assumptions had led him wrong was assuming "guy" was synonymous with "human". In the span of a single day, he was face to face with the second beastman he'd ever hoped to see in his life, having just this morning himself denying the likelihood of their very existence before Tark's emergence at the Assay. The shoes he'd seen stomping down the steps were not shoes at all, but the sturdy crescent shaped soles of a pair of hooves. Hooves jointed by slender ankles leading to bony shins to supremely muscle-packed thighs that rippled visibly even through the mostly loose-fitted silk bottoms of their owner. An open robe framed a washboard of steel-pitted abdominal muscles, and higher still, the thick corded neck balancing a long and angular skull. Despite the inhuman appearance, the expression on the beastman's face was anything but unrecognizable, the crooked eyebrow of surprise and bemusement cresting the solid brow of the equine's big eyes.

The powerfully built horse spread his arms, the loose flappy sleeves of his oversized bathrobe falling to crumple around his elbows, revealing enormous hands that looked as if their carved knuckles could separate boulders in two. Despite Brann's shock, the only response the horseman gave was:

"Hey, buddy—we *have* room service!"

Just behind the towering horse, Nestor at the bar had turned to watch the scene, and even without taking his eyes off the horseman Brann could see the engineer doubled over on his stool in fits of laughter.

*

"Eighteen fights, eighteen wins, all by total knockout, the longest running streak in the history of the sport," Boomer was saying as he poured a frighteningly dark brew of hot liquid into the strangely shaped glass in front of Brann, the horse having spent the last few minutes introducing himself and his illustrious career to his newly met Geihan escort. "Shame they don't let you kids have holoscreens in training, personally I lobbied to make my regime part of y'all's workouts—because, I mean, well, just look at me—" Boomer motioned to his open robe, sidestepping from his spot behind the bar to begin pouring into Nestor's glass, "—But, hey, what do I know, I'm only prizefighting champ of the world, what do I know about combat, right?"

He grinned, showing off a bleached smile of massive block teeth Brann caught himself staring directly at. He'd seen pictures of horses in old military history books, but never dreamed that they'd ever stood on two legs and spoke the same language as him; apparently the books weren't as comprehensive in their coverings as Brann's instructors had led him to believe.

The rest of Boomer's entourage had been waved away by the celebrity fighter, leaving just the three of them to chat at the bar: Nestor was a contractor but apparently had a long-running relationship with Boomer as a client of his, Brann having surmised this by the way Nestor didn't budge from his barstool when Boomer shooed off everyone else, and the casual way Boomer would recall moments and direct Nestor to retell them.

"There was this other chump, had a big ol' hookjaw and a *fanny ackshent loik dish,*'" Boomer was saying now, jutting out his lower lip and bumping his fist against his cheek as he mimed his former opponent, "Never could understand what he was saying—tell 'im, Nes!"

"He had a funny accent," Nestor said, lifting the glass to sip.

"Yeah exactly! Funniest thing I ever, heard, anyway," Boomer continued, already laughing at his own story. "Ugly sonuvabitch, had to have been almost as tall as I was—not a bad size for one of your own, I gotta admit," he pointed at Brann for emphasis, likely meaning humans. "He made for my title in the Saltwash Finals, and, I mean, whoof, he came as close as any ever did, except, see, Saltwash and Geiha, two different species entirely—no pun intended," he added with a wink, pushing the steamy glass closer to Brann. "C'mon buddy, drink up, it ain't gonna kill you, not like that wacky pink shit you were boutta drown in—I mean, did you see the SIZE of that bottle, Nes? Wasn't that thing giant?"

"It was a giant bottle."

"Yeah, exactly! Anyway..." Boomer stopped dead, hands in the air. "What was I talking about?"

Brann stared into his glass, not trusting it. He'd never had a hot drink before. "Saltwash."

"Yeah, Saltwash! Yeah, so, this guy, big guy, did I say—" Boomer swung a questioning pointer finger to Nestor who nodded silently, answering his question before it was even said. "Yeah, I said he was big, but, these Saltwash guys, they're good guys, I sold out every fight I had there, great crowd, great stadium, love the acoustics. But, they're just not..." He frowned, searching for the word with a wobbly shrug. "...They're not like Geiha. Their fighters, they got no bite, no thirst for blood, y'know? See, most people, lotta media guys anyway, they like to write that I'm the best because I'm a horse—" Boomer paused just long enough to throw back his boiling hot glass and croaked approvingly, continuing speaking at a mile a minute without even reacting to the blistering heat. "—But, I think, see, I think it's got everything to do with you boys over at Geiha," he said as he leaned against the bar, close enough to Brann that the young man could smell the beastperson, his somewhat funky aura landing comfortably in the middle of a locker room and a muddy field after a rain. "I think, see, your outfit, you boys know how to fight, you're serious about the whole up close and personal shit in a way that a lot of those other Houses, they ain't worried about it anymore because they forgot how to fight in a war. My being Champion of Geiha, that's like—I think it basically imbues me with your whole fighting spirit, y'know what I mean? Don't these boys at Geiha have a real fighting spirit, Nes?"

Nes turned slowly with a flat expression to stare at Brann. "Real spirit."

"Yeah, exactly!" Boomer slapped the bar, moving to pour himself another glass of brew. "I think me being your guys's...es..." He frowned again, counting on his fingers.

"Guys'," Nestor said helpfully. Maybe Boomer wasn't a native to human language after all, Brann thought.

"Your guys' Champion," Boomer corrected, looking as pleased with himself as a boy getting an answer right when called by the teacher, "I think it's sorta given me an edge in the ring. I'm like, sort of an honorary soldat, you know, just being out there, the face of the whole Empire on top of being the best of all time...I'm sorta just as much of a real killer as you are, even though I didn't go through the same training," he beamed. "Maybe even better!"

The warm smile instantly fled from Boomer's face, and an expression of abject horror sunk into its place, Brann instantly becoming uneasy. He looked around, wondering if some awful monster was standing behind his stool, and Brann wondered if he should reach for his rifle.

"You haven't drank it yet," Boomer moaned pitifully. Brann realized Boomer was actually looking at him that way. He turned to Nestor for help, who lifted his own glass for another sip demonstratively with his eyebrows raised.

"Oh, sorry, I was just—" Brann stammered, sitting upright in his seat and leaning towards the glass. "I meant to ask what it was; I don't think you...mentioned..."

"Oh, it's coffee, you dummy!" Instantly, as if he'd never known the word, the sadness vanished from Boomer's face and he was back to his rapid movements and bright smile, even his ears perking back up. Everything about his way of expressing himself and speaking was enhanced above that of a normal human—Brann found Tark's demeanor comparatively cold and impassive back at the Assay, though he wondered if that had less to do with being a kuaneach and more to do with his status as a military leader. "What, they don't let you boys drink coffee in training? Shit, that should be illegal."

Brann peered again into the glass. It was a sort of foamy brown terminating in a banded orange sediment at the bottom, the smell rising from it decidedly spicier than he was comfortable with. "What's it made of?"

Boomer's hands dropped to his sides comically with his robe fluffing up from the whoosh of air, and he looked to Nestor pleadingly. "Where did you find this guy again?"

"Assigned to protect us helpless peaceful folk against the cruel and violent criminals that may detain us on our perilous journey," Nes rasped with a wry smirk that wrapped itself around a freshly lit cigarillo.

"Was that sarcasm? I still don't know how to tell." Boomer tilted his head, then shook it, turning back to Brann. "It's a drink, obviously, ground up flora beans soaked in steamed goma milk, and when you let it sift together for a minute and then filter it all out, you get this..." He lifted his refilled glass, gazing at it as if he held the kingliest of treasures in his hands.

"The secrets of the universe itself, making all things possible, and giving you the power..." He slugged it back, and exhaled in bliss, eyes closing with reverence. "...To crush all who stand in your way. Their families too. You'll be poppin' children like ripe little tomatoes."

Brann opted to not offend the horse further, lifting the warm glass by the crooked handle and pursing his lips tightly to allow only the barest sip past. He jumped a little from the heat, but was surprised by the taste: he'd remembered once they'd given the recruits a congratulatory breakfast of roasted bison shavings with a sort of sweet and smokey syrup poured over the whole plate—this was the closest he'd come to tasting something similar to that, and while he didn't know if he loved it as much as Boomer appeared to, he definitely didn't hate it.

"Wow, that's, yeah, best cup I ever had," he lied, setting it back down and licking his lips. "Sorry, we just call it something else back at base, but...yeah that's the good stuff."

Boomer's eyes grew soulful, his shoulders sagging, and with his hooves barely even leaving the ground he shuffled around the entrance to the bar to bring himself beside Brann's stool, arms spreading wide and wrapping himself around the young man so tightly Brann thought his brain might pop from the horse's bulging muscles.

"I love this boy." Boomer was patting Brann's s head like a dog as he looked to Nestor. "Can we keep him?"

"'Fraid this one's just a loaner," Nestor replied, quaffing off the last inch of his coffee and pushing away from the bar to his feet. "We're gonna be dropping him off at the embassy at Belljar so he can get a ride back to base on the next flight out. Just a day assignment."

Boomer released Brann, who felt instantly sweaty. The resting body temperature of the horse was wicked hot. Boomer leaned back on his elbows on the bar, looking confused as he insistently slid the glass back into Brann's hand. "I thought there wasn't an embassy at Belljar? Think you're thinking of Bellevue, Nes."

Brann turned to look at Nestor, who had frozen in place for a moment, before recovering by nodding in realization. "Oh, right, my mistake—yes, Bellevue. Belljar doesn't have one, you're right. We'll just have to find him a chartered flight at the port."

Boomer pointed and laughed at Nestor, shaking his head. "Look at you forgetting shit in your old age, ya big dummy. No embassy at Belljar, duh!"

"Duh," Nes repeated, making the briefest of eye contact with Brann before turning to walk away towards the stairs. "We'll be landing shortly, I gotta get the boys ready to offload."

Boomer chuckled to himself as he watched the engineer leave. "Oh, Nes, great guy, great guy—isn't he a great guy?" He asked Brann to confirm for him.

Brann blinked, then nodded, beginning to understand the routine. "Yeah, great guy," he repeated. He was starting to feel like what a parent must feel like raising a child.

"Yeah, exactly!" Boomer tousled his blonde mane, the palomino yawning and stretching, vertebrae crackling audibly. "Glad you're with us, by the way, uhhh..." He was looking at Brann's ranking badge now, that same furrowed brow reappearing, his expression whenever he was attempting to identify some sort of human idiom or word.

"Specialist Corpsman Brann," he said, holding out a gloved hand. "Happy to be here...civilian."

Boomer shook the hand eagerly, not noticing Brann's near-omission. "Oh sure, sure, happy to have you guys on board anytime! Hey, I tell you what, I got a big match coming up, that's where we're headed now—we'll be in House Cheneye territory for the semifinals, I'll be fighting aaahhhh..." He snapped his fingers, trying to remember this word as well. Looking up to remind himself Nes had already left, he shrugged it off. "I'll be fighting somebody, match nineteen—finals will be the big twenty, maybe you wanna be a temporary assigned escort for more temporary than you were s'posed to? I can pull some strings, get the guys back home to maybe extend your orders for a few more months to be my personal valet till the big night?"

Brann was tempted. Legitimately tempted. A few months of worry-free time spent aboard this luxury pleasure cruise, eating good food, not worrying about where to find work next...then, souring on the idea, he realized it wasn't possible without directly alerting Tark to his whereabouts if it involved Boomer contacting Barrier City on his behalf. Especially since he was dumb enough to tell Nestor his real name when coming aboard.

"Thanks, really, but you know." He patted his rifle. "Gotta be ready to fight for the Empire at any time. No time for fun trips."

Boomer's mouth was agape. "That is the coolest thing ever. Buddy, you're a real inspiration." The sandy-gold horseman stuffed his hands in his wide robe pockets with a wistful sigh. "Man, I wish I coulda joined up. They only let humans in obviously, but, hey, I can throw down when the call of duty rings out, y'know?"

Brann found this statement interesting. "But the Marshal isn't human, someone had to let him join up at some point when he was younger, right?"

"Hm?" Boomer turned back, then shook his head. "Nah, that's different, he's—those dragons, you know, they just swing in from the rafters and say 'hey losers! This is my land now, suck my dick,' and then put themselves in charge. He never would have enlisted, he probably helped conquer some big important city for Geiha and they just let him run the show after. That's their whole thing, the art of war and conquest and all that...cool shit," he finished with a cough, frowning again. "So, was it? I couldn't tell."

Brann was lost. "Was what...what?"

"Sarcasm. What he said." Boomer motioned towards the stairs where Nestor had left.

This threw Brann for a loop. Talking to a member of another species and the way they processed speech and information was going to take a lot of getting used to—for as disarmingly familiar as it seemed to be, like chatting with another recruit back in the barracks, the compounding quirks and nuances in the way the horse jumped back and forth in conversation must require some navigational skills. "Oh, right, yeah, that. Yeah, that was sarcasm."

"Still haven't gotten the hang of that one. Nes tries to help teach when he can, but you tell me 'This guy is here to protect us' and show me one of the coolest guys in the world wearing your super cool armor with a super cool gun, I'm like, 'of course, yeah!' Then it turns out he was lying when he said it, except it's not a lie, because that IS why you're here..." Boomer's eyes popped. "There's some complicated shit in your culture; I tell you what."

Brann laughed a little. For all the strangeness, he felt far more at ease talking to Boomer than he did to Nestor. "If it helps to make more sense of it, I think he wasn't saying it as a lie so much as saying it in a way that meant he doesn't like me very much."

The look of hurt and disbelief on Boomer's face was worth a lifetime of remembering. "No! How could anyone not like you! You're so brave and tough! I'm gonna go talk to him, and you know what, he's not getting any more of my private stash of coffee for a month." Boomer stomped off in a huff, his big loud hooves sounding like cannon shots against the glasswood floor. "Gonna keep making fun of his bad memory some more, too! Forgetting there's no embassy in Belljar, what a dope..." he trailed off as he ascended the stairs, leaving Brann alone once more, sitting in silence at the bar as he pondered this too.

It was a little suspicious, if Nestor had been doing this as long as he'd claimed, and had such familiarity with Boomer's tour route. Had he been playing along with Brann's bluff all along just to find a way to jam him up later? Was there going to be a troupe of Uhlen at the ready with cuffs and chains to take Brann into custody when they landed? Brann couldn't help but sweat a little, even as part of him was confident that if the plan was to get him caught, Nestor could have just as easily not let him on board to begin with. Whatever was going on in the older man's head would have to come to light naturally, as there was no sense in trying to get too familiar with anyone and their habits while he was here—Brann wouldn't be around them long enough to get close.

He looked down at his coffee, taking another sip.

Shame. He could get used to this.

5. The Gunner

The next morning came all too soon, Brann regretfully snapping on his breastplate as he prepared to deboard, having spent the most comfortable night of his life in his room curled up under that gloriously heavy bedspread covered in the discard wrappers and crumbs of his purloined snacks. Of all the promises the service had made to him about fame and prestige gleaned in the name of Geiha, the pitch always ended with him 'dying honorably'—admittedly a slightly less appealing alternative to a cozy bed in a nice room. The further away from home he got, the more uncomfortable Brann's armor felt strapped onto him, like a budding realization that if it were a natural part of life, he would have been born with it. Still, as he looked himself up and down in the mirror, tucking his visor under his arm, he had to admit he looked better in uniform than he ever did in his dirty street clothes.

The rest of the crew had already been working the morning away, having been unloading cargo since the sun came up. As Brann stepped off the ladder in the cargo bay, the actual number of workhands clustered on and around the ramp surprised him: the *Myrmidon* was staffed by a relatively threadbare crew, barely a dozen hands on deck finishing up the offload. Nestor was waiting for him just inside the bay, joining Brann at his side as they stepped off the ship.

"Every fighter in the GLFF—that's the Global League of Fortune Fighters, which Boomer didn't have time to mention last night in his rush to tell you how amazing he was—gets appointed to represent their chosen House in broadcasted, non-lethal combat whenever a need arises between Houses to settle petty political disputes that could be aggravated and potentially turn violent." Nes launched into this explanation as he walked together with Brann onto the rickety looking pier where the Donnie had moored, the daylight stilted by a surprisingly cold arrangement of clouds that had gathered overnight, not yet fully dispersed by the warm sun and instead clinging to the surface of the wide river around them in a dense fog. "Most just pick from within their own Houses, but some like Geiha, they draft promising fighters from others, usually because they'd rather train real fighters to go to war than play pretend. So, when these 'fortune fighters' aren't settling trade or social disputes for money paid out by the generous citizens of House 'Whatever' sitting comfortably at home in front of their holoscreens, they gotta scrape a living between fights going on tour all over the continent and hocking their merch to the fans."

Nestor pointed to a passing laborer who was wheeling away a pallet of open-faced crates, holding what looked to be a collection of packaged apparel in colors matching the *Myrmidon*'s paintjob. "While obviously this would be easy enough to just have a manager or a PR spokesman do a lot of this instead, our boy likes to make every stop personally on his routes, so he can kiss mugshots and sign babies himself. He's a very congenial sort, if you didn't notice last night," Nes said with an eyeroll. "Loves his fans almost as much as himself. But hey, he sells tickets, and pays his crew well, so I say sure, 'gimme another box of junk, I'll carry it for you.'

The view of Belljar before Brann as they stepped off the long pier was both somehow impressive yet depressing: a nearly entirely vertical town assembled on struts and linked rope bridges, the height of the cheaply constructed building rising partway up the side of the great cliff that towered above it all. Were it not for the scatterings of neon signs marking public areas and shops at ground level lining up and down riverbank as far as Brann could see before the cliff turned away and the town curved to follow with it, the entirety of Belljar would look as though they'd never entered the modern age. The loose smatterings of people going about their chores high above the main population below by the river's edge appeared to get more densely clustered at the upper levels while the houses became more like shacks: maybe the closer to the river and to the businesses you lived, the wealthier you were. This seemed to be supported by how the housing blocks got wider and more brightly lit the lower the stacks got, the ones resting on top of the ground level shops often looking like a continuation of the shop itself. There was a prevailing sense of shared hardship among it all, however, the main gaggles of people entering and leaving the shops seeming to have humble and kindly interactions with each other even if they were crowded or had to wait for a passing rickshaw to cross an alleyway. It was towards one of these alleys Nestor was directing Brann, giving a little more clarity to their destination in the meantime:

"While Boomer is off at the exhibition stage in the center of town, I took the liberty of hiring a charter ship for you. Given that this place is miserable for ships taking off—the steep cliffs—most people just land upriver like we did, float down between the cliffs to dock here, then keep on floating down to the coast where the cliffs break away then take off there. The Donnie's about as big a ship as'll fit between the cliff walls, so I had to find you someone running a smaller craft. Not the most personable sort. She's likely a skyfisher, or a disgruntled tour guide..." He shrugged. "Or maybe even a pirate. We'll see."

The alley narrowed as it curved around into a particularly deep-running fissure in the side of the cliff before opening up again into a sort of cul-de-sac, string lights illuminating the more sunlight-averse space where the shops became less flashy looking and more hewn. Restaurants, bars and antiquities seemed to occupy most of these older looking shack-fronts, though one in particular was where Nestor was heading: a more spacious looking stack wedged between the rock faces, with a neon sign bearing only the letters 'QM' above its broad doors.

"Any town you visit, find the local Quartermaster, and make friends with every stupid bastard you meet inside," Nestor instructed Brann, like he was giving him advice before sending him off on a school trip. "The big Houses may like to think they run the world, but it's the little guys in between who make the real connections and get shit done. Plus, not a bad place to polish up that fancy armor of yours."

Pushing past the heavy doors, the two entered a dimly lit rotunda of stairways, each leading up into an isolated mezzanine of open offices and minor storefronts. The occupants crossing between mezzanines were a far less friendly-faced sort than the bulk of the population outside this place, and Brann took that as a sign this was where the outsiders and mercenaries travelling between major cities probably came to find work on the road.

Ignoring the stairs, Nes took Brann across the rotunda and underneath the central mezzanine, where a collection of small tables and chairs were scattered, like a casual meeting spot. One couple sat across a table from a grizzled old man in cold-weather gear, listening to him explain some paper charts he was laying out for them. Another table had a surly looking woman stabbing into a plate of fried fish, a tall seabag packed to the brim leaning against the table. One man had pushed three wicker chairs together and draped himself across them to nap, snoring loudly with a crude "FORe HIRe" sign folded over the edge of the table next to him which itself was covered in an array of pelts and hooklike armaments.

"It was slim pickings today, good news for you," Nestor said quietly to Brann. "Most days this place is packed with yuppies trying to buy a trip to see some big monster from a flashy safari guide. The real tough nuts tend to tell those kinds of customers to piss off. Means they know their worth."

Brann raised the visor to equip it but was stopped, Nestor wagging a finger. "No, keep it off, they won't trust anyone they can't see. Now, that one over there, she's the one." He was pointing to the woman eating. "Met her on the waterfront earlier this morning. Your fee is taken care of. Just show her some of that famous soldat respect and she'll get you where you're going."

This was goodbye, then. Brann raised a hand to shake, which only prompted a chuckle from Nestor.

"Take it easy, kid. You're gonna make it."

And with that he withdrew, leaving Brann to make his journey alone. There was an air of certainty in Nestor's final words that told Brann he'd never been fooled, but any help to get Brann out of the clutches of the Geihan service was gratefully accepted. He couldn't help but feel his face blush in embarrassment coupled with a small smile to himself—Brann knew his secret was safe with the old contractor.

He turned on his heel back towards the tables, navigating a path that kept him away from the ones that were occupied, lest he disturb one of the more unstable individuals. There was a lingering air of desperation among these people, something he'd been all too familiar with back on the streets of B.C.—in a way, despite the uncertainty ahead of him, he felt right at home.

The woman was finishing up the last few bites of her meal, wiping away flakes of fish from her chin as Brann stopped next to her table. Brann opened his mouth to speak, realized she likely wasn't the sort to respond to him identifying rank, and decided against doing just that in favor of keeping it simple.

"I believe I'm meant to catch a ride with you, ma'am."

She tossed away a crumpled napkin, kicking out the chair opposite her from under the small table. "Sit. We have some things to cover first."

Brann stifled the urge to talk back, reminding himself he wasn't paying for this ride, and besides—he didn't know how much Nestor had let her in on. He set down his visor, taking the seat as instructed.

"You're on assignment out of Geiha territory, you got a blank check from your benefactor the prizefighter, and you have a bad case of being absolutely precious. I've seen it before, and I'm gonna let you right now, I ain't got time for precious. Back home, you strut around with your ass all polished up in that shiny armor like some prize pig for your parents to brag to their friends about you—out here, the Wilds will rip you open and spread you out all over the goddamn dirt if you so much as blink. You ride on my barge, you don't just sit back and feel the breeze, you follow my orders and you stick a bayonet into anything gets too close. You put me or my equipment in danger because you want to play soldat, I'll shoot you myself."

She pushed aside her plate, arms crossed across her chest as she leaned in close. Her dark hair arched low into her face like glistening obsidian claws, her eyes piercing into Brann unflinchingly, her voice never wavering from a flat monotone delivery that entire speech. She wasn't making idle threats, that was without question.

"You may be the one with the badge, but on my craft, you're to refer to me as 'Captain'. Is this going to pose a problem for you..." She turned her gaze lower at his badge, giving a slow blink. "...'Specialist?'"

Brann knew one thing about responding to an authority figure, as all his time in training had instilled a single philosophy into him as ironclad as his armor:

"Captain 'Who?'"

Maybe she just wasn't expecting that answer, or had a hidden friendly streak, but this made the pilot's crack a bit into a small smile. "That is the correct answer." She leaned back, keeping her arms crossed. "Captain Zaydat, House Kadzhieva. Former House, I should say. No real associations since I left home, younger than you are now. You?"

Brann straightened a bit, happy to have made a good impression. "Brann. Specialist Corpsman Brann." He cleared his throat a bit. "House Lachlan. Also left home."

There was a strange moment between them. Something in Zaydat's demeanor, the way it changed—or, rather, didn't change. Her body remained stock still, and for a second, Brann wondered if she was even breathing. The smile she wore even appeared painted on. This moment dragged on for a few seconds, and he almost wondered if that was the wrong thing to say.

"House Lachlan," Zaydat repeated finally. Her tone betrayed nothing.

"Yes. Conscript, not naturalborn to Geiha."

Her eyes drifted away from him, and Brann sensed that this information meant far more to her than it did to him. "Tell you what, Brann Lachlan," Zaydat said, not making eye contact with him now. "Call me Zay. Captain Zay. Let's keep things light, shall we?"

This was a small surprise, but he knew better than to press for answers. Brann nodded. "Captain Zay, then."

Zay stood. Brann stood with her. The cumbersome seabag was hefted up and swung over her shoulders, the motion looking completely effortless, save for the clenching of her impressive arm and neck muscles. She cut a stiff figure, battle worn and tested, no doubt, and when her other hand lifted the heaviest looking automatic weapon Brann had seen this side of the Geihan armory from its resting spot behind her chair, there was no question as to why Nestor had chosen her to lead Brann through the wild.

"I've been told to take you wherever you need to go, within reason. I'll leave that last part to my own discretion, based on how well we get along en route, but stay on my good side and I may just get you most of the way there." Zay motioned to the exit. "Let's get moving, army boy."

*

The water level had risen significantly with the arrival of an oversized passenger ship shaped like an inverted whale, as broad as it was tall and white as paper, making a painfully slow show of its journey through Belljar's waters. A few dockworkers were shouting and making obscene gestures as their own smaller ships were lifted in the obnoxious cruise liner's wake, the cleats of its own massive floats threatening to even scrape against some of the other vessels. Zay spat in distaste at the sight, walking just ahead of Brann in the opposite direction of the flow of the water past the beleaguered dockhands.

"Fucking tourists. Some rich jackass and his buddies on a scenic trip down Belljar Canyon paid the captain to ignore the size restrictions. That's a Saintmarie ship, I'd bet on it." She tossed her chin to motion ahead of her. "This is us, the second to last pier. Ten to one says that giant piece of shit waterlogged the VTOL when it shoved past."

Zay's craft was a sight humbler than the gaudy *Myrmidon*, looking more like a conjoined pair of wafery half-moons swept back along the sides of a roomy four-seater fuselage. The low-profile, almost rectangular cabin reminded Brann of an air taxi he'd seen hopping between the further reaches of the shipyard and the main terminal at Barrier City's airport. This one was far more utilitarian, however, its backside segmenting off into a cradled cargo bed that rested on the surface of the water with a set of independent floats strapped to either side. Wedged in between the passenger cabin and the cargo bed was an ungainly looking barrel engine, likely the VTOL that Zay was concerned with—in fact, definitely so, as even from a distance Brann could see dirty water swirling about its upper intake.

"What'd I tell you. Can always count on the rich to piss on your head. This is gonna slow us down, we'll have to separate the fuel lines and drain the intakes before we can take off, otherwise the whole thing'll flood. Two sets of hands should make short work of it—you don't mind getting a little grease on your nice armor, do you?" She was back to her original prickly tone, putting Brann back on the defensive, making sure he didn't speak out of line—or much at all, truthfully.

"Just tell me what to do," he said, following her lead and setting his rifle down beside her gear as she let it fall to the ground just in front of the start of the pier.

Zay stretched her arms behind her back as her heavy boots clopped down the wood pier, tugging a pair of fingerless work gloves from the back pocket of her cargo trousers and donning them, motioning to the underside of the ship. "Hold on tight to the cowling and climb underneath it. You'll have to crouch but as long as you keep your feet on the cleats and don't let go you shouldn't fall in. You're gonna have to reach across and detach those two big yellow veins tucked under the housing, but you'll need a hand-clamp to do it, so just give me a second to grab it." She strode confidently right across the sturdy crescent shaped wing, the material sounding hollow underfoot, climbing up the sloped surface to the lip of the cargo bed. Brann followed behind and stood at the other end of the wing while she popped open a small mounted tool locker affixed to the cargo bed's exterior and removed a round claw-tipped hand tool. When she swiveled in place to toss it suddenly, Brann barely caught it. Unimpressed, Zay pointed back towards the engine.

"See the clamp release lever? Squeeze that against the handle hard as you can to open the clamp. Let off once you've looped it around the line coupler, rotate hard counter-clockwise till it snaps loose—it might spray back, so keep your eyes closed just in case. Then just release again and let the open end of the fuel line go slack so it can drain. That's one down. Afterwards, swing over and do it on the other side. Once they're both loose let me know, I'll be up top ready to purge the intakes."

Brann wordlessly set to work, lowering himself to wedge the cleft of his boots just along the cleat running along the wing's floater, stuffing the tool in his breastplate to free up his hands to grab the cowling and letting himself swing under. Shimmying back under the wing towards the engine, he had to clench his core to keep gravity from pulling his center of mass straight down into the water, relying on his own abdominal muscles to function as a bridge for the rest of his body while he scraped his way down to his objective. The surface of the water lapped at his boots, the dirty green ripples casting painfully bright reflective sparkles up into his eyes and decorating the underside of the wing with wavy bands of bouncing light. He halted himself just beside the engine, stretching out one foot till his boot connected with the housing and gingerly stepping across, the ship rocking a bit from the shift in weight and letting his rear dip close to the water. Once he was satisfied, he still had a good grip, he removed a hand to free the clamp from his breastplate and squeezed as hard as he could—he was no slouch, but even his grip strength barely gave enough pressure for the release switch to click down into the handle, the clawed end snapping. The yellow tubing he was looking for was impossible to miss against the oily black mess of cabling and metallic assembly of the engine, the metal coupling forming a tight seal between the fuel valve and the hose itself. Reaching down slowly to keep his balance, Brann slotted the clamp into place around the raised ridged of the coupling and released, the claws slamming shut in a perfect lock. It was difficult to provide enough torque to twist it free while his arm hung so low beneath his waist, so reaching back up to grab the cowling with both hands again, he used his boot to push on the handle steadily till he felt it about to give, then quickly gave it a final kick while reaching down to yank the handle back up in the same motion so the tool wouldn't fall into the water.

Zay was right, he did nearly get a faceful of water and oil as the loud clang of the fuel line being released sent a cannon shot of liquid arching up against the underside of the wing before splashing back down into the water below, the loose tube swinging free and letting the rest of what was stored inside splash directly below. The bulk of the liquid seemed to be dispersed in that initial release of pressure, with the stream slowing to a gentle drip in a matter of moments after Brann had uncoupled the line. Satisfied he'd done his job, he watched for a moment longer before moving to climb around to the other side of the engine, but stopped cold when something else appeared beneath the splashing surface of the water. The reflecting sparkles of light made it hard to get a good look, so he leaned in closer, wiping some of the spray from his face to open his eyes wider and peer below.

Where previously he couldn't see the riverbed below, presumably because of how deep the water ran, the muddy undercurrent seemed to have risen up significantly, the rugged dark sediment visibly flowing with the current of the water coated in a thick layer of algae and detritus. Brann grew apprehensive—the river hadn't been displaced THAT much from the larger cruise ship, had it?—but the moment he looked away to call out to Zay the torrent of mud vanished, letting the bouncing sunlight from above shine down through the mostly opaque dirty water as far as it could reach before going dark again. Maybe it was simply a displaced mudbank that had sent a slurry upwards towards the surface, Brann reasoned, getting back to business.

"Move with a purpose, soldat," Zay called down from below, her shadow filtering down from the gaps in the wings as well. Brann ignored her and let gravity rotate him around till he could reach the opposite cowling, making a small swing after releasing to grab at it, his wet boots threatening to slip free of their hold on the engine housing for a moment but otherwise holding true. Steadying himself once more, he moved to repeat the process with the second fuel line, having to clench even harder this time with his gloves now wet before the clamp released—though this also let the second coupler disconnect with less resistance than the first, with Brann able to keep a firm hold of the handle the entire time without needing the help of his boot. The initial burst of gunky water missed him entirely this time, aiming straight down like a faucet opening up and dumping its unwelcome contents directly into the river.

"Both lines open and draining," Brann called, spitting away some droplets clinging to his lip. He spun to latch onto the cowling and step onto the opposite floater, sidestepping until he felt sunlight on his face and swung his arm up to clamber up onto the wing. Bringing himself onto both feet, he shook free some remaining liquid from his arms and wiped his face again in the crook of his elbow, watching Zay with both her boots planted firmly in a wide stance on either side of the engine reaching down to grip at a rubber-capped lever just beneath the intake.

"Alright, this is gonna be loud," she said beginning to twist the small lever away from herself. The air filled with a steadily increasing hiss, the sound becoming piercing in no time at all, and Brann covered his ears in response. Barely had the sound been blotted out before he pulled his hands away again, a sudden surging wave buffeting the ship from below, prompting him to hold his arms out wide to keep his balance. Zay too had pulled the lever shut, waiting for the sudden seismic activity to die down and the water's surface to calm again.

"Biggest wake I've ever seen a ship that size leave," she commented in response, shaking her head. "Rich people."

She twisted the lever sharply, the air intake yawning wide and sending a deafening blast of steam straight down into the water.

Brann and Zay were launched skyward by the explosion of a geyser from below the ship, the vessel rolling up onto—and into—the pier, crashing down through the wooden planks in a splintery haze. Brann was sent sprawling across his front, feeling shards of wood flying around him at sonic speeds, deafened to his own cries when he felt shrapnel lodge itself in his leg—meanwhile, Zay was hurled even further down the pier, her already curled stance giving her time to tuck in and roll on impact, landing on her shoulder before spinning away across the planks. The skyborne expulsion of water rained down onto them moments later, the surface of the river where once rested Zay's moored ship now a chaotic bubbling cauldron of white and green. The moment his hearing returned, Brann could hear a distant shrill alarm blaring across the waterfront between pained gasps as he attempted to get his breath back. For a moment he thought the ship's engine had simply combusted, and had been terrified he'd made some kind of mistake in the process of following Zay's instructions.

Screams of fleeing people brought him back from those thoughts, however, Brann pushing himself over off his stomach to look back towards the water. Rising from the surface like an uncurling finger that pointed at the shore, a disgustingly matted body of scales and what looked like fur formed itself into the neck of an enormous creature that gazed back at him from sunken eyes of black tar, pinpricks of yellow in their center betraying the terrifying stare of a cold-blooded predator. The unsightly snout of the aquatic beast split wide and screeched in outrage, the bony jaws like that of a disfigured barracuda displaying rows of needle teeth so sharp they became nearly transparent at the tips.

Barely had the sight had time to register with Brann before he felt arms looped around him dragging him to his feet roughly, Zay's gloved hands yanking him back towards the shore. "Arch eel! We gotta kill that fucker, else it'll wreck this whole town! Pick up your gun and start shooting!"

The first combat scenario he'd been tossed into and the last thing he'd expected it to be against: a giant river monster. Brann was blinking away the stunned swirls in his eyes, adrenaline having numbed him to anything but what Zay was telling him to do. Feeling the wood give way to solid ground beneath his boots, her hands let go of his shoulders and he slipped free—though no sooner did he turn to reach for his rifle than he collapsed again, a stab of icy magma twisting into the nerve endings of his calf. He rolled himself to look down at the culprit: a fractured spear of jetty wood had buried itself in the meat of his leg, the fabric of his trousers tattered to show off a starburst pattern of flowing red wounds bleeding profusely around smaller fragments. The shrapnel of the dock had turned his leg into a pincushion.

Zay hadn't noticed Brann had fallen again, nor heard his pained bellow that accompanied it—when he searched for her from his prone position, eyes scanning between the countless sets of legs fleeing from where he lay in a blur of colors, he finally spotted her when the white of her simple muscle shirt popped up from the crowd. She'd strapped her massive gun to her back and was scaling a rope ladder that ascended along the broadside of a butcher shop, looking like a soaked cat scrambling to higher ground. She pulled herself up onto the slotted tin roof of someone's shack and disappeared, leaving Brann far below on the ground, helpless and bleeding.

He looked back down at his leg, then to his gun several yards away.

"Shit!"

Brann would have to drag himself the distance, and fast: the river monster—the arch eel, as Zay had called it—was swirling about in vicious circles in the bay, head fixed in a hunting posture as the rest of its enormous body remained mostly hidden underneath the waves. Weaving a sort of figure eight pattern on the river's surface, the neck of the beast flexed before the pier directly next to Brann exploded, the moored vessel there simply bursting open around the barbed tail of the arch eel that had swiped upwards from the water below. The lifeless bodies of the crew that were below deck, likely sleeping unawares in their bunks, tumbled down into grisly heaps onto the pier just as Brann had—albeit, in more than one piece.

Brann squeezed his eyes shut before he could get too good a look at the gory sight, turning back to set them on his gun when they reopened, and dug his fingers into the wet concrete of the river wall. Pulling himself along inch by inch, driving his elbows down to gain more traction, he combat-crawled as best he could with one bad leg dragging uselessly behind him til he could almost wrap a hand around his rifle's barrel.

As if sensing danger, the frantic swirling of the water ceased, the arch eel raising its head even higher above the surface of the river and turning its gaze back to shore. Eyes of stupid hunger snapped to and fro, watching as further down the dock, a scattering of armed men were moving against the surging mass of the fleeing crowd. Orders were shouted uselessly above the din, and a few stray shots of small-arms fire popped off like fireworks echoing between the canyon walls.

The enraged serpent's eyes lidded over with glassy, sheath-like lids, and around the base of its skull a pair of fleshy winglike appendages flared open, cupping forward around the eel's face. Its lower jaw hung slack for a moment, twitching rapidly, before it cracked open wide at almost a ninety-degree angle.

Then, the jaws slammed shut.

A supersonic wave of force blasted forth, the air searing around an invisible beam of pure kinetic energy across the surface of the water and into the side of the stacks. The approaching men were blasted off their feet by the wall of concussive force, some of the more unfortunate ones caught directly in its path simply being vaporized in a violet burst of maroon mist. Like an artillery shot had been fired into the cliff, the shacks around the site of the blast were scattered like shredded leaves, a backblast of granite dust from the cliff itself firing back towards the direction of the eel and sending a plume of dark smog down to settle across the river wall.

Brann had never seen such carnage, and yet, despite himself, found his training provoking his unwilling hands to wrap themselves around his gun and stand it upright, using the butt of the weapon to support his weight and raise himself. He knew he couldn't kill a creature that size himself, let alone with just a simple mid-caliber service rifle, but he had to at least draw its attention away from the fleeing civilians. Deaf to his own moans and gasps of pain, he planted one boot, then the other, and stood as best he could with his weight on the good leg, racking the slide on his rifle and hobbling towards the eel, having to half-step the entire way to keep from doing more damage to his impaled leg.

A brief observation of the scene, and Brann could see the monster would snap its head to and fro at lightning speed whenever a gunshot went off, often responding in kind with a smaller concussive blast by quickly snapping its jaws again, firing back at its tiny human assailants with unimaginable ferocity. The militia of Belljar were firing in a panic, doing what they thought they had to in order to protect the citizens, not realizing that their own actions in such close proximity to the crowds were putting them in immediate danger. Shooting at it himself should be enough to draw its gaze towards him, Brann concluded, hoping that he could connect enough shots from this distance to present a sufficient threat to the beast.

He dropped to his knees behind a stack of toppled shipping crates, ignoring what looked suspiciously like a human ear making a dark and sticky smear down the side, and swung his rifle around to rest the butt of its pistol grip against the flat surface, the bullpup design allowing the magazine to curve back below the edge of the crate and provide another contact point of support. For good measure, Brann reached up to snap open the recon grip, a small nub of a handle jutting out at an angle away from the barrel of the gun just behind the muzzle brake. He had to keep it steady, because as big as Brann's target was, the arch eel was also impossibly fast, its movements unpredictable.

Lining up his sights, Brann clicked off the thumb safety. Part of him—no, most of him—had hoped he'd hear the report of Zay's much more deadly weapon from above, saving him from having to shoot himself. There was no such luck to be had, and for all he knew, she had been pulverized in the stacks when that first shockwave was fired. His moment of hesitation had a cost: another shack high above burst, the half-disintegrated carcass of a sharpshooter splattering across the balconies below, followed by the muffled screams of onlookers inside. Every second he didn't act, more people would get hurt...and he hated it more than anything in the world, but Brann knew he was a soldat. This was his job.

Blinking away a final rivulet of water (or was it sweat?) before resting his cheek against the rubberized comb of the riflebutt, Brann inhaled deep, then slowly, steadily, exhaled.

His finger squeezed the trigger and, for the first time since his live-fire exercises in training, the rifle beneath him rattled off a burst of copper jacketed rounds in an arc towards the creature. He waited just the briefest of moments to see any sign of impact—the second he saw the eel flinch and the neck muscles recoil around three pops of shattered scales, he resumed firing in full. Pull after pull, deliberately paced, a steady rhythm of ear-popping volleys shooting the fiery purple cross pattern before his eyes from the gas vents of the gun's muzzle brake.

Bright and colorful tracer rounds like laser darts arced slightly from the distance, the eel staggering back from its onslaught and spinning to shriek defiantly across the water back at Brann. Every shot didn't need to hit—just enough to feel like an annoying finger repeatedly tapping at the beast's flesh, like Brann was speaking through his rifle, saying *hey, look, pay attention to me, I'm over here, asshole.*

The arch eel's attentions were pried away from the rest of the population at last. Brann's plan wasn't the best, but it was all he got: once the beast prepared another kinetic blast, he'd stagger towards the stacks for cover, hopefully finding a dense enough rock wall he could roll behind in time to dodge the worst of the blast. His dumb young idealism told him it was possible, and though logic said otherwise, it was all Brann could do to beat that logic back down and keep from choking him.

What happened instead was not figured in Brann's calculations. The arch eel snapped its jaws shut, the wide leathery fins slapping back against its neck...and the serpent simply dove back into the water, barely even making a ripple on the surface despite its size and speed.

Brann blinked. The stacks swayed and loose rubble crumbled from above, but otherwise Belljar was silent.

Shit. It was swimming back upriver. Back towards him.

It wanted to attack up close.

Releasing the magazine, Brann unclipped a replacement from his belt and jammed it up until it clicked into place in the magwell, yanking on the slide again to clear the final casing stuck in the ejection port. He stood again as best he could, looping the strap over his head till it dug into his neck, the rifle hugging against his body as he shuffled backwards away from the water.

"Hey, kid!" A shout from high above, a woman's voice. Brann looked up, but couldn't see her among the stacks. "I got him on approach, coming directly at you!"

"I kinda figured that, yeah!" He shouted back, not finding this at all helpful.

Zay ignored his retort. "Any second he's gonna pop up, and you're gonna have zero-fuckall seconds to get out of the way before he takes a shot at you—so, listen carefully! Here's what you do—"

The water was beginning to stir, a rising wave headed closer and closer, split by a jagged dorsal fin.

"—Don't!"

Brann was at a loss. What was she saying?

"Don't what?!" He shouted back.

"Don't move!"

No, he heard her right the first time.

"That doesn't really work for me!" He raised the barrel of his gun, aiming it towards the water to ready himself. "Why would I do that?!"

"He's gonna ready another shot at you, and when he does, I'm taking mine—just trust me, or we're both dead!"

The wave of water disappeared just at the river wall directly ahead of Brann. He stamped his foot in frustration, almost wishing the eel would just get this over with, but despite his fear he resisted the urge to run. Zay was right, they were dead either way.

Brann lowered himself to take a knee, gripping the rifle with both hands again, taking another deep breath to get ready.

The spiraling jet of water as the arch eel shot upward into the air sent streaming trails splashing across the dockfront, its black eyes already fixed on its prey before Brann even saw them emerge from behind the watery blast. The earlike fins flipped open wide, the jaws separating and beginning to vibrate again—this close, Bran could hear the rumbling in its throat and the tendons clicking around its jawbones.

"Don't you dare move!" Came Zay's repeated command.

This was all so bad, Brann thought, shaking uncontrollably. He sobbed a little to himself.

The arch eel's vibrating jaw snapped open wide. The eyes glassed over. Brann could almost see his reflection in them. A soft pocket of flesh in its throat expanded wide just as it fired.

Except, it didn't—the swelling in its gullet burst with a thunderclap, shreds of heavy machine gun fire spinning into the eel's exposed neck, Zay's perfectly timed shots like a white-hot beam of phosphorous boring a gaping bloodied portal into the eel's underbelly. The kinetic blast dissipated like a misfire, echoing outwards in a ring of bloodied smoke from the base of the beast's head as its following scream was muted by the raspy sounds of its gutted vocal cords. The head snapped backwards in shock and pain, eyes still fixed to Brann, looking back at him from an impossible angle in its broken neck.

Zay stopped firing just long enough to shout down to Brann:

"Go for the neck! Now!"

The rifle against his shoulder was suddenly steady, his shaking gone. He exhaled, and pulled the trigger.

A second beam of glowing bullets joined Zay's from below, Brann aiming directly at the destroyed throat and soft palette of the creature, carving into its tenderized underside like their conjoined gunfire were a pair of knives cleaning an oversized fish. Red slices cut from the initial wound, lacerating the neck of the arch eel until they peeled away and were pulverized by the crossfire; soon the serpent's throat was gushing spouts of blood and gristle from its still-gurgling sonic pouch. The head, no longer supported by the destroyed neck muscles, lolled back further, the eel's slack body languidly sliding back into the water away from shore.

As the gunfire died off, the arch eel sunk a bit before its stiffened spine touched bottom and, like a toppling tree cut down by lumberjacks, the eel's neck fell lengthwise to splash down into the river, its barely attached head bobbing like a colossal cork on the surface.

The arch eel was dead. Brann had fought his first battle—against a monster no less—and survived.

He let the rifle clatter to the ground, moments before he did, falling back on his ass.

Everything was quiet in the canyon once more, until the wails and relieved cries of the townspeople rose up from amidst the swirling dust. The limp body of the great serpent began floating gently along with the current, its lifeless head bumping against a dark object—Brann recognized it as the barrel-shaped VTOL engine of Zay's ship, severed from its original body much like the head of the arch eel itself. The engine, still sputtering it's dying gasps, gently swirled about for a few meters downstream before being pulled below the blood and oil-streaked surface of the river.

6. The Deal

"That big floating tumor that came through the canyon must have stirred up the arch eel in its oversized wake," Zay was saying as she let her waterlogged seabag slap wetly against the deck of the cargo bay, pulling her hair away from her face—her arms were streaked with a metallic grease that terminated near her elbows and dried into flecks of powder. So much gunsmoke had been expelled during her sustained machine gun fire that it had clung to her soaked body, mixing into a paste on her skin and turning her once-white shirt a shiny, ashen grey. "Those happy, wealthy pigs just continuing on with their sightseeing tour downriver none-the-wiser as they literally destroy towns in their fat-assed boat's wake. These Belljar folks are just lucky we were here, otherwise this whole place would be underwater right about now."

She perched herself atop a stack of now emptied crates, plucking gingerly at a thick shard of metal that presumedly used to be part of her ship and had now embedded itself in her arm. "So. Who's the captain here? Who owes me a new glider?"

Brann had set to tending his own wounds with Nestor's help, the rest of the crew making preparations for an early departure. Boomer would be back any minute and they'd be off, leaving Brann stuck as a fixture onboard the *Myrmidon* for the time being until he'd made a full recovery, or until other arrangements could be made to see him off, whichever came first.

Nestor didn't look up from his work, tugging a particularly stubborn splinter of dock from Brann's leg as the young man prepared one of his magick-silica first aid sachets to seal the shredded meat of his calf, but nonetheless responded to Zay with respectful firmness. "The ship being destroyed by the eel was a tragedy, no doubt. But holding us responsible isn't helpful to anyone. It was a wild animal that had its territory invaded. Nothing we did provoked it, you said yourself—it was that sightseeing ship. Take it up with the rich people who can afford to reimburse you."

Zay wasn't impressed with this reply, grunting as the metal shard was freed, letting it clatter to the deck with a few droplets of her blood spattering around it, a much cruder solution to her medical needs in the form of engineer tape being slapped over the gash to staunch the bleeding.

"Only reason my ship got trashed was because I was giving your kid here a ride. Without you two hiring me as a babysitter, I'd still be riding a cot at the Quar'master's. That, and my fees cover travel and expenses, and this—" She kicked the bloodied hunk of shrapnel towards Nestor. "—Counts as a mighty big expense, one not sufficiently covered by your deposit. So, way I see it, I'm due a chat with your captain, '*Re:*' the rest of my fee."

Brann was sitting on the tatters of his trousers, the garment ruined from the countless punctures and the blood soaking into it. He'd need some new pants before the day was out. "I didn't mean to put you through all this trouble," he said in a low voice to Nestor, tearing open the sachet.

The older engineer's face was stony, but his tone was dismissive. "Nah, shit happens, kid. You got put on the ship to protect it, and you did just that, right?" He slapped Brann's knee, already unfurling the papery sealant to prepare to wrap it around the currently crystalizing silica spiderwebs filling in the wounds. Brann handed him the anesthetic, his face sweating from pain and nausea, never having sustained such grievous injuries in his life. He hoped this wasn't going to be a regular occurrence outside the walls of Barrier City, otherwise he almost wished he'd stayed put.

Nestor injected the numbing fluid and wrapped the leg, needing little instruction from Brann, almost like he'd done this very thing once or twice himself. "Twist once sharply and pull, right?" He verbally confirmed, and Brann nodded, sitting back to look away.

Nes sparked the flare tip, and Brann's entire leg felt not hot, but icy cold, itchy lightning bolts of discordant sensations lancing up his back along the channel of his nervous system and making erratic patches of nerves all over his body feel like they were being microwaved—even his gums felt tickled and his nose felt like pins and needles were stabbing into one side of it. The magicka flame died off and his leg went totally numb, the nausea passing almost in an instant. He looked back down, and was morbidly fascinated by the sight of his newly rejoined calf muscles replaced in part by that off-white rubbery flesh. Nestor must have seen his expression, and poked at the silicone skin, making Brann giggle nervously. "God that feels weird."

"Good as new," replied Nes with a sympathetic smile, punching the restored calf and sweeping up the discarded first aid materials. Zay was watching the process as well, the sight likely completely alien to her.

"Hey soldat, didn't think I might need some of that fancy doctoring over here?" She said indignantly, likely to mask her amazement. She tossed aside the bloody rag she'd wiped her arm with stepping down from her perch atop the crates just as a clopping of hooves on the cargo ramp signaled Boomer's return.

"Remind me why I don't come to visit you more often where you work, Nes," the horse said, removing his expensive looking sunshades with a flourish. He'd ditched his lazyman's robe from the evening prior in favor of a decidedly more tailored appearance, a tight burgundy undershirt tucked into satin pants with the neck buttoned low to show off his pectorals and an ochre jacket of some kind of slick artificial material draped over one shoulder, held there by a single finger. If this didn't strike the figure of wealth he intended it to, his golden scarf wrapping itself around his broad neck definitely pushed his outfit over the edge firmly into "lavish" territory.

"Damn kid, you okay?" Boomer's eyes went wide at the bloody sight of Brann's naked leg, pushing right past Zay before she had the chance to speak and tossing his expensive coat aside as if it were nothing. "Or no, don't tell me, 'I should see the other guy,' right? The security guys down on the dock told me you killed a giant snake all by yourself or something, is that true?!" He crouched down beside Brann before waiting for a response and was squeezing the boy's calf in his hand like appraising a ripe piece of fruit. "And all he got on you was a little cut like this? Nes, I think we gotta keep him now, this guy's almost as tough as me! Oh here, let me help you up man," Boomer said as he caught Brann's arm, the young man attempting to stand, gingerly putting his weight on the leg to test it. It was like the pain had simply evaporated, feeling no worse for wear than he did when Brann had gone on a long hike marching with the division on the palace grounds.

If Zay took offense to Boomer's initial appearance, she definitely made it known she was repulsed by his personality. "Hey, rodeo clown, eyes up," she barked, stamping her boot to grab his attention. "You the captain of this shitheap?"

Boomer's ears swiveled a microsecond before his head snapped around towards her, the horseman stepping-to with urgency that would make a soldat proud. "Yes, my queen, that is I, King Captain. King Captain Boomer, actually," he winked, seemingly both smitten by being addressed with such directness and admiring of Zay's own appearance in a manner that was not reciprocated. "And may I say, whoever your personal trainer is, that man deserves a raise. I would use those deltoids to slice my morning bread and spread it with butter, my word." He tossed the bangs of his mane out of his eyes, looking the woman up and down without any shame whatsoever.

Zay stepped forward briskly, invading Boomer's personal space in a way he must not be used to considering how far back he leaned in surprise. He leaned on Brann's shoulder to steady himself, as if he was the one who had the leg injury now.

"Oh, hello to you, too." Boomer's grin widened.

Swiping her hand across her still-bleeding arm, Zay smeared red across Boomer's chest in an X pattern, staining the soft looking burgundy material with an offset of complimentary rust. "You and your crew here owe me a new ship," she spat, shoving his shoulder for emphasis with two gloved fingers. "And I'm collecting payment direct from you right now, today. So, we understand I'm not interested in any kind of layaway plan."

Boomer's hands were raised in a surrendering posture, but it was at this moment Brann saw a new side to the horseman, one he didn't expect given the absolute warmth and chipper demeanor he exuded at all times.

Bringing those hands together slowly to clasp Zay's own, Boomer chuckled and lidded his eyes, his head crooked to the side as his voice lowered to a seductive pitch.

"Babe, I have been accused of a lot of things in my time, but 'cheap' has never been one I'd dignify with a response. I'd be happy to work something out with you to get you made whole again," he said, leaning in close to whisper his next words:

"But let me tell you. Any man puts hands to me the way you just did, he's looking to add himself as a statistic to my career card. So, if you're curious as to why they call me 'Boomer', I'm happy to give you a demonstration with my famous 'broken skull combo'.

The air had gone chilly in the cargo bay as Brann watched in stunned silence. Boomer's hands were shaking from how tightly he was gripping Zay's wrist—and the female gunner's other hand was snaking towards her belt in kind, reaching for a holstered combat knife there. "Nothing would make me happier than you paying me to turn your rich playboy insides out all over your own ship, bronco boy," she smirked in reply, eyes pinned wide open in a challenging stare. "Gimme a reason to call today a blessing in disguise. I fuckin' dare you."

"Boomer, take a step back son, right now." Nestor was at his side, gripping the horse's mane firmly and pulling him away, staring down the still-grinning beastman with authority above his own humble station as a contract worker.

Despite his nostrils flaring in anticipation, the pugilist recognized the words of his old friend and released his grip on Zay's hand, his grin as wide and sparkly as ever even as he snorted, the whites of his eyes betraying a crazy look of bloodlust. Nestor replaced himself in front of the mercenary woman, arms crossed and chin forward. "Don't mind him, please. He's only acting captain because he fired the real one. I can assure you we can arrange a new ship to be paid out to you, the only condition being that you're civil enough to keep that blade sheathed until we ferry you to our next stop."

Zay never broke eye contact with the battle-roused Boomer, her free hand flexing and popping the joints loudly. "By all means. Happy to tag along for a while, so long as you know whichever room you put me up in on this dickless animal's flying wreck of a boat is gonna have a helluva room-service bill I'll need comped during my stay."

"Whatever you need, we can take care of it," Nestor said, perfectly amenable to her demands as one hand was held behind him to point at Boomer and direct him to stand down. "We're on our way through Cheneye territory next, and there's a lovely ship depot we have a longstanding relationship with. They'll be happy to fix you up with whatever you need."

Zay reluctantly broke her steely gaze from Boomer and fixed it on Brann instead, who suddenly felt very unjustly maligned in the woman's sights. "A decent sized freighter. With a crew. I'm thinking I've saved up almost enough to start my cross-continental delivery service. The horse can match what I've earned to cover the rest."

Nestor bowed in a manner that nearly seemed patronizing, also looking to Brann. Was it his imagination, or was everyone suddenly blaming him for everything that happened?

"I'll show you to your quarters, then," said Nes, directing Zay to step around Boomer towards the ladderwell, keeping himself wisely between the two of them. Once he'd seen her off and the cargo bay was silent again, Boomer's hackles instantly relaxed and he turned back to Brann, that same excitable personality bubbling back to the surface.

"Man, I am just having a blast on this tour, kid," he giggled, leaning back against a locker next to Brann, elbowing his new pal roughly. "You get to come along with us after all, how's that for lucky, huh?" He paused. "Or, did you still need to get back to base? I know you were pretty set on it before..."

He'd seen more comfort and hospitality the night before and more gory violence this morning than he'd ever expected in his entire life, and the fears of the pursuant Marshal were all but assuaged now, given how quickly his view of the world around him was expanding—Brann wasn't sure where his journey was going to end up, but he wasn't about to end it prematurely, not with how overstimulated he felt at this moment.

"Actually, I uh, I called my DC just a minute ago before you got back," he began lying, staring off into the distance. "Turns out I'm good to go as long as you need me—since this ship definitely seems to need more protection than previously thought," Brann added, patting the rifle standing up next to him.

Boomer's grin widened even further, his arm draping over Brann to pull him in close. "Best news I've had all day. I cannot wait for you to see my next fight. Barrier City's gonna look like a backwater pit stop compared to the places you'll see on the Donnie, trust me. I've always wanted a real soldat bodyguard of my own—play your cards right, I might uhh..." Boomer's expression became mischievous, voice becoming that of a hushed schemer. "I might be persuaded to introduce you to the captain's personal harem chambers, if you need some time to unwind after today's excitement."

Brann stared back at him. "Harem, like, you have..."

Boomer nodded excitedly like he was discussing a bug collection. "Whole heap of ladies, beauties too. Don't worry, they're not like indentured concubines or anything, they're free to come and go as they please. But you know how it is with chicks—who would want to go out for hay when they got a barrel of prime oats back home on the Donnie?" He motioned to his partially exposed chest, and Brann was simultaneously awed and repulsed. For all the friendly aspects of Boomer's childlike personality he was warming to, he was also beginning to sympathize with the less charmed point of view from someone like Zay.

"I don't know if...that's really my scene. If that's okay for me to say without offending you," Brann said carefully, remembering the scene Boomer had made over the coffee. "Us soldaten, we sort of like to keep to one lady at a time. Keeps things simple for us humble warfighters, you know?"

Boomer's eyes popped and his big boxy equine mouth formed around a silent 'ohh', and he nodded in understanding, to Brann's relief.

"Yeah, yeah, I getcha buddy, gotta keep the whole combat sense sharp and at the ready. Can't have a bunch of mares distracting you when you gotta take that hill tomorrow morning. Say no more, you know me, I totally respect the whole serious business vibe, for sure," he said with a wide wave towards Brann's armor.

"Mares," Brann repeated dumbly, again at a loss. It seemed so obvious, but hearing it spoken aloud so casually by the self-preening horse was nonetheless a shock.

"Well, yeah. What, you thought I was joking with that honey?" Boomer pointed back over his shoulder at the ladderwell, meaning Zay. "I'm not picky or anything, but, the horse gals from back home are perfect for me; I need ladies who can take me in the ring just as easily as in the sheets after all—"

"Yeah, okay I get it, you're right, enough," Brann interrupted, pushing past the inappropriate horseman. "I'm starving, let's hit the galley."

He picked up Boomer's discarded coat, feeling the smooth, leathery material under his thumb a moment before tossing it back to the horse. He'd stayed quiet so far for the most part on his journey, letting everyone around him do all the talking while he simply soaked in the sights and sounds like a sponge, but today's events made Brann feel invigorated in a way he hadn't since he'd been among his young friends on the streets looking out for each other. He ventured a joke, feeling emboldened enough to do so. "After all, I gotta keep up my strength to protect you again in the event of another monster attack, right 'bronco boy?'"

Boomer guffawed at that, clapping his muscled hands together loudly like sheets of rock, his coat draped over his shoulder once more. "This trip is gonna be a BLAST—you're the most fun guy I've met since Nes, kid," he said, leading the way to the ladderwell. "I'll have the cook slap together a special spread for us and we can chat it up tonight during the flight, get a chance to know each other better!" He lifted his massive bulk with ease onto the rungs and ascended, Brann following just behind.

"You know your outfit matches the inside of your ship, right?" Brann ventured curiously.

"I know! Isn't it just THE BEST?!" Boomer bellowed back.

*

"No! No way, Nes, you're mental! Out of the question, bro!"

Nestor's arms were crossed inflexibly. "We have no choice. Just how it is."

Boomer stamped a hoof like a child having a tantrum. "Not fair! I have a schedule too, I'm more important!" He stuttered. "I-I mean my fans; my fans are more important! Who is gonna take care of them, they need me!"

"This is why public relations guys exist, and you fired the last ones."

"I didn't FIRE anyone, no fire," Boomer retorted, waving his arms. "They all quit involuntarily due to circumstances I didn't like, is all."

Brann was walking into this newest spectacle, rounding the stairs after testing his weight on his recovered leg, making the trip from his quarters down to the galley again. He'd changed his outfit, abandoning the armor entirely in favor of a casual outfit that hung loose and breezy—he'd forgotten how long it had been since he'd worn clothes he could think of as "comfortable". Zay and Nes both had their arms crossed sitting at a table, bringing some apparently bad news to bear for Boomer's consideration. He was not taking it well.

"We'll wire the fee back for you, send a nice fruit basket to apologize, and ask them to find someone else. There's no stopping this train we're on, sugar, sorry!" Boomer was looking down his snout at Zay, hands on hips, expressive muzzle pulled in an exaggerated frown. Brann appreciated how easy it was to read Boomer's moods, between his long features and swiveling ears that would stand up, out, or flatten back at a moment's notice to match the tone of whatever he said. It made relating to him much easier for Brann than anyone else on this journey so far, given how reserved and private he'd resolved to be to avoid giving himself away.

"They paid half up front with scales, in person, and their one half was bigger than all you've already paid me so far, which still hasn't cleared my account," Zay said in her signature monotone, not batting an eye at Boomer's churlish display. "Your manager here already promised I'd get everything I'd need—this is what I need, so make with the keys."

"He's not even my manager," complained Boomer.

"Yes, and you fired your last one of those, too," was Nestor's dry riposte.

"It's a short detour that runs not far afield of your existing flight path and gives you enough time to make your next stop before your next little scrap," Zay resumed, listing off points in her favor on her fingers. "You have no immediate financial need to hock your merch right now; you have no captain to keep your ship moving and largely rely on these public appearances to decide where to refuel anyway; you have enough empty beds—I presume from all the 'involuntary quitting'—that space isn't an issue for you; and, lest we forget, you still owe me a ship, the loss of mine being a direct result of your unscheduled detour to begin with."

Nestor looked sideways at Brann quickly, then back again—Brann suddenly got the feeling he knew why Nes had so readily assumed responsibility to pay Zay back.

Boomer fumed. "That all may be well and good," he allowed, "but that doesn't explain why I have to let YOU be the one to FLY my ship to do it!"

"Because your last pilot was fi—"

"Involuntarily quit!"

Nes sighed. "Boomer. I can't be pilot and head of personnel while still having time to oversee the in-flight maintenance we're gonna need on this next longer leg of the trip. We need a dedicated pilot on the wheel to keep us on track, one whose first name isn't 'Auto'. Zaydat here is qualified, has a need, a purpose, and sufficient motivation to keep us on our original schedule, save for this one deviation from it." He stood, obviously exerting more authority over the celebrity than the other way around, as Brann was coming to slowly learn. "We let her fly until she has a ship of her own, and in the meantime, we make up the losses incurred at Belljar by assisting in her passenger flights. One cancelled stop in Cheneye means a mutually beneficial relationship for the near future." He cast an eye to Brann. "For everyone."

Boomer stared at Nes, then Zay, then back, then even to Brann, who shrugged. *I'm just along for the free ride too, man,* he thought to himself.

There was no victory to be had here. The horse snorted in exasperation and resigned from the conversation, dragging Brann away with him to the lounge side of the common area. "Well, you two mutineers have fun destroying my reputation. The cool guys on board are gonna be over here being served fine cheeses and watching my old fights—you know, looking after the things that matter in life," he shot back at the table behind him.

"What did I miss?" Brann asked, looking back longingly over his shoulder at the row of snack coolers that were drifting further away from him.

"Queen Usurper there is commandeering the Donnie to turn her into a commercial flight craft, and I've been cast from the throne." Boomer flopped across a reclined loveseat, wrapping his arms around a pillow to sulk. "The king is dead. King Captain Boomer no more. I'm a prisoner on my own flagship. Don't look at me kid, I'm a fraud."

Boomer reached up weakly with a slack wrist to tap repeatedly at the crew service button on the loveseat's arm, a cheerful little buzz and flash of a small bulb giving feedback on each tap.

"Cheneye isn't a city, though," said Brann diplomatically, trying his best to be sensitive to the horse's woes. "So, it kinda sounds like you didn't have an original stop planned anyway?"

Boomer pouted. "I just let Nes pick where we go next, I like the cities he picks. He knows my taste in crowds."

This was a level of self-insuffiency hitherto unknown to Brann. He took pity on his new friend, sitting cross-legged on the seat next to the dejected horse. He had an idea. "You know," Brann said, drawing himself up straight. "Some of us boys from Geiha, we get to pick our own assignments, from time to time." He neglected to namedrop the Uhlen, opting for a half-truth over an outright lie. "Go where we want, do what we want, as long as at the end of the day we make the mission a success."

Boomer looked up hopefully with puppydog eyes. "Yeah? You don't gotta do what you're told all the time?"

Brann nodded with authority. "Yeah man, it's a sweet gig. Even with the big man in charge telling us what to do most of the time, the rest of the time, he actually works for us. Cool, huh?"

Boomer elevated himself upright as well, enraptured by this story. "Whoa. That is cool. You still go where you need to fight, but the rest of the time, you just do what you want? And no one but you is in charge?"

"No one else," Brann repeated with a warm smile. "You and Nes are good friends, I can tell, but he might like it if you decided where the ship went sometimes."

"Yeah, exactly," Boomer nodded.

"Of course," Brann continued, as if deep in thought on this complex matter. "You can't make the decision all the time, what with your fighting career and all. You've got other concerns to keep your focus on, like your..." He coughed. "...Your delts, and your meals, and that other important stuff."

"The stuff that MATTERS," Boomer said, understanding. "So, someone who isn't me, but isn't Nes either, someone who can also help fly the ship sometimes!"

"Right!" Brann pointed. "You've got a good point there. Like, what if there was someone else, like...a pilot, someone you hired, to help share the load of leadership when you need to keep your mind on other things? And what if that pilot could make those decisions for you, because just like us boys at Geiha, we still get the job done in the end even if they go where they want without bothering you about it?"

Boomer threw up his hands. "I've got it! I can use Zay as our pilot and let her decide where to take us between fights, because I'm actually the one in charge, which means she gets to leave me alone to take us where we're going without asking me first!"

It seemed there could be peace between the warring nations of Boomer and Zay after all.

Boomer leapt up from the seat and beamed down at Brann. "You know what, from the moment I saw your stupid, gawky look coming down those stairs, I knew you were a smart guy! Next time we're on the ground, I'm taking you shopping and buying you the biggest present you can carry." He spun on the spot as the kitchen door bounced open back in the galley, a mealcart being wheeled out by a crew hand wearing a headset, responding to Boomer's wordless call through the service button. "Before that, though, let's eat—you've earned yourself a meal today, my good comrade-in-arms."

Brann had a thought. "Earlier, down below. You were saying something about why they call you Boomer."

Boomer turned. A moment in time slowed, and Brann didn't understand why nor had the presence of mind to ask the question, but this would be a defining memory in years to come to him. The horse's signature wry smile cocked itself, one bereft of his usual self-aggrandizing charm. "You wanna know why they call me that?" His voice spoke in the low drawl of a seasoned sports announcer.

His arms were held high above his head, and with the slightest of bow's, Boomer's torso tilted so one hand could point a finger at Brann, the other raised above his ears clenching itself into a fist.

"Because when you step to me and demand my name, the only response you'll hear is the 'boom'."

7. The Pilot

The flight only lasted a few hours, but the daylight was already fading fast when the Donnie touched down in the next shipyard—or at least, touched down, as calling this next stop a shipyard was a stretch of anyone's imagination. A flat outcropping of sand and volcanic rock, like a beach with no ocean, a single stubby path with exactly two small wooden buildings that easily could have been home to single families but were instead so packed with bodies pouring in and out it made it impossible for anyone to feel safe from light fingers picking their pockets. In no organized fashion were the small ships parked on the sand, forcing the *Myrmidon* to put down chocks on the far edge of the lot so her massive amphibious floaters wouldn't flatten any smaller ships beneath their expanse. Zay had gone on ahead to make contact with her clients, the rest of the crew stowed away in their bunks for the night—except Brann couldn't sleep from the day's excitement, Boomer didn't want to touch down without introducing himself to the local population, and Nestor was on Boomer duty putting together an assembly of merchandise in a single hand crate to accompany his belligerent friend on his impromptu public appearance. Boomer's jacket was actually on his body instead of draped over his shoulder like a cape now as the evening air chilled, cool drafts buffeting the sand in small waves at the trio's shins as they crossed the sandy lot.

"Cheneye doesn't have too many outlier cities to speak of, considering how deep into the Wilds it sits, so these little holes in the wall are the best we got for meet and greets," Boomer was saying, his hooves almost silent when they sank into the sand, his flashy outfit making up for the lack of noise in his stride. "I love it. Reminds me of the days coming up in the underground. Cutting my knuckles on the illegal fights, touching teeth with other would-be contenders—the good old days before the weight of glory's crown sat atop this head." He breathed in a massive lungful of cold air and sighed happily.

Brann didn't need Nestor's nonplussed frown and shake of the head to tell him that Boomer was never an illegal underground fighter. He was catching onto these antics quick.

A few scattered claps could be heard from the mingling crowd as Boomer entered the fray of travelers and vagrants, standing a full head above even the tallest people—but unlike the ports at Barrier City or Belljar, 'people' was a term that was complicated to the point of challenging Brann's idea of the definition of the word itself. Humans, yes, but as they drew closer to the standing structures, Brann saw more variety in species than he ever thought possible scattered among them, and he knew they were further into the Wilds than he ever would have gotten as a humble corpsman in the Geihan infantry. An ornate rug laid out on the sand decorated with twinkling jeweled knobs probably meant to cap a ship's flight stick—in the center of them a coiled serpentman using the flexing of his own elongated body's muscles to make the rug undulate and the custom knobs sparkle appealingly as a result. The human merchant on the rug beside him held aloft a staff that looked like a hat-rack, the rungs all decorated in colorful strings looped around what Brann recognized as holoplay cards, these ones likely bootlegged—but the human merchant had to keep waving away the probing beak of a feral quaggabird that kept sifting through them. The long-necked avian stood on all four scaly legs amidst an array of pikes capped with roasted meats, the bird's eyes rapt with fascination at the sight of the holoplay cards dangling just before him, his wings flat along his back and the greatbow he'd used to hunt the prey he was currently offering to hungry customers looped around his teardrop shaped body.

Not selling any wares but simply passing through the crowd as any other traveler, Brann also saw the back of another kuaneach with a start but regained his ease when the female turned to show a face decorated with glittering scales of bronze quite unlike Tark's dark pitch tones. In what might have been the strangest sight yet, the few streetlamps were being lit by a man who seemed to be assisted by a pair of long fireworms draped over his shoulders—but with a shock, Brann saw the man's arms *were* the fireworms, and his face gleaming in the newly sparked lamplight a false one, a hooded mask of rudimentary human features barely disguising the writhing mass of smoldering nematodes within a set of night-worker's clothes.

Being led in a daze at the sights, Brann had to wonder just how much of the world outside Barrier City was human at all, and how much of the world the Wilds actually composed, given the absolute lack of surprise shown by his cohorts. Boomer simply greeted each fan who recognized him with a firm handshake and bleached smile, and Nes would pass him a pair of replica gym shorts or a signed mugshot to usher the fan along, taking the scales passed back to him in payment to deposit in a small slotted bank within the handcrate.

To Brann, this was a day at the circus—to them, this was a day like any other.

When the crate had run dry, and Boomer disappeared among the crowd to socialize, Nes and Brann pulled themselves to sit on the lip of one of the two buildings' elevated decks to wait for Zay's reappearance. Brann noticed something about the street vendors and nudged Nes to inquire.

"They're all on this side of the street," he said.

"Hm?" Nes didn't quite understand, taking notes of their earnings on his holoscreen.

"The sellers. They're all on one side of the street. How come they don't sell over there?" Brann pointed to the building directly across from them.

"Oh." Nes finished counting and pocketed the screen. "Because this is the Quartermaster," he said, thumb over his shoulder, then pointed at the opposite building. "And that is a brothel. They're selling something altogether different."

Brann's eyes wandered over the crowd, and sure enough, he saw what Nes meant. There were indeed vendors on the patio of the other house, though they weren't selling meats or baubles—at least, not in the obvious sense. A demonic looking caprine doe in matron's garb was ushering in customers, led by the eye-batting partners tugging them along by the arm: a heavyset woman, a gem-studded and genderless mechagolem, and a bottom-heavy gooseman with gaudy eyelashes—Brann looked away with a blush, suddenly very self-aware with how obviously he was staring at everyone around him. Maybe the best course of action was to get used to how things worked here quick, lest he be caught gawking.

He turned to other and more local matters instead, watching Nes slip a few scales from the bank into a small spring-loaded hand-device that looked like a cigarillo lighter. "You know, back in the city," Brann said, clearing his throat, "We only used to pay for the small stuff with scales. Junk food, drinks at the galley, things like that. Out here it's like the only thing anyone uses to pay for anything."

"That's because it is," said Nes, pocketing his scale charger once his merchant fee was taken from the rest of Boomer's bank. "Scalenes are the main form of currency everywhere except Barrier City, where you all rely on work credits to pay for your lodging and your bills and all that nonsense. Scales are basically worthless everywhere except on the street to buy you a snack, because the city is counting on you staying in debt to them and using the work credits you earned this last week on next week's electric bill, or that fancy new holoscreen, or the fuel that goes into your ship. If you all could pay your way out of work with an independent form of currency—like this—" Nes unpocketed his charger and waggled it in the air for emphasis, "—Then there would be no reason for you to stay in the city, and you'd all simply leave for the Wilds to make a living out here with the commonfolk."

Brann frowned at this. "But the Wilds are dangerous," he said, resisting the urge to point at the less humanlike travelers milling about. "There's...monsters. Like that arch eel. It's safer in the city, closer to Geiha."

This seemed to be a conversation Nes was dreading, and the older man sighed, replacing the scalene charger in his hand with an actual lighter, a wrapped joint of yamweed having appeared from nowhere to fasten between his lips.

"Kid, this is how it works," he said, clicking on the flame and puffing at the cigarillo to get the cherry going, familiar spirals of blue smoke pouring out of his nostrils. "You're born in a place. Some big fancy town with a lot of nice buildings and nice amenities. They tell you that you fucked up by being born there, that you owe them with work, and you're gonna have to get started as soon as you can to pay your way, because only criminals live for free. So, you get yourself a job in that warehouse—it's hard work, but it pays well!—or you sign up to get yourself killed for the military's furthered goals; but it pays well! Or you study your whole life to get that degree so you can build rockets and bigass guns that kill people your city doesn't like. But it pays well," he reiterated, blowing a cool stream of weedsmoke upwards. "'Pays well.' 'The pay is good.' At least I get paid.' All these things we tell ourselves so we don't have to butt heads with the fact that just because someone else a hundred years ago had this idea that their neighbors living well and owning property wasn't benefitting them enough, so they created these rules where in order to just be yourself, you gotta make with the coin."

Nes pointed at the brothel across the way, the cherry glowing between his fingers as he did. "See them? You see how well they're living?" He meant the sex workers, and Brann's eyes wandered back, watching closely. The horned caprine woman was being kissed on the cheek by a polished woman with masculine features, the two joining hands like old friends, chatting it up while the revelry around them drew into the house where no doubt warm beds were waiting to receive the night's dues.

"They have everything they need, right there on this little patch of land, far away from anyone's rules. We still pay each other to get by, of course, because we're still part of this world as a whole and we need to help each other out—but at the end of the day, when the work is done and the coin is earned, what do you do? You say hello to good friends, you share a good meal, you open up your bed and fall asleep when you're spent. All the best of life's prizes, won at the cost of no more than another day you survived under the sun. We pay for what we want as a courtesy, but what we need more than anything, that will always be free." He replaced the cig, taking another long draw. "You're young, and I ain't saying you did anything wrong. You got pulled into one of life's big lies, just like we all do. The lie of cost, the lie of service, the lie of war. Whatever it is that you believe, the thing we all come to realize is that you can get everything you need to be happy in this life by giving up what you don't need at all. And if someone else who has more than you do is telling you that you need it..."

Nestor flicked away the still burning cig. Brann watched it tumble down into the sand below, a lone lantern in a tiny sea of volcanic gravel.

"That's a sure as shit sign that you don't."

A gust of wind drew another wave of sand over the small ember, snuffing it out, the dying puff of smoke blowing away into nothing. Brann hadn't heard Nes speak this much since the two of them met, and didn't know what prompted such an event, but smartly opted not to ruin the moment by commenting. The message was clear: Barrier City was just one self-important neighborhood among many, and he had a lot to learn about the rest of the world outside its walls.

Nes looked around for a moment, the chatter of the crowd filling the space between them. He stood, wiping his hands together to dust them off. "Sun's about to go down any second now, this is taking longer than it should. Let's pull the village idiot out and go find Zay so we can keep moving—I'd like to avoid having to pay out today's profits to some bullheaded jackass what picked a fight with a champion fighter's big mouth."

*

Inside the Quartermaster's house was more like the inside of a bar— in fact, Brann suspected the entire place had been fitted to be just that, given a distinct lack of any kind of shops or services within its walls save for the tavern-like assortment of stools and tables decorated with inebriated patrons. Nestor carved a path through the drunken din towards the easily spotted top of Boomer's head, those palomino ears flicking astride his shampooed blonde mane. Brann kept his eyes forward to continue his resolved decision not to stare, even if he felt a pair of antlers dig curiously into his shoulder or antennae tickle his shin. He was just another nondescript traveler in a crew, no home port and no fancy set of shining armor to set him apart from anyone else—the less time he spent wearing his service uniform, the less naked he felt.

The crowd parted around a table where Boomer sat, and at first, he was the center of the attention as usual, but it was actually the one sitting across from Boomer that Brann realized had drawn the eyes of onlookers. The man—man? Brann paused. The creature—the being...was not organic. At least, not apparently so. His garb was human enough, tailored to fit and ironed free of even the slightest wrinkles; his voice was smooth and honeyed like a fine liquor poured over ice; his demeanor was casual, relaxed, and altogether inviting like a favored uncle. His face was cold, shiny, and layered with plates of chrome that slid and clicked together in such a way his features reminded Brann instantly of a great big synthetic mantis. Eyes of artifice illuminated anyone he cast them on, perfect iridescent halos glowing from within set sockets that would click shut with rapid precision beneath horizontal lens cleaners that served every purpose a human eyelid would. The robotic man's articulated, clawlike hands flipped a deck of carousel cards so quickly and effortlessly without even needing his eyes to supervise that the sight was a blur to Brann; meanwhile, the other arm of the automaton was looped around the waist of an attending waitress, tickling at the bare space just above her belt with all the sauciness of any real human rogue.

"I tell ya, my man, you drive a bargain harder than any freight captain," the android was saying to Boomer, cards being dealt blindingly fast from that deck between his shuffling to the two of them. "You know I got everythin' I need right here in this fine upstanding establishment, and anythin' I don't, I can get across the street at Mother Superior's." He pointed at the door, and despite his face essentially composed of matte painted paneling and those chromed mouthparts, he was just as expressive as any real human Brann had known. "Ain't never had trouble makin' money, ain't never had trouble gettin' where I was goin', and now you wanna impose this life of servitude on me, I mean c'mon..."

Boomer spotted Brann and Nes, waving them over cheerfully to their table, even as he continued his negotiations. "I know, believe me, I totally get where you're coming from—if I had this sweet a gig, I wouldn't want to give it up either!" Boomer leaned in close, swiping up his cards to look at them briefly before fanning them facedown again. "This town—this outpost, they can always get a new sheriff, but how many times you get offered a deal as sweet as mine? Piloting the Donnie, of all ships—I mean, it sells itself. You wouldn't just be set for life; you'd get to see the whole world and would never have to break up another barfight again to do it!"

The—sheriff? Brann didn't understand this word fully—gave a sigh that, for all its humanity, carried with it a distinct electronic echo. "The world ain't as impressive as you make it sound, I've seen it all before, believe me." The android's eyes didn't even break contact with the waitress beside him as his hand flipped up the cards he'd dealt himself before slapping them back down just as quickly, barely regarding the game he was playing with Boomer.

"Tell you what, friend. Your hand beats mine here, I sign on; if not, you get me free box seats to your next five fights along with spares for me and—"

"Sativa."

"—Sativa here, thanks doll," the automaton regarded the waitress, thumbing a scalene patronizingly down below her beltline. "'Course, the rest of the boys here—" he motioned to the onlooking crowd, "—We don't gotta tell you who the winner of these obvious little wagers always ends up being. I mean..." He leaned back, letting his black trenchcoat fall open wider to show off his golden silk shirt and dark trousers. "...How do you think I pay for these legendary suits?"

"You do wear nice suits," Boomer allowed, visibly jealous.

Brann pieced together things quickly: Boomer was following "his own" advice from earlier and recruiting a pilot for the ship. The horse wheeled the young man around to stand next to him at the table, Nes falling back to light up another cig in the meantime. "Hey, kid, this is my new friend, goes by Hawkshaw," said Boomer, motioning to the automaton, "but only because his birthname is so impossible to say."

"Listen, if you meatbags all walked around having to introduce yourselves by numerical designators like 'S-I-C-A-TWO-SEVEN' at all your family reunions, then maybe getting together for the holidays wouldn't be so miserable to y'all," Hawkshaw retorted, mimicking Nestor and lighting up a cigarillo of his own—though Brann didn't see any open flame on this one, the tip glowing in a similar fashion to his own artificial eyes, and the smoke he breathed out was more like an opaque purple fog than the bluer wisps of Nestor's yamweed. "You'd be forced to have a conversation with each other longer than two goddamned seconds, wouldn't that be something," he finished with a laugh, dealing another pair of cards to himself and to Boomer.

"SICA-27—I mean, uh, Hawkshaw here," Boomer said mockingly, correcting himself only after the cocked brow of Hawkshaw's side-eyed blink, "Has agreed to be our pilot if I can beat him at carousels. Of course, what he doesn't know even with that magic encyclopedia jar-brain of his is that not only am I the best fighter on the continent, but I've never lost a game of cards. Least of all to a walking microwave."

"Nor I!" Hawkshaw proclaimed triumphantly with another bellow of purple vapors, tucking his electronic cigarillo back behind his (ear? fin?) and rotating his torso to finally face Boomer at the table. "So, let's begin. Six-card meld, three hand draw, should be easy enough even with those big sausages bending my nice cards—hey, take it easy big fella, seriously."

The two of them were ribbing incessantly, but it made Brann feel immediately at ease in the busy bar; they'd become instant friends and it showed, despite their jabs. What Hawkshaw didn't notice was that Nes had drawn away from the table and receded elsewhere into the bar—through a gap in the crowd, Brann could see him slip a pair of carousel cards into one patron's rear pocket casually, standing aside to watch what happened next unfold.

The man had come to his feet to celebrate his own winnings,

swiping a handful of scales across the table towards himself and away from his defeated opponent, a red-faced poemole who looked completely crestfallen. When the winner turned to clap his wingman on the shoulder, the poemole spotted the ears of those cards peeking out from the man's back pocket and immediately stumbled to his feet with a cry that the entire bar could hear:

"Oi, prick, gimme them fackin' scales back! You done cheated me, ya fat cunt!" With that, he swiped his claws across the man's face, turning his jaw into red ribbons before being tackled by another bystander.

The riot broke out instantly, chairs splintering as bodies were hurled, the hapless winner falling to the floor and clutching his face as it pooled red onto the dusty wooden boards beneath him. Immediately Hawkshaw was on his feet, cards flat on the table as he excused himself from the game and the waitress with a courteous bow. "Sirs, ma'am, all apologies, back in a tick."

The poemole was standing over his fallen opponent, pummeling him with a leg of his own stool, then came to a stop when he realized the noise all around him had silenced as quickly as it began—turning his head, his bloodied snout met with the tall blocky barrel of a compact autopistol. The whine of the electronic magloader was the only sound audible now, Hawkshaw's calm demeanor never waning even as he prodded his weapon into the rowdy patron's face.

"Now now, lads, let's keep things down to a dull roar, if'n you please," he crooned, the lidded eyes of the android betraying a killer's smile in place of his friendly roguish glow. "You're interruptin' some important business opportunities I'm negotiatin', not to mention my date with Saliva—"

"Sativa."

"—Sativa over there," he corrected. "I'm hopin' we can resolve this amicably. Let's say you deduct your fair winnings from the cost of this cheater's medical bill no doubt incurred by your mistaken departure from your civil self. I'd say that's an even deal for everyone here that keeps Mother

Superior from havin' to come over and intervene herself, wouldn't y'all?"

The poemole didn't answer right away, just enough time for the man with the bleeding face to sidle up behind Hawkshaw with a sawed-off rifle being drawn up to his waist—and faster than Brann could shout out a warning to the android, Hawkshaw's opposite clawed hand had smoothly unholstered a second autopistol, rotating himself to lean back with arms akimbo pointing both weapons at both cardplayers, every motion he made bearing all the cool swagger of a seasoned gunslinger who knew he could draw faster than any living person.

"Unless I'm bein' asked to just settle this my preferred way in the here and now, given I don't recall provokin' such ill intent on *your* property, gentlemen," he drawled smugly, the air stiff with the sound of his charging twin pistols.

"I didn't cheat shit," the bloodied man hissed through clenched teeth, tossing aside the crumpled cards he'd pulled from his pocket. "This coward planted those cards on me before the game started so he could swindle me later out of my fair win, knowing he'd lose. I keep it all," he challenged, though he dared not raise his rifle any higher.

Like a disappointed father, Hawkshaw furrowed his metal brow at the poemole. "That true, Ginny? You cheatin' this cheater's cheated winnin's?"

Ginny spat. "Loik 'ell I is. 'E's a fackin' cunt who cain't take an' 'onest loss. Shoot 'im."

"Much as I'd enjoy obligin' that tender proposal of shootin' cunts, 'fraid I'll have to let this one off the hook, as I have more pressin' engagements to keep me from doin' the paperwork on this unsolved mystery after the two of you have been put under the sand," said Hawkshaw in an almost disappointed tone, flicking the barrels of both pistols to indicate both Ginny and Shredface should drop their weapons—both did sullenly, to which Hawkshaw politely curtsied and holstered his own.

"There, see? Decency in a world gone mad. You two have shown commendable restraint despite a truly unknowable enigma of shithead diplomacy tonight," the automaton sheriff said with the red tinge of killer's light fading from his piercing yellow eye lenses. "When we can't see our way to the truth, let's see our way to the bar for another round of cheap, disgusting swill, what do you two say?"

The two combatants grumbled, Shredface handing over a stack of bloody scales from his own winnings to Ginny, deciding he'd rather walk away with a few scars than losing the entirety of his gains. The two walked at an arm's length together back to the bar, and a few muted claps of appreciative admiration announced the resuming of the rest of the noise of the night's revelry, Hawkshaw swaggering back to his seat across from Boomer. "Your indulgence is forever appreciated, my compatriots," said Hawkshaw as he dropped himself back onto his stool, giving a disappointed double-take at the sudden unexplainable absence of his loyal waitress friend. "Six card meld, was it?"

What Hawkshaw hadn't noticed was right about the time he'd drawn his second pistol in the prior commotion, Boomer had snuck a peek at both hands and replaced one card from his own with one from the middle of the deck, then moved the top three cards to the bottom, taking care to tuck the displaced cards back in to straighten the stack together. With his muzzle sitting atop both hands, he gave a comical performance of unrestrained awe at Hawkshaw's display of conflict resolution, the horse's eyes wide and doey.

"I'm so impressed I can't even speak real words, my goodness," he lied, never having trouble speaking in his life. "You gotta join my ship now, you and the soldat here could turn the Donnie into a real crew of hard knocking killers before the week is out!"

Hawkshaw bathed in the fake worship, batting aside the compliment with a bashful hand. "Please, all in a night's work. See how these shitheads can't get along without me to keep the peace? By week's end they'd be pulling each...other's..."

His swagger dropped away as he drew his three cards from the top of the deck, Hawkshaw knowing he'd lost before even letting Boomer have his turn to draw.

"...Balls off." He let his six cards fall to the table face up, the suits matching about as well as his own. "Well shit."

Boomer elbowed Brann gleefully and drew his three, cackling like a madman all the while. Hawkshaw clicked his eye lenses shut to wipe them and pinch his elongated face as if he had a nose, giving a defeated sigh and standing to button his trenchcoat. "Well, I know where this is going, and as much as I can't abide them, I suppose spending the rest of my life bumpin' off cheaters ain't as rewardin' as bumpin' elbows with good, honest types like yourselves." Hawkshaw offered his hand to Nestor who had appeared wordlessly with a face that could have been carved from stone, shaking the automaton's hand with a nod.

"More honesty you could not find among this crew, believe it, friend," Boomer chuckled, still elbowing Brann with all the subtlety of a jackhammer.

Nestor held out his holoscreen for Hawkshaw to sign, the android's clawed middle finger splitting open around a stylus to do so. "Welcome abord, Captain," said the older man, giving a small salute to the ship's new permanent captain.

After a small time spent cleaning up after themselves and Boomer finishing off his drink, Brann pulled Boomer aside as the four of them made for the exit. "I thought Zay was still the captain for now?" He whispered to the horse.

"Shhh," Boomer hushed him, waving down the comment to the floorboards. "Don't let him hear, I picked him out for more than just how well he can fly the ship, just trust me."

They'd crossed the threshold of the door now and stood out in the twilight, looking out at another fight that was about to break out in the street in the middle of the crowd.

Although Brann didn't think this one would end nearly as

peacefully.

121

8. The Chaperone

The street had cleared out around a recent display of violence, the crowd encircling the scene with gasps and whispered condemnations of what they saw—somewhere between Boomer's crew entering the Quartermaster and now, a more lethal confrontation had taken place than the scuffle back at the bar. In the center of the ring of bystanders, a man was spread eagle on the ground, with the biggest and broadest looking spear Brann had ever seen in his life driven straight down through his abdomen—the design of the weapon immediately recalled to him the strange design of Marshal Tark's great battleaxe, hinged and segmented in odd ways. Next to the corpse crouched an oversized dog sniffing at the man's shocked face. A brilliant, crimson tricorne hat with the bill arched forward like the beak of a bird of prey was clutched in the man's hand, a snowy white feather as tall as the hat was long gently swaying in the breeze.

The fingers of the dead man relaxed just enough to release his hold on the cap, and the wind lifted the red garment, sending it rolling end over end towards the crowd like a tumbleweed. The hat came to a sudden halt at the tip of a pointed boot so polished it gleamed even in the faded evening light, and the owner stooped low to retrieve it, white gloved hand smacking away the dust before placing it atop their head. When the tip of the hat's forwardmost point was straightened in place, the figure strode forward gracefully, boots crunching audibly on the sand over the muted chatter of the crowd. Ruby red coat hanging low, matching the hat; a saber in a dark polished sheath, matching the boots—no more striking an outfit could be seen in this traveler's humble outpost tonight, save for that of Boomer or Hawkshaw, as the woman held her pale chin high with all the pomp of a noblewoman. The blood-red corsair tugged away a few errant strands of platinum blonde hair and came to a stop at the corpse, looking down at the body distastefully.

"Look what you've gone and done, you great oaf. This close to our own salvation, no less," she purred with all the regret in her voice of a cat who had swiped open the belly of an invasive rat. Brann didn't understand, however, why she was talking to the dog, when clearly someone had killed the man with a spear.

He had his answer immediately, and with it, another reminder to expect the unexpected out here in the wilderness of the world. The oversized dog stood to its full height—and not to all fours, either, but its FULL height, the great canine rising higher and higher until the bipedal beast toward even over his human companion. His face shielded from Brann's view, the young man could still see the gunmetal blue-gray fur of the canid rising and falling across his shoulder-blades, the dangerous growling breaths of the beast reaching Brann's ears. A muscled arm, vascular enough the thick veins were visible even through the thick pelt, reached out to wrap impossibly lethal looking claws around the spear and—with all the resistance of an apple being plucked from a tree—yanked the weapon free of the corpse's ribcage. A geyser of still-warm blood jettisoned from the wound and sprayed directly across the front of the canine, who didn't even bother to react. The rest of the crowd, however, understandably gasped in shock, one man even keeling over to retch at the sight of human innards spilling out onto the sand.

The ruby red noblewoman tsked and drew a handkerchief from her coat, leaning in close to the beast to mop up some of the blood. "Honestly, you're worse than me, and I deal in the stuff by the barrel," she was fussing under her breath, and Brann felt a breeze at his back blowing towards her. "You simply cannot outright murder every fool who makes a grab for my hat," she continued, pocketing the handkerchief and reaching up to hold the canine's still-soaked face with her immaculate white gloves—as if the act of using the kerchief were simply for show, those gloves immediately soaking in blotted ruby red that matched the rest of her outfit.

A moment of silence, that ragged breathing fierce and rumbling, and then a reply was rasped forth:

"Watch me."

The beast spoke—of course it did. Those back muscles heaved once more before stiffening, and Brann heard sniffing—then saw the noblewoman's eyes dart in his direction.

A scent had caught the beast's attention. His hunched shoulders rolled back and the back of his head raised with it, before the entire frame of the creature lurched, causing the crowd—and Brann—to startle. Vibrant amber and black eyes of tragic fury blazed out from underneath a furred brow that nonetheless could cut steel with its permanent frown. Those eyes locked directly onto Brann, and no one else—and Brann knew he was the target, those eyes the most honest of any creature alive, and fear as cold and slippery as that fear he'd felt on the day of his Assay squirming up his colon and alongside his spine.

The great wolf exhaled, a breath powerful enough to knock the ghost free from Brann's skeleton, and raised his spear to point directly at the young soldat in a manner that said, uncompromisingly, unmistakably, *I know who you are, and I know your sins. Be ready for me.*

The crowd shifted backwards, away from Brann, who realized he could be next to fall under the wolf's spear—before an incredible thing happened that spared him. A single finger, bloodied white satin, touched with the gentlest of sensibilities against the very tip of the dripping weapon...and like a leaf in a storm, the broad bladed head of the weapon fell away, slamming into the sand with a loud chunk. The corsair woman stood beside the wolf now, also staring at Brann, but with far less murder in her eyes—though they were no warmer, Brann saw, those irises an icy blue as deep as the most frightening ocean.

"Save thy fangs for worthy prey, my love," said the woman, that same hand as delicate as a porcelain doll's lifting the wolf's chin with a soothing stroke. The beast's brow softened ever so slightly, and though he never took his eyes off Brann, his shoulders relaxed as well, retaining their more natural looking hunched appearance. "This one means no ill, nor should you him. Just a young pup on the road, as you once were."

The crowd muttered to each other still, yet despite even among them several bearing fearsome looking armaments, none dared step forward to challenge the two blood-soaked outsiders. The wolf's eyes flickered, and

Brann sensed some form of recognition sparking behind them, before he heaved another great inhuman sigh and swung his spear up to rest it across his shoulder—again, in a manner strikingly similar to Tark's own posturing at the Assay. The lady let the wolf sag against her, bumping foreheads and whispering soothing words to him even Brann couldn't hear above the wind, and the ferocity of the killer animal melted away before his very eyes until he was as complacent as a common dog.

The silence was finally broken by a strangled laugh Brann recognized as Boomer's. "Holy shit everyone, there's a werewolf right here in town," he guffawed, his laugh as ripe with fear as Brann was. "You guys seeing this?"

Nestor collided angrily with Boomer to shut the loudmouthed idiot up, but it was Hawkshaw who made the first move, the inorganic being stepping forward with confidence that matched the noblewoman's— not to confront the two, but to Brann's surprise, to stroll right on past as if they weren't there and instead cross the street to the brothel. The click of Hawkshaw's boots on the wooden steps roused the attention of the establishment's owner, and from just within the bead-curtained entryway, the devilish looking caprine floated forth to greet Hawkshaw with open arms.

"Sith culva, my darling Hawkshaw," the caprine rasped, her pronunciation indicating this was not her native tongue she spoke. "Howth reckon sie spactickal, hmm?"

"Actually, I was gonna ask you just the same thing, ma'am," Hawkshaw grinned back, speaking with the same respect and reverence he would his own mother. "My new friends and I were distracted by other nefarious goings-ons inside the bar, I was hoping you could fill me on this here scuffle."

"Ack ack! Nith sie," she croaked, her jangling earrings swinging all about as she waved away Hawkshaw's inquiry, crossing both hooved arms over her more-than-ample bosom. "Carryin' oon hik-way and hak, noth sie den manners—sie den grabbin' dem doe's cap," she said, motioning at the noblewoman. "Non spake die wulfen. Sie den gotten ill-good whatkonin, reckon sie." She spat, jabbing a finger at the corpse. "None spake, none."

"Now, that wasn't very nice of him, was it, Mother?" Hawkshaw said appreciatively, looking back at the dead body none-too-impressed with the story being laid out to him. "Reckon I'd have done the same, were our places in time contrary to one another." He motioned to the werewolf.

The cross demeanor of the caprine faded, and she glowed up at Hawkshaw, raising her hooves to clap them against his metal-plated face in much the same way the corsair woman did the wolf just moments ago. "Sie spake nith, darling, den whatkonin raised upsen right."

"Well, I have you to thank for that, ma'am," Hawkshaw said with a kiss on her wrist. "One regret I have for you on this fine day of days, though, I bring to you with a heavy heart. My friends and I will be departing this eve to visit places far hence, and it's my fear I may not be back for some time."

Mother Superior tutted and knocked a hoof gently against Hawkshaw's forehead. "Nith sie. Gent den hence, sie foal, nith spake none sooths. Ein giventh sie all den giventh, nith 'regret', nith sadth. Allen love, darling Hawkshaw, allen love."

The quietude and vulnerability with which Hawkshaw responded made Brann almost imagine he could see a tear rolling down the automaton's plated cheek. "Allen love, Mother," he whispered, giving her wrist another kiss before releasing her. The android kept his glowing eyes on her before turning to clop down the wooden steps again, drawing his coat about him as a melancholy wind swept it open, his clawed hands jamming themselves in his pockets as he returned to the violent scene in the street.

"Mother Superior explained the whole situation to me, so you've nothing to worry about," Hawkshaw addressed the corsair woman, keeping a respectful distance from her wolf bodyguard. "Had to about enact a similar course of street justice inside the bar not a moment hence, else I'd've been here to intervene on these proceedings my good self," he said, motioning to the body of the man that not a person in the world seemed too interested in defending. "My associates here, they're travelling with a smalltime trader who is accompanying two as-of-yet-undiscovered folks to places decidedly more civil than this. Might I guess that'd be you two?"

The noblewoman drew one hand up to bow, the other on the hilt of her saber. "I've an accord with the mercenary Zaydat Kadzhieva, myself and my champion here were to be returned to a safe port of my saying outside the Wilds. If she travels with you, we are indeed your wards."

Hawkshaw crooked an eye at Brann, who nodded. "Yeah, Zay's with us, she's uh..." He swallowed, noting that the werewolf was still staring directly at him. "She was meant to meet you here, actually, we just came down from the ship to look for her when we realized she'd been gone longer than expected."

Hawkshaw queried: "And you still haven't made contact with this mercenary?"

"Nay." The lady in red removed her bloodied gloves—and with an impressive level of foresight, drew a pair fresh from her coat, freshly white and unblemished, drawing them over her skin that was almost as pale as the gloves themselves. "The miscreant in the street introduced himself as an associate of hers as well." She too noticed Brann still fixed in the wolf's stare, and added, "You must forgive our suspicions as a result of this. Were we to have been greeted directly, no doubt we'd have departed ages ago, before any threat of violence had been raised."

Hawkshaw turned back to Brann. "And you haven't seen Zay since she left your ship earlier this afternoon?"

"Not once," Nes replied in Brann's stead. "Said she'd have been back in minutes. Only thing keeping us from finding her sooner being a short interfacing with this fine crowd of pilgrims to spread our leader's merchandise," he said with a less-than-gentle backhanded slap on Boomer's chest, who pouted.

"Zaydat Kadzhieva, anyone recognize the name?" Hawkshaw called out to the crowd, scanning their reactions. "Anyone seen her, spoken with her today?"

There was silence. Then, a single voice, quiet and humble.

"I have, yes."

The crowds parted a bit, and a man approached Hawkshaw. No more assuming than any other travelled street vagrant, his old clothes vaguely resembled the garb of a holyman on a pilgrimage. His round wide-brimmed hat shielded him from even the most inclement of weather, everything about him dusted and worn. Even his hands seemed bandaged as if from long-forgotten injury, Brann noticed.

The man continued speaking with an eloquence quite unbefitting his raggedy appearance. "I spoke with a Miss Zaydat just up the road. She described a rendezvous with two clients she was meant to travel with, though I fear one or both of us must have spoken in error, as I mistakenly directed her to wait at my parish beyond the radish fields. Had I known more about the identity or, indeed, unmistakable appearance of her intended liaisons, I certainly would have asked her to remain in town," he said, bowing regretfully. "While I have no wish to intervene in what is no doubt meant to be a private matter, if one or both of Miss Zay's clients wish to accompany to my parish, we would no doubt find her waiting with thumbs twiddling."

Hawkshaw turned back. "I can vouch for Emrys myself; he's been a forthright visitor in his short time here, and has been eminently helpful whenever called upon. Any objections to this arrangement?"

Ignoring the low growl of her canine guard, the ruby red woman held up a parlaying hand. "In relative candor I regretfully must not be allowed to leave the safety of the town until my hired pilot makes her return, as we must retain some..." She regarded her companion's bloodied fur with irony. "...Discretion. More dangerous than a common vagabond is the nature of our pursuant. I am confident the rest of Zay's party may make a suitable temporary replacement for my good friend here, who would be happy to see you safely to your parish to retrieve our contact."

The woman bowed again. "Forgive me. I must similarly keep an air of anonymity about our journey. You may call me The Lady Red, and my guard The Wolf. I wager no greater need for memorable monikers than what simple appearances allow will be required in our short time together."

The Wolf looked between Hawkshaw, Nestor, and Boomer, immediately disapproving of them as worthy guardsmen to Lady Red, but nonetheless respecting her decision to accompany the holyman to his parish. One more turn, and The Wolf's eyes once again locked onto Brann. Brann did not stare back.

"Then we'll make a short trip of it," said Emrys, motioning to the street. "With all sensitivity and respect for his proven killing prowess, may The Lady Red direct the Wolf to accompany me, the understanding being that I mean no harm?"

The Wolf didn't wait for a command and lurched forward, elbowing past Hawkshaw to stand behind the holyman, hunched low with his spear at his hip. The Lady Red nodded. "Speak as respectfully as that and with direct intent, you'll have no trouble as a guest to his obedience," she said, rattling her own saber as well. "He worries a great deal for me, but despite an overprotective nature, he knows as well as I the killing prowess shared between us is complementary."

Boomer leaned in close behind Brann to whisper quietly, "I really don't understand all these big words flying around, man."

"Then the Wolf and Emrys will be off," the holyman said, giving a bow of his own. "Likewise, apologies for not introducing myself sooner, but I deign not presume any familiarity when bodies are in the street. We will retrieve this Zaydat and see you all off before the moon peaks tonight."

The crowd shifted again, all the silent bystanders like an audience at an engrossing holoplay watching the Wolf and Emrys depart. Brann turned as Emrys brushed past, an incomplete thought forming in his mind before he felt something heavy on his shoulder.

He turned his head slowly. It was The Wolf's pawlike hand, draped there as if by mistake.

"Him." The beast beside him growled, the sound low and rumbling, vibrating Brann's sternum.

All at once, Emrys, Hawkshaw, The Lady Red, Boomer and Nestor all turned simultaneously to stare, all equally taken aback by this. None moreso than Brann himself, who was suddenly very aware of how much he was sweating despite the cold evening air.

"Him?" One or more of them said, Brann couldn't tell which.

The Wolf didn't repeat himself, once was enough. He tapped the butt of his spear impatiently on the sand.

The Lady Red seemed to have more insight into this than was obvious, though even she seemed confused. Nonetheless, she leaned in to whisper something to Emrys, who adjusted his spectacles and cleared his throat.

"Yes, of course, this won't be a problem. Two strangers may make an ill-advised pass at bringing Lady Zay around back to camp. Better to be accompanied by a familiar face. Yes, let's bring the young man along. I trust you are appropriately armed for a short hike through the fields?" Emrys said with a tilt of his head, the merest of gestures sloping his broad hat at the most extreme of angles.

His rifle was still comfortably stowed aboard the Donnie. Brann was about to say no before the Lady Red herself stepped forward, unlooping the snowy sash keeping her saber strapped to her belt and offering it up hilt-first. "My blade will make do. No threat that has slipped past The Wolf's spear has bested my saber in turn. I only ask that you..." She cleared her throat. "...Try to wield it with some dignity. Not as a blunt instrument to be swung about willy nilly."

Brann almost retorted with a comment that included his military training, but, seeing Nestor's face, toned it down significantly. "I'll do my best. I've been given the best in close quarters combat training the instructors at Geiha have to offer."

The Wolf bristled, and The Lady raised an eyebrow, but otherwise did not acknowledge this. "See our guide back safely, a goodly sum of money was paid to ensure this journey was carried out safely."

A small sound, the rapping of a hoof against metal, made Hawkshaw turn in muted surprise. Mother Superior had sidled up behind him like a ghost, regarding Brann with a fixed stare not unlike the same one The Wolf had been giving him. Brann was very uncomfortable with how many people found him so interesting all of a sudden.

"Hearen layway, sith, on momenth," the caprine said, the goat speaking in a somewhat authoritative manner to the automaton. "Dem foal nieth hoolen Mudar Superi's takken tarry. Sooth sayen, himmen nieth."

Hawkshaw shrugged, then regarded Brann to translate. "Mother Superior would like a moment to speak with you before you leave. Or, more accurately, demands it. She's something of the mayor around these parts; I'd do what she asks. It won't take but a moment. Gives us some time to put together a more complete picture of what went down here."

The older caprine woman stood at about Brann's height but nonetheless conveyed great import, tapping her hooved fingers expectantly against Hawkshaw's arm as she waited for an answer.

"I don't see why not," Brann finally relented.

The goatmother grinned wide, beckoning him to follow her into the brothel. "Kommen. "

*

The bead curtains parted around them as the caprine led Brann into her home and business by the hand, her hooves clamped somewhat uncomfortably around his wrist, despite his protests that he could follow without aid. The dim lights of the pleasure den cast spiraling clouds of dense smoke down on Brann's head, the oil-infused vapors making him feel somewhat lightheaded, a prickling sensation on his skin —he did his best not to look any of the onlooking patrons in the eye, the main hall of the house leading off into a half dozen different passages and stairways all lined with their own locked doors and curtains, some with a waiting courtesan just outside.

Mother Superior guided him past the mostly empty couches of the waiting area, into a side hall with no doors of any kind, culminating in a sort of open floor study where a desk stood in the center of the chairless room. The circular walls were all lined with paintings and pictographs of various subjects, mostly nude—and at first glance they had Brann already blushing, seeing not just humans, but all manner of species and genders, some even hybridized in a way he didn't think possible: features both male and female blended into one another, defying his natural understanding of sexuality, and it took all he had not to stare agog at the dizzying array of strange eroticism.

Mother Superior paid no mind to his visible discomfort, however, leading him to stand before the desk and taking her place opposite him, leaning forward to examine Brann closely. "Spaketh die tonguen 'Zoic?'"

Brann blinked. "What?"

She scoffed, her silky robes a flurry as she waved his ignorance away dismissively. "Stupid! Allen love, sie foalen. Ekk spaketh ein die simplath, orren tryth." She took a breath, jawing at the air as if chewing cud, then spoke again—slower, obviously outside her native language, labored in a way that Brann could better understand. "Yewen—ach, nie, 'you'—have kommen from..." She tapped her hoof against his breastplate. "Die House off 'Geiha', Barrier City, yessum?"

Brann clapped his heels together in the proper manner. "Yes ma'am. Corpsman regiment."

Mother Superior laughed at this, the sound rattly and stilted, more akin to the bleating of a real goat. "So strong and big, yah?" She chuckled, crossing her arms, looking him up and down. "The wolfen out dere. You know why he stare so curiously?"

"I don't, ma'am." Brann felt his face flush red a bit, obviously not impressing her with his rigid display. "Because he wants to eat me, I'd guess?"

Her fingers were at his cheek, digging into the flesh painfully, and Brann flinched with an offended cry of shock. "What he do, braise die foalen in whiskey? No fat! No flavor!" She reached into a drawer on her side of the desk, fishing out a long cigarillo—the longest Brann had ever seen—and held it to the solitary candle that stood without a holder in the center of the desk, held upright by the melted remains of countless candles long past, the wax forming a small mountain that spread outwards and infused itself into the surface of the wood. Her weed lit, Mother Superior chewed thoughtfully at the end of the cig, still appraising Brann in her own mysterious way, letting the smoke swirl around her in a blue haze. "Where you go?"

Brann was about to respond by relaying the plans made outside to act escort to the parish, but realized she meant in a more general sense. "I'm accompanying Boomer to his next fight, acting as guard to his ship on behalf of Geiha. After that, I don't..." He frowned, then shook his head. "I don't really know what I'm doing, where I'm going." Something about the vapors in the air, they wore him down, lowered his guard—he didn't feel as nervous about keeping up appearances in front of this woman, feeling drawn to her despite her somewhat alarming appearance he still couldn't quite reconcile.

Mother Superior didn't like this, her wrist crooking to one side, her head to the other, squinting at Brann. "You run," she said, catching Brann entirely off guard. "From someone—nay. Summat more. Youself."

Brann shifted in discomfort, feeling sweat begin to run down his back, mind feeling somewhat foggy from these aromatics coating his lungs. "I don't know what you mean, I'm task—I'm on a mission, on task, to escort—"

She silenced Brann with another unconvinced wave, fanning the smoke around her head in the process, the caprine not buying his act one bit. "You have business, not mine, not concern," she said, meaning his desertion. "I deal in dis...this...place, this people, suitors, men, beast, and other. Dis ein home of...pleasure, yes," she said wryly, gesturing behind herself at a rather flattering painting of a caprine woman that looked suspiciously like her, albeit several decades younger, the stylized brushwork denoting features on her naked body Brann would have guessed belonged to someone closer to his own gender. "Pleasure hist nie purpose—purpose, I want to give to allen their self." She pointed two fingers accusingly at Brann. "Their truth. Foalen wear shining armor, color of House proper— wear no truth on you, I see." A tug at the cigarillo, and smoke was blown back into Brann's face, making him blink, but otherwise he didn't protest.

He felt ashamed, exposed. Brann cast his eyes low—not just to avoid staring at the pictures, but because he found himself looking inward, despite himself. "I mean no one any harm," he pleaded, feeling like a child being scolded by his own mother. This must be why she carried the title. "I had to get away from that place. Those people." He swallowed, finding painful memories welling up inside him unbidden. "Not just Geiha, not just the military. All of them. That place, that city. All that...shit."

Brann kept himself from elaborating further on that, but the near-admission was not lost on Mother Superior, who nodded in understanding, despite her scrutinizing gaze. "Truth ist nay painful. Pain come from looking for truth, looking for self." She replaced her hooved hand on his breast, gently this time, patting the armor. "Run from self, run from pain— run from truth. No. Run to truth. Run to pain, and when pain finds you, raisen fist. Howl, and bark, and show pain self. When pain is gone, you will find truth." She removed her hand, taking another drag of the cig. "The other one you run from. The kuaneach."

Brann raised his eyes to meet hers, trying not to let the tears fall. "The Marshal."

"Mhmmm..." She nodded knowingly. Mother Superior seemed to know everything, Brann began to feel, the longer they spoke. "The greaten Axe of The Roost. The Iron Tark. Allen rage, allen war. Hundred battles, he foughten, hundred years he rise." She pointed to her own ample bosom. "Almost olden as Mudar Superi, him. Spent many nights together, himmen and dis old momma."

Brann coughed in shock, nearly falling over. "You had sex with Marshal Tark?!"

Mother Superior's hooved fingers snapped at his ear faster than a striking viper, the sound loud enough to feel like a slap across his face, Brann flinching and falling silent. "Hikk, stupid foalen! When yewen offren pleasure of body uppen tie nieth amouren, interm die sith privvy, hikk faithless, cor!"

She spat on the ground, then inhaled deeply to calm herself, adjusting her tongue once more to resume speaking more patiently after her bilingual outburst.

"All apologies. Young, stupid, yes, but. Still run, you are. Still run from pain. Pain follow." She jingled her wrist bracelets, placing a hand on her breast. "Pain teach. Pain is a master. Learn to respect...the truth of others. The love of allen, even if only one night. One day. Allen love, we say, allen love give us the way to live true." She prodded at Brann's shoulder in gentle reprimand. "Even when allen others mean those we fight. Those enemy chase us, harm us."

"Sorry, you're right, I shouldn't have asked," he said sheepishly, clearly infringing on a sore subject that was none of his business. Still, he couldn't imagine the commanding officer ever removing those Geihan colors, least of all to bed a woman. Putting this image out of his mind, Brann was at a loss—he wasn't sure what a conversation with the caprine woman would have entailed, but the absolute whirlwind of emotion buffeting him was nothing he could have prepared for, standing here in her brothel—her home.

"Why am I here?" He cautiously ventured.

She took a particularly long drag, the goat's eyes narrowing once more, looking almost sorrowful as she spoke again, this time much quieter. "You run from pain—great pain. Not just Geiha. Fear of war. Yes?"

Brann swallowed, and nodded. "Yes."

Mother Superior blew the smoke out of her slitted nostrils, her leathery dark lips pursing as she regarded Brann now as tenderly as he felt she could manage. "Then great pain you must find. Run toward. Not from. Run with allen might, raise fist high. And prepare to lose."

She inhaled more smoke, leaving Brann to process this. "You mean to say," he said after a few moments, his brow furrowed. "You want me—I'm supposed to stop running from Tark, and...face him? Fight him?" He was baffled by this notion, eyes blinking rapidly. "Have you seen the size of him? That axe? Yeah, no shit I'd lose."

The caprine shook her head, frustrated at his lack of understanding. "Sieth foalen, allen love, allen love," she said soothingly, attempting to speak her meaning into him. Brann sensed her limitations of their language barrier were being reached, and her face was cracking into an expression that regarded him with a kind of remorse that sent chills through him. "Nay, nay, foalen, nay. Allen fall away—yewen run, when fear guide you—fight when fear turn to face you. The Iron Tark, he chase, always, his way, his truth to find you: you, no truth, only run, always run. Until allen you hold in dem hands be dat fear, dat pain—allen lost. You will lose..." She put the cigarillo out in the wax, quietly snuffing out the ember. "...Everything. Allen."

Brann set his jaw, growing impatient. Who was she to tell him what to do, to tell him that he would lose everything? There was nothing to lose if he kept running, kept riding Boomer's coattails comfortably, never having to show his face in Geiha again.

"I don't get what you're trying to say at all, I'm sorry," he said, doing his level best not to sound rude. "I don't think you know enough about me to say that."

Mother Superior rounded the table slowly, coming to Brann's side, resting a hand on his shoulder—then her chin on that hand. The golden arrowhead irises around her black, slitted pupils widened as she took in his face, vision seeing through him, into him. The sage old goatmother's bearded chin tickled him as she spoke now, so close to his own face, her breath smelling of warm pastures and berries.

"Don't be so sure," she whispered, pronounced with almost perfect diction now. "Mother sees much, knows much. And Mother knows best." She let her other arm wrap around his waist—a gesture that would have seemed forward and make Brann recoil, were it not for the turmoil of emotion within him, past and future at odds in a bloody conflict that registered as a stony jaw and a rivulet of tears down his cheeks. "You need not run to Iron Tark. The blade that seeks you will find you, when time intenden. When you have lost all, when you and pain remain alone, you will know your truth."

Her scratchy lips met his cheek, kissing away a salty tear, Brann crumbling into her warm embrace. "You will know yourself. And allen left for you will be the love you deserve."

Brann nodded, still adrift in uncertain thoughts and unease at such prophetic inclinations, but he nonetheless found a small warm comfort in the center of himself as she spoke, a tiny beacon of purpose. "Am I a coward for running away?" He asked.

She sighed, the goatmother holding his head in her hands. "Yes," she admitted, prompting a nervous chuckle from Brann, not expecting such bluntness. "Yet, also think on: no foalen, no boy, young and lost, is no coward. Only dem fool heart never runs, and will surely stop beating afore his time kommen, when learning to run must kommen just as learning to walk. When your legs give out, when your breath is dagger in dem chest: when run as far as dem can, then a coward dies, and dem—you—are born at last."

Mother Superior released him from the hug, leaving Brann feeling somewhat cold, strangely missing her touch. "You frienden—they allen distant, frayed, unkind in turn," she said with caution, walking towards the main hall. "You, alone, will be—allen is well, foalen, I 'seech you bide and endure. When the coward is gone, they always learn to love, but barbs and cold eyes will prick all the while."

She turned to bow. "Matter not, worry not. Only you matter. One day, allen love." She smiled, disappearing into the haze of the brothel, her voice calling out from afar:

"One day, you love yourself."

Brann stood there, feeling overwhelmed, like he'd been cut open and sewn back shut by the kindest and yet sadistic person he'd ever met, and may ever meet. He took the moment of silence to compose himself, wiping his eyes carefully so as not to rub them red—he'd been apart from the group only a few minutes, and it wouldn't do him any favors to reemerge looking as if he had been crying.

He looked up at the paintings and the pictographs on the walls— lewd, yes, uncomfortable, no doubt. But, a newfound understanding, if not appreciation, was forming in the depths of Brann's tumultuous young mind: though he may not yet understand it, as he gazed on high at the painting of the intersexed young Mother Superior, it was an important lesson embedded within the strokes of that painting that he was meant to learn from.

The way the caprine's eyes, lidded and inviting, gazed back down at him seemed to agree. When Brann first entered the room and saw the portrait; in his shock, he thought the image intended to arouse him, attract his gaze. Now he knew better: where Mother Superior stood at her desk, her line of sight was directed at the portrait of her younger body. It was meant for her eyes, not the eyes of others.

It was as much a mirror as it was a portrait. A reminder to love who she was, just the way she was.

"Yeah," Brann said quietly, shaking his head and staring at his boots, "I don't think I'm ready for that yet."

*

Emerging from the bead curtains, Brann was nearly blinded even in the low evening light, not realizing how dim it had been inside. The smell of herbs and vapors followed him for a moment, clinging to his clothes, and he took a breath of fresh air: realizing only then he'd likely been inhaling

138

some special cocktail of incense specifically formulated by the goatmother to break down inhibitions and allow someone to overcome their fears of the flesh.

Or of their own thoughts.

Emrys bowed stiffly to Brann, looking somewhat bothered by the delay, but keeping it to himself as he spoke only kindly words. "I pray it was a fruitful conversation shared between you two and nothing more distracting, given your armor remains intact and blouse unruffled?"

Brann didn't feel his usual need to defend himself from this gentle ribbing, watching from a distance as Hawkshaw once more leaned in to listen to Mother Superior whispering something in his ear. Though neither of them looked in his direction, something about the way the caprine patted the automaton's shoulder as she spoke made Brann think they were talking about him—if not what was said to him inside.

"Just a few words of warning as to what I can expect up ahead," Brann said, technically being honest. "I'm all set now, if you'll lead the way. And, you are correct," he added, a small burst of self-confidence rising unbidden to bolster his image of a dutiful soldat on the job. "We should avoid any and all delays on the road—my party is honorbound to see The Lady and her..." He nervously nodded to The Wolf. "...Friend...safely to their destination. Word is an assassin has tracked them to these parts, as I understand it, and we should give no reason to draw his attention."

"On that, we are in absolute agreement, Specialist," Emrys said with a tip of his rumpled hat. "If the canine protector and your good self will follow me, we shall be in the company of your missing friend before last call at the bar."

The trio struck out, the crowd parting around them as they went. Brann looked back, but didn't see Boomer or Nestor's faces before the lake of people converged on itself again. He did, however, see a pair of helpfuls carrying off the body of Lady Red's assailant, directed by Hawkshaw who pointed them outside of the town and towards the wide expanse of sand past the shipyard.

9. The Parish

The night was young still, the moon having yet to crest the treeline the three followed. The sand turned to dusty soil beneath Brann's crunching boots, his stride matching Emrys while he did his best to resist turning his head, keenly aware of the werewolf padding along almost silently behind them. His curiosity as to why he was a subject of interest to the creature was no greater than his desire to not be disemboweled for making any sudden moves or showing fear. Ultimately, he doubted conversation would get him very far to begin with. This he saved for the holyman, Brann looking Emrys up and down as they walked.

"I don't mean to criticize—you got any newer clothes than that? I know the outpost isn't the best for shopping, other than what those travelling merchants have, but I'm sure there's some spare threads back on our ship..."

Emrys tilted the brim of his wide circular hat, giving Brann a good look at the man's bandaged hands in the process—even those handwraps seemed ancient and tattered. "My thanks young sir, but truthfully I need little in the ways of personal goods, certainly not when it comes to putting on airs. All respect to your exceptionally well-dressed friends back there."

Brann rolled his eyes. "Trust me, I'm not the biggest fan either. Never really understood buying expensive clothes when it doesn't cost much to get something comfortable." He tugged at the hem of his own borrowed jacket, grateful he'd thought to leave the ship with warmer clothes than his own standard issue uniform. "Even so, you gotta want to, I mean..." He cleared his throat, searching for a polite way of saying this. "Clean up sometimes?" He offered.

Emrys slowed in his gait for a brief moment before holding up his hands sheepishly as he realized Brann's meaning. "I understand, being out on the road as long as I have, I suppose I am all but benumbed to my own hygiene. Rest assured, it is not a lack of shame, but rather an abundance of it, that keeps me a fringe citizen to these small settlements. I will confess, being humble and being unpleasant can be a fine line to walk when your mind is as prone to roaming abroad as your physical form."

Behind them, the mostly silent Wolf snorted. Apparently, he agreed with Brann on this matter.

"You can always come back with us and have a night to just take it easy, just have a reset, so to speak," Brann continued to offer, wondering how much his reach in inviting people aboard the Donnie extended. "Have a good meal, change of clothes, shower up. Let your humility take a vacation from you."

The bedraggled pilgrim pushed his spectacles up his nose and clasped those bandaged hands together softly. "A tempting proposal, and your kindness is a welcome balm to this weary wretch. I fear I must put aside any desires to oblige you, however, at least until the matter at hand is resolved—I've left this business too long unattended, and must atone for my negligence."

Brann didn't think it was that big a deal, Zay couldn't have been left alone waiting for too long—this Emrys character sure lived up to the stereotype of a self-flagellating man of the cloth, he thought. "Is this it up ahead?"

The path turned sharply around a steep bend, and a crumbled stone fence where a warped gate had curled in on itself gave way to the sight of a small ruined structure no bigger than the two houses back at Mother Superior's Outpost. The roof was long rotted away, and a sizeable portion of the wall facing them as well, the parish unfit for gatherings without a complete rebuilding of the foundation. Whether by earthquake or storm or other means, the stone floor had cracked apart in dozens of discordant directions, every gap filled in by mushrooms and weeds that sprouted like a fur carpet from below. There was more care paid to the cemetery that served also as a garden of sorts to the parish, the path crossing between carefully pruned and cultivated graves, flowers of all colors in freshly plucked arrangements placed across their marbled cylindrical surfaces. Better to attend to the dead than to the absent, Brann figured, noting the stark lack of interest in maintaining the church itself with the same devotion.

"I don't see her down there," said Brann, and indeed he imagined that Zay would be easy to spot waiting inside a building with no real roof or complete walls to speak of.

"Yes, I fear something may be amiss," agreed Emrys, his attitude becoming more cautious as they descended towards the parish. "Best be on our guard. Even this close to safe haven, a night in the Wilds is still just that."

Brann raised Lady Red's saber to keep close to him in case of danger. Behind him, he heard a yawn—The Wolf definitely didn't feel the same. Likely he didn't even know what fear meant.

The three formed a single file line on the narrowed path through the graveyard. Emrys's visage disappeared behind his raised and crooked collar, and Brann dared a glance behind him—The Wolf had his great spear on his shoulders with his powerful arms draped over them like a yoke, totally at ease. A unique configuration of human and animal hybrid, unlike the other inhuman races Brann had seen earlier, Boomer included—where Boomer managed to affect a decidedly familiar way of relaying entirely human emotions, as if it were a language class taken in primary school, The Wolf veered off into a comfortably bestial manner of carrying himself. The humanlike traits he exhibited were, as a result, that much more shocking, particularly when he vocalized or otherwise toyed with his spear as any seasoned human vanguard would.

The Wolf noticed Brann's glance had become a stare, and he returned it in kind, tilting his head with his ears perked in a way that challenged Brann to say something. He hadn't been unkind thus far, so Brann hesitated before testing the waters a bit.

"You holding up okay back there?"

Stupid. That was the best he could come up with?

The Wolf didn't verbalize his reply, but rather flicked his snout up sharply, the motion applying enough pressure to his neck from the spear yoked over his shoulders that a series of loud pops could be heard.

"Yeah, you're doing fine," Brann said mostly to himself as he turned back, unsure what he expected. Best keep chatter to a minimum, especially now that Emrys had come to a stop.

The holyman was at the top of the collapsed stone steps where the floor of the church just met them, not crossing the otherwise invisible threshold to enter the space properly. He had a hand crooked upwards by his waist, as if cautioning silence, the wobbly brim of his wide hat turning this way and that. Did he hear something they didn't?

The Wolf didn't think so, stepping forward and unshouldering his spear, pushing roughly past Brann to approach Emrys. His own ears were swiveling this way and that, his expression even more stern than normal—if a human could pick up some faint sound, there's no doubt he could as well. The werewolf's snout began to likewise turn to and fro, wet nostrils flaring as he sniffed the air.

"No one else here," he grumbled. If Zay had been here earlier, she'd departed by now.

Emrys turned back to face the two of them, his face somewhat puzzled. He reached into his coat, removing a small leatherbound book, the accessory just as tattered and worn as the rest of him. He opened and thumbed through its pages, brow furrowed thoughtfully, as if searching for a lost note he'd jotted down. Page after page he turned. Paper crinkled quietly, the slight sound carried on the wind to Brann's ears. Emrys didn't speak this entire time, simply searching his little book for some kind of answer.

The Wolf didn't have the patience for this. He raised the spear directly at Emrys, the tip pointing just below the man's chin. He snarled, and in proper fashion, spoke with the fewest words needed to convey his thoughts.

"Go."

Emrys looked up from his book. The kindly warmth had receded from his eyes.

"Yes, let's."

His bandaged hand clutched at his chosen page, tearing it free of the book and crushing the paper in his fist, which ignited in a shower of green sparks—then with no hesitation, laid that same hand flat alongside the spearhead as if shaking hands with a friend.

The weapon exploded with those same green sparks, Brann falling back to shield his eyes from the blinding burst, seeing through his fingers as the weapon spiraled away in the opposite direction of its owner, The Wolf being tossed aside like a ragdoll and being hurled bodily against a gravestone. The cylinder crunched from the impact, fissures appearing up and down it, and The Wolf's normally impassive face was overtaken by pained surprise.

Emrys stepped down the crumbled stairs, flipping to another page in his book, the bandaged hand sizzling with flecks of plasma as the ashy remains of the page spiraled away on the gentle breeze. He turned to regard Brann, his back to the werewolf, and spoke in that same agreeable voice as if this were no great matter at all.

"I did in fact lead Miss Zay to this parish, if only on a slight detour before sending her on her way—and in the spirit of honesty, I continue to speak true to you now, my young friend," he said, tearing another page from his spellbook. "I will indeed lead you to her in good time, once I've finished the task at hand. You'll indulge my apologies for delaying your journey. Rest assured; this won't take but a moment."

Brann saw the blur of a seriously pissed werewolf lunging at the turned backside of the holyman—who had already clenched the page in his fist. The Wolf's jaws were practically at Emrys's neck when the man spun to bring that fist up into the beast's jaw, dazzling sparks making a thundercrack of light and sound as the magically augmented blow sent The Wolf again through the air, hurled now directly into the ruins of the church. A line of pews was flattened and sent scattered in wilted splinters beneath the bulk of the wolfman—there was no doubt about it, Emrys meant to kill the beast, who was now realizing this as he brought himself up onto his shaky arms.

Blood streamed in a thick river from a cracked fang, curling down his creamy neckfur and staining it freshly red, and his glowing amber eyes practically smoked with his locked gaze of fury. Spitting a wad of chunky red, the werewolf rose to his hindpaws, hunched as a predator would when circling his prey.

"Spear."

Brann blinked away the spots of colored fuzz in his vision, realizing he was being addressed. The Wolf didn't budge from his spot, Emrys standing at the entrance to the church with his hand hovering over a third page, daring The Wolf to try another attack.

On the one hand, Brann knew The Wolf was a brutal killer, having cut down a man in the street just an hour before for little more offense than grabbing at a woman's hat.

On the other hand, he thought, remembering the absolutely polite and friendly way Emrys had lured the two of them here—Brann *really* did not like being lied to.

The young man lurched forward to reach for the spear, nearly tripping over a grave as he did—and just as Brann felt the weapon's steely butt under his palm, the entire spear was enveloped in a neon green aura, before slipping from his grasp and hurling itself in the opposite direction. The missile embedded itself into the stone pillar where once a front door was hinged, and The Wolf once again was deflected from a leaping attack, being clotheslined by his own telekinetically displaced spear and giving a sharp yelp as his momentum carried him forward to land flat on his back at Emrys's feet.

Two glowing green fingers pointing at the spear where he'd directed it to fly moved to now point at The Wolf, Emrys casting a gesture of condemnation down at the beast laying prone before him, paying no mind to the sputtering coughs that speckled his face with wolfblood.

"Unholy, your make, and be it sin or saint that laid this curse upon you, I stand before you blessed with divine purpose."

The glow of his fingers condensed, small vines of sparking light tying knots around those frayed bandages until his fingertips burned like an evil pair of disembodied eyes.

"To unmake you and release you from this evil spell. Your soul will be cleansed in a purifying fire, and with it, the curse that lives beneath the soil of this once beautiful parish. Your sacrifice will once again consecrate this broken house of holy promise."

The Wolf sneered up at Emrys, his thoroughly battered appearance not suppressing his bloodlust, his claws already swiping away the blood from his eyes before digging themselves into the mossy stone foundation to ready himself to rise again. "Boring shit," he growled, licking his bloody chops in a feral canine manner. "Fight or talk, pick one."

Emrys gave a small nod of impressed approval. "To brevity, then."

His arm shot upward, and with it, The Wolf again shooting back into the opposite wall, the fur all over his body tipped with that same green glow. The invisible hand of manipulation had bodied him with as much resistance as a piece of lint, and the already concaved ceiling fell in further to bury his curled form in more planks of wood, and as a cloud of dust settled around him The Wolf remained still this time.

Brann had seen enough. The whole fight had taken only just under a minute, and another spell would surely be the deathblow. He drew the blade at his side from its sheath, the saber gleaming blue silver in the moonlight, and like a switch had been flipped he was back on the training grounds of the Geihan Palace. Dominant hand just under the guard, single finger pointed flat against the hilt to keep it steady. Second hand just below, loose enough to direct the direction of the saber's edge while his main hand stayed stiff. He brought the blade low, and with no words spoken, exhaled in the same moment he sprinted forward.

Emrys had stepped forward towards The Wolf, giving no thought to the young man behind him. Perhaps he had been underestimated as a threat, or perhaps Emrys simply believed he'd be allowed to kill The Lady Red's werewolf companion unimpeded, but Brann's swiftness carried him forward into an offensive stab that wasn't noticed until it was far too late. Emrys had just barely heard the clatter of boots behind him when he spun around, his eyebrows shooting up in surprise—the sound of pierced meat froze Brann in place, having run the holyman through.

Warm liquid trickled onto his fingers, soaking the saber's hilt. A scrape of bone reverberated through the metal beneath Brann's grip; he suspected he'd severed the spinal column. Emrys hissed an agonized grunt between his pursed lips, nostrils whistling as he sucked in air, then stumbled back. Whether by his own movements, or the professional manner in which Brann tugged the saber back to regain his stance, the blade slipped free with a disgusting crunch of parted flesh and sprayed steaming arterial violet all down Brann's face and chest.

The mortally wounded Emrys lilted, still clutching his book, his other hand reaching out to Brann in defeated confusion. For a moment, a flash of the sentry lying on the grass in his mind's eye sent a lance of guilt through him and made Brann reach for his belt—but he'd left his corpsman kit back in his room. No medicine on hand to save this one. Emrys was going to die.

The wet slap of his blood-soaked coat against a patch of wall still wrapped in yellowed wallpaper, and Emrys slid down a bit, smearing his escaping lifeblood against the surface. Beside Brann, a plank of wood rolled to stop at his feet, and he felt a warm body breathing—The Wolf had come to, and was hunched beside Brann, appraising the young soldat's work. With a bubbling blow of his still-bleeding nose, the werewolf leaned in close—too close—and Brann was just about to raise the saber again to defend himself before his face was being sniffed at. The Wolf's ears were perked, eyes softened, and for a moment he almost seemed friendly: no words spoken, he was acknowledging Brann's intervention, if not outright thanking the young human, even if he left a stringy trail of bloody mucus against Brann's cheek. Trotting forward past him, The Wolf leaned up to grasp at his spear, the leverage allowing him to crack his back loudly before he yanked the embedded weapon free. Clods of disintegrated stone fell in dusty puffs from the mechanized paneling of the weapon's edge, but otherwise it was unblemished, the tool of war forged from far sturdier stuff.

The Wolf gently pushed aside Brann, taking his place, chest heaving as he continued sucking in air with shrill wheezes. He hefted the spear, feeling the weight and judging the distance for a second before he launched it with a twist of his torso and a feral bark. The short distance it flew didn't even give Brann enough time to blink before it had buried itself in the wall—that is, after it had burst through Emrys's ribcage, the wide spearhead turning the precise wound of the saber into a craggy fracture of gory carnage, Emrys's dying breath little more than a startled gulp as he was pinned in place. His wide-brimmed hat tilted forward to hide his face, body going limp, suspended in his half-crouched position partially dangling above the ground.

The would-be assassin was no more.

Wolf huffed with a stiff nod, his pawlike hand slapping against Brann's back a couple times—it was time to return where they came from. Brann looked on a moment longer at Emrys's corpse as it drained its lifeblood onto the floor, then turned away, not wishing to see what a mess it would make when that spear was dislodged from it. He stepped down the ruined stairs onto the path, looking up at the moon that had risen in full above the trees—unanswered questions left this a less than satisfying encounter, and he still had no idea where to find Zay. With a shake of his head, Brann swiped the saber in a downward arc through the air to clean it, sending a wash of blood airborne to splatter against a gravestone and the flowers decorating it.

So much for a well-kept garden.

Wiping the remaining blood off with the corner of his jacket, Brann walked down the path as he sheathed the saber. An abominable crunch behind him signaled the removal of the spear, and the sound of a body toppling to the floor followed. The Wolf would be close behind, he was sure of it, so he didn't look back.

But something stopped him, just at the edge of the graveyard. He wasn't sure what, but he was being held in place. Like there was unfinished business here.

Brann looked around, the trees quiet, the fields beyond the path empty, their high stalks of grass swaying. Something was amiss. Something cold, and foul, was in the graveyard with them.

Something holding him back. Actually holding him back, physically.

The hand gripped his ankle, pulling the weight of its owner forward—Brann looked down in slow realization, his worst fears confirmed by the sight. A fetid corpse, eaten partially through, too fresh to be a skeleton but too long buried to be intact. The hand oozed gelatinous soft tissue onto his boot, and shriveled eyes drained of vitreous cast their dead gaze up at him. The jaw hung agape in a silent moan, no sound issuing forth, save for the repulsive clenching of its decayed lungs.

The Wolf stopped in his tracks as well behind Brann, and barked out a warning, assuming a hunched defensive posture in Brann's peripheral vision.

Emrys had been telling the truth. This parish was cursed after all.

With a wide swing, Brann pulled the saber free again to bring it down hard, yelling out as he severed the hand grabbing his leg. "What is this shit?!" He yelped out, kicking away the gooey hand. All around the garden of the dead, occupants of their graves had quietly dug themselves out from their rest, awakening beneath the watchful moon.

"Undead!" The Wolf aligned himself with mechanical precision to thrust forward and obliterate the yawning face of a zombie, giving a small twirl as he ripped the weapon free to send the top of the monster's head bouncing away. "Cursed graves! Don't get bitten!"

Like I needed to be told that, thought Brann in a flurry of panic, spinning around to look for any other encroaching bodies crawling towards him. The once-lovely grass of the graveyard was now squirming with rotten bodies dragging themselves about like glistening worms, the air crackling with wet noises of decomposed vocal cords and open chest cavities.

The saber cut low, cleaving the front of the skull of the zombie that had grabbed him, Brann separating the face of the vile thing from the rest of it. He had every freedom to cut and run, nothing behind him but the open path back to the outpost—and if it weren't for the muted respect The Wolf had shown him, Brann might have considered doing just that. As it were, the zombies were pulling themselves up onto unsteady feet, all of them ignoring Brann and moving towards the werewolf—he'd be surrounded in seconds, the weakened hybrid no match for a dozen foes. There was nothing for it—they were stuck together.

The Wolf kept low, shifting his weight with his back to the church, making sharp retreating thrusts anytime an undead got too close. The jabs kept them at bay, but only just—the piercing spear cut through their sloppy flesh easily, but with no nervous system to feel anything, the stopping power was minimal at best. An arm flopped to the dirt, a jawbone, but the zombies didn't slow, giving no reaction to losing these valuable pieces. Brann fought down his terror as best he could, reasoning that they were too slow to turn and face him if he moved quickly and made his attacks from behind. Inching closer, he readied the blade, immediately forgetting his instructions not to swing it like a club: the first blow cut through nearly the entire torso of the decomposed horror, halted only by the intact spine, which cracked from the impact and sent the top half of the zombie folding inward on itself. As it rolled on the ground to gnash its teeth up at Brann, a second swift stab to the forehead freezing it solid.

Meanwhile, the werewolf had adjusted his strategy somewhat— rather than thrusting forward, he planted his footpaw against the steps behind him and, leaning in, held the spear from just below the center of weight to wave it in a wide arc before him. While his power was reduced, it kept the forerunner zombies from getting too close, especially when the flat end of the spearhead slapped one aside to stumble away in the grass. The church behind him was a dead end, so retreating further inside wouldn't serve as anything better than a last resort. Roughly a dozen zombies still stood, only three or four being totally dispatched between the two living fighters: Brann and The Wolf couldn't cut them all apart at this rate, not without one or both of them falling.

The next zombie was more stubborn—Brann brought the saber

down across it's back in an attempt to repeat the act of breaking its spine, but the blade didn't swing true and bounced off a protruding bone spur. The creature spun, a hand swiping at the air just in front of Brann's nose, the fingers decayed to the point the bony fingertips were exposed like claws. When the stinging vibrations in the blade settled, Brann rotated with the momentum of the failed attack and brought it back around again, this time aiming upwards. The spine above the zombie's shoulders was snapped, the neck falling away and taking the head with it, the rest of the body instantly dropping into a squishy heap.

Too slow, still too slow. Brann threw a look to The Wolf, who was cut off from view save for the small gaps in the congregation of walking carcasses. There wasn't time to kill them all before they'd be on him, and even the angry snarls of the werewolf had been replaced with frustrated sharp gasps of air.

He felt a sudden pinch, like his toes were caught in a vise—Brann looked down, disgusted, seeing the severed head of the zombie was *biting his boot*. The teeth were blunt and cracked, but with enough gnawing, it could surely sink them through the leather and into his foot. With a startled yell, Brann kicked at the air in vain to free the stuck parasite, but to no avail—so, with a summoned burst of adrenaline-fueled logic, he kicked up his leg to drape it on a gravestone and sliced just above where he felt he would connect with his own boot. The scalp of the zombie popped free, and the jaws released, the head's eyes rolling back as it dropped to rest on top of the gravestone.

That was his one-time freebie. There wouldn't be such luck next time he left one of these monsters alive, and it took twice as long to kill that one as the previous. Brann called out to The Wolf, giving a command he'd hoped would be respected:

"Get inside the church! You're about to be overrun!"

Whether from his urgent tone or simply because he had no other options, The Wolf acknowledged: he shoved forward off the steps to slip his spear free of the bodies that had impaled themselves on its length in a stack while trying to get at him. The zombies fell backwards into the others behind them, giving enough breathing room for an egress, Wolf scrambling up the steps behind him with a quicker corpse snapping its teeth at his tail. Rather than climbing the steps like living people would, the zombies simply walked straight into the elevated foundation and dug in, clawing themselves up onto the surface and rolling back upright slowly.

Brann took a shot at the legs of one such climber, lopping both feet off at the shins. The splintered bone dripped rotten marrow, but otherwise the zombie didn't notice, simply crawling forward towards The Wolf inside regardless of whether or not it could stand anymore. This wasn't gonna work, they were simply too relentless.

"Just hold on, I'm trying my best," Brann called out, his voice shaky to his ears. He wasn't convincing himself. They'd fall onto The Wolf, rip him apart, then turn on Brann and do just the same. He had to run. He had to get away, now, while he still could. This wasn't his fault; he didn't make the werewolf provoke a murderer to corner him. He would be guiltless—he could get back to the others at the ship, and they'd take off after it was decided Zay was gone too. What was he still doing here, inches away from an infectious bite on his neck?

The Wolf didn't answer. Someone else, however, did.

"I can do better."

Green sparks shot up from the dirt at Brann's feet, and spikes of luminescent energy sprouted before him in a dizzying display of light. The outstretched arms, legs, and necks of the shambling undead were skewered from below in the ectoplasmic trap, all of them lodged in place, twitching helplessly—and from the shadows within the church, a bandaged fist showering green sparks onto the floor opened wide like it was releasing a lever.

The spikes of energy, all facing upwards like stalagmites, simply inverted. In the span of a nanosecond, the tips of the spikes all turned inward like the gaping mouth of a great leech snapping shut, pulling all of the trapped corpses into the center of the trap and pulverizing them faster than could be visibly observed by the naked eye. One moment, the zombies were frozen in place, and the next, a giant meat grinder of magicka was sending a pillar of pulpy meat and bone skyward, the disintegrated mash of bodies blanketing the floor of the church in a disgusting slurry.

The Wolf stood still, spear still extended, the head of a zombie chomping away on the blade of his spear where it was pierced—the only identifiable piece of corpse to indicate the foul pool of masticated goo was ever a horde of undead. He blinked away his own surprise and, with a deft twirl of his hands on the spear's pole, split the disembodied head into three parts that plopped onto the floor.

Brann kept his blade drawn, drawing measured breaths to quell his panic as a different kind of living corpse emerged.

"It is beyond my expectations that I may be forgiven," Emrys was saying, wiping away the green plasm from his hands on the torn shirt soaked in blood—the gaping wound in his chest completely disappeared, as if he'd never had a scratch on him. "I do however hope you'll understand what I'm about to tell you, and why it was sufficient motivator to mislead you and your friend here." Emrys turned, eyeing The Wolf, before giving them both a bow. "Please. Indulge me for a moment, and I will return you to your friend the pilot, as promised."

10. The Witch

It had taken more than Brann's fair share of negotiating skills to work The Wolf down to a state of calm, or at least, a state of restraining himself from driving his spear through Emrys a second time. Behind the parish, a smaller footpath hidden by the long grass led away into the trees, and as Emrys quickly explained himself, the wind had begun to quietly sing in an ominous dirge that snuffed out the usual nighttime sounds of crickets and nocturnal birds.

"You can imagine as a former man of spiritual leadership, it would be altogether unwise to introduce myself as a practitioner in the art of necrotic magic," he was saying as he led the two of them on, keeping his hands spread wide with his book of spells safely stowed to indicate he meant no further harm—though with both The Lady's saber and The Wolf's spear prodding him along from behind, he had sufficient motivation to keep the peace. "I acted in haste—that blade, it's of Vampyr make, is it not?" He tilted his head back over his shoulder, indicating the saber Brann held.

The Wolf answered for Brann with an affirming grunt, not even allowing himself to blink as he stared fixated on Emrys's back, still dripping blood freely from his snout.

"Thought as much," said Emrys, giving a slight cough that sounded wet and pained. "Excuse me, when you've had a weapon wide as a frying pan through your lungs, even a regenerative body pact has to run its course healing the internals in due time. Now, as I was saying," he continued, using a hand to indicate the path curved ahead, "Vampyr steel channels summoner magic in similar fashion to my own necromancy; if the blade of a Vampyr summoner spills the blood of a living man on deconsecrated burial grounds, the dead beneath the soil will have themselves a lovely nighttime stroll as if they'd been merely napping these past years. That saber was borrowed from The Lady Red—the second half of the quarry I was pursuing in this region."

Emrys turned slightly to wave a passive hand to The Wolf, who growled. "You were the other half, pardon me. I'm only human despite my otherwise elevated clinical conditions, and to err is to be me. Had I known that the werewolf and the Vampyr I pursued were, in fact, themselves of sound mind and uncorrupted soul..." He shrugged apologetically. "I'd have offered my hand in aid on your journey, sincerely."

Brann spoke now, interrogating Emrys mostly for his own benefit, feeling entirely out of his depth with this subject matter. "Werewolves and vampires, and you're wearing priest's clothing—I take it you're a monster hunter of sorts? Which means you thought you were protecting the people back at the outpost—especially when one of them turned up dead the moment these two entered town," he gestured to The Wolf beside him.

"Oh yes, and quite an accomplished one at that," Emrys said, his attitude snapping back to his former polite self faster than he'd resurrected. "In matters of undead, exdeath and aldeath, I am by all accounts likely the longest surviving agent enforcing the extermination of all afflicted creatures that may spread their unholy ailments to the daywalking world." He lifted his hat, stopping a moment to bow to The Wolf, showing off a receded hairline that spiked into a frantic mess of thinning hair. "It is under that sacred mandate I perform the duties of the cloth, and with the honored tradition of protecting the world of living men I extend my deepest apologies to you, my good sir." He took a knee, one bandaged hand held high. "A more contemptable display of foolish haste I could not have made in carrying out my duties towards you, and a great debt is owed, to which I intend the repayment be made in compounding interest."

Careful not to upset The Wolf further with his next question, Brann asked: "He is a werewolf though. What convinced you he wasn't just some undead monster like any other?" This did earn a disapproving side-glance from the canid, but otherwise Wolf was silent.

Emrys paused, his smile one of a patient teacher who believed the answer to be obvious. "Well, the spear," he laughed, "Or to be more specific, the adherence to its purpose." He held his tattered robe wide, showing off the bare chest where once he'd been ripped open. "You see, a creature of the night, well—the need to kill will always overcome the need to remain human. And even caught in the vain trappings of believing themselves still counted among the living, a deathblow will come without hesitation when easy prey is presented." He let his robe fall closed, an open hand waving towards The Wolf. "Not only did he choose not to tear my throat out at the moment I was at my weakest, brought low by your blade—oh, to wit, I bear no hard feelings to your actions either, young man," he hurriedly said to Brann, "But our calculating friend here saw fit to satisfy his desire to kill in an honorable fashion at the end of his chosen weapon. No truly cursed being absent of their humanity could have made such a distinction."

Brann's saber lowered a bit as the conversation drew on, looking The Wolf up and down, who largely appeared entirely unimpressed but made no outward signs he was disinterested in what Emrys had to say. "So, a werewolf who was really undead wouldn't have been smart enough to go for his spear and take his time killing you."

"Ahem. Aldead, actually; apologies young sir," Emrys corrected. "Undead would refer to the rotting corpses you so valiantly held your own against back there. Aldead would be more in line with those who, while once people of intelligence, succumbed to transformative blight that stains or otherwise interrupts the natural cycle of their lifespans." He nodded. "But, yes, you are correct—and if this insufficiently explains away my change of heart, a storied history in slaying these vile beasts allows me to also impart upon you the knowledge that if he were indeed aldead, our werewolf friend here would have been ignored by the walking dead at the church same as you. In fact, I suspect the only reason they did not divide their ranks to make you a meal as well would be the removal of that Vampyric saber from its sheath." He paused. "Always a student of the arts, I can safely learn from this encounter that not only is our unfortunately wolf-shaped friend here not truly an aldead, but that the Vampyr companion I—erroneously—intended to snuff out separately is similarly intact when it comes to the human condition?"

The Wolf snapped his jaws together with a curt nod. "Not a vampire."

Emrys seemed relieved by this, letting his arms fall to his side. "Then truly, I have wandered astray and become lost in the thicket of spiritual warfare's dense undergrowth. Speaking of, I must insist that we make for the trees and continue to our destination away from these fields—the blood I shed that brought alive the dead will almost certainly reach the foul nostrils of those awaiting revival in the fields beyond. " He cast a hand over the long grass. "A battle of some import long ago laid low at least a hundred young souls defending their homeland in these meadows, and I suspect even I may have a difficult go at returning them to rest in numbers that great."

The low moan in Brann's ears didn't seem so natural anymore, as he too looked out at the long grass, convincing himself he'd see the silhouette of another horde of corpses emerging from the fringes any moment. "Yeah, let's get going," he agreed, choosing to sheathe the saber. The Wolf didn't lower his spear for a second.

"From this moment hence, my most honest foot forward will lead us to your misplaced pilot, and believe me when I say I have the most trustworthy of sanctuaries keeping her warm in wait." Emrys rose and replaced his hat, waving the soldat and the werewolf along behind him into the forest. "Quickly, my friends, quickly."

*

The way through the moderately dense proved uncomfortably dark for Brann, with the moonlight filtered heavily by the branches overhead, stripped as they were of leaves for the most part. The Wolf likely saw just fine in the dark, and Emrys led the way with utmost confidence leading Brann to think he may have some form of augmented vision as well—never before had Brann's visor been missed so much.

"Not to be a pain, but I can barely see where we're going," he spoke up finally, after the only thing he realized he was following was the noise of footsteps, which he didn't trust fully.

He heard Emrys stop ahead. "Oh, of course, my apologies, how thoughtless of me." A crinkle of his little books pages made The Wolf shift warily behind Brann. After a second, a tearing was heard, and then with a spark a beam of suffused green light shone forward from Emrys's upturned hand like a guiding lighthouse. Even the shadows retreated, like a lime-tinged portal into daytime had opened before them, banishing the night within the light's reach.

"Too bright," The Wolf snapped, blinking with discomfort and rubbing at his eyes.

"Ah." Emrys took notice of this as well, flipping a page with his illuminated hand, which waved the light about hurriedly. With another torn page, the light recast itself. It was far more muted this time, like the light was being diffused by a thick cloth. "Better?"

"Kinda hard for me again," said Brann.

Another tear. The light returned, somewhere between the two. "Now?"

"Still too bright." The Wolf chuffed.

Emrys grunted haplessly. "You—I understand it's not ideal, but, please, I can't find a perfect brightness for everyone. Can we all at least proceed forward this way without getting lost?"

Brann sidestepped a bit so a healthy amount of the light bouncing off the bark of the trees was shielded by his body, keeping The Wolf in his shadow. The Wolf nodded in thanks at him. Brann turned back to similarly nod to Emrys. "Yeah, we're good now, sorry."

Emry shook his head impatiently. "Good to hear. Onward, then."

Save for that brief faux pas, the hike up the path as it seemed to wave an almost crescent shape back west, towards what would have been the way to the outpost, was an uneventful one. The nightlife within the safety of the trees was vibrant and chattering, quite unalike the disturbing stillness of the fields where the zombies roamed. Brann felt entirely at ease here, despite the pitch black surrounding them, finding comfort in the bravery of the two quasi-immortal beings he found himself between. In fact, this subject further piqued his curious nature, and he decided to relieve himself of some burden of ignorance.

"What exactly is the difference between the types of undead?" He piped up. "I don't quite get what the names mean."

"Well, to be revived with necromancy, or to have been infected with a carrier of necrotic blood, that is undead," replied Emrys, his words punctuated with pauses where he breathed as he trudged up the steepened path. "While it is the most rampant and toxic of deathless curses, it is also the most easily repressed, given that physical damage to the carrier in extensive dealings is enough to end the blight. The trick is simply to keep one's distance when rooting out these nests of sick, as they transmit their curse easily as a stray cough. The second, less manageable of the curses, is the aldeath."

The Wolf mumbled something to himself, but Brann didn't interrupt.

"Aldeath is a more sinister condition, dealt in equal parts passage through prolonged contact with a carrier, as well as allowing the victim an unfortunate illusion of hope that they themselves remain in control of their better selves, even as they often seek to feed on the flesh of their loved ones. Entire communities have been warped by the will of an angered aldead, proving a rather unconcerned populace may indeed maintain some semblance of civility once everyone in their lives has been turned...though, woe befall any outsider who stumbles upon the den of hungry aldead, as they and their children are just as likely to be torn apart as to be themselves served a warm meal. Werewolves, vampires, red shades, mollusks—they walk on two legs, speak our tongues, maybe even enjoy a polite conversation or two...but won't hesitate to pull their next meal from within your flesh. I will undoubtedly be a willing student to investigate the circumstances in which your passengers here have avoided such a fate, despite their inhuman tendencies," he added, speaking over his shoulder. "It's not every day that you encounter a person or persons of reason and mercy who nonetheless have taken on the physical traits of an aldead."

"And the third one?" Said Brann, intervening before the clinical ramblings of the holyman risked upsetting The Wolf again.

His voice became less cooperative, the excited scholar losing his luster for the conversation. "The exdeath, yes. The most grievous of the three. None have been so lucky to have lived with this curse and seen an end to their stories as merciful as having their earthly souls ejected from their living flesh like an undead, or the chance of a peaceful existence outside the reaches of living society like the covens of aldead." He sighed once, then again, masking the sound as his heavy breathing from the exercise. "Prayer is the only anodyne for those unfortunate souls. For theirs is a tragedy each as worthy of legend as any conquered kingdom or reticent God."

"So, what happens to those who have it?" Brann persisted. "When they're cursed with exdeath, what do they become?"

"We're here," said Emrys curtly. This conversation was at its end. Likely for good.

Though even in the dim light, Brann couldn't see what Emrys meant. No structures to speak of, no humble shack or curls of inviting smoke rising from a warm chimney. Just a cleft in the path where a tree had been split down the middle, as if by lightning, its innards laid bare and scorched.

Was this another trick? "Yeah, I'm not seeing anything, man." Brann didn't waste time voicing his concern, mentally warning The Wolf to prepare for another spat, his own hand going to the saber. "There an invisible house or something you're gonna wave your hand in front of before it appears?"

"Something of that nature," was the cheerful reply, Emry stepping lightly right up to the tree. He stood at the lip of the severed trunk, arms flat against his sides, and then: "Look out below!"

He tipped his weight forward, and vanished, falling straight down into the earth. The light vanished, leaving Brann and The Wolf alone. Brann blinked frantically to regain some of his vision in the absence of his guide. "Where the hell—?"

"Below," was The Wolf's flat reply, clearly understanding more than Brann. "Into the tree. I'll stay."

He was being given a command. Brann blinked in the werewolf's direction—was he seriously more trusting of Emrys than Brann was? Clearly, they knew something he didn't.

"You and I gotta spend some time on the ship together, this whole shorthand communication, I'm not so good as you," Brann said, pointing to the beastman as he felt his way forward to the tree stump.

The Wolf shrugged, leaning on his spear. "Get good."

"Yeah, right." Brann folded for now, deciding there would be time later to make friends with his new shipmate. For now, if Zay really was down below, he needed to bring this nighttime adventure to its end. Holding his breath in anticipation as if jumping into water, he stood atop the trunk just as Emrys had and leaned his weight forward.

Once, as a very young child, Brann had been living in the fostered care of a sickly old woman in Barrier City's skidrow. Her house had a closet, locked off upstairs, and Brann had picked the lock one afternoon in his explorations, much to his peril: falling through the dark, catching himself on an outstretched leg, he had found the floor opened up beneath him. A laundry chute, invisible in the unlit closet, forgotten for years. He'd screamed and cried for hours before he was found, hoarse and soaked in his own piss, trapped there between worlds. This was the closest he'd felt to returning to that memory from his youth, and his stomach flipped as he simply fell straight down through the stump, the rings of wood separating with the same ease as that laundry chute. The wind rushed all around him, the walls of the tunnel inches from his nose, and a scream rising was caught in his chest by the quick arrival of a sharp bend in the tunnel. At once, his back scraped along—was that moss? A painless transition into a slide forward, body buffeted by a most comfortable surface that sent him sprawling out horizontally into an open space, and immediately his eyes were stung by the vivid array of chromatic spirals all around him. He'd fallen into a chamber of bioluminescent undergrowth, fungus of some kind perhaps, undulating waves of welcoming rainbows filling the tiny chamber.

Brann swallowed down his fear, raising himself up on his palms, staring straight ahead at a curtain of tendrils as alight as the rest of the chamber. One way in, one way out: whatever called this place home was well-hidden indeed, though it was a wonder the glow of the luminescent moss and toadstools didn't penetrate the tunnel above. Brann stood as best he could, finding the low ceiling making it impossible to reach full height, and moved forward into the curtains of twinkling cilia. The curtains parted around him, tickling at the hairs on his arms but never touching his flesh bare, as if magnetically repelled just off the surface of his body. Another tunnel heading straight in, and with so much color and light dancing around him, Brann felt he was in the middle of a winter festival show, something cheery and joyous, even his body feeling warmed from within to stave off the bitter cold night of the forest above.

The curtains floated away before his eyes, and at once Brann was home.

No, that wasn't right—he blinked, feeling numbed a bit from the tunnel behind him. Not his home, someone else's home. Did those lights have some kind of pacifying charm on him? He had never been in this place, but at once felt like this was a domicile he was welcome in, even one he was considered a friend. The walls and ceiling were streaked with vestiges of that same luminescent moss, but the light was stilted in the glow of a smaller, brighter source of light: a single candle within a glass orb on a table no bigger than the ones in the *Myrmidon*'s galley. Around this table, three figures sat at ease, two familiar, one new. Zay was digging into a bowl of steaming meat and tubers, and the bowl itself even looked to be made of a crusty bread. Emrys was hunched low before a woman opposite Zay, his smile wide and kindly once more and his hat nowhere to be seen, hands out to clasp the gloved hands of their host. Seeing Brann appear over her shoulder, Emrys nodded to the young man, inviting him in. "Yes, there you are, I was afraid you had run off! We've been expecting you, young sir."

Emrys outstretched his bandaged hand towards Brann, once again looking back to the mysterious woman. "Meet the lovely young steward of these woods: my darling Grishka."

The raven hair of the woman facing away from Brann shifted, her entire form seeming to wobble and wave just as the tendrils of light had in the tunnel. In fact, her raven hair was not hair at all—feathers spread, flipping up in an alert crown, and her neck spun at an impossible 180 degrees—her entire body was raven hair. No, feathers. Raven feathers.

Brann had to steady himself and blink away his confusion, as well as a wave of warmth surging through him again. Raven feathers. Raven face. A raven in whole. There was no woman, no pale skin with rosy cheeks, only tarlike dark pitch, a black beak set below black eyes like a doll's, black feathers shivering over a black tunic. Or was the tunic made of feathers as well? The longer he stared at her, the less he understood, and the more uncomfortable his eyes felt: he closed them for just a moment, resetting his expectations. Then opened them again.

The woman was, indeed, a raven. Perched upon her stool, legs drawn up to her chest, not much bigger than an oversized carrion bird of nature, but no less intelligent in the way she peered at the boy before here. Everything about the way the colors on the walls gently reflected off her silken feathers confused and slowed Brann's thinking, an illusion of both sight and mind: she was a woman, as much as she was a bird, and yet what Brann saw settled on neither. When she spoke, however, the illusion was lifted, and Brann breathed freely: her defenses were lowered, and he was allowed into her space of understanding.

"Nith sie. Given hark den boyis younglen, chikk-sen?" Brann couldn't tell if he was the one being spoken to, or if Emrys was, but either way Grishka spoke in the same language he recognized back at the outpost, the harsh and inhuman tones Mother Superior had engaged Hawkshaw with. This must be the common tongue of the Cheneye region, and humans its visitors, not its indigenous people. Emrys responded in kind.

"Yes, I know, he's not much to look at, but trust me when I say this young lad has proven himself more than capable of great deeds this night, showing a resolve in the face of danger that would make generals of time-honored wars blush." Emrys stood, circling around Grishka to stand at her side, watching Brann's face closely. "If you're feeling that sense of disorientation and nausea, remain calm, it will pass—our gracious host here, a witch of the forest, Grishka is a matron of magics beyond yours or my ability to understand and carries with her the innate ability to conceal any weakness to predators. Even this, her home, is designed to ward off hungry foes," he said, motioning back to the colorful tunnel. "In fact, though I've yet to see it firsthand, I have it on good authority from Grishka here that should someone enter uninvited, they may find themselves, well..." He cleared his throat with a wry smile. "Wondering where their skin had gone, as their internals heap themselves on the cavern floor. Pardon the macabre image," he said to Zay, acknowledging she was still eating.

Brann also turned to Zay, still not quite ready to look Grishka in the eyes yet. "Zay, it's me, we—I—we found your clients, uh, I think," he stammered, somewhat perturbed that she'd spent the entire day missing yet had resigned all urgency in her task. "You okay? You've been gone a long time..."

"Shit yeah, I'm great," she said, wiping her mouth on her arm. "This is the best meal I've had in like...ever." A thankful spoon was raised to the raven witch. "Keep your pants on soldat boy, I only left a few minutes ago, I can take care of myself."

Brann kept addressing her, but looked to Emrys, worried. "Uh, no, you...left hours ago. You've been missing for at least half a day; we had to come find you. There were..." He took a beat. "Some casualties, even."

Zay paused mid-chew. "Whuzzat?"

"Klick ten die day yah, den holmslow-slow." Grishka ruffled her feathers as any bird would, and from the corner of his eye, the movement reminded Brann of a woman tossing her hair over her shoulder. This was fuckin' weird.

"Yes, what she means—or, rather, what happens when you've spent time with a forest witch," Emrys translated, "We're in her safe space here. Her home environment. To ensure her crafts and duties are carried out safely and without interruption, time can behave...strangely within this den." He lifted his hat from the floor behind his chair, and Brann noted in that moment a distinct lack of any kind of shelving or hooks on the walls, everything resting at ground height save for the table itself. "In what must have been mere seconds before you fell into the trunk, Grishka and I had time to prepare this lovely meal and catch up on stories of our travels." He smiled warmly, once again taking her—wing? Hand? Talons?—into his own and kissing at it. "There's no host more soothing to a weary traveler than an omahkaiikii."

This word was the first word he'd heard that instantly made sense to Brann—not because of the phonetics, but because Emrys so obviously intended Brann to hear it being used to denote Grishka's race—a raven witch. Woman and bird filling the same space; entirely both yet never fully either. What was most fascinating to Brann, now that the more defensive aspects to her disguise had receded, looking directly upon her now...she simply was that, a woman and raven, partway between both just as The Wolf and Boomer were entirely complimentary hybrids to both man and animal. Where Grishka differed entirely was a sort of aura, or maybe even an impression on his naked eyes as a new taste on his tongue; like he'd lived too short a life to learn the language of seeing her properly. If Brann concentrated hard enough in one direction, he felt he could see a human woman, as familiar to him as his own mother, despite never knowing his mother's face: yet, the second he pulled back from this, her image likewise recoiled, and a simple raven as curious and unassuming as any perched on her stool would be. The trick, he learned, was to focus too hard on expecting neither, but rather appreciating both, like unfocusing his eyes or swallowing back the taste without swilling it about too much: then, he felt he saw her, or rather, a more honest version of her.

Grishka tossed her feathers again, or rather, shifted her winged shoulders so the feathers resembling her flowing hair rustled about the fluff on her neck, her puffed breast giving way to a hand-stitched tunic of leather as closely resembling the flesh of her own legs as any garment could. She swept away the forgotten breadbowl with her wing—the feathers wafting in her aura, lifting the edible dish as any fleshy fingers would despite their flat weightlessness—and tossed the bowl into a small trough of compost. "Omahkaiikíí," she corrected, with much the same patience as Brann found Emrys correcting him. The difference was negligible to his ears, but apparently not to Emrys's, who bowed apologetically.

"You'll have to forgive me Brann, far be it for me to teach you improper pronunciation, as I myself am still a young student in this language."

"'-Kíí' nith sie den gibbeth qwan heark den rightsup," explained Grishka to no avail, Brann's head spinning has he completely failed to grasp these words. Was she just making up words as she spoke? "Spaketh 'EE' den sie washen Grishka-wa sie den boysup, hek-hek!" Her beak clacked together, the rattling sound reminding Brann of a young woman's cheerful giggle, humored as if by a funny joke she told herself.

Emrys also laughed at this. "No, we certainly wouldn't want that," he said. Was HE also pretending to just understand what she was saying?

Even as he looked upon her, Brann heard a loud flutter of wings behind him—turning, he felt the talons clutching at his shoulder, and, though the rational part of his brain understood this to be impossible, saw the raven perched there. She resembled any other bird of her species now, her eyes peering back at him, then at his chest, her head tilting quizzically.

He looked down—his platinum corpsman pin, fixed above his breastplate. The single shiniest part of his uniform.

"You like it?" Brann asked, pinching it between his fingers to better allow the firelight to glint off it. He saw a mischievous intent in Grishka's intelligent little eyes, and he knew she did.

Then his vision blurred, and the weight on his shoulder was gone— she'd returned to her seat, once more assuming her hybrid form. No one else seemed to even notice how she'd teleported from one end of her den to the other then back so quickly—was it in Brann's head? Had he inhaled some kind of killer fungus?

Zay finally swallowed her mouthful of food. "Shit, we gotta get going!" Was her only contribution to this exchange, bolting upright and nearly hitting her head on the ceiling. "I was supposed to have flown all night to get my clients all the way across Cheneye by now, we have a deadline to meet!"

"I promise you, no one will be late to any previous engagements," Emrys calmed. "Though you are correct, it is time we be off. Losing oneself to even an hour of chatter down here with our dear hostess could cost us a day up above." He patted his hat back into place and raised his arms to usher Zay and Brann towards the exit, the former moving briskly, shouldering her heavy weapon. "In due time, I trust our paths will cross again, and an entire day in your home will give us a year's worth of friendship's tithings." Emrys retreated back towards the tunnel of light where Zay had vanished.

Grishka remained in place, head tilted off to one side, peering again at Brann curiously. Those dark little glassy eyes—no, rather, eyes of radiant violet, irises sparkling like gems around pupils that swallowed the very light reflecting off them—they asked him to stay, so she could learn his name, hear his voice, but no such luck. Brann hadn't so much as introduced himself, and he feared the opportunity was past. "Thanks for watching out for my, uh, friend," he offered instead, struggling to find a word to describe Zay, not quite subscribing to the one he chose. Regardless, her wings spread in a young woman's pleasant curtsy, phantom toes with painted nails dangling off her stool where only the tar-black talons clutched the hewn wood.

"Jikseth sie den gowan, boysup," she replied, her tone flecked with disappointment, but never hostility. "A-hawai'll gowan sie den sooneth insth die thanken."

Absolute gibberish, Brann thought, though he only smiled back politely. "Er, yeah, same to you, miss."

Her eyes never left him, he felt—or, more likely, the shiny pin on his chest—even as he crawled back through the chromatic tunnel. Here beyond the expectant reach of his comfort and understanding, Brann was beginning to very rapidly bounce off the ceiling of what he thought was his own intelligence: the world was growing quickly, faster than he could keep up with, and the rules of what was normal and what was alien were blurring into a pasty mess of fragmented thoughts and missing information. No more than a few days removed from the moment he'd stepped onto the cargo ramp of Boomer's ship, and yet his life's experiences were compounding to a growing mess of enormity.

Barrier City was always so formidable to him. Now, he was beginning to suspect the city of his youth was not so large after all.

He'd pulled himself up the mossy chute of the trunk with far less trouble than he'd anticipated, the mossy walls giving easily to allow his fingers to sink in and his boots to find hold in the stiff wood beneath. Just as his hair felt the cool touch of open air, a pair of arms hefted him free, and he had to blink away the surprising light of mid-morning. "Shit, we lost the whole night down there," he said, rubbing at his lids. Once he'd adjusted, he saw Emrys standing alone, Zay and the Wolf nowhere to be seen.

"They've gone on ahead some time ago, they'll surely be awaiting us back at the ship," Emrys was saying, the priest yawning a bit and cracking his back. "Our trip back will be downhill, and generously shorter than the path that led us here from the parish, so we won't be keeping them waiting long."

This made Brann somewhat nervous—with Zay back at the ship along with her passengers, there was no concrete agreement spoken at any point that he was also expected back. In all honesty, he was still something of a stowaway, one who didn't have the same obligations owed to his travels as the rest of the party. In fact, he still had no destination laid out for him, other than Boomer's expectation to bring him along to the next fight in the tournament.

He again swallowed down this fear, donning his professional act of militant procedure once more, nodding impassively. "Yes, let's hoof it back, got a schedule to keep," he said in his best attempt to mimic Zay's curtness. Bran was hoping against hope now that he wouldn't round the bend back into the street of the outpost only to see a blank space in the sandy clearing where once the Donnie had landed.

*

It was nearly noon by the time they saw the wooden roofs of the outpost's twin buildings peeking out from behind the fringe of trees, and the ground beneath their feet again softened into bright sand. There was nowhere near the same bustling crowd filling the sands as there had been the night before, and in fact most of the ships in the yard had taken off— not, thankfully, the *Myrmidon*, which came as a wash of relief down Brann's sweaty back. If they hadn't simply expected him back as a member of the crew, Boomer likely had stayed Zay's eager hand in taking off. His affinity for Brann may very well be the most valuable tool in his survival kit right now, and Brann was not about to take it for granted.

"Well, I wish I could say thanks for seeing us safely back, but," Brann started, pausing a moment as he and Emrys stood on the street. "To be perfectly honest...you did almost get me killed, and not really on accident either. I guess I'll say thanks for eventually coming clean, and leave it at that." He stood at attention, giving a somewhat half-hearted chest-salute as a uniformed soldat would to a civilian, though his heart really wasn't in it.

Emrys took this in good humor, laughing it off. "In the interest of complete and open fairness, where I merely misjudged your companion, you did in fact successfully end my life, let's not forget." He tapped on his chest, his bloodied coat still torn and ragged. "The world of the living may yet be owed a great debt in my name, but rest assured, there is no quarrel to be had between us and both our ledgers have been balanced free and clear of any red." He held out his hand for Brann to shake it. "All that's left now is to see you aboard your ship and on your way, young Master..."

He paused while leaning in, and Brann realized he'd never told

169

Emrys his own name. He stood to, taking the offered hand in spite of himself. "Brann, Specialist Corpsman Brann, of Lachlan. Though I currently serve in the Geihan infantry."

Emrys had that same strange faraway look in his eyes that Zay had when Brann introduced himself to her. The same look of confusion, of peculiar expectation, like there was more to be said—come to think of it, both reactions recalled a specific gaze that had been cast his way by another party before. The way Marshal Tark had looked at Brann at the Assay, when he too had namedropped House Lachlan.

"You don't say," Emrys finally said, mystified.

"Okay, what is this," Brann said, not buying it. "What is it about Lachlan that has everyone giving me this 'you don't say' act every time I say my name, it's starting to get on my nerves." He broke the handshake. "How about we balance that line in my ledger real quick, because I'm seeing red everywhere I go when it gets mentioned."

He hadn't meant to sound upset, but he couldn't help but raise his voice some, and Emrys was slightly cowed by it. "All apologies, I was unaware you hadn't the knowledge of your House history, of course as a conscript of Geiha you would have been forfeit any communication with the outside world during your time in the service behind their walls." Emrys shifted his weight, looking to the *Myrmidon*. "I pose this offer: with my time in the Cheneye region coming to an end in lack of a noble quarry to pursue, I will be turning my hunt of judicious purpose towards lands far beyond, wherein other rumors of the occult draw my ear. Let's say I take you up on your previous kindness and spend a day or so under a hot shower and warm blanket, and I tell you everything I know about your heritage between meals. What say you, young Brann of Lachlan?"

He did have a point. Brann had made that promise, and technically even if The Wolf regarded Emrys with hostility, he wasn't required to spend any time in direct contact with them aboard the ship with its widely spaced living quarters.

"Fine. Just, maybe don't stir up any trouble with the other passengers," he said, continuing on towards the extended ramp of the Donnie. "I can talk my way into getting you a room on board, but I don't know how long they'll want you there, especially when the Lady Red hears that you were planning on taking her out after nearly killing her guard dog. She's pretty dangerous herself, from what I hear."

"A more complacent and humbled bunkmate she will never know," said Emrys, his verbose charm wearing somewhat thin on Brann. Somehow, he didn't think that was the end of all this nonsense, despite the holyman's repeated promises.

In typical fashion, Boomer welcomed Brann aboard in the cargo bay, and made no efforts to resist Emrys coming aboard as well ("Any friend of my friend is my friend too, friend!" Was Boomer's response to Brann's pitch,) and though they were a full night behind schedule the Donnie was back in the air with an increasingly full dossier of passengers filling her beds. In fact, though Brann's first instinct was to make for his room to get some sleep, he reasoned he'd actually only been awake a small portion of the duration of the elapsed night and wasn't entirely tired yet, so he made for the galley where one more surprise awaited him.

There, in the corner closest to the bar, between it and the beverage coolers, a small candle burning within its glass orb had been placed on one of the dining tables, the floor around it wreathed with grassy weaves and decorative bone charms. Locked in the same posture she had been in watching Brann leave her home, Grishka stared at the young man as he came down to fetch a snack, giving a squawk at his startled cry on seeing her on board.

The amount of decorating she'd done in her little corner of the galley, the wallpaper peeled away in small bits by what looked like a beak, talon marks gouged into the soft padded stools all around her table, Grishka looked as if she'd been staying there for months, despite only a morning having passed between Emrys saying goodbye to her and escorting her guests out of her forest home. "Gowan, sie den boysup, ken hek-hek?" She inquired sweetly, giving another rattle of her beak that echoed the amused laughter of a mischievous woman.

Emrys was coming down the stairs now, rounding the bend to come to Brann's side, giving him an encouraging clap on the shoulder. "I told you, time works funny with these witches," he said, laughing along with the Raven as Brann simply stared.

The world he travelled was just getting far too weird for his tastes.

Brann reached up unconsciously, his fingers running along his breastplate—then, a patch of smooth fabric. Something was missing. He looked down, surprised.

"What is it?" Emrys asked. "Everything alright?"

Brann frowned, shaking his head, still not quite getting it. He looked back at Grishka in her makeshift nest as he answered:

"Yeah, just—my pin is gone."

The raven cooed back at him, pretending to have no idea what he was talking about as she set to preening herself.

11. The Morning

Within the span of merely a day the once sparse population of the ship was beginning to feel quite packed—the crew at their workstations in avionics or maintenance would be surprised to end their shift, bumping into a fully-fledged werewolf snoring on a heap of chewed pillows in the common area or the fiendish raven who would peck belligerently at their hands as they tried reaching for a sandwich in the cooler. Brann had awoken far later in the day than he'd intended, beginning to feel the soreness in his muscles from the stacked fights with monsters he was being drawn into—in fact, unconvinced that the ship wouldn't suddenly be caught in a storm of tentacles emerging from some airborne portal mid-flight, he had taken to wearing his breastplate over his street clothes, cutting a somewhat more tailored image of a combat ready young man serving his role as the ship's unofficial escort through the Wilds. Emrys hadn't emerged from his own quarters since they'd come abord, however, leaving Brann's questions as to the history of Lachlan still in wait for the time being—until then, Boomer had again attached himself to the young man at the hip, making Brann feel like something of a small pet being touted around by the tall prizefighter.

"He singlehandedly cut the head from an arch eel at Belljar, and laid low an army of undead in the outskirts of Cheneye territory, cutting a warpath of carnage through the continental Wilds," Boomer was saying to Nestor over coffee, mimicking his favored sports announcers again. "The mad lad simply cannot be stopped! He'll have taken the world by storm before the week's end and come toe to toe with The Champion himself, by God!" He mimed a right jab in slow motion at Nestor's cheek, eyes wide in mock surprise, the engineer simply waving the slow blow aside like a lazy gnat flying about. "Best get ready, old man, you may be managing two prizewinning fighters soon!"

"I'm not your manager," Nes repeated flatly, swiping the page on his holoscreen with another sip of coffee.

Brann was sitting at a table nearby—not so close as to impose on the two friends, but not so far as to appear as if he wanted to keep his distance. Boomer was the only one he felt totally friendly with at the moment, and didn't want to further put into question his role on the ship right now, let alone his expected timeframe to stay. Looking directly at the question of when he had to leave scared him somewhat, like confronting it would result in the worst possible answer then and there. Best to leave it to chance and not speak up on the issue at all. "So, the next stop," he said as his entry into the conversation, having not yet touched the coffee served to him by Boomer as well. "Which comes first, the fight or letting Zay's passengers off?"

Boomer froze mid-punch, his false expression of pretend focused violence dissipating. "Actually, good question," he said, letting his fists go limp as he regarded Nes with this same question. "Which is first, you old dickhead? We aren't really on our scheduled route anymore after last night."

"I'm also no longer the pilot," was the next flat reply. Nes never looked up from his screen, reading the morning news with devoted interest. "Go ask the two you hired and find out yourself."

"Uh, excuse you, I hired one, you hired the other, quite against my wishes," Boomer retorted with a wag of his finger. "Only one of them is on our payroll, the other one might as well be my boss with the deal you cut with her."

Nestor ignored this, and instead raised his voice to interrupt Boomer. "So, Mister Escort, when were you planning on leaving us?"

His annoyed tone caught Brann dead, the cold grip of embarrassment in his stomach turning the taste of his breakfast sour. Brann took a moment to digest this sudden hostility, realizing maybe he wasn't going as unseen as he'd like as a free passenger. "Well, I'd been told by Boomer, he wanted me to watch his next fight," he finally responded, trying not to let himself sound too confrontational. "Other than that, I guess I would just get off wherever was most convenient after that?"

"Well, we appreciate your service, but ship's startin' to rack up a hefty water bill." Nestor swiped another page, still not looking up. "Think

I can hear duty calling you away somewhere else, so I'd start thinking about your next port of call."

Boomer was stunned. "Nes! You can't be serious, that's so rude!" He stepped between the two humans, shielding Nes from Brann's view. "Don't listen to this grump, as far as I'm concerned you can escort us as far as you want, buddy. We wouldn't have gotten this far without you, *obviously*."

Nes let his coffee cup clatter a decibel too loud against the bar, thumbing off his screen with an irritable stab. "If I'm the manager here, then it's my job to manage your irresponsible ass into keeping expenses low between fights," he said, turning his baggy eyes to Boomer. He looked like he hadn't slept a wink. "That means not hiring everyone you trip over in a backwoods parking lot, and especially not giving up free rides to folks for no reason other than keeping your fragile self-image as a well-liked public personality intact." Nestor looked to Brann, then to Grishka for emphasis. Brann sunk a bit lower in his stool. Across the galley, Grishka simply croaked, rolling a cherry squash back and forth on the bar.

There was some tension here on both sides, something Brann had maybe missed in his night away from the ship, a conversation unheard between the two old friends. Boomer's response was equally nasty. "Then don't put me, your friend, your employer, in a position where I have to choose between you not stressing out over our treasury accounts and replacing the essential crew you're always complaining about me firing. Come to think of it, I seem to remember you giving me permission to make decisions aboard my own ship, isn't that right buddy? Or does that only apply to decisions you think I'm not smart enough to make?"

Nestor stood, staring down the much taller horse with legitimate anger. "You know what your problem is, old friend? You got all the balls in the world and nowhere to stow 'em, and it's up to us lesser creatures you like to rope into your dumb little escapades to carry them for you, because what good are we to you otherwise? Every decision you make you cry about turning out wrong and at the end of the day someone has to come behind you and clean up your mess, while you sniffle and wipe your nose on your nice velvet fuckin' shirts—that someone being me. Then when I do make your shitty decisions right again, you find some creative new way to undo that and set us back even further."

"Then maybe you'd be happier on another ship." Boomer crossed his arms at this.

Nestor scoffed, not taking the bait. "Happier? Definitely. Your sorry ass would be grounded in a month. First champion to lose the title because he couldn't get a ride to the fights anymore. Imagine that." Nes elbowed past Boomer—and, surprisingly, Boomer did not respond, remaining silent as Nes departed.

The room was silent. Grishka didn't seem to care much for this squabble, but Brann was definitely feeling the prickle of discomfort. He got the feeling if anyone but Nes had bumped Boomer like that, they would have been laid flat. Instead, the horse simply turned sullenly to the bar, the straw-like ends of his tail lashing against his leg.

"You know, Boomer, man," Brann began, breaking the silence if only to have it broken. "It's okay if I need to get out of your hair. I know I'm not really doing much to pull my weight as far as flying the ship is concerned, so if it's too much trouble covering my expenses, I can always find another duty station. I've been aboard several days longer than I expected anyway," he said, leaning back against the bar to look sideways at the horse.

Boomer didn't raise his head, tapping a fingertip on the bartop. "Nah. Ignore that old rag, he's just in a mood. You're right, anyway, I should've been taking more responsibility on earlier, choosing my own crew. He acts all pissed like I can't make sensible choices for the ship, but he doesn't get that me keeping him around was the most sensible thing I could think of. I mean he's another friend, another one of those people I rope in, like he says," the equine grumbled, turning away to lean on the bar as well. "He was a contract worker, started as one job, then became another, and eventually it turned out he knew everything about everything and everyone and it would have been stupid to hire anyone else to run the other deckhands on the Donnie. I mean if he's the best, and I like him, why replace him?"

Boomer scratched himself. "The same time, though, yeah, it's like...how can you put all that pressure on someone you want to keep as a friend for the rest of your life and expect them not to be put out when you bump them out of the driver's seat? He wanted a pilot to get us moving, we ended up with two—you don't even wanna know the spat Hawkshaw and Zay got into last night in the cockpit when we were trying to take off. He wanted more hands on board to go with us in landing parties, I found you," he said, motioning to Brann. "Or, rather, you found him, and I kept you. He may not like it because he's used to everything done all proper, but, if home base says it's cool that you keep flying with us, what's the big deal? I really don't see it."

Brann stayed silent at this.

"As for the other two," Boomer continued, "The priest guy is your guest for a bit, not like it's the end of the world to host a friend of a friend for a bit. The bird there, well..." He squinted a bit. "Truthfully I don't know who let her on or when she got here, but someone told me she maybe is gonna help cook a few meals? We have some good guys, but they're all borrowed maintenance workers, since..."

"The head cook voluntarily quit," Brann finished for him.

Boomer snorted, shaking his head. "Yeah, nah. I fired him. Easier to take your hand off the wheel and say people quit because it wasn't working out the way you wanted instead of saying you made the decision. If you aren't the one who said the words, how can they be mad at you, right? They'll still like you at the end of the day, won't they?"

Brann leaned forward to scoop his cup of coffee from his table, bringing it up to stare into it, swirling the cup apprehensively. "It's really important that people like you, huh."

Boomer stared at him dead on, blinking. "Well, what else is more important than that?"

Brann stared back. Boomer was being serious. Was it a matter of ego? Intelligence? Upbringing? The subtle differences in their species were rising like little snakes from the grass, cautioning Brann to tread carefully.

He searched for an answer to that question. Maybe there wasn't one. To buy himself some time, he took a sip of coffee.

Boomer smiled widely at that, breaking into a small laugh. "See, that's why I like you, kid," he said, elbowing Brann none-too-gently. "You know exactly what to say every time. I don't care what any of them say about you, you're great."

Brann swallowed hard, coughing a bit. "People are saying things about me?"

*

Up above in the main thoroughfare of the ship, on his way back to his quarters, Brann overheard low voices in a side passage. Keeping one ear close to the bulkhead to reduce the echo, he crept forward until he made out the speakers to be Zay and Red—the former of whom sounded quite agitated. Lady Red, however, was as cool as ice, just as the one encounter Brann had with her. He couldn't make out exactly the topic of conversation, but "payment" and "convenience" were decipherable through the metallic walls. Deciding not to let himself get caught eavesdropping, Brann stomped his feet in gradually rising volume as if he were walking closer before turning the corner, giving the two women time to break away from any sensitive subjects he wasn't meant to hear.

Zay was turned away with her arms crossed, but Lady Red stood anticipating Brann, hands folded together. "I had heard from my pet you stood by him in a battle of some evil dealings," she said in greeting, bowing slightly. "A very brave fighter you make, he tells me, though without much in the way of grace or experience."

Brann nodded sheepishly, sort of half-shrugging. "I mean. Things happen. You gotta be ready." What was meant to be humble just came off as cocky and smug, he realized too late. When Lady Red didn't respond, he realized with a start, "Ah! Right, this is yours." He unfastened the white sash from his belt, handing over her saber hilt-first, giving a kind of slight bow

178

of his own. "Sorry, should have gotten it back sooner. Wild night, I guess."

She twirled the weapon on its axis and refastened the sash to herself, drawing the blade smoothly to examine it, nodding to herself. "He also tells me you've brought along a rogue element, something of a caustic persona," she continued, almost as if half-speaking to Brann at all. "One lowly vagrant who sought to claim our heads, yet despite inflicting a killing blow, he rose from the dead and charmed you into some sort of personal arrangement. Did I hear all that correctly as well, young man?" She purred these words, as sweetly as she had to Wolf back on the street, standing over the corpse of the dead man.

Brann stiffened. "He...we talked. He gave me his word, he wouldn't cause trouble for you, and would keep to himself."

Lady Red nodded. "The same man who gave his word he was leading you to our mutual friend, here?" Her eyes flicked to Brann, but otherwise she was stock still, saber still held before her nose. Zay's shoulders rolled back uncomfortably, but otherwise she didn't turn to join in, remaining the silent bystander.

Brann paused. "He did, though." Another pause. "Eventually. Just took some...convincing."

Red smiled, her scarlet lips shining in the dim light of the passageway, looking almost black against her bloodless cheeks. "Convincing, you say. That is certainly one perspective."

She twirled the saber in a singing silver moulinet that made Brann flinch, housing the blade comfortably in its sheath in a deft subversion of momentum with the professed ease of an expert bladeswoman. "Without your presence there, indeed The Wolf may have met his end, I confess." She stepped forward, her polished boots clicking on the paneling, then stopped as if struck by an afterthought. "Though, considering it was my borrowed blade that kept the two of you alive, one does wonder how much a hand you truly played in last night's turn of events." She brushed past Brann, barely touching him, yet the motion still made him stumble. "I may yet need 'convincing' of my own, young pup," she called back to him around the corner, her voice bouncing daggers off the walls.

Brann was, again, crestfallen. Why was everyone acting like he'd done something wrong? He looked to Zay, who was lost in her own thoughts.

He recalled what Boomer said about her fight with Hawkshaw in the cockpit, and cautioned a friendly probe: "So, you're in charge of the ship now, huh?"

Zay spun, her eyes burning. "Bite your fucking tongue, kid," she spat, stomping past him and very intentionally pushing him into the wall.

Wrong thing to say, then.

Brann let himself vibrate from the impact a bit, then slid down, gravity pulling him into a fetal position, legs against his chest. He may be wearing a soldat's armor, and he may have fought a few monsters, but never before in his life did he feel like a kid more than he did now.

The young man wrapped his arms around his knees, choking back a lump in his throat. This whole adventuring thing was beginning to suck.

12. The Brace

Hawkshaw's voice rang out like a smooth holovision personality, crooning ever so lusciously over the PA system throughout the spaces on the ship. "It is with great pleasure I welcome you all to the next stop on our voyage, the ever-verdant city of Mongillo, nestled within the bosom of House Saintmarie territory. Though her borders may be cramped, her towering skyline of marble majesty challenges even the skies above, and her stadium gives even the fabled Broken Heart Temple of House Ito a run for its money with how resplendent it is. A perfect venue for witnessing tonight's bout of pitched combat between our very own champion fighter and his challenging opponent. Please enjoy your stay, and be sure to tip your pilot," he finished, signing off with a chuckle that even grated on Brann. He'd stowed himself below the main deck, finding a small porthole just astride one of the Donnie's overly large clawlike floaters to look out over the landing pad, the city stretching away on either side of them towards the stadium in question.

Saintmarie was reputed for its vast wealth and successful trade agreements longstanding between most of the major houses, and it came to no surprise now why Recruit Caleb was always so insufferable when speaking about his homeland. The city of Mongillo, despite not even being the capital city of the House's region, looked every bit as lavish as Hawkshaw had advertised in his little pilot's memo: towering white structures that looked as if they'd been chiseled out of towering mountains rose from the ground, a series of spiraling windows climbing upwards around their spirelike designs, as if the insides of the buildings were one continuous slope rather than a series of divided floors. Even with the tinted window shielding his eyes, Brann still had to squint from how bright the angelic structures looked beneath the high sun, the needle-shaped skyscrapers framed by even patterns of colorful flags and balconies that housed vibrant foliage on every structure. Some of the tallest buildings looked to even have whole parks at their peaks, trees with golden green leaves sparkling in the daylight from high above, casting their warped shadows down across the landing pad below.

The ship itself was being lowered by a great elevator built into the landing pad, the entire raised platform flattening itself until the ship was beneath roof height of even the shortest buildings in the city. The Donnie was a large craft in a desolate outpost of the Wilds, but here in Mongillo, she was dwarfed by more craft than not, even some civilian ships: one aircraft in particular that was being wheeled onto the pad by a tuglift looked as if the owner had simply taken a civilian's personal commuter skiff and blown it up to a scale of twenty times larger, the single pilot cockpit looking like a comically tiny head atop the body of a great fat bumblebee. Brann thought of what it would feel like piloting such a monstrosity, and felt embarrassed on behalf of the owner, who no doubt thought it a symbol of his own worth.

The Donnie was swiftly carted off the enormous pad, sidelined into a pigeonhole bay where she fit snugly, twin mezzanines running alongside it where service workers could inspect her before her next flight and refuel her elevated tanks. In the meantime, the cargo ramp opened directly into a welcoming hallway shrouded by dark red lights and strobing holoposters lining the walls. It was down this hall the entire crew of the Donnie made their way, and for the first time since being aboard, Brann saw the entirety of the staff that filled her spaces: a meager dozen alongside his named companions, recognizing only those he'd seen in passing on their way to their shifts, each dressed in matching jumpsuits streaked with patterns alongside their arms that mirrored the paintjob of the Donnie herself. Besides those in maintenance garb, only one of Boomer's personal trainers had deboarded as well, though from the way he was speaking angrily into his headset back to those left behind with the horse himself it sounded as if he may as well have stayed as well. Interspersed with the flight crew, the other passengers were walking to the stadium as well: Lady Red and The Wolf, the former wearing her same outfit, the latter having donned a surprisingly handsome brigandine that he wore with no small measure of pride, white and red matching his female companion. In fact, everything about him seemed groomed and clean, and Brann reasoned this was the first time he'd seen the werewolf not soaked in blood. The spear was draped appropriately over his shoulder, however, a white satin sash waving behind it as the pair walked. His attempt at making the weapon look less menacing, perhaps.

Some yards ahead of him, Brann also saw Hawkshaw, leaning in close to one of the female crewmembers, her grease-speckled arm looped around his own as she accompanied the automaton. Not far from them, striding on ahead with her signature impatient march, Zay cut a zigzag pattern around the slower civilian workers, still with that massive autocannon hanging off her back. Apparently, there were no real restrictions on self-arming in Mongillo, as Brann noticed the passing walkers going in other directions paid her no mind. In Barrier City, such a heavily armed woman would have caused quite a stir, probably bringing down the entire Nightwatch force on her head in moments. This put him immediately at ease—he himself had brought his rifle along as well, and fastened his breastplate over his street clothes, giving him the desired appearance of private security. Something about this city, despite its glamor and allure, had cautioned him to take protection along; Boomer had assured him he was clear to be armed when watching the fight according to the rules of his private box seats.

Grishka was nowhere to be seen, nor was Boomer. Emrys had promised he'd be at the fight and wanted to explore the shops beforehand; otherwise, Brann was left to pretty much just follow the flow of foot traffic to decide what to do before the big event. Deep down he'd hoped to have Boomer or Nes alongside him killing time, but obviously that wasn't possible, all things considered: in fact, if it weren't for the fact that this massive pedestrian tunnel only led between the ship bays and the stadium grounds itself, he'd almost wished he could simply disappear into the crowd and find his own way. Brann wasn't entirely sure what it was exactly that had begun to sour everyone towards him, but, given his status as a fugitive, it seemed the universe was calling him away to his own path away from the *Myrmidon* and its crew. Mongillo was well outside the easy reach of any arm of the Geihan military, Brann figuring Saintmarie to be nearly half a continent away based on charts he'd seen in class—what danger could he possibly be in at this point?

In fact, looking around him at the flashing lights of the holoposters, which depicted a stylized artist's rendition of Boomer promising a night to remember from the big fight, Brann really had gotten away, he decided. A deserter free and clear, there was no sense in expending all the money and resources it surely would take to track down a wandering young man with no real home to speak of: of course, Tark would have threatened to chase him down, that was his job as a military leader, to be intimidating and make big statements to keep his troops in line.

There were no security guards waiting for him any time he'd stepped off the Donnie.

There were no soldiers patrolling the footpath, interrogating the city's population.

There were no spies milling about scanning the faces of the crowd.

Brann was completely free to go his own way.

The pathway split off into a cross junction just before a great spiraling ramp that promised the stadium grounds were overhead, the opposite paths going to his left and right following an underground road brightly illuminated by the glow of hundreds of shop entrances, the signs all as foreign and visually taxing as the next. Brann felt like he could get lost down here forever, between the sparkling entertainment clubs, the hypnotic holoarcades, and the assault of appetizing seared meat and candied treat scents clawing for his stomach from the roaming food carts. In fact, in his sulking on board the ship this morning he'd neglected to have a proper lunch, and one particularly savory siren's call had rooted itself in his nostrils.

The pathway to the left—there was one wide cart being wheeled along by a kindly looking automaton, a slender monitor lizard no larger than a housecat basking on a raised panel in the steam rising from below. The cart seemed far less high-maintenance than some of the other flashier looking treat stands, the painted text across the side simply reading:

BRACES
CLASSIC or SPICY!

The smell was coming from this cart, he was sure of it. Brann flagged down the automaton, the mechanized clerk casting a blinking smile from its holoscreen face, likely no more than one or two responses programmed into it.

"Siksimassura?" A tinny speaker warbled out as Brann approached the cart.

"Sorry?" He leaned in, not understanding.

The automaton's little vicegrip hand clicked at an upward facing arrow button on its chest before waving to the cart.

"Siksimassura?"

"Oh, this, yeah—I'll take one," he replied, guessing his way through the transaction.

The person-sized mech clasped its little gripper hand around a slide mechanism and pulled until the overhead door of the cart slid open, a cloud of that meaty steam billowing out and bathing the monitor lizard in its aromas—the reptile lidded its eyes and tasted at the air rapidly, beads of condensation from the steam forming on the colorful scales of its snout. Reaching in, the robotic server produced a tightly wrapped bundle of foil sealed shut by a sticker marked with a 'C'. "Keshe, oo-spanna?"

It must have been programmed in some other language. "Yeah, that's fine, classic—uh, yeah, 'keshe'", he repeated, nodding and holding out his hand.

The lizard lunged at his hand with a warning hiss, Brann snatching his hand back at the last second to avoid a bite—"Shit, sorry, what!" He yelped, regarding the reptile fearfully as it slowly leaned back onto its perch of steamy delight, maw kept slightly open to show off those tiny teeth.

"You gotta pay first," came a voice behind him. Brann was casually pushed aside, Nestor reaching into his coat pocket to withdraw a gold-plated charger, clicking in the plunger four times to send as many scales clattering into a small tray being gripped by the small claws of one of the lizard's forelegs.

"Ti keshe, ti spanna," Nes said to the automaton, holding up two fingers. The tray tilted back towards the lizard and the scalenes fell into a hidden bank underneath the steamy tray, and a gleeful ding from the mech's chest indicated thanks for payment. Lifting a second foil wrap marked 'S', the clerk-bot handed both to Nes, and the treads of the food cart spun back up so it could trundle on its way—the lizard still glaring back suspiciously at Brann.

Nes handed the classic brace off to Brann, peeling open the layers of foil and paper on his own spicy. "You leave your charger back on the ship?" He asked, biting in.

"Not really a charger, more like just a sort of compartment on the breastplate to keep scales in," Brann replied, cautiously regarding Nes in case he was about to come under the older civilian's crosshairs again. "Mine was empty when I left the city anyway."

Nes nodded, not surprised by this news, making Brann feel even more like a bum. "Eat up, fight's not for a few more hours," he said through a mouthful of food, wiping his lips on the ball of his wrist. He slowly drifted back down the street, keeping an eye on Brann sideways to indicate the young man should follow.

Brann did so at arm's length, picking at his own wrapped brace. The foodstuff had definitely been machine-wrapped by the automaton, given how tight and clean the creases on the foil and paper were, giving him some difficulty in opening it. He didn't look Nes in the face as he strolled alongside, but decided to speak directly. There wasn't much to lose at this point by being blunt, but reticence was not earning him any favors.

"You want me to shove off once the fight's done, yeah?" He asked. He tried not to sound too much like a lonely child, but it happened anyway.

All he could do was be himself.

Nes swung his legs in exaggerated swirling motions to either side as he walked, despite his slow progress down the street—Brann wasn't the only one dealing with some uncomfortable thoughts apparently. The only response for a few seconds was some thoughtful chewing, wet and crunchy, piquing Brann's curiosity even further as to what mysteries lie within this new mystery meal.

"The thing about Boomer," Nes finally said through a swallow. "Thing is. He's never gonna be on the same page as anyone around him. He's never gonna grow up, and he's never gonna stoop low. There's no way to be the straight man to his antics, and there's no way to relax and enjoy the quiet when he means business. No matter what, we all get pulled into his wake. Like a...like a big ugly ship floating through a narrow canyon," he said, calling back to the incident at Belljar. "And it isn't until a big snake jumps outta the water and bites you in the ass does he realize maybe he's taking up too much space."

He took another bite, but didn't wait to swallow to continue speaking. Nes needed to finish his thought like the other night at the outpost, and like then, Brann didn't want to interrupt. "But fr'all the wreckage 'e leave behi'," he mumbled impolitely, "You c'n always count on 'im t'be 'onest." An appreciated swallow. "He'll never bullshit you—I mean, he will, but not really, not when it matters. Like a kid who doesn't know how to lie, all he really wants is a friend—if not that, someone to tell him that he's doing a good job, and keep doing whatever it is that he's doing that's making such a mess."

Brann was still listening, but Nes interrupted himself to reach over. "Here, just, quit peckin' at it and tear it open," he said impatiently, roughly ripping the foil lengthwise so Brann could finally get into his food. "Anyway. What I'm saying is, it can make it hard for someone who has to wrangle him in when he's bouncing all over the damn place for months and months at a time," Nes continued, nodding as Brann gave a small 'thanks' for opening his wrapper, "It can make it hard for someone like me to tell when he's the one actin' the fool or when you're the one just letting him piss you off. It's easier to get pissed and blame the guy who acts like a kid all the time than it is..." He took a bite hesitantly—a big one.

Brann stared at the brace with sullen interest before biting in. "Than it is to admit when you're acting like one yourself?" He offered.

They had woven a path through the crowd before coming to a stop before a set of open glass doors, the more formal lettering of the neon sign beckoning in the mature clothes-shopper into its aisles. Nes wiped his mouth a few more times, even though it looked perfectly clean to Brann.

"We have no shortage of beds on the Donnie, is what I'm saying," Nes negotiated uncomfortably. "That, and Zay coming along, she still has the deposit I paid for you, which—much as I could easily get it back—wasn't that big to begin with." He was struggling. "Boomer likes you, and he likes everyone—it's just his way. But he likes you like he likes me. He needs a friend, one who isn't acting captain, or like his dad, telling him what to do all the time. All his life, he's never been in charge of himself, and I think we all fucked up in just being okay with that."

Nes cleared his throat. "Well, I'm not okay with that anymore. He's not getting any younger, and we always expected the time was coming he would be done as a fighter—I sure as hell ain't getting any younger. He missed out on a normal life outside all this, just like you—he got squeezed under the thumb of the great House Geiha, and thought he was gonna live forever as their poster boy fighter. You and I know better than anyone that's a load of shit, and with that true-blooded warlord in charge of it all, they aren't ever gonna be happy letting some outsider settle all their big conflicts for them. Conflict's coming their way, or they're going out lookin' for it, but when that time comes that The Marshal decides to conquer another big region they fell out with on their last trade negotiations, it won't be a proxy war Boomer will be fighting for them."

He stared off, steam rising lazily from his half-eaten brace. "Boomer is gonna get set aside in favor of direct armed conflict. They have no use for all this ceremonial champion shit, and just kept him around to rake in the easy economic stimulus his image cultivated for them. Geiha has always taken their fights head on, and when next that happens, Boomer—and everyone he's surrounded himself with—we're all cooked. No more sponsors, no free rides, no comped stays at the local bed and breakfasts." Now he addressed Brann with direct eye contact at long last, and it startled Brann how sad and tired Nes really looked. "The kid who always got his way and never had to grow up is gonna be on his own, and we all have to decide on our own if we're really his friends, or if we just like the steady paycheck."

Brann was beginning to see the picture. "But he doesn't know the difference."

Nes nodded with a heaving sigh. "He couldn't know. He's just...too honest. He'll have a whole lifetime of his special collection of friends disappear without a trace, and no home of his own to go back to. And every time I make up another bed for one of his new pets he's brought home with him from our last pit stop..." Nestor swayed awkwardly, hoping Brann was getting the message.

Brann turned, leaning against the support pillar just beside the open clothes shop's doorway. "Look, I get what you mean. And—" He paused, realizing that for the first time, he was about to say out loud what only he and Nes knew, his secret being exposed between them in a hushed tone. "—And, yeah, with me ditching the military and all, I'm the first one who would split."

He kicked the heel of one boot back against the toe of the other, Brann staring at his feet—saying it out loud was too weird a feeling, like rolling over in bed onto an ice cube. "Yeah. I wouldn't trust me either." He didn't necessarily see his way to accepting this as an apology for Nestor's attitude at breakfast, but he at least understood a little more now about why things were shaking out like this. "I don't wanna lie and say I think we're gonna be best friends for life, I just met you all like, what, a week ago, less? I like it on the Donnie, and I don't have anywhere else to go—I don't know where I'm going now."

Nes added a detail Brann hadn't even considered: "No House Lachlan to go back to, anyway."

"Right." Brann turned his meal this way and that, still not taking a bite. "Least on the ship I have a bed, and—food," he pointed at the brace, "Which is about all I ever expected from being in the service, that and being threatened with some heinous punishment if we didn't go along with everything they told us to do."

The truth of the matter was a simple one, and Brann was suddenly happy to be so young, realizing he had a better hand to play here than he thought. He looked back at Nes, shrugging, his best idea of a solution being no more complicated than his basic needs. "I never had a friend either. Not a real one. I like Boomer too, and I have just as much reason to stay with him as go on alone. At least he keeps things interesting."

He paused, smiling. "That bed is also...absurdly comfortable."

Nes looked down his nose in mock smugness. "Only the finest mattresses are worthy of the legendary *Myrmidon* and her crew."

The space was empty on the wall next to Brann, and Nes decided to fill it, leaning against it shoulder to shoulder with the wayward young deserter. "C'mon, eat, I paid good money for your broke ass to try this."

Brann had gotten enough of an eyeful of the brace already: some sort of crusty bun that even so yielded under the touch, a golden skin crackling gently and concealing soft fluffy bread and fillings within. Brann craned his neck to bite down at an angle, tearing away a mouthful of steamy goodness: tender flakes of buttery meat split like paper in his teeth, a mixed arrangement of thin slices, fatty and salty. The spoon-soft meat needed no help, but nevertheless a thick and satisfying wash of tangy sauce burst between bites, punctuated by the crispy pops of fried string vegetables collapsing into a fruity and peppery sideshow.

He had to work at chewing his mouthful, barely containing his surprise at how much the street food jolted his tastebuds to life, Brann nodding and vainly trying to lick away a smear of various sauces from his upper lip. "S'fuckin' good," he mumbled, grinning through his full mouth.

"Right, this stuff's how you loosen a fuckin' screw or two," Nes nodded back with a hearty chuckle as he took another overly large bite of his own, nodding alongside his shipmate in their shared moment of simple satisfaction. He clapped Brann on the shoulder, waving to the doors of the shop. "Finish up, we'll go in and get some new threads."

Brann barely swallowed that first bite before he descended on his next hungrily. "Yeah, first time seeing you in regular human clothes, by the way," he joked, referring to Nestor's coat and distinct lack of greasy jumpsuit.

"Least I can afford my own, ya freeloading, smartass little twink," the engineer rebuked, snorting with laughter as Brann had to pause mid-bite so as not to choke.

13. The Tournament

The piercing, nasally wail of a soaring guitar seared electric waves of noise through the chests of the roaring crowd, the uplifting intro track bringing to life the already boiling armies of people crammed into the stadium as Boomer's walk-on music sent them into a frenzied overload. Overhead, the wildly flashing beams of laserlight burned flashes into the smoky air itself of symbols that announced the impending entrance of the champion: the emblem of Geiha, a pair of crossed fists, spread wings, and of course: a stylish 'B'. The countless fans screamed and applauded along to the rising chorus of their favorite fighter's classic intro song as the spotlight lasers all began to converge and fold inwards towards one fixed point far below the globe of the stadium's arched ceiling: the black mouth of the tunnel extending out from ground level towards the elevated platform three or four stories up from the low center of the stadium's basin. Sparks of crimson, ochre and gold began to shoot from the archway of the tunnel, and just as the crowd cheered the final words of the chorus and the name of the song itself, Boomer leapt from the darkness of the tunnel to stand at the platform's edge with his arms raised high. The subsequent guitar riff was drowned out entirely by the hurricane of noise he pulled from the masses, the entire world alight for him tonight.

Brann had to pop his ears and yawn to keep from losing his hearing, the buzz in his ears becoming a ring. The balcony overlooking the platform was close enough a person could probably fall and land in the fighter's pit without serious harm, though he was in no hurry to test this—their box seats jutted out from a beveled platform to tell everyone else in the stadium they were the chosen few accompanying Boomer tonight, an identical balcony likewise overlooking the opposite end of the platform, though from this distance Brann couldn't make out the occupants. Boomer's opponent tonight was a member of another species Brann had, unsurprisingly, never heard of, and was accordingly curious—apparently this was the toughest fighter ever produced in that particular corner of the continent, from a nation notorious for being unwilling to partake in showy politics. Or so Emrys had told him: the priest sat to Brann's left, freshly trimmed and scrubbed in his new pressed outfit of black and white, even having rewrapped his hands in bright and clean new gauze. Nestor hadn't changed, but had picked out a new outfit for Brann as well, one that more appropriately suited the style of the Donnie's crew—a combination of a long vest and high-collared undershirt with its sleeves rolled up just under his elbows, along with a utilitarian looking scarf coiled tightly around his neck and ending in a similar over-the-shoulder drape as the capelets of the Geihan uniforms. The look was completed by his newly polished breastplate once again fastened over the whole thing—it was beginning to look a little worse for wear, scrapes of paint missing and some dents visible from the fight with the arch eel, but overall, he felt it gave him an air of toughness: he was fashionably ready for a fight, should one arise.

He knew what it meant to dress comfortably—but never before tonight did Brann knew what it meant to look good doing it.

Down the row of seats, Hawkshaw and his female companion leaned in to hoot and scream out with the crowd—Brann still didn't recognize this woman, yet couldn't shake the feeling he recognized her from somewhere, like a passing face among the crew who had nodded politely at him while passing onboard the ship at some point. Zay sat silently, arms crossed across her leather-clad chest, though became considerably less unhappy looking when a server approached and offered her a tall jar of some kind of sizzling candy.

Turning the other way, diplomatically sitting as far away from Emrys as possible, The Lady Red was clapping one hand softly against her dainty wrist with the utmost of politeness, looking as vivid as ever in her immaculate red outfit—meanwhile, The Wolf was hunched low in his own seat, looking equal parts anxious and excited, ears pinned back against the noise that was likely the single thing keeping him from engaging in the same merriment as the crowd. Brann surveyed his travelling companions and their reactions to the whole display, finding it all as enthralling as the noise and splendor of the stadium itself: he was already giddy from experiencing this overload of fun, but knowing that he wasn't the only one being pulled along in spite of themselves made it all the better, even the famously stony Nestor clapping as he looked down at his longtime companion jabbing at the air in anticipation of the fight.

Boomer's lightly-padded fists were still waving in the cheers of the crowd when the lights died off briefly before rising up in a wave of swirling purple and white beams spotting the opposite wall of fans in shifting star patterns. The music too was cut off in favor of a new, far more sinister track of twangy strings and harsh sounding drums in a rapid beat of rising urgency. The opponent's intro music was far more alien to Brann's ears, and he leaned forward to see what kind of fighter would be worthy of facing down an enemy as sizeable as the towering equine man below.

The opposite tunnel had already extended to the platform, a pair of gemstone-faceted filters beaming up those swirls of bright white and purple haze across the stadium on either side of it, like a great insect with the proboscis probing for the fighter's pit. From within the inky depths, a hunched silhouette slunk forward, staying low until a beam of purple light fell from above to freeze it in place.

The fighter stood tall, raising a single fist in an uproar that rivaled Boomer's fans, the opposite end of the stadium sparkling with holoscreens and laserlight. Brann had to take a moment to fully understand what he was seeing, as this was no kind of creature he'd ever seen: lanky, lithe, yet shifty with taut flesh that shifted and flowed around its neck and shoulders, the torso and abdomen not hidden by those fighter trunks coated in some kind of short, oily fur. The arms, legs and head of the creature were bony, plate-like even, like a beetle or a suit of armor, and the head was a fearsome sight even among all the outlandish people Brann had encountered thus far—like the skull of a beast somewhere between lizard and dog yet belonging to neither, the face alive and expressive as any but deceptively camouflaged by a protective bony mask and fangs that cupped its jaw. The fists uncurled, revealing hands that bore only three fingers in a Y formation that Brann realized with a start ended in gigantic claws that had been padded as well to prevent injury to the horse during the fight. Likewise, those feet with their trio of talons gripping into the cushioned floor would likely have torn the surface to shreds without the buffer of those soft sleeves wrapping them, and just when the appearance of the beast couldn't appear stranger to Brann, he caught sight of the twin whiplike tails lashing energetically at the air behind the bipedal organism with all the fervor of a centipede's agitated antennae.

Nestor leaned in to yell something to Brann, who couldn't hear a word of what was said. He assumed Nes had seen his fascination and was trying to tell him the name of the creature, but to no avail. Brann was awestruck by this newest example of just how sheltered things were back in his home city, and by simple strangeness alone he suddenly wasn't as doubtful any other living person could challenge Boomer in the ring.

Boomer, meanwhile, was feigning fear at the intimidating display of the other fighter's grasping claws pointing in his direction, but nonetheless let the facade fall away with his boyish grin beaming back out into the stands, his hands waving away the challenge much to the delight of the rowdier stadiumites.

Something was nudging against Brann's arm—he turned, seeing Nes had penned something on his holoscreen. A single word:

KLIKUSHKI

Brann read this, shaking his head with a complete lack of understanding, then looked back at Boomer's opponent when Nes pointed. This must be the name of this fearsome looking race. Brann nodded and made an 'o' shape with his mouth to signal understanding, then Nes wiped away the word and wrote something else:

NAME IS RAUM. GOOD MATCH TONIGHT.

Nes was making a face like he was impressed by Raum's reputation, and Brann nodded again. Probably he wouldn't have bothered saying anything if this were just another run of the mill bout.

Raum was rolling his shoulders and rocking his hips to and fro, and even through the wall of sound Brann could swear he heard the klikushki's entire bony body clicking with each movement. The two fighters finally drew together in reserved stances as if summoned, standing inches apart in the center of the pit; Brann realized though he hadn't heard it, the giant holoscreen above the platform depicted the fight's live broadcast, where the empty space between the two fighters in real life was occupied by an electrograph image of a referee relaying rules to them both.

Another nudge. Nestor's screen read:

BONE CONDUCTION MOUTHGUARDS

So the fighters could hear the callouts above the noise of the stadium, Brann reasoned. And so no living referee would risk serious injury intervening in the potentially devastating fight they were about to witness.

The lights came up and cleared away the clashing opposite spectrums of color, bathing the whole enormity of the stadium in a blanket of soft white, the flesh and bone bodies of the two combatants below as crisp and easily visible against the dark padding of the pit as any laserlight. The final words by the invisible referee must have been spoken, because both pugilists nodded stiffly and raised gloves to give each other chest salutes before bumping them together respectfully, though Boomer's was definitely not without his usual saucy air of arrogance. The two spread apart, slinking back and lowering themselves into ready stances, wrapped fists raised and at the ready.

The crowd seized, the chatter low, and a horn blared out from the rafters—the fight was on.

Light bounces on his hooves brought Boomer into the center of the ring, engaging the klikushki head on, no real strategy that Brann could see in his approach. The demon-like Raum simply awaited the horse's onslaught of blows, ducking low with arms raised to absorb Boomer's rapid fists—Boomer broke off quickly, and as he shook his hands, Brann realized that it must hurt like hell punching into what looked like solid bone. He adjusted his approach, lowering himself as well to Raum's height, stepping in with his hooves sweeping forward to lunge for Raum's shins before Boomer twisted himself into a wild hook at Raum's head as the klikushki danced over the low sweeps.

Raum was no doubt far more cautious than calculating, anticipating this as well, punishing the quick high and low with a vicious riposte—spinning so quickly he went airborne for a moment, Raum's upper body whipped his lower half around so fast his leg looked like a blade cutting the air, slamming directly into Boomer's gut and sending the horse stumbling back with the accompanying howl of the crowd. Boomer didn't let his fists fall, but was visibly winded, shaking his head in frustration: shouldn't have been so flippant. He snorted, expelling the pain from his lungs, and approached Raum again—slower this time.

Raum moved to the offensive with a feinting maneuver that Boomer fell for, dipping to one side to expose the horse's neck and shoulders when he moved to mirror, then a trio of lightning quick blows from his wide-arcing right pummeled Boomer's upper bicep. Shouldering the attack gave Boomer the opening needed to come close, absorbing the grievous assault to unleash a punishing response of his own; with quickness defying his size, the barrel chest of the horse heaved upward, followed by a surprise knee directly up beneath Raum's chin, bashing the lighter man back into a recoil that broke his stance for only a second—and that second was all Boomer needed, speeding forward to wipe away those fists that attempted to close Raum's guard and unleashing a blinding flurry of chest high jabs directly into Raum's body.

If the energy of the crowd could be measured in light, the arena would be arcing white hot beams into the air, the rising screech of shock and delight at the velocity with which the fight had escalated so quickly in the first round enough to power a whole city. Raum was bullied backwards several meters on the platform before his rear foot found a steady foundation to dig in and he curled in sufficiently enough to halt Boomer's furious attack. Still taking heavier swings at the lowered Raum, Boomer kept the pressure on, making sure there would be no respite until the horn—which blared two short bursts, signaling the round's end as Boomer immediately pulled off.

Brann ignored the urge to holler out with the crowd as another nudge of Nestor's holoscreen brought him around:

3 ROUNDS MAX

1. TESTING EACH OTHER

2. SHORTER, BUT THEY GO ALL OUT

Brann mouthed to Nes silently: "What about three?"

Nestor just nodded to the ring, signaling the next round was about to start after this short interlude.

He was right, round two was no joke: where a moment ago the fighters were more quick and agile, dancing around each other to move in and out and take their quick shots, this second horn immediately put them together head-to-head in a startling display of absolute power.

Boomer opened with a roundhouse that looked to go too wide when Raum ducked low to avoid, then quickly turned lethal with a pivot that paired with Boomer flexing his knee to extend his leg like a switchblade and kick directly into Raum's skull. The face of any human would have been instantly mulched by this, but the bony plate shielding his head surely saved Raum's life, though he nonetheless fell back stunned—and, when he blinked, a second set of eyes popped open just behind the first, making Brann flinch in surprise again. This klikushki race was just full of surprises.

Something Boomer was about to learn up close and personal, as his repeat of round 1's dual assault did not go as intended. When Raum stumbled back and Boomer dashed forward again, Raum didn't stop himself—instead he simply rolled, taking Boomer over one shoulder and flipping his center of mass so gravity brought the klikushki down hard directly into Boomer's stomach again on the mat, making the horse's eyes bulge. Raum wasted no time, spinning to the side to continue rolling, sweeping up Boomer's arm between those bony legs and pinning the horse—and in an impressive display of flexibility, while his legs locked, his upper body twisted back to throw a brutal volley of elbow strikes over and over again into Boomer's face, the horse unable to shield himself with his pinned arm adequately while still keeping his elbow from snapping, eyes squeezing shut as each elbow sent gradually larger spurts of blood spraying across the mat.

The crowd on Boomer's side rose in boos, but the maneuver must not have been illegal, as no attempt was made to end the round early by the horn. Boomer simply endured, head snapping back and forth three, four, six, a dozen times, until his large nostrils were a geyser of red and the palomino fur was awash in it. Finally, once he seemed this close to going limp, the horn clenched twice and Raum withdrew, though not without a cocky roll of his shoulders acknowledging the side of the crowd rooting for him.

Boomer stayed prone on the mat for a moment, and Brann was gripping the arms of his seat in a panic—then the horse rose at last, somehow, impossibly, smiling even still. He wiped away the heavy flow of blood from his snout, thumbing one nostril shut to blow air through the other, sending a healthy glut of clotting red splattering disgustingly across the padding. He turned up to look at his balcony, the entire audience on edge—even Zay seemed somewhat concerned, having forgotten to keep chewing her candy.

Again, he just smiled, and with a wink Brann could swear was meant for him, the horse punched himself reassuringly in the side of his head a couple times before returning to face Raum, his mane tousled with blood and sweat.

"Round three?" Brann repeated silently. Nes put pen to screen to hastily scribble his longest note yet, then turned it around:

IF NO ONE BOWS IN TWO,

THIRD DOESN'T STOP TILL ONE GOES DOWN

He turned it around again, adding another word, which he underlined aggressively:

<u>PERIOD</u>

This truly was a sport to settle conflicts for good, then. Brann turned back, looking up at the giant screen. A pair of announcers were chatting inaudibly, no doubt regarding the fight itself, and in this extended pause Boomer and Raum had also turned their attentions to watch in anticipation. The way they both moved, their posture and energy, Brann doubted either fighter wanted their towels thrown in.

The screen changed, showing two separate zoomed in shots of the fighters cut together as if they were standing shoulder to shoulder and not several meters apart. Their faces both slicked with blood (though Boomer's definitely moreso), chests heaving and bright sweat speckles glistening under the lights, the names of their respective nations appeared beneath the collarbones of the two. Beneath Boomer, "GEIHAN EMPIRE" shone on its green backdrop, while "HOUSE KLIKUSHKA" in purple lettering mirrored it with white borders.

The image hung there expectantly, then Boomer's side flashed red: The Geihan Empire did not concede, and Boomer renewed his grin with a fist in the air, waving back at his fans who wanted to see a total knockout. After a tense moment with no immediate response, at last Raum's electronic banner also flashed red, and the entire stadium was roaring again: neither side would forfeit, and only complete defeat would name the winner.

Brann shuddered as goosebumps rolled over the flesh of his arms: he couldn't tell if this excited him or filled him with dread, but he definitely felt queasy knowing more blood was yet to be shed. If he knew anything about Boomer yet, he knew the horse wouldn't let up, and nothing about the challenger's attitude said he was disappointed by this decision either. He hadn't thought to ask before the fight started, but suddenly Brann was wondering to himself if this would be to the death or not.

The horn blared a third time. The fighters moved in.

Almost wishing he didn't have to watch, Brann raised his hands, feeling moments away from covering his eyes. He was glad he wasn't, though, as what happened next came so fast and unexpectedly, he wouldn't have believed it if he hadn't seen it himself.

Raum went high at Boomer's head, looking to capitalize on his bloodied face, Boomer's fists held low as he seemed to expect another mid-body assault. A swipe from Raum's left connected, Boomer's neck tightened to keep his head from rolling, and it was in this moment that the challenger realized his mistake.

Absorbing the slap, Boomer's body carried the momentum of the blow around, and up, down the length of his leg in another roundhouse kick that this time aimed true and brought his hoof straight into the back of Raum's neck. Feeling the entire weight of the horse channeled into this one powerful strike just below his brainstem, Raum nearly collapsed on the spot, legs giving out from under him as all four eyes blinked without seeing. He went low, taking a single knee to steady himself, preparing to rise again.

Raum didn't have the chance. Where he had went slack and slowed, Boomer carried that same momentum around and spun the opposite direction—where Raum kneeled, Boomer was waiting with a full-bodied right hook that hugged his body until the last second—and like a meteor launching from orbit, plowed so deeply into Raum's face that Brann COULD hear the crack over the noise of the crowd.

Like he'd been shot from a cannon, Raum flew backwards from his stagger, going horizontal and spiraling away to land face down in the matt, nearly a full three bodylengths away.

The moment of silence was deafening, and then the crowd responded in kind. Hands over his ears were all that stopped his eardrums from bursting, Brann dazed from the absolute explosion of full-throated cheers from thousands of viewers, tasting blood on his tongue before realizing he was one of them screaming into the whirlwind. Everyone in Boomer's box was on their feet at the balcony, leaning over the edge to reach and clap at the horse—even The Wolf was howling out, swept up in the chaos, lights beginning to flash all over the stadium in the colors representing Boomer as well as House Geiha.

That fist, still extended, raised skyward. Boomer turned, his pained smile now one of relief, and he looked upwards at the balcony. He tilted his torso, that fist raised above his ears, while his other hand pointed directly at Brann.

That was why they called him 'Boomer,' thought Brann, his face feeling like it would split in two with his wide smile, and he returned the point, his own free hand raising into a matching fist.

It was then, at the peak of the noise and fervor and glee, the sound of an intercom speaker crackled, severing all the joy and electricity with the cold blade of fear that made Brann's blood freeze and the smile disappear from his face in an instant.

"Recruit Brann of House Lachlan. Step forward, if you would."

*

The entire stadium was illuminated with the full bearing of thousands of lights, casting every face human or otherwise in maximum exposure where none could hide in any shadows. The crowd was murmuring amongst themselves, confused, some stray applause still peppering the air from those who might see it all as part of the show still. The voice of Marshal Tark carried every note of menace it did back in the palace grounds, but on a loudspeaker for all to hear, it was positively damning to Brann's soul. Raum was being carried from the platform back towards his entrance tunnel by a host of his fellow klikushki, Boomer dropping his showman's display and looking around overhead to locate the source of the voice.

Brann himself was caught in the cold gaze of everyone in the box with him, all their eyes demanding answers with silent expectation. He looked back behind the seats, towards the entrance to the box—the stairway beyond was locked off to prevent rowdy fans from getting past the general seating areas, and the recessed ceiling of the balcony left no room for him to hide. Slow as a glacier, Brann drew his eyes up to the giant holoscreen, and sure enough, his expression of panic was caught in exhausting detail in the eye of the unseen cameras that were showing his sweat-beaded face to the entire world in real time.

There was no running this time.

Brann took a few more unsteady breaths, peeling his eyes from the screen above, and stepped forward to the edge of the balcony. He'd leaned his rifle against it earlier when taking his seat—he demonstratively raised it now, cradling it in the crook of one arm as his other gave a mock salute. He looked around at the faceless thousands, the tiny dots of light and flesh tones scattering the walls separated by hundreds of meters of empty air. Wherever the Marshal was, he was not immediately visible, likely to make another grand intimidating entrance.

Frankly, Brann didn't want to give him the satisfaction. Something inside him, stirring beneath his fear, reached up from below—the smell of Mother Superior's incenses in his nostrils, a phantom scent memory. Swallowing the knot in his windpipe he cleared his throat, jutting his chin out, looking directly up into the array of lights overhead where he assumed the cameras were and called out loud enough that he hoped the microphones would hear:

"Why don't you step forward, Marshal? I'm not hiding from anything, what about you? I thought we were supposed to be the pride of the Geihan empire—isn't that why you make us wear all that pretty armor? Or what, you don't want your ugly mug up on the big screen? Camera shy, that must be it—the big badass kuaneach afraid of the spotlight after all. Come out where we can all see you, why don't you?"

Down below, Boomer was throwing a thumbs up with a giant grin, but beside him, Brann could tell Nes and the other crew were palming their faces in embarrassment. Not only was Brann probably about to get arrested live on continental holovision, but he was likely to drag everyone into his mess with him.

The speaker crackled again, and Tark replied thusly: "As you wish."

A wrench of metal, a powerful smash of steel on wood, and the balcony doors exploded inward towards the seats—a pair of limp security guards were tossed forward through the air like wet rags, and through the yawning jaws of the destroyed doors came the Marshal in a full battle rage as swift as the storm. His gilded horns nearly gouged the low ceiling, platinum mask shielding his visage against the hailfire of Hawkshaw's twin autopistols in showers of sparks and smoke. The balcony was small, and the furious kuaneach practically glided forward to cross it in seconds, coming straight for the paralyzed Brann.

One powerful hand gripped his enormous axe just below the head, the other crushed the tiny speakerphone he'd likely lifted from one of the guards and waved away the dust, Tark's entire body wreathed in smoke as he spoke aloud to Brann while ignoring the others.

"You owe me a life," he snarled, the most hate-filled words Brann had heard him speak yet, even without raising his voice by more than a shade.

The occupants moved to protect Brann, none so swift as The Wolf—with practiced ease of a veteran warfighter, that spear was already splitting the air towards Tark's heart, the werewolf lunging behind it with his fangs bared. Tark was a breath away from Brann when he was forced to dodge backwards, swiping up his axe to knock away the stabbing spear as it glanced off his pauldron, catching Wolf by the throat in the same motion with his free hand—his claws dug into the soft brisket of The Wolf's collar, and Wolf gasped, the breath being squeezed from him. Brann saw Tark's luminescent eyes narrowing as he leaned in, examining the creature.

"You and I, we have shared a battlefield," he said with quiet recognition, grunting as he hefted the entire massive weight of the werewolf off the floor, those broad footpaws dangling helplessly. "My quarrel is not with you—now, heel."

He spat this last taunt out with a grunt as he rolled his entire body to the side, throwing the Wolf over the balcony's edge with his full weight behind him, sending the lycanthrope sprawling in a tall arc through the air to land flat on the platform far below. The crowd audibly gasped, hundreds of onlookers watching the display unfolding before them while the rest were fixed on the holoscreens above, watching it all in high definition.

The next was Lady Red, and as Nestor pulled Brann away from the balcony's edge by the arm, he saw the corsair noblewoman unsheathe her blade and engage in combat for the first time, to devastating effect: Her white glove gripped the hilt of the saber and, with a small focused cry from Red, a twist of the handle sent a hidden needle long as her finger spiking directly into her wrist with a spray of arterial steam. Like a torch coming alight in a searing flame, the mirror steel of her saber was doused in a coating of her own lifeblood—nearly a foot of length was added to the weapon's profile, the entire elegant sword warping into a horrific bloody display of body magic. Lady Red gave another one of her twirling moulinets to ready herself before charging forward.

The assault was one that would have taken any other weak stomached man off guard, but Tark showed no signs of being impressed by the vampiric blade, simply twisting his body and dancing out of the way of each of her impossibly fast swordstrokes, the sound of thick liquid splashing against nearly every surface as she swung. The more she concentrated, the more the Lady Red's saber grew with scarlet rage—and Brann could see the rosy blush of her cheeks fading pale: she was literally draining her own blood to corner Tark with her attack.

Not for long, though, as the saber had grown so long it began to cut like a viscous scythe through the seats and the carpet, streaks of steaming blood gouging the surfaces of the box all around the swift kuaneach. Tark kept himself low and flexible enough to avoid each strike narrowly until Red overstepped the extended reach of her weapon and he was on her, slapping away her blade and sending it too flying out over the edge of the balcony, the woman gasping as the intravenous needle was suddenly yanked from her arm. Tark spun in a crouch, and like a giant snake whipping through the air, his massive tail collided directly into Red's back—the corsair was airborne, disappearing out of sight over the railing.

Hawkshaw had abandoned his attempts to fire on the Marshal and instead wrapped himself around his woman companion, shielding her from the frenzy with his long trenchcoat before leaping with her off the balcony willingly. Only Nestor, Emrys and Zay remained behind with Brann now, and with Zay still struggling to load her stripped machinegun, Emrys was the only one up and ready to fight.

"My foolish son, no greater a mistake could you have made," he was saying, already crumbling a page from his spellbook in his bandaged hand. "These good people? They walk in the company of death itself."

The green sparks from his arm spattered wildly, and with an uppercut of his glowing arm, a burst of light shot forth into a web—no, not a web, Brann blinked, watching a ghostly pentad of skeletal arms materializing through the jettisoned wall of ectoplasm and wrapping themselves like serpents around Tark. Their bony clawed fingers dug in, tearing at his scales and face, the ghostly light howling angrily and clenching tighter around him in a concentrated vise of necrotic energy. He came to his knees, axe falling aside—and Brann leapt up from behind Nestor with joy.

"You got him!" He shouted, Emrys already readying another page.

Nestor wasn't so sure—the engineer pushed at Brann, backing him against the railing of the balcony again. "Jump," he whispered.

"What?!" Brann was incredulous. "He's down!"

"Jump, idiot!" Nestor threw his weight against the young man, and Brann was falling, the lights of the stadium overhead for a lurching moment of surprise before he saw the platform below heading up to greet him rapidly.

With all the litheness of a junglecat, a dark furred shape leapt from the dark mat, snatching Brann bodily out of the air and landing with him cradled safely—The Wolf had caught him, and was steadying Brann onto his feet, dizzy from the fall.

Up above, Nestor was already falling feet-first, The Wolf nearly knocking Brann over as he pounced again, only barely catching the older man in time and spinning to slide against the padded floor with Nestor on top of him. Red was being helped up by Boomer, and Hawkshaw and once again unsheathed his pistols—beside him, the dark-haired woman shuddered before her disguise was liquified in a haze of fog, and Grishka stood beside the automaton with her short body held low and wings spready defensively. All stood and waited as the balcony above was becoming dangerously bright with its green glow, the howl of the dead becoming unbearably loud.

Brann heard Zay curse, and a sound like a guillotine falling cut the howl of energy short, a second of silence before the explosion came: the necroplasmic nova burst out in a wide tidal wave and two dark bodies were swept along on its skeletal crest, Emrys and Zay tumbling down headfirst. The fall would have killed them both as they landed—but the plasm bathing their bodies turned the ground to gelatinous puddles, the two of them pulling themselves out of their small pools of energy with pained moans.

The entirety of Boomer's party was now joined with him down in the fighter's pit, and as they stood and readied themselves for more, the holoscreens above captured their battered resolve in panoramic view: nine companions all standing at the ready, waiting the re-emergence of the Marshal Tark from the balcony overhead, weapons singing as they were primed and aimed.

Tark eventually did reappear, and Brann was struck by the unexpected sight of him: the black and fuchsia scales all over his hide had crystalized into vivid purple growths like feathery blades, the boiling hiss of necrotic green turning to steam all over him as it was washed away. The Marshal gazed down over the platform, raising his axe and rolling his neck to crack it loudly, those serrated translucent scales slipping back into his body and returning him to his mostly armorless organic self.

"I've no patience for the vain flourishing their toys in hopes of scaring me off," he began speaking, loud enough now that a great many in the stadium could likely hear him even without the assistance of the hidden microphones catching his voice, "As if I were some toothless kobold recoiling at the sight of a magician's parlor tricks. There is a singular purpose to my existence, and that is the pursuit and cultivation of higher warfare." He brought the head of his greataxe down in a sudden burst of fury on the railing of the balcony, an earsplitting clang and another burst of sparks emphasizing his rising anger. Tark raised his hand, removing that decorative mask to once more reveal his face fully, those rugged scales still smoldering their dangerous purple hue.

A moment passed, purple steam dissipating about his visage—he closed his eyes and inhaled to center himself, and when he opened them again, he had reclaimed his composure once more.

"Recruit Brann," he began, taking a moment to dust off his capelet. "You're out of uniform, son."

He looked to each of them in turn, eyes settling on Nestor. Brann could swear he saw a flicker of surprise for a brief moment slipping through the gaps in Tark's hardened expression.

"Nestor, old friend." Tark's voice betrayed neither sincerity nor sarcasm. He simply spoke as plainly and stiffly as if he were addressing the troops. "I admit, of all the unlikely faces I'd expect to see among this lot, yours is an unfortunate one, if not entirely unwelcome."

Brann shot a look at Nes, eyes wide. Nes didn't return the look, simply crossing his arms and speaking back up to the kuaneach with the same disdain he showed Brann back on the ship the morning earlier.

"Marshal," he drawled, a half-smile threatening the corners of his mouth. "We really need to catch up one of these days, have a drink together. Get to know more about the kinds of company we're keeping lately." He spread his arms wide. "Though I have a feeling in a contest between the two of us in that respect, I'd probably win."

"Of all admirable qualities I attribute to you, Nestor, the ability to judge the character of another is not one of them. All apologies, but that drink will have to wait."

Tark returned his gaze to Brann. Once he locked in, that same cold fear began spreading from within the young deserter's gut. A dragon's eyes were like a father's eyes: there was no staring back without the urge to blink becoming unbearable.

"I have conquered foes greater than the sum of any gaggle of miscreant bandits you may surround yourself with, young soldat," Tark continued, and like a silent host of shadows the Marshal was surrounded by a dozen Uhlen casually watching everything unfold with their same familiar smug posturing. "I promised you a debt would be collected—did you regard my words as faithless? Did I not stake my claim over your life entire?"

He was working himself up, growing visibly angrier, his normally placid and understated exterior crackling with black rage. Tark was nothing less than Brann's angel of death, and this was his sermon.

The Marshal broke his thousand-mile stare at long last, looking up to the rafters of the high stadium ceiling, speaking into the cameras and addressing the audience. "Good, honorable people of Saintmarie, of Klikushka, of Geiha, of the world entire," he bellowed, a dragon's primal roar tinging his fanged words. "The Assay of a coward is underway, before you the young soldat pledged to my own great Empire's service who abandoned his call to higher meaning. Brann, a conscript of a fallen house worth no mention of any consequence, fled before me on what was to be the proud day of the reclamation of his life's purpose, out of the gutters of his youth's vagrancy." Tark looked back down now, casting a judgmental hand over the platform. "Aligning himself with what can only be a suitably treacherous outfit of bandits and lowly villains, he rejected a life of dignity and noble sacrifice in favor of taking our very own House Champion hostage on board a ship of luxuries and easy living, choosing to leech of the accomplished to satisfy his soft palette." Tark let his hand fall to his side, head shaking. "An honest living defending his homeland sent him scampering off to find a stocked pantry to hide himself away in. A more abhorrent blemish on my own reputation I could not fathom, and to all who have been taken advantage of by this young toad, I offer my most humble of apologies."

Through the hot shame swelling in his ears, Brann could hear Boomer shouting indignantly about being taken hostage, but the microphones weren't interested in what anyone in the fighter's pit had to say: all eyes were on The Marshal now, and his proclamation was made manifest for the world entire in these harrowing minutes he spoke.

"Recruit Brann and his unruly compatriots, living off the gifts we give to our Champion—" Tark paused slightly, almost as if he'd forgotten the name, "—Boomer, to whom a lifetime of service in resolving disputes on behalf of our great nation in ritual combat has been rewarded." He wrapped a hand around the pole of his axe, twisting it free from its embedded fissure in the balcony. "Look at them, now, my friends. Remember their faces. This band of terrorists have been joined by this young failure of a soldat to interfere in the honored traditions of our society—to steal from you all the promise of an honest and judicious way of life, and to cut their ill-gotten gains from the purse of our collective House treasuries."

The air swirled in dissatisfied murmurings, and as the nine stood in judgment of the onlooking audience, Brann realized the terrible truth: the world was agreeing with Tark.

For all intents and purposes, everyone standing with him was a thief and a terrorist. The most powerful warlord in the world had just decreed it so.

Marshal Tark crossed his arms, locking eyes with Brann again, who stared back in open defiance. The challenge had been issued. The bounty had been made public.

"They owe us all a great debt," Tark said quietly, dangerously. The image on the holoscreen above zoomed in on the oligarch as he concluded his speech.

"Shall I collect on your behalf?"

The crowd's response was unanimous. A smattering of applause drowned out by the cold roar of approval—they had turned in no time at all, still revved up from the energy of the fight. They wanted more blood, and needed little convincing to expect it.

The Wolf readied his spear, The Lady Red her saber. Hawkshaw reloaded his pistols, Grishka quivered in an ominous aura, Boomer clenched his fists. Zay raised her machine gun to her hip, Emrys tore a page from his book, and Nestor lit a cigarillo with a low sigh.

Brann racked the slide on his rifle, and looked to his accidental allies, trusting they all knew what they had to do now.

Once more, it was time to run.

ACT II

GOD HATES A COWARD

14. The Fugitives

There was a time in Brann's life, not so long ago, when there were no problems that couldn't be solved by simply running. Swiping the charger full of scales on the edge of a diner's table at an outdoor cafe before bolting into the nearby alleyway—if he were caught, he risked an ass-beating. Sneaking into the bedding department of an outlet store in uptown Barrier City to sleep overnight on their display mattresses, before being discovered by a roaming Nightwatch patrol—if he were caught, he risked conscription into the ranks of Geihan military service. And, finally, once he did get himself caught when one particularly bitter spell of cold turned what should have been a night of respite into a nightmare, the punishment for abandoning his basic training was always on his mind—if he were caught, he risked lifelong imprisonment, or worse.

Brann couldn't help but think back to that night now, catching glimpses of it through the noise and smoke, the memory rearing up to remind him of his first step towards his current journey. The stadium around him chilled, and he heard nothing but his own thoughts speaking back to him *on that precarious cement ledge, no bigger than the span of his own barefoot heels that dug into the freezing surface. The street far below beckoned him to fall, the night breeze brushing his face threatening to send him there, feeling as powerful as a hurricane for all its gentle whispers.*

The windowsill beside him cast a waterfall of golden light out over the edge, the window itself sliding upwards on a gloved hand—the Nightwatch patrolman leaned out slowly, taking care not to alarm the young man lest he be responsible for Brann slipping.

"There's no reason to tell you there's nowhere to go," the patrolman said, tilting open his visor and leaning against the sill. "You knew that when you climbed out here. I think you're smart enough to know to climb back in, so I won't tell you to do that, either."

Brann's fingertips were like climbing hooks against the brick, frozen stiff like a gargoyle fixture on the ledge—the winter cold bit into his flesh, fusing his body painfully to the side of the tall apartment building.

"Then I won't tell you to come out and get me yourself," he replied with false bravado. He'd gotten pretty good at faking confidence when cornered.

The patrolman produced a cigarillo now, sparking it quietly and rolling himself onto both arms, looking out at the tops of the buildings before him. He breathed out a long, slow cloud of smoke after his first drag, thumbing at the fold of smoking paper between his fingers. "We don't get as many calls like this one as we used to," he said, speaking half to himself and half to Brann. "At least not downtown. Edge of the city, closer to the wall, maybe, when someone wants to leave without papers. Lot of people wanting out, thinking they're being held here, thinking they're trapped. Truth is, we don't stop anyone from leaving." He turned to look at Brann, and at the tiny ledge he was perched on, watching the boy's bare heels turn white against the brick. "Or stop them from jumping. Same thing, really. You wanna go out there and get yourself killed in the Wilds, by all means."

He took another drag, and Brann ever so cautiously turned to look at the Nightwatchman, fearing even his neck twisting too quickly could cost him his balance.

"You wanna get down from that ledge, I won't stop you either way— just, one of those ways is much quicker than the other." The bright cherry burned, glinting in the Nightwatchman's dark eyes. "Though I won't lie, son, the other way...might be more painful."

Brann didn't respond, simply staring, daring only the lightest of breaths. He sniffed, the frozen rivulets of tears on his cheeks long since dried into icy flakes. Out here, in the sky, he was free with nowhere in the world to go but this little ledge of safety. Back inside, he was trapped like an animal, with limitless possibilities.

The gritty flesh of his dry heel crumbled a bit as he rotated his body back towards the window, reaching sideways to shimmy towards the light. The Nightwatchman nodded, pursing the cigarillo between his lips to free his hand up, reaching out towards Brann.

Brann reached back, the weight of his body transferring to one square inch of flesh beneath one foot, the other raising itself to let him stretch towards safety.

> *His fingertips touched the patrolman's glove.*
>
> *His foot twisted, legs sprawling out into the night air.*
>
> *Brann lurched forward—*

—Falling to the pavement as he was shoved out of the way of a crackle of gunfire, the bullets whizzing into the shop wall above his head and showering him with dust and plaster. The burly arm of The Wolf was dragging him back to his feet before he could even register he'd been pushed and Brann was again running, keeping low in case of more gunfire, ears ringing from the sound of screaming chaos all around. The fighter's entrance tunnel beneath Boomer's viewing box led the nine of them into what should have been a killbox before Zay had shredded through a wall of solid concrete with her huge autocannon, opening a portal of escape that led directly into the streets below. No sooner had they jumped to the street below than the Uhlen were on them, firing from overhead as they ran for the underground stairs that would lead back to the *Myrmidon's* docking bay. There was an expectation that Brann held, that surely if Tark had tracked him on the *Myrmidon*, the ship itself would be sealed off from them under the Uhlen's guard—but at no point did he have the chance to shout this to the Wolf above the gunfire or the screams of the fleeing crowd all around them.

Emrys had been the last to jump, and as the rest of the party made for the stairs, he was unnoticed by the Uhlen overhead—a page of his book burning into green ash, and he slammed his palm into the wall of the stadium, sliding it upwards quickly with purposeful aim. A fissure of neon ectoplasm raced up from his hand towards the gaping hole in the wall before encircling it—and the Uhlen leaning out the furthest had to jerk himself back inside to avoid the skeletal hand clawing for his throat. Like budding flower petals, skeletal arms reached forth from the destroyed wall to clasp around each other and form a tight barrier, ghostly fingers interlocking into dozens of layers of quasi-corporeal bone. The Uhlen trapped within, illuminated by that lime glow, bashed the butts of their rifles and swords against the wall of bones, to no avail—the arms simply flexed outwards from the impacts, but held fast, denying anything from getting through.

The grip on Brann's arm relaxed, and he turned, the Wolf already running ahead on his own to the stairs—they had a chance now, thanks to Emrys, who himself was now pushing through the frenzied crowd to cross the street. They were all on their own now to make it back to the ship, and it was not outside Brann's scope of thought that they might leave him behind if he lagged, just as he feared they would at Mother Superior's outpost.

Then there was no reason to wait around.

Ducking low, rifle out ahead of him in both hands to help shovel aside bodies, Brann elbowed his way forward through the crowd and pushed back against any resistance, being knocked this way and that a few times himself. He couldn't see the way ahead and had to trust he was still making for the street exit—and, indeed, when the butt of his rifle clanged against metal bars, he reached forward to grab the railing of the stairwell, hefting himself over and falling feetfirst to the steps below. It wasn't far, but still his knees popped from the impact, feet stinging through his boots—no time to complain as he caught himself gasping, gritting his teeth to descend those stairs. The ramp greeted him just around the corner on the floor below, and he fell forward as he was shoved from behind, a few stray runners from the mob following his egress.

The rampway opened up, leading down into that illuminated tunnel, the honeycombed entrances to docking bays still at least a half mile of velvet carpeting and bright advertisement holoscreens away. Brann came to his feet again and, remembering his training, broke into a combat run straight forward with his elbows tucked in, rifle bouncing left and right in lieu of his arms swinging at his sides. The quick tug of his trigger finger spat a warning shot overhead into the ceiling, a lightbar exploding over his head, warding away the panicked mob to give him enough room to run unimpeded. Through the blur of wide eyes and yelling mouths, Brann could see familiar shapes—the spindly frame of Nestor, the glint of

Hawkshaw's paneling, the red of the Lady's coat—no one was watching out for each other down here in this stampede, and the best he could do was keep up.

The rapid thumping of his boots against the carpet and the deliberate measured breathing in his ears drowned out the rest of the noise—Brann was putting his endurance running ability to the test now, knees nearly knocking his rifle with each long stride, his run gaining momentum into an all-out sprint for the safety of the *Myrmidon*. Adrenaline gave him wings and the foresight to strafe this way or that to dash out of the way of the rogue civilians still cutting in front of him. A black shadow swooped low by his ear and prompted him to jerk to one side—the moment he realized it wasn't a projectile aimed at him, Brann saw the wings of a huge raven beating just above the heads of the crowd, zooming down the tunnel to lead his way forward. Grishka's talons had nearly taken off his ear, a nonverbal warning for him not to make any more overheard warning shots—Brann relaxed his finger above the trigger guard in response, watching the huge bird frantically flapping her black wings against the backdrop of bright ceiling lights.

The tunnel branched off into a T-intersection just ahead, the same one he'd came to before—turning left here would lead directly towards the main bays. Brann yelled out commands for the crowd to make way—but just as he made the intersection, the world inverted, and his teeth rattled from the blow he'd taken to the side of his head.

Brann bounced on the carpet, his shoulder breaking his fall painfully, and reflexively he rolled over to bring his rifle up—the barrel flashed in a trio of shots that just missed the Uhlen fighter who swiped it away like it was nothing, the bullets sparking against the ceiling and bursting another lightbar. The Uhlen above him brought a fist down, Brann narrowly avoiding the blow that cratered the concrete floor through the carpeting—that fist, the same fist wrapped in chains he'd seen back at the Assay. He didn't know his name, but this Uhlen's appearance was unmistakable, those high pauldrons silhouetted against the flashing overheard fixture, his entire form strobing between shadow and light.

Chainfist again batted away Brann's rifle when it was again raised to aim at him, those enormous forearms rippling with muscle hard as the iron-wrapped gauntlets he bore. His expressionless visor stared down at Brann, the mouthpiece hissing static—seeing it up close now, something about the subtle curve of the face: whoever was beneath that helmet likely wasn't human.

"Tired of running yet?" The voice garbled, likely run through a translator, harsh and distorted.

"I could go a couple more laps around the country," Brann taunted, anticipating the punishing reply: he rolled to avoid another downward strike, ejecting his vibroblade from the shoulder of his breastplate and spinning it around to slash at the arm—the superheated filament of the knife spat bright flecks of plasma against the chain-wrapped gauntlet, but otherwise was ineffective, other than making the Uhlen fighter lurch backwards to avoid the stab going any higher. Brann sprung to his feet, his recessive hand taking hold of the pistol grip of his rifle and the knife held aloft in front of him, making enough room between himself and Chainfist to allow a proper faceoff.

"Shame they don't teach you rickeys how to fight with your hands," Chainfist's bassy voicebox boomed, his gauntlets hefting up to curl into fists, the steely hands looking like great thick piledrivers capping his black sleeved arms.

"Funny, I was just thinking the same thing," Brann shot back smartly, taking another step back as he readied his rifle.

Chainfist kicked forward, slamming his elbows together with a ringing clang of his chained gauntlets, shielding his face from another burst of gunfire from Brann—the warped steel made easy work of deflecting the molten lead and knocked aside the gun's barrel a third time with ease as it was held in Brann's weaker off-hand grip. Brann spun to bring the knife in close, the air around its glowing edge searing hot as it glanced off Chainfist's shoulder, the wide pauldron protecting his otherwise exposed chest; the butt of the Uhlen's palm came up directly into Brann's collar, smacking his entire body aside as his spine followed the momentum of the blow, and Brann stumbled backwards several feet to stay upright. The gun would do him no good in one hand, and the knife was useless against that armor—with no regard to aim, Brann launched the vibroblade at Chainfist who again slapped it out of the air. His hands exchanging places, Brann took the pistol grip in his right hand and twisted the rifle at his chest, quickly assuming a canted stance to fire from.

The trick worked, but only just—spattering bullets against the hunched Chainfist who took to a crouch to hide behind the wall of his combined pauldron and gauntlets, Brann was only afforded a few seconds of sustained gunfire before the clack of his ejection port signaled the depleted magazine.

Chainfist heard this too, and was on his feet in a flash, barreling towards Brann, who had no time to reload—but the massive metal fist that pulled back never found its mark, as another body sailed through the air to slam into the Uhlen warrior, one taller and bulkier than either of them.

"Shit!" Brann turned down his rifle to avoid aiming it at Boomer as he reloaded, fearing he'd have shot the horse given the time to replace magazines. "Say you're coming next time, Boomer!"

The horse was crouched, still bloodied from the fight, grinning ear to ear as Chainfist stood opposite him. "That's what my entrance music is for, kid," he clapped back, not losing his arrogant swagger for a second even as he faced down this armored challenger.

Chainfist shook his head, but clanged his fists together anyway, raising them again to engage. "Playacting as a fighter doesn't make you one," he growled darkly.

"Funny, I was just thinking the same thing," retorted Boomer, and in an instant, they were on each other—the ironclad gauntlets smacked wetly into Boomer's defending forearms, the bare-knuckled pugilist showing no signs of pain despite the massive blows, pressuring Chainfist back into a slight retreat as he absorbed them. Ducking low with almost psychic speed, Boomer feinted in a mirror to Chainfist's sudden changeup and elbowed downwards to diffuse the energy from an incoming uppercut—before unleashing his own, his open palm bashing the metal visor to keep from breaking his fingers. Whatever species was beneath that helmet definitely had a weak jawbone, because the Uhlen nearly toppled then and there, falling backwards in disorientation.

The chained gauntlets were up to his chest to protect him from a follow-up, but Boomer didn't give him the chance to raise them higher, kicking off the ground to bring his elbow down from above, nailing the soft spot between the pauldron and Chainfist's visor. The pained cry from his electronic mouthpiece made clear the severity of this injury, and when he recoiled, the arm on that side of his body hung limply at his side. Still he stood, however, bringing himself low with his good hand lowered, poised like a cobra ready to strike.

Strike it did, as Boomer danced his way in close, attempting a knee to Chainfist's lower body but finding it met with a solid jab directly into his kneecap, which put the horse into an off balance kneel as he too cried out in pain.

Brann was still fumbling to reload, only seeing through one eye now, the other swollen shut from the punch to the face he'd taken—everything felt hot, and he didn't know what it was, but something was leaking from his nose. Still, he had to try to help, Boomer surely weaker than he was letting on from the last fight.

Or, so he thought. Chainfist jabbed rapidly, again and again, elbow leaping from his waist to bring that fist into Boomer's already bloodied face once—twice—but, metal reinforcement or not, the distance was simply too short for any greater force to build up behind that heavy hand, and Boomer's skull was made of sterner stuff. Smiling through the weak punches, Boomer let his injured knee fall—and with it, the weight of his whole body, save for the opposite leg that popped up as he cartwheeled it directly into Chainfist's belly. The Uhlen folded, static spitting from his mouthpiece as no doubt he sprayed something from his lips within his visor—and, sure enough, a second later there was a telltale red waterfall flowing from the speaker holes, dripping his internal injury all down his front. Even at half power the kick of a horse was lethal, and Boomer had every intention of fulfilling that promise: standing to full height now, covered head to toe in violent purple bruises and bloody smears, his smile never let up for a second.

A short jump forward, and his hoof shot out from his body again, lightning fast directly into Chainfist's gut a second time—then a third—Boomer's leg like a switchblade popping in and out over and over to impale his enemy with powerkicks. Chainfist crumpled, falling to his knees and sagging, head heavy and low: those chain-wrapped gauntlets shuddered, the knuckles dragging the carpet, every mote of strength he had sapped from him. He simply couldn't raise his arms anymore.

The normally playful horse calmed, steadying himself with lidded eyes, a sudden detached look washing over him—Brann had only just finished reloading, racking his slide back, when Boomer ended the fight decisively. Like a ballerina from hell, Boomer pirouetted on the spot faster than should have been physically possible, that raised leg again snapping out at the exact moment his hoof found Chainfist's helmet.

The head snapped backwards—literally. So powerful was that kick, the spine simply separated within his neck, and short of decapitating him entirely Chainfist's head was now hanging loosely from between his shoulderblades. Those hands spasmed for a microsecond, then his entire body was limp, propped up on those same huge and heavy gauntlets—a sickening knot of destroyed vertebrae forming a lump in his folded neck where once his head stood straight up.

A choked scream from an onlooker reminded Brann they were still surrounded by fleeing citizens, and there was little time to make it back to the ship safely. He hurried forward to grab at Boomer's arm, tugging him back towards the bay—trying not to look at the horrifically decollated corpse as he did, lest he lose control of his gag reflex. "Let's go, we're almost to the ship man, we gotta move," he said warily, trying not to sound scared.

Boomer stood a second, then turned to look at Brann, and his eyes were cloudy. Brann was quiet, waiting for him to say something—then the horse just gave a small smile again, and this one didn't feel as arrogant as normal.

"You're with me now, kid," he said, speaking at a volume that pretended the noise of the crowd didn't exist around them, yet still Brann could hear every word. "Anyone steps to you, I'm pulling their card. Nobody tells me who my friends are."

The Marshal's words to the audience had fallen on Boomer's deaf ears, and Brann felt a little lump forming in his throat. He couldn't think of anything smart to say in reply, so he simply nodded, and repeated himself:

"We gotta go man. We gotta."

The distant echoes of renewed screaming down the tunnel turned both their attentions towards the source: despite the great distance between them, Brann could still spot the towering kuaneach striding deliberately towards them, his head like a guided missile above the crowd as his unarmed hand shoved aside bodies left and right to ensure he wouldn't be slowed for even a second.

"You're gonna have to help me, then, because uh..." Boomer leaned on Brann, raising his opposite leg, his knee visibly dislocated from its socket where Chainfist had slammed it. "You're a little better than running away than I am, especially right now."

Brann cringed at the remark, but obliged with an arm hooked around Boomer's lower back, supporting his weight. "You don't know the half of it," he joked bitterly, letting the horse hop a few times to get his balance before the jogged forward, finding a rhythm enough to keep them both moving forward at a steady pace back towards the ship.

*

The entirety of the crew had made it on board before them, with Nes waiting in the cargo bay to beckon them in, slapping the ramp extension switch to draw it up behind them and keying the intercom to tell whoever was at the controls of the Donnie to take off. It was a two-man job, helping Boomer up the ladder, his strength fading quickly—Brann was nearly flattened beneath him at one point when he stumbled drunkenly off the bottom rung. Eventually Nes had coaxed him over the edge of the ladderwell into the hallway above, however, just as the engines had begun spinning up and Brann felt the ship rolling forward behind the tuglift. Boomer couldn't raise himself off the carpet, though, nearly passed out as his head was cradled in Nestor's hands.

"Goddamn moron," Nes hissed down at him, using a blackened greasy rag to wipe away some of the blood coating Boomer's face. "Brann, get to the cockpit, tell whoever is at the controls we need to stay below the tops of the buildings—leaving the city is gonna be a foregone conclusion if Tark activated the anti-air measures before he tracked us down here which, since he wasn't exactly in a hurry following behind us, I'm guessing he did. Under the skyline, tell them that," he repeated, ignoring the fresh bubble of blood that popped against his nice coat.

"Below the tops of the buildings, okay," Brann said back, taking a second to reorient the ship's layout in his mind's eye and turning around to hurry down the hallway—the cockpit was straight on from the ship's main corridor, but he remembered a side hatch where Boomer had emerged from at one point after remarking he'd just come from the cockpit. Rounding the corner, Brann faced what looked like a set of double doors to someone's personal quarters, albeit much larger than the others. He reasoned if it were Boomer's room, then it was possible there was a more direct passage connecting it to the cockpit than the rest of the common areas. Confident in this logic, Brann grasped and pushed wide, swinging the door open and stepping in.

Like a self-contained burlesque club, the space within was generously swathed in all manner of velvet drapes, throw pillows, and knee-high beds looking as soft as clouds with not a hard surface in sight. A single occupant had poured herself over an especially plush bodypillow and raised her attention to Brann's intrusion—looking back over her shoulder at him, the mare looked to be so well groomed as to glow in the low light of the room, her chestnut pelt shining almost like polished glass around the supple globes of her pronounced rump, naked in all but the most literal sense as her flimsy nightie could have been painted on.

"Help you with something?" She crooned sweetly, not budging an inch or otherwise making any effort to cover up.

Brann stared. He caught himself staring, then stared a few seconds longer, realizing if he made it obvious he was staring it would look like he was staring, so he simply leveled his eyes to hers and pretended he was in the right place. "Just...trying to get to the cockpit," he stated with all the professionalism he could muster.

The chestnut harem mare sighed in frustration and craned her head back, that soft mane washing down between her shoulderblades like liquid, her tail lashing against the pillow. "Champ was supposed to be back by now, all the other girls went into the city so we could have the alone time he promised me," she said with a chuff, adjusting the microstrap of her nearly invisible panties. Her eyes once again met Brann's, and she smiled wryly. "Don't suppose you're in too much of a hurry to get up above, though?"

Brann watched her fingers tapping against the fatty curve of her ample gifts and gritted his teeth, hard. "Nope. Official business. Gotta get up quick—up to the cockpit," he stammered.

The mare's eyebrow raised in amusement, but nonetheless she gestured an open hand towards the opposite set of double doors. "Through there, big boy," she said with a honeyed chuckle behind her breath.

Brann's feet never left the ground an inch as he shuffled through the pleasure room with all the grace of a stone golem, gripping his rifle for emotional support—he had to make a curving path around the mare, as she acted as centerpiece to the entire space, and he found he nearly had to step over her just to get around.

"Sorry. 'Scuse me." He whispered, trying not to look down at the busty horse.

"Don't step on me, killer," she cooed up at him sweetly.

Brann reached the doors, turning to give a polite thanks only to jerk his head back in whiplash as he saw the mare had risen to follow him, standing above him nearly as tall as Boomer did, his upturned chin coming dangerously close to her chest. He slid backwards, unlatching the door as it groaned with a deafening squeak of the hinge.

"Gotta oil that," he joked, meaning the door.

"You promise?" She didn't.

He was through the gap, but the mare was leaning against it, her forearm sliding up and down the wood surface as Brann tried desperately to push it close without hurting her. "Just, gotta—gotta get up—"

"I bet you do."

"—Gotta tell them—to stay low—"

"Oh that sounds fun."

He pushed with all his might, and the mare simply batted her eyelashes at Brann through the gap in the door. "Up in the...cockpit..." he mumbled.

"Ooh, say it again slower," the mare teased.

The door slammed, and Brann flattened himself against it to keep it sealed, fearing the concubine might burst through like a hungry monster. His face felt so flushed he couldn't see straight. After a moment, the low rumble of the ship's thrusters sent vibrations through the walls, and reminded him of the task at hand.

Before him was a short passageway leading to a utilitarian looking hatch. Brann stood straight, adjusting his armor and straightening his shirt beneath it one too many times, then trudged forward on his way with his fists clenched white at his sides. There was a lot he had to learn about his new friend Boomer, but this was not one of those things he was in any rush to discover just yet.

The hatch opened up to a small ladderwell, and climbing up,

Brann's head popped into another open space—the lights of the cities poured gold over his face, and he knew this was the cockpit, the wide view of the windshield giving him a clear view of the ship's steady ascent. They hadn't lifted off but a moment ago, and given how close Tark had been behind them, part of him feared the Marshal may have actually made it on board. "We're going?" He called up, more to announce his presence than to ask the question.

"Obviously," Zay shot back over her shoulder—she sat at the starboard controls, while Hawkshaw occupied the captain's seat, both of them gripping at their respective flight sticks tightly. She stopped, glaring at Brann as she studied his face. "Why are you so *red*?"

Brann froze. He struggled to find a convincing response, and eventually just said:

"I ran here real fast."

Zay frowned, but let it slide, turning back to Hawkshaw to redirect her anger.

"Loosen up on the top flaps, we aren't gonna get off the ground fast enough with them fully open," she snarled at her rival pilot.

"No offense, darling, but I happen to have an entire set of transistors in my head dedicated to aerospace and fluid dynamics, I'm pretty confident in my ability to tell a ship to go *'up,'*" Hawkshaw shot back sarcastically, his metallic fingers clicking up a flurry on the panel of switches next to him.

"Call me darling again and that head'll be my new hood ornament." Zay similarly flipped her own set of switches, and based on the way she watched Hawkshaw's hands, Brann suspected she was undoing a lot of the things the automaton was doing.

"Guys," he called out, stepping up into the cockpit fully, his head low to not bang on the ceiling, "Maybe we shouldn't fight right now and should just get out of the city?"

"I gotta imagine it must have been quite the rush waking up this morning and saying to yourself, 'gee, you know who I'm smarter than? The fuckin' robot who didn't even need to go to flight school because he was literally built to communicate with advanced computing systems and predict patterned outcomes in ballistic physics,'" Hawkshaw continued, ignoring Brann. "How intoxicating, your sense of self-importance must be!"

"Predicting ballistics, huh?! You see this coming, then—" Zay was reaching clumsily for her autocannon, the weapon sliding this way and that as it leaned against the lilting flightboard.

"More threats! How original!"

"GUYS!" Brann shouted, his voice betraying the smallest of cracks in it. The ship was beginning to rise fast now, the rooftops growing dangerously close. "Nes says we need to stay below the skyline, it's important that the Donnie doesn't go above the tops of the buildings—"

The ship lurched to one side—Hawkshaw's side—and Zay cursed, a gloved fist bashing against the android's shoulder. "Prick! Keep it steady, you're gonna put us into a building!"

"Violence!" Hawkshaw whined, recoiling as he insisted on tugging his stick the opposite way, "Nestor's right, we'll trip the city's anti-air defenses if that big dragon brute told the security forces we would try to escape!"

The angle of the ship's ascent leaned far too deep in, the nose nearly pitched down, and Brann saw the vibrant green blur of tree foliage from a balcony whizz by. "We're too high, Zay, we have to get out of range first—"

"You stay out of this, twerp, you have NO fuckin' room to tell any of us what to do," Zay shouted over him, smashing down a set of flap switches, and the starboard engines coughed in an uneven surge of power, the Donnie overcompensating in her lilted trajectory—

The air around him screamed in red alarms, and Brann raised his arms as if to flee, beginning to panic. "The hell is that?!"

The automaton in the pilot's seat reached up and grabbed at a hanging bar-switch, keeping his other hand on the control stick. "They've already locked on, we went too high, we gotta lose some height and hope they don't risk firing into civilian buildings," he confirmed, his eye-panels spread open wide to give him an unobstructed view of the integrated HUD that sat just above the flight panels in the center of the windshield. Brann leaned in and squinted, seeing a little glowing 'Y' symbol that represented the Donnie at the center of a rotating 3D radar, the axis tilting to show a rising cloud of red dots rapidly closing in on the ship's tail.

"No good, they already started firing," Zay yelled, pulling back on the center thruster levers to slow the ship, "I'm gonna put us in a dive then pull up quick to bring up her belly, then you loose the chaff!"

"Appreciate you giving me permission to activate the ship's defenses, big thanks 'Mom,'" Hawkshaw replied snidely, even his inhuman voice tinged with anxiety despite his snarky attitude.

The ship, already nose-down, began to plummet, the streets far below rushing up faster and faster, and Brann felt his stomach fly up into his chest—he grabbed a nearby seat's headrest and pulled himself towards it, working against gravity to swing himself around and sit down painfully, buckling himself in. The view of the HUD was mostly obstructed from his seat, but given how he could still see the cloud of angry red fireflies swirling towards the Donnie, the projectiles must be close—

"Pulling up, when the nose clears the horizon, you release!" Zay yanked back on her flight stick with both hands and kicked up to slam her boot into the thruster levers, bashing them into the forwardmost position and making the ship shudder from the engines firing up to max so quickly.

Hawkshaw didn't bother responding this time, instead turning to look at Brann, his insect-like faceplates stiff and lacking their usual fluid expressiveness. "Kid, listen, I've already done the math and we can't stop them all, they're proximity darts and the slowest ones are gonna cut straight through our chaff," he said urgently. "When they detonate, the ship is gonna roll to the side, and Zay is gonna have to cut the starboard thrusters—"

"What!"

"—In order for us to keep rolling and avoid going inverted,"

Hawkshaw continued over Zay's shocked reply. "When we get level again, she'll put 'em back to max to stop the roll, but the maneuver is gonna cost all of our height and speed—so to keep from going straight into the ground you're gonna have to help—help—"

He didn't repeat himself—the android's vocalizations simply skipped as if a record were scratched, the premature explosion of one of the faster darts rattling the ship from behind. Hawkshaw cut himself off and yanked the bar forward, and like a glowing pair of angelic wings, Brann saw the 3D radar light up with waves of white fanning out from both sides of the Donnie—the chaff was free, and like hornets that had been caught in a rainstorm, the red dots began spinning out wildly and chasing the streams of white. Brann was pinned back as the force of the ship's sudden pitch upwards smeared him against his seat, the whole world shaking from what sounded like thousands of firecrackers being set off beneath his feet.

"Get ready to cut power!" Hawkshaw's voice had returned, both hands now flying over the switchboard, opening every flap he could on the port side of the ship. Zay had similarly abandoned her combative attitude and obliged him with her hands steady on both thrusters and flight stick. "Ready!" She responded, and a starburst of light from below reflected the sweat on her temple for Brann to see.

The cloud of red had mostly dissipated amongst the wings of chaff, but just as Hawkshaw predicted, the straggling dots had avoided the deployed flares entirely and were beelining straight for the Donnie with nothing to stop them. An almost friendly beep accompanied their small pop on the HUD, and with an earsplitting screech the Donnie was buffeted upwards from the force of the airborne fireball, the skyline spinning sideways as the ship entered a forced roll.

"Now!"

Zay yanked the thruster levers closest to her back to neutral, and the spin increased rapidly, the entire world going upside down. Above them, colorful sparkles rained upwards from a blossoming orange and black airburst, the fire and smoke quickly collapsing from the air's density—

Brann, though his head felt squeezed in a vise, opened his eyes long enough to see a glowing red orb fall away from the nose of the ship: one of the darts that never detonated, illuminated by its tracking light in the night air.

"Brann, you ready?!"

Hawkshaw was yelling at him now. Brann groaned in response, even his lips feeling heavy. "You didn't finish telling me what to do!"

"The big yellow bar next to you, pull that until the seals break, hard as you can!" Hawkshaw was nearly sideways in his seat, pushing the flight stick to keep the ship rolling—the horizon was righting itself again, now free of the lights of skyscrapers, only the black night and calm grey of the earth beyond. "Zay, you too, push now!"

Zay's boot once again came up and shoved itself into the thrusters, pushing them as far as she could manage, crying out in pain as the G-forces tore into her leg's hamstring. The vertical thrusters fired back up, but again as Hawkshaw had predicted, the compensating push back against gravity made the forward engines whine as they lost power suddenly.

"Brann, pull now!"

The yellow bar in question was a bulky round cylinder embedded in an extruding block on the side of the auxiliaries' panel Brann was seated at. With the waning force of gravity releasing him from his seat at last, he reached up to wrap both hands around it, pulling so hard the veins in his forearms bulged through his shirt—the stiff polymer seals keeping it locked in were like steel locks, and he had to break through with nothing but sheer willpower. Biting so hard he felt his incisors cut into his cheeks, Brann's whole body shivered with the strain of his muscles, and finally—

The seals snapped, the bar popping out of its recess in the wall, and a sound like a great elephant roaring below the ship caused the nose to rise sharply, the engines screaming back up to maximum force in no time flat.

"The hell did I just do?!"

Zay turned back now, her face furious. "You severed the floaters, you idiot!"

Brann was mortified. "He told me to do it!" Was his weak cry.

Far below the ship, a distant booming impact, then another—the great metal floats had slammed into the earth like torpedoes, cutting the ship's weight nearly in half and giving it the thrust it needed to keep flying instead of falling. The Donnie was still vibrating from the maneuver, but otherwise everything had calmed at last, the alarms silent and the engines whining steadily. Just through the windshield, the nose was nearly even with the horizon, albeit dipped slightly under it, signifying a slow and sure descent.

"You've crippled the ship's landing capabilities, you absolute DICK," Zay complained at Hawkshaw, throwing the flight stick away from herself in disgust and pushing her chair on its sliding rails away from the flight panel, arms crossed.

"We either go facedown into the ground, or we take a hard landing on her belly somewhere flat and soft, I made the only choice there was," Hawkshaw replied with his own artificial sigh, leaning back in relief.

Zay stood, leaning forward to point out through the windshield at the rocky ground below, the ship gliding over what looked like the foothills of distant mountains. "*Asshole*. There IS nowhere flat and soft. We could have at least found a nearby body of water and risked an uneven landing there, worst case we could have just swum to shore—*in one piece!*"

Their bickering continued, and Brann unbuckled himself, rising to his numb feet and wobbling back out of the cockpit's main hatch, letting the angry pilots fight between themselves as he let their voices fade behind him as he closed it. Feeling like his lower half was made of cotton, Brann sagged to the floor, then rolled onto his side, pressing his hot, sweaty face to the cold metal beneath him. Recently—very recently—he'd discovered a newfound fear of flying, and the closer to the ground he felt, the better.

15. The Inkwell

The tunnel had been cordoned off by security, gaggles of curious onlookers pressing earnestly against the deployed hologlass barrier as it gently pulsed a yellow message of caution from within the transparent shield—there was a regiment of security standing by to block the crowd's view, but to little avail, as the determined (and taller) citizens simply looked over their heads at the gruesome scene beyond.

Tark beckoned over the head of this security unit, leaning in to give a hushed command: "Sergeant, if you'd oblige me—don't waste manpower doing what your barriers can do on their own."

The officer blinked, then nodded in delayed understanding as Tark's meaning registered, and he turned to call out a command to the other officers: "Boys, let's put up the shades, get to work cleaning up back here, yeah?"

The uniformed guards all nodded, breaking ranks behind the barrier as one of them flipped a breaker on its control panel—the glass darkened steadily until it was completely opaque, a matte black wall now separating the violent scene from the bystanders, that yellow warning still flashing quietly. Satisfied, Marshal Tark turned back to survey the gory scene of Chainfist's demise, the disproportionate body of the iron-handed fighter still kneeling, propped up by the balanced weight of his armored shoulders and the dense gauntlets keeping his arms vertical against the ground.

Tark circled the corpse, peering through the hooded grooves of his mask with an eagle eyed intent, collecting every perceptible detail of how this duel had played out as best he could. Arms crossed over his chest, one fist thoughtfully tapping a hooked finger against his chin, the kuaneach oligarch was somewhat taken aback: one of his most capable fighters, dispatched so easily when pitted against an already exhausted civilian and a young, inexperienced recruit. There'd be a discussion later with the rest of the Uhlen about letting their egos get the best of them, if this was the performance he could expect in the coming days on their continued hunt.

"I can see the smoke coming out of your ears, Boss." The Speaker appeared beside him, also looking over Chainfist's mangled body. He gave a noise of disgust. "Puh. Big guy pulled his punches, I see. Not like him to hold back."

Tark sighed, shaking his head. "No, it's not. He didn't hold anything back; he misjudged his opponent. Which means so did I. The Champion isn't just good at putting on a show for the mob, apparently—he knows his own strength better than we do, and even half dead he can fold us in half." He paused, turning a hesitant eye sideways at The Speaker, and shrugged apologetically. "Well, most of us. Sorry, son."

The Speaker laughed it off, clapping the great leader on his thick arm. "Think nothing of it, Boss. We weren't all so lucky as to be born with dragon magic. Though I don't mind telling you to your face you don't use it as often as you should—all the times I've had to scrape your fat ass off the field when you put yourself out there. You know how heavy you are, you big idiot?"

Tark let his arms fall, hands on his hips as he tapped his footclaws, mulling over his frustrated appraisals of Boomer and the rest of the crew safeguarding their quarry. "All that time you clowns spend flexing in front of each other in the fitness hall? My fat ass shouldn't be any trouble for you at all." He turned away from Chainfist's body, motioning for his underling to follow. "Besides, I have no need to resort to relying on a genetic crutch in exigent circumstances—there's no honor in holding the warrior in front of you responsible for your natural advantages. Give them a fighting chance." Tark waved back over his shoulder as they walked. "Just don't forget to show respect to their own abilities, like our mutual friend did."

The landing bay where the eyesore known as the *Myrmidon* had previously docked was now occupied by Tark's own personal vessel—a humble, sleek craft of precise engineering and luxury taste, the pilot's cabin retracted above its curvaceous lower fuselage and its extendable wings pulled back over its tailflaps. The profile resembled a great, elegant waterbird at rest on the surface of a pond, the landing gear supporting its weight looking far too delicate to be able to do so. The Viola had been the one concession Tark had made in his usual reticence, his tendency to deny himself pleasurable ownership of any kind of showy trinkets having melted at the first sight of her. No ship in the Geihan Empire had ever been so fast, so maneuverable, and yet so beautiful all at once: she truly was the gem of his fleet.

"Viola will close the gap between us and these bandits in no time," Tark remarked, running a caressing hand over her mirror-shined black surface. "I'm not concerned there's any chance they could evade or outrun us. What I am concerned about," he said, turning serious as he addressed The Speaker directly, removing his facemask and rubbing at his spiked temple, "Is how the rest of the men intend to proceed, now that they've seen one of their own killed."

The Speaker shifted his weight, expressionless visor crooked to the side—it was his turn to cross his arms. "Not sure I follow, Boss," he said, sounding guarded now.

The Marshal stepped around the breast of his ship to come to the boarding ramp, unfastening his enormous battleaxe from his lower back and climbing aboard, dropping the heavy weapon into its vacant rack just beside his uniform locker. When he spoke again, not looking at the Uhlen, his words were gentle—careful, even.

"The art of warfare is not inert, as a painted canvas might be," Tark said, stripping off his scarce pieces of armor, "But alive and vibrant, as a symphony—open to interpretation by the performers in the orchestra and their own hopes, emotions.... prejudices." He opened his locker and stowed his armor carefully, using his fingers to gently straighten his capelet as it dangled. "Often in spite of the measured considerations of the conductor."

"You know this poetic shit doesn't fly with me," The Speaker said with an insubordinate tone that would guarantee any lesser soldat a savage reprisal. "Spit it out, Boss, none of this junk about music."

"I'm saying," Tark continued patiently, disengaging his harness and letting it fall away, those restrained wings shuddering as they resisted the urge to stretch, "I cannot have any of my chairs playing to a different tune than the exact notes on the page." Once the harness was on its own hook, Tark pushed the locker door shut, turning to look The Speaker full in the face now. "I need the boys—all of them—to toe the line, and stay within set protocols. My intent is to bring back every dissenter on that ship alive, and deal with them in my own way. No mishaps, no...collateral damage." Tark narrowed his eyes at this last part. "Do we understand each other?"

The spooled wire of tension tightened between them, like anglers standing shoulder to shoulder, vying for the same catch: The Speaker may be addressing his commanding officer, but the familiarity and history between them armed him with far more insolence than should be tolerable...and yet tolerate it he did, even as Tark was met with the following dismissal:

"None of us got any designs on going against orders, Marshal, but with respect, just let us handle things our way." He stepped backwards off the ramp, hands spread wide, a suspicious drop in his voice making his mouthpiece crackle with amplitude. "The dogs are out for blood—don't set them on the scent and then crack the whip when they decide to take a bite for themselves."

Their conversation over, the cocky Uhlen gave his Marshal a half-hearted salute and pulled the ramp's release lever behind him, Tark watching the soldat vanish—the lights clicked on automatically in the small space, leaving the warlord alone in silence.

*

The engines had hummed to life just as Tark climbed the ramp into the cabin, the immaculate space occupied only by the pilot—an automaton of humble design, lacking much in the way of personality in its plain assembly, save for the almost cute way it wore its captain's hat. Tark couldn't remember if he or another member of the Uhlen had put it there, but either way, he appreciated the mock representation: it made for a better illusion of company aboard the ship.

"Evening, Germaine," Tark greeted the bot, hunched low in the space as he placed his talons against the autopilot's, giving a small smile. "Haven't yet decided to fly away without me, then?"

The heavily processed voice that responded lacked any kind of charm, synthetic or otherwise. "All is as directed, Marshal. Diagnostics performed returned two minor system errors resolved with software commands; no further flight risks detected. The Viola will depart at your command."

Tark nodded, still forcing the smile. "Glad to hear it, Germaine. We'll take her up, perform another grid sweep—access codes to Saintmarie's geographical survey sensors are ready to download, just connect to their main gateway and—"

"Download complete, building graph nodes now," the bot responded coldly, already sweeping its ball-jointed arms at lightning speed over the flight console to begin the takeoff procedure. "Grid scan will take approximately twelve hours of suborbital flight, adjusting for inclement weather and tectonic activity. We will depart immediately."

Tark gave a small sigh, but nodded again, slipping back towards the cabin's hatch and palming the electronic lock open to step onto the stairwell beyond. Hesitating, he turned back. "Thank you for all you do, Germaine. What would I do without your guiding hand at my side?"

The automaton did not respond, save for the mechanical whirrs of its hydraulics as it input commands on the switchboard, the captain's hat on its angular cranium lilting off to one side. The bot made no efforts to straighten it.

Tark cast his eyes down, his smile turning to a remorseful frown. He stared into space, the kuaneach quieted as if by a cold wind blowing through him. He could feel the powdery snowfall of long-dormant sorrows dusting his shoulders: there was work to be done, and no blood to be drawn from this particular stone. Shaking off the imagined slight, the dragon-blooded warrior descended the stairs, leaving the unresponsive machine to its tasks.

The single living space afforded by the Viola had become a second home to the Marshal, with his interests in stagnating back at the palace in Barrier City providing little in the way of opportunities to further his goals. Here on his ship, his simple oversized cot, compact cooking station and writing desk were all he wanted: that, and the most important accommodation of all. The high ceiling within his roomy cabin provided just enough room for his cramped wings to finally spread and crack their compressed joints, Tark giving a low rumble of satisfaction as his bat-like appendages reached skyward in much needed relief. It had been a long week, and few chances to slow down and collect his thoughts presented themselves: twelve hours alone on the Viola was like a year's vacation paid out, and he intended to collect.

The normally rigid dragonman rolled his shoulders to discard the dogmatic colors of his brigandine, a soothing cold wash of air conditioning seeping through his slightly damp undershirt: an elastic turtleneck with cutoff sleeves that provided cushioning for his scales, meant more to keep them from cutting through his leathery vest than to protect him from irritation. Nevertheless, he appreciated stripping down from his nearly permanent uniform, folding the lightly armored garment and squaring it away at the foot of his cot—no, that wasn't quite centered. Tark saw a small crease in the angled fold of his sheets, and smoothed it out, tugging lightly to tighten the tucked corner. There, much better: the brigandine was now perfectly aligned with the sharp corner of the thin mattress.

Everything in its right place.

Tark pulled his chair back on its suspended tracks away from the desk, sagging into it with another appreciative sigh. Age wasn't a concept he tended to dwell too much on, the lifespan of the average kuaneach that survived any given period of war being as of yet lacking a document of final expectancy. His body had definitely grown these past decades in the service of House Geiha past where he assumed it would have before he had left the service—or, rather, when the House itself no longer had need of his service, or had otherwise fallen to invading forces. As it stood the Geihan Empire boasted the longest ruling period of any prior house in history, thanks in no small part to Tark himself, given how since his promotion to Marshal no successful attempts to repel Geiha made by hostile territories had succeeded in saving them from annexation. Tark's net was cast wide and encompassed all, snaring the weakest and most wanting within—it was no interest to him, the diplomacy of starving nations baring their fangs at him. If the citizens of a dysfunctional House had a chance at a better life under the warm wings of a dragon, then Tark would displace any misfit politicians more interested in bearing a flag than feeding their population: bloodshed was simply their decision and their expense, should they fight back.

But the time spent. Time was the tax paid by Tark, the wages of his campaigns paid in increasing dividends. He examined his hand, where it rested on his desk—this desk, when he'd purchased it from the bazaar in House Coltour's outlying territory all those years ago as a freshly inaugurated oligarch, a clear horizon of possibilities before him in an otherwise troubled world ready for his intervention—it was so much...

...Smaller, now.

Kuaneach back home at The Roost would always undergo immense change over long stretches of time as they led their chosen lives of purpose. Some grew outwards, opulent and soft, as they acted caretaker and creator to nurture the younger generations of drakelings; others, the nomads, often grew lanky and serpentine in their travels, almost like they were blessed with the mirrored image of the revered Godheads themselves. Tark, however, was a warfighter. A honed tool in the carefully selected ranks of combat acolytes trained to act ambassador to those nations weaker than their own—he was fated for something altogether...larger. His eggmother, given up to the Aether before he'd bedded his own broodwife, she'd sneak into the undercroft where the acolytes would sleep cut off from the sun above and whisper fables to comfort him as he nursed his bruises and bloodied knuckles.

Tark leaned in close to the desk, closing his eyes, pressing his snout directly into the oiled wood and breathing deep: the perfume of sandalwood and volcanoflower seed oil rolled back into his lungs like a hit of a powerful drug, the nostalgic profile of familiar smells both cooling his head and warming his sore back muscles all at once. He could hear her now, smell her close by, her voice carried on the scent and breathing memory into him.

"...And when the Tower of Shirra fell, Rigel met with the thirteen kings at a table in the middle of the city, a table of simple wooden build—they sat in wooden chairs, ate from clay plates with their hands, and under his watchful eye, they had their first meal as peasants. If they complained, or stopped eating their cold bread and stiff meats, Rigel would welcome the townsfolk to pelt them with mud until they continued. Their colorful robes and shining crowns were caked with mud by the time their plates were clean, and Rigel himself bade them to wash their plates in the river, still wearing their robes and crowns and finest jewelry. After their meal, your grandsire then sent them into the town as ordinary citizens, paid only what they earned fairly cleaning the homes and tending the gardens of the townsfolk: a full year they toiled, never allowed to remove their kingly outfits, even as the jewels turned to brass and the robes became soiled and torn."

Tark wiped his wrist against his snout, sniffing as he left behind a bloody smear. The young acolyte was little more than a kobold in stature, the vibrant purple of his underscales often bringing the mockery of other acolytes down on his head, suggesting his colorful appearance be better served seeking to pleasure the elder kuaneach in the pleasure houses. It would be many, many seasons of hard training before his armor hide grew in, and given his lineage, his family's scales were famously smooth and soft. He'd even been horrified to himself wake up one morning early in training to find a broad streak of luminescent blue running up his snout: the most feminine of colors according to the older acolytes, certain to make him the prime target of their cruelties. He'd taken to disguising it with a thin layer of paste he'd made from mixing the volcanoflower seed oil they collected to make ink with the caulking he'd dug from the walls of the undercroft—better to look as if he were growing in his armor early on his face than to risk the alternative.

His mother continued her story as Tark picked unconsciously at the dried scab of paste on his snout—Ula's sandalwood scented scale lotion drifted through the small burrowed hole above his bed, the rat-sized tunnel leading up to allow air in from the higher levels closer to the surface. "Rigel gave his strength, his body, back to the world and all peoples of all lands, giving everything he had until the end of his life almost a millennia later. The drakeling he sired, that became my husband, your sire, Turroch. Though he was taken to the Aether before you hatched, he was as noble in spirit as Rigel himself, giving his life in battle to win a pyrrhic victory against House Geiha: their leader, a hateful despot who feared death and proclaimed himself messiah named by a Godhead, died alongside Turroch—though, that is a bedtime story for another night, my love."

Tark had heard that other story before a dozen times, not nearly as interested in his sire Turroch as he was the mythical Rigel. Impatiently, he whispered back, trying not to wake the other sleeping young warriors, lest he risk his belly being sliced: "You promised tonight you'd tell me what happened to him after Shirra—Rigel, I mean. After he sired eggs."

"I did, didn't I?" Ula sounded hesitant, but even though her voice was mere echo, Tark could imagine her thoughtful expression blossoming into a reluctant smile on her smooth snout. "Rigel had only one eggchild, in Turroch. Your sire was delivered back home here to The Roost, promised to wed to another family—my family—as soon as he was of age, raised by another so Rigel could continue seeking out evil unhindered by his brood. Rigel so pledged to continue his campaigns, but having brought about an age of peace that spread from Shirra like waves all up and down the Blackfire Coast, there were no more tyrants to overthrow—no House pledged war, no monarch dared speak a wicked word. Rigel had a choice: return home and train the next ten generations of young warriors, or continue seeking out the root of all that is wicked and terrible. Wander not astray, but of purpose, singular and righteous: walk the Path of the Ascendant. So, wander he did."

Tark felt he could sense a tinge of regret as she continued, but continue Ula did, and he decided she must simply be speaking with reverence, given how the next part of this story left him awestruck: "Every town he visited, he sought out the strongest fighters, teaching them not just technique but principle. Should they have wicked designs, he would cut that wickedness from them, until only goodness remained...or nothing remained. His campaign took him far and away—over hills, then mountains; over rivers, then lakes. His deeds grew, and along with them, so did he: centuries of battles, of hardships, and like a great tree he stretched ever skyward, until he himself could climb the hills with a single step and tower over mountains; until he could drink a river dry and bath in the lakes. He became one of the proudest forms of kuaneach: the Goliath, a great titan made servant to the planet itself, defending not just people but entire nations, as every new century gave rise to another corrupt nation exploiting its people. Some even say," Ula grinned audibly, and Tark grinned with her, "His Godhead gift of Heartfire became a great pulsar of holy light that could wipe away an entire blighted city with a single breath."

Tark wriggled on his warm cot with pride: those other drakelings wouldn't dare pick a fight with him if they knew he was sired by the son of a legendary Goliath.

"He was just like me, then—he knew there was nothing more important in life than strength and honor."

Ula tutted disapprovingly. "Careful your understanding of this story remains aligned with his perspective," she chided gently. "Your grandsire brought all of Shirra out of the age of monarchy, showing its people that those who call themselves kings can be made as pawns, just the same as all flesh and blood people. Rigel's gift to the world was no monument to his strength, nor temple to honor him, nor great mural of his deeds: he simply gave the gift of perspective to a defeated people who scraped and bowed at the behest of overfed tyrants. He showed them the truth that had so long been shrouded in the darkened souls of greedy men: that though we all may live and die as pawns, we too could be kings—given time, the last shall be first, and we will find our strength in the beating of sovereign wings. Rigel gifted this lesson to not just the people of Shirra, but to all peoples of all nations, all creeds and races, all who suffer beneath the stroke of the sword, or the judge's gavel, or the tax collector's claws. Most of all, he gifted this to you: for it was in the stables of

Shirra your sire was conceived, and christened with Rigel's words of promise."

The memory faded when Tark opened his eyes, and they flicked upwards to the corner of his desk. Beneath a stack of wax-stamped letters addressed to him from various House diplomats, which he swept aside carefully, a message he'd carved to himself in the hard wood, glistening with the oils that had seeped into it over many years of polishing:

AND THOUGH THEY SERVE AS PAWNS

THEIR SEEDS BEAR FRUIT OF KINGS

LEND WEAK AND WEARY STRENGTH

THOUGH SOVEREIGN BE YOUR WINGS

Tark dug his claw into the grooves of these old letters, centering himself with their meaning, their generational significance. He'd never met his sire, nor grandsire Rigel, but all acolytes who survived the Assay would bear the weight of their families' missions on their shoulders, their backs growing armor and their bodies expanding with muscle to carry forth these promises of generations past.

His gaze turned from the scratchings now to the tome above his desk. The accursed text that fouled his mind and turned his mouth dry as sand. Tark, for all his strength and purpose, still found himself hesitating whenever faced with the prospect of opening the book's pages again—yet, purpose and strength came with it a responsibility he had promised an age past to devote himself to, and open the book he did. Letting the weathered spine strain as he flattened the book open, the pages fanning out as he turned to his saved page, withdrawing the shaved fang that acted as bookmark.

The pages were all filled in with his own neat print, decades of study and thought poured into the wrinkled paper which had become so worn and softened from constant use they had turned almost to cotton. The page he turned to now—not a passage, but an artistic rendering of a creature. A creature he'd seen only once, a fated encounter he'd give anything to forget, and the features of whom had etched themselves forever on Tark's soul.

A head like a great reptilian bear, jaws wide in an agonized roar—yet, favoring a horror of biological mutation, a second pair of jaws themselves yawned open from within, layers of needle fangs pressed together into a sort of evil baleen. The beast's head was wreathed in a pentad of lightly curled horns, the bony platelike forehead splitting around a third eye, much larger than the original pair, the pupil slitted and diseased looking. By all measures, it was the face of a giant demon, furious and in pain.

The page had only a few words scrawled on it, just beneath the beast's face:

Goliath (NAME UNKNOWN)

"THE FALSE GODHEAD"

Tark pulled open a drawer in the desk, withdrawing a thin plastic sheet—a laminate dossier, which he dropped onto the open book before him, partially obscuring the drawing of the False Godhead. The unremarkable details of a soldat recruit were printed in fine lettering beneath a small pictograph of the subject, nothing about the document indicating any measure of importance concerning the man, save for one word that was underlined with ink:

LACHLAN

Giving the bio a cursory scan, the contents so bare they weren't worth remembering, Tark looked into the eyes of the young man he'd been hunting this past week—and, longer still, been appraising for the past several months before his Assay had gone awry.

"Brann of Lachlan," Tark said aloud, barely above a whisper. He said it with some discomfort, like he was rolling a shard of glass on his tongue, his eyes narrowing as he stared back into the hapless young man's nervous face. "Would that you knew how vexing you are to me, and how crucial you are to this puzzle: I wonder, could you have been as quick to flee from me, then?"

The pictograph was as responsive to his query as Germaine. Tark closed the book with the dossier still inside and rose from the desk, reaching up into a shuttered cabinet to remove a small hexagonal tin—popping off the cap, he wafted up the heady aroma of his favorite sleep aid tea before dipping his claws in and taking a hefty pinch of the leaves out to fill his percolator. The small cylindrical device began whirring as he replaced the lid and, just as he fitted a tall metallic cup into the dispenser, hissed in a rising cloud of steam as thick and murky brew splashed into the cup. Once it was nearly entirely full, the weight sensor switched off the boiler, and the percolator gave a small electronic chirp of success—Tark removed the steaming cup barehanded, not minding the heat through his tough scales, and ignored his chair to sit on the moderately softer cot.

The mirror opposite him made an honest man of him. Tark's dragonblood had chosen him for greatness, and he bore the appropriate gifts outwardly on every inch of his body. The gentle shine of the indigo beneath his black scales, channeling his gift of stoneskin. The smooth, imperious wave of his fierce horns. The way spikes of keratin had formed an intimidating backswept frame around his jawline, and his long snout—

Tark leaned forward, staring intently, honing in on a particular detail.

The bridge of his snout, where his mask rested. A small patch of soft, pearlescent blue, peaking out between the crevices of jet black scaled ridges.

He appraised this detail of himself with a lifetime of turmoil and decisiveness behind his eyes, his furrowed brow cracking in restrained sorrow. There was a lifetime of choices concealing that blue marking. A lifetime of regret.

Tark gently set aside his tea, reaching into the desk drawer closest to him beside the cot and removing a tiny bottle. Uncapping it, he dipped a single clawed finger lightly into the inkwell, pulling away once his clawtip shone wetly.

Turning back to stare himself in the eye in the mirror once more, he stroked his finger softly, deliberately, over the patch of blue, painting in every tiny bright millimeter of the intruding markings under a coat of pure black ink.

The crags of blue soon no longer gilded his entirely black snout. His visage, refreshed, unwavering in its dark determination.

Everything in its right place.

Tark sniffed the air. The ink had no smell of seed oil, no familiar tang. It was simply harsh, chemical, and acrid.

He once more held his cup of tea, lifting it partway to his slightly open maw. Then stopped.

His lips pursed. Tark set the cup down on his desk and clasped his hands together as he receded inward, letting the tea go cold and its rising steam to fade in silence.

He'd lost his taste for it.

16. The Malaise

The stack of handcrates clattered down the ramp to heap themselves in a pile of disarray, Zay clenching at her wrist and grimacing as she screamed out:

"Fuck!"

The ever-helpful co-pilot she resented sidled up beside her, his yellow beams clicking behind rotating lenses, Hawkshaw appraising Zay's arm with little regard to personal space.

"Ouch, looks like a fractured radius there, skin-sister, you might wanna see a doc about that."

Zay elbowed the snarky bot aside and stomped down the ramp, kicking over the lopsided crates to rearrange them beside each other and form a level surface. "Is that the best you got, 'skin-sister,' really?"

"About as creative as 'metal-man' but you've been throwing that one at me like a rock nonstop all afternoon. Time permitting I'd like us to get to know each other more intimately, if only so these less than friendly exchanges can expand the limits of our respective vocabularies?" Hawkshaw joked as he leaned against the frame of the ramp, the metal plates of his face sliding to imitate a smirk, though the expression managed to make the artifice of his design look more like a locust than ever. "By ours, I mean yours, obviously."

"Can it, can-opener," was the reply from within the cargo bay, Nestor appearing with an unrolled holomap hefted over his shoulder, his greasy jumpsuit having replaced his finer attire.

"See that's what I'm saying, Zay—get on Nestor's level here!" Hawkshaw bounced a finger back and forth in the air as he repeated the cadence: "'Can it,' 'can-opener,' get it? An artist at work!"

Nestor crouched next to Zay as she sat back on the ramp, the two of them unrolling the thick plastic sheet of the holomap on the arranged handcrates, the gentle glow of the beige surface lighting up as it blinked with a few lines of code before the whole screen conjured a topographical chart. The inky pixels arranged themselves on the sepia-toned holographic plastic as if by the hand of an invisible cartographer, and soon a map of the region was completed for them. Zay clicked a switch on the side of the extended screen and the topography blurred slightly in displaced layers to give itself the illusion of three-dimensional space, which allowed her to center and rotate with her fingers around the miniature model of the Donnie.

"We probably cut through the entire southwest corridor of the continent overnight, which places us on basically the ass-end of the coast we were supposed to be following north, so you can thank the can-opener for that," Zay said aloud, tracing a finger along the route the Donnie had made since last night's near-crash.

Hawkshaw gave an electronic click of the tongue. "Okay, but Nes just used that one? You can't just steal someone else's creativity—"

"Which means," Zay continued, raising her voice to speak over her rival pilot, "We now have two passengers that are even further away from their destination than where we picked them up, and I am even further away from a paycheck than I was before you fine people wrecked my perfectly good ship." She glared at Nestor, then at Brann, who was sitting quietly on his own solitary crate some distance away, watching everyone else take stock of their situation. "So, really, just, a sincere thanks from me to you. Care to add your thoughts on things here, 'Recruit Brann?'"

His secret was out now, and like crows circling a fragrant carcass, Brann felt his skin prickle under the eyes of his companions who were all beginning to settle on him as the one to blame for their misfortune. The Donnie had embedded itself in a mudbank in a wide valley separating two distant plateaus, possibly the remains of a dried lake—the air was still smokey from the fires that had been put out in her lower decks where the hull was splatter-painted with tiny shrapnel punctures. The already sparse crew was down to its last workhands, a pair of exhausted jumpsuits sitting in the mud, faces blackened by smoke and oil—the only ones who had remained aboard while the rest of the flight crew had stayed overnight in

Mongillo, left behind when the nine fugitives made good their escape. Emrys had just returned from a nearby grove with bundles of dried wood under each arm, having set to digging out a pit to create a campfire, with Grishka perched on his shoulder in her most true raven form—she was entertaining herself by swiping some of the smaller branches out of his hands before he could place them. Above in the cargo bay, Red and Wolf were sitting in opposite deck-chairs, The Lady's legs crossed and her boot impatiently bouncing in the air while her lupine bodyguard was using his fangs to rip at the armholes of his vest and give his powerful shoulders more room to flex. The only ones not present were the mare Brann had met in Boomer's den last night and the fighter himself, likely still recovering from last night's beatings.

Which left Brann alone to speak up for himself, something he was finding himself increasingly at odds with doing whenever addressed by Zay. Where previously she seemed content with avoiding him during their shared flight, now she was spitting daggers at him anytime she spoke to him—and Brann had already come to realize he didn't have any more bluster in him like he'd tried showing Tark in the stadium. Zay—and everyone else—saw right through him now.

Brann decided not to give a direct answer, instead reaching for his belt to open his medipack. "Zay, I can fix that arm for you if it's hurt, I have a splint here and plenty of numbing vials left—"

"No. I'll get someone else to fix it." She obviously wasn't going to let Brann off the hook this time. "Someone who isn't just pretending to be qualified at their job. Now, how do you plan on fixing this mess, soldat? You got a new engine in that little purse of yours?"

"I can fix the engines, Zay, they aren't in that bad a shape," Nes interjected, a hand offered up in Brann's defense half-heartedly. "You can let Brann set your arm, he's still a trained corpsman, and right now the best qualified we've got for medical—"

"He's not touching my goddamned arm," Zay snarled, on her feet suddenly, circling around the crates to stand before Brann and loom over him. Brann did not return her gaze. "Since I took your money—no, correction—since you broke my ship, this little tumor has been at the center of everything that's gone wrong these past few days, and now we know him for what he is: a criminal, a deserter, who had us all played for fools thinking we were under official watch of the Geihan Empire. Only now we know that not only was that the opposite of the truth, but he's gotten us all branded as terrorists—terrorists!—by the single most brutal House on the continent, who has built a reputation on absolutely merciless warfare. On top of that," Zay continued, her voice rising and becoming progressively angrier, her words begin to stumble into one another, "He managed to personally piss off probably the most bloodthirsty motherfucker still living this side of the Arbitration Wars, who probably has a higher body count notched in his axe than all of the people any of us have met in our entire lifetimes combined."

Zay kicked Brann's boot, opening his legs roughly to plant her own between them, shoving her knee forward towards his chest and putting her hands on her hips—his personal space was now her space, and she wanted him to know he was danger. "Hey. You. You listening to me? I'm talking about you."

"Zay," Nestor warned.

"Let him speak, Nes," she motioned back, not breaking her stare for a moment—Brann could feel her eyes burning holes in his skull above him, his own cast down at her boots, paralyzed by fear and shame. "He's a soldat, yeah? Big tough warfighter, yeah? Maybe he wants to get dropped off back on the palace steps, we fly over Barrier City and push him overboard? Or maybe," Zay hissed, her voice becoming low, and unambiguously threatening now, "Maybe we just deal with him our own way. Send a special package addressed to the Marshal ourselves, with this little ratfuck's peeled face inside—"

"Zaydat, step back," Nestor was saying now, also on his feet. Though they made no attempts to similarly intervene, everyone else was watching quietly now, all eyes on Brann and the mercenary woman.

Brann swallowed, his face searing hot, fat teardrops beginning to splash onto his hands as they clenched themselves together. His whole body was shaking, and he simply couldn't speak, no matter how hard he tried. Try as he might, he had no rebuttal, no words to assuage Zay's fury: she was right on all counts. He'd been selfish, and had endangered everyone he'd met since coming aboard the Donnie, even bringing along some volunteered passengers of his own for the ride.

He didn't know what to say, and he didn't know what to do. Helplessly, pitifully, his shaky hands once again slowly moved to open his medipak, fingers slipping as they grasped at a packaged splint within.

Like a snake striking at a mouse, Zay's fingers clamped onto Brann's throat—the same hand attached to her broken arm, and yet, she squeezed as hard as he could in defiance of her own injury; Brann choked out a sob, and Zay just clamped down harder, growling—"I *told* you. Don't you *dare* fucking touch me."

Nestor nearly tripped as he leapt over the crates, lunging forward to loop both arms around Zay's waist and shove back, the much skinnier man summoning all his strength to heave her away and off of Brann—who was tossed to the side as a consequence, Zay's nails scraping into his throat as her hold was released from the force, the young soldat tumbling into the mud facedown. Zay and Nes fell together, though she landed on top of him and winded the older engineer, his eyes popping as he locked his hands together with all his might to keep her restrained.

"Get off me, you old bitch, I'm gonna kill him," Zay gurgled through her teeth, her lip dribbling blood down her chin as she struggled wildly, having bit her own tongue in the fray.

"Then you're gonna have to kill me too," was Nestor's muffled reply into her shoulder, desperately trying to wrap more of himself around the merc as they became soaked through with mud, keeping his legs from getting a good hold on hers.

"Fine by me!" Zay lurched forward and rolled, elbowing upwards into Nestor's chest and breaking his grip—and, when he landed on his back, she drew back a fist and sent a right hook cracking loudly against his jaw, screaming out from the impact as once more she'd used her injured arm. Nestor was nevertheless stunned from the blow, just long enough for Zay to scramble once more to her feet, nearly slipping and falling several times from the slick mud in the process.

Brann hadn't moved from his spot on the ground, and simply clenched his eyes tight when Zay grabbed for his shirt collar, yanking him up and onto his side so she could see his face.

"Get up, you little piggy," she breathed, voice hoarse from her scream of pain, no doubt using her own broken forearm as an excuse to vent her outrage on him. "Show me how a coward fights."

Brann's arms were held just above his head, partially to shield himself, partially to keep his face hidden, still audibly sobbing—his hands stretched up, fingers dripping cold mud, pleading to Zay. She held him there, that injured arm cocked back ready to strike again, both of them shuddering from the cold and wet, and from the overwhelming emotions surging through them.

But Zay's next blow didn't come. Brann couldn't see anything, but felt it when he was roughly shoved back down into the mud, nearly cracking his tooth when a hidden pebble connected with it.

"Just like that," he heard Zay say above him. "Exactly like that."

Her boots slopped away from him wetly, and Brann pulled his face up from the mud, opening his bleary eyes to look back through his streaked vision at everyone else watching: no one had budged an inch, not Hawkshaw, nor Emrys, nor the Lady and her Wolf—even Grishka had stayed silently perched on Emrys's shoulder, her dark little face turned sideways to peer down at the boy. No one but Nestor had made any attempt to stop Zay, and as the winded man lifted himself from the wet dirt unsteadily, Brann knew Zay probably would have killed the both of them if she hadn't relented.

And they all would have let her do it.

"So, what," Brann began to speak at last, his voice rattling loose from the scrap, propping himself up on his hands: what a miserable sight he must make, that nice outfit paid for by Nestor, that armored breastplate paid for by the Geihan military, his entire mud-covered existence a courtesy of those he'd leeched off of since his days as a street urchin. "None of you ever ran away from a fight? No one here, you never got stuck somewhere you didn't wanna be?" He wiped an arm across his face, only smearing it with more mud, sniffing as his nose began to run. "You all just had perfect luck, perfect lives, growing up exactly where you wanted to be?"

Brann spat out a wad of muddy saliva, looking around at the group, hoping to see any shred of sympathy or compassion from even one of them. "I don't know who I am or where I'm going—yeah, you all have it figured out for yourselves, you all know exactly what you're gonna do with your lives," he said with an accusing finger. "I didn't have a family, I didn't have a home, I didn't have anything—and even when I had something, when I became a soldat, I had even less. I didn't choose it, I never wanted it, but I was stuck with it anyway—and everyone says hey, congratulations, you're so brave and tough, taking the hard road none of us could!" He wiped his hand on his mostly dry shoulder, displacing enough mud so he could use the knuckle of his thumb to dry his tears. "I didn't say any of that shit, I never wanted to be brave or tough, I just wanted somewhere to live and have a bed and be normal like everyone else!"

Zay had climbed the ramp, her back still turned to him, shoulders high and rigid—Nes had dragged himself there as well, arms crossed as he listened—even he had a look like he had once more been soured, like it hadn't been worth the effort to stop Zay from pummeling Brann. Emrys, Grishka, Red, Wolf, Hawkshaw—all their eyes, as Brann searched them, held nothing for him. At best, they looked at him with a detached sort of pity—at worst, they held judgment.

"Who's in charge here?" Brann asked. His finger moved to point at Hawkshaw, then Nes, then Zay. "You? You? Her? Who's the captain? Who's the pilot? Who runs the ship? I've had to listen to you all fight each other for a week and still don't know—everyone wants to be in charge but no one wants to lead? You're all a mess! You couldn't even stop fighting each other long enough to avoid getting us shot down!"

Hawkshaw scratched his metal claws awkwardly against his neck, and Zay's shoulders sagged a little. Nestor looked away from Brann, rubbing at his sore jaw.

"It's Boomer's ship—no, Nes, no, the pilot decides where we all go, no, because you don't even know who the pilot is, so it's my fault we're stuck here—what, because I ran away from the service, because I didn't want to be a soldat?"

Still, no one responded.

"Why don't I get to decide how I live?" Brann challenged them, sounding to his own ears as much like a petulant child as he ever did. "Why don't I get what everyone else gets, to go live where I want, do what I want? Why am I the bad guy for wanting a place to sleep without having to worry about going off to die tomorrow fighting someone I don't even know for someone else who doesn't even care about me? What makes any of you better than me?"

Zay's fists had unclenched, and she turned—and, where moments ago was unbridled rage, Brann saw to his surprise her eyes had become glassy and moist. She responded with only two words.

"You ran."

She turned once more, disappearing into the ship. Nestor quietly regarded Brann with a look of regret, but followed behind Zay soon after. Even Lady Red and The Wolf stood from their chairs to retreat inside—though, the latter stood for a moment to appraise Brann, his predatory eyes beneath that sharp brow no more warm or kindly than ever, before he too padded along behind his partner. Hawkshaw almost looked as if he was going to say something sarcastic, but thought better of it and just shrugged, then he too went inside.

Brann stood and watched them all vanish. Sniffing a few more times to try and clear his nose to no avail, he dragged his heels through the mud towards the ramp before turning and dropping limply to sit, elbows on his knees as he brooded to himself.

Emrys set aside the remainder of the firewood and cleared his throat, choosing to speak when everyone else remained silent. "Look, kid," he began, lacking his usual flair for overly syllabic speech. "Far be it for me to tell you your life isn't yours to live. All of us, myself included, we all face trials, challenges, and we have all lost or been made to lose when faced with choices we didn't want to make."

He stood from his crouch next to the firepit, wiping his hands free of bark debris before unpocketing his little leather spellbook and tearing a page from it, crumpling it with a small green spark before tossing it in and letting the fire roar to life. Emrys watched it grow for a moment before finishing his thought. "We all know where we're going, but more importantly, where we came from," he resumed, looking up at the sky as the afternoon light began to wane as twilight drew closer. "Having that perspective makes it easier for us to say we know what's right, and what's good, and what's not. We're not on some mission of noble intent, or vainglorious purpose to seek out some evil. We're simply passengers on a ship that, until we met you, largely had no designs on fighting for our lives."

Emrys let the fire burn and reached up to give Grishka a reassuring pat on her beak, then walked away towards the ship, passing Brann on the ramp. "Like it or not, we're all stuck with you now," he said back over his shoulder. "And none of us, not even Zay I imagine, know if any of us are gonna have a life to go back to now. For some people that's medicine that's just...a shade too bitter for them to swallow."

Brann heard the holyman's shoes clicking against the ladder rungs, then the sound of the hatch closing. The lakebed was silent now, save for the crackling of the fire. He stared forward, eyes unfocused, his vision filled with the blurry ink and sepia colors of the forgotten holomap.

The wavy lines formed ridges, mountains, tiny rivers crisscrossing through it all. A line of no texture, simply an imaginary barrier, cut through the middle—the word "Saintmarie" in opaque font running perpendicular to the line. Brann reached out his cleaner hand and tapped curiously at the map, watching it bounce and wobble with his touch, then found he could enlarge the areas around the ship with a pinch of two fingers. Zooming out, that line intersected with other lines, the finer details of the topography disappearing under the borders of other nearby regions, all marked with the names of their own Houses.

Brann's eyes drifted lazily this way and that, the depressed young man simply taking in the size of his surroundings, having not even zoomed the chart out far enough to see the entire continent. He'd come so far without even realizing it, this past week having put him hundreds of miles away from everything he'd known, and yet he knew no matter how far he fled, Tark likely had a map just like this one with Brann's name on it, his every move charted to the inch as long as he was still on board the *Myrmidon*.

He continued toying with the chart a moment longer before stopping sharply, his fingers freezing over one particular area. Brann stared, unblinking, then zoomed in, rotating and panning the map to give himself a better idea of what he was looking at in terms of distance from where the Donnie had landed. He looked to the holomap's built-in compass, then oriented himself north, raising a finger to aim it towards this point of interest. Brann looked up from the map, following his finger where it led straight away towards the distant grove of dead trees Emrys had collected the firewood from.

*

The small pen-shaped commlink was vibrating on his desk, its light blinking a piercing blue starburst in the dark room. Tark snapped out of his half-asleep stupor, the movement setting off his motion lights, reawakening the soft glow of the overhead lamps gently. He halted them from reaching full brightness by reaching over his bed to click the manual switch for them, his other hand grabbing for the commlink and depressing the activator button with a soft rubberized click.

"Go for Marshal."

The communicator device spun its frequency wheel against his thumb with a quiet whine, adjusting to optimize the signal before static gave way to a tinny voice. "Marshal, your packet just came through, we downloaded and got an immediate ping on their location. Standing by for orders now."

He looked over through drowsy eyes at the hatch to his chambers, still sealed—he hadn't sent anything; likely Germaine transmitting on his behalf on an automated protocol. Tark would have to remind himself to turn that off later. "And? One thing at a time, what is their location?"

The static phased in a bit for a moment, before The Speaker's voice returned. "They sure made a go at it, but couldn't quite make it outside Saintmarie's borders, so the scan got them having landed right at the runoff point of the Old Dam. It's a straight shot from where we are now, but you're still a ways off overhead—should we wait for you to proceed?" There was another brief wave of static, and possibly a scoff—Tark couldn't quite tell. "Under your supervision, I mean. Marshal."

The Old Dam. Tark recalled the friction between himself and the Uhlen Speaker earlier in the day. He mulled over this information: where the recruit was headed, what his intentions must be. If he thought he would find answers, or perhaps if he was seeking shelter.

Of course, there would be no shelter. Nor answers. Only the realization of his last mistake.

Tark looked at his desk. In the low light, he could still make out the shadowed features of Recruit Brann's face staring up at the ceiling, next to the obscured drawing of the Goliath. At the uncapped inkwell still sitting there, shiny and black and cold. As cold as the tea sitting next to it.

He spoke into the commlink once more. "No. Proceed without me, as you see fit. Take a leader's initiative and let's put this matter behind us. This hunter has other prey to pursue."

The Speaker chuckled appreciatively. "Glad to hear you talking sense again, Boss. You know if he ever heard you let off the accelerator in chasing him down, he'd never be scared of you again."

Though it was the truth, in unusual fashion, this irked Tark somewhat. "If you handle this decisively, then he'll never have to hear about it," he replied, maintaining some semblance of cold imperiousness in his voice—though he didn't convince himself it worked.

"Copy good, Boss. We'll take it from here. Rest up and we'll see you on the trails another day. End comms." The link went dead, the light dulled.

Tark rolled the pen communicator between his fingers, then tossed it aside, back onto the desk. He looked to Brann's dossier once more before snatching it up between two claws and tossing the small plastic sheet into the wastebin below with a clatter, then slammed the research book shut.

The Geihan military would scantly lose sleep over the unceremonious execution of a single deserter. In that spirit, he honored those who served under him, Tark clicking off the overhead lights and heaving himself fully up onto his cot, taking care not to let his heavy tail roll off the side as he laid himself down to the rare treat of a sound night's sleep.

*

The sun had mostly disappeared behind the horizon, only the sliver of dying red light keeping the purple night sky above at bay when the sound of hooves filled the cargo bay. "Yo, kid, we're about to serve dinner," Boomer called out hoarsely, his face bandaged and purple as he emerged from the dark bay, stepping onto the ramp. "Grishka said some weird shit about cooking something over a fire but I ain't eatin' whatever that is while we still got a perfectly good kitchen, so we're just gonna have some sandwiches or something else more..." He slowed as he stepped off the ramp. "...Normal."

Boomer looked east, then west, eyes scanning all around the ship, searching the distance reaches of the lakebed. Brann was nowhere to be seen. The fire burned high, sparks rising above it, but no one sat beside it. The young soldat had just vanished into the night—no trail could be made as to which direction he made, given the rough scene the mud recalled, any semblance of even footprints lost in the scrapings and slurry of the scrabbling bodies that had been rolling about in it this afternoon.

"Bunch of animals," Boomer said quietly to himself, his expression growing concerned. He scanned his immediate surroundings for any more clues, then looked straight down, where the map still lay spread out with its faint beige glow. He blinked, then crouched, the tall horse bringing himself lower to get a better look at it.

"Ah, shit."

The 3D effect of the map had been disabled in favor of a flat overhead view, where the small pin that represented the Donnie had been rotated to align itself beneath the northernmost bordering region. Where a small ovular convergence of borders met on the map, a humble oblong territory sat nestled between the outer reaches of Saintmarie where the Donnie sat and the other encroaching regions, with almost its entire surface area filled in by a single word:

LACHLAN

17. The Coward

The dead trees all around did little to shield the bright moon above from guiding Brann's feet along an old footpath, his trek illuminated with nary a threat of any hidden dangers that might spring out at him—there was almost no sign of life to be had here, only the barest distant call of a creature or flutter of a moth's wings. The ground itself was packed hard and firm, as if once it had been verdant and lush but was salted, the moisture leeched entirely out of the soil. It made walking easy on his legs, but hard on his feet, his boots feeling like they were marching on cement—but, this didn't deter him one bit. Brann was no stranger to the long hikes the recruits would often be subject to, and this was if anything easier than those, considering he had no Division Captains giving threats. Only the quiet night air and his thoughts—his tears had run dry, the knot in his chest unwound, replaced by the stiffness of his lower back and tender feet.

It must have been hours since he'd set off—the moon had elapsed its peak overhead already, and if he looked up at only a slight angle, he'd be face to face with it: while he didn't have an exact distance to Lachlan's borders from where he'd started, he was sure he was well within them by now, given how close the Donnie had landed to it. In fact, the more he dwelled on it, stewing in his own frustration and self-pity, the more he convinced himself that they had been heading there on purpose all along to leave him behind once they'd landed within its borders. Knowing Tark and the Uhlen would be chasing them down, it would make sense for Nes and the rest to simply deposit Brann at his place of birth and be on their way, a sure way to guarantee their escape while as much as hand delivering him up to Tark without risking their own safety in another fight. Where this thought began as suspicion in the back of his mind, the more the size of Lachlan versus the rest of the nearby regions they could have travelled to versus the straight line away from Saintmarie they'd flown proved theory to be fact in Brann's perspective. It was simply too much of a coincidence to be one at all—they'd definitely been flying him there to ditch him.

Well, now he was just saving them the last leg of the trip.

The trees had been stretching on for miles, and as the moon dipped lower above his head, beginning to peek into his field of view if he so much as tilted up his chin, Brann caught the faintest of scents on the breeze. Sweet, almost floral, although...something else behind it, something more complex. The further he marched, the more whiffs of it he caught, and soon it was there to stay: sweet, yes, but in an almost unpleasant way, like sugared ammonia, something unhealthy and rotting that had been masked by a perfume. He didn't know why, but the stronger the smell became, the more Brann was reminded of something...recent. A plant—no, a flower. He thought back to the graveyard at Emrys's parish, and something began to click, a connection of sensory memory forming. This smell definitely harkened back to the flowers that decorated that graveyard.

The sparse sounds of nightlife had disappeared entirely, the only thing he heard now the beating of his feet against the packed dirt and the repetitious breaths hissing through his cold nostrils. Brann squinted, and sure enough, the trees ahead became denser, growing closer together and blocking out more and more light, though no less dead and bitter their bark. The vanishing moonlight may have concerned him, were it not for the reassurance that the path itself was actually more visible, more beaten and hewn—the foot traffic here was far more regular. He was closer to civilization now, he was sure of it: in fact, just as he questioned his resolve in moving into the heart of the darkness ahead, Brann could swear he saw the faint outline of an old boot print outlined by the smallest of shadows cast by its textured imprint.

There was a town nearby, or maybe even a solitary homestead in the wild of the forest—in any case, there was no reason to stray from the path now. He'd be among members of his own House soon enough.

This idea didn't register as particularly exciting to Brann before tonight, but now, cast out from under Boomer's watch, he did feel a strange surge of trepidation—would he be welcomed back as some lost wanderer, possibly forgiven his desertion? Would anyone even know who he was or where he'd run away from?

Another thought struck him, this one much more alarming.

Would he have family there? Parents?

Suddenly, Brann wasn't so sure he wanted to find out. Not that he wouldn't welcome the idea of a home of his own to return to, if he had parents still, then surely having left him behind to fend for himself so young in Barrier City must have been no mistake. If they didn't want him as an infant, why would they welcome him now as an adult—as a soldat, no less?

These questions sprang forth unbidden, bouncing around inside and twisting his innards—the possibilities of what may await him beyond this dead forest were as frightening as they were exciting, and Brann was resigned to simply accept whatever he may find as what was meant for him regardless—anything, even a tepid reception by complete strangers, would be better than continuing to live as a fugitive, branded a coward and a terrorist.

Anything.

The path dropped off sharply, into the darkness of trees that bowed on an incline, and Brann found his steps quickening at gravity's insistence—he was descending now, the path following a sharp decline of altitude, and the further he went the more he could see light beyond: the trees were thinning. His pace began to pick up now, not just from the sloping path—there, ahead, a gnarled old tree was almost horizontal as if it had been bent in half in some great storm, but continued to grow still...and the branches were visibly trimmed where they otherwise would have blocked the path. This was it, whatever it was, wherever he was: his destination was just past this grand old tree.

The incline smoothed itself out, and once again Brann was on flat ground as he past beneath the tree's earthbound canopy. Like a natural archway, welcoming him home, to this—

—Place.

Brann cleared the fringe of trees and stopped dead, blinking. His first instinct was to be disappointed—his second, to be confused.

His third instinct, the one he pushed down and ignored in favor of his curiosity, was to flee. To run back as fast as he could the way he came.

There was a village here, yes, but only in the past tense. Brann walked slowly, cautiously, between plots of land where houses once stood, now bereft of light or warmth...or even solid walls. Like the parish, all of the humble homes here had caved inwards on themselves, as if a great force had collapsed their roofs and walls from without: stone and lumber, ashen and splintered, all as dead and drained of color as the forest surrounding this place. There was nothing here waiting for him, no one.

Brann groaned to himself, coming to a halt at a point where the path curved, obscuring the rest of the village ahead behind a row of ruinous cabins. He'd walked all this way for nothing, and he was exhausted.

At worst, if not a warm bed to be welcomed to, he'd hoped for some unattended bale of hay to rest on before the sun rose. Now, he'd be lucky to find anywhere that even had a roof to cover him.

The moonlight was still fading, and Brann knew dawn would be here soon—the prospect of continuing on to find somewhere else habitable that may or may not even exist was not an enticing one. Turning to one of the nearby cabins, Brann stepped off the path, crossing over the threshold of the broken home: the highest walls all terminated at about waist height, but the furthest corner of the structure looked promising. Where the roof had fallen in, there was an intact section that had propped itself up between the wall and the floor, forming a sort of accidental awning—just big enough for a person to squeeze under, it was as much a shelter as he needed tonight.

There was a rotted-out bureau nearby—this may have been a bedroom at some point. Brann searched as best he could for something, anything to create impromptu bedding with—there was no furniture visibly intact, only more shriveled planks and broken frames, nothing usable. Until one patch of wall gave way around an even square of empty space, a small door having fallen away from it with its hinges rusted. A cabinet—and sure enough, just next to it, its paired door was warped inwards, something visible in the dark gap. Tugging with one hand only made the wood creak—Brann had to put his strength behind both hands, leaning his weight back until the cabinet door gave and cracked, coming apart under his fingers in a splintery mess of termite dust.

What unbelievable luck: a single water-stained pillow, and an equally filthy looking set of bedsheets, tossed and rumpled with withered leaves clinging to their greyed fabric.

With a few strong shakes, the worst of the detritus was freed from the bedding materials, leaving scattered curls of leaf fragments and flurries of dirt and dust streaking the floorboards. Brann bundled up his treasure under one arm and returned to the small patch of fallen roof, spreading out one of the sheets on the floor with no particular care to keep it straight— tossing down the pillow, he'd made himself a veritable fort against the cold night, and one discarded breastplate later he was ready to tuck himself in.

The sheets were gritty and the pillow smelled of mildew, but once he rolled over with the second sheet wrapped around him, Brann was warm, and the pillow was soft. He'd been in worse sleeping situations than this, and despite himself, he found a sort of welcome relief in this artificial bed of his: not a teenth as comfortable as his quarters onboard the Donnie, but alone out here in the woods, in this abandoned village, he was feeling somewhat nostalgic. The abandoned housing projects on the outskirts of Barrier City weren't so different than this, save for the roaming bands of Nightwatch who would often scare off trespassers like himself.

Not here, though. Here the night was quiet, still, the entire township empty and barren. No one to disturb him, or scold him, or scrutinize and demean him. Here, he could get a decent night of sleep, free of any fear of imposition or obligations to anyone else.

Brann stared at the patterns in the cracked stone wall before closing his eyes, slowly—the moment they shut, however, he was out, taken by a deep sleep.

Tomorrow, he'd figure out where to go next, who to seek out. Tonight, he was free.

*

The smell was back, and stronger than ever, sickly sweet perfume coating his throat—strong enough to wake him up, and yet he slept still, plagued by bizarre visions. The wall before his eyes seemed to sprout moss that withered and died as quickly as it grew, turning to dribbling rot that bled downwards in cold streaks that shone in the moonlight before hardening, crystalizing, reaching out like the spindly legs of a spider towards his face. Turning away weakly, Brann rolled onto his opposite side as he slept, his mind's eye still wide open to look beyond the limits of his shut eyelids. Hair, thick and dark and wet-looking—like a woman's, one who had recently stepped out of a lake—hung from the nonexistent rafters above, silently floating over the floorboards, dripping brackish liquid from their dense tendrils. The sheer walls of hair stretched upwards, far above where he could turn his head to see, and the closer the creeping vines of hair came to him, the louder the sound grew: rasping, heaving, scratching, the sound of a dying breath caught in stasis, repeating and rewinding and repeating at the exact moment the soul escaped its fleshy prison. Inhaling nothing, exhaling its entire life, air caught in pierced lungs sucking air through them uselessly. Soon the hair was encircling him, blocking out the world behind its black curtain, that sugary ammonia smell practically choking Brann in his sleep. Then the hair began to pile on top of itself, the dripping coming to a halt as curls upon curls of impossibly black hair condensed together: the source of the hair was drawing nearer, lowering itself, its giant head—and, as if falling through the sky, the dream lurched, and Brann saw only the wide and accusing stare of a pair of bloodshot eyes as familiar as his own yet as anguished and stomach-turning as the most brutally flayed of cadavers—lifeless, soulless, pitted and veined, blinking through shredded, lidless skeins of bloody tissue emergent from a gored skull turned inside out. Those eyes stared at him in the dark, only at him, Brann becoming the sole fixation of their very existence, and though he couldn't scream, he felt his mouth agape nonetheless—and the giant dead face mimicked his expression, jaw gaping wide around sawed down, blunted teeth, that black tongue curling up as the entity's head began shaking uncontrollably, screaming silently right along with Brann, mocking and sorrowful and as terrible as the end of all life itself.

18. The Spillway

The dam guarded the village from the morning sun rising behind it, standing sentinel over the valley below. Where once water flowed downstream, a large concrete spillway separated the southern border of the ruined township from the forest beyond, and now seemed little more than a footpath up the side of the small mountain where the lake above had been dammed off. In the tentative glow of dawn, Brann could survey the village entire now, and having climbed atop one particularly steady looking wall of toppled bricks, the view was even more dour than first impressions gave him last night.

The majority of the village proper had been sunken into a bog, the structures that still stood primarily skirting the dry fringes of the swamp; almost no homes or buildings remained upright where the earth softened into a fungal pit of opaque mudwater. Scattered patches of fallen brick walls could be seen rising from the marsh, decorated in stringy algae and slime mold of varying colors, all of it reeking of that same rotten sweet smell Brann had endured through the night: undoubtedly this was the source of it, the pit of decayed earth swallowing the village into its decomposed epicenter. No one had lived here for months, years even. Circling the precarious edge of the boggy village instilled in Brann a sense of unease— though the footpath was on steady, solid ground, the visions that plagued him in his sleep returned to him in fresh bursts of acuity every time he took a particularly deep breath of that fouled air. As if the nightmares had visited him from within that sunken bog where the world had swallowed this once living place.

Eventually the footpath veered off to the right into that marsh, and Brann abandoned it in favor of a new objective: the clearest and quickest way out of this village was to follow the spillway up the side of the mountain to its point of origin—maybe there were people still living around the lake, at a higher elevation obscured from his view. Either way, he decided a single village was hardly a fair indicator of Lachlan's population as a whole: surely somewhere within its borders were still-living Housemembers who would give him an idea of where he could head off to next.

The slope wasn't unbearably steep, but given the steady rise up the mountain and the distance he'd have to travel, Brann definitely had his work cut out for him—if he didn't want to wear himself out, the climb would take at least an hour. Standing at the concrete lip of the spillway, he lowered himself down carefully, finding enough of a grip with his backside and his elbows to let himself slide down and land upright on the dry surface of the spillway's relatively wide channel. Adjusting his armor and reshouldering his rifle, Brann took stock of the steep climb he was to undertake with a resolute sigh, then turned to look to where the spillway terminated.

The concrete channel burrowed directly under the dry ground, and below a reinforced barrier, a gaping black hole in the earth stared back at him like an unseeing eye: even as early daylight was cast directly back it, nothing but black abyss could be seen within, and though he could only guess Brann wouldn't have been surprised to learn if deep within that chasm was where some catastrophic internal collapse had caused the earth around it to flood and create the bog that sank the village. The longer he stared into its depths, the more nervous it made him.

Something about this entire place was just...wrong. Brann couldn't place it, but something terrible festered within the soul of this ghost town, and he wanted very little to do with it any longer.

So began his climb, away from the bog and the spillway's chasm. Brann found a good steady grip in the sloped concrete by leaning forward onto the toes of his boots, and upwards he went, taking measured and even breaths along the way. If nothing else, training in Geiha had prepared him for this with the endless hikes the recruits had taken, and he quickly found himself receding into a state of mental quietude just like he did when he marched in formation. He recalled with a small breathy chuckle one night in particular; the recruits, after being worked a long and hard day daisy-chaining supplies between the stockhouse and the galley, were marched back to barracks in the small hours of the morning. Brann had woken with a start to realize he had been marching in his sleep, still in perfect sync with the rest of the formation, his legs moving completely independently of his waking mind. Such a thing didn't even seem possible until—

The order of events became jumbled in a hazy moment of chaos, but the first thing Brann saw was the spray of blood against the concrete, and the second was the stinging white cloud of concrete dust and fragments that blinded him in a sudden explosion. Falling forward onto his belly, the pain in his shoulder made itself known to him on a delay; the second he felt it, however, was the same second he heard the echoing crack of the sniper shot that had sent a high velocity aluminum rod into the spillway next to him at nearly the speed of light and disintegrated a healthy section of the concrete wall beside him. Brann found his voice just long enough to loose a strangled scream as his shoulder burned with liquid fire, and on instinct, rolled into the wall and flattened himself along the ground, making himself as small a target as he possibly could.

The marksman that had fired at him either couldn't see him from this angle, or otherwise didn't intend to immediately follow up with another shot—regardless, a familiar crackle of pressurized electronic audio rang out overhead, and the amplified voice of The Speaker addressed him from an unseen vantage point, loud enough that it could be heard anywhere in the village.

"If you're still alive to hear this, just know that we handed off our favorite toy to the soldat with the worst aim here to take that shot—we don't even need a direct hit to kill you." The muted chuckles of Uhlen rang out through the air briefly before the Speaker continued: "Electromagnetic rounds—fun fact, when fired at close range, if they impact before travelling far enough to build speed, can create sonic blasts that are as devastating as an arch eel's—speaking of, settle a bet for us, if you don't mind. The boys and I heard a rumor that you actually killed one of those yourself back at Belljar, is that true, or is that a load of horseshit?"

Brann started crawling slowly on his elbows, making forward progress up the spillway as carefully as he could without lifting his head more than a few inches off the ground, his breathing punctuated with grunts of pain as the partially cauterized wound in his arm left a trail of dark blood on the concrete below.

"If you're saying something in reply, we can't hear you," joked the Speaker sarcastically. "Why not stop playing possum and come out where we can see you, and we can settle the bet back home in the city over a cuppa tea with the good Marshal? Who knows, if that story is true, maybe he'll be so impressed with you he won't turn your skull into his new favorite codpiece."

Fuck, why did he run away from the Donnie? Brann cursed his poor judgment, his childish emotional response—so what if they didn't like him, was it really worth it to go off on his own and get killed, no one to intervene on his behalf now? Worth it to be turned into a pulpy smear on the concrete in this godforsaken place that reeked of the dead?

"Tell you what, I'm gonna give you the benefit of the doubt, and assume our boy here had better aim than we thought, and you're just taking a moment to catch your breath. But in a few seconds, if you don't surrender yourself, we're gonna demolish that entire mountainside and bury you where even the swamp rats can't find you. Consider this your final warning, but don't get me wrong, Recruit—we sincerely hope you don't comply."

At this rate, he'd never clear the top of the spillway, more than a half mile of climbing to go—he had to get up and move, fast, and take his chances giving them a clean shot, otherwise that EM rifle would cut him down before he even had time to realize he'd been obliterated. Brann sucked in a harsh, deep lungful of air, gritting his teeth and saying a silent prayer before he came to his feet, ducking low as he ran, hoping against hope they still couldn't see him from their sniper's chosen nest.

A few seconds headstart was all he had, before a distorted buzzer was fed through the broadcast, and the cheerful voice of the Speaker returned one last time. "Damn, looks like we won't get to hear that story about the eel. Recruit Brann, you are hereby subject to summary dematerialization. Thanks for the memories, kid, this was a fun chase."

The microphone's whining echo vanished, and then Brann was tossed feetfirst into hell.

The spot where he'd fallen vanished behind a cloud of plasma and dust, the ultraviolet rings of laserlight that spiraled outwards from the EM rod the only indicator of the direction the shots were coming from before they disappeared in a second explosive impact. Brann stumbled, nearly caught off balance from the shockwave, and abandoned any notions of caution: sprinting up the mountain was his only hope now.

Another blinding neon burst of red and purple spread out around a blast that plowed into the side of the mountain like an artillery shell, inadvertently creating an overhead cover of smoke and raining dirt that kept his head low but sheltered Brann from direct view. Up and up and up, he scrambled over the concrete, nearly falling to all fours many times but never stopping, the young soldat denying himself any ideas that he wouldn't make it, even as the explosions came at a consistent and unrelenting rate all around him. Above, below, the entire spillway became a radioactive purple river of dust and light and heat, the superheated particles of dust that wafted all around burning his cheeks and boiling the air in his lungs. And still Brann climbed, hands reaching out to heaven above as he sprinted, eyes squeezed tightly shut to protect his vision from the ultraviolet beams.

There was a slight pause in shots, and with a jolt, Brann realized he must be in their sights, the sloppy marksman firing at him taking a moment to align his sights. A second later, the ground beneath Brann's feet became a geyser of magma, and the blast sent him tumbling upwards through the air—landing with a bodily thud against the concrete, Brann's boots sizzled, the rubber soles melting into the cement beneath his feet. He groaned and looked skyward, finally accepting he'd been had—he'd run as far as he could, and this was as far as he could go. The crosshairs were on him now, and any second everything would go black. It would be mercifully quick, he knew, and he began to tremble, tears pouring down his cheeks.

Except the shot never came, even as he remained prone, in full view on the concrete with the sunken village plainly visible down below. And in that moment, another noise could be heard around the fading echoes of the

EM rifle's cacophonous blasts—a familiar screech, that of a set of an airship's engines, circling around overhead to prepare for a landing. Brann craned his neck upwards, fingers curled as they blackened and burned in a coating of sulfuric earth, turning his flesh to melted wax, and what he saw was as much a relief as any medical treatment.

The gold and rainbow-streaked hull of the *Myrmidon* hovered just at the crest of the mountain where the mouth of the spillway began, and from an open side hatch, the long barrel of Zay's autocannon emerged like a proboscis—before it took aim at the unseen sniper and responded with a hail of its own, the thunderous tattoo of sustained gunfire signaling Brann's salvation.

The responding shots from the EM rifle went wide of the Donnie, and did not have nearly the same rapid eagerness as they did shooting at Brann—the Uhlen down below in the village were moving to avoid being hit, their sniper providing covering fire but having no real opportunity to take a clean shot, the bright lasershow the EM rifle made creating a direct tracer back to their position. Nevertheless, Brann knew there was no time to waste cooking here against the ground, and he crawled to his feet with great pained effort—his entire body felt like he'd been crisped in a great oven, and though it made the flesh of his burned fingers crackle, he swung his own rifle off his shoulder to join in with Zay and let loose his own defiant bursts of gunfire back down onto the valley below.

He was nearly there, the top of the spillway so very close. Just another few minutes, and he'd be safe back on the ship.

He'd be home.

*

Morning light almost blinded Nestor as the cargo ramp split open the Donnie's belly, revealing the village down below, Brann somewhere unseen in the concrete channel of the spillway beneath the ship. He'd spent nearly the entire night laboring to fix the ship's crippled engines, and just before dawn had broken, the old engineer had taken the liberty of descending into the bowels of the ship, into the long-forgotten main storage hangar, where he'd spent the rest of the morning toiling away on one of his many personal projects.

The grizzled old machinist pulled a safety harness over his head, fastening the buckle between his legs snugly, settling into the compact pilot's seat he occupied. The leather was still supple and a little oily beneath his fingers—once upon a time, Nestor practically lived in this seat, and he was comforted to know it curved so perfectly around his worn frame that it was as familiar to his older self now as a beloved relative, welcoming him in its embrace.

"Hey darling, did you miss me?" He said to himself, looking around at the canopy as the switchboards lit up. The oxygen mask above him with its automatic fitted straps dangled suggestively—Nes wouldn't need it, he decided, opting instead to pull a cigarillo from his breast pocket. All the oxygen he'd need.

The switchboard blinked, and a radio hummed to life, with Hawkshaw's voice filling the canopy. "Zay's got them pinned for now, but Brann isn't gonna make it by himself—in a few minutes they'll have set up a clean shot on us and will have taken out our engines. Nes, we need you on the ground, it's now or never, buddy!"

Nestor's hands slid smooth as silk into a pair of gloves, tailor fitted to his hands, the leather matching his seat. Through lidded eyes, the veteran machinist sparked up a light, casually bringing the flame up to his cigarillo—as blue haze filled his view, his fingers flexed, the old joints cracking before he wrapped both hands around a pair of control sticks just above his knees.

"Fire in one hand," he recited to himself, the old mantra of a former life dancing across his tongue, lips bouncing that cigarillo between them. "Steel in the other. Mind the afterburn."

Nes wrenched the control sticks up, and he was engaged.

*

Brann let his spent magazine clatter to the cement, pulling a spare with shaky hands from his belt just as down below, he could see the dark shapes of several Uhlen troops pouring into the spillway. They'd chosen to pursue him directly, and at least a half dozen were now climbing up the destroyed channel, making a direct line for the wounded young man. Even if he turned and ran directly for the Donnie, there'd be no assurance he could make it on board in time before they reached him—and as flashes of cross-shaped muzzle flares were followed by the distant clatter of gunshots and the scattered pops of bullets that whizzed into the cement all around him, Brann knew they weren't gonna waste time trying to apprehend him anymore. They simply needed a lucky shot to put him down for good.

Luck was not on their side, though, as another low rumble overhead matched the sound of the Donnie's engines—something big was occupying her cargo ramp, and before Brann could turn to see, an earth-quaking boom of something enormous falling to the earth sent lightning bolt fissures racing down the spillway around him. Brann steadied himself as the impact tremor faded, and looked back over his shoulder, awestruck at the sight.

The chassis of the great machine blocked out the rising sun, the dark silhouette of a challenging iron angel spreading its twin cannons outwards from its bulky hips—the center torso pushed outwards from the main body into something like an airship's cockpit, albeit without wings to lift it into the sky. The shoulders hunched like a werewolf around boxy missile racks with flaps lifted to reveal the countless yellow-painted tips of their waiting payloads, and with the groan of enormous hydraulics, the colossal machine drew itself up to full height on a pair of thick, metal-muscled digitigrade legs, the backwards-facing joints hissing around a pair of rectangular pistons that extended themselves back like the dewclaws of a giant bird of prey. Wide, nearly flat steel talons dug into the concrete, and with those two cannon-decked arms now fully deployed, the huge warmech stood at the ready to defend both the hovering ship behind it and the young man on the slope below.

A distorted speaker crackled to life, the frequency of its voice almost identical to that of the Speaker, but instead it was Nestor who spoke to Brann from his unseen seat behind the tinted canopy glass of the mech's snout-like cockpit. "You're gonna want to cover your ears, Corpsman," came the official sounding order of an old warfighter.

Brann obliged.

The hexagonal shielded barrels of those boxy arm-cannons whirred up before firing, the air filled with a deafening blastbeat, the precise rapid-fire drumline raining heavy metal death down on the spillway below. Ionized beams of cadmium green waves of light rippled through the sky above Brann's head, the much higher-powered EM rounds causing less explosive damage to the concrete structure but at an incomparably faster rate of fire, sending the unlucky vanguard of charging Uhlen scrambling for cover helplessly. The walls of the spillway were too high, though, and their reaction time too slow, and within seconds their bodies were shredded in arterial bursts of viscera under the focused fire of Nestor's mech—a landslide of pink-tinged concrete complimented their demise, wiping the very earth they stood on clean, leaving no trace of any living persons behind.

Brann, equally sickened and emboldened by the gruesome sight, redoubled his efforts to climb up the spillway towards the mech and the Donnie waiting just beyond. "Please just don't step on me," he said aloud, adrenaline carrying him past the limits of where his injury-ridden body otherwise would have permitted.

The surviving majority of the Uhlen forces responded in kind, the lower frequency red light of their EM rifle streaking up just over Brann's body to burst against the mech's midriff, a surface explosion scoring the armor plates with carbon but making the body of the war machine yaw to one side. Small arms fire may not pose a threat to the metal giant, but even a single EM sniper definitely would, a patchwork of glowing orange holes melting around the impact zone of the charged round.

Nestor's mech tilted to compensate from the impact, legs remaining firmly rooted in place, before Brann heard a follow-up command directed down at him: "Run between my legs, and don't get too close to them, I don't want to stomp you!"

Suppressing a laugh at the idea that Nes might have actually heard Brann talking to himself, he diligently obeyed this command with self-preservation at the absolute top of his priorities—the young man darted between those twin towering legs, feeling like an insect beneath a dinosaur, the legs tensing before the mech accelerated and began striding forward down the spillway. Each slam of its massive feet sent shudders up Brann's skeleton and made his teeth rattle, and once he was sure he was free and clear of those stomping legs he turned to watch the machine descend towards the village.

Re-engaging those EMACs, the arms swiveled on its elbow axes to aim into the scattered buildings, letting loose another renewed rhythmic barrage of colorful tracer fire. Though Brann couldn't be sure, he imagined he could see the tiny dark bodies of the Uhlen far below scrambling to escape the fanning gunfire that blanketed the boggy town with an even crisscrossing pattern of white-hot microbursts.

The ship hovered several meters above Brann's head—the updraft of earsplitting wind that held it aloft send dust swirling all around him, and he waved his arms up at any visible porthole he could see, hoping to catch someone's attention.

"You're too high, I can't reach!" He shouted uselessly into the noise, hoping someone, anyone, might extend a ladder or otherwise offer a way for him to ascend. Nothing came, however, save for the conjoined fire of Zay's cannon from her protected aperture.

Someone did respond, however—or rather, something. The machine gun fire overhead ceased, and even the gundecks of Nestor's mech cooled—there was another sound filling the valley, something that cried out from the hells below, loud and anguished enough Brann even heard it drown out the scream of the Donnie's engines.

Keeping his head low, he turned back, looking down at the village below and scanning for the source of the sound. He knew where it was coming from. He just didn't want to look, the nightmares from last night resurfacing—and though a black shudder ran through his soul, Brann turned anyway, casting his gaze down to the very end of the spillway.

The black chasm of the drainhole seemed to vibrate in his gaze, the heat rising from the cement creating an illusion of watery waves, blurring the sight of what was emerging. The spindly grace of a spider, and the cold-blooded assuredness of a reptile—a single arm, reaching from below, hand stretching out to the sky in a display of skeletal fingers that had far too many joints and far too little flesh. The bizarrely humanoid hand came down to earth and curled those clawlike fingers in, another arm emerging from the blackness above to grip the edge of the drain.

There was a great devil emerging from the dark beyond, and all bearing witness stood in horrified silence—not just Brann, but Nestor in his cockpit, the rest of the Donnie's crew, and the Uhlen alike, all watching the terrifying scene unfold, those slender arms pulling up the body of a horror still unseen. A third limb—a hindleg, like a mutant dog's, crooked and pawlike yet still tactile in the way it flexed those long toes, which gripped an opposite edge of the drainhole as coldly and deliberately as the hands did. Impossible to discern in the way its body seemed to contort in such disgusting ways, the mouth of the drain was soon filled by the creature itself.

Curtains of black, wet hair obscured the head and face, pooling onto the cement as it fell from the hellion's pale shoulders, and Brann felt he wanted to vomit, suddenly very aware his nightmares may not have been imagined after all.

Nestor's voice was a harsh whisper over his mic, his own fear palpable despite where he sat in his own great armored death machine. "What the fuck is that thing?"

The creature rotated in strange and discordant ways as the limbs and body realigned, until it had fully emerged from its den, hunched low on all fours—the slick flesh seemed wrong, wet and pulsating in a way that seemed to suggest it was still decomposing yet never deteriorated. Gray, vascular, disgusting—the quadrupedal beast stood on the clenched knuckles of its bony hands and raised its neck that seemed all at once far too long and yet too short for the rest of its proportions. No matter which way it turned, slowly examining the world around it bathed in the light of the morning, the living horror never let its face be seen behind that waterfall of oily hair.

And all at once, with a great crack of bone that could be heard all over the valley, the head snapped directly towards Brann.

Not the mech before him, not the airship above him. Brann, and Brann alone.

It saw him. Though he may only be a distant speck, it saw only him.

And it roared. Screamed. A rising wail of animal fury, buffeted by the soulful dirge of damned souls, like a choir of dead men and women were all at once engulfed in fire, their rage and agony becoming the howl of a monstrous beast.

"Climb."

Brann stood rooted to the spot, barely even hearing Nestor's voice being cast down to him through the mech's speakers.

Another roar, the monstrosity's arm lurching forward, pulling the rest of its bulk free of the drain, never quite looking completely steady even as it rose to its full height on all fours—it looked as a woman drowned might, crawling towards the light of the morning sun, the face hiding unbearable sorrow and anguish behind that impassable wall of inky hair.

The EMACs on Nestor's mech, dipped low as they reloaded, snapped upwards to reseat their ammo boxes once their internal magazine feeds completed their cycle. The mech adjusted both legs to widen its stance, planting itself firm as it prepared yet again to unload.

"Brann, climb, now," Nes repeated through the mic, and the great corpse wailed.

The mech let loose, sending streams of liquified metal rounds downrange into the body of the beast, and like the starting shot of a footrace, it Brann snapped back into reality—he cast aside his rifle for good, letting the issued Geihan weapon cartwheel against the concrete as he scrambled up the side of the mech's leg like a squirrel on a tree. The exposed cabling between the joints and the angular armor plating made for a swift ascent, the young soldat ascending as fast as he could to get atop the mech's shoulders—the Donnie still hovered low, and must have seen him beginning to climb, drifting ever so carefully closer to put the cargo ramp within range for him to get on board. The world was nothing but blinding noise all around him, and Brann wished dearly he'd left with his visor and its hearing protection sensors, his eardrums being assaulted with the engines of the airship and the fully automatic magnetic cannons joining together in a hellish deafening duel.

He caught himself just beneath the mech's torso propulsion engines, Brann's burned hands clinging to the oily lattice of mesh that protected the side vents, pulling himself bodily up onto one of the flat engines that jutted out from just beneath the mech's shoulder—he could see Nestor's reflection in the cockpit now, the engineer locking eyes with him and nodding; it was time for both of them to get the hell out of here. Nes threw his safety harness clear and pounded his fist against the canopy release mechanism—the trapezoidal glass windshield began slowly rising upwards and Nes helped speed things along with a high kick up into the polyglass, making enough of a gap for him to climb out onto the mech's center fuselage. The EMAC's continued firing at the rapidly approaching monster below, the bright maroon lances of superheated aluminum phasing directly through its flesh and doing little to slow the horror—it didn't even bleed, simply spraying misty chunks of bloodless gristle behind it as the EMAC rounds passed through, like there wasn't even a beating heart to speak of behind those ribs that were practically shrink-wrapped in glistening pale skin.

Nestor had locked both triggers in place on their respective control sticks, a built-in feature that allowed a mech pilot to briefly take their hands off their stick to operate their switchboard without interrupting their fire against an opponent—the unintended function being that Nes was now free of the cockpit entirely to help Brann and himself evacuate on-board the Donnie. The two of them were hunched low, buffeted by the downdraft of the ship's engines, the cargo ramp fully extended as the ship dipped ever so slightly—Hawkshaw in the pilot's seat with an android's steady and unwavering hand meant the ship could reverse its hover with absolute precision, but even so, Zay awaited them both now on the ramp. The mercenary had wrapped her gloved hand with the cargo netting that hung from the side of the bay's walls, kneeling to steady herself as she reached out, beckoning Brann and Nes to jump—she shouted as much, but no voice could be heard, drowned out in the hurricane of sound.

Brann felt Nes clap him on the shoulder, the signal for him to go first—rocking his weight back and forth gingerly to test the sturdiness of the mech's engine, Brann took a step back before taking a running leap into the air, both hands locking themselves around Zay's wrist as his feet slammed into the cargo ramp's rough-textured surface, the rubber grip of his boots keeping him from sliding back down the ramp; Zay heaved, pulling him up and giving him the momentum he needed to run the rest of the distance up the ramp and into the safety of the bay. Brann planted himself behind her, rotating just in time to see the cockpit of Nestor's mech engulfed in oily black hair.

Nes had hesitated for only a moment before he jumped, and it was enough to lose his balance as the giant carcass slammed into the mech—his jump went askew, and Zay would have fallen to the earth with him had Brann not been there to launch himself forward and catch her belt—Nes slammed into the ramp chest-first, Zay's gloved hands hooking him beneath the armpits, both of them clinging on for dear life as the Donnie's engines whined in a climbing pitch. The ship kicked into gear and ascended at a blistering rate, Brann helpless to do anything but cling to Zay's belt and the netting on the wall, watching as the mech was overcome by the rotfleshed monster—the EMACs were snapped off simultaneously by both of the creatures' hands, sparking electrical bursts in its torso.

The cargo bay was bathed in the flash of a plasma explosion—the dead giant had brought both hands together and locked its fingers in a disturbingly human fashion before slamming those conjoined fists down so powerfully into the torso of the machine that the mech's core was breached with no more effort than a tin can being flattened; the fireball rose to fill Brann's vision, nearly engulfing the open cargo bay, were it not for the swiftness with which the *Myrmidon* made a sharp banking maneuver to avoid the blast.

The centrifugal force of the ship's curved ascent kept the three of them pinned against the ramp, both Brann and Zay watching the spillway below ignite in a river of orange fire that quickly blackened and carbonized into plumes of smoke. They had a clear view of the valley below, seeing the distant and tiny figures of the surviving Uhlen fleeing for the treeline of the forest beyond—and the hunched shoulders of the giant undead creature rise from the burning wreckage of its mechanized kill. The head turned up on an impossibly twisted neck, face still unseen behind the tendrils of air lapping up at the sky on the updrafts created by the fire burning all around; like thousands of spindly black limbs reaching up into all directions, the hair of the beast spread outwards from its shoulders and lashed into the sky wildly.

And yet, despite never once revealing the entirety of its face, save for only the barest glimpse of its yawning maw, resplendent with sawn down and blunted teeth, Brann knew as the creature screamed skyward at their ascent that the great rotting Beast of Lachlan was still staring directly at him—and only him—as the Donnie flew up and away into an ember-soaked dawn.

19. The Confession

The life was being choked out of him, Brann's lungs being crushed between mountains of cruel muscle, everything going black as his vision swirled—

"Boomer, let the kid go, you're strangling him, look."

Brann gasped for air as the horse released him from the powerful bear hug, the bandage-covered face of his benefactor filling his view, hands on both of Brann's shoulders.

"Don't you ever," the horse gasped, face contorted in a teary-eyed grimace, "Run off again, that is a direct order from me as your employer and commanding officer or master or whatever you guys call it back at base—"

"Commander is fine," Brann started, but was just as quickly silenced—

"—I NEVER want to hear anyone saying a word against this kid again," Boomer called out over Brann's head, addressing the rest of the team. "You know how many times he's saved all our lives now, and you all want to thank him by, by what, by driving him out, by attacking and driving him away—"

"He didn't save our lives, we had to save his, again!" Zay replied indignantly, wiping the soot and gunsmoke from her face with a damp towel.

"Nevertheless, irregardless, overruled," Boomer shot back with a shake of the head. "He is an essential member of this team, and he deserves our respect, no matter how badly he screws up everything for us all again, period!"

Brann pulled away from Boomer coldly—the crew was gathered in the common area in a circle on the various couches and seats, and it was to them Brann now spoke in spite of Boomer's defense of him.

"No, we're not a team, and I'm not anything to any of you," Brann said, arms crossed, still nursing his hurt pride from Zay's attack on him the night before. "We aren't family, we aren't friends—this isn't even a working crew, you all know it, and I know it."

He turned to Zay. "You were right about me, I admit it. I can't fight, I can't keep anyone safe, least of all myself—all I know how to do is run away, and there's no place I can go, not anymore. Not back to Geiha." Brann paused, watching Zay carefully. "Not Lachlan."

She flinched, almost imperceptibly, but enough to tell him his suspicions were likely on point, so Brann pressed. "Lachlan's gone, isn't it Zay? All of it?"

Zay remained silent, looking away. Brann turned to Nestor instead. "You knew too, didn't you—after everything, the only reason you let me stay on the ship was because you all knew that the only place the deserter from House Lachlan could return to didn't exist anymore. It wasn't just that one village. All of it, it's all been erased, right?"

Nestor looked as if he was going to say something to the contrary, but just sighed and nodded, putting his hands together apologetically. "Yes. It's all gone. Wiped off the map years ago."

Brann swallowed, knowing where this was going. "During training, they told us the history of Geiha, we had that—military history class. I never could get the hang of remembering all of it," he said apprehensively, almost regretting to steer the conversation in this direction. "All those different Houses that volunteered or got annexed into Geiha to make the first Continental Empire. All of it was just so neat, so...clean. Going down the list, this House surrendered without bloodshed, that House submitted their territory as willing tribute. Then they got to Lachlan, and it was just..." Brann mimed the sound of a puff of air with a wave of his hand. "Never a word spoken, it was just gone. I never met any other recruits from Lachlan. I never got an answer when I asked the DCs about it."

He took a breath resolutely before continuing. "That village—that wasn't the only one. I figure we're still flying over Lachlan; if we landed right now, let's say in the capital, there wouldn't be anyone left there either, would there Nes?"

Nestor shook his head.

"Lachlan wasn't annexed, or surrendered, or any of that. So where are all its people? Where did everyone else go?"

Before waiting for an answer, Brann turned to Emrys now. "That thing, that monster—you're the expert on undead and aldead and all that shit. Last night, I thought I had a dream—that thing was watching me. And down there, in the village, it wasn't coming for the Uhlen or for Nestor or for the ship—it wanted me."

Emrys nodded in agreement. "Yes, I believe that is the case."

"Now, hang on, wait a second," Hawkshaw interrupted, raising a hand incredulously. "Sorry to be that guy, but the way I saw it, we just woke up some big ugly organism that was pissed off and just went after the biggest thing it saw on its turf—which, by the way, it probably didn't have a lot of love for Nestor after he started shooting it unprovoked." He spread his arms questioningly. "Help me out here, what exactly about that is meant to make us think it was coming for one person?"

Emrys rose from his seat, regarding the room as a professor teaching a lesson might. "What we saw was, though I cannot quite determine the specifics of its taxonomy, based on such a brief encounter, undoubtedly a creature touched in some way by the influence of exdeath." His bandaged hands waved in the air, seeming to reach for answers as he suggested them, like he was as much educating himself as he was everyone else. "A flesh and blood animal, a living person even, will always have unconscious reaction to stimuli in its environment—driven by hunger, or fear, or sexual inclinations, it cannot help but respond in appropriate measures to whatever it encounters, willingly or otherwise. In my pursuits of higher knowledge—you see, though I am not at my most proud of self to admit it, it may come as some shock to you all to learn I may have strayed into some darker corners of the world in my studies of the nature of life and death—"

"No shit."

Everyone's head snapped around—lounging on a pillow with disinterest, present only to accompany the Lady Red, The Wolf had spoken up. Brann made a note of this; apparently, the werewolf knew what sarcasm was.

Emrys winced, giving a submissive shrug in reply, but continued nonetheless. "Where I turned to the learnings of necrosis and the occupation of living souls in the planar magics—that is to say, when I drew closer to learning the distinction between a living person and a dead one, and where in between the existence of intelligent thought and spiritual matter converge..."

"You're talking about whether or not souls are real, and what happens to them when we die," Lady Red offered.

Emrys pointed a bandaged finger at her. "Precisely. Unaccounted for though such spirit matter may be in the husks of aldead creatures such as yourself and your lycanthropic companion here—"

"Excuse me?" The noblewoman rose to her feet, haughty and imperious, taking immediate offense to this. "You refer to myself and my companion as 'husks' at your own peril, sir, and I advise you tread very carefully."

"I assure you my intent is only in the most clinical of regards," Emrys offered as a non-apology, seemingly puzzled by this anger. "Intelligent and beautiful as specimens as you both are, you've no more understanding of the evacuation of your own souls from your bodies when you met your untimely deaths as the lack of moral comprehension of the starving crane that feeds on his own young to survive a harsh winter, simply the means through which biology—"

Red was on Emrys in a flash, her elegant flintlock pistol drawn from her belt faster than Nestor could leap between the two, the engineer finding himself backed down in an instant with both hands up as the tip of The Wolf's spear threatened to bury itself in his throat. The rest of the crew recoiled in their chairs, all but Grishka, who sat cross-legged in Emrys's chair with rapt fascination at the scene unfolding, pecking hungrily at a bag of colorful candied fruits.

"Toe the line with suggestions that my pet and I lack a soul," Red said dangerously, barely a whisper, "Cross it with insults that we are as but animals feeding on the dead. I will not abide your presence on this ship a moment longer."

Emrys stood shoulder to shoulder with Nestor, slowly raising his own hands. "I fear I've failed to communicate my thoughts in a...shall we say, a manner that is sensitive to inclusive language," he said slowly, making no effort to reach for his own spellbook to defend himself. "If I speak in a way that is beyond your...reach...I apologize for misrepresenting my interests as a scholar, and will gladly invite you to a session where studying your perspectives may bridge any gaps in my knowledge?"

Wrong answer. Lady Red slipped her thumb backwards to depress an unseen mechanism on her pistol, and much like when she drew her saber against Tark back at the stadium, a previously invisible needle lanced into her wrist with a tiny gasping spray as her artery was pierced. The polished wood of the gun was suddenly wreathed in vines of liquid scarlet, the barrel of the pistol glistening bright blood red to extend outwards to nearly double the original length—Lady Red didn't move an inch, but her antique pistol was now pressing its dripping tip right between Emrys's eyes, a hot rivulet of her own blood now running down his face.

"Consider the gap between us bridged," she said coolly, cocking back the hammer of the pistol, her white gloves quickly soaking through with her own blood. "Apologies if my own perspective was not communicated..." She tilted her head thoughtfully. "...Inclusively."

Brann slowly edged forward, readying himself to attempt a diplomatic solution to things. "Miss, uh, Miss 'Lady,' he didn't mean to sound like..."

Emrys raised a finger to quiet Brann, shaking his head. He drew in a breath and blinked slowly, then stared Red in the face, meeting her gaze with newfound humility. "There has indeed been a lack of perspective on the matter, to which I take full responsibility. I admit to a regressive attitude towards the clearly nuanced nature of yours and your—associate's—existences, and though I may claim a wide breadth of knowledge in this field, it is as always the personal responsibility of a scholar to educate not only others but himself when he finds personal bias leading him astray from the path of a willing student." Emrys slowly—while giving a nod to The Wolf who growled as he removed his hat—leaned forward into a bow. "I have spoken out of turn, and can only offer ignorance as the stationary upon which I pen this sincere apology. Of course, a conversation of other matters must be had before we resolve this misunderstanding between us, but I shall be ever patient and eager to learn from your own experiences, dear Lady."

Brann's eyes darted between Emrys and Red, hoping this satisfied her anger. The Lady's face was as smooth and unreadable as a porcelain doll—she turned to look sideways at her werewolf bodyguard, pursing her lips in inquiry.

The Wolf drew his eyes from Nestor to stare Emrys in the face, those piercing golden beams on high as he studied the priest, before giving an accepting nod and lowering his spear. Taking a step forward, The Wolf hunched low over Nestor who still remained frozen in place—and lapped his longue canine tongue against the man's forehead.

Nestor blinked slowly, reaching up to wipe his face, looking at the strings of saliva between his fingers, then at Red, completely baffled.

"His way of apologizing," Red explained. "He was trained only to ever put his weapon to the throats of an enemy—in your case, he acted in haste to defend me. He means no ill will."

Nestor nodded, frowning as he wiped his hand on his shoulder. "Outstanding."

Lady Red turned back to Emrys. "You, on the other hand, are another matter. I accept your apology for now, overwrought though it may be. We will indeed speak later, when we reach my House and home— though we may still find ourselves beyond reparations of mere words."

Emrys let his hands fall to his sides as Red's pistol lowered, watching with a childlike awe as the weapon shrunk back to its usual length, leaving the flowery etchings in the pistol's wood stained in arterial red. "Of course, I look forward to it, come what may," he said, replacing his hat atop his balding head. In the meantime, I will continue with a renewed sense of self-mediation."

Brann took a step back, sighing in relief, as did Nes—everyone else, save for Zay, seemed to find whole thing entertaining. Grishka had nearly finished her bag of candy. Boomer stared at the carpet, frowning.

"Gonna have to get those bloodstains out, that'll cost a fortune..."

"That's another problem with you all," Brann said. "I don't know who is or isn't 'supposed' to be here anymore than you do, other than Boomer or Nestor—everyone else, we all just got...tangled up in everything that's been going on. We're all just stuck here, so why are we always fighting?" He looked accusingly around the circle. "Shit—why do some of you guys seem to want to fight all the time? You all almost witnessed a double murder, and nobody stepped in to stop it, except Nes and I? Same as yesterday, you all would have let Zay beat me—beat us both—to death. Why?"

Hawkshaw shrugged. "I don't know any of you, but, frankly, I haven't gotten paid to be here yet, so...honestly, I'm not a bad guy," he said, lounging back in his seat, "And I sure don't like murder, hell I spent my fair share of nights getting in the middle of spats just like this back at the bar."

Brann waited. "But?"

Hawkshaw frowned, and gestured to Boomer. "Tell the truth? I just haven't gotten paid to be here yet. Speaking only for myself, of course, but my willingness to save a life usually scales with the size of my last paycheck."

Brann stared at him. Then at Zay. Then Boomer. "Is money all this is really about? So, the question of who lives or who dies—who gets left behind, who gets rescued—is all just about getting paid?"

Hawkshaw, Zay, and Nestor all nodded. "Pretty much," said the automaton.

"Then why did you all come to save me?" Brann spread his arms. "I left. I was gone. Problem solved. Tark wouldn't have come for any of you ever again, now they'll probably never stop chasing any of us until we're all dead. Why bother?"

There was a twinge of hopefulness in his voice. A yearning from within, reaching past the boundaries of his self-doubt, asking for the simplest of connections.

Hawkshaw put those notions to rest with a regretful admission.

"Boomer promised to double our pay if we came after you."

Brann's hands fell to his sides.

"I mean...wow." He nodded, genuinely impressed. "Here I was, thinking to myself I was the biggest scumbag on the ship."

Emrys laid a comforting hand on Brann's shoulder. "Son," he began, behind a long and wistful sigh, "I understand your frustration, and believe me, I know the life of the solitary man comes with it the hopes you have that these fine people may yet become more to you than just passengers beside you—but, in the spirit of putting aside personal resolutions, we'd better serve the needs of the crew by continuing our conversation in regards to your home of origin, before I derailed it with my inadequate manners."

Brann wasn't satisfied leaving things where they were—any chance at vindicating himself among the rest of the team was one he was eager to take—but he nodded, stepping aside to give Emrys the floor again. "You were saying. Lachlan, and the exdead. That monster."

"Yes, our automaton pilot very wisely questioned our mutual conclusion that the Beast of Lachlan pursued you, specifically, with intent, young Brann," Emrys resumed, once again assuming a professor's candor. "Living beings have needs of a primal nature, but assume intelligence in that they may choose to deny those needs. Undead beings, though obscure to our typical understanding of what they may entail, also have needs, lacking the ability to deny themselves even the most reflexive of urges." He extended a hand to Red and The Wolf, once again giving a small bow. "As I have been graciously educated under the tutelage of this merciful maiden, I will so alter the parameters under which I define the needs of 'aldead' such as lycanthropes or Vampyr—and instead, we must look to where the beings touched by the influence of exdeath diverge from the pattern we have outlined."

Emrys licked his lips, furrowing his brow. "The contact one may make with exdeath, even under the most remote and controlled of conditions, is subject to the contradiction of any evidentiary claims that establish what we previously accepted as fact in regards to these unholy organisms. Devoid of souls, no doubt, the only single defining trait that I, or any self-learned researcher of the Exdead, have come to accept as fact is that..." He struggled with his own words. "...They simply do not have urges. There is no balance of id and superego; where a ravenous zombie seeks the id's satisfaction of flesh, and shrinks from a flame; where a reasonable person may look to their ego to tip the scales between their desire for pleasure and their desire to adhere to moral resolve; in the case of the Exdead, we find...a contradiction of consciousness."

Brann was only barely following this. "What does that mean?"

"It means," he said, still speaking cautiously, his explanation verging on tedious and frustrating. "A living creature is a balance of desire, of the needs of its nature, and of its ability to decide between the two. An undead seeks only to satisfy the reflex of its nature. An Exdead...desires nothing, and needs nothing. It exists only outside our perception of life and death, and seeks only to deny both."

He looked around at the blank expressions in the room. "They are beings of absolute hate," he finally said simply. "A mistake of nature, or perhaps the antithesis of it. Whatever we want, whatever reason or purpose we were placed here for, be it simple science or the will of a higher power— to the question of why we are here, they are the spiteful rebuttal, a deferred answer."

Emrys folded his hands together. "They are beyond death itself. They are our doom. The end of all things."

*

Emrys withdrew a handkerchief from within his coat, wiping the partially dried blood from his face. "A moment ago, a weapon was placed between my eyes, right here," he said, tapping his forehead with his finger. "The Lady Red exhibited an emotional response to stimuli—be it instinctual, be it conscious, she was faced with a choice that only she could make for herself. Albeit with the helpful suggestions of others," Emrys conceded to Brann with another small bow. "Should she pull the trigger, paint my brains all over these lovely plush seats and beautiful carpeting—"

"No, she shouldn't," Boomer said in alarm.

"—Or should she exert a higher judgment, and allow me lenience, despite having—at the time, and I say this with all sensitivity—ample provocation to act on these urges?" Emrys paced in a circle, hands behind his back. "The important idea we give credence to is not which decision she made, but rather that the decision was made at all. She did not shoot me, and in choosing not to do so, she knowingly influenced the outcome of future decisions she will have to make, should such a choice be presented for her again."

Emrys withdrew his spellbook. "You'll beg my indulgence, but I assure you this will be a completely safe demonstration." He flipped to a page, the delicate paper nearly transparent, save for the incomprehensible scratchings and runes penned in blood-red ink—finding the rite of choice, Emrys ripped the page free and crumpled the paper in his hand, giving a deft twist of his wrist as the green sparks birthed a small orb of ectoplasmic fire on the tip of his finger, which he raised so everyone could see. "Consider this: the soul. The body of the flame itself, the id, the simple existence that is bound to what is required to nourish it—oxygen, fuel, the things we all need."

He waved a hand around the orb, letting it grow bright, then dim in turn. "The light that is emitted from the flame, the influence, that is the superego. Given purpose, to heat the fuel required by the id, or to provide it oxygen to grow—but is, in itself, the manipulation of the id, regardless of wants or needs. A dim flame may yet be called on to light the blackest night, a strong flame may yet burn the flesh of a child. Both are purpose, subject to what we call..."

Emrys gestured toward his finger that balanced the flame. "The ego. Our decision, our own process and presence—what some may call destiny, or others choice. At any time, I may snuff out this flame—knowing I may be lost in darkness, or freeze to death. Knowing that it is a denial of the purpose of the flame, which is to burn. I choose if the id or the superego deserves satisfaction, between pleasure and pain or purpose and protection. I decide. Me."

Emrys curled his finger inward, the flame dissipating in an instant. When he extended it again, the bandages glowed with the gooey embers of the plasm, but otherwise all that was left was his own finger. "The Exdead are simply the ego in absence of need or purpose. A hand without a flame to warm it, a decision without a goal or a consequence, save for one: to snuff out all the flames of this world we struggle so hard to set ablaze and protect, to undo all decisions of all intelligent and spiritual creatures."

Boomer raised a hand. "Yeah, I totally understood all that, definitely."

Hawkshaw wasn't convinced. "That doesn't explain why you and Brann think it was after him."

Emrys looked to Brann for help. "You said you had dreams of this creature, yes?"

Brann nodded. "Vivid. Like it was there, watching me sleep—maybe it was."

"There's not a doubt in my mind it was," Emrys agreed. "A hungry animal would have made easy prey of you. An intelligent person, seeing you as an intruder, may have quietly slit your throat, or otherwise woke you, or exerted any number of actions based on decisions made as a result of your presence. Instead, it simply...watched."

Emrys paused, then explained further. "When you slept, you could only dream, no sensible or reasonable decisions made because of or in spite of the Beast's presence. When you awoke, and faced it as it emerged in the village, it acted exactly to the contrary of what you wanted, or needed, or otherwise had the ability to influence with your own judgment."

"It wanted to kill me," Brann said.

"No. It didn't want anything. It simply...was compelled to exert exactly what you did not want to happen. To manifest your greatest fear. In fact, we don't know killing you was its goal at all. Perhaps it simply...had to have you for its own." Emrys shrugged. "To assimilate you."

Hawkshaw was about to interrupt again, but Emrys was one step ahead, already raising a hand. "Where this specifically concerns Brann, and why I believe it appeared directly and solely as a consequence of his presence here today, is linked to that latter idea. It could, and would, have killed any one of us. The Beast of Lachlan was focused on Brann, because..." He took a breath. "...Because I believe that it *is* Lachlan."

It was Lady Red's turn to look dumbfounded. "Pardon?"

"I must speak with care if we are to continue this subject," Emrys said, turning to invite Nestor and Zay into the conversation. "These two may have already seen the dots connecting, and might be better suited to matters of such...delicacy." He gestured to Brann. "As it directly concerns this young soul."

Brann looked to Nestor, and Zay, already feeling his stomach flip, hoping what he was about to hear wasn't what he thought. "Help me make sense of this," he pleaded. "I know you didn't know any more about 'exdeath' than I did before I met Emrys, but I know you two know why it was here, why it was coming for me."

He finalized the query with as much directness as he could muster. "What happened to the people of Lachlan?"

Zay, having remained silent the entire time, finally rose and turned heel, half-running out of the common area and up the stairs, disappearing out of sight with the loud clang of the hatch above. Nestor stood in to answer the question now, leaning forward in his seat to rest his elbow on his hands.

"The reason you never met any other people, any recruits or otherwise, who were also born in Lachlan," he said ruefully, "Is because

Lachlan wasn't just annexed or conquered. The people, all of them, everyone...they were all exterminated. On order of Marshal Tark." Nes shook his head, looking up at Brann. "Genocide. Not because of a war, or because of some political dispute. Just...as a matter of economical inconvenience."

Brann felt his jaw might drop. "Economical what?"

Nestor shook his head again. "I didn't say I agreed with it, just that it shook out that way. Lachlan was never on the up and up as a rising force in the major Houses—they never had the wealth of trade routes like House Saintmarie, they never had the warfighting zeal or strength in numbers as House Geiha—they were a minor region that had a small patch of land, right in the middle of some of the most prolific territories among the Houses, wherein they had the means and motivation to live humble and self-sustaining lives for as long as they found it comfortable." He leaned back in his seat again, crossing his arms. "Remember the outpost? I told you those people living there had everything they needed, and were happy—no need to expand, no need to pay for better roads, no reason to invite in outside commerce or conflict. They just...were. Lachlan was much the same—a small region of hills and lakes, surrounded on all sides by a forest full of life, a natural barrier to the outside world. Sure, they sometimes indulged in the minor enhancements of society—a shipment of holoscreens here and there, allowing a network station to be built in each village to allow intercontinental communication and socializing. Otherwise, they were happy to just...exist on their own, unbothered by the rest of the world."

"So how could that be an inconvenience to anyone?"

Nes pointed to Brann. "You answered your own question earlier. If they were out of the picture, what was the problem? Money, of course. Not necessarily that Lachlan was particularly wealthy—no, they'd never be worth the expense of a scale invasion from Geiha to be stripped of their resources or have their treasuries plundered. No, they simply didn't contribute to the accumulated wealth of their neighbors. They stimulated no real trade, they almost never responded to Geiha's demands for conscripts."

The hatch overhead opened again, and footsteps stomped down the stairs—Nestor turned to watch Zay reappear, but otherwise didn't stop speaking. "You have to understand, the world is trying to move away from the idea of wartime solutions being the final solution," he said, "When not all the Houses who rely on wartime solutions to keep them wealthy have discovered—or otherwise opted for—other means of economic growth and prosperity for its citizens. Any House that shows weakness or friction against the needs of its neighbors is subject to a vote of proxy war." He waved to Boomer. "Geiha was the last House to sign the Arbitration Treaties. They would have gone on waging war on any other House that got out of turn if they had less resources and warfighting potential to stave off Geiha, and it was only a swing vote that kept them from becoming the sole empirical power that assumed control over all other House—most of the Houses opted for a more peaceful solution to their ongoing problems: let an anointed champion settle disputes in single combat, build an infrastructure of entertainment and financial dependency on these fights between champions..."

Zay was holding a long, heavy case, metal and clasped with buckles looped with leather straps—she let it clatter loudly to the floor, right at Brann's feet. "And absorb all the profit cut from citizens who were financially dependent on this entertainment to keep paying for their invisible wars and campaigns against rival houses."

Brann looked down at the case. "What is this?"

Zay didn't respond. She seemed angry at first glance, but her body language suggested something entirely different. More vulnerable.

Brann crouched down, lifting the box from the floor to set it on a couch, undoing the metal clasps and sliding the leather belts free.

"I said Geiha was the last one to sign," said Nestor, "Not that everyone else signed. There was one House that didn't."

"The small House in the middle of the world that never helped anyone but themselves, and never hurt anyone either," Zay continued for

Nes. "The House that wasn't valuable enough to invade, but wasn't interested enough to advance the goals and ambitions of the other Houses. The stronger ones."

The hinges creaked as Brann lifted the lid of the case, staring at the contents."

"The House that just needed to go away, so the rest of the Houses could say nothing was left to stand in the way of world peace. The House that disappeared overnight in a tragic series of natural disasters that devastated its population and rendered the land unlivable."

Brann looked up at Zay, and saw tears running down her face. "The House that, by never standing against anyone, stood against the new Empire—so, to avoid a political incident and jeopardize the impending time of peace, House Geiha simply recruited an army of raiders and mercenaries, paid them just enough to motivate a ceasefire against their usual prey of merchant ships traversing the Wilds, gave them weapons..." She swallowed hard. "...And ships. And sent us in to move from town to town in the dead of night and kill every civilian of House Lachlan."

"Disguising it by draining the region's dams and aqueducts, coming up from under the ground to send the waters directly into the crowded population centers, calling it a mass flood caused by unstable geological activity in the region," Nestor added. "Even drained that huge lake in Saintmarie's borders to prove it, knowing they wouldn't hurt from the loss too bad."

"And from the sunken earth, the mass graves, touched by an unknown Exdead presence that likely lurked far underground, the drowned bodies of the citizens of Lachlan surrendered their souls into the manifestation of their betrayal, the monument to their genocide which watches over their grave...and awaits any who carry the blood of House Lachlan to welcome them home for good. The Fellbeast of Lachlan," Emrys said with solemn realization. "Who today awoke from its slumber when it sensed the presence of the final living human who carried its name. Recruit Brann of Lachlan."

Brann reached into the case before him, lifting free a large ceremonial sword—the blade was very nearly as tall as any claymore, but had a shape unlike any weapon Brann had seen in the armory of Geiha, the weapon seeming to curve back slightly before it became wide and rectangular at the tip, a longsword designed for hacking and slashing, not thrusting. All along the edges of its squared-off blood channel, the symbols of a foreign language Brann couldn't read but knew instinctively must have been a forgotten tongue of Lachlan were etched with the care and precision of a master calligrapher. The weapon was resting in a velvety mold within the case, a message in that same foreign lettering printed on a platinum plaque that adorned the inside of the lid of the case—except this one had a translation meant for common tongue, one Brann could understand:

ON SOVEREIGN WINGS WE LEND OUR STRENGTH

The hilt of the weapon had a small red sash looped with the utmost care around the guard, adorned with a simple platinum charm: the spread wings of a small bird.

"That was the sword taken from the home of the Lachlan's chief enforcer of civil protection and anointed diplomat who spoke on behalf of its people," Zay said. "The leader of their people who exerted no personal will over them, but acted at their behest to correct any criminal doings or defend them in the courts against the outside influence of nations or Houses that may otherwise seek to exploit them. They called him 'The Sparrow.' I took that from him after I killed him and his family in their sleep."

Zay lowered herself to her knee beside Brann, head low in a plea for forgiveness. "In my final days as a raider from the Wilds, I led the extermination of Lachlan's citizens, acting on behalf of Marshal Tark and the vested interest of The Geihan Empire and her allies. I am very certainly responsible for the death of any family members you may have had left in the years prior to your conscription in the Geihan military."

The common room was stunned into silence. Even Boomer said

nothing, at a loss. All bowed their heads—except for The Wolf, who continued watching Brann with unwavering intent. Like this was nothing new to him.

Brann rose from his seat, letting the case close quietly. The crew waited with baited breath for him to say something, to react, to give some kind of emotional outburst.

All the young soldat said, however, was:

"Thanks for coming back for me, Boomer."

The horse looked around, waiting for someone else to speak first, then just nodded. "Of course. You're my friend. Always."

Brann stuffed his hands in his pockets, walking away and climbing the stairwell, the hatch closing quietly behind him.

No one else moved, and no one else spoke, save for one: Grishka had finished her bag of candy, watching Brann as he went with her head tilted to the side, her avian gaze soaking the entire drama that had just unfolded before her with an unusual reverence.

"Very sad story," she cawed, ruffling her wings sympathetically.

20. The Beach

At this hour of night there was no real crew presence to speak of, leaving Brann to wander the passageways of the ship unworried about possibly crossing paths with anyone in an awkward moment—after a trip to his favorite spot, the food coolers, he trolled the spaces looking for a more cozy area to enjoy his midnight snack of choice, not wishing to be discovered in the common areas by anyone else who might be similarly afflicted by sleeplessness. He'd arrived at the hatch leading into the cockpit, whether unconsciously or otherwise, but once he found himself there Brann couldn't quite come up with a reason not to go inside, as he'd likely be in the company of the only other ship occupant not dead asleep. Ear to the paneling of the hatch, he couldn't make out by sound who it was inside—if it were Zay, he'd be afforded the opportunity to resolve the day's earlier revelations away from curious onlookers.

This wasn't a particularly comforting idea of how he wanted to spend his night, but then again, he couldn't sleep for good reason, and this may have been the way to reacquaint himself with his pillow. Shrugging off any imagined concerns, Brann clamped down and opened the hatch, swinging it open loud enough to announce his presence but not so much so as to startle the pilot.

With mixed feelings Brann realized there wouldn't be any late-night reparations made, as the pilot seat swung around and Hawkshaw's bright yellow irises beamed back in the low light at him. "Oh, look who it is, the public enemy himself," Hawkshaw joked, his expression that of a muted surprise. "Looking for someone?"

Brann hesitated, but entered, closing the hatch behind him. "In a manner of speaking," he offered, hunching to keep his head from banging on the low hatchway ceiling before stopping next to one of the jump seats. "You mind?"

Hawkshaw waved a welcoming hand towards the seat. "All means, sir. Never turn down a chance at hearing myself talk."

Brann flipped the safety harness over the headrest and sat, rotating the seat to face the pilot's and setting down his vittles—another fizzy glass bottled drink, the contents clear at the top and settling into a gradient opaque pearl at the bottom, and a bag of name brand sugared oat lumps. He tugged open the back of crunchy snacks, fishing out a handful and gesturing out at the night sky ahead with his chin. "Where we headed next?"

"Well, with those exciting distractions out of the way, we can finally deliver Zay's cargo to their destination, we'll be landing in Jan-Jito hopefully before dawn—or our best approximation of landing, anyway, ah," Hawkshaw scratched at his metal jaw thoughtfully, "As we don't actually have any ability to do so in the strictest sense. Wasn't really at the forefront of my mind when I had you jettison the ship's landing floaters the other night. But, hey, every day brings with it a new learning experience, no?" He eyed Brann's bag of treats, then extended a hand. "Can I get one of those?"

Brann didn't think twice, just mumbling agreeably through a mouthful of oats and plucking a glazed lump from the bag, giving it over. Hawkshaw held the snack between the metal clawlike tips of his fingers, examining it at arm's length, then stared at Brann wordlessly.

His chewing stopped, and Brann stared back, confused. Then, when it dawned on him, he had to swallow his mouthful of food to keep from choking, laughing behind his hand as it covered his mouth. "Yeah, okay, good one."

Hawkshaw chuckled and handed the snack back to Brann, spinning around to face the windshield. "I usually get everyone once with that one. Zay didn't fall for it, though, I don't think she was born with a funny bone in her body." He reached up to switch off the overhead lights, casting the cockpit into almost complete darkness, letting the natural moonlight creep in and illuminate them booth. "I'll admit I'm envious of the living, getting to enjoy the things you always talk about that bring you all such obvious joy—a good night's sleep and a tasty meal always top the list whenever I ask what it is that you all enjoy the most in life. That, and the pleasure of another's company, though I can't say I'm entirely a stranger to that one, given the extent to which my maker allowed me to relate to organic creatures," Hawkshaw said with a wry smile. "I did spend half a decade in the company of Mother Superior and her lovely tribe of courtesans, after all."

Brann became suddenly very interested in his drink, watching the bubbles rise to the top of the glass silently. Hawkshaw took notice, and turned back, tilting his head. "You don't enjoy that topic, I've noticed," he said, sounding somewhat sympathetic now. "Permit me to ask why that is? Seems like every young man your age I meet is jumping the bones of anything with a pulse that catches their eye."

Brann shrugged. "It's not that I'm not interested. Just, you know." He gave a non-committal wave of his hand, and Hawkshaw's eye panels blinked.

"Not really, no." The android said flatly. "Far be it for me to pry into such personal matters, but I can always change the subject, I'll be the first to say I don't have the lightest of touches when it comes to probing the minds of the naturalborn."

"No, it's fine." Brann set aside the bottle, bringing his legs up to sit crisscross in the seat. "You don't seem like the type to be offended by me saying I'd be more comfortable telling you than anyone else on the ship, given that you aren't really..."

"'Real?'" Hawkshaw finished for him, feigning hurt. "Well, aren't we presumptuous! I guess I deserved that for bringing it up in the first place, though," he admitted, tapping a few keys on the flight panel before pushing away from it, sliding his chair closer to the young soldat. "I get it though. I spent many nights in Mother Superior's listening to the quiet admissions of the stricken when they found themselves confronted with the truth of their own flesh. I doubt there's much you could say that hasn't been confessed to me a hundred times over by some drunken sap looking to offload their burden on the metal man who wouldn't judge them."

Brann sighed, scratching his chin. The sound was a bit gritty; he'd need to start shaving regularly soon, finding stubble growing in more frequently now on his normally boyish smooth face. "Let me ask you this," he said, navigating his thoughts in real time. "Is it possible to have technically had sex and still be a virgin?"

Hawkshaw's head dipped forward, his yellow beams going somewhat cross-eyed. "You're gonna have to do better than that, that's the kind of question that'll make my artificial brain explode trying to calculate," he pleaded.

There was a brief moment of doubt that he should continue, but Brann soldiered on. "I don't remember exactly when or how I ended up in Barrier City as a kid, I just know I wasn't always there, but when I was, I was always alone," he explained as best he could. "I don't know if you've been there, but it's supposedly the most lavish city in the Geihan Empire, and everyone there—well, mostly everyone—lives pretty well. They take care of their citizens for the most part; you don't use scales to pay for the things you want like your house or your furniture or your holoscreen, you use work credits to buy all of those. As long as you have steady work, and you put in the hours, you can have the nicest things in the city delivered right to your door, so everyone's pretty comfortable."

"I don't mean to interrupt," Hawkshaw said, "But, 'work credits' just sounds like a roundabout way of saying indentured servitude. You don't get paid free and clear, you just owe time and energy back to the city with labor to get the things you want, right?"

"No one ever really leaves the city," Brann agreed, shaking his head. "They're all pretty happy, at least I think—everyone is always busy and in a rush, working nonstop, but isn't it kind of worth it if it means they get to come home to all the nicest things?"

Hawkshaw frowned, but relented. "Anyways, go on, apologies. You were on your own."

"Having a home, having steady work, these all require registering as a citizen of Geiha through official channels," Brann continued, "Which wasn't really possible for me."

"Can't change citizenship if your House of origin doesn't exist anymore," Hawkshaw said.

"Right. No Lachlan embassy in Geiha anymore, no way to officially move in, so I was on the streets all my life. Wasn't all bad, plenty of people who were happy to let me sleep in their bed while they were off at work—only thing is, the Nightwatch had to start cracking down on all the refugees that were flooding in from the other Houses that didn't submit to Geiha's rule, and eventually it became too much of a hassle for a lot of citizens to take in all these streetwalkers and look after them for free when it meant more work for them to get the credits to afford it. So, the problem sort of took care of itself, and only the more..."

He trailed off, and Hawkshaw studied Brann's body language, beginning to formulate a conclusion at inhuman speeds. "I think I know where you're going with this. It had to be worth their while to risk getting their doors knocked in by the Nightwatch, so some of the less savory residents of Barrier City began putting a price on letting in desperate young men off the street."

Brann nodded solemnly, and Hawkshaw's metal cheek panels puffed out in an artificial sigh, the automaton leaning back in his seat and rubbing at his temple. "Boy, that's one thing I'll never understand about the living, you all have such an easy time at hooking up with each other, yet some of you always gotta turn it into something vile. I used to always think the point of intimacy was sharing something special with those closest to you, but I got set straight a long time ago, sad to say." He shook his head, and leaned forward again, holding up a hand. "You don't have to finish that story; I get it now. You had to do what was necessary to stay off the streets, but you don't feel like you had a fair shake as a real player in the game."

He didn't expect this level of support from the automaton who, seemingly only a day or so ago, would have been happy to see Brann flattened beneath Zay's heel, but he appreciated it nonetheless. Brann pushed down the more uncomfortable memories of his time in the city before speaking again. "When I said before that all I ever wanted was a normal life, that's a big part of it—I do want that, to feel normal, and to be close to someone like that. It's just that the only times I've ever...done that...was for the exact opposite reasons than I wanted to. So, I just can't help but clam up whenever it comes up."

Hawkshaw bounced his wrist against his chair's armrest, and hummed thoughtfully to himself. "I don't blame you, honestly, given how much you have to trust someone in order to be comfortable with that, and seeing all these horny freaks around you giving it up with barely a wink and a nudge to provoke them. I could tell you for a fact," he said, giving a wide mischievous grin, "There are two of our mutual companions on this ship right now who are probably boinking like rabbits as we speak, and you'd never know it being in the same room as them—but, I have the gift of augmented interpersonal cognition, and not even the most micro of facial twitches and vocal cues escapes my notice. For the sake of respecting their privacy I won't name names, but, take it from me, kid: you aren't the only one who would prefer to keep their sex life out of the public eye." He outstretched his hand, and Brann, having resumed picking at his bag of sugared oats, almost offered another lump—but caught himself, breaking into a bashful smile. Hawkshaw smiled with him, raising his arms to signal he'd been caught.

"All that noise aside," the android said, folding his hands together with a series of metal clicks, "I don't think anyone on the Donnie, even the less personable of us, would hold it against you for not rushing into figuring that part of yourself out just yet." He paused. "Did you happen to give any thought to where you were going when you finally decide to part ways with this band of boneheads, though?"

Brann again could only shrug. "I had only one real option worth considering, and I think I'd rather stick with a bunch of bullies for a while than have my body assimilated into some kind of giant exdead mutant spirit of revenge."

Hawkshaw giggled nervously, the sound like a cricket caught

laughing at something he shouldn't. "Wouldn't blame you there, either. Seems like no one here but Red and her dog really know where any of us are going. We all just need to get ourselves as far away from your friends from Geiha as we can, and hope there's somewhere still left in the world that'll take us in, now that we're officially on the continental 'most wanted' list. Reason I ask, though, is I have a feeling Zay is going to want to become the permanent pilot on the Donnie, and I've never been one for being a third wheel—going back to Mother Superior's outpost will suit me fine, and I don't imagine Emrys or Grishka will find much reason to say no to coming with me. Emrys tells me you invited them to come along to Boomer's fight at Mongillo free of charge?"

The young man nodded sheepishly, wordlessly indicating he didn't necessarily have permission from anyone to do so. "So, I tell you what, Emrys and I go back a-ways, even if we aren't the best of buds," Hawkshaw offered, "And I'd be willing to repay that debt on his behalf by giving you my old room in Mother Superior's lodge. It's a *private* room," he said quickly, noting the speed at which Brann stiffened nervously, "But if there is any one person alive who is the most caring and understanding when it comes to the subject of identity and the pursuit of sexual catharsis, it is the old goat herself. Think of it as like a sort of...bed and breakfast and intimacy therapy combo. She's had all manner of abused and wayward souls pass through her doors, and there's not a doubt in mind she'd have exactly the right thing to say to treat those old wounds." Hawkshaw extended a hand once more, this time offering to shake it. "Least we can do for the young menace who almost got all of us killed by a homicidal kuaneach. What do you think?"

Brann knew there was little reason left for him to continue living on this ship, an arrangement that couldn't continue forever no matter how much Boomer liked his company, and this was the closest thing to a realistic place he could hide from Tark and the Uhlen without being discovered— he shook Hawkshaw's hand gratefully. It was the first time he'd touched an automaton, and though the metal itself was cold, there was a surprising warmth to the grip, like a static energy just under the surface that could only be interpreted as a feeling of friendship. "You and Boomer also seemed to know each other pretty well, so he's travelling through that region pretty often, I take it," Brann conceded, "So it's not like he wouldn't get to see me ever again."

"Exactly. He's got no object permanence anyway, he'll forget he's sad that you're gone in a day, and it gives him something to look forward to next time he's selling cheap merch to his fans at the bar." Hawkshaw released Brann's grip, satisfied. "She likes you, you know. Mother."

Brann blinked, remaining stoic. "She does? We barely spoke." Not necessarily a lie.

Hawkshaw nodded. "After she met you, we had a little side talk. She said—oh, what were her exact words," the android pondered. Brann wondered if this was a reflexive behavior to make the robot seem more human, since it was unlikely that supercomputer brain could ever have trouble remembering anything. "She told me: 'That boy is like a fragile young bird in the nest, unaware of just how far he will fly once he finds his wings at last.'"

Brann thought to the reclaimed sword of Lachlan in his quarters, and the small bird charm hanging from its hilt, and in spite of himself a sudden ache in his chest made him tear up. Hawkshaw pretended not to notice, saving for himself a small smile.

"'When he finds himself', you mean," Brann said.

Hawkshaw just waggled his eyebrows.

"Told you she was good with words."

The ship's engines droned on, the sleek profile of the recently amputated *Myrmidon* gliding high above the coastal waters below, the two newfound friends sharing their journey in silence as they watched the earth turn slowly around them by the paths the stars cut above through black space, sliding beyond the horizon on their own ordained paths into the unknown future.

*

It was only a few minutes after dawn that the translucent HUD in the windshield glass had flashed a soft yellow with an accompanying electronic chirp to alert them that the Donnie had entered Jan-Jito airspace, and it was time to awaken Lady Red. As the cabin hatch swung open and Nestor entered with a tray of tin coffee mugs balanced on his slender fingers, Hawkshaw was already tapping at the ship's PA system panel to sound the reveille call to the crew quarters, undocking the microphone arm to call Red's room directly. The small speaker burbled a small tune as the line connected, before it clicked off and a less than enthusiastic Zay opened the call.

"Yeah?"

"Good morning valued customer, rise and shine, this is your scheduled wake-up call greeting you to a new day— approximately 10 minutes until we touch down at Jan-Jito Intercontinental Shipyard, we'll have you on the ground in no time at all," Hawkshaw crooned into the mic in his best commercial pilot impression. "Expect the morning to be overcast in the mid-aughts but with a windchill factor at play that you may want to account for with an extra layer; should you require additional amenities, I'd be happy to release one of our valued room attendants to your quarters with an—"

"Suck my dick," Zay interrupted before ending the call.

"—Extensive menu of our in-flight—hello?—oh, yeah, welp, she hung up," Hawkshaw pouted, immediately keying another room number with a carefree whistle as Nestor's slender fingers delivered a hot mug into Brann's grateful hands, the young soldat rubbing the sleep from his eyes. The call waiting tune resumed before again clicking off, met with silence, save for a low rumble. Hawkshaw's mouth panels were open expectantly, waiting for some greeting on the other end before launching into his scripted joke again, but none came.

"...Auuhh, Wolfie, is that you, bud?" He cautioned, checking to ensure he'd dialed the right room.

"Speaking."

His fun ruined, the android pilot nodded in defeat before resuming, "Hey, just wanted to get our esteemed Queen Crimson on the line and let her know we're landing shortly, so, no rush, but we could use her up on deck here to have those authorization codes at the ready whenever her people hail us. Mind passing along the message, hero?"

There was only a grunt in reply, and the call disconnected. Hawkshaw slapped the microphone arm back down into its cradle, shaking his head in disapproval. "My word! The manners of some of our guests, good graciousness." He looked back and saw the tray of coffee, leaning backwards in his chair to address Nestor. "Ah, thanks Nes, mind passing one this way?"

"Real boys only, sorry," Nes replied from behind his own mug as he sat in the jumpseat beside Brann, Hawkshaw foiled once more as he spun back around to the controls with his shoulders sagging and mumbling something about a sense of humor to himself. "Couldn't sleep?"

Brann grimaced, still not a fan of the taste of coffee as he set aside the mug, then realized Nes was talking to him. "Hm? Oh, no, not really." He looked down at himself and brushed off the crumbs from his midnight snack in embarrassment; surely there was a hand vacuum somewhere in the cockpit, he thought as he started looking around for one. The hatch opened behind them again, and Zay entered, wearing an all-weather parka liner with the outercoat removed, as utilitarian a look as ever.

"Well, look who didn't waste any time, welcome welcome," Hawkshaw began, but was shut down instantly as Zay dropped her travel satchel in his lap, cutting him off from launching into another rehearsed gag.

"I've seen you land once before, you're taking the 'co-' seat this time, partner," She grumbled, already fitting her fingerless gloves onto her hands as she took the second set of controls. Hawkshaw's chair spun around quickly as the automaton gleefully wiggled in his seat.

"You hear that, Nes? She called me partner, finally!" He chirped.

"Please don't drag me into this, it's far too early."

Winking at Brann, Hawkshaw rotated back into place again, and Brann caught Zay eyeing him from the corners of her vision, the stoic mercenary pretending not to be addressing him directly when she spoke again. "We all good up here, otherwise? To land, I mean?"

Brann ignored her, Nestor still taking a long drag on his mug. Before Zay could speak up again, the hatch swung open a third time, and the dull padding of Wolf's wide paws stomped in, his massive hunched frame filling the entire space of the entryway.

"Where's Red?" Hawkshaw asked in surprise.

"Sleeping." The manwolf spoke between clenched teeth, then opened his jaws to let a small, flat holodrive fall into his hand, stepping forward to offer it to Zay instead of Hawkshaw. "Have codes instead."

"Ah, well, sufficient as they may prove, the assumed intent of her being present herself was so we could have a familiar voice on the line once the hail comes through, but, hey, Princess knows best I suppose," Hawkshaw said, looking somewhat annoyed at how cramped the cockpit was becoming. "You don't have to stick around yourself, you know."

Wolf had already clambered awkwardly into the chair behind Zay, his bulk making the jumpseat sag and his massive paws making one of the mugs of coffee disappear behind his furry knuckles, clawtips clicking against the tin vessel.

"Or, hey, pull up a chair, there's plenty of room!" Hawkshaw turned to Zay, switching off the sarcasm. "So, plans on how we're gonna land this bird, I'm open to your suggestions."

Barely had the hatch closed itself before it swung wide yet again, and the loud metallic clop of hooves on the paneled floor announced Boomer's arrival, his bandaged snout ducking underneath the low ceiling and peeking into the cabin. "Eyy, I knew I smelled Nestor's coffee—we got ourselves a real party up here this morning, don't we?"

Hawkshaw was prepared to voice his indignation at another visitor until he saw who it was, the automaton instantly changing gears and lighting up. "Finally, a ray of sunshine! Please, save me from these mirthless goblins, I beg you," he moaned to Boomer, looking around the crowded space in dismay. "Kick someone out before our combined weights makes the ship take a nosedive, yeah?"

"Ooh, shichyeah, oats!" Boomer paid him no mind and instead honed in on a stray sugar lump caught in the wrinkles of Brann's shirt, clapping his young friend on the shoulder as he plucked the sugary treat up and tossed it into his mouth. "Sorry, no-can-do, Shaw. I had to send my escort home in the Donnie's lifeboat, so I am starved for company this morning. We landing soon? I need to stretch these legs or I'm gonna *die*."

"I'll handle the landing, you just keep a hand on the throttle and make sure we don't go nose down," Zay was saying to Hawkshaw, inserting the holodrive as the HUD flashed again, signaling the incoming hail from the Jan-Jito shipyard. She fixed a headset on her ears and keyed the mic to reply—and the cockpit hatch once more swung wide.

"Has the hail come through? Allow me the chance to speak to them," Red was calling from the entryway, and Hawkshaw looked like he might short circuit.

"I—hey—you're supposed to be asleep—look, I was fine with one or two, but we don't have the space up here for seventeen of you meatlings!" He craned his neck back to glare at Boomer. "You couldn't commission a full freighter cabin plan in here? It's starting to smell like a gym and hairspray in here."

"Nah, had to keep her profile looking sleek! Isn't that right, Nes?" Boomer said through a mouthful of oat lumps, elbowing the engineer as he leaned on Nestor's jumpseat.

"Aerodynamics."

"Yeah, exactly! Aerodynamics!"

The Lady Red peered at the empty tray. "I take it an insufficient amount was brewed this morning, as usual?"

Brann offered up his own mug to the prim diplomat. "Here, take mine."

"It hasn't been tasted yet, I trust?" She looked at the cup with her upper lip wrinkled a bit.

Zay's hand was tapping on Hawkshaw's shoulder. "What's the ship's reactor class?" She mouthed silently to him.

Brann shook his head innocently. "No," he lied to Red, who accepted the mug and glided away to take her seat on Wolf's lap.

"We don't have functioning gear, just remember," Nestor said, interrupting Hawkshaw and Zay's exchange.

Hawkshaw was being tugged in two directions at once. "It's—what? Class G—" he said to Zay before turning back to Nes. "Tell Zay, she's landing—look, can we—"

"Who designed the ship and decided not to have a backup set of landing gear?" Brann asked, brow furrowed.

"They were damaged when we came down in the lakebed back in Saintmarie," Nestor explained. "Only meant for smooth vertical drops, we came down at an angle in rough terrain—"

The Wolf had leaned over between them, cutting Nes off as he stared Brann in the face, sniffing at him dangerously. Brann recoiled in shock, then, realizing, produced the unfinished bag of oat snacks from between his legs and offered it up, the werewolf snatching it by the corner in his teeth and reclining back to share them with Red.

"Bro, not cool, share and share alike!" Boomer complained, reaching uselessly for the bag.

"Pay attention," Zay said loudly at Hawkshaw's side, holding the headset mic in her fist to mute herself. "Set approach vector, glideslope at seven percent—"

"Is that coffee I smell?" Came a voice from the ladderwell.

Zay was still repeating instructions from the call. "—Then sync localizer signal, final approach fix is three thousand feet at four AM—"

"No, no more coffee!" Hawkshaw whined back at Emrys, trying to yell him off before the priest could enter. "We're closed, come back tomorrow, flight lounge at max capacity!" He punched in Zay's commands on the instrument panel with one hand, glaring at her as he did. "Aren't you supposed to be doing all this?"

She simply pointed at the headset and shook her head dismissively, indicating she was otherwise occupied.

"Can we have some of those when you're done?" Brann said hesitantly, pointing at his bag of oat snacks in Wolf's claws.

"No." The werewolf crunched down on his stolen goods, offering the bag up for Red to slip her dainty fingers in and scoop out a lump.

"Did you explain to them we have no functioning gear? That's a mite steep for our ship's current abilities," Hawkshaw said, clawed fingers hesitating over his next set of button commands.

"You wanna talk to him?" Zay barked, lifting up the headset to let the complex commands from a very hostile sounding flight controller fill the cabin.

"I said I will speak with them," Red offered, holding out her hand to take the headset.

"I'll talk to him," Brann joked. Only Boomer laughed.

"Are you sure there's not more coffee? Sounds like the whole crew is up there!" Emrys called again, sounding hopeful. "I'd have to refer to some of my older journals, but I think I wrote a spell of Everflowing Waters once, and while I haven't yet tested it on other liquids—"

"That reminds me, I gotta piss like—" Boomer coughed, the horse not finishing his thought. "Are we there yet?"

"He writes his own spells? How does that work?" Brann asked no one in particular, confused.

"That's how all magic works, it's a skill, like poetry," Zay said, apparently hoping to catch Brann's attention now that she was off the call, the headset perched delicately on Red's head as her tricorne hat was placed between Wolf's ears. "Strictly speaking, anyone can learn magic, but it usually involves dedicating your entire life to it and costs more money than anyone can earn in their lifetime—"

"That's not a problem for Emrys, though, since he's basically immortal," Boomer piped up, still wistfully eyeing the bag of oat snacks. "Didn't Brann say he saw him sprout his head back like a lizard after Wolf exploded it with his spear—"

"We'll be setting down on the Queen's Heart Beach," Red said, handing the headset back to Zay. "Likely I will be immediately apprehended and the rest of you summoned to court before the Queen herself; I'd suggest conducting yourselves with some..."

"Civility?" Zay finished, making Hawkshaw snort in spite of himself. "With this bunch of reject lowlifes? Not likely."

"I take umbrage with that," called Emrys from below. Zay's eyes went wide, whispering to herself, "How did he hear me?"

A wild flutter of wings startled everyone present, Grishka in full raven form flapping wildly into the cabin through the open hatchway and snatching an oat lump from Wolf's paw—his jaws snapped shut with a clap inches from her tailfeathers, the werewolf looking just as taken aback as anyone else. Grishka glided up and landed on the headrest of Nestor's jumpseat, making him slide down to avoid the beating of her wings as she settled in, proudly showing off the catch in her beak to everyone in the room with soft croaks.

"That's cheating," remarked Hawkshaw, noting the witch's ability to successfully find a chair despite the lack of available jumpseats. "I confess a lack of familiarity with how things are done in the courts of Jan-Jito, but I'll agree with my partner here—" He winked at Zay, who rolled her eyes, "—We seem to be less of a cohesive unit of single-minded individuals pursuing a common goal, more of a...flying zoo." He avoided eye contact with Wolf, whose hackles raised at this comment.

"Why would they be apprehending you when we land? I thought this was your home?" Brann asked Red.

"Reasons I have neither the patience nor inclination to impart upon you at this time, young sir," she replied coldly. "Given recent events and how your folly has waylaid our journey here, I will also be expecting you to be on your best behavior for The Wolf, and abide by his commands during your time—as blessedly brief as it may be—in Jan-Jito."

"What does that mean?" Brann looked to The Wolf nervously, who was staring him down yet again.

"When I am summoned to court, you will be escorted everywhere you go by him, as if you were his prisoner." Red's silvery white gloves rolled their fingertips together to free them of any oat dust clinging to them. "For all intents and purposes, you are—so long as you are a fugitive from Geiha, with whom House Jan-Jito has little reason to provoke an invasion, you will have either myself or my companion at your side at all times acting as overseer in lieu of confining you behind bars. A notion, I assure you, did not go without extensive consideration on my part prior to agreeing to continue travelling with not only you but our very own assassin welcomed on board by your own foolishness."

Brann was crestfallen. It seemed not everyone had yet been won over to his side yet, even after everything that had happened. Red noticed his reaction, and lifted her chin, adding what was not entirely a heartless afterthought. "Consider my decision to be a mercy, as your bloodless body's extradition from Jan-Jito's shores directly back to the palace of Barrier City in a golden box as a peace offering was not outside the realm of possibility." She laid a hand on Wolf's shoulder, looking fondly at her bodyguard. "None, not even the most battle-tested of Jan-Jito's corsairs, would ever dare go against my wishes—and certainly not when facing the wrath of this hound would be their reward for doing so."

The ship was beginning its descent, gradually, the morning light shifting to cast shadows over Brann. On the bright side, that meant he wouldn't be tempted to run again. The Wolf licked his chops hungrily, those golden lupine eyes never seeming to blink, and never allowing Brann any hope of escaping their gaze.

"I hate this ship," Hawkshaw grumbled, sagging in his seat.

"I can brew another pot, if need be," Emrys called up weakly.

*

The Donnie made a less-than-optimal landing on the cold Queen's Heart beach, the marine layer blanketing everything in a dense and pillowy cover of fog that Brann felt he could almost reach up over his head and touch with one hand. Stepping off the ramp onto the seafoam-draped sands, he came to the realization in the span of a single moment that he'd never actually seen the ocean in his life, a concept that should have been obvious until he stood before it in person: once the expanse of cold purple water stretching beyond his ability to see into the cloudy horizon was before him, he'd never again make the mistake of comparing it to the River Geiha or the lakes he vaguely recalled from his forgotten youth in Lachlan. He felt he could see the exposed heart of the planet itself in those waters, their foreboding promise of fears unknowable lashing at the shore with foamy tendrils, and for a moment that compared to losing his balance on a flight of stairs Brann almost convinced himself he could feel the very real eyes of a god staring back at him from beneath the black sheen. The moment faded quickly, though, when the rough shove on his back from behind prompted him onwards, The Wolf already fully immersed in his role as Brann's de facto parole officer.

"I bluff my way on as the ship's escort, now I'm the one being escorted," he remarked to Nes beside him, the engineer bundled up in what must have been the biggest, puffiest, pinkest jacket Brann had ever seen in his life. The cloud layer above had descended to swirl around Nestor's head in the form of blue smoke, his face almost entirely obscured by the puffs of his hot cigarillo. Apparently, he did not like the cold.

"Look at it this way," Nes responded stiffly, his lips pursed so tight around the cig he sounded like he was already frozen inside and out. "You made it almost two weeks without being sold down the river or stabbed in your sleep by any of these reprobates who have graciously commandeered the ship I've spent half my life maintaining for their own personal gains—as a direct result of you meddling in or otherwise upsetting their lives, I might add," he said optimistically. "Even knowing you will continue to do so as long as you are in close proximity to them hasn't been enough to convince them you're worth a late-night call to the good Marshal's private hotline. I'd say things are looking up for you." Nes clapped Brann on the shoulder, taking a peek at the spear that nudged at the small of Brann's back as he did. "A few days of convincing The Lady's clan you're not half as bad as you seem, they'll be just as enamored with you as our friend The Wolf here."

The lycan grunted in acknowledgement, that speartip so precisely hovering against Brann's back that he could feel it tickling his skin through the blouse. "One can dream," the young man replied sarcastically.

The entire party was greeted by the expected dispatch of Jan-Jito's finest, a trio of officiate corsairs all appropriately dressed in their own ruby red jackets shining like dark blood in the low light of the cloudy morning. Their leader stepped forward, drawing a shining white-silver dagger as curved as the moon and offering it hilt-first to Lady Red. She spoke in a clipped manner, reciting what must have been a formal greeting among their people:

"Be it blood, or be it blade?"

Red stood to, one hand on her saber's hilt, the other outstretched as if to shake. "A bloodless blade is barbarism: blood it shall be."

The moment hung silent between the two, then—to Brann's utter horror—the welcoming corsair did not shake Red's hand as expected at all. Instead, with practiced ease, she twirled the curved dagger and struck downward through the air, slicing through the Lady's wrist so cleanly that it took several seconds before it began spitting hot, steaming arterial fluid against the cold and muddied sand.

"The fuck?" Brann heard Boomer whisper quietly from somewhere nearby, mirroring his own thoughts.

The corsair sheathed her blade on her chest, following up with a more recognizable greeting and bowing to Lady Red—the guard to her right stepped forward dutifully, already unrolling a length of gauze to wrap around Red's gushing wrist. "If you'd told me when you left us this would be the manner in which you returned, I'd have resigned my post on the spot," the leader said, looking equal parts saddened and relieved. "The merest chance of having to lock blades with you is a thought more devastating to my nerves than I feared I could bear these past few nights."

"Let it not be said you never had it in you to spill my blood in my own home, Bosun Neve," Red replied, returning the bow with her own slight curtsy, though she kept her chin high. "Put yourself at ease, your trepidation matches my own: a more skilled opponent I dare not imagine." Red gave a nod of thanks once the guard finished bandaging her arm. "I suspect one among us has a more toothsome greeting waiting for me above, however?" She tilted her head up at the high marbled walls rising behind the trio, and at the curled incline of rough stone that served as a ramp off the beach and into the city.

The bosun gave a regretful nod. "She waits on the throne as if turned to solid ice—we've seen her move not one inch since news came you would be landing on the morrow." Neve clicked her white-gloved fingers together, and the two accompanying guards stepped forward to appraise the rest of the group, their weapons sheathed but poised at the ready. "Along with the offending prisoner who still travels with you, I expect."

"Aye." Red turned, locking eyes coldly with Brann, who did his best not to look too defiant staring back. "This young lark, a refugee from his sworn service. Though he has much to answer for in his homeland, he's proven not entirely without his uses on our journey here—my champion in particular has taken to him, a considerable feat."

Brann turned slowly to stare in absolute disbelief at The Wolf, looking at the spear-wielding werewolf through squinting eyes.

Bosun Neve shook her head. "Regrettably I must respect my Queen's wishes, and see him to the brig myself. No intruder enters our borders free of royal judgment, no matter their vouching party—you know this better than any, love. You and your wolf," Neve added, clearly in reference to some unspoken history.

"Then you three be witness to this: I stand in defiance of Mother Dearest, and I alone." Red raised her bandaged arm, and Brann felt the speartip removed from his back—only to have the heavy shaft rest itself on his shoulder, the dangerous razor edge of the weapon's huge head practically singing in his ear, and behind him he could practically feel Wolf's chest rumbling as the beast growled in warning to the corsairs. The two women froze in place, daring not challenge the animal without direct word from their bosun.

"Not you."

Red's eyes were deadlocked with Neve's, and while Brann didn't yet understand the complex relationship between these two reunited women, he knew at this utterance that Red was just as willing in this moment to die here on the sand as she'd ever been.

Neve paused, her inner conflict ever deepening. "She will not be pleased, my Lady," the Bosun cautioned, though she made no move to draw against Red. "So long as you take heed of the possible consequences; I cannot promise she won't have your entire crew executed for such a mutinous act."

Red dropped her hand, and The Wolf relaxed his spear, withdrawing it entirely from Brann's back. "So heeded, old friend." She said this more than a little bit snidely, though Brann took it as aimed at the Queen's orders, rather than at the Bosun herself.

Neve snapped her fingers again, and the two subservient corsairs bowed in retreat, returning once more to their bosun's side. "We're awaited in the Pavilion," she barked at the assembled crew of the Donnie over Red's shoulder. "Stow your shitty frowns and give respect when called to court:

our Queen is owed what little graces you lot possess, and she will have it, so help me."

The procession moved onwards behind the Bosun, though it took the agreeing nod of Lady Red to encourage them along: Brann was relieved to hear everyone grumble sullenly at being treated with such hostility, feeling for once he wasn't the only one unaccustomed to this strange land.

"What was that all about?" He nevertheless asked quietly of Nes, nodding towards the blood-soaked sand as they passed it, meaning the initial exchange of greetings between Red and Neve.

Nestor leaned in to speak quietly. "Jan-Jito is famously war-hungry, their reputation exceeded only by Geiha, and the oldest of their customs all reflect this. By cutting Red, she—" He pointed to Neve, "—Was saying 'I could kill you if I wanted.'"

His finger moved to Red, the profile of the Lady cutting a royal figure indeed as they walked, head still high despite their precarious situation. "And by letting herself be cut, she said back: 'I know, and I don't care.'"

Brann watched the Lady's haughty strides up the stone ramp, and shook his head. "Pretty brutal for someone who buys white silk gloves in bulk."

Nes gave a muted chuckle behind his nose, elbowing Brann in the ribs. The group moved on in silence, following the path onwards and upwards to the Pavilion.

21. The Imprisoned

Calling it a mere pavilion was reductive to say the least—polished stone pillars rose up to cradle the arched ceiling so high it seemed a giant could stand beneath it comfortably, the narrow walkway leading up between mirrored sets of decorative stairs to an expansive platform—Lady Red, Neve, and all the others in the party ascended to this platform, the bosun issuing nonverbal commands to the rest to arrange themselves shoulder to shoulder at the edge closest to the steps, the two other guards taking their place on either end facing inwards. The view behind them looked over the city walls at the beach below, the coastline stretching out seemingly to infinity into the shrouded distance—as if the white foam where ocean met sand was a path leading out of the fog directly up these steps to stand audience before the Queen of Jan-Jito.

Neve clicked her heels together in the center of the audience platform, bowing before the balcony overhead, another platform suspended above the one they stood on—the circular dais that gave the Pavilion its name. "Queen Mother," Neve said, "The Absentee Viscountess and her Champion come to heel before you, along with her six found companions and one captured dissident of the Geihan Empire." She held aloft the same blade that cut Red's wrist, showing off the dried black blood along its crescent edge. "The blade was offered, and blood was so given." She sheathed the blade, spinning in a tight about face to address Boomer's crew. "You stand now with privilege in the court of our most revered Crowned Commodore of the Jan-Jito Corsair Legions, and Reigning Monarch of House Jan-Jito: Queen Hester. You've but one courtesy warning: keep thine tongues stowed, eyes forward, and hands out of pockets."

The Bosun gave a quarter turn to bow slightly to Lady Red, then another to bow once more to the balcony overhead. "Bosun Neve stands as bailiff: court is in session." She about faced once more, Neve crossing her hands behind her back to stand at ease, keeping her face to the crew of the Donnie. Lady Red stepped forward now, eyes up, arms crossed in an impudent fashion befitting an annoyed child. "Credit given where due," she sneered, "I didn't think it possible to be even further removed from the Queen's favored embrace—I stand corrected, and at the mercy of your tribunal, no less. Well done, Mother."

Above, a single figure sat on a white marble throne as white as the snowy robes dressing its occupant—nary a glimpse of color escaped the layers of brilliant silk and cotton, save where the tight cleft collar cut away just beneath the Queen's chin, her own flesh nearly as colorless as her garb. In stark contrast to the white throne, her hewn features were framed by midnight black feathery locks, her wavy hair cut with such jagged grace above her shoulders it looked as if it may have been the work of the most skilled barber wielding a hacksaw. Darkly troubled eyes stared back at Red, shadows cast beneath the Queen's brow such as it made the ice green of her irises seem to glow—like a dragon waiting to unleash bolts of lightning upon the earth. Queen Hester was not only the most frightening woman Brann had ever seen, but the most beautiful as well: her angelic face stood challenge to the rest of the world, looking back at the infinite coastline beyond, daring the foolish ships of stricken men to land at her shores at their own mortal peril.

For several moments, Queen Hester said nothing—Brann wondered as he examined the fury creasing her features if she had been petrified by the sheer rage she seemed to be suppressing. If she removed her gloves, Brann suspected her knuckles would be so white as she gripped the arms of her throne that one could seldom tell the difference.

"Bosun Neve," Hester finally spoke—deceptively calm and cool, reminding Brann of Tark addressing the troops back at the Assay. "My mind flags. Memory is not what it used to be. I did see, not within the space of a breath past, the offered blood of my wayward daughter upon your blade, yes?"

"Aye, Queen Mother," Neve responded, still staring straight on. "Your memory is as sharp as your saber, Marm."

The saber in question was balanced on Queen Hester's upper knee, the stillness with which she sat cross-legged on her throne not letting it wobble even one inch. Brann's eyes roamed over the snowy sheath, the pressed leather awash in the pattern of a reptile's scales—the material matched the Queen's boots, which themselves otherwise appeared nearly identical to the size and shape of Lady Red's own. Clearly, even the Queen of Jan-Jito had seaworthy legs, and Brann wouldn't have been surprised to learn if she'd crafted her sheath and boots from the flesh of a kuaneach she'd killed in combat.

"Then I must beg your indulgence, daughter—why, when my Bosun says you come to heel, you instead yap as an insolent dog demanding kibble?" Hester crooked her head to the side barely an inch, the most Brann had seen her move this entire time. "Did the meaning of 'blood or blade' escape your own failing memory? A solemn tragedy, demented at such a tender age."

Red didn't back down, and if anything, her stance became even more sullen, shoulders hunched and hip jutting like a rebellious teen. "I've neither the time nor inclination to entertain this crude form of masturbation, Mother," she said, her words dripping acid. "Nor do your theatrics serve to threaten any of my companions, who politely endure this embarrassing display, not knowing you as I do."

"No?"

Hester's gaze turned, those eyes fixed on Brann now—as piercing as The Wolf's and as condescending as Tark's. "Not even this—the coward you consort with? I showed mercy when you took the company of this...creature..." She said, spitting the word with the smallest of nods towards The Wolf, "...But we have underestimated each other's ability to disappoint, clearly. You deny the embrace of your own kind and the noble purpose we stand for in favor of throwing what value your life has away...over a deserter? A frightened child who dares not cross blades with his own shadow?"

"At my lowest and most disappointing, you sink even further by your own doing, in failing to live up to the barest promise of a fitting mother," Red shot back, her face looking flushed—her own fury was rising to match the Queen's, unknown years of friction between them threatening to spark a fire in the court. "Could you draw YOUR blade in my defense, if it meant nicking your perfectly tailored gown? Could you shed YOUR blood on my behalf, if it meant insulting the lecherous tithes of another foreign ambassador, hoping for nothing more than a chance to 'negotiate trade' between Houses?" Red's chin quivered, her eyes wide and unblinking, searing with hot anger. "How cheap would the ink cost him with which you'd sign, I wonder, Mommy Dearest?"

The Queen was on her feet so quick Brann missed it entirely, her boot heels clapping so hard against the marble balcony they could have cracked it. Her white fist was tight around the hilt of her saber, which remained sheathed, though it rattled within so all at court could hear. "Speak not of the appraisal I give to the value of one's blood and kin, my young bitch daughter," she spat, voice raising to a commanding pitch. "Would that you were not my own, I would have festooned this court with your entrails after such a lowly taunt and made practiced deck swabbers of your crew as they cleaned what remained of you up with filthy mops."

This prompted an expected reply from one amongst the assembly: The Wolf nearly knocked Brann over as he lunged forward to Red's side, hunched low with his spear at the ready, the butt of the weapon held aloft behind his head as he assumed the dragoon's stance—Bosun Neve and her guards all cried out in unison, hands on the hilts of their sabers, but the Queen brought her silver-tipped sheath down with a loud clang against the marble to halt them.

"Nay!" She called out, and the corsairs stilled, all frozen at the ready to attack The Wolf if needed, though Red herself didn't even flinch, the only corsair at court who didn't have her hand on her weapon. "The dog is of no concern. That he stands here breathing at all is at my grace, the crime of his transgression already paid in full by my own daughter's blood, a waste though it was." Hester leered down at The Wolf, as if regarding an unwelcome pet brought home from school. "I am, if nothing, adherent to even our most obscure of customs, and invoking an ancient binding rite—distasteful as it was—will be so recognized by this court."

The Wolf's jowls pulled back, and for a moment, Brann thought the werewolf might actually be grinning, taunting the Queen with his exposed fangs.

"I spent decades devoted to every ash-crusted and waterlogged text filling our disgusting library, poring over texts I'd wager even you yourself would be hard-pressed to recall in detail, Mother," Red said. "I was to be your successor, and I aimed to exceed even you—and you still find it surprising I used your own crippling weakness of your slavish service to this dusty old dogma against you, one which you yourself exhumed from forgotten centuries past?"

"We are not so primitive as your tale would describe us, my dear," Hestor crooned sarcastically. "I'm well aware of the advances and the follies of circus diplomacies the other, lesser Houses have fallen to—we have the holonet here now, after all."

"The most unified and collaborative society has ever been in centuries, and you reject the most peaceful and prosperous ways in favor of this facade." Red laughed mirthlessly. "You don't call such self-destructive piety a weakness? Ha! I thought you an expert tactician, Mother."

"Life of honoring the beliefs and traditions of those who carried your mothers generations past in their wombs is strength, not weakness," Hester replied, holding up a gloved hand reverently. "Your failure to grasp this was your weakness, and ultimately your failure as my successor. This is not a monarchy of birthright, nor was your seat in my court or on my ship ever promised to you, Lorna."

Brann blinked, realizing that for the first time he'd just heard Red's real name. Red—or, Lorna, rather—seemed to wilt slightly, possibly not expecting this informal namedrop. She looked to the werewolf next to her, placing her hand on his shoulder, fingers gripping his fur pelt tightly. "All I ever wanted for you, Marm," she said softly, "Was a long life ruling fairly— with an open mind, and open heart. I read the same texts, performed the same rites and oaths, slept under the same stars and traced the same constellations out on the sea. I sailed on every current, every headwind, every stormcursed route out on those waters as you." Red—Lorna—turned back to regard her mother with wet eyes. "Nowhere did the seas take me, nor passage did I commit to heart, that taught me anything about the hate that has taken root in you so. Beyond my reach, you drifted not into clear waters, but a swamp—and you became ill. You don't live in accordance of our beliefs at all, you live to spite them. I could not see my own mother fall so far: so, I left."

Lorna stepped forward, The Wolf relaxing under her touch, his hunched shoulders uncurling somewhat. "I once thought you the most powerful and beautiful creature, the inspiration to my very purpose," she continued. "You didn't just fail your people, your culture—you failed your daughter. You let me down. You abandoned me, as if rescuing even one poorly translated page of Jan-Jito's tenets from a fire you yourself started meant leaving me behind to burn." She paused. "You became the thing you hate the most: afraid. You saw death beckoning, and sought refuge in your faith, misplaced as it is. You're..."

She turned, looking at Brann now, and he saw regret in her eyes meant not for her mother, but for him. "You're the biggest coward I've ever known, Mother," Lorna finished, and Brann felt a strange warmth reaching out to connect the two of them. "If I had stayed, if I hadn't gone off to see the world, to meet these people—my friends—I would have become just like you."

Queen Hester's eyes scanned the Donnie's crew. All remained silent, heads bowed somewhat, even Boomer showing uncharacteristic self-control. "And what would that be, my sweet daughter?" She said this with all the love and admiration of a stone.

Lorna broke eye contact with Brann, looking her own mother, the Corsair Queen, full in the face as she replied:

"A sad, scared, and lonely old cunt."

Even Bosun Neve looked shocked, not knowing if she was supposed to draw her blade at this. Boomer, for all his restraint, finally broke with a strangled cackle, clapping a hand over his muzzle to silence it.

Hester did not react with fire and brimstone, nor did she call for their summary execution. Instead, she simply, quietly, but firmly, issued one command.

"Get out of my city."

Bosun Neve clapped her heels together once more. "Court adjourned, turn to." She beckoned her pair of corsairs over, the two guards standing at her side, facing Lady Lorna, The Wolf, and the rest of them in silent dismissal.

"House Geiha will have known we were here," Lorna cautioned.

"The Empire of Geiha," Hester corrected, "Has no quarrel with us, nor we cause to invite it. Take your prisoner and go, I've no desire for the headache that would come from such entanglements."

Lorna laughed, rooted in place even as the Bosun and her corsairs began ushering the party out of the Pavillion. "You honestly think when the Marshal Tark lands on your shore and hears you allowed us safe passage, he would see that as anything but a betrayal of Jan-Jito's accord with them? He wouldn't spill a drop of blood on your sands, not when the blade is offered to him so willingly."

"Stop."

The Bosun and her guards froze. Brann turned, his toes at the edge of the platform, very much ready to return unmolested to the Donnie and get out of this city.

"What's wrong, Queen Mother?" Lorna spread her arms wide, her words finding their mark. "Something else you're afraid of? Surely you wouldn't take a knee at the behest of a lone invader."

Queen Hester seemed to be calculating something, her expression becoming more puzzled than troubled. "The Marshal of Geiha. The Iron Tark. He is coming here? Himself?"

"Did you not hear?" Lorna waved a hand towards Brann. "This deserter? Insulted The Marshal directly. Tark is personally seeing to his retrieval, and has pursued us across the continent to do so, at great cost to his own personal regiment. Recruit Brann here is the lone survivor of the fallen House Lachlan, and all of House Geiha now moves to lasso him back into their stockades to make an example of him for the ages."

Queen Hester inhaled sharply, her eyes going wide in understanding. Something clicked in Brann's mind as well, finally, something he hadn't quite been able to articulate all this time, but was stated so plainly now by the Queen that it felt like he was being slapped across the face with how obvious it was:

"The entirety of House Lachlan now stands in defiance of the Geihan Empire," Hester said in realization. "Reduced to a single man, his desertion is not just an act of cowardice, but a declaration of war on behalf of his entire clan. A challenge issued directly..." The corners of her mouth twitched, threatening to form a smirk. "...To the famous warlord, The Iron Tark, Marshal of their armies himself. Who has conquered every House who dared challenge him."

Brann felt weightless, a ringing clarity echoing through him now. All eyes turned to him, and in that instant, feeling so many people examining him—among them, those familiar burning amber lamps of a certain lycanthrope—the young soldat suddenly understood why The Wolf was so obsessed with him, and likewise, why Tark was as well.

Recruit Brann of Lachlan was, in the eyes of the Marshal, a sovereign nation unto himself, who—by fleeing from the Assay after pointing a gun at Tark—had declared war on all of House Geiha.

He spoke, briefly, barely a squeak. All he could muster was: "Oh."

Queen Hester's aura shifted in an instant, and a renewed sense of purpose took the place of her previously compromised emotional state. "Bailiff, remand this prisoner to the brig. He will act as offered tribute to The Marshal upon Geiha's arrival in Jan-Jito, and will be cared for accordingly until such time." She nodded, the corsairs immediately surrounding Brann, their gloves gripping his arms tightly. "It seems my daughter's visit to court today was not as shrill and fruitless as previously thought. Well done, young Lorna."

"Hey!" Boomer stepped forward, pulled back by Emrys and Hawkshaw, while Nestor got between him and Brann just shaking his head. Lady Lorna didn't seem surprised by this new command, her expression defiant as ever—Brann was now thoroughly confused; did she want him to be captured by Tark after all? Was this her plan all along?

"As you said, Marm, you are nothing if not adherent to our customs," Lorna teased, like there was a private joke only she knew the punchline to waiting to be spoken aloud. "All the choices you face—fighting for your own family, or submitting to the whims of other nations—never could you make the right choice. The choice of a loving mother."

"On the contrary." Hester nodded, and Brann was dragged away by the Bosun's guards, leaving the rest of the crew awaiting their own sentence. "All your need to stand apart from me, revel in the glory of waving your own colors instead of obeying your captain's simple orders—it has you fooled into thinking that what I do, the choices I make, no matter how heartless, how..." She tilted her head, scoffing to savor this pun: "...Bloodless. It is, and has always been, the most pure, abject, and resolute expression of a mother's love for her daughter. My love for you." She allowed herself a small, victorious smile, watching Lorna's hands clench into fists. "And make no mistake, Viscountess: you will, as you yourself said, endure it."

The Queen waved her audience away, turning to depart the Pavillion, still clutching her ceremonial saber at her side all the while. "You are free to wander the city at your leisure, but I will expect you and your crew at my table for dinner tonight. Oh—" She stepped back, turning to scan everyone's appearance with a look of distaste. "They will be dressed appropriately, of course. The House tailor will appreciate the challenge of fitting such an array of curious bodies, I've no doubt."

Hester disappeared, her white robes slipping out of view behind the throne. The Queen had spoken, and Brann was gone, leaving everyone awaiting Lady Lorna's orders.

"Listen, Princess, you may be rich and all," said Boomer, raising his own fist, "But you paid to have two passengers delivered to their destination—not three. You better start working out a plan to get him back, because a few less scales to my name is the last thing on my mind right now, because if that kid gets hurt—"

"Weren't you listening?" Lorna interrupted, looking somewhat smug. "I know my mother—I know this city—better than anyone. Trust me, my knucklebrained friend," she said, a calming hand wrapping around Boomer's fist to lower it soothingly. "Not only will I have my satisfaction, but you will all leave Jan-Jito's shores before the sun sleeps tomorrow's eve—fully intact, and with more scales to your name than you could have ever dreamed." She nodded to The Wolf, who nosed at her ear affectionately before padding off, disappearing down the steps after Brann and the corsairs as swiftly and silently as a ghostly breeze. "The Queen has fallen for this very trick once before, and by her own admission, I have always been the better strategist."

*

The majority of the city was comprised of winding stone stairways in lieu of streets—there was definitely an aged, time-forgotten air about Jan-Jito, Brann unused to the distinct lack of ships screaming overheard to land at the local port or being able to walk through the streets without sidestepping motorized rickshaws. The Bosun followed just behind as he was nearly lifted off the ground by the two corsairs, and in his best attempt to sound cooperative, he pleaded: "Can we—can I—you're holding me very tightly, I'm happy to walk on my own two feet, really, I'm not gonna try to run—"

"If you did, you'd be reduced to a smear on the pavement, make no mistake," Bosun Neve replied. "But I take your point. This boy is as much a diplomat as prisoner, and should receive the appropriate treatment. Let him hoof it."

"Aye, Bosun," the guards both replied, and released their grip on Brann, who straightened his blouse and rubbed at his sore bicep.

329

"Do you usually let prisoners keep their weapons? Not a threat," he added quickly, turning to nod courteously to Neve, hands up, "Just, you know—I do have a sword on my back and all, doesn't that make me dangerous?"

Neve stared at him impassively. "No."

Brann sighed, but nodded, turning to walk on. "Alright, just asking. Lead on."

Given the apparent size of the city when they'd first landed, Brann estimated it wouldn't take long for them to reach the brig, and sure enough after only a few minutes of walking they had arrived at the outer wall opposite where they'd entered from the beach side. Instead of seeing the imposing bars of a gate, or a great wooden door barred by a heavy plank, the entrance to the brig was altogether different from what Brann expected.

"A mine?" He asked, having arrived at the wood-buttressed hole that had been bored into the side of the mountain, just within the protection of the city's walls. Likely the mine had existed long before Jan-Jito did, given how worn and diminished the entrance was, a lantern swinging from creaky hinges just above the dark chasm.

"Only one way in or out, same as on board a ship," Neve replied. "Unless your sword is magic and can carve a tunnel through an entire mountain?"

"I dunno, I haven't really given it a go just yet," Brann joked, prompting a chiding shove from Neve.

"Don't be an ass, boy. You are being shown courtesy far above your station as a prisoner else would be—give respect, and thanks."

Brann nodded sheepishly, the dark of the mineshaft washing over his face as they entered. "I'm—you're right, I don't have a lot of time outside of Geiha, all apologies," he offered. "Lady Red hasn't been the best conversation partner on our trip here, so I didn't have a lot of time to learn about your customs. I'll do my best, I promise?"

"Who?" Neve queried, and then laughed softly. "You mean Lorna the Lamb? Goodness, what a title, 'Lady Red,' so mysterious. What a darling."

"Right, like it's some kind of cool alias protecting her secret identity?" Brann was feeling relieved that he wasn't being escorted in cold silence, and was actually conversing with the Bosun—friendliness was never expected from Geihan sentries, and to be treated so humanely despite the Queen's hostility was a welcome curiosity among the corsairs. "Lorna, huh? She never told us her real name. And what's—'Lorna the Lamb', what's that about? Gotta be a story there."

The mineshaft, despite its imposing entrance, was more than sufficiently lit by rope lights strung along the ceiling, nailed to each buttress in so they never let any shadows darken their steps—though it was a relatively straight path, and would likely remain so, assuming they weren't eventually going to be following along some other side passage that spiraled off deeper into the bowels of the mountain. Neve entertained Brann's request, speaking with fondness as she recalled the story.

"All corsairs give themselves to the sea on a small vessel, their first journey out on the waters—small crafts, no more than three to a crew, barely fit to be called dinghies," she said, speaking with measured breaths as the slope steepened. "But more than just surviving the crossing of the channel to the continent beyond, they have another challenge: keep alive a beast of their choosing on their journey across. Feed it, clean it, keep it placid, avoid conflict with the other animals their crewmates have chosen— and if, by the time they reach the opposite shore, they and their chosen beast have survived, they earn the right to enter ship's officer training."

"So, three people, and three different animals, all stuck on a tiny boat crossing the ocean for who knows how long it takes?" Brann echoed, baffled by this. "I'm guessing they have to share their food, too, and don't get extra provisions to account for the animals?"

"Aye. It's an exercise of balance—keeping yourself alive, keeping your charged animal alive, and making sure by the end of the journey neither of you have killed one another," Neve confirmed. "Much like an officer and her sailors—to show nobility and self-sacrifice while being able to assert control in uncontrollable circumstances. A most valued rite among Jan-Jito's corsairs. Thing is," she said, directing them when the path split, taking the tunnel that stayed level—Brann eyed the opposite path as they moved away from it, how it descended further into darkness—"There's a saying in the crew camps, those awaiting selection for the next batch to sail out. More a rumor or flight of fancy, no doubt invented by generations past to scare the youngins; they say that once you cross the channel, your challenge isn't over, for the animal you've brought with you must also stand by your side and face another cruel test. Naturally, this scares many of the girls into bringing with them beasts of war—a nihiloraptor, or a deywolf, for example, something with teeth and fangs."

"And Red—Lorna—she brought along..."

"A lamb." Neve chuckled. "We about pissed ourselves when she showed up, petite little waif, arms around the wailing little woolen ball. Big as she was, and she practically disappeared into it—she'd taken it from a nearby farm, and it had never been shorn, so there was more wool than lamb."

The passageway flattened out even more, and on either side of them, man-sized holes in the tunnel appeared—each leading to a small, hollowed out bedchamber, all of them lit and sparsely decorated with wooden furniture. No gates, and no bars: the corsairs truly feared no escaping prisoners. Likely, anyone who posed a threat was never taken prisoner at all.

"So, Lorna is chosen, along with two others—myself, and a third, can't remember her name, rest her soul," Neve continued. "She didn't survive the journey across—a wave hit us during the night during her shift standing watch. Gone without a trace when we woke, her jackal yapping up a storm with a broken leg. More rations for the rest of us."

"What animal did you bring?" Brann asked politely.

"A sand viper." Brann shifted nervously, and Neve explained, "Small, doesn't eat much, can survive the harshest conditions—when they're older, they're calm like you wouldn't believe, and almost never bite. Still venomous as shit, though—I, like the other girls, assumed we'd need our beasts to protect us on the other side, so I cheated a little," she admitted. "Something that I could mostly ignore, but would still pack a punch if I needed to throw it in an enemy's face.

"Lorna, bless her, would have made a farmer proud. That soft little lamb never once went without a meal the whole trip, even when Lorna had to go hungry—she split her rations with the jackal as well. 'But he's not yours,' says I, 'Wouldn't you want to throw him overboard, or cook him up for yourself?' Lorna didn't mind though—said he deserved a chance to walk warm sands again, same as us. I never understood. Anyway, we make it across, nearly two weeks adrift—Lorna, she's skin and bones by the end of it all; meanwhile a gob of meat every other day has my snake fat and happy, and the jackal bolts for it as soon as we touch dry land, right off into the snow. We'd landed in the very start of a coastal blizzard, you see, so it was coming down hard, and the longshoremen waiting for us all said it would go on for days—we were proper fucked."

They came to a stop outside of one of the hollow chambers. Neve, kindly, decided to wait a moment before finishing her story. "We spent the week shacked up on that beach in a hut, barely bigger than this room here. I was shivering so hard my skeleton threatened to bust right out of me, could barely keep a fire lit. And Lorna..." She chuckled, finally arriving at the end of her story. "There was so much wool on that puffy little fucker, when he got his first shear right there on the cabin floor, she had enough to knit herself a warm little coat and a blanket to cuddle him underneath."

She nodded ruefully. "That was Lorna, through and through. Never understood a thing in her head, none of us did—we were always making her out to be the gaff, but in the end, it was always her having the last laugh right back at the rest of us. She never did much care for the insults that came as a consequence of being born to royalty—but showing up to her first command ship as a newly commissioned officer, wearing her new bosun's jacket lined with sheep's wool...well, she set the lot of us straight, no doubt. And when she abandoned her last post, well..."

Neve glanced at Brann briefly, and he took her meaning.

A deserter. Just like him.

"Why would she run—I mean, just leave her duties like that?" He corrected himself when Neve's eyes flashed at the word 'run'. She left it alone, however, remaining silent.

He approached it from another angle.

"What happened to the lamb?"

Neve's face soured a bit at Brann's question. She clicked her tongue before answering.

"Lorna's mother ordered him fed to a wolf."

Brann winced. There was nothing left for them to discuss.

The Bosun waved him in, gesturing at the cell. "These will be your chambers until summoned once more—a cordial invitation to stay put is extended on behalf of the Queen Mother, and should you feel need for food or drink, there is a holopad on the desk that will send a telegram directly to the warden's screen: write down anything you need within reason, and it will be brought to you at the earliest opportunity. Understand, young Lachlan," she said, her words turning cautious, "Your stay here is as a prisoner, despite any kindnesses extended to you. Should the desire to take a walk back up the tunnels and get some fresh air become too much to bear, rest assured it is not the Queen you will be standing before next, but the undertaker. Do we have an understanding?"

Before Brann could reply, Neve's eyes snapped up over his shoulder, and she reached for her saber. "Steady on, there," she said in alarm, and Brann and the guards spun around to face the intruder.

"Peace," came the gruff, single word reply of The Wolf, who stood hunched low with his forepaws pressed to the dirt, his spear slung across his lower back. Brann watched his jowls flex and lips curl on the other side of years of practice relearning human speech as he attempted a rare verbal parlay.

"Lady says...to stay with...boy." It would be almost cute, were it not for the absolute lethal display of his lycanthropic jaws clicking together between syllables. "At...Bo...Boswwunn's...p—perm...puurrrrmmmrgh..."

"Permission?" Brann said to himself quietly. The Wolf grunted with a nod.

"Lady asks her...friend." He chewed on this word to himself thoughtfully, then nodded. "Friend," he repeated in self-satisfaction, looking pleased with himself.

Neve softened a bit, hand withdrawing from her saber hilt. Apparently, she was as unused to the Wolf asking for anything as Brann was. "If Lady Lorna wills it, then it shall be," she replied, stepping aside to invite the werewolf into Brann's cell alongside him. "I remember the last time you sat at dinner across from The Queen—best for all we make a compromise on this matter."

The Wolf padded forward, keeping low and nodding politely before entering Brann's cell...and immediately stepping up to drape himself over the single bed in the chamber, settling himself in comfortably with a chuff.

Brann grumbled. "Would a request for a second bed be within reason?"

"Afraid not." Bosun Neve clicked her heels together, signaling she was off. Brann stepped into his cell, his boots crunching as they touched down from his short hop out of the tunnel, and the three corsair women disappeared in silence behind him.

"So," he said after a moment of silence, being left alone with the Wolf for the first time since the night they killed Emrys together. "You're my bodyguard now too, huh? That's nice. Seems like the sword doesn't really impress much anyway," Brann said dryly, swinging the aforementioned weapon off his back and resting it against the edge of the nearest buttress.

The werewolf didn't respond—probably he'd exhausted his interest in human speech for the time being. He simply yawned, tail lashing slowly, eyes as ever fixed on Brann.

The small table in the center of the cell had a single unlit candle and a stack of playing cards on it, and nothing else. Brann pulled out the small stool and sat himself there, scooping up the deck and shuffling. "You play carousel?"

Again, no response.

He nodded his lack of surprise, cutting the deck in an attempt to remember the fancier tricks he'd been shown in training by the other recruits. "So, Lady Red—Lady Lorna, Lady the Lamb. The princess who never runs," Brann said with some relish, "Ran away from home—and from military service, too. Huh."

The Wolf crooked an eyebrow at him.

Brann continued, emboldened. "You know, you don't have to try so hard to scare me. You, and the rest of the group—back on the Donnie, everyone likes to act so big and confident, and yet..." He began fanning out cards, slapping down two hands in an alternating fashion with the faces down, "The more we all travel together, the more it seems like...we're all just a bunch of liars, and runners, getting all cozy judging one another for the same things..."

Brann slapped down the last card a little bit too loud, watching to see if the Wolf reacted. He didn't.

"That we all seem to be equally guilty of."

There was a barrier of communication between them, and Brann was feeling determined today to get through it, if only once. "I'm gonna be handed off to the Marshal here in a few days," he tried reasoning, "So it won't be long before you may never see me again. We can at least get to know each other a little before then."

Silence. Wolf lapped at his nose, swiping away some debris clinging to his nostril. Just staring, forever.

Brann sighed. He lost interest in the cards before even turning a single hand over, tossing them loosely down, leaning back on the stool to stretch his back. "A werewolf, huh." He pondered this concept. "Neat.

Spooky, but you know. They always show them as being like dumb monsters in those holoplays I'd see as a kid. Never expected to meet a real one, let alone one who didn't want to kill me." He paused. "Or, well, maybe you do, I can't tell—one who was smart, I mean. Like, human smart."

The Wolf snorted, annoyed by the comment. So, he was listening after all. Brann allowed himself a mischievous grin.

"They'd always show you to be mindless killing machines, but I guess you had to have been human too at some point a long time ago, so it only makes sense you remember certain things." He thought back to his time as a youth, watching the cheesy plays that would air on late night holovision, bundled up with other young men in some anonymous benefactor's apartment in Barrier City. "Is it true if—well, hang on, let me rephrase," he said, thinking out loud to himself. "Would I turn into a wolf too if you bit me right now?"

"Yes."

Brann blinked, then leaned forward. Did he imagine it, or were they actually breaking ground on a conversation?

"No shit?"

The Wolf just stared, unimpressed. Brann thought, then tried again.

"So, then, what would happen, I'd just...transform right here on the spot, grow a tail and get all big and tough too," he asked. "So, then no one would recognize me, and I could run away and get out of here, and no one could stop me—just like you?"

"Yes."

This was a revelation to Brann. He laughed a little, slapping his hands together. "Alright, cool, well," he said, rubbing them together. "Should we get started? I mean how does it work; does it have to be like—I assume you have to break the skin. Can you maybe just do it like on the ankle or somewhere that it won't hurt too bad—"

"No."

Brann frowned. "But you just said—"

"Asked if it would work." The Wolf chewed on his words, much like he did with Neve. "Not if I would."

"Oh, well...would you?"

The Wolf snorted. Nope.

Brann blew a raspberry, disappointed. "Thought you were here to do what I say, like a bodyguard is supposed to."

"I am."

Pause. Brann said that with some measure of sarcasm. He didn't expect that to be the case in actuality. He stood slowly, crossing his arms behind his back.

"So..." He looked at his feet. "You won't turn me into a werewolf because I asked...what if I ordered you to?"

"No."

"What!" Brann was indignant, and confused. "But you just said—!"

"Asked already. Should have told first."

"Goddammit, you mean if I gave you a direct order before asking your opinion on it, you would have bitten me?"

"Yes." The Wolf spoke as bluntly and honestly as anyone Brann had ever met.

"Okay..." Brann considered this. "Then...what if—no, that's a question." He took a breath. "I order you, on behalf of Lady Red—Lady Lorna—to tell me all about yourself. Who you were before you changed, where you came from, how you became what you are now."

The Wolf growled a bit, though it carried no threat behind it. He raised himself to sit, hunched like a large child on the bed, the small frame sagging a bit from his weight. He regarded Brann with an expression that looked less than enthusiastic, and said:

"Don't wanna."

"Ah ah ah, that's not how that works," Brann chided, wagging a finger. "You said you have to follow my orders. So? Tell me everything, it's the rules." He cackled, then added, "Your Lady said so, remember? You have to do what I say."

Wolf's eyes narrowed, and with contained glee, Brann bet to himself the lycan was wishing he'd have just bitten him before when he was asked.

"Words," said the beastman slowly, "Too big. Too many."

Brann considered this. "Can you draw? Write?" He remembered the holopad, and pointed to it, sitting on the bedside drawers. "On that, maybe?"

The Wolf, to his surprise, leaned over to swipe up the holopad in his hefty paws. It clearly served a real challenge to him, using his lips and tongue to manipulate the attached e-pen to scrawl out some message on it, which he turned to show Brann, written there on the sepia surface as crudely as a toddler might have done:

B l o db bo ll

"That's...yeah, no, good story," Brann said, blinking. "I get it now."

Wolf snarled, wiping away the words, then trying again. Brann stifled a laugh; he didn't mean to make fun, clearly this was a genuine struggle.

After taking it a bit slower, more patiently, the Wolf turned the pad—and this time, Brann could see something resembling real words:

BL O OD

BOOLL

"Blood...bool?" He twisted the second word on his tongue a bit. "Bowl? 'Blood bowl', is that it?"

Wolf chuffed again, his tail slapping the bed. Affirmative. He held out the pad to Brann, bidding him take it. "Ask. They send."

"So, I ask them to send us a...blood bowl, and they'll know what you mean right away?"

Another slap of the tail. Affirmative.

Brann took the pad, wiping off the wolfscratch and penning cleanly the message to send:

Can we have a "BLOOD BOWL" sent to us? - Brann

He turned to show off his neat recruit penmanship to Wolf, who just rolled his eyes, unimpressed. Brann clicked the send button, and the words were wiped away automatically in a wave of ink dots that fled from the electronic page to signify the message was dispatched. "Now we wait," he said, setting the pad aside.

22. The Mines

The bowl in question was delivered within the hour—a humble basin of pewter, the rim adorned on four sides with small spikes, each of them leading down into small channels carved into the bowl that all spiraled together into a strange symbol in the basin's center. Along with the bowl, a small leather chest was also delivered, and inside Brann uncovered a set of four matching surgical tubes capped with long, silver needles. There was not much else to any of it, and it was no real mystery why the device was called a "blood bowl", Brann figuring the mechanics out pretty quickly.

"I mean, I did get trained as a corpsman, and no offense," he said with some hesitation as he lifted one of the needles free, watching the tubing dangle. "But typically blood transfusions are meant to be done a little bit more...safely? Professionally?"

The Wolf sat hunched next to the table, setting the bowl between them and extending his forearm to Brann. "Too big," he said gruffly, holding up his paw; Brann knew he meant that those thick werewolf pads couldn't do such precise work.

"Other end goes on the spike, then we bleed together into the bowl, that it?" Brann asked, pointing out the order of rudimentary steps with a finger.

Wolf nodded.

Brann sighed unhappily. "Outstanding."

He capped the spikes closest to himself and to the Wolf with two of the rubber tubes, their open ends rolling snugly into place with the help of some plastique rings that clamped down once set. Brann leaned forward to insert Wolf's needle—realizing he didn't even ask permission first, startling himself when he touched that furry arm.

"Carrreful," Wolf growled in alarm.

"Sorry, sorry," Brann apologized, trying again. He had no difficult locating a vein, the vascular flesh bulging visibly once Wolf's fur was parted, his inner elbow just as rife with waiting veins as any human. Probably not much internally changed when one was turned into a werewolf. Steadying his hand, Brann tapped the chosen vein a couple times before smoothly sliding the needle in. "Hold this," he ordered Wolf, using his thumb to demonstrate. As Wolf obliged, Brann reached into the small chest to retrieve a satin red strap, which he looped around Wolf's arm to keep the needle in place.

"No anesthetic or anything, just great," he complained to himself. "You'd think a whole religion of blood magic users would know a thing or two about medical safety."

He loosely looped another satin strap around his own arm, flexing and clenching a fist to make a vein appear in his own smooth flesh, tapping it a few times as well. "So, I guess it won't do me any good to ask what I should expect will happen," he said, exhaling to calm his nerves. He didn't wait for an answer, slipping the needle in, his eye twitching a bit at the feeling of his flesh being pierced. Once the red rushed up the tubing, he tugged the loose knot of the strap tight, finishing it with his teeth while his thumb held the needle down to ensure the most secure fit possible.

The Wolf stared in at the basin, and Brann followed suit, watching with admitted fascination as the stone channels painted themselves red with the flow of their blood like an invisible pair of ink pens were swirling together in unison. As the twin streams rushed closer and closer together, staining the shape of the runic symbol, Brann felt a small twinge of disgust, apprehensive of what the results of his blood mixing with a beastman's would be. It came as some relief, then, when the symbol was complete, shining for a brief moment in reflecting the low light of the ell before it disappeared beneath the rising blood that pooled together within the basin.

"Here." Wolf pointed a claw at a small arrow shaped figure carved about midway up the bowl's insides. "Stop when here."

There were four gauze pads at the ready in the chest—Brann watched until the blood's rising level just about met the arrow, and made to grab the pads.

Wolf stopped him silently, shaking his head. "Wait."

Brann frowned, about to protest, when he saw why. The blood rose to fill that small symbol as well, then—simply stopped. As if their veins had been closed off, no more fluid flowed into the basin.

Instead, it seemed to be...retreating. The volume of blood was shrinking.

"Uhh, is that..." Brann watched with consternation. "That's not supposed to happen..."

The falling level of red liquid left the inside of the pewter shining wetly, the blood indeed draining, and to Brann's horror a warm rushing sensation that turned his stomach cold signaled that the blood in his arm was flowing the wrong way. The Wolf made no indication that anything was amiss, simply watching as the basin emptied as quickly as it had filled, before all that was left were the dark dregs that receded until only the symbol remained filled with their blood.

"Now," he said, tugging free the needle with a wayward spurt before holding out his paw to accept a gauze pad from Brann, who handed one over nervously.

"I'm gonna be so mad at you if I get some kind of weird canine disease from this," Brann whined, tamping his own pad in place and re-tightening the strap to keep it there.

"You complain too much. It's safe, don't worry."

Brann froze. He looked up at the Wolf, studying his face. "Say again?"

There seemed to be a disconnect between what he was seeing and hearing, and what he understood—Brann was reminded of the sensations of first meeting Grishka in her home, how he couldn't quite focus on her shape. The Wolf was not actually speaking more, but within the span of the few words he chose, there was a string of conscious thought that seemed to unravel from their center, filling Brann's mind with their truest meaning.

"I've seen this ritual done before," the werewolf was saying, the words seeming to sweep through Brann as if on a breeze, though he heard them in his ears as plainly as if they were spoken aloud. "We've shared our blood, and now there can be no secrets between us. The corsairs use this when signing agreements with other Houses—there is chance for them to lie when they can sense each other's true thoughts."

Brann's head was swimming. "I'm not sure I like this—you're saying we can read each other's minds now? I never agreed to that."

"No, fool boy. Only when we speak together alone, we can speak plain, our words translated in spirit." Wolf gestured to himself. "You commanded me to speak, this is the only way, if you mean to understand me."

Brann tried to examine this new ability as if from afar, but simply couldn't—his brain had just been rewired in an instant, and Wolf spoke just as clearly and deliberately as any human. "Do I sound any different?" He asked.

"Yes. You sound younger. More afraid."

That wasn't what he'd hoped to hear.

"So, okay, it's safe. Weird, but, safe." Brann scratched himself behind the ear. "So, when I ask you, say...what did Lorna mean when she said earlier that you had taken a liking to me?"

"That's a question I can only answer in part," Wolf said. It was strange to Brann how much like a human he sounded, despite those unblinking eyes still staring at him like a hungry animal. "It is not my decision to keep certain things I know to myself, but I'll respect my Lady's wishes nonetheless. All I can say is that within your fear, I can smell something else, something that the rest of your friends can't."

He exhaled, chest rumbling. Even with this blood magic enhancing his speech, there were things he still found trouble communicating. "Ask another question. Be more specific. I do the best I can but I have parts of me...missing. Unknowable even to me."

Brann readjusted himself on his stool, sitting a bit more

comfortably as he leaned in closer. "Back at the stadium, Tark said something to you," he recalled. "Something like...you two had fought before?"

"He said we had shared a battlefield before," Wolf corrected. "I have no recollection of him, save for the barest of scents I can almost recognize. More certainly he and I crossed paths before I changed."

He held aloft his spear, showing off the complicated looking head of its blade. "This weapon—I woke with it, the day I was reborn an animal. Whoever I was, it stayed at my side, along with my memories of how to wield it. A place, a people, some part of me long ago that belonged. If ever the lizard you and the others call 'Tark' and I cross paths outside of combat, I would ask him the same thing."

Brann was a little disappointed by this. "So, you really don't know anything about yourself, then?"

"I didn't say that." Wolf set down his spear. "I woke with Lorna at my side. When I changed, whatever the reason or cause, I did not completely disappear inside the beast. Her knowledge of blood magic kept something intact, something human. But all the things you would call memories—images. Words, names, places. Faces. Those all left me forever. All that remained were...sensations. Scents. Something in here," he said, paw against his chest. "Hurt. Something that followed me, that aches, and taunts me to remember, knowing I can't."

Brann hoped he wasn't coming off as rude with these questions. "Does she speak to you like this," he said, waving a finger between them. "Did you share a blood bowl?"

"We had no need. Lorna is simply who she is, someone who understands things deeply." Wolf bowed his head. "I never need to speak a word more than what is said between us, once she retrained me to understand human tongues. She just knows and accepts me, and that's all there is to it." He examined Brann's face. "There is another question you've had on your mind since the Bosun told you Lorna's story. Ask it now."

Brann obliged, though not without reluctance. "She said the lamb was fed to a wolf." He broke eye contact, not willing to stare Wolf full in the face as he asked. "Meaning you?"

"Yes." The answer was tinged with regret. "Before I awoke, there was a time during my change was as mindless and without hope as any cursed lycan. My Lady tells me she was forced to watch it happen—perhaps a punishment for what I had done as a human, or a punishment for her, she will not say. Her only word on the matter is that it is not my fault. For my sake, I believe her."

"Why do you stay with her and do everything you're told? Is it also some kind of magic?"

"If you call manners 'magic,' then yes." Glib—there was a sense of humor peeking out from the depths. Brann liked that. "I'm no more bound to her than I am to you, but by doing all she has to protect and comfort me, I follow her and carry out her wishes because I simply choose to. As I choose to follow your commands now, out of respect for her."

"Comfort you?" Brann paused. "You? You're like...a killing machine. Almost invincible, from what I've seen."

"I spoke of pain already," Wolf reminded. "I don't know where it comes from or why I can't be free of it, but it stays with me, always, never letting me free. It has a grip inside my chest, and will tighten whenever I am in moments of quiet."

Brann fiddled with a playing card. "We call that sadness, I think."

"If that word helps you understand. I don't understand it any more than I understand why you would run from your duties, when you are protected by armor and a functioning weapon," Wolf replied, and Brann knew this was sincere confusion, his voice carrying no contempt.

"That why you always stare at me?" Brann looked back up in Wolf's face. "You don't understand me?"

"Why run?" Wolf repeated. "I know what fear is. It is what happens when you lose your balance, your weapon, and you are exposed to a killing blow. I have felt it, but never when I am on my feet, spear in hand."

Brann challenged this question with one of his own. "Why did Lorna run? If she wasn't afraid, if her own mom was the Queen and she did so well in the academy—why abandon her command?"

"So, she would not lose me." Wolf quirked his head, as if it were obvious. "As she lost the lamb. She fights with her mother, and I cannot help—if I tried, as I have once before, we would both be killed. Lady Lorna left home to have me at her side, always."

"Then why come back now?" Brann spread his arms. "Sure, isn't doing me any favors, you either, from the sound of it. If this was where Zay was hired to deliver the two of you all along, then something's not adding up."

"That I also cannot say. I simply came along because I chose to." Wolf dipped his head. "Why did you run? Tell me."

There wasn't any way around it, and even though Brann felt like he'd answered this question half a dozen times before, in good faith he couldn't recall what reason he may have given. So, he tried another.

"Lorna ran so she wouldn't lose you," he said, speaking softly. "Like she lost the lamb. I guess if I had to compare, I'd say I ran...so I wouldn't lose me either." He nodded. "Kind of like how you lost your old self."

Wolf was silent, save for his quiet, deep breathing. He blinked slowly, his tail lashing against the dirt. Like before the ritual, Brann had no idea how to interpret what was on his mind now.

"I will not bite you," he said finally. "Becoming a werewolf—if it means you will have the same sadness I live with, then that is something no one can command me to do, not even my Lady. But," he said, rising to his paws, "I will help you with your other request—to escape from here."

"Well, actually," Brann stammered, raising a hand to stop Wolf, "I didn't mean it seriously, not if it gets someone hurt or killed—"

"I said you worry too much," Wolf interrupted, his spear once again in hand. "You answered my question, and I am happy to understand you better now. I would not help you flee otherwise if it were done out of cowardice. You will return with me to Lorna's side, but we must not harm

347

any corsairs—so we will use the other exit from these mines, where we will not be seen."

"Won't the fact that you helped me escape be reason enough to make the Queen snap?" Brann tentatively picked up his own sword. "I'm not seeing the big picture here, help me out."

"Lady Lorna will make it right." Wolf nodded with a huff. "Be patient."

"The Bosun was really nice," Brann said, resisting. "I don't know, I feel like whatever Lorna's plan is, springing me from jail after all that would just make things worse..."

Wolf stared down at him. "As I said. Young and afraid. Stupid too."

"Hey, that's not nice."

"We leave the mines," insisted Wolf, "We make for Lorna, she will get us out of the city before Tark arrives. You mistake her intentions. She was never giving you up to him. Her mother will help us in the end." He pointed to the exit with his spear. "Go."

There was nothing for it. Brann shouldered his weapon, rubbing at his needle-pricked arm as he climbed up out of the cell, turning the opposite direction from where they came. "Shouldn't have swapped blood with you," he griped, descending down the path as the Wolf followed close behind.

*

The tunnel had begun to tighten and twist at a steeper incline the further they went, the lights growing farther apart and the cells looking smaller and less frequent—-likely these deeper chambers were meant for less desirable inmates. It didn't escape Brann's attention that, save for himself, the entire prison seemed empty.

"This is just taking us deeper into the mountain, isn't it?" Brann asked, beginning to pant from exertion. "How is that escaping, exactly? They were pretty clear there was only one way in or out."

"The mines have many tunnels," Wolf replied from behind, "And the corsairs are a sea people. They sealed off the main exit—the dark tunnel you saw, back near the surface—but any number of prisoners over the centuries have tried to dig their way out. Almost none succeed, so Jan-Jito never tries to stop them. When Lorna was young, a troupe of raiders was captured attempting to sneak into the city one night—the Queen was more merciful then, and let them live, sentencing them to a decade down in the brig. What she didn't know, as Lorna discovered, was that before they were raiders, the men were all a mining crew who were lost at sea and crashed on these shores without a captain to lead them. So, using the materials they requested very slowly over time, they crafted tools from the small items they requested from the warden during their sentence—aluminum cups, wooden chair legs—they dug their own exit in their final years through existing, forgotten tunnels in the mines, never once attempting to make for the main entrance in Jan-Jito. Most of them escaped when they dug through into a natural cave that led out of the mountain, just outside the city walls."

"'Most of them?'" Brann repeated.

"There were some accidents," Wolf replied flatly. "We are close. Look for a diamond carved into a stone overhead."

The tunnel had become less neatly dug, the walls becoming rougher and rockier, the buttresses less stable looking. There were even points where wooden planks had been laid in the dirt to cover small holes, likely natural formations that had been discovered, proving hazardous to the ancient miners. The downward slope of the curling tunnel had Brann jogging, finding it easier than trying to walk at an incline. He took care to duck whenever a particularly low part of the ceiling descended on him, but otherwise Brann was throwing caution to the wind: if the exit was as assured as Wolf said, he had little reason to waste time.

"There," he finally said—a limestone boulder jutted from a higher point in the dirt ceiling, framed by a square of wood, seated just above another side tunnel that branched off this main path. In the flattest surface of the limestone, clear as day, a diamond was drawn in the surface by some sharp tool long ago. "This is the way, let's—"

The world went black, and Brann was a child again, falling into that laundry chute in that dark closet, but this time he couldn't catch himself in time. His feet had found a hidden plank of wood, long since rotted by time and obscured by the dirt of the tunnel floor, and he simply fell through it—and all he knew was dark, and the air rushing up past his ears and up his nose, choking back his scream—the walls around him were so close he wasn't just falling past them, he was sliding down them, with them, through a vortex of stone that curved and sent him shooting forward—

The momentum built up by his fall had carried him into an open cavern, and Brann was falling now, but this time launched horizontally from the tiny gopher hole that had been bored in the ceiling, and he found his voice finally as he tumbled through the air. The light and shadows bounced all around him, and knowing any second he'd be splattered against the stone, he instead was jolted by the stinging slap of icy water: everything spun, bubbles buffeting him about like a million tiny fish, and in his shock, Brann could see the pool of the cave was illuminated all along the bottom by glowing algae. He bobbed in the water for a moment, then—reaching down within, grasping at a straw of logic—looked up, seeing the black. The surface. He swam, flopping his arms weakly, kicking upwards and forwards, until his head met that black ceiling and air rushed into his lungs once more, his shoulders breaking the surface of the glowing stone pool.

The cave was nearly entirely illuminated by the glow from the subterranean pond, the light reflecting off the stalactites and clusters of crystallized quartz in a dazzling disco of color. Brann paddled there, treading water as he collected himself, feeling his heart bashing against the inside of his ribs—up above his head, where the pool disappeared under the rock wall, dozens of small holes ranging from man-sized to looking as if they could barely fit a worm passing through pocked the stone surface. One of those had been where he'd fallen from, and he knew without having to even consider the question that none of those holes were big enough for the Wolf to pass through—he was not going to be followed. Brann would have to escape this cavern alone.

He kicked forward, swimming to the edge of the pool, where the sheer lip met his freezing hands—he pulled himself up, out of the frigid water, shaking as much of it from himself as he could. With a start, Brann checked his shoulder—the sword was still there. He could still see, thanks to the natural biolumescence. He hadn't been seriously injured, only suffering a few stray scrapes and abrasions on his face and arms—and his tailbone hurt something fierce, likely from his rear taking the brunt of the impact when the rock chute had curved horizontally.

He was alive, and could stand and fight. It was, all things considered, a miracle.

"Fuck."

He laughed, beginning to shudder from the cold and the ebb of adrenaline. Brann took a few deep breaths, getting his bearings and looking about the cave. There was a good chance this was the same cavern Wolf had mentioned the miners had found—which, if it was, meant there was...

There. An exit tunnel which, to Brann's immediate relief, was also supported by wooden buttresses and had dim lights running along the ceiling within. He may not have been meant to fall as he did, but clearly, he wasn't the first, nor the first to survive—there was an escape route, and no doubt would lead him back to Wolf, then to the surface.

Travelling this tunnel was different—he didn't know how far he'd fallen or how much deeper under the surface he was, but the air was heavier, almost as if it had been suffused with the weight of the mountain above, pressing against the inside of his sinuses and goading deeper breaths out of him. Brann found himself moving significantly more cautiously now—not only to avoid any more pratfalls, but because the light was much sparser here, the ceiling lights powered by unknowable means—the cabling that connected the individual bulbs seemed to stretch on forever in this tunnel, no beginning and no end, and the further Brann went the dimmer they grew.

And the smell.

The space between his footsteps grew shorter and shorter, his pace slowing to a crawl. Brann recognized this smell, something that began as a faint tickle on his nostrils—now, having been walking for almost ten minutes, there was definitely something pulling itself in and coating the back of his tongue.

A sort of...sweet ammonia smell.

The light was crushingly dim now; almost like the actual bulbs were holding their glow back, keeping their range within only a few feet, the shadows pooling together ever closer and darker by the minute.

Brann could even hear less ambient noise—the deeper gut of the mountain was blotting out the cavern sounds, the breeze that drifted lightly through the higher tunnels. Down here, everything receded, the way ahead becoming a black curtain that closed in on him and denied everything else. He stopped, the echo of his footsteps gone—holding his breath, the silence was painful, making his eardrums hum with deprivation.

This might have been a mistake.

The brisk pace he'd made so far had mostly dried him, save for the damp fringes of his clothes his body heat couldn't quite reach—even so, as he pressed forward despite his foreboding, Brann almost thought he detected a sort of wet, slippery sound—not something dripping, necessarily, just...like the sound of mucus sliding along stone, the sound a slug might make if you held it to your ear and listened closely—except it was all around him, growing more audible the darker the tunnel became, until by the time he could barely even see the dying bulbs above it was making his teeth itch.

Just as Brann was about to convince himself to turn back, return to that cavern and find another way out he may have missed in the panic of his fall, there, ahead—the lights were growing brighter again, and he could see the vague shapes of the wooden buttresses re-emerging from the clotted black air. He exhaled in relief, feeling his hands shake a bit—for a moment there, his imagination was starting to run away with him. A few more minutes and he might have started hallucinating voices.

The tunnel widened, a chamber visible ahead—not what he would call brightly lit, but significantly more illuminated than the length of tunnel behind him: Brann could even see a few abandoned wooden crates, mostly intact, with some rusty looking tools leaning against them. He was on the right track after all; if he picked up his feet, he might be out of here before dinnertime just as promised.

Brann stepped forward confidently into the chamber, the heavy air around his ears almost making them pop as the pressure changed noticeably—he chuckled a bit, the sound comforting him more than it should, simply hearing another living thing in the tunnels with him making it—

He slowed, taking a few beats, until he found himself standing stock-still.

Brann furrowed his brow. Why did he stop?

The breath died in his throat, and he swallowed, his skin prickling, muscles tense all over. A quickening in his chest—Brann's heart was pounding, the drumbeat rising into his ears.

He turned. Slowly. So slow his knees creaked, and he could hear a few stray droplets drip from his hair onto his shoulders.

The first instinct he had was to imagine the word 'man.' Though that shifted, warped into something else. Creature. Though even that seemed unfitting in its description.

The skin—no, not the skin...the flesh, the almost gooey cellulite...was white. Grey-white, like the lack of sun didn't just sap pigment, but turned the cells rotten, like a skinned animal that had been left in the heat far too long. The joints were visible, bent and twisted at such distant and uncomfortable angles, the bones themselves seeming to have warped to account for the off-kilter way in which the limbs of this thing had joined together: it hunched low, close to the ground in a sort of crouch, but in doing so almost looked like it had broken something to make such a position possible. The face—

Brann felt the rising knife of dread tickle his esophagus, the sunken eyes looking back at him not with hunger or blankness. No, the most terrifying thing was just how human those eyes looked, how intelligent, how...aware. The lids had long since withered away, the lips having dripped off like melted butter, leaving behind a humorless grin framed by its gory red gums that clenched together a set of perfectly intact, horrifically ingrown teeth, more teeth than a human should have.

It wasn't just looking at something, at someone. It was looking at, studying, acknowledging Brann. Those dark pupils, pools of tar bleeding into white globes of blue veins that practically bulged from its decayed orbitals.

It didn't make a sound. It didn't growl, or howl, or scream. It just stared. At him. Unwavering eye contact, as if it expected Brann to speak or run or attack. A stone-dead corpse, as lifelike and alert as a child.

The seconds ticked by like hours. Brann felt he was in the sights of some predator, some great jungle cat—that moving first would trigger it to pounce.

He moved his foot. Slowly, so slowly, scraping his boot against the ground.

IT didn't move.

A small pebble was kicked away, his muscles so stiff with fear that the slightest exertion made him lurch—Brann froze again, the pebble clacking against a nearby crate.

IT didn't move.

Brann blinked, then blinked again, feeling so scared his eyeballs were sweating—he couldn't help it—his arm wiped over his eyes, squeezing the moisture out between his lids, streaking against his damp sleeve. He opened them, instantly regretting this sudden movement.

IT still didn't move.

The stupidity of what he did next would haunt him forever:

"Uh, hello?"

Nothing. IT just stared.

Brann couldn't even hear breathing.

He slid to the left, slowly, non-threateningly, hands raised partially as if to signal peace.

Nothing. He'd think the thing properly dead, if those eyes didn't swivel in their gluey sockets, fixed on him absolutely.

The corpse had no immediate interest in Brann, yet never did those eyes leave him. IT simply...watched. Waiting.

Brann cautioned a step back, then another, facing the dead thing as he continued his journey on into the tunnel. The further away he grew, the more his confidence dared assure him he was not in danger, the rotten thing not budging an inch from its spot.

A final test. Brann waited until the thing was just within view, inches from disappearing behind the tunnel wall—and, quickly, hand on his sword hilt, Brann spun about, readying himself.

Turning his back on IT did nothing. IT still didn't move.

Satisfied that IT meant him no harm, Brann watched IT disappear behind the wall, and turned, stepping further into the tunnel.

No sound of footsteps behind him, no hungry breathing. When he checked over his shoulder, nothing followed. Brann watched, looking back towards the chamber, his eyes fixed on—

An errant rock, and Brann stumbled, crashing hard down onto his knee. He grunted in pain, rolling himself onto his hand to push himself back up, looking back once more—

IT was in the tunnel.

Silently, it stood, the black silhouette framed in the spaces between the shadows cast by the overhead lamps, those huge white eyes practically glowing in the dark—it had moved too fast, faster than any living thing possibly could, and yet was as stock still as a statue.

Brann's heart did a backflip into his stomach. The fucking corpse was following him.

He whispered a curse to himself, not daring to take his eyes off IT again, not even blinking—never more had he wished he'd kept his rifle, Brann drawing his sword from across his back for the first time since he'd taken ownership of it, doubting any ability to wield it with the same self-assuredness his training with firearms had given him. The speed at which IT had appeared in the tunnel made it clear Brann would not have the reflexes to defend himself against a charging attack.

Yet, even as Brann was back on his feet and balanced, stepping slowly backwards and leveling his sword forward ahead of him, IT still remained frozen in place, the gleam of its pupils like tiny stars in the dark.

"Don't come any closer," Brann breathed. He'd meant to say it loud and intimidating—instead, it was barely a whisper. The air in the tunnel was sucked from his lungs, pulled from him by the presence of this decaying creature.

When he put enough distance between himself and the corpse, Brann turned away again, this time steadying his nerves before deciding— against his better judgment—to run. The tip of his sword down, he broke into a jog, keeping his breathing level and checking over his shoulder only every few moments while ensuring he didn't lose sight of the tunnel ahead.

Once more, IT disappeared behind a gradual curve, the tunnel beginning to move at a slight incline upwards, emboldening Brann. There was no downside to getting closer to the surface in his mind, and it looked as if the ground was becoming rockier again, much like it had been back at the start of this tunnel—

One such rock gave way sharply beneath his foot, and Brann managed to catch himself, landing in a spin on both feet with the sword immediately swishing upwards to point back at the tunnel.

Nothing. No corpse, no glinting eyes in the darkness. No drifting smell of sweet ammonia following on the breeze.

"Okay," he sighed, nodding. Sweat dripped from the tip of his nose; he didn't realize he was even sweating. Brann swallowed down his fears as best he could despite everything. "Keep moving forward, don't look back, and it won't follow. Simple enough." At this point, it might as well be his motto.

Brann pushed on. Up ahead, the light grew brighter—a much larger lamp, suspended just above a hole in the ground in warning, the way ahead blocked by a stone wall. Likely the diggers couldn't blast through or get over the obstruction, so they went underneath. Brann came to the edge of the hole, carefully testing with the toe of his boot—the lip of the hole was sturdy, a series of metal hooks dug into the vertical surface, a makeshift ladder made possible by the small iron bars slotted into the hooks.

Brann looked behind. Nothing in the tunnel.

Brann looked down once more. Nothing but dark ahead—the way below was shrouded in dark. No telling how deep it went before rising once more.

It was only a few yards down—if it led to the way out, there was no other choice. Not if the choice was to return back down the tunnel and face the corpse head on.

Brann turned, putting his back to the hole and—unblinking—sheathed his sword. Staring straight ahead of him, back where he came, he slowly and carefully reached back with one foot, letting it dip low until he felt the first metal rung catch his weight. He balanced there, making sure it was steady enough to hold him—it was—and, crouching slowly, Brann put both hands to the dirt.

Nothing emerged in the tunnel.

His other leg slid backwards, down, then straight—the next rung. He tested it, keeping hands in place. So far, so good. The ladder was sturdy. Both hands hooked on the packed dirt atop the wall, Brann lowered himself bit by bit, until only his eyes peeked out over the edge, still staring down the tunnel.

Empty. Safe.

One hand moved to grip the rung. The next. Taking a breath, Brann climbed down. One foot after another, one hand, then the next, his palms stinging a bit from the caustic rust that coated the rungs. Rust wasn't good, rust meant—

The bar under his right boot snapped, and Brann fell back into darkness, slamming hard against the cold dirt. The dust swirled around him a bit, and he coughed, regaining his breath, seeing stars for a moment. There was a cool breeze coming from behind—Brann blinked away the hard landing, and looked up once more.

IT stood at the top of the ladder, staring right back down at Brann, once more a black silhouette blotting out the lantern behind it that cast an evil shadow down from above. Only those gleaming, bloodshot eyes staring back down at him. In the span of seconds, it had closed what must have been at least a quarter mile gap between them in the tunnel, and Brann didn't hear it make one sound.

This thing was fucking with him, and it wanted him to know it. IT grinned wide, humorless as ever, but now those teeth were beginning to chatter as if in anticipation.

Brann screamed up at it—he didn't know if it was human speech or not, just a guttural bellow of primal fear and rage, the frustration of being stalked like a mouse by this horror choking the sound of life from his lungs. He slapped away the sweat from his eyes and spat into the dirt—staring back defiantly, he met the thing's gaze.

"You won't stop me," he challenged, his voice gravelly and hoarse, speaking from the most bestial part of himself, unwilling to let this thing have the satisfaction of a terrified plea. "I'll cut you—I'll rip you the fuck *apart* if you come any closer, I'm getting the fuck out of this place. *Watch me.*"

For the first time since he'd met the thing, IT moved within his sight—the slightest, gentlest tilt of its crooked head, as if finding Brann's words curious. Those teeth ground together, the only vocalization it made, the sound like pebbles crunching beneath a shoe.

Brann stood upright, clenching his fist around the hilt of his sword once more, and breathed deep. He let the sickly stench fill his lungs, allowing the aura of this dead thing in, opening his lungs to whatever he could learn from being this close to it before outright challenging it. No matter how frightened or panicked he became, something deep within, a steely and unwavering part of his constitution that was being chipped away beneath years of fear and selfishness—it spoke to him, clear as day, and told him under no circumstances should he draw his sword once more.

He couldn't show fear. He couldn't fight. He couldn't stay put, and he couldn't flee.

Brann thought to the day with Mother Superior. Her words tickling his spine.

He laughed bitterly to himself. So dearly he wanted to live, to get out of this mountain, to see daylight. See the Donnie again. His friends.

Brann let go of his sword hilt. He still had too much to lose, and a far bigger threat than some slimy dread zombie was still approaching. This wasn't his time.

"Watch me."

Brann stared IT full in the face once more and—making sure he let no fear show on his face—turned away, to the darkness. He stood there, exposed, vulnerable, those grinding teeth above, and ignored the pursuer...but, more importantly, let IT know IT was being ignored.

With his jaw set, hands balled into fists, Brann walked.

Forward into the dark, only the cool breeze guiding him. The lamps were gone now, nothing overheard to illuminate his way. All that awaited Brann was absolute black. Absolute nothing. Behind him, death followed—there was no sound of feet landing in the dirt, but the chattering teeth were there, close enough to remind him of their presence.

Brann walked, even still, until his eyes were shrouded. Nothing before him, and nothing behind—he was cloaked in oblivion, and still he walked. No, he jogged. His legs, quivering, begging him to stop, to take care, to get his bearings—he ignored this, and sped up, the tunnel growing darker still, impossibly so, as if he was disappearing into the waiting void of the universe itself. The faster he ran, the closer those chattering teeth were behind him—if his pace slowed for a moment, or if he broke into a sprint, he knew he was dead.

From his mind he banished images of hidden pits or jutting rocks. He spat out thoughts of being ripped apart by pale, bony fingers. He ran, as if it were a day in the ranks of his fellow recruits, and for the first time ever Brann felt a pang of guilt. When he deserted Geiha, the service, he didn't just leave behind the military—he left behind his fellow young soldaten. Jefette, and Groose, and Caleb, and any other street urchin who had their freedom stripped away, replaced by a rifle, wishing they could find the courage to find their fear and run as Brann had.

Brann ran, unstopping, unfearing—he could practically feel the sticky rot of the creature on his back, the grinding teeth at the nape of his neck. The friends he had, or could have known—the friends he'd made, Boomer and Nestor and the rest. The risk of dying in battle, the chance he may have earned his freedom another way, a chance he wasn't willing to take. The choice to strip himself before a lecherous old man, to let himself be probed and mouthed and filled by a half dozen of society's worthiest, most valuable and deserving of citizens, if cutting his dignity from himself meant seeing the morning sun once more. A lifetime of choices made to survive until the next day, that led him here, deep underground, dooming him to die in the black forgotten by all, disappeared into the gaps of the earth's memory.

Fuck that. He pounded dirt, hard, fast, running like he'd never run before, breath metered with complete control and discipline, and with the grinding teeth in his ears and cool breath in his face, Brann opened his eyes.

And saw, ahead. The dimmest of lights. Cold, grey, but light nonetheless, reflecting off the buttresses, the stone walls. He didn't even realize he'd shut his eyes during his run until they were open again. The tunnel had become a steady slope upwards, and the dirt ceiling curved, until he saw it: the pinprick of daylight above. And exit.

The most critical timing was required. Brann wasn't there yet, couldn't see the sun or breathe the open air. To let himself break the pace now would be fatal.

But he would surely be dead before he was allowed to reach it.

The voice in him spoke again. Urging him to prepare. To breathe deep, not choke, and get ready for the final stretch. The sweat poured off him, splashing on his face, almost blinding him—he made no move to wipe it away, blinking through the curtain of moisture. He was alone in this tunnel, there was no creature behind him, and he would be free.

The daylight was near, the cold grey wind blowing against his face. Cooling his sweat. And at the exact moment the vomitous odor of death was tempered by the first breath of open air, the voice in him spoke.

NOW.

Brann roared his challenge, purging himself once and for all of the hateful fear clinging to his flesh, and spun in place—a mere stride away from feeling daylight on his skin, the very moment he crossed the threshold from death to life, he stood to face the corpse with his sword in hand, slicing it through the air directly at those maddening, grinding teeth.

Those eyes filled his vision for only a fleeting nanosecond, close enough that his own dead soul reflected back into his face in their bloody, veinous orbs, and then his sword cut through only air: IT was gone, retreated back into the dark of the tunnel as blindingly fast as IT had pursued him. The corpse was disappeared, banished back into the dark, and Brann stood fearless, ready to die.

The tunnel was silent, those grinding teeth no longer in his head. Instead, he heard the steady drip of fluid, and the woosh of the wind in the leaves, even a bird or two whistling up the mountain.

Brann exhaled. He looked about for the source of the sound, feeling the dirt splash between his boots—the dripping fluid was dark, and red. He saw his wrist, and the gouging clawmarks in his flesh, like those of a human's bony fingers that had reached for him before snapping back.

A memento of his hike beneath the mountain, they would turn to scars in the years to come, living proof of the terror he'd seen. Death itself had reached out from the dark to seize Brann, and had let him go for now, but with the reminder of its promise dripping from his arm.

"Watch me," Brann repeated back quietly, still facing the dark.

Though IT was gone, he knew that his words were heard nonetheless.

23. The Audience

The exit from the mountain had led out onto a flower-lined path, the deep purple and white blossoms slightly withdrawn in the cold, sunless day, saving their skyward praise for a warmer sky. Brann had followed this path until it curved out onto a much larger road, what he assumed would lead back to Jan-Jito—he found himself finally returning to reality when his feet touched this road, the draining adrenaline making him shake all over, his breathing alternating between nervous laughter and restrained sobbing.

"Soldat!"

The call came from the roadside, between the trees—Brann wobbled around to face the source, and saw Wolf bounding towards him in uncharacteristic delight, the great beast on all fours as it sped up the road.

"Oh, yeah, hey," Brann called out weakly. "How's shit, man?"

Wolf skidded to a halt, nearly bowling Brann over, his snout immediately going to the young man's injured arm to sniff at it. "You've been attacked," he said, ears upright. "Who did this, are they still following you?"

For a moment the clarity with which Wolf spoke caught Brann entirely off guard, and he almost forgot the ritual that had linked them together hours ago. "How long was I gone?" Brann asked in a daze, looking about.

"I lost you in the tunnels before the night fell," Wolf replied, still sniffing all over Brann to check him. "You've come back to a new morning—I had almost lost hope you would come back at all." He paused, head snapping back, tilting curiously. "Why do you stare at me like that?"

Brann was staring, he realized—Wolf's demeanor was like that of a loyal dog, and in this moment, for the first time, he saw in the werewolf what Lorna must see in him. A great, concerned pup, happy to see his friend.

"Your tail is wagging." Brann grinned.

Wolf blinked. "What?"

Laughing, Brann wrapped his head around Wolf's neck, tugging the great animal in for a hug, collapsing his full weight onto the lycan. "That was so unbelievably scary," he sobbed between giggles. "You should have seen that thing, I nearly died so many times!"

Wolf was stiff, but allowed the affection, his great muscular arms reluctantly wrapping around Brann. His embrace was warm, his fur smelling like a musty, sweaty old towel, one that had been used to dry a dog after a bath. "I'm—glad you made it," he said, still wagging his tail in obvious glee, despite his stern face and surprised tone. "What did you see down there?"

Brann released the great canine, looking to his arm. "Shit, it really got me, huh?" He swiped away some of the oozing blood, showing off the clawmarks. "Not positive, but I think I might have found one of those...exdead."

"A zombie...?" Wolf's fur stood on end. "Were you...infected?"

"No, this wasn't like those others back in the graveyard," Brann said, shaking his head. "I'm fine. This was something...else. It had a..." He waved his hand, searching for the right word Wolf would understand. "...An intelligence? A purpose? It didn't just attack me, it stalked me, it..." He steadied himself. "It was...playing with me. Testing me."

"For weakness," Wolf clarified.

Brann nodded. "Chased me out of the mountain, could have killed me anytime, but...it let me go." He held his arm aloft. "With this."

Wolf stood up on his hind legs, a head taller than Brann even when he was hunched low, looking over the young corpsman with renewed curiosity. "I have seen you say and do a great many things that I do not like," he finally said after a pregnant pause.

"Oh, okay, thanks?" Brann frowned.

"However," Wolf continued, circling Brann, "No more confident have I been than I am now that you conceal yourself beneath yourself." His heavy paws fell softly against the dirt, examining his companion all over.

"There is a man of worth waiting for you to call on him, and wield his blade." Wolf emphasized this line by tapping a claw on Brann's sword hilt. "I should like to meet his man someday."

Brann wiped his forehead. "Wolf, I'm sorry, I'm still not used to hearing you talk like this, you sound like Emrys right now," he said. "No offense, but for all the people I've met lately who like to stare all amazed at me like 'wow, what an important person you'll make someday, wait and see,' I gotta be honest, I'm really not convinced. Feels like you might just be trying to make me feel better about running away from everything like a little kid all the time."

Wolf stopped in front of Brann one more, his familiar stern gaze returning, but no more did Brann feel apprehension beneath those golden beams—rather, he felt the appraisal of a father consoling his son, or as close to it as Brann felt he could imagine. "The creature in the mountain let you go; you said it yourself. I can smell on you the stink of the profaned grave. Something wicked pursued you, and you denied it its prey."

A wide paw lifted Brann's arm, the wounds still fresh. "The mouse that escapes the hawk does not go free, not entirely. Snagged by the talons, even when it wriggles free, it is forever marked. Forever changed." Wolf released Brann's arm. "You, young friend, have escaped many hawks, not all of them so willing to go without a meal. A boy evading a kuaneach such as Tark does not do so out of simple cowardice. What people see in you—what I see—I may not yet know, other than to know it is more than what I see."

Brann took a breath, feeling the last of his shakes leave him. "Wolf, buddy," he said, clapping a hand on the broad, furry shoulder before him. "I don't have a clue what you are on about. I just want to get back on the ship and get out of here."

Wolf grunted, but relented, turning and fixing the spear on his back. "I suppose I should leave the metaphors to the smarter humans," he said, though it sounded more sincere than bitter. "I am not sure I will fully grasp the strange way you all speak of each other."

He trotted off, towards Jan-Jito, and Brann hesitated before following.

"A bird," he called out after the wolf.

Wolf paused, and turned back, his expression puzzled.

"A small bird. Escaping a hawk," Brann elaborated. "Not a mouse."

Wolf shook his head. "I don't see why not—but why would that matter, a mouse or a bird?"

Brann felt the weight of the sword on his back, the strap on his shoulder. His fingers rubbed the leather a bit, seeing the decorative emblem on the sheath in his mind's eye, a small bird spreading its wings. "Just something said to me a while back," he replied. "Didn't really know what they meant until now." He looked to Wolf. "You just reminded me, is all."

The werewolf shrugged in resignation. "If it makes more sense to you that way, then I suppose." He continued on, beckoning Brann to follow him. "We've got more important things to deal with now than birds or mice. Lorna is waiting for us."

Brann took another moment to himself before he started after Wolf. In the trees, the birds continued chirping, preparing to leave their nests for the day.

*

The gate opened to them without resistance—behind the great wooden doors, Bosun Neve awaited, her face a dark omen, no doubt having awaited their return.

"You left your cell," she said simply, standing alone without her usual guards—but her fingers tapped her saber impatiently. "I stood watch all night myself, watching the mine entrance from that gatehouse," she spat, pointing emphatically at the small structure nearby, "Yet here you are. Tell me how you got past me, and I may let your executions be carried out at the Queen's discretion, not my own."

Wolf's response would surely be overly aggressive, so Brann took point, stepping between them to attempt to talk down the Bosun. "First off," he started, cutting off the beginning of Wolf's snarl, "Believe me when I say that it was not our wish to disrespect the hospitality you showed me. I would not have escaped if it weren't of the utmost importance that I do so."

"What could be so important," Neve retorted, "That a night in a comfortable bed, the envy of many a seasick corsair, was too high a price to pay for your own life, short at it will no doubt be?"

Brann stammered, then turned to Wolf for help. "I—we—there's something we have to tell the Queen," he said, watching Wolf's expression carefully, reading it for clues. "Something we can only tell her in person..." Wolf frowned a bit. "...With Lorna—sorry, Lady Lorna present." Wolf nodded curtly, satisfied.

Neve looked between the both of them. "I'm inclined to deny you such an outrageous courtesy, given how little you thought of my earlier kindness," she said hesitantly, "Except I don't have at this moment the inclination to send my mates down into the mines to trace the route you took that led you to freedom, as you surely didn't dig your own way out." She pointed to Brann's arm. "Did the dog try to stop you, at least, in respect to Lorna's orders?"

"This wasn't Wolf," Brann said. "I'll only tell the Queen herself—and you can't afford not to hear it." A nudge from behind. "Lorna too."

Neve didn't correct him this time for forgetting Lorna's proper title—she clearly was distracted, thinking things over. "A late breakfast is being served in the audience chamber," she said. "Lady Lorna declined to attend dinner last night, speaking of a sour stomach. They've not been in each other's company since yesterday's court—if I can plead your case, I will do so, but understand that ultimately my affection for my Lady will not overrule the will of my Queen."

"All we can do is ask," Brann said, clasping his hands together pleadingly. "You said yourself, I'm no real danger, right?"

"Surely not," Neve said, hand on her hip. "In all my days I'd be right fucked to conjure a memory of a prisoner crafty enough to escape our mines yet stupid enough to turn right back around and surrender himself within hours of tasting free air."

Brann deflated a bit, but spread his arms. "Then hopefully you take that into consideration when making our case...?"

Neve scoffed, but nonetheless jerked her head. "Follow. I make no promises, save that this will not end well for you no matter what you have to say."

Brann gave Wolf a thumbs up, getting only a dismissive snort in reply. Clearly, he wasn't a fan of following anyone's lead.

Neve led them on a straight path at a purposeful pace, largely retracing their steps from yesterday, where they'd come to court after stepping off the ship. Instead of following the path up towards the Pavilion, however, they instead took a branching path off into a grand, carved marble archway, mirrored on both sides by stairs leading up into the tower.

"Audience chamber this way, thataways to the royal garden," Neve said, taking them up one flight as she pointed back at the opposite stairs. "A thing of beauty, if you're lucky enough to see it." She paused, remembering her present company. "In your case, I wouldn't hold my breath."

The stairs broke off into a high mezzanine overlooking the city, and across it, an open banquet hall concealed by no doors or windows to appreciate the morning air. This was the audience chamber in question, no doubt, currently populated with the Queen's dining table and chairs—a relatively humble assortment, given the size of the chamber itself. Neve bade Brann and Wolf halt, crossing the mezzanine alone to enter the hall— from a distance, Brann could see everyone seated, and made out the familiar profiles of the Donnie's crew. Her back was turned to them, but Brann recognized Lorna's silvery hair, sans her signature tricorne hat. Neve came to a halt just within the hall, bowing to her left—the Queen must have been seated just out of sight at the head of the table—then stepped forward to lean in and speak to Lorna.

Brann turned, curious. "The exdead wasn't part of the plan," he said.

"You never did tell me why we had to escape in the first place."

Wolf nodded at the hall. "Lorna is going to challenge her mother to single combat today. Your escape was to be the inciting incident that convinced the challenge to be taken seriously."

Brann hoped his expression made Wolf intimately aware of just how he felt every time the lycan had leered at him. "You might have mentioned that before I agreed to an impromptu blood transfusion and a prison break," he said through gritted teeth. "Why exactly does she want to fight the Queen?"

Before he had his answer, Neve had returned, heels clicked together. "You will attend breakfast," she declared, "Then, if your message is not of the most critical of importance, the Queen has decreed your blood and marrow to be used as fertilizer in her garden."

Brann began slapping Wolf's arm furiously. Wolf ignored this, nodding in acknowledgement.

The Bosun held out her hand, and Brann's first instinct was to reach out and shake it, but was interrupted by Wolf handing over his spear—feeling foolish, Brann followed suit, unequipping his own sword and giving it to Neve, who carried both weapons away to a nearby rack on the mezzanine, just outside the chamber. Stepping into the makeshift banquet hall was discomfiting to say the least: nobody spoke, the only sound being the subdued clinking of silverware. There was a moment where, spotting Brann, Boomer looked up from his plate and seemed about to call out in delight around a mouthful of food, but was halted by a sharp elbow in the ribs from Nes; the older man tilted his head slightly, motioning Brann to look to the end of the table, where the Queen sat with stone-carved imperiousness, not looking up from her plate.

"You'll pardon my hesitance to consider you 'esteemed' guests, though I would be loath to entertain any pettiness the viscountess has invited to breakfast along with you this morning. I'm afraid I just cannot find myself in a balance of good humor without my morning steak, so please: find a seat, join us, provided prior arrangements aren't keeping you."

The Queen stabbed at the empty seat next to her, the only other space being the opposite end of the table. Since Wolf had already chosen this seat for himself, clambering up onto the small chair to balance awkwardly on his hindquarters, Brann knew the space next to Queen Hester to be intended for him. Circling around the table, looking the rest of the assembled party in the face and nodding in turn as they wordlessly greeted him, he took note of how they had all been dressed in their own custom outfits of red leather and white cotton—even recognizing the raven-haired woman sitting beside Hawkshaw to be Grishka in human form, her attention wholly fixated on the bread she tore into with her fingernails that curved like talons.

Feeling more naked than if he had actually torn off all his clothes, Brann smoothed over his sweaty, rumpled blouse, suspecting he may have been the only person in years to be welcomed (albeit reluctantly) into the Queen's presence outside of acceptable Jan-Jito attire in years. The chair beside Hester was deceptively heavy: Brann pulled it out slowly, the legs screeching extraordinarily loud against the marble floor.

Save for the Queen herself, the rest of the table froze in place to stare at him, horrified by the earsplitting noise. Brann bowed his head sheepishly.

"All apologies," he mumbled. "Heavy...heavy chair."

He sat himself down quickly, equally unprepared for just how soft and plush the cushion filling the seat was: the moment he bounced on it, the motion made his entire body discharge an enormous cloud of orange dust, the filth of the mines swirling around him like a great cloud in the morning light.

Queen Hester's knife froze in place, the frightening woman just watching the rusty particles of dirt settle around Brann, staining the otherwise perfectly white satin tablecloth the same color as his unwashed face.

Brann couldn't even blink from the shame. For a moment, he was more frightened than he was facing the corpse back in the mines underground.

His saving grace was the Queen's spiteful mood, however, the angelic monarch simply returning to carving the steak on her plate undeterred. "I am remiss in not delaying our meal this morning to ensure everyone attending had proper time to groom and redress—my mind was elsewhere," she offered, strategically sidestepping apologizing to her intrusive young guest. "Though of course, I can only endure so much self-effacing, given the manner in which my breakfast plans have been commandeered by a certain young, saltless lamb."

"Pen yourself all the droll letters of assurance you'd like, mother, all here blessed with the barest of educations can read my name as the intended addressee," came the quick reply from Lorna, who likewise never allowed her gaze to break blue, simply looking into space as she forked a boiler onion delicately from her charcuterie board. "Unbefitting of a queen to retreat behind such defanged behavior when her dignity is at stake."

"The guilty offer their smugness in substitute for the barest of courtesies and civility when their own defense has been loaded with dampened gunpowder." Hester didn't skip a beat, already mid-response before Lorna had finished her sentence—they had all the rapid-fire disdain for one another as a mother and daughter should.

"Admitting your intent of offense by circling on a public map your enemy's defense," Lorna sent back flatly. "You'd make an appalling spy, my Queen."

"I am reminded suddenly of the shame I felt the day your telegram arrived with your final exam results from the academy," Hester parried, "Namely the shriveled digits that comprised your navigational mapmaking score—what was the word your instructor used in her notes? 'Haunting,' I believe."

"A loving tribute to my dearest mum, given my fondest memories of the way she would glide through my studies like the ghoulish widow in the moors, her spirit stalking wayward travelers—that trailing white gown makes for a chilling sight to a sleep-starved dibbun."

Queen Hester's fork screeched on the plate—Brann watched as her steak was becoming shredded, so intent to cut the meat into pieces she had forgotten to actually eat any of them.

"No doubt," was all Hester could muster, visibly irked by the comments shifting to target her physical appearance.

Lorna just sipped at her juice cutely. Brann's eyes wandered down the table to look at everyone else in turn—for the most part, everyone seemed to be keeping their head low, trying not to get caught in the crossfire. He did a double take after seeing Hawkshaw, though: the automaton was apparently amused to no end, and was entertaining himself by silently miming the act of cutting into food and taking comically big bites of it as he watched the show, his plate entirely clean. Catching Brann looking at him, he waggled his metal eyebrow plates and grinned, then went back to eating his imaginary meal with renewed enthusiasm.

"Soldat," Hester suddenly snapped, bringing Brann's attention back to her in the quick. "You had a message for me, I believe? We're all present now—ordinarily I would have denied your request for an audience outright and bled you from the bannisters for such presumptions. However, while I have little taste for these bickerings, the Lady Lamb has bemoaned to exhaustion how critical it is that I set aside our squabble to hear you out." Her eyes flicked up and down the young man briefly. "Go on, then. Step to it, while I remain your captive audience."

Brann looked to Lorna, then to Wolf, both of them nodding encouragingly. He cleared his throat lightly, an immediate error.

"Do not take the liberty of wasting my time with coughing and hand-wringing when you could have instead delivered your words promptly," Hestor barked, her eyes glowing icy green. "Find your tongue or my blade will find it for you."

Brann winced, beginning to feel sweat on his neck again. "All apologies, Marm," he said, doing his level best not to emit any more errant vocalizations. He inhaled deeply, then let loose his words in the span of his following exhale as clearly as he could in as little time as possible.

"There's an exdead presence in your mines and it almost killed me, and there's nothing stopping it from coming up to the surface and into the city." He bowed respectfully, the message delivered, and immediately set to stuffing his face to avoid being asked anything further.

Hester's eye twitched, the Queen studying Brann for a moment before looking down the table. "I've been away from my library a spell too long, I fear," she said. "Make sense of this word for me—'exdead,' the prisoner says."

"Oh, allow me, your grace," piped up Emrys, who stood halfway out of his seat and bowed. "I am merely a stray traveler lucky enough to have been gifted a temporary stay among present company, but despite only a brief time spent with these wonderful souls, I do believe my—if you don't mind my saying—substantial expertise is of particular value to you in this matter."

The Queen tapped a finger against the table, but nodded curtly. "Thank you for your candor, you may speak."

"No, thank you, Queen Mother," Emrys replied humbly, bowing even lower, before pushing out his chair and beginning to pace around the table as he began his monologue. "I am a scholar of the matters of all things unholy and aethereal, and I have specialized in the study and removal of all unclean beings that walk alongside, but not within the boundaries of, the natural cycle of life and death—"

"Here we go," Zay muttered quietly to herself, tossing down her napkin.

Emrys frowned slightly, but continued anyway. "Scores of cadavers beneath my instruments have given very clearly defined separation in the taxonomies of these unnatural beings, and while I'd discriminate between none of them when it comes to the removal of their corporeal bodies from our world, one genus of fiend in particular is the clearest threat to the living day." His hands waved through the air demonstratively, as they always did when he was allowed to sermonize on his favorite subject. "Now, young Brann here, would you kindly show us your arm?"

Brann pulled back his sleeve a bit to better accentuate his wound, raising it for the Queen to see clearly. She was not impressed.

"A poorly manicured vagrant could pose as much a threat," Hester said dismissively.

"Yes, of course it is not so much the physical wound my companion has sustained that is of concern—given his training in field dressings, no doubt he could patch himself up in a cinch, were his medical kit restored to him," Emrys conceded. "No, Queen, it is less of the physical nature of this threat that should worry you, but rather the purposefulness of it." He had nearly circled the entire table now. "You see, biological and anatomical profiling aside, there is a characteristic of defining significance that gives a being cause to have itself classified as 'exdead', as we necromancers have come to define the term. In layman's terms, the simplest of identifiers is...a manifestation of evil, or rather, a quasi-living vessel in which spiritual decay may more directly and drastically influence the world of the truly living." He stopped just beside the Queen, who was listening intently.

"They are creatures of unknowable malevolence, your Grace," he said, bowing once more to speak more directly to her than to the room. "A cancer to life itself, indestructible in all but the most literal of meanings...and they are woefully intelligent enough to infect and consume a chosen populace well before countermeasures may be plotted to repel them."

"We have encountered one already, er, your Majesty," Hawkshaw joined in, taking the opportunity now that Hester was thoroughly engrossed in Emrys's words to allow an open forum. "I barely pulled our ship out of its warpath, and respectfully, I have reflexes far beyond the limitations of your average living pilot. Thing was as big as a building, and had assimilated an entire village of poor sods—no offense, Brann," he finished, nodding respectfully.

Hester turned to Brann again. "You had cause to be of interest to this beast, then?"

"I did," Brann replied, forgetting to add any formal recognition of the Queen's title. She didn't notice. "The village was in the Lachlan territory—the people there who had been executed," he said, glancing at Zay, "They couldn't truly pass on. There was an exdead infection under the dam, and when the place was flooded to destroy any evidence of the massacre, they were just..." He struggled. "Made a part of it. Grew it into a giant walking mutant corpse."

"You were intended to be added to this...abhorrent assemblage, then," Hester concluded.

"Yes, Marm."

The Queen tilted her head inquisitively. "Why would the creature in the mines beneath my city not do the same? It clearly came close enough to leave its mark," she asked Emrys.

"It didn't want him," Lorna interrupted, staring at her mother directly now, forgetting her snide tone. "The Beast of Lachlan wanted the last survivor of Lachlan—the creature beneath our mountain is, by all accounts, a former citizen of Jan-Jito. Maybe even a corsair of repute," she added, urging the Queen closer to recognition. "Someone we knew. Someone who served you, sailed with you, even."

"If indeed, as your daughter and our friend the viscountess says, this is a creature that has taken hold of a host that lived a natural born life here in your great House," Emrys resumed, "Then much as the Beast of Lachlan hungered for the living spirit of your young prisoner here..."

"So too would the infection in our tunnels seek to expand its domain and pull my people into its deathly embrace," Hester finished, her expression softening a bit as she came to terms with this reality.

"I implore you, Queen Mother," Emrys whispered, displaying genuine concern. "Grant our young soldat his freedom, allow him to pass through your city intact, and we will draw the approaching Marshal away— while you evacuate Jan-Jito territories until such time as we can return to lend our aid in suppressing this inevitable doom."

"Mother," Lorna said, her voice growing pleading, standing now to approach the Queen's side as well. "I have my grief, I have my grudges, and I do not see a future between us that can exist while they remain unresolved. Believe me when I say, truly, that none of that matters as much as your safety and the safety of all our people. When we—when I came here—it was to confront you, once and for all," she said, motioning around the table, "But travelling with these friends I've made, the path we took to get here, we have seen more than enough reason to believe there may be a greater threat to not just our House—but to all Houses." Lorna shook her head. "There is no quibbling match between us warrants turning a blind eye to what could become a true danger to all civilization."

"These things, these exdead, encountering one in a decade would be considered poor luck by even the strictest of scholars of the unholy," Emrys added. "We, within less than a single calendar month, have made physical contact with two, mere days apart from one another as our ship flies. There is coincidence, and there is providence, and I believe truly that we should begin to assess this as the beginning of a widespread threat, if only until the elimination of evidence to such a conclusion."

"I know I'm not in a position to say this," spoke Brann, much to everyone's surprise. "I have less pull to make decisions here than anyone— and I know sooner or later Tark is gonna have his day with me. But until then, if it's possible," he said while leaning in close, "I think I can say all of us here who have been travelling on Boomer's ship don't really have a compass pulling us any which way—and if we're the only ones who know about this possible outbreak of exdead, and we only discovered it by accident, then maybe..." He paused, but decided to risk it anyway. "Maybe we're in a position, being that we're public fugitives right now, we could help shine a light on it, even convince the Marshal to call off his pursuit and help us—help you—stamp out these exdead things. If the whole world is watching the holonet right now to see where we pop up next, maybe we pop up somewhere else where people are in danger, another House capitol city. Make it public that there's something bigger to worry about than a few supposed terrorists flying around the countryside."

Lorna looked almost as if she was going to dispute this, but instead seemed to find the sense in what Brann was saying. "We have the resources and the warfighting prowess, mother. We could send the corsairs abroad, help search out more of these evil things and where they're hiding in the world, try to contain them. The next Lachlan may not be such a small, remote territory," she reasoned, "It may be somewhere bigger, a much higher population count. If another horror as big as the Beast of Lachlan were to wreak havoc somewhere else, the death toll could be...unforgivable."

Hester looked up, eyes narrowed. "Unforgivable?"

Lorna nodded—she may yet have broken through to her mother. "If we could have acted, and chosen not to. It may be a tenuous peace at best, but the Houses have not fought in a great war for a century: there's any reason that suspicions may turn against each other, and if it's discovered that either Jan-Jito or Geiha knew of this threat—and didn't act, leading to the death of innocents—they may seek cause to spark another never-ending war, one none may survive as long as the exdead remain to grow in strength as they plunder the battlefields we leave behind."

The Queen seemed to be examining Lorna's face, and Brann hoped she had been sufficiently convinced—if not about the exdead threat, then convinced enough to allow him to go free. She opened her mouth to speak, and Brann's heart leapt, then—

"You came here to confront me?" Hester repeated.

Lorna blinked. "That was..." She frowned. "Before we knew your city, my city, was in danger, yes. I wanted to face you, try to convince you one last time to see how you were becoming blinded by your faith in these ancient practices. Convince you to let me come home...so we could be a family again." Her eyes glistened wetly.

"I see." Queen Hester seemed to forget everyone around her, standing to her feet. "In that case, I accept your challenge, daughter."

Everyone recoiled, none moreso than Lorna herself. "What are you talking about, Mother?" She was utterly baffled. "Did not we speak plainly about something far more treacherous darkening your door as we speak?"

"A well-crafted, well-educated, and thoughtfully worded attempt to parlay for mercy, but an obvious distraction all the same." Hester nodded to Bosun Neve, who crossed the chamber to bow, ready to accompany the Queen out. "We will not deny the Marshal his prize, and by his example I will so address the crimes you have committed against this House and against your family, which you suddenly speak of with a great deal of piety. Would that you have shown my teachings and the teachings of the Dhampir that came before you such respect, we may have avoided this unfortunate day."

"Ah, 'dhampir,' this is a term I am admittedly less familiar with in my travels," Emrys interjected with abysmal timing, "Though if the looser classification of such an organism may be re-evaluated, perhaps it may make a great case for the absence of aberrant behavior in the people of Jan-Jito as would be prominent were they afflicted as the more traditional Vampyr—"

"All this time, after all we've said, you weren't listening to a word of it?" Lorna cut off Emrys, her lip quivering. "You truly don't value a word I say to you anymore?"

Brann caught sight of Boomer—the horse had occupied his habitually loud mouth with a tall glass of juice, taking the slowest, deepest pull from it possible, his eyes darting between Lorna and the Queen in sheer terror.

"Quite the contrary, viscountess," Queen Hester said in rebuttal, already stepping away from the table with Neve at her side, "I have learned a great deal today, and have been blessed with great fortune by your arrival, unpleasantness aside. The Marshal Tark of Geiha will arrive to claim his prisoner, and after I have dealt with you and your treachery, I will scour the texts of the Dhampir libraries to find some rite or tool to turn this 'exdead' you speak of against the once mighty Geihan empire."

Lorna stumbled in place, shocked. "You mean to say war with the other Houses was your intent all along?"

"I never made criticism of your innate ability to grasp politics and social climates," Hester said, pausing for a moment to turn and look back at her daughter. "You were quite right about the Houses seeking cause against each other, and you've given cause to ours. Tark will seek to apprehend this prisoner, the sole survivor and regent heir of the House Lachlan, and under the terms of the treaty signed after the Arbitration Wars, I will declare Tark's actions against the boy a clear and present act of war against the welfare of all shared peace between Houses. Young Brann will be executed, Lachlan will have fallen for good and all, and linking the atrocities you described having taken place in the Lachlan territory will be the pyre upon which we set the ill-bled corpse of the waning House Geiha alight." Hester bowed regally, the hostility all but evaporated from her voice. "My dearest daughter, you have allowed our great House to seize control of the world's prime warfighting nation and its assets, and have done so with such ease and swiftness that we will be able to etch the tenets of our faith on the mantle of every home in every nation within a fortnight."

On her heel she spun, striding out of the chamber quickly and with purpose. "I trained you well," she called back loudly, voice echoing in the stunned silence of the hall. "I may yet allow you to survive our duel this afternoon. You've the hour to prepare."

24. The Bloodletting

The clouds hadn't let up—if anything, they'd grown thicker, descending closer to the coastline as the day went on, blotting out the sun entirely. The royal garden was, to Neve's promise, quite a beauty indeed: the same purple and white flowers growing wildly along the side of the mountain had been cultivated here with the utmost care and attention to their precise placement, forming a vivid display of perfectly symmetrical crescent moon shapes facing one another opposite a stone dais not unlike the one the party had stood on when first meeting the Queen the day prior. A waist-high barrier of carved marble separated the innermost circle from the flowers beyond, and it was behind this barrier the group had been assembled, shoulder to shoulder—flanked on both sides by Neve's corsairs, who encircled the entirety of the garden, forming a seal around the exits with their bodies, all standing at parade rest. A red ring of witnesses, even Brann himself having been given the opportunity to shower and dress in a simple crimson jacket—now, he wasn't the only one out of uniform, much to his relief.

The inner ring was occupied by the two combatants: Lady Lorna, wearing her familiar garb, and the Queen, who had undergone a radical change in her choice of fashion: the white gown was nowhere to be seen, her well-toned body bereft of any ornamental, flowing materials. Her torso was practically shrink-wrapped in a carefully tailored dueling jacket that fit her to the millimeter, the red leather tapering down to a point where the jacket met her beltline, meeting the hem of a much less restrictive pair of loose, almost billowy leggings, the thickly corded cloth pants ending in almost bellbottom style ankles around her slim, pointed corsair boots. Shoulder to toe, Hester was a blood-red model of battle-readiness, save for her single white adornment: a silk scarf, wrapped around her neck in a tight bundle, a pristine band of frosty brightness concealing her bare neck. Her feathered black hair had similarly been somewhat pulled back, brushed along her temples so no errant bangs would obscure her vision. For being so meticulously pampered and regal only an hour ago, every inch of her now invited the challenge of cold steel, even her face completely wiped clean of makeup. There was nothing left to suggest she was anything less than a trained killer, her saber already unsheathed and held low at the ready, the silvery tip pointing directly between Lorna's feet.

"There's no need to stand on ceremony today, Bosun," Hester said loud enough for all in attendance to hear. "No solemn words or grandstanding need be shared. We've had a lifetime to speak our minds."

Bosun Neve, who had stepped forward from behind the marble barrier, bowed courteously. "Aye," she called back to her Queen, returning to her place in the ranks.

Lorna looked out across the garden at her mother from beneath her tricorne hat, the tip tilted downwards to shield her eyes from any distractions overhead, causing the long white feather that adorned it to flag upwards. "First sensible thing you've said since we arrived, mother," she called, assuming her own similar ready stance, though her saber tilted itself up to an angle that her blade may defiantly break the symmetry between the two fighters, an almost impudent gesture on her part. "As you would remind me, bloodlessness is barbarism, my Queen."

The wind swirled around them quietly, the delicate flowers making waves as they bobbed in unison, the garden otherwise silent—none dared speak, lest they invite the fury of the Queen's blade, which seemed sharpened to the point it could cut the stone dais they stood on clean in two.

"Then let this Bloodletting be a monument to civility." Hester made the slightest of adjustments to her stance as she said this, then fell deathly silent, eyes locked in on her familial opponent.

Neither of them moved, the two corsair women silently plotting their strategies, predicting each other's every minor decision in every possible scenario. The seconds ticked by, agonizingly slow, becoming minutes—neither dared be the first to break the stillness, and the world around them seemed itself to slow, the wind quieting until all that remained was the mother and her daughter, eyes locked in a fatal staring match.

Then, at the world's most still, they met.

Their speed would have ripped flesh from bone, had they been of lesser matter, their blades whistling in swift disharmony—scarce did they meet that the crack of steel ice against its mirror made the onlookers blink from the display of blinding sparks. Lorna's saber made a figure eight of moulinets that, despite their ferocity, never came close to meeting their mark: Hester retreated at a leisurely pace on her back foot, yet seemed in absolute control of their conjoined fury, her own spiraling blade moving so quick and so precise that Brann felt a jolt when he realized the Queen was on the offensive, not the other way around. Lorna applied pressure, moving forward, but her wide flourishes and lower stance were indeed to keep herself alive—every flick of Hester's wrist made for a killing thrust at her daughter, and Lorna couldn't afford a single gap in her defense.

They must not have been engaged for more than mere seconds before they were buffeted apart: Lorna twisted her boot, lowering into a crouch and leaning back just enough to let the tip of Hester's saber breach her guard before shoving up at Hester's drill-like motions from below, blowing them apart from the opposing force of their blades. Lorna stumbled backwards to put enough distance between herself and her mother that she could catch her breath: and in that moment, Brann learned never to trust his own eyes again. The viscountess, so composed and unfettered every waking moment Brann had known her, was panting like an animal...and, like a painting peeling in the heat of a fire, a dozen imperceptible cuts in the flesh of her face and neck began running with thin streams of bright red.

Brann hadn't seen Hester's sword touch Lorna even once.

Hester flexed her ankles to bounce slightly in place, bringing her heels together once more to reset her stance, that shining blade speckled with the lightest dusting of red droplets. "Oh, I would not speak now, little girl," Hester said, her own corset heaving as she too clearly felt the exertion, "If that piss-warm show of vain flourishing is how you thought you would humble me." She didn't look amused or pretend to preen herself: Brann saw in Queen Hester the same lack of patience he saw in Tark, the day Recruit

Caleb was put on his ass. Lady Lorna, for all her airs, was meeting this fight with the same disregard to decorum that a young and angry woman would, and her bleeding micro-cuts were the punishment.

Lorna waggled her sword at Hester in nonverbal acknowledgment, then abandoned her ready stance altogether, turning her back to walk in a few circles as if she were recovering after a spring, her lips shining with saliva as she sucked in air. It may not have reflected in her eyes, but there was an uncharacteristic fear in her body language that Brann knew meant she was beginning to realize this was a mistake.

"Red," he hissed quietly, trying to draw her attention as she paced close to where he stood, forgetting her real name for a moment. Lorna's eyes flicked towards Brann for a moment but otherwise she ignored him, occupied in her own thoughts, hands on her hips.

Hester didn't budge from her place in the circle, but did quirk her head, eyebrows wrinkling together. "Has the Lady recalled terms of engagement from her studies that the rest of us overlooked? The Bloodletting affords no pauses, Lorna," she called out, raising her voice. "We've spilt nary a drop to prompt such a withdrawal."

"Spare me, mother," Lorna shouted back in frustration, and wiped her nose as she sniffed: Brann felt in that moment more of a connection to the Lady Red than ever before, knowing exactly what was going through her head.

"Red," he said again louder, insistently.

This time, she locked eyes without looking away. Brann mimed breathing out slowly, signaling her to relax, which was met with an annoyed shove from behind: Wolf did not appreciate him interfering.

Lorna's eyes narrowed, but she exhaled nonetheless, expelling her lungs to slow her breathing, returning to her place across the dais from Hester. She ground the toes of her boots into the stone to embed herself in place once more, resetting her stance: this time, she did not hold the saber at the impudent off-angle she had in the previous bout, but held it at the respectful and proper height, hilt at her waist while she leveled the tip directly forward at the other duelist.

"All apologies, Queen," she said. Then, after a pause, she couldn't help but crack a smirk. "I seem to have forgotten where I was."

Brann chuffed through his nose: she couldn't help it. Lorna was just not going to take this match as seriously as she needed to if she meant to survive. Once more, he thought back to Caleb, and the way he approached the second round with Tark.

The sour feeling in his gut told Brann history was about to repeat itself.

He looked around at the crowd: to his left, Wolf hunched beside Emrys and Boomer, who clearly didn't understand the stakes, given how fired up and excited he seemed to be as he watched the duel. To his right, Nestor and Zay watched with wide-eyed concern, while Hawkshaw once again had his arm looped around Grishka's, the witch still assuming her unshifting human form, though no amount of illusory magic could hide the devious curiosity with which she regarded the world around her.

As the two combatants stood apart once more, sizing each other up, Brann leaned in close to Nes, waving the older man's eyes down at him. Nestor frowned, baffled as to why Brann would dare distract from the proceedings.

"My bag," Brann whispered. Nes just furrowed his brow. He didn't understand.

Brann pointed down the ranks at Grishka, then at himself.

"Tell her," he mouthed, "My bag is on the ship."

A corsair in his line of sight shot Brann a dirty look. She was not pleased that someone would dare speak.

Nestor shrugged, spreading his hands wide pleadingly.

Brann mouthed his words as wide and emphatically as he could.

TELL. GRISHKA. TO GET. MY. MEDIC BAG.

Now he understood—but wasn't exactly convinced, either. Nestor squinted at Brann and shook his head slightly to show he did not like this idea, but nonetheless, turned reluctantly to pass the message down the line, whispering into Zay's ear. Zay likewise gave a disapproving squint, but did the same, leaning across to mutter the message to Hawkshaw and Grishka together.

"Again," Hester called out, and all eyes snapped back to her. The circle of bystanders once again fell silent.

Save for one: the moment of peace was broken by the loud flapping of wings, startling several in the crowd, and a black missile shot up into the sky above as Grishka took flight, the shapeshifted raven releasing a burst of black feathers above the heads of the crowd.

The feathers drifted and spun about as they descended like an ominous snowfall to earth, and the moment the first dark mote of plumage touched the stone dais, the Bloodletting recommenced.

And the ceremony lived up to its name in spades.

*

Lorna's red coat was a blur as she streaked towards Hester—the Queen, however, did not wait for the gap to be closed this time, a clockwise spin of her saber matching her sidestep as she lunged forward to Lorna's immediate right, the momentum of her flourish carrying her sideways sharply into a full body slam against Lorna, only the last-minute defensive upswing saving the viscountess from a vertical blade in her sternum. Reeling from the bodily collision, Lorna quickly leapt back in to deny putting herself back on defense, instead carrying through with a sidestepping thrust of her own, locking the both of them into a spin. Circling each other with their heels scraping the stone loudly, Hester and Lorna met their sabers time after time, far slower but with far more power behind their swing than the inhumanly fast fencing of round one. Their movements mirrored each other with almost preternatural synchrony: a low swing met with a low swing, a high stroke met with a high stroke, always meeting in the middle like a choreographed dance.

Brann would have forgotten this were a duel to the death, were it not for the free-flowing stream of blood streaking down Lorna's jawline, the way this second round of engagement seemed so much more restrained and almost rehearsed. The illusion would not hold long, though, with one of the fighters far more intent in causing pain than the other: like an alligator reversing its deathroll, Hester awaited a moment where both sabers went wide in their arcs before kicking back on her heel and spinning the opposite direction, Lorna's blade swinging through the air where Hester's would have clashed with it. Hester's leg spiked upwards in a fierce high kick, her heel stabbing downwards into Lorna's exposed elbow, causing her daughter to cry out in shock as her saber wobbled out of control from the blow—

Brann winced, seeing Hester whipping up her sword arm from a low angle, knowing what was coming next—

—Except Lorna, knowing she wouldn't have time to regain her grip and block the attack, anticipated this already, and with a deft twirl her flintlock cartwheeled up from her belt and caught Hester's blade inches from her shoulder, the pistol grip hooking it to shove the saber away before riposting with a powerful crack against Hester's jawline. The Queen gasped and jerked to one side, and in that instant, Lorna recovered the grip on her saber just fast enough to shove the blade forward like a woodcutter and saw a deep gash directly under Hester's arm.

The crowd winced audibly, and unlike the dainty, stinging cuts Hester had left on Lorna's face, this wound was singular and brutal: whipping her sword arm back, Lorna sliced even deeper on the backstroke, and a whip of ruby wet launched from the arc of her saber and splattered loudly behind her, painting a bloody streak across the stone dais.

This time, Hester recoiled, her black hair plastered against the sweat of her face, hiding the shock in her eyes from the crowd. She hugged her arm close against the wound, elbow to hip, the darker red of her own body's drippings running down the glistening red leather corset.

Brann wanted to shout out, to warn Lorna not to act rashly, this being the exact moment she was liable to let her guard down—there was no willing her way through this fight—but he wouldn't have been fast enough even if he tried. A reverse twirl of her blade and, with a gesture even the young recruit could see coming, Lorna stabbed forward directly at Hester's midriff with the decisiveness of someone who had already won this fight.

Not even close.

The askew angle that Hester's saber had fallen wasn't from injury, it was for leverage—like a viper snapping up a mouse that stepped too close, Lorna's thrust was sideswiped away in a vicious parry, and without even having to move her whole arm to swing, Hester's wrist snapped to and fro rapidly, the saber swiping in an X shape before her face, and suddenly Lorna disengaged. There was a pregnant moment of anticipation before Lorna faltered, almost falling to her knees—and there, between the collar of her jacket, the white fabric of her blouse became soaked in the surge of blood that seeped from the cross-cutting slashes just beneath her throat.

The two duelists stepped back now, in mutual regard to each other's nearly fatal wounds, Hester still hugging her arm to her breast as blood washed down her side, watching as Lorna clutched at her collar to confirm that her throat hadn't just been cut wide open—though, mere inches higher, and it surely would have, every patch of white cotton and silk being blotted out in growing blossoms of dark blood.

Around them, the stone ground was growing darker itself in streaks of spattered scarlet, a chaotic scatter of flower petals, black raven feathers, and bloody paint.

Both Lorna and Hester were injured, but far from finished, and far from settling their grievances: Brann could see it in Hester, the Queen had no quarter to give; he could see it in Lorna, she had no satisfaction with only the one wound left in her mother, no matter how deep it may cut.

"It's been too long since the sea," Lorna giggled quietly, donning the mask of an irksome child doing her best to annoy her parent. "You can't practice only against your own subjects—they all had the same training as you, you old cow!"

Hester spat in a decidedly unqueenly manner, a lance of bloody saliva slapping against the ground, her lip curling to wipe up the red dribbling down her chin. "What churlish tediums you love subjecting me to," she sneered. "You taunt when you should attack, you twirl when you should stab—I'd have married a wild boar if I had known the union would have borne me less of a slobbish pig for a daughter—"

The earsplitting crack of the gun cut Hester's words short, and the garden echoed the report far and wide, an explosion of purple and white swirling up in a hurricane of color. Queen Hester's eyes were wide as she stood straight, having snapped her head back and to the side: a gruesome channel was carved into her cheek where the bullet had ripped open her face before cratering the flowerbed behind her like a cannonball had struck the earth—and, looking on in his shock, Brann thought for a moment the garden itself was bleeding, the impact site as bloody as any gunshot wound in a human.

It was not the earth that bled, however, but rather the one who had fired the shot: whether out of strategy, or falling for the Queen's taunt, or simply having run out of patience for the fight, Lorna's flintlock pistol was raised to aim directly at Hester's face. The hidden needle of the siphon mechanism had plunged itself into her wrist, which dripped profusely, the elegant pistol already having been wrapped in the gleaming crimson artifice of Lorna's blood summoning magic. Nearly as long as a full musket, the extended blood barrel of the flintlock stretched out like the judging finger of a demon, hot steam from the heat of Lorna's veins rising from it in the cool air to mix with the blue of the gunsmoke.

"Point taken, mother." Lorna's face was impassive, emotionless, and completely coated in smeared sanguine.

Hester's lip quivered, her hand curled around the split cheek, the pale flesh of her wrist becoming dotted with blood that dripped from between the clenched fingers of her glove. "You would break terms of engagement to shame me, child? You doom yourself to die, use of anything but a blade or club in a Bloodletting duel is—"

"—Completely and utterly subject to the agreement of the participants," Lorna interrupted, wagging her pistol in disappointment. "And you, dear Queen, in your haste to make a dramatic exit from this morning's repast did not settle terms with me before our duel begun."

Lorna canted the pistol to the side, a tendril of gleaming blood magically cocking the hammer forward to disengage. She lowered the weapon, but only slightly, so she could lean in and ask: "Do you agree now to set such terms as to allow the use of not only gunpowder, but our own blood itself, as suitable weapons?

"The alternative being, of course," she said, thinking out loud to herself sarcastically, "That you decline and I am summarily disemboweled on the spot for having breached such terms, having only decided them after I committed the offense in question."

Brann watched Hester carefully: the Queen knew Lorna was right, but was loathe to speak it aloud, her glacier blue eyes radiating fury. No question in her mind: Lorna had planned this all along, and her own emotions were being used as bait to tempt a rash decision.

"No," Hester finally said after a long moment, tonguing at her wounded cheek from within. "I agree. They will be permitted. Carrying out an execution on a technicality in the middle of a duel? I am not the cowardly tyrant you would have me known as, my dear."

"I'm glad to hear that, Marm," Lorna replied sweetly, cocking the hammer of her pistol back and once more turning away, striding back with her head high to her starting position in the circle. "I'd hate to die to prove myself right—I'd never get to enjoy your shameful tears as you eulogized me."

*

The minutes had ticked by as Queen Hester and Lady Lorna reset, both now looking a proper mess: bloodied and tired, streaked from battle's claws, they readied for a final round of conflict. Not even a participant, Brann was exhausted from watching them go at it, and had foregone his hope that they may find a diplomatic excuse to cut the duel short the moment the gunshot had rang out in the sky. He had watched both their moves carefully, the decisions they made in the quick, which were driven by the logical fighter seeking victory and which were made by an emotional reaction...and, with defeat, Brann admitted to himself that the latter was skewing the majority of Lorna's performance in the fight, with Hester only allowing her personal feelings to be voiced in the spaces between their flurry of blades. In a straight one on one, it was no question that the Queen was the superior swordfighter and had greater tactical command of the field.

On the other hand, Lorna's entire strategy seemed to be rooted in the same dismissiveness of a headstrong teenager, and yet she still lived. Brann saw her once-gleaming white gloves rub tenderly at the crossed gashes in her neck, Lorna's entire front soaked red, her outfit ruined. If she was acting so rashly, fighting with such disregard for appearance of skill, why was she still alive?

He hoped his hunch would come through as correct, and Brann kept looking back nervously at the sky, in the direction of the beach. Grishka was taking a long time to return with his medical kit, and this third round would surely be the decisive one.

Brann tapped his fingers nervously against the marble, willing Lorna to come closer once more. She held her head low, not looking up from the ground, the blood-infused pistol still in her hand despite having sheathed her saber temporarily: she was once more lost in thought deciding a strategy, and her posture betrayed her feelings that such a decision wouldn't matter in the end.

He whistled, quietly—Brann wasn't very good at it. Didn't work, Lorna kept pacing, head down. Brann tried again, louder, tilting his tongue to give it a little melody.

Her head snapped up, and now Lorna looked as perturbed as the corsair had when Brann had started passing notes earlier. She clearly did not feel there was anything to be shared between them at this moment.

Brann felt otherwise. He didn't say anything, but rather mimed a very specific set of motions. Lorna watched his hands, attempting to decipher—then, she stopped in her tracks. She didn't quite get the message, and she raised her eyebrows at Brann in disbelief.

Come again? She was asking.

Brann repeated the motions. This time, though, he mouthed along his meaning as he repeated them.

Palms face-up to submit. *LET.*

Pointing now at the Queen. *HER.*

A downward stabbing motion. *KILL.*

Finally, pointing at Lorna emphatically. *YOU.*

There may have been an ocean of personal differences between them, but Lorna must have seen the affinity Brann felt for her now, because his meaning registered in moments. Her eyes went round in recognition, and she nodded ever so slightly, the solution clicking into place. There was a small, warm spark in Brann's belly when Lorna returned his suggestion with the thankful smirk of someone who had underestimated him, and her face became serene, accepting of her fate. Knowing how this duel would end, her next moves were clear, and Lorna spun in place with renewed confidence.

"I've decided I can no longer show you to reason, mother," Lorna sang, alight with an almost gleeful energy, despite her gore-drenched appearance. "Seems you were right all along, in part, and there is simply no way to bridge this divide." Her saber once more slipped from its sheath, and Lorna assumed her stance a final time.

"I'm sorry mum, but you have to die."

Brann felt a slap against his shoulder—Zay had reached across to scold him incredulously, nearly knocking Nestor over in the process. "Did you just tell her to let herself get fuckin' killed?!" She rasped as loudly as she could without the entire assembly hearing her.

Brann's shoulder stung but he held up a hand placatingly, nodding back at Lorna. *JUST WATCH.*

Zay was not convinced, but stood back nonetheless, her old, familiar contempt for Brann threatening to shine through for a moment before losing out to her willingness to give him a chance, turning eyes back to watch the duel's conclusion.

Two sabers, speckled red, shining against the dark stone—Lorna held her pistol aloft and at the ready. Hester, hand outstretched, accepted her own polished flintlock from the offered case brought before her, Bosun Neve bowing slightly as she once again departed the circle. Hester eyed her own firearm with fondness, tracing her thumb over the pearl grips that were bolted into the polished butt.

"There's often times," she said to herself, but loud enough all could hear, "I feel a sense of regret that I did not intervene more directly. Take a harder line with you, all those years ago, anytime you strayed or spoke your dissenting mind." Hester clenched the grip, and the mechanism activated, the needle driving itself from the curved handle and into her wrist—she didn't even flinch, and the pearly etchings along the gun's length were filled with the pumping of her heart, red runes humming with ancient cursed energy before the barrel shot out like a switchblade. Nearly twice its length, the lip of the pistol's summoned muzzle wept bloody tears in lieu of Hester's own, the Queen's face darkening as she once more looked back at Lorna.

"My mistake was believing there was anything I could do to fix you." She lowered the point of her saber, pistol held aloft behind her turned head in an identical match to Lorna's stance. "You were never mine to lose—you were simply a test of my faith. I am sorry I could not have seen this sooner, my lamb, and spared us both this life of sorrow."

The two corsairs were locked in at last, and for the last time, the air went silent, save for the sizzle of their enchanted weapons dripping hot animus against the cold stone dais. Brann's fingernails dug into his palms as he clenched his fists, praying to an unseen deity that he was right, knowing he'd never forgive himself if Lorna were to lose.

Like mother, like daughter: their first moves were synchronized down to their very heartbeats. Both women twisted sharply at the hip and arched their backs to the side, pistols leaping forward and bursting in misty red clouds of bloodfire—their bullets, slick and wet and casting spirals of arterial magma, passing each other like ships in the night, seared the air and missed both targets by the breadth of a hair. Opening salvo met with its twin, Lorna had already clenched down to pump the needle in her wrist to reload when she sprinted forward: Hester held her ground to read another shot, but the only way to survive was to get in close...and Lorna had every intent on survival.

The second shot barely missed, popping open the seam of her shoulder on Lorna's leather jacket, the dark red vapors of her new wound splattering her silvery blonde hair. She clenched her other hand—holding her saber—and a second needle introduced itself to her bloodstream. All the speed her legs could afford brought her across the stone dais just before a third shot could be fired, and in the broadest, most distracting twirl she could manage, Lorna's saber carved a trio of shining ruby crescent moons in the air, streaking skyward in a dazzling display of her own gushing lifeblood.

The flashy maneuver worked, and Hester pirouetted out of the way to avoid them, the fluid projectiles indiscernible from the blood-wreathed saber itself that Lorna struck out with. Hester came full circle, face to face with Lorna, who had leveled her flintlock once more between her mother's eyes.

Tragically, the speed of Lorna's blade could not be matched by the speed of her trigger finger. It was over in a flash. Hester's raised pistol smashed downward, knocking Lorna's barrel off to the side just as it fired, and the bullet scarce had left the length of that long muzzle before Hester's saber spun like a sawblade before stabbing forward triumphantly.

Directly into Lorna's breast.

Another concussive blast blanketed both women in a menagerie of bloodied flower petals, a snowstorm of finality obscuring them briefly from view, before the unfortunate truth was once more laid bare for all the audience to see: Hester, elbow straightened, her saber's completely scarlet blade protruding from between Lorna's shoulder blades, her daughter on her knees before the Queen.

Even Brann, knowing what would happen, couldn't help but avert his eyes from the gut-wrenching sight. He stepped to one side, throwing his arms around Wolf before the beastman could leap to Lorna's aid, barely even encircling the werewolf's waist—the rest of the party joined in to help as best they could, their own cries of shock masked beneath the low, guttural howl of anguish that ripped through Wolf's chest. There was no hope in holding him back physically: only his own, dimly aware connection to Brann's words as the young soldat whispered in his ear kept him from ripping the Queen apart.

Lorna reached up, weakly grasping her mother's wrist, holding it in place—Hester had tried to release the saber, her face suddenly aghast with horror, only now finally realizing the unspeakable thing she'd done.

"Lorna, wait, Lorna," Hester was chanting in a rising panic, "Wait, wait, wait. Stop, wait, wait, stop this, go back, I didn't—this wasn't what—"

Lorna said something, but no one understood, the sound a wet gurgle. She smiled, gulping visibly, rivers of blood rushing from the corners of her mouth.

Hester fell to one knee, still holding the saber at Lorna's insistence, the queen abandoning all pretense of stern decorum as she dragged herself forward on the ground to embrace her child. "Lorna, my girl, my lamb, my baby, wait, I'm sorry, I'm sorry, I'm sorry, wait—"

The beating of wings and an urgent caw overhead, and Brann released Wolf, turning his eyes skyward just in time to see Grishka shooting past and loosing the medical kit from her talons and into Brann's waiting arms. The young corpsman acted with all the trained confidence he'd retained from his time in basic, vaulting over the marble wall and crossing the stone dais with unstoppable purpose, even the watching guards staying their hands as they watched in shock as their Queen cradled her dying daughter.

"I can help, Queen, let me look—"

Brann didn't even get a complete sentence out before the bleeding barrel of Hester's pistol was raised to his lips, her lips clenching so tight they turned white as she glared at him with wide-eyed outrage, daring him to get between her and her offspring.

Swallowing and lowering himself to her height, Brann raised his medical kit, kneeling beside Lorna as he pointed to the pack. "I can stabilize her, but only if we act quick—please, let me do this for her. For you."

Hester's tempestuous eyes could have lanced hot bolts of lightning through his body. Instead, she slowly, unblinkingly, shuffled backwards, not lowering her pistol an inch.

"Save her."

Brann needed no further encouragement. Swinging himself around to Lorna's side, he unfastened the pack of supplies and fished out a packet of congealing silica, as well as two tinctures of anesthetic.

"Now I'm gonna need your help," he said, abandoning any pretense he was addressing royalty as he spoke to Hester firmly, but with a tone of optimism, speaking over the pained coughs and sobs of the wounded Lady. "As soon as I tell you, with your arm perfectly straight, I need you to pull the sword directly out—not yet!" He reached out to halt Hester's quick hand, the Queen already prepared for the task. "I need one of these in her first, or she might struggle and cause even more internal injuries," Brann cautioned, showing off the small vials of clear liquid. "I'll tell you when, you just stay ready."

Hester whimpered, lip trembling, but nodded, shaking her hand to relax the jittery muscles before taking hold of the saber's hilt once more, keeping her elbow straight as she awaited the signal. Brann scootched in close on his knees, leaning in to speak encouragingly to Lorna, one vial in his teeth as his hand fished out the cutter tool from his pack.

"Hey Red," He soothed, doing his best to smile down at her, "This sucks, I know, but we're gonna fix you girl, I promise, just try to stay calm and let me do my job, we'll get this thing out of you before you know it." He deftly swiped the horseshoe blade through her already shredded blouse, exposing Lorna's bare breasts with an apologetic nod to Hester, who didn't protest—sure enough, the blade had pierced at an askew angle, just left of center, leaving a nasty gash on the underside of her bloodied mammary. Brann studied the site of the wound, calculations running through his head at a rapid pace as he recalled his holobooks, and made a snap decision: rather than injecting the bony breastplate, he steadied the vial just above the wound, where the flesh softened around fatty tissue.

"Miss—I mean—Queen Hester, I need to ask your permission before I proceed," Brann urged, pointing out his intent. "I need to inject this are with the numbing fluid, and help it along by rubbing it in, which will mean I need to put my hands on her breast. All apologies, but this is how we save her life—"

"I beg your PARDON—"

Before she could finish, Lorna's hand shot up to snatch her mother's sleeve, twisting it tightly. "Stop," she gurgled, coughing up another bubble of blood, before looking up into Brann's face and nodding—it was her decision, not Hester's.

"Alright, get ready to pull that sword out, Marm," Brann warned, jabbing the vial in and immediately discarding it: with professional care, Brann kneaded the lower breast in a downward, sloping motion, urging the fluid into Lorna's veins and warming the site to open up her circulation. The moment he saw white droplets mixing with the oozing blood around the wound, he knew it was ready, and Brann used his lips to rip away the paper seal of the silica crystals.

"Ready?" He eyeballed the stab wound, laser focused on what he expected to see once the steel was removed, his vision completely tunneled in on saving Lorna.

"Pull, now!" Brann barked.

The pained wail that followed was not from Lorna, but from Hester, who yanked the saber back smoothly and swiftly—the outer tissue may have been numbed, but there was nothing Brann could do internally, and the feeling of a meter's length of freezing cold metal slipping out of her body prompted a horrendous sounding moan of discomfort from Red—the pain was short lived, though, the packet of silica upending directly into her exposed chest cavity the moment Brann saw bone. The geyser of blood was stymied when the crystals solidified into a mass of scabby mana, and Brann already had the second vial at the ready, jamming it directly into the crackling, glassy material.

"There we go, there, we did it, you're through the worst now, girl," Brann said, cradling Lorna's torso and gently lowering her to the ground, meeting no resistance from Hester when he took her daughter from her arms. "Just like you planned it, Red, just like I told you," he laughed nervously.

Lorna, for her part, was no longer gasping for air, a low sigh escaping her throat, her eyes closing tight as she frowned, mumbling something inaudible.

"What was that, honey?" Hester said frantically, leaning in close. "What is it, talk to me."

Lorna swallowed, her throat sticky with blood as she spoke.

"Knew it."

Hester shook her head rapidly, dripping sweat and tears. "Knew what? What—I don't understand—" Her eyes darted to Brann. "What did you say to her? What were you planning?"

Lorna, slowly, shakily, raised a hand to tap against her bare chest, and grinned devilishly, teeth stained with rust.

Brann exhaled, throwing away the spent vial dramatically, the empty tincture bouncing and rolling on the stone with a faint tinkle.

"You just missed her heart, Queen," Brann declared, as if he were addressing her back in court. "Lady Lamb called your bluff, and you spared her—which means you forfeit the duel."

Hester was aghast. Her head snapped back, face contorted in horror, her daughter laughing wickedly back at her through the pain.

Brann wiped his hands together, standing to his feet, Bosun Neve and her guards rushing in now to attend to the royal family. Brann stood aside, watching as they lifted both mother and daughter to their feet—she still required a real doctor, but the fast-acting field medicine had done its job well enough that she could already walk again, albeit only leaning against someone for support. It was only for a moment, and then the two disappeared from view behind a wall of red leather, but for a fleeting second Brann saw Lorna and Hester's hands clasped together tightly.

The host of corsairs vacated the garden, following their Queen no doubt to wherever the two duelists would have their injuries treated. The stone dais was left a frightening display of utter carnage: nearly every inch was stained dark red, the flower petals drifting about sticking to the hard surface and curling as they absorbed into the larger puddles. Brann turned to look at the remaining crowd: the rest of his companions, staring at him in disbelief.

Curious. He furrowed his brow, then looked down at himself.

His forehead, where he'd wiped it—his face, chin, his entire front—was as soaked in shining red as Hester and Lorna had been.

Brann hadn't even noticed it happening.

25. The Pardon

The eight outlanders stood outside the doors of the royal clinic, an unusual amount of modern looking equipment being shuffled by on wheeled carts—given the fairly medieval appearance of the rest of Jan-Jito, Brann had expected less impressive technology, though it stood to reason that their way of life need not impede their ability to effectively heal their sick and injured. Boomer was massaging at Brann's shoulders like a proud father, the rest of the party awaiting news with quiet patience—all save one.

Wolf sat back on his haunches, directly in front of the clinic doors, ears pinned and a low whine emitting from his chest. Brann had attempted, briefly, to speak to him, soothe the lycan with his newfound ability to converse with the beast: there was no conversation to be had, sadly, as he reached out and felt only confusion and sadness meet his words, tumbling about in a jumbled mess of disorganized thoughts no human could parse. In this moment, the Wolf was all alone, awaiting the return of his big sister.

The doors at last whisked open with a bright chime, and a bedraggled Hester—removed of her dueling jacket, white undershirt tattered and stained—stepped out into the stone hall, coming to a swift halt as she was now face to face with Wolf.

No one dared breathe. The Queen stared directly into the glaring amber lamps of the monster, her gaze just as steely and fierce as his. Brann clenched, feeling a sickly apprehension in his stomach.

Hester didn't blink, didn't speak, and didn't back down—instead, to the shock of everyone present, her hand raised to rub up and down Wolf's snout, the frayed and bloodied Queen giving thanks to her daughter's faithful hound with affectionate pets.

Everyone breathed a collective sigh of relief—not just because disaster had been averted, but the Queen's demeanor meant Lorna must be doing fine now, Wolf's tail even wagging in appreciation as he grasped the gesture's meaning.

The Queen gave a final stroke under Wolf's chin and excused herself, stepping around to step towards Brann, the heels of her boots clapping against the stone as she stopped once more. Brann stood tall, hands behind his back, only just remembering to give a slight bow of his head as he waited to be addressed.

"You acted enabler to a dangerous and foolish gambit on my daughter's part," Hester said sternly, looking down her nose at the young corpsman.

Brann bowed again. "Yes, Marm."

"In quite a literal sense," she continued, "You took her life in your hands—and your own, for that matter." Hester tilted her head. "A fugitive, branded terrorist by his own people, risking his own life for an enemy nation, knowing full well they planned on moving against his House."

Brann shook his head. "With respect, Marm, I don't belong to House Geiha." He sighed, crossing his arms. "I don't belong to them, to Tark, to Lachlan—no one. I would have done that for Red no matter where she came from."

"Because you care for her?" Hester was puzzled.

Brann turned, facing the rest of the party. Facing Wolf. "Because they do," he replied. "To be honest I don't even think Red—sorry— Lorna—likes me all that much. I just know..." He fumbled for the words, then turned back to face Hester when he found them. "I know we're all kinda stuck together now, and I get the feeling when she's better, Lorna would say that includes her, too."

Hester scoffed, turning her eyes away. "Hmph. You won't have to wait that long, I fear, she's already made up her mind." The Queen stood rigid, but the way her hands clutched her elbows, hugging the air—Brann knew she was hurting. "Lorna did not return home to stay. She says she's found herself a job to do. One what warrants the help of her new friends." Hester cast her eyes on the party behind Brann. "Her new family."

"What a big softie," Boomer cackled, punching Nestor in the shoulder gently. "All that hard leather and prim princess attitude, and she's writing about us in her diary at night all along!"

Nestor didn't shut Boomer up this time, but rather Zay, the merc's boot whipping up to find Boomer's ass, the horse guffawing mischievously before quieting down.

Hester took no notice, returning to Brann. "I would go amiss, telling you the words shared in private between a mother and her daughter, so I'd ask you to avail yourself of such questions. However," Hester said, blinking with just the slightest of nods, "I am nonetheless grateful for your actions, and should you ask anything else of me, I will do all that is within my considerable reach to grant your requests."

"There is one thing," Brann blurted out, startling himself with how quickly his response came. "Sorry, Marm—but, yes, there is something—"

"Of course," she interrupted, already anticipating this. "I cannot pardon you for crimes committed outside our borders, but neither will I detain you further. You will not be delivered to the Marshal when he arrives—and furthermore," Hester added, threatening the faintest ghost of a smile at the corners of her lips, "I look forward to disappointing the arrogant lizard, presuming himself above negotiating entry into our territory and demanding our prisoners with nary a coin in return as payment."

Brann paused, choosing his words carefully. "All due respect, but we've seen him up close, and Tark isn't especially fond of disappointment," he said dryly, scratching his face nervously. "Especially when it involves me running away from him again...kind of a sore spot for him."

"Pardon me, your Grace, I mean no offense by my intrusion," Emrys piped up awkwardly, stepping to Brann's side with hat in hand. "I believe my befuddled young friend here, rattled as he is by the excitement of the morning, has overlooked the root cause of our mutual problem."

"The creature beneath the mountain, you mean," Hester intoned quizzically. Brann tilted at Emrys, eyes narrowed as if he, too, expected an explanation.

"Indulge me, if you would, dear Queen," Emrys explained, his bandaged hands articulating his meaning. "Earlier, at breakfast, we delivered to you news of this creature's existence, and—frankly—I detected in your reaction somewhat of an...absence of surprise?" He motioned to the clinic doors. "More immediate matters drew your attention, naturally, but I don't believe I'd be off my mark to infer your pre-existing knowledge of the matter."

Hester gave a curt nod. "You would not. Of course I knew."

Brann recoiled a bit. Unexpected.

"The creature you call 'exdead,'" Hester conceded, "Posed no immediate threat to our city, and has—almost certainly against my better judgment—been allowed to live, provided none of my corsairs are taken by its hunger. You'll recall no significant presence of guards standing watch in the mines," she remarked to Brann, "As is by my design. The only known disappearances we have attributed to the monster were all intruders and marauders who held no value in being kept alive."

Brann opened his mouth to speak against this, but stopped when Emrys waved him down with one hand. "This creature, this exdead being," he questioned, "Did not originate within your borders, did it?"

"Indeed not." Hester uncrossed her arms, hands going to her hips. "I think little of those who give credit to coincidence when the roots of schemes grow where planted by scoundrels."

"You believe this monster to have been...planted, then," Emrys prompted.

The Queen took a breath, speaking openly now. "Years past, I'd wager near as many as this young man has lived," Hester said with her hand motioning to Brann, "An emissary of House Geiha kneeled in my court, inviting himself to a luncheon. He droned on and on about the conception of an Empire, joined under the colors of Geiha's banner, a union of the strongest and worthiest houses seeking to rail against the treaties handed down from the Arbitration Wars. An invitation to return to a time of directness and decisive leadership." Hester snorted. "The pursuit of war as a necessary function of diplomacy, amending the treaties to allow conflicts sustained by the indecision of bureaucrats to once more resolve themselves on the open battlefield.

"House Jan-Jito, of course, declined. No treaty, nor union, nor the self-proclamation of an empire of any sort will dictate when and where we choose to draw our blades." Hester waved dismissively. "I stood mute, and honored the emissary with no pledge, no response. Within the month, prisoners began disappearing from the brig, starting with the deepest cells in the mine."

"It has been there for quite some time, then," Emrys said, looking as surprised as Brann felt by this revelation. "You believe it placed there in retaliation—more to the point, placed there by House Geiha, by Tark himself, even?"

"In my youth, the stories of the Iron Tark would have banished the thought. None doubted the honor with which the dragon stood before his enemies when challenged. In recent years, however..." Hester snapped her fingers. "A change—imperceptible, perhaps, to nations and journalists less loyal to the warrior's code. The Marshal Tark has nonetheless shown a new side of himself, one he never would have allowed billed to his name in his prime."

"What that might be, Marm?"

Hester stared at Emrys as she replied coldly: "Mercy."

Brann shifted uncomfortably.

"It is your opinion, then, Tark has lost the taste for bloodshed," Emrys said. "Deploying more insidious methods as a means to avail himself of direct conflict?"

"It would seem in his mind a mercy to let the ravenous dead take their meals from the bones of those who would defend our people, allowing us avenue to—as you said—evacuate. In the years since this visit from House Geiha, I have taken a litany of meetings with diplomats from every corner of the continent. Each has heard rumor, has shared a morsel of gossip, speaking of unholy creatures that deny a place in the natural world." Hester pointed at Emrys. "Your 'exdead.' Each one of them recalling, shortly before these ghoulish sightings, a similar meeting with Geiha: whether they responded favorably or not."

"I'm not sure I get it," Brann said, perplexed. "I've seen—I mean, I was in—Geiha's military. They don't need to sneak around and plant monsters to get their way. They could just storm in and take any capitol they wanted." He took a beat. "Other than, of course, you know. Jan-Jito. Marm."

Emrys scratched his chin. "With your blessing, my Queen," he said ponderously, thinking some private thought to himself as he spoke, "May we perhaps beg another favor?"

Hester nodded. "You may."

Emrys looked over his shoulder—at Boomer, much to the horse's confusion—and leaned in, whispering something not even Brann could hear to the Queen, holding his hat up to shield his lips from being read. When they parted, Hester considered something for several moments, visibly concerned. Nevertheless, she nodded.

"I accept."

Emrys replaced his hat and skated on over to Boomer like a child about to confess to a broken vase. "My dear friend, may I say your contribution to the cause is a tremendous gesture, and I'd like to thank you on behalf of all of us blessed to be in your company and care," he said gently.

"Certainly!" Boomer didn't even wait for Emrys to finish his thought before puffing up in a heroic stance, hands on his hips. "Anything I can do to keep my employees happy and safe." He flared his nostrils. "What exactly am I doing?"

Emrys couldn't help but grin mischievously, wringing his hands together. "Your suggestion that we leave the Donnie parked on the beach to allow us an exit from the city on foot, making our way out of Jan-Jito territory enshrouded by forest cover, of course. An inspired idea, good sir."

"Yes, yes it is—no. What, no, that's not good, not good at all."

Boomer's entire attitude reversed dramatically, the horse looking horrified. "Why would—my ship? Why would we leave it behind? I spent so much money—!"

"With respect to our gracious host," Emrys interrupted, looking back to Queen Hester with his arms outstretched, "I believe we should allow her to explain why we would find mutual benefit to such an action. Please, if you would, Marm?"

Hester raised a finger to crook it. "Follow."

*

"The North Forest fills the valley between the Harrowed Peaks," Hester said to the group as she led them into a small chamber lit by wall sconces, the floor filled with desks arranged in a circle, where a professor may deliver a lecture to a surrounding mass of pupils. "The peaks separate northern Jan-Jito from the wildlands, and beyond the valley, the coast rises from the sea level to create the Bloody Northern Cliffs." She pointed with a gloved hand to the tapestry map that covered the wall closest to the chamber doorway, looking to each of the members of Boomer's party in turn as they filed in to listen. "The cliffs sit at what would be considered the safest edge of the Wilds—the Goliaths, as best we know, prefer the inner continental lowlands as their hunting grounds. Where you would travel is here—" Two fingers tapped against the embossed image of an imposing tower, sitting at the highest point of a cliff jutting out towards the ocean waters.

"Where is that?" Hawkshaw asked, stepping forward in rapt curiosity.

"The Dakhma," Emrys answered quietly, looking over the map carefully. "The monument erected by the Great Houses in the wake of the end of the Arbitration Wars, where the treaty they signed rests—and where it was amended," he said, turning to face everyone, "To include a very important passage."

Hester recited a stanza from memory, quoting as if she had been there to witness the signing herself. "'No one House acting in unilateral cause, and outside the summary decision of a tribunal of no less than eighty-nine percent of declared and duly appointed House representatives, may seek the removal, annexation, or other hostile engagement of an equally recognized House, under penalty of severe sanctioning and reciprocity.' The amendment that required a majority decision by all the Houses to allow one nation to declare war on another through means of direct and targeted violence." Hester waved at Boomer demonstratively. "The reason we have conflicts that cannot otherwise be resolved meet their resolutions via proxy combatants."

"Hey, that's me!"

"This amendment," Emrys continued on Hester's behalf, ignoring Boomer's gleeful outburst, "Meant that in order for any war to be officially sanctioned, then eight out of the original nine ruling Houses that were formed following the wars would all have to come to a unanimous agreement that such action was necessary. Previously, all nine would be required, but—" He smiled wryly, "—No war would vote to allow itself to be attacked by another, would they?"

"It seemed a small, rather inoffensive decision at the time, barely warranting a full signing ceremony," Hester added, also looking over the map—it seemed this particular tapestry was an ancient one, indeed only showing off nine regions separated by their stitched borders. "A House standing alone against the others, be it for reasons of self-aggrandizing or for evoking disfavor—this would be reason for their judgment to be of ill-consequence in a decision to have their territory disciplined." She pointed out the names of the original Nine in turn. "Jan-Jito. Saintmarie. Geiha. Cheneye..."

"...Kavorcka, Jacques, Thaddeus, Klikushki." Emrys stood beside the Queen, likewise pointing out the regions in turn. "No single nation held advantage over another; no magic or school of science, nor religion or medicine, imposed on another through means that were not mutually agreed upon in official parlay." He scratched his chin. "All seemed to be at peace, and today, despite relatively minor conflicts—Jacques dissolution into smaller territories, the addition of other sovereign states that lobbied for House recognition—all war has been a thing of the past."

"Eight." Brann raised his hand.

Hester and Emrys turned to look at him.

"You said nine Houses," Brann explained, nodding to the map. "You only said the names of eight. Who was the ninth?"

Emrys stood aside, dutifully giving a small bow as he laid his hand upon the region that sat directly in the middle, surrounded by all the others, the name of it written in a runic font that was barely legible to Brann, but one he translated almost instinctively:

-LAOCHAIL-

"Lachlan," Brann muttered.

Queen Hester nodded. "The nation besieged on all sides, and the one most grievously weakened in the wars."

"But strategically placed to be the keystone that held the lands together," Nestor added. "No one House could seize it by force without it being perceived as a tactical maneuver against the others. It survived the wars not because of the strength of its forces, but through willpower, and because of the influence it held."

"Until Geiha decided to take matters into their own hands," Brann reasoned. "When they decided Lachlan couldn't be bought or conquered. So, if I'm understanding this right, what the Queen is saying is if there's any proof that Geiha was working against the other Houses all along, and Lachlan was at the center of their plans, then we'll be able to find it at this... what was it called?"

"Dakhma," Emrys repeated, holding up a hand. "Forgive me, we did get a bit off the trail there, though I'd scarce live a day longer calling myself a scholar without investigating this matter further at the nearest opportunity. Yes, this is where we should head now, all of us, once Lady

Lorna has made a full recovery. I believe we will find an answer to all of our mysteries there: the nature of this potential exdead menace, the reason for Geiha's possible subterfuge, and Tark's vested interest in young Brann."

"The obvious answer to this latter question being, of course, your status as the last surviving member of Lachlan," Hester offered to Brann. "Though I cannot help but find a lack of rational thought behind the decision to allow your escape in the first place—certainly there must be more at work behind the curtain, for none with the reputation and resolve of Tark would simply stand by and let the sole living representative of a vulnerable House train as an ordinary recruit under him." She shook her head, jabbing a finger at Brann. "You are more than a target to conquer to him, and it is beyond my sight to fathom what that may be."

Nestor leaned against one of the desks. "To the Dakhma, then. An empty spire in the Wilds, surrounded by colossal monsters and other fiendish anomalies—so that we can discover...what, exactly?"

They all looked between each other. Grishka, having assumed her human form, finally engaged in the conversation, saying only one word.

"Purpose."

Hester nodded. "The witch speaks true. I am a servant to my beliefs, and they have guided every plotted course I have sailed. Belief in divine purpose or fated unions matters not—the only thing that matters is what you do once set on your path." She looked to each of the eight of them, one by one. "I know not why Lorna was meant to travel with you, but to stand in her way now, in the face of these implications of the foreordained..."

"Would be proving her right—again." Brann grinned confidently at the Queen, in spite of himself, trusting she'd see the humor in it.

She did. After a moment, her stern gaze broke, and the frigid monarch's giggle brought a light into the dusty chamber that warmed every corner of it. She composed herself, but pursed her lips in a wide smile, those sea green eyes twinkling back at the young man she'd seen as her prisoner only hours ago.

"We certainly can't have that."

A joke. The entire room breathed a collective sigh of relief.

"That's all fine and good," Boomer said, still visibly distraught, "But why in the hell would we need to leave behind the Donnie? We could fly straight to the Dock-mom or whatever in less than a day; why walk all that way? What if we get there and there's nothing? We gotta haul our sorry asses all the way back here? I'm all for a good bout of cardio, but come on—"

"There's a pissed off dragon flying right for us as we speak," Nes answered impatiently, assuming his familiar role as Boomer's counsel. "Likely with a whole heap of equally pissed off sociopaths who have been embarrassed by us giving them the slip several times already. We fly off now, they pick us up on the holonic, or more likely, on their sensors if they're close enough. We make for it on foot, we can give them a clean break in the forest, and make them guess where we come out. Or where we're going next, for that matter."

Boomer thought this over. He seemed deep in thought. Then: "But why do we have to leave the Donnie behind?!"

"Queen, thank you eternally for all the patience you've shown us," Emrys said, bowing to kiss at Hester's gloved hand courteously (but turning his head to the side, Brann saw him quickly wipe away a smear of congealed blood on his upper lip after doing so.) "My companions and I will away now, provided your daughter is well enough to travel once more—should we ever be invited into your home once more, I cannot predict the depths of gratitude we will show on that happy day."

Hester looked at her hand where she'd been kissed, but said nothing, visibly confused by the gesture. "Of course, you will be welcome, with far more hospitality than I so callously denied in my myopic behavior." She addressed Boomer, now: "As for your question, the answer is simple: when the Marshal boards your ship to retrieve his prize, and finds it empty, he will disembark to find no prisoner awaiting transport."

She grasped the hilt of her sheathed saber, the polished ruby leather glinting in the light of the wall sconces. "Instead, he will be held accountable for his impositions at court: not of a Queen's diplomacy, but a mother's wrath. One who has severely neglected her duties in protecting her daughter against those with such ill-mannered declarations of their own supremacy."

Brann didn't think there had been reason to assume Hester wasn't a capable fighter before. Now, however, streaked in her own blood, and the blood of her own daughter, a rising fire of adjudication in her eyes...there was not a soul alive he'd wish the Queen's displeasure upon.

"One last thing," the Queen proclaimed, clipping her heels together. "Though you represent the vested interests of House Geiha's decisions, I cannot recognize you as an enemy of my court, as long as you stand alongside my daughter in her travels. Therefore," she said, bowing to Boomer slightly, "The full weight of Jan-Jito's significant financial influence is at your disposal, should you require the need of an ally in mercantile matters."

Boomer stumbled backwards. "You mean—"

"You're rich baby," Nes chuckled, clapping the horse on the shoulder. "Or, richer, anyway, not like we ever needed a sponsor..."

"What does that mean for the rest of us?" Brann couldn't help but feel a surge of excitement at this—thoughts sprung unbidden to his mind, images of even bigger ships, softer beds, more colorful fizzy drinks in giant glass bottles...

"While you still have time on your side, I bid you all pay a visit to our armories and our tailors, who will no doubt equip you with a wealth of supplies befitting a royal flagship." Hester clapped her hands together once—they were dismissed. "Bosun Neve will see you to the gates once you've been fitted for your journey. You all walk now under the watchful eye as allies of House Jan-Jito, and all that implies."

The party bowed to the Queen as they once more filed out of the chamber, headed back towards the clinic to check on Lorna. Being the last to leave, Brann took one step out of the door, then stopped—he was halted suddenly, a tug on his back. He turned, seeing Hester directly behind him—

her white scarf nowhere to be seen.

Brann reached around, feeling the hilt of his sword, spinning it around to look: the scarf had been knotted just under the guard, like a decorative plume, two white wings spreading out from the handle.

"You have my thanks, young Brann of Lachlan, and with it the Queen's favor." Hester kissed her filthy fingertips, the nailbeds stained dark red, and planted those fingers against Brann's forehead. "It is beneath a Queen's station to apologize for her actions—but it is her duty to make right that which she has wronged. You will always have a home here, should your own path lead you back to my city."

Brann thought for a moment. He could have bowed, or thanked Hester. Instead, he took the liberty of one last question, one he hoped wouldn't sully him in the Queen's eyes.

"The Bosun, she told me a story," he began, his voice low. "About a lamb. About how you fed it to a wolf." He looked back over his shoulder, at the backside of the werewolf plodding after the rest of the group. "Was that..."

Hester took his meaning immediately. "Yes. I may yet come to regret such an action, as it no doubt cut the love of her mother from Lorna's heart. To recall my previous statement, however—it is not a Queen's job to apologize for such things. Were I transported to a time past, I would no doubt make such a decision all over again unflinchingly."

Brann looked the Queen full in the face now, without fear.

"Why?"

Hester, for the first time, averted her gaze. Instead, she looked down the hall as well, watching the sorrowful gait of the werewolf draw further away from where they spoke. "As repayment for your actions today, I will allow you this one concession, though I will deny any further questioning of royal decree." She inhaled deeply, slowly, lost in her own thoughts. For a moment, it seemed she'd forgotten Brann was there. Finally, she answered.

"A mother's love for her child is a vulnerable idea, a living creature, of soft flesh and a reckless gnashing of teeth, frightened and frightful in equal measure. Should you cradle it close and tight, you will bleed—should you intimate its presence to your child, you draw their blood instead." Her lips tightened until the wrinkles at their corners turned white. "Yet to avert bloodshed is to have never loved your child at all. The most brutal and cold thing a mother can do is to live in such a way to sidestep altogether the possibility of violence—for how can a mother say her heart beats for her daughter if it does not bleed?"

Brann let this sink in for a moment. He thought of Wolf's actions and behaviors, how his entire attitude seemed to change once they'd performed the transfusion ritual. How tender a side was revealed to him once he'd been taught how to listen.

"I think I understand what you mean," he replied after a moment. "But, without assuming too much...sometimes, maybe all it needs—all it wants—is just..." Brann fumbled for the words. He remembered standing outside the door of an apartment on the streets of Geiha, wishing the person who opened it was a kind soul, one willing to help without drawing their payment from his body in turn. Then, he thought back to a few moments earlier—witnessing Hester scratch beneath the werewolf's chin, the way she saw him as she cradled his snout. The simple act of acknowledging him.

"Maybe all it needs is a friendly pat on the head, now and then." Brann finished flatly, not even convincing himself with his limp metaphor. Really, he should have just kept his mouth shut.

But when he looked back at the Queen, though she wouldn't return his gaze, he saw her eyes watering a bit. She understood his meaning fully.

"Lorna has always been a willful girl—I cannot begin to imagine how this day has changed her, but one thing I know to be true: she will be looking desperately for a way to repay you for your kindness. I pray that when that day comes, you will both have the sense to stop her from doing something unforgivably stupid. She would sooner walk off a cliff than allow one of her favored pets to come to harm."

Hester swallowed, then motioned for Brann to get going, the rest of his attachment disappearing around the corner down the hall. "Lorna will be waiting for you. I trust you will stand beside her when called to arms, young soldat."

Brann stood at attention, mimicking his facing movements from training. The most comforting thing he could say to the Queen of Jan-Jito now, in his most official tone of voice, was—

"Understood, Marm." He saluted in earnest, then went on his way, jogging after his companions, knowing he had been officially pardoned.

The eyes of the watchful Queen Hester were on Brann's back, all the way down the hall, until he rounded the corner and disappeared from her view. Even still, he knew she was there, always just behind him, always present, wherever he may go.

A mother's love for her child, wrapped in a bow around Brann's sword, snowy white and silky—stained with the cherry red droplets of mother and daughter alike.

ACT III

A WORLD AWAY

26. The Skidrow

Autumn had come to the North Forest, the high treetops trapping the late morning fog beneath their canopy where the sun could not banish it, errant leaves of copper decay tumbling to earth all around the party as they hiked single file on the infinite path carving ahead through the trees and fog. Rays of amber light shone through at an angle, the sun not quite reaching its zenith in the sky above in the later months of the year—all the forest was a hazy glow of gold around the travelers, wrapping them in warm bloom that made the red leather of their Jan-Jito attire glisten. At the back of the procession, Zay watched their rear with her autocannon held at waist level, ready to engage but at rest, her whole body swiveling this way and that to scan the trees for encroaching threats. Hawkshaw trudged along at a stiff pace just ahead of her, his shoulders locked in place as he hunched forward, an enormous twin set of equipment crates carried on his back. Though he made no indication of physical discomfort as he walked, even whistling a quiet electronic tune to himself, his softwire joints creaked and hissed in hydraulic strain more than usual; Hawkshaw had swallowed his pride when he agreed to act as pack mule for the party, though not without a sly comment about humans using robots to do their heavy lifting for them.

Ahead of him, Emrys was entrenched in the pages of his spell journal, mumbling to himself as he jotted down symbols every so often, flipping pages back and forth to review—every so often a small spark of green would crackle at his fingertips on the page, a new spell effect slotting itself into place on the page. Brann was upwind from Emrys in the lineup, watching over his shoulder in curiosity, wondering just how the journal worked to himself—though he was periodically distracted by the raven clinging to the hilt of his sword, Grishka's beak plucking at a strand of his hair or jabbing at his earlobe mischievously. She'd taken to roosting on his head and shoulders now, and though Brann couldn't think of a single time he'd exchanged words with the introverted shapeshifter since she'd been travelling with them, he sensed a newly plotted interest in him on Grishka's part: picking at him playfully, like a child might, and for what it was worth he reacted in kind by giving mock cries of anguish, which prompted a rattling avian chuckle from her every time.

Shoulder to shoulder, next in line were the reunited Wolf and Lorna: though she was back on her feet, the viscountess had remained mostly silent since they'd crossed the border of Jan-Jito, her face and bare arms covered in at least two dozen small adhesive bandages: wearing her heavier travelling jacket was too painful against her healing wounds, the garment instead draped over Wolf's spear like a signaling flag, his burly arm wrapped around Lorna's waist to help keep her upright in case she got dizzy. Brann watched the two from behind during their walk, and though they never spoke aloud, every so often Lorna would lean in to press her nose into Wolf's neckfur, prompting a small wag of his tail only Brann could see. Just beyond their stride was Nestor's bony frame, making wobbly progress, the older man visibly challenged by the long trek: though he too remained voiceless, his breathing was labored as he attempted to regulate it, sweat pouring from his head and soaking all down the front and back of his undershirt, having wrapped his leather jacket around his waist to cool himself. At the head of the line, like a proud father goose leading his goslings, Boomer marched with his head high and arms swinging in exaggerated fashion, his sparkling gold satin shirt practically acting as a headlamp through the fog for them from beneath his scarlet vest.

There were no separate compartments for them to retreat to, nor divergent sleep schedules: the troupe moved now as a single unit, bereft of the luxury of privacy in the Donnie's absence, and so far, no one had stepped up to the plate to be the first to take a swing at a conversation they may all partake in. The silence was broken only by the crunching of dried branches beneath their feet, or the distant swirling chirps of birds in the canopy far overhead. They may have been walking in the same direction, but something about having everyone together like this with only each other's company to occupy their attentions made Brann feel like there was more distance between them all than ever.

This gave Brann an idea. The young man, still suffering under the assault of light pecks, held up a hand to halt Grishka's teasing for a moment—his other hand reached into his jacket pocket, retrieving a small bag of dried lichenfruit, doing his best to keep the paper from crinkling too loudly to give himself away.

"Here, let's try something," he whispered to the raven, her beady eyes watching the bag of snacks with equal parts hunger and anticipation, waiting to hear this scheme. Brann pulled a piece from the bag, holding it between two fingers as he directed Grishka's line of sight with it, pointing up to the head of line—at Boomer, specifically. He motioned to the raven with his hand spread like wings, miming the action of the fruit arcing downwards, then tapping it against his head and pointing at Boomer once more.

"Wanna give it a shot?" Brann asked beneath his breath, the corners of his mouth pulled into a devious smirk. Grishka cooed appreciatively, nodding before plucking the fruit from Brann's fingers, then gliding silently away to stay undetected before beating her wings to climb at a generous distance. The witch disappeared up into the obscuring fog overhead, and for a few moments, everything remained quiet. Then—

"Hey, what—!" Came the startled cry at the front of the line, Boomer's head jerking about as he looked up to the sky, feeling at his forehead with a hand in his confusion. "Something hit me!"

"Probably just a twig," Nestor huffed, not interested in entertaining the horse.

The quiet woosh of wings above signaled Brann to pull another dried fruit from the bag, his arm slowly raising above his head, the black blur snatching it deftly before taking to the sky once more. Several more moments passed, Brann watching Boomer with an expectant grin, waiting for the next strike.

It bounced off of Boomer's snout this time, the horse whinnying with a jolt, his lightning-fast reflexes kicking in: his hand snatched the fruit out of the air before it could fall to the ground, the frightened equine opening his hand to see the dried snack in his palm. He gasped in awe, the fear melting away, replaced with childlike wonder.

"It's raining fruit!" He exclaimed, and Brann ducked his head as he snorted out loud, biting his hand to keep his laughter quiet. Quickly, he rearmed with another fruit, fingers jabbing upwards just in time for Grishka to snatch it on her next pass. The raven didn't wait so long this time, letting her payload drop almost immediately, the fruit falling directly into Boomer's open, waiting maw, his teeth clacking together around his catch.

"Oh, it's a bountiful season of harvest this year, everyone!" The horse laughed, twirling about to keep watch for more fruit raining down. "The forest will nourish us on our hard journey, praise be!"

Brann didn't wait for Grishka's return, pulling a fruit from the bag and aiming it himself, launching with an overhanded toss aimed directly at Boomer. The dark little shape of the snack arced through the air haphazardly before bouncing off of the horse's leg, causing Boomer to double over and chomp at the ground uselessly in a failed attempt to catch the snack. A quiet cackle from far behind reached Brann's ears—Zay must have seen his throw—and Nestor's head swiveled about to locate the culprit, raising a brow at seeing Brann laughing to himself with the bag in hand. Caught red-handed, Brann gave an innocent shrug, eyes wide as he mimed searching the trees for the mysterious assailant.

"How much further until we reach the cliffs?" The silence now broken, Hawkshaw spoke up, his voice pitched down a bit from the strain of his load. "Not complaining, but I'm starting to think I bit off a bit more than I could chew here..."

"We're not heading directly for the Dakhma," Nes called back, panting a bit between every few words. "Mercenary Row is where we're heading first—it's in the other direction, but we can get a vehicle and speed up the trip through the Wilds, save us some risk of being caught out in the open by some giant predator. Not to mention get those crates off your back," he added.

"Oh, goodie," Hawkshaw replied, sarcasm masking genuine relief. "As much as I'd love to haul everyone's underwear across the wildlands..."

"What's Mercenary Row?" Brann asked.

Emrys joined in now, lifting his head from the pages of his journal. "You'd be forgiven for thinking it less of a town, more of a slum," he said. "Another outpost, at the border of the Wilds, something of a 'last stop' for desperate travelers to hire a guide or refit themselves for a journey into the brush."

"Why'd the fruit stop?" Boomer whined.

"We wouldn't survive a day on foot in the Wilds," Nes continued. "We'll buy whatever cheap armored crawler we can, head for the Dakhma, and hopefully by the time we find whatever it is we're looking for there, Tark will have moved on from Jan-Jito and it'll be safe for us to return for the Donnie."

A flapping of wings at his back and a familiar weight tugging his sword down signaled Grishka's return to her perch on Brann's back.

"She's starting to like you," Emrys remarked behind him.

"Yeah?" Brann spun about, reaching up to offer a few fingers to the raven, who plucked at them affectionately with her clattering beak. "I noticed. You and Hawkshaw seem to know her best—how come she almost never speaks? She seems to have no trouble in human form."

Emrys shut his journal, pocketing it for now and giving a thoughtful shrug. "She is a creature of many mysteries. Honestly I have travelled the world entire, and have no doubt experienced a longevity far beyond what should be considered fair for a man, and I can tell you she is undoubtedly one of the oldest and strangest beings I have ever met—far older than myself, even." He held up his hands, showing off the bandages. "Scholars of my kind aren't born to long lives, we achieve it through careful study and ritualistic commitment to our craft—at the cost of great personal sacrifice." He let his hands swing freely, nodding to the raven on Brann's back. "Grishka is a wildling witch with true earthly mysticism imprinted on every cell in her body, and channels unknowable and untranslatable abilities that would make even the most proficient of my order seem a mere apprentice. Her choice to remain in animal form—or transient between the two—no doubt affords her more happiness than remaining human. Considering all that we inflict upon ourselves, and all that we must labor for," he chuckled, "I don't blame her for finding that less than appealing, when she can live a life so free."

Brann cautioned a finger to stroke at Grishka's underside—the bird cawed lightly, her breastfeathers puffing out in response. "Then I guess what I'm really asking—why travel with us at all? We didn't ask her along— no offense," he added hurriedly, Grishka stabbing her beak at his ear. "She just sort of showed up on the ship and never left, even though she's only putting herself in danger by tagging along. Seemed like she was perfectly safe and happy back in her den in the woods."

Emrys adjusted his hat before pocketing both hands as he walked. "You two would benefit from a proper conversation with each other, I'd wager, next time the luxury of peace and quiet finds us. She is, in many ways, much like myself: never happy to remain sedentary when curiosity plants its hooks. If she attaches herself to any band of merry folk, it is because she feels she has something to learn from them—something to learn from you, that is," he indicated by twirling his finger about in the air. "Everyone else here? Hawkshaw and I, she finds our company familiar, but the others she's pointedly avoided, keeping herself isolated on board Boomer's ship. You're the only other member of this happy tribe she's decided makes for a good perch."

Brann appraised the raven for a moment, studying her expressionless face, the dark little eye of the transformed witch staring back at him with rapid little blinks. "I'll have to keep that in mind, then. Though what she finds interesting about me, I can't imagine."

The holyman tipped his hat respectfully. "If I may say so, young Brann, I do believe that is one thing the rest of us all have in common. We may have our differences—some, undoubtedly, more malcontent than others—but I don't think for a moment there's a one among this group who doesn't think they have reason to learn from you, whether or not they care to admit it."

Brann turned back to face ahead, not letting Emrys see his face sour a bit, the young soldat unconvinced. "Learn how much of a nobody I am, you mean. I only seem to be making everyone's life miserable." He looked over Red's profile as he said this, at the bandages covering her, at the shaky way her knees bent as she walked alongside Wolf.

"We're all nobodies, young friend," Emrys responded warmly. "It's only when we find other nobodies to walk alongside that we discover we can be somebody."

The leaves continued to twirl about in the fog overhead, dampening the sounds of the forest around the procession, this rare spell of silence a comfort to them on their long journey.

*

The lion's share of the daylight hours had passed them by before the forest had thinned, the loamy undergrowth giving way to rocky shelf and uneven footing. At the threshold of the trees, the horizon dipped, and they could see out over an expanse of lowlands ahead—and below them, after a relatively steep climb down the declining path, an absolute mess of tightly clustered shacks of all manner of mismatched size and shape spread out almost a mile in every direction. Large enough to be a city, yet no single structure ever seeming to rise higher than another, the impoverished looking favela nonetheless had an air of industriousness about it as circling rickshaws and freighter haulers encircled it on all sides as they ferried their cargo to and fro. Very tellingly, no ships capable of flight were visible anywhere in the area: anyone who could afford to fly would have little cause to visit these slums, apparently. Steam rose from countless sets of piping jutting up from between the shacks, creating an almost cloudy layer over the slums, the air smelling strongly of iron oxide and engine fumes.

"We'll probably have to stay the night," said Zay, shouldering her autocannon with some relief. "No telling what kind of nightmares roam the Wilds after dark, if the stories of what can be seen in the light of day hold any truth. If it's a choice between keeping company with lowlife scum or giant monsters, I know which I'd feel safer with."

"Agreed," nodded Nes, who heaved a massive exhale and wiped his arm broadly across his face, throwing it out to scatter sweat drops across the rocks. "Frankly I don't mind saying I'm done walking for the day, either."

"Weeeak," Boomer drawled, teasing at Nestor with his hands on his hips. "Should have been using my training holotapes years ago, old man, get you some muscle on those twigs you call bones."

"First thing's first," Emrys joined in, patting his stomach. "First trolley I find, I'm procuring myself a big greasy brace, who's with me?"

This made Brann's stomach rumble—he didn't realize how hungry he was until Emrys pointed it out. The young man's eyes went wide with hope. "They have braces there?"

"Oh, most definitely," Emrys grinned, teeth gleaming white. "No self-respecting den of inequity sells anything less than the most authentic street braces you ever did taste."

Nestor laughed knowingly at Brann. "Someone's got a new favorite food, huh? Told you they'd change your life."

"Where's he going?" Remarked Hawkshaw. Everyone else turned to see what he meant. The automaton was pointing down the slope, where Boomer was already at a full sprint, beelining directly for the favela.

"Oh fuck, looks like someone else was hungry," Nes guffawed, nearly doubling over in mirth. "Come on, let's follow him. If we're quick enough, the first round's on him—I know he's got designs on buying up a whole dozen for himself."

Needing no further encouragement, the party set off once more down the path, with Brann quickly moving ahead of the pack—Zay had moved out ahead as well, and the two found themselves in an impromptu race, making eye contact just long enough to meet each other's challenge and try to outpace one another, giggling all the while. Giving a startled caw, Grishka took flight, circling about overhead as she was nearly knocked off her perch by the jostling of Brann's sword on his back as he took off.

Boomer had already disappeared into the shacks by the time they reached Mercenary Row, Brann having just barely slipped past Zay and into one of the many alleys, squeezing into the tight corridors and jogging ahead as best he could while sidestepping the many denizens occupying the narrow streets. Faces of all manner of person and creature alike were a blur to him, along with the hundreds of tiny neon signs and dimly lit stalls where shopkeeps had set up to hock their cheap wares, the entire favela bustling with the sound of clanging metal and shouting salesfolk. There was an allure, a comforting sort of familiarity to Brann, being in a place like this, entirely distinct from the sort of crowds he'd find in Barrier City—where the proud citizens of Geiha were a haughty, entitled bunch, the lower class of the territories that filled these sorts of outposts all had a far more colorful and endearing sensibility to them, even those with the more hostile outward appearance. Bickering and snapping at one another, the humans, insectoids, automatons and other beastmen alike all had nonetheless a far more intimate sensibility about them, preferring to be in each other's personal space and sharing their time together, rather than the distant and disinterested attitude the average pedestrian of Geiha would have had. Brann couldn't help but admire them, a warm appreciation rising in his chest, being here in the streets of this slum: like he was among friends, or at the very least, his own kind, those who had lived in poverty and struggle and knew the value of social commerce, the way they would shout in each other's faces before immediately breaking into hearty laughter. Though he was running between bodies like a child might as he raced Zay, Brann could even swear he saw a kuaneach leaning against a stall, a white and gold specimen of gleaming polish, the dragon's arms and legs bound in tight fitting black leather while his torso and midriff remained completely exposed.

If he spent the rest of his life evading the forces of Geiha in places like this, that notion didn't seem too terrible to Brann.

"Hey! Zay! Zaydat, whassup girl!"

Brann slowed to a halt, panting as he spun about, looking for the source of that shouting voice. Zay had fallen behind where he couldn't see her through the crowd, so he began retracing his steps, before coming to a small gap in the alley—a pair of tables had been set up beneath a bright light post, and several card players sat at stools, one of the games having paused. A completely bald and tattooed man was standing beside his stool, cards in hand, arms spread wide as he grinned and beckoned someone in close. Zay had frozen in place, having caught sight of the tattooed man, and all the joy had evaporated from her—as Brann drew closer, he saw her face drain, and it wasn't difficult for him to surmise that the man was much happier to see Zay than she was to see him.

"Don't be such a dry slit, get over here and say hello, bitch!" The man's remaining teeth were all capped with shining metal, his scarred lips peeled back over his gums, everything about his physical appearance indicating he'd lived a life of violence. His torso, bare except for a snakeskin vest, was covered in more scar tissue and ink than actual human flesh, and his belt was lined with enough grenades to bring down a skyscraper. Mercenary Row didn't get the name for no reason, as this was a killer through and through, joined at his game of cards by a crew of equally rough individuals all armed to the teeth as well.

Zay looked as if she might turn and run, but something beyond Brann's scope of understanding compelled her to step forward towards the man, her gloved hand gripping the strap of her machine cannon so tightly the exposed knuckles were white. Brann stepped close enough to listen in as she spoke, but not so close as to get in between the two, deciding it unwise to interrupt this reunion.

"Been a long time, Lovejam," she said, straining to sound pleasant. "Thought you were dead by now for sure."

"Nae quite," he chortled, pulling back his lower lip with a blackened fingernail. "Only missing a few more teeth, is all, but still kickin'. We'd heard you'd been made ground meat by those—whadja call them, uhh," Lovejam said, furrowing his brow as he snapped his fingers. "Cannae 'member, that job you took for those fackin' hosers up in Geiha, what was their name..."

Zay bristled, her eyes darting to the corners of her vision—at Brann—before she stepped closer, attempting to silence Lovejam with a raised hand. "Yeah yeah, I know who you mean, but what about you, where have—"

"Ach! I 'member now, Lachlan!" He slapped his knee, leering crudely at Zay. "Those slobs up in the high lakes, you and your boys did a real number on 'em, from what I hears—they were findin' pieces of 'em floatin' all the way downstream in Saintmarie's reservoir, they tell me."

His phlegm-thick laugh sent chills through Brann. Zay, too, had fallen silent, her face hidden from Brann's view by her long bangs. "Wish I'd been there, I tell ye, couldae used the practice!" Lovejam continued, sounding wistful as he patted the machete at his belt. "Hackin' up those poor fackin' pigs, bet you pulled a real pretty fackin' penny from that job, you greedy slag—"

The mercenary's words were cut short by a meteoric right hook to the temple, the skinny tattooed man cartwheeling sideways into the card table, sending his compatriots diving out of their chairs to avoid being struck by splinters of wooden shrapnel. Zay was on top of Lovejam in a flash, like a lion pinning a sheep, one hand at his throat while her fist continued to pummel into his head over and over and over. She said nothing, her breaths punctuated by primal snarls between each punishing blow, punching the merc's face into the dirt with the force of a sledgehammer. The surrounding mercs just stood back, watching in shock, not daring to intervene—even as their boots were streaked with their friend's blood, one of them lurching backwards in disgust as a gleaming metal tooth bounced off his shin.

Eventually, Zay had her fill—her fist, drawn up between blows, dripped with red water, her shoulders quaking—and she jerked herself away from Jovejam's prone body, standing tall over him. Brann couldn't see the merc's face, likely for the best, but were it not for the twitch of his boot the man would appear dead.

Conversation over. Good to see you again.

Zay hooked a glove around one of the bystander mercenary's shirts, wiping her bloodied fist on it, shoving him back roughly with her posture daring anyone to make a move. When no one did, she spat on Lovejam's body, then about-faced to walk away in a hurry. She stopped as she made eye contact with Brann, standing directly before him now—her frightening eyes, burning with outrage, immediately were doused, becoming mournful. Her chest rose and fell rapidly, entire body shaking, wracked with adrenaline and an overload of emotions.

She tried to speak—her words missed their mark, lacking context.

"Look, kid. I know that—if you can't forgive—" She shuddered, drawing in a breath. "I get it. I know what I did. You don't have to pretend anymore."

She meant Lachlan.

"We didn't ever really resolve...that." He nodded, looking at his feet. "I'd be lying if I said it's all good. I don't really think you can ever fix something like that."

Zay's shoulders slumped.

The two shared this pained silence, the noise around them growing dull, the battle-weary woman and the fresh-faced young soldat ignoring the murmurings of onlookers. There was, it seemed, forever a gulf between them: a lifetime of regret and sin, repelling the two souls across a broad river of blood: the blood of Brann's family, the people he'd never had the chance to know.

People that, as far as he was concerned, would forever be strangers to him. Whereas this woman, for all her failings, was willing to share this moment with him, here and now, despite all that had transpired, despite all he had done to her in return.

"Buying me a brace, though, I'd say," he pondered, biting his tongue a bit. "That might get us pretty close to being even."

Zay's eyes snapped upwards, and she saw Brann biting back his wry smile—there was no hate in his face, no bitter accusation. Only a young man looking back at her, at someone he considered a friend.

He reached up, shoving at Zay's shoulder playfully. "Maybe two," he joked, squinting at her through his suppressed smile. "Two braces, I think. Yeah, that'll work."

Zay crumbled, choking back a sob as she laughed hoarsely, and shoved him back. The gruff woman clutched Brann's shoulder and kneaded it roughly, inhaling with a sharp hiss to try and compose herself, fighting back the tears.

"I'll buy myself one, and let you have a bite, if you don't piss me off," she responded, forcing a pained smirk. "Two—maybe two bites."

Brann patted her on the forearm, giving a mercantile nod as the bargain was struck. "Kind of a shitty deal, but I'll take it, for now. You caught me on a good day."

The pair walked away from the scene of carnage together, disappearing out of sight down the alley with their arms across each other's backs, not even bothering to check on the fallen man they left in their bloody wake.

There were more important matters at hand. Like lunch.

*

Boomer's arms were cradling no less than ten foil-wrapped bundles as he sat himself down at a nearby table, the braces spilling out over the aluminum surface, the horse cackling in delight.

"I'm gonna have to do so many laps in the pool after today," he said quietly to himself as he latched onto the first bundle—before he could unwrap it, however, a hand reached across to snatch one of the stray braces, causing Boomer to recoil in shock. "Hey, what th—"

"Oh, thanks man, appreciate it boss," Nestor said sweetly, sitting alongside Boomer to unwrap his stolen meal. Before Boomer had a chance to object, a half dozen arms suddenly descended on the table, swirling around the horse like the tentacles of a hungry seabeast as the rest of the party joined in on the heist and steal away their own lunches.

"Aw, you shouldn't have, Boomer—"

"—So gracious a host—"

"—Damn, can't believe you bought us all food, thanks man—"

"Fuck all of y'all!" Boomer whinnied, his eyes turning sorrowful as his meal was reduced to a measly three braces. "Bunch of freeloading leeches, I swear, no respect for the working man...!"

All the seats around the square table were quickly filled by the scavenging members of Boomer's crew, Hawkshaw pulling up a stool to sit close to them as the rest of them unwrapped their ill-gotten gains. It had been almost a full day since they'd left Jan-Jito, and making quick progress of their hike to the border came at the cost of taking any breaks for a meal, so it didn't take any time for everyone to tear into their piping hot pastries.

"You gonna share any of that?" Hawkshaw queried, eyeing Zay's brace with a soulful glow in his lenses.

Not falling for the bait, Zay simply stared back at him, taking a slow, exaggerated bite, too big for her mouth—letting the dark sauce drip down her chin as she gave a satisfied grunt.

"Gross," Hawkshaw said, turning to the person sitting directly next to her. "What about you, sport, you gonna let me starve?" He said, addressing Brann.

Brann thought about this a moment, then—adopting Zay's impassive expression—leaned in close to the mercenary, taking an even bigger bite of her brace, giving a comical moan of almost orgasmic satisfaction as ribbons of meat dangled from his lips, never once breaking eye contact with Hawkshaw.

"You know what, you two are going to hell," the indignant automaton accused with a finger pointing at them both, Brann and Zay nearly choking on their mouthfuls of steaming meat as they fell together in hearty laughter, having successfully sabotaged Hawkshaw's attempt at his familiar tricks.

Emrys had set his hat on the table, his wild hair standing nearly straight in sweaty peaks as he raised his own half-eaten brace, letting Grishka tear away flaky clumps of the breading from her seat on his shoulder. "What's next on the itinerary, then—go shopping for a vehicle, make Boomer pay for that too, even though we've been given a generous donation from our royal benefactor?" He emphasized this with a dutiful nod to Lady Lorna sitting across from him, the still-recovering corsair raising her own brace to toast the sentiment before letting Wolf steal a nibble from it.

"We passed a pretty big lot on our way in, looked like they had a good variety of carts for sale," Nes responded between bites, wiping his mouth with a thumb before sucking it clean. "Didn't see one big enough to seat us all, but maybe they got some in the back worth checking out—we'll grab one before finding somewhere to board up for the night; hopefully we'll get lucky and nab a place with running water that still has open beds."

"And holonet, please," Zay added, still working on her oversized mouthful. "I'm in dire need of entertainment. All due respect to you boring yuppies."

"Just come with me and Brann to the fight," Boomer replied, already down to the end of his second brace. "I signed up for a few rounds at the local ring."

"Oh, I'm coming to a fight with you?" Brann said, eyebrow raised in surprise, only hearing about this for the first time.

"Uh, yeah, I need my valet, obviously," came Boomer's nonplussed response. "It'll be fun, flexing on some of these backwater rubes, show them what a champion fighter looks like."

"Like Zay said, they do have holonet here, I'm pretty sure they know what you look like," Hawkshaw rebutted. "You'll be lucky if anyone agrees to face off with you."

"Already got a challenger lined up!" The horse beamed, looking quite pleased with himself. "Get this—he's a drifter who has made a name for himself in local circles, supposed to be something of an urban myth. A kuaneach, no less—always wanted to fight one!"

Brann paled, and the rest of the table stopped eating, instantly alarmed. "Boomer—" Nes began protesting.

"Shh, stop it, I know what you're thinking, it's not him," Boomer dismissed. "Goes by some other name—I forget it exactly, 'Child of Something,' but it's not Tark, trust me. If it were a trap I'd never have signed up."

"Don't be so sure it isn't," Nes said, his tone dubious. "How can you know for sure it's not him?"

Annoyed, Boomer set down his third brace before he could bite into it. "Nestor, old buddy, just trust me on this one, I looked into it. They say he's been coming here for years, he'll show up once in a blue moon to hand out the thrashings then disappear again, some kind of nomad."

Brann remembered seeing the white and gold kuaneach lounging on the stall earlier, when they first entered Mercenary Row. "No, I actually think I might have seen him," he said in Boomer's defense. "Passed by a kuaneach on our way in. Didn't look anything like Tark, but definitely looked like a tough sort."

Boomer splayed his hands, his case rested.

Nestor, still frowning, just shook his head. "I dunno. Still can't be too careful. Besides, even if it's not him, you gotta be ready for the championship fight...assuming you'll still be allowed to attend."

The horse just rolled his eyes. He leaned away from Nes, speaking in a hushed voice to Brann across the table. "'Mother may I,' am I right?"

Brann just shrugged silently, preferring to keep eating. There was an unusual sense of ease towards his presence about the table, he thought to himself as he rubbed shoulders with Zay while they ate.

Frankly, he wasn't in a rush to upset that.

27. The Duel

"Here." Nes handed Brann the small device, like a tall, somewhat heavy lighter that filled the young man's palm, plated in dulled copper. "This is just an old junky one, but we can shop for something more personalized somewhere down the road."

Brann just stared at it. "What is it?"

Nes blinked. "What do you...oh, right." Having forgotten himself, he took the device back, holding it up. "Called a charger. It's what you carry scales in." He pressed against the back with his thumb, a button clicking in and releasing a pearl scalene into his open hand. "So you can have a little spending money to carry around."

The two of them stood outside the paneled glass door of the inn they'd rented out for the night, waiting on Boomer to come out and accompany Brann to the fight, everyone else having taken to their rooms. Nes wore his cold-weather coat, the chilly winds of the wild beginning to whistle between the metal shacks as the night drew down on them. Nestor thumbed the scale back into place, then handed the charger to Brann once more. "Gonna have to get you familiarized with the outside world, kid."

"Yeah, having 'spending money' isn't really something I'm used to, so thanks," Brann replied, examining the charger a moment before pocketing it. He'd left behind his sword, not wanting to risk having it lifted, deciding a low profile was the best strategy in navigating these unfamiliar streets. He looked around at the alley, watching the passers-by for a bit, thinking to himself before speaking up once more. "We have money," Brann repeated, "We have a decent team of people—none of whom seem to be going anywhere off on their own anytime soon. We have a ship, probably not the lowest profile, but it can also get us just about anywhere in the world, I bet. Why don't we just..." He motioned to Nes with a wave of his hands, like he was performing a magic trick.

"Disappear, you mean?" Nes interpreted. He shook his head, crossing his arms as he too looked around the alley. "Nice idea, honestly I wonder that myself too. I don't think it's that simple at this point—we have our faces all over the holonet, and it's only a matter of time before some opportunist decides to have a go at locking us up. We've had a good streak of luck so far, especially with the Queen letting us go, but that won't hold up forever—it's only a matter of time before they really apply the pressure on the territories and raise the bounty to something anyone's grandma wouldn't want to turn down."

With his signature deft hands, Nes made a rolled cigarillo appear from nowhere, lighting up his favorite blend of yamweed to warm himself against the encroaching night air. "Much as I'd like to think we could just spirit away to some distant fringe town, we'd be stupid to split up, get ourselves picked off one by one—sticking together keeps us pretty high profile, but at least we can look out for each other. With this whole 'exdead conspiracy' Emrys has dreamt up, it looks more and more every passing day like we're gonna have to see all this through to...some kind of end, I dunno." He took a long drag, hissing out the blue smoke between his lips. "Damned if I know what we're even trying to do anymore."

He offered the cig to Brann, who looked it over once, then shook his head—there were only so many new things he was willing to try just yet. "Join up with Emrys as monster hunters, maybe?" Brann offered, drawing his jacket in close. "Rid the world of the rising exdead menace, become famous heroes, clear our names? Take a stand against Tark, put him down for good, go free to live our lives in peace?"

Nes gave a humorless chuckle, puffing on the cig once more. "Yeah, I get it. Quite a shit deal we've been handed. Not a lot of room for us to maneuver. Something's gotta give, and soon."

"Just roaming the continent together not a good enough reason for us to keep going, huh? Gotta be some big important mission for us to carry out," Brann joked bitterly. "I know that's been the case ever since I stepped onto the Donnie, but it doesn't make it feel any better to say it out loud— all I ever wanted was a normal life, y'know?"

"Don't we all." Nes flicked away his ash. "Not really a choice anyone gets to make for themselves—a normal life is what you get while you wait for what you actually want to do to come your way. 'Normal' doesn't really exist, I don't think."

The door swung open behind them to reveal Boomer in his daily workout joggers, the least flashy outfit Brann had seen in his wardrobe. Fists pumping at his waist, the horse was already heading down the alley, not even waiting to see if Brann was following him. "Let's get a move on, I feel the NEED tonight!"

Giving a rushed glance back at Nes to see the engineer saluting Brann farewell, the young man hurried after Boomer, resigned to his fate as Boomer's own personal `attendant. "Hold on a minute man, wait for me!"

The pair wove their way between the bodies filling those narrow corridors, Brann only just barely able to keep up, the shampooed blonde mane of his employer gleaming in the overhead streetlamps. For a moment Boomer vanished—then, breaking free of the crowd, Brann came to a steep flight of stairs, ancient looking stone bricks practically melded into the dirt slope, curving down in between mirrored rows of flimsy looking structures decorated with a mishmash of metal and wooden sidings. Where the curved path ended, Brann emerged into another busy street, this one running perpendicular to the other alleys, the largest and least crude building he'd seen in the favela yet opposite him. Boomer was conversing with— someone?—at a makeshift box office of sorts, the window standing empty at first glance, save for what appeared to be some kind of oversized seashell left at the table. When Brann drew closer, though, he realized with a shock that the shell itself was manning the box office, a giant bivalve that yawned open and stretched out it's thick, gooey looking arm to depress an illuminated amber button on a panel beside itself. The sound of a buzzer came from somewhere behind the mollusk, the button it had pressed labeled "FIGHTER" in crude lettering—next to a button marked "BETS"—and a heavy metal door swung open beside the box office, which Boomer stepped into. Before disappearing entirely into the lit hallway beyond, the horse turned and beckoned Brann to follow urgently, the young man doing so with his neck craning back to get an eyeful of the bivalve creature while he had the chance. He couldn't be sure, but in the brief second before the shellfish disappeared behind the door that swung shut behind him, Brann thought he could read a message written across the smooth shell that read:

DON'T FUCKING STARE AT ME

"We're up next, they don't really have timers on these fights, it's just an 'until one goes down' sort of ruleset," Boomer was panting, sounding excited as a puppy. "I haven't been in a good old fashioned cage match since before I got scouted as a proxy fighter, this is gonna be a good time, you just wait, kid!" He stopped short in the hallway, nearly collapsing Brann's lung as his arm halted the much shorter human man, causing him to wheeze.

"By the way, it's been a minute since we've had a chance to talk, how are you?"

Brann rubbed at his chest tenderly. "In...what sense?"

Boomer cocked his head curiously. "Dunno! Nes tells me sometime I don't take the time to stop and listen enough, so I'm trying to do that more. I guess he means I should say 'how are you' whenever I remember to?"

Brann gave an amused nod. "Yeah, something like that, sure! Good job."

The athletic equine beamed, ears perked up as he spun about to move on. "Great! If that's all it takes, that's a lot easier than I thought! Nes sure does like to make everything out to be so complicated with you humans."

This made Brann smile as he followed his tall, dopey friend. He found it easier to let Boomer navigate their conversations any way he could find ease of doing so—no point in stepping backwards to burden the horse with all the emotional turmoil Brann had experienced since their last conversation, before they'd landed at Jan-Jito, even.

Best to just follow Boomer's lead, and go where the path took them.

The hallway opened up into a grungy waiting area filled with benches, most of them unoccupied save for a couple unsavory looking potentials sitting in their respective corners of the room. One man, nearly as tall as Boomer and with body hair like a shag carpet, was bicep curling a pair of rusty old paint cans—the other waiting fighter, a skeletal looking sphinx cat jingling with every slight moment from the amount of gold bangles hanging off its pierced body, pointed at the opposite exit before Boomer could open his mouth to speak.

"Already gone in, mate, best step to."

"Damn, I wanted to make my entrance first!" Boomer clapped Brann on the shoulder, the sound of a crowd erupting in cheers echoing down the hallway ahead. "You're gonna have a good time, trust me, just try not to say much if you're standing in my corner—some of these less civil country types can get a little sensitive when it comes to their wagers, don't wanna say something that comes across as 'giving me an advantage,' y'know?"

Brann frowned. "Isn't that just what coaches do?"

"Yeah, but, you know, one man's coach, another man's conspirator, you know how it is," Boomer replied with an endearing scoff, as if he found the distinction quaint. "Just have a towel at the ready in case I get a little wet on my knuckles, alright?" He clapped Brann's shoulder once more, and the two set off down the hall.

The light disappeared into a void of black curtains that reached all the way to the ground, the heavy fabric muffling the sounds of the audience behind it. Boomer rolled his shoulders, flexing his neck with an audible crunch, throwing his fists up to his chest in rapid succession to loosen up his elbows.

"Announcer says good evening, runs down the stakes, calls out your name," he was whispering to himself, "Then...cue walkout music."

Though not a note was played, Boomer's eyes lit up as if he could hear the wailing melody in his head, and like he was stepping through fire he burst through to the other side of the curtains with his hands aloft, welcoming the mixed dirge of yeahs and boos like it was confetti raining down on him. Brann slipped through the curtains just behind, the sight that greeted him about as far from the gaudy stadium of Mongillo as he could have imagined: Little more than a dirty prison cafeteria, chairs pushed to the walls as the audience preferred standing, gathered in bustling clusters around a ground-level cage that had been erected around the center of the shattered tile floor. The ceiling had almost no paneling whatsoever, loose ventilation piping and hazardous looking bundles of frayed wires dangling like the vines of a dead jungle just overhead—if ever there were such a thing as safety in this place, the meaning of the word had long been forgotten.

Bodies stepped aside to part around the pair, some of them sizing Boomer up while clapping their approval—while those less than impressed weren't shy about shouting in his face, swearing and threatening him themselves, though this didn't seem to bother the horse in the least. The seasoned brawler just grinned right back at them all, jogging up to the cage with the practiced showmanship of a true entertainer, even doing a little dancing spin as he rotated for the crowd once he reached the gate.

The other fighter was nowhere to be seen, and even through the smiling, Brann could see the confusion on Boomer's face. He didn't voice it, but instead gave exaggerated nonverbal signals to the crowd, miming like was looking about for someone hidden.

"Water break!" Came the reply through a host of mismatched voices, apparently meaning Boomer's opponent had stepped out momentarily—Boomer rolled his eyes and nodded his understanding broadly, knocking his knees together as if he were scared, prompting some raucous laughter. Brann couldn't help but chuckle a bit himself, somewhat relieved—kuaneach or not, any fighter truly hoping to make a name for themselves would surely hesitate at the thought of facing off against the title champion of the world, whether or not they had the skills to prove worthy.

The relief was short-lived, however, as once more cheering and clapping broke out, heads turning to face to Boomer's left—Brann's right—the other fighter having obviously rejoined the crowd. Whoever it was, they must have been an impressive sight in their own right, some of the onlookers quieting as they stepped aside for the approaching challenger—then, eventually, the clapping subsided as well, the faces of the rowdy bunch looking a mix of puzzled and disturbed.

Brann looked to Boomer with concern. The horse, much taller than most present, could see over everyone's heads, and already spotted the other fighter.

His face was like an open book to Brann, his expression saying it all.

"All apologies, gentlemen," came the familiar rumble of that smokey, relaxed voice. "My throat was parched like you wouldn't believe."

The last of the crowd skittered out of his way, some of them even falling backwards into each other, a fully fitted warlord in combat ready attire stepping out to stand before Brann. Swinging it round once like a deadly windmill, his colossal battleaxe pounded into the tiled floor, sending up a burst of shards and dust that wafted around his clawed feet like a smoke machine.

"Would you like to step out for a drink before we begin?" The Marshal of House Geiha asked Brann casually, rolling his shoulder back to fix his thin capelet, the shadows cast by the harsh overhead lights painting his face into a hideous draconic skull beneath that gleaming platinum mask. "It's only fair."

*

"I don't mind admitting my intent behind stealing away your big entrance," Tark continued, turning away and peeling away his pauldron, handing it off to a hapless bystander who accepted the heavy piece of armor with fearful eyes. "Frankly it wouldn't be fair to let the recruit here walk out to your song—it's his fight, after all." Continuing to strip, Tark calmly and with storied ease worked himself out of his combat attire bit by bit, not even looking to see if Brann and Boomer were trying to escape.

They knew better, the two fugitives frozen in place, along with an unwitting audience of mercs and travelers who had no idea what was unfolding before them. Brann already felt soaked in a cold sweat, catching another of Boomer's glances, the horse just shaking his head back at him. Wall of bodies surrounding them or not, they were trapped in here with Tark, and there was no two ways about it.

Eventually, Tark was left in nothing but his undergarments—a nearly skintight pair of fitness wear, the muted green turtleneck almost as dark as his outermost black scales, save for the pearly wash of indigo that reflected off them in the right light. Even at his most vulnerable, the thin fabric rendering the kuaneach all but naked, the draconic warrior was the most intimidating creature alive to Brann.

And likely to everyone else in the room.

"That's pretty low," Boomer finally spoke up, sounding downright angry, rather than scared. "Making up a fake reputation for yourself to lure us—to trick me into a fight with you."

"I'd say that's weak as shit," Brann confirmed, his own shaky voice far less confident than Boomer's. "Unbecoming of an officer, even—a dirty trick like that? Cowardly, even."

This last accusation made Tark pause, the corner of his lips pulling back into a small smirk, before the kuaneach turned to face them finally, sweeping off his mask and letting it hang from the hilt of his axe in one smooth motion. "You've both mistaken me entirely. I forgive you, of course, you couldn't have known, but it falls to me to correct these errors all the same." The meaty footfalls of his broad-toed feet thwacked against the tiles, unbothered by even the most jagged of cracks, Tark closing the gap between himself and his prey with the urgency of a glacier. "Tonight, you are facing off against none other than God's honest truth himself, the Nomad of the Lowlands: The Child of Rigel."

Tark stopped mere inches from Brann, staring down at the young man just as he did back at the Assay, what felt now a lifetime ago to the trembling soldat. "A servicemember of Geiha's armed forces cannot enter into any official prizefighting circuits, true—but this is no official fight, and I assumed this alias years before ever enlisting." He spread his arms placatingly. "It may not be with my own name, but there is no fiction behind my reputation as a fighter: I have indulged in these backroom brawls for decades before either of you were born. Call it...a hobby.

"As for who I'll be fighting tonight," He said after a pause, head lolling to one side to look to Boomer, addressing him as one might an annoying child, "I did not speak metaphorically. You aren't going to be in the ring with me."

Brann flinched, the heavy hand of the kuaneach suddenly clapping itself against his shoulder, not unlike the way Boomer had done mere moments earlier—he could feel those wicked claws, like the predatory talons of a raptor, tickling against his back even through his blouse.

"The recruit here is. We have a previous engagement long overdue."

Swallowing down a lump, Brann stared back at Tark defiantly, his face burning hot—no matter what he said to excuse it, nothing about this felt anything less than an underhanded ploy to Brann. The luminescent, acid green eyes meeting his gaze held absolute power over him, the Marshal's victory at long last all but complete now.

"I hesitated once. I allowed myself a single moment of mercy, sending my Uhlen to capture you in my stead. I will not make such a mistake again. Tonight, I will execute the design of my forebears myself, young recruit," Tark growled, vapors of ice in his lungs as he spoke.

"You will submit to me tonight. Alive or dead, you will submit."

Just then, Boomer spoke again:

"What if I were in the ring, though?"

Boomer drew Tark's attention back to himself with this question— Brann, too, looked to his companion, seeing the horseman's arms crossed, seeing his eyes squinting as if he were working through a complex problem in his head, something just out of reach of his ability to fully articulate the solution to.

"A recruit must be judged on his own merit in the Assay," Tark retorted coldly. "There can be no substitutions."

"I'm not talking about that, dumbass," Boomer spat, the first time Brann had ever heard anyone speak in such a way to the Marshal. "I'm saying here. This isn't Barrier City, and you said it yourself, tonight you aren't...yourself. This is one fighter challenging another, and backroom or not," he said, looking to the crowd for approval, "You have to accept—or forfeit." He leaned forward, encouraged by the agreeing murmurs of the audience, some of them even clapping once or twice. "That means you get the fuck out."

Tark took a deep breath, and Brann knew the strategy was having some desired effect on the warlord's tactical mind, the hand on his shoulder eventually withdrawing itself—it felt like a boulder being rolled off Brann's back.

"I suppose you have a point." Tark turned on his heel, nearly cutting Brann's feet from his ankles with the low sweep of his heavy tail as he did, the dragon approaching Boomer now to negotiate the terms of this engagement. "Though you'll see the logic when I point out—in good faith, of course—you are still the elected fighter of House Geiha, pending any orders for your removal from the House Tournaments." He crossed his own arms, mimicking Boomer's stance. "An order that I, standing in as regent ruler in the Emperor's absence, have not yet given."

"Right, I can't enter a fight with someone representing the same House as myself," Boomer allowed, frowning—Brann could see the horse losing ground, his plan backfiring. Tark was simply too smart to let the laws of government be used against him, underground fight or not.

Yet, it seemed this would not deter him, much to the surprise of both Boomer and Brann. Tark stretched his arm back, torso twisting to follow.

"House Lachlan. The sole living heir to its governance," Tark offered. "As superior officer to Recruit Brann, I can, with his consent, anoint myself the incumbent ruler of his House, and thus serve as his champion in his stead."

The logic clicked into place now—Boomer couldn't see the forest for the trees, but now the map through it was drawn up for him plain as day. He grinned triumphantly, winking at Brann over Tark's shoulder, as if this was his plan all along.

"Right, exactly what I meant to say," Boomer lied. "It's not Geiha against Geiha, it's Geiha against Lachlan—we fight to settle a House dispute. I win, you release Brann from his service, and clear his name along with it." He paused, then added, "Uh, all of our names, I mean, our entire group—you stop chasing my ship, is the point, and let us all go free."

"I can't let you go free," Tark corrected, still staring at Brann, "Though I do take your meaning—your entourage will no longer be pursued as enemies of House Geiha, though you will still be expected to carry out your duties as proxy fighter in official bouts." Tark pointed at Boomer, wagging it thoughtfully. "But, yes, of course that would be the first order I give, should you manage to put me down."

"And if you put me down..." Boomer hesitated, like he didn't quite want Brann to hear the alternative spoken aloud.

"I will still release Recruit Brann from my service."

This was the last thing either of them expected to hear.

"Wait, really—" Brann began, eyes widening.

"Having thus transferred rulership of the entirety of House Lachlan and all its remaining territory," Tark interrupted, clarifying his position, "I would countenance his surrender by allowing him to go free, no longer bound to service...the moment he completes the final stage of his training by means of the Assay."

It was Boomer's turn to interrupt. "Now wait, that's not fair—"

"This is the best I can do. My hands are tied by military law." Tark shook his head. "I assure you. This is a mutually beneficial path to resolving this conflict, pithy as it is, between our Houses," he said, nodding to Brann. "There is no personal grudge at work here: not even I, the Marshal, can release a recruit from his service contract before he has fully graduated from training, and that cannot happen without being subject to the Assay."

He approached Brann now, and, in a manner entirely unlike himself, crouched down to meet the human's gaze at equal height. "This is my considerable gift to you, recruit, and I need you to understand the depths of my generosity in offering it—I am not deaf to the rumors, I know all about the stories they tell in the barracks, teenagers gathered in their undergarments to scare each other after lights out—Caleb survived his examination." Tark took a beat. "Intact, for the most part. You, on the other hand, were to be the one to die at my feet, if the rumors were to believed. Fairytales, all of it, the inventions of mischievous young men.

"You have my solemn vow, as both your commanding officer—as well as your anointed champion, should you have me—you will not come to any harm, save for the lightest and most minimally expected scrapes and bruises you may suffer under the barest of expectations for the Assay to be determined as having been successful."

Tark drew tall, and despite himself, Brann couldn't help but feel somewhat softened by this—trick or not, there was a sincerity being spoken here, one that resonated deeply. The Marshal meant every word.

"Only then, Assay complete, can I terminate your contract—after which, you will be free to live your life, your contract dismissed." Tark's hand offered itself, palm up. A rare sign of compassion. "Knowing this, do you so accept me as your champion, Brann of House Lachlan?"

Brann looked back to Boomer, who was completely agog. There was, in both of their minds, no immediate downside to this. Whether or not Boomer won this fight, Tark was allowing Brann—no, not just Brann, all of them—their freedom.

Had Brann underestimated Tark's bloodlust and uncompromising reputation? Had he really just been exhausting a disinterested Marshal this whole time, wasting enough valuable resources that he was no longer worth the chase?

It seemed one of these possibilities must be true. At this moment, there was nothing to suggest otherwise, no one to find fault in Tark's offer.

Brann, slowly, reached his arm out, hand opening to take Tark's.

"Before you accept," Tark cautioned, stopping Brann momentarily. "Think on this, recruit: You are the one who deserted in the first place, and any other solution that may be offered ends only one way. You know what that means."

Brann knew what he meant. His eyes narrowed as he took Tark's meaning, but still knew this was the best thing for everyone.

He grasped the kuaneach's hand, and shook it.

"Aye, sir."

Tark nodded curtly. "I accept as well. Thank you for your service, soldat."

He released Brann's grip suddenly, marching off towards the cage, pushing open the gate to invite Boomer in.

"Shall we?"

*

Fingers woven through the chain links of the cage, Brann's nose prodded against the cold knots of metal, eyes darting between the two towering combatants.

Boomer, lithe and limber, bouncing lightly on his hooves and jabbing out wildly to flex his elbows, his fighting form dependent on elasticity and confidence—the mane being tossed out of his eyes that glinted with their signature cocky gleam. Palomino coat loosely cradled in his crimson joggers, his sweat jacket partially unzipped, sleeves rolled up past the elbow in thick bunches of fabric: everything about him was loose and quick and disorganized, touting his arrogance, his exuberance in awaiting the fight to come.

Tark, still as the dead and cold as the grave, streaks of indigo outlining the dark of his stone scales, the barrel-chested kuaneach standing apart from himself as much as from his opponent. Black matte mesh fabric tightly clinging to every inch of him, ankle to throat, not a crease visible anywhere—save for the moment he leaned forward to raise his elbows until they almost stabbed outwards at Boomer, clawed fingers curling into themselves to create blades of his compacted knuckles above his open palms. His tail held aloft almost perpendicular to his body, and he was the image of a serpent, coiled and ready to strike, not wasting even a single breath.

The crowd, having recognized their local champ now that his armor was stripped away, began jeering and catcalling in earnest: overworld circuits held no interest to the country folk, these mercs having about as much interest in seeing a celebrity interceding on their underground sport as they did in regular showers—though, there wasn't a complete one-sidedness to their sentiments, as chargers began appearing and clicking scales into hands at a frantic pace, bets being passed around like candy, as this was likely the first time in recent memory they'd seen the Child of Rigel squaring off against someone his own size. There was always room for greed between the cracks of loyalty.

The gate swung open once more, and a stout man wearing a fur coat that nearly reached his shins waddled into the cage, pulling the crispy bangs of his stiff, sprayed hair out of his eyeliner-thick gaze. Raising his hand to hush the crowd, the announcer cum laude spoke in a harsh bellow like that of a lifelong smoker, flecks of spittle shining against the bright violet of his lipstick.

"Alright you blistery cocksuckers, don't say I never did nothin' for you—the bonus match of the evening puts two surprise entrants together, giving us a much-needed break from the usual bunch of hicks having a slap fight here in the Row. Both champs in their worlds: our returning undefeated, the Child of Rigel—"

The announcer's painted nails sparkled as his hand waved in Tark's direction—

"—And the so-called 'world champion' up in the more bourgeois circles."

He crooked his wrist limply towards Boomer. A few onlookers guffawed at this.

"Everybody gets a fair shake in the cage, even the prissy boys from up top. Both fighters paid top coin to be in the ring here tonight, so I don't wanna hear no fuckin' bellyachin' later about rigged fights when youse all lose out on your shitty bets," he barked at the crowd, manicured finger stabbing outwards in all directions. "Any of you give my bookies a hard time at the window later, I'll personally come down there and slit your fuckin' nutsacks down the middle with a sugar spoon."

Tossing his bangs once more, the announcer listened to the anticipation build for a few moments before his other hand shot up, gaudy bracelets clanking loudly against one another in a simulation of a starting bell. "Bets are now closed! Are both fighters ready to get to painting, or what?"

Tark's snout dipped slightly in a nod.

Boomer just laughed, and looked back over his shoulder, at Brann. His right fist raised above his ears, and his other hand pointed directly at the young soldat.

Just as he'd done before his final round against Raum. For some reason, the gesture didn't comfort Brann—if anything, it sent a chill through him, like something was amiss, a warning deep in the back of his mind.

This wasn't the even matchup Boomer thought it was.

"Alright, gents," the announcer rasped, letting his jangling arm fall, retreating backwards out of the gate before slamming it in his own face.

"Get to it!"

The crowd hollered, and the fight was on.

Brann sucked in a deep breath.

Tark was faster than the speed of sound, lancing forward before Brann could even hear his claws on the tile floor, coming up from a low pounce with a flying knee that could have bruised God, if Boomer hadn't narrowly avoided it by feinting to one side with trained reflexes that betrayed his vanity. Brann could see his own surprise reflected in Boomer's eyes, neither of them expecting the patient and calculating kuaneach to make the first move—and certainly not the next, with the dragon hissing out a beastly kyup as his momentum tornadoed into his tail, which whipped around and into Boomer's upraised forearms, the deafening crack of scale on bone making the crowd wince. Boomer was beaten down into a low crouch with this blow, his face contorted with enormous pain—his arms surely would have been broken, had he the bone structure of a smaller man.

Brann clenched hard on the fence, wanting to cry out. Boomer locked eyes with him for a moment and just shook his head—then, still crouching, his hands spread and his fingers fluttered outwards, like he was shaking off excess water.

A couple mercs snickered, warming to the horse's swagger.

Brann knew better. There was trouble.

The arch of Tark's back as he readied to attack once more, the delay with which Boomer stood to his hooves to ready himself—everything was wrong about this fight, everything so misaligned. A nanosecond before Boomer could anticipate it, Tark once more closed the gap between them, and machine gun palms rained down on the horse's arms in an offbeat pattern of unpredictability. It took his entire body rooted in place to defend himself, Boomer's torso bouncing about like he was caught in a hailstorm, absorbing every blow he should have slipped, bending when he should have pushed back. Tark didn't stop unloading those palms on Boomer until the horse's leg shuffled backwards and his hoof found the cage—seizing the opportunity, Boomer elbowed forward powerfully and broke the cresting wave, creating a gap in Tark's hands just wide enough for him to cup upwards and inwards, both arms exploding away and forcing Tark to leap backwards. Catching himself on the back foot in much the same way as Boomer had, Tark snapped his arms back together like a praying mantis lest his chest remain exposed, already meeting Boomer's incoming fist with a response of his own: a downward strike of his wrists, sending Boomer's hook wide, before cutting into Boomer's defenseless inner circle, head craned backwards—

—His head slamming like a battering ram against the broadside of Boomer's skull, those bony spines gilding the ridges of his eyebrows tearing Boomer's cheek open, a spark of bright blood spattering both combatant's faces as Boomer was sent toppling over to one side. The crowd lurched with excitement at the brutal blow, all but Brann, who couldn't help but cry out when Boomer's shoulder crashed into the tiles. Dazed, the prizewinning fighter had a moment of self-realization as he peeled his body out of the shattered crater in the floor, blinking away the healthy flow of blood that dripped from his eyelid—there was no time for showmanship or ego here, and it had cost him dearly to learn this, already hitting the ground only a few moments into the fight.

Tark, to his credit, retreated to one corner, allowing his enemy the honor of standing upright once more before they continued. Boomer, pushing himself up onto all fours, wiped away the wet from his vision before doing so: he needed to see his target with fresh eyes now, his head cleared of the fog of self-assuredness. He snorted, wiping an arm against his broad nose as he did, the boxy muzzle of the horse downturned in a focused grimace; when his fists raised once more, they were clenched around diamonds, ready now to crush Tark's face.

The kuaneach acknowledged this, recognizing the respect Boomer showed him now with a courteous bow of a duelist: now, they could fight properly, with ego banished from the ring.

Boomer stepped to it first this time, sprinting into a forward kick, aimed low for Tark's legs. Where another fighter may have hopped out of the way, Tark did the opposite, and dove forward face first—at the last second, his hips twisted, and he caught Boomer's leg in a scoop over his shoulder. Then, he lifted.

Boomer spun in the air, suspended in a horizontal barrel roll for a full second before landing square on Tark's knee, the crowd cringing—doubled over, Boomer wheezed, eyes popping, having no time to recover before he received a punishing elbow against the back of his head that nearly caved it in. That same arm rocked upwards into Boomer's face from below, the uppercut launching him up off of Tark's knee and opening his body up to a meteoric stabbing kick from the kuaneach's other foot; Boomer, on his feet once more despite stumbling backwards from the combination of dizzying blows, had enough sense to duck just in time to avoid the follow-up swipe from Tark's claws. His shoulder heaved upwards to bash into Tark's arm and forcibly crook its elbow, hooves stomping down to steady himself, before Boomer's offset fists had their shot: one two three, fast as daggers, pounding into Tark's belly in triplicate; Tark curled in, stomach tightening, just as expected. His guard down now, Tark's head was snapped back from the cannonfire of Boomer's arm, a tight left hook bouncing him backwards and out of Boomer's corner.

The mercs all yelped and shouted once more, finally getting to see a decent response from the underperforming challenger; Brann, still holding his breath, couldn't blink if he tried. Misguided though it was, Boomer couldn't help but grin once more, allowing himself a moment of prideful reprieve as he saw Tark recoil.

The kuaneach, cupping his jaw, processed the pain of his blow with almost clerical calmness. Not enough to seriously injure, but enough to prove a more accurate measure of Boomer's strength: he was already centering himself into a new stance now, this time with his arms bowing outwards, palms facing low, away from his hips, feet apart. He denied Boomer any expression, verbal or otherwise, simply enduring the pain and returning to the ready, calibrating to anticipate their next exchange.

Boomer, on the other hand, had a simpler design. He dashed forward now in a crouch, fists up, already swinging them outwards in another repetition of his previous bodily assault—perhaps not anticipating lightning to strike twice in the same spot, or maybe in a turn of strategy, Tark once more had a downward arcing strike deflected, and once more received a healthy barrage of fists to his gut, though not without his abdomen tightening reflexively this time, and denied another hook to the face by grappling Boomer about the shoulders and jabbing downwards with his elbow repeatedly. Though the horse gasped with each strike, he let his kidneys take this abuse, just long enough for him to settle his weight in and bend Tark's knee.

A weak spot—another charged left hook blasted against that crooked knee, collapsing Tark's sturdy form, and Boomer was free to launch his own knee skyward and up into the dragon's chin, pairing the brain-rattling blow with a well-timed spinning kick, the horse's blonde mane and tail billowing outwards like triumphant flags as he roared, eyes wide with furor.

Tark's body bounced. Tiles shattered. The crowd bleated.

Brann pumped a fist—there was hope yet, if Boomer could keep the pressure on.

The feeling was mutual, and as if reading Brann's thoughts, the horse didn't wait for Tark to regain his footing—no sooner had the kuaneach rolled onto his back, crushing his own tethered wings beneath him, before Boomer's same leg sliced downwards in another spinning kick into Tark's ribs. The dragon's arms, not raised in time to shield his chest fully, nonetheless helped absorb much of the impact, and he was left with breath in his lungs enough to roll out of the way of Boomer's follow-up stomp. The ferocious hoof turned a floor tile into powder, narrowly missing Tark's face, and in the dragon's roll he found the presence of mind to whip his heavy tail up at the ceiling—it, in turn, also barely missing Boomer's face. The maneuver gave him time to leap up onto his feet again, the bruised Tark stifling Boomer's forward advance with a surgically timed backhanded strike at chest level.

The timing was perfect, and his open hand slapped away Boomer's jab, nearly snapping the horse's elbow with the misdirection of force.

Boomer was unbalanced, catching himself on his forward leg, chest nearly folding into his knee. His defense was evaporated.

Tark followed through, his torso spinning, building momentum off his initial deflecting jab, and he pirouetted on one clawed foot—then, he was airborne, kinetic energy leaping from one arm to the other, windmilling through the air above Boomer's head—

—And he dropped the hammer, earthbound like a shooting star, a brutish snarl of fury bursting from his lungs in primal exultation as his fist pummeled into Boomer's skull.

When Tark's feet hit the ground, Boomer's head jerked backwards, and for a stunned moment Brann thought maybe the fist had merely grazed the horse's face, judging by how little he seemed to notice. Then, his body reacting on a delay, Boomer crumpled backwards in a paralyzed heap, the life evacuating his legs.

The crowd had fallen silent, strangely, their bloodlust having been sated, replaced now with a discomfiting tension—Brann's ears were ringing from the silence, Tark standing over Boomer, who would have appeared unconscious were it not for the way he had propped himself up on one elbow. Head sagging, red goo dripped from Boomer's face, pooling darkly beneath his agape lips—the will to fight was oozing out of him in streams of saliva and blood, all of his remaining strength being channeled into merely remaining conscious now.

The fight should have been ground to a halt. Someone should have intervened.

None dared move, or breathe a word of protest. Some mumbled in confusion, wondering why Tark didn't simply accept his winnings and leave.

Brann just watched, frozen, unbelieving.

The draconic warfighter dipped low, arm looping around Boomer's almost tenderly—the horse was upright once more when Tark stood, eyes seeing nothing, not even the thunderous fist that crashed into his world once more, Boomer cracking backwards like a tree that had been cut down; he would not hit the ground again, though, instead meeting the upwards sweep of yet another one of Tark's devastating elbows. Boomer went vertical, spine straightening, head cocked at a disgusting angle as a geyser of blood splashed up into the destroyed ceiling. Raindrops of scarlet rolled off stray wires and pipes above their heads, Tark unleashing an absolutely godless series of strikes against Boomer: cupping the horse's neck from behind, the butt of Tark's scaled palm drove itself over and over and over into Boomer's face, each meaty crack paired with another beastly snarl from Tark's straining lungs, each time the dragon catching his already defeated foe by the mane and guiding him upright once more.

All present just watched, cowed into humble quietude, witnessing the brutality play itself out beyond the outer limits. Brann, once more, felt the helpless child, terrified and weak, unable to do anything, unable to even speak.

His best friend was being slaughtered in front of him, and he did nothing.

Tark, soaked at this point in red water, chest heaving, had all but satisfied himself—though, impossibly, Boomer still stood, knees quaking together as they supported the lifeless upper half of the punished horse. Painful, inarticulate croaks, bubbling with an absence of sentience—the only vocalizations he could manage, an abominable sound, one that made even Brann wish it would stop. The sound of a dying animal.

Yet, still, Boomer stood. Hooves clattering against the tiles below, sticky with the puddles of his own blood, he stood, head hanging low. One awkwardly clenching hand reached up, slowly, pleadingly, to rest against Tark's chest. He had no voice to speak it aloud, but he made it clear: the fight was not over for him, either. Boomer didn't know how to lose, and with all the strength of an infant, his knuckles rapped against Tark's pectoral. Even now, on his last breath, Boomer refused to pull his punches.

Unfortunately for him, Tark understood.

The dragon reached up to clasp Boomer's hand in his own, patting it gently, soothingly. Though Boomer's eyes were hidden from view by his blood-matted mane, stuck to his face like a veil, Tark did his best to meet his gaze. There was a warrior's spirit trapped within the preening, self-aggrandizing horseman, and the kuaneach sympathized with it now, at the end of Boomer's struggle. Tark leaned in, his pointed snout whispering something into Boomer's tucked ear, something not even Brann could hear despite his straining to do so.

The warlord embraced the defeated champion, as one might a brother. Then, taking a step back, Tark inhaled deep and raised his foot like a scorpion's tail, readying to sting.

Tark executed the final blow impossibly fast, his heel a guillotine that cut into Boomer's neck, so explosive in its delivery that its shockwave sent up pulverized shards of tile from the floor around Boomer's lifeless body where it struck.

The fight, at long last, was finished.

Tark, bowing slightly to the motionless horse, rolled his shoulders to crack his neck once more and immediately made for the cage's exit, pushing aside the gate with ease. Striding past Brann, he paused for only a moment, long enough to say only a few words:

"I will complete your Assay, at another time of my choosing. For now, House Geiha thanks you, and accepts House Lachlan's surrender. Be well, little recruit—for now, you still belong to me."

28. The Sickness

Swatches of blood stitched themselves across his front, skin and clothes alike a patchwork of red sheen. Brann sat hunched against the bulkhead, much like he did in his times of quiet reflection during training, knees drawn up to his chest to act as a makeshift chinrest. The Donnie's engines quietly droned in a single held note that whistled all about the ship's pressurized spaces around him, too quiet to be uncomfortable but too loud to be completely ignored. The steely passageway of piping and bundled cables made for undesirable acoustics compared to the padding of the common areas or plush carpeting of the passenger cabins. Similarly, the metal floor beneath him was an icy excuse for a pillow, his ass having gone numb quite some time ago.

He pressed his fingertips to the cold surface, flexing the digits at the knuckles, then lifted—ghostly spots of condensation misted over where his warm fingers had been. The speckles of dewdrops that formed reflected a sort of matte sheen in the dim artificial light of the maintenance passage; Brann bobbed his head this way and that to see if any points of reflection formed in them.

None did. The microscopic droplets of moisture almost looked like little grey ants dotting the floor, and he huffed in amusement through his nostrils, entertained by the slight illusion.

Weird.

It was then he was confronted with just how humid it was beneath the ship's main spaces. Brann didn't know the first thing about aviation or how the Donnie stayed aloft, but he was sure something about how the engines operated were causing the humidity, and likely the cold temperature as well, given how warm the night air had been when they had taken off—

The crushing dead weight of Boomer's upper body across his shoulder, his legs practically kicking back against the ground as if he were swimming to stay upright, the barest of consciousness present to keep from flattening Brann on the spot—the narrow alleys, teeming with impassive bystanders, parting like drifting leaves around them.

"HELP US," Brann was screaming hoarsely, summoning the strength of his whole body to cry out from the depths of his crushed lungs as he dragged his dying friend between the shacks. "PLEASE HELP ME, SOMEBODY, ANYBODY—"

Boomer withered against him, the horse heaving, expelling a fresh gush of bloody bile directly across Brann's boots. The packed dirt ground turned to muddy death beneath his feet.

Brann's voice choked upwards to a desperate pitch, a childlike wail of terror, the unheeded words coming as a thoughtless mantra at this point as he pleaded:

"SOMEBODY, ANYBODY, PLEASE, HELP ME, HELP ME—"

The hatch directly to his left squealed open, Brann's head swiveling to look, surprised to see nobody there. He blinked, confused, then from his right came a pitter patter of talons.

The raven peered up at him in a gawky fixation. Brann felt he was being sized up.

"What's up."

Grishka puffed her throat feathers out in response. A shimmer of unfocused vision, and she sat upright beside him, mimicking Brann's posture in a decidedly more humanoid form, though her beak remained a fixed point between the young man's eyes.

"You've grown," she finally croaked after a shared moment of appraising one another's appearance.

"Really?" He was surprised to hear her say that. That kind of observation, coming from the typically mute witch—it softened something in him. Brann shrugged meekly, hoping it didn't come across as dismissive. "I sure don't feel it. Feel like the same scared recruit—no, scratch that; the scared kid that ran away from the home all those years ago. Doesn't feel at all like I—"

"No," Grishka squawked, interrupting him with an annoyed shuffle of feathers across her shoulders. "Taller."

"...Oh." Brann's gaze flickered up towards his own forehead briefly, as if he might see a height marker floating just overhead. He cleared his throat sheepishly. "Right. 'Grown.' Thought I was done, but I guess not."

The witch tossed her beak aside. "Tch. Never done growing. Alla time, we all grow, never stop. Stop growing, then die."

Brann nodded—so she was attempting to speak metaphorically after all. "Guess that's true too. Every time I've thought I've seen all there is to see, you all have some new wild place to show me, some new piece of advice to share, and I think to myself—"

"No," Grishka repeated sternly, once more silencing Brann. "Taller, I said. *Taller.*"

Maybe not. He stared at the shapeshifter, utterly nonplussed. "You're saying that we literally just grow upwards and get taller and taller forever until we die."

Her returned stare challenged Brann silently. *Did I stutter?*

Brann sighed and reset his gaze forward, suddenly a lot less confident in this conversation being the deeper heart to heart he was expecting. On his right hand, the knuckles were aching—he rubbed at them tenderly, slipping slowly back into his own muted thoughts.

Grishka had other plans, apparently. "You talk funny."

"Thanks, you too."

Brann's annoyance was lost on her, the witchy avian leaning in close to investigate his features, those big glossy eyes roaming over him with critical absorption. "Dress funny. Act funny." She flipped up his collar with her long beak. "Wear clothes when still dirty? Tch tch."

Brann took her meaning, the comment aimed at the blood still soaked into his blouse. "Changing wasn't really at the top of my list of priorities."

"Always change." The raven shimmered beside him once more, leaving the impression of the dark-haired witchy woman in Brann's peripheral sight, the ash of ephemeral feathers drifting around him. "Me? Always change. Change good. Make what you don't like better."

He wasn't in the mood for more of these transliteral exchanges, so he didn't respond. Brann only had one thing on his mind—anticipating when the hatchway opposite him would open, Boomer standing there, giving his signature wry grin through bloodied teeth.

It had been seven hours, and the hatch remained firmly sealed.

His ear tickled, like a roaming insect was caught in his hair—Brann brushed at it, knocking something aside; a small twig rolled off his shoulder, and Grishka caught it deftly in her beak before it could touch the ground. She bobbed her head at Brann's hand, indicating for him to hold it out. Reluctantly, he obliged, and the twig fell into his palm.

"Old twig. No more grow, no more change." Her beak tapped his thumb. "Bend twig."

Furrowing his brow, Brann rolled the twig between his thumb and forefinger, using his middle finger to apply pressure, doing his best to bend the twig without it breaking. A foregone conclusion: it snapped easily, leaving crumbles of woody dust in his hand.

Grishka plucked away the offending debris, and her beak slipped between the feathers of her wing, rummaging about as if looking through a purse, before she withdrew another twig. This one, however, was far more supple and green, even sprouting a young flowering bud near one end. She placed it in Brann's palm once more. "Bend," she commanded again.

Brann paused, then did as he was told, repeating his movements. In his fingers, the younger twig refused to break, even as a whitened crease formed along its length.

"Still growing," Grishka noted, indicating the small flower. "Still changing. Can't break.

Brann took her meaning, thumbing gently at the flower, causing Grishka to give a satisfied nod. A thought struck him, eyes drawn once more to the snapped twig at his feet.

"What happens when we stop growing?" He looked at Grishka imploringly, the young man burdened with an unfamiliar weight of dread in his chest. "What happens when we die?"

For all her communicative quirks, she seemed to understand Brann fully, and her demeanor shifted ever so slightly. She mimed a deeper tone of voice, someone no doubt having asked her this very question before:

"'Where do our thoughts go,'" Grishka said, throat puffing out a bit as she flexed her vocal cords. It almost sounded like someone Brann knew.

Brann nodded. "Yes."

Perhaps he simply had expected too much of her mysticism, or maybe it was just a deeper question than could be answered through the haze of their shared language barrier, but Grishka's answer was less than Brann had hoped for. The raven witch reached back into her feathers to search for something—had she always had that bundle of necklaces clattering about?—and withdrew a small object, affixed to a string of leather loops, placing it in Brann's outstretched palm.

It was a small wooden totem, carved from some sort of hard wood—or perhaps it was polished basalt—in the unmistakable shape of a perched raven.

Inwardly he frowned, but outwardly Brann just nodded, pretending to understand, handing the small fetish back. "Ah, right," he said, looking away once more. "Of course."

Another thought struck him, and Brann's gaze swiveled back towards Grishka. His thumb jutted back at the hatchway across from him. "Wait, weren't you supposed to be in—"

The sound of the hatch creaking open snapped Brann's head upwards, his forehead stinging from the welt left by his forearm where it had rested, the young man blinking the sleep out of his eyes. Perched on Emrys's shoulder, Grishka's beady little eyes winked back at Brann from beyond the threshold—Brann stood to greet the two of them, rubbing a knuckle into his eye. "How is he?"

Emrys stopped short, surprised to see Brann waiting for them. "Far be it for me to question the loyalty of the Geihan infantry, but surely I would have retreated to my quarters by now." He wadded up a tissue wet with red and let it fall into a wastebasket just behind the hatch before stepping out, using his hand to protect Grishka's head from bumping against the upper frame, the raven responding by nipping his fingers. "Coming from anyone but myself, these words would surely prove ill tidings, but I would bid the young sir to take them in the spirit of optimism in which they're given..." Emrys pulled the hatch shut behind him tightly, dusting off his hands before turning to face Brann with a hopeful smile. "He is far beyond my reach."

Brann stared at Grishka curiously, still somewhat murky on whether or not the exchange he'd just had with her had really taken place. "So, he's gonna be okay?"

"I wouldn't go so far as to say that," Emrys cautioned, motioning for Brann to walk with him, leading the three of them back up the passageway towards the ascent to the passenger cabins. "I mean only to say that my influence reaches beyond where its effects can be felt by the living, and in the fields of aether where the dead and dying speak their last rites, no whispers did I hear spoken by our equine friend. Despite the Marshal's best efforts, Boomer remains firmly rooted on our side of the Ghostfence—he possesses an admirable defiance towards death I've not seen in another living soul."

Brann followed Emrys up a ladder, emerging into the warmer and decidedly more comforting passageway above, the familiar sight of crimson carpeting and amber light fixtures greeting them. "But you don't think that he's ever going to fully recover?"

"It's no small admission that you've far greater knowledge of the realm of corporeal medicine than myself," Emrys conceded, helping Brann up to his feet. "The precipice between life and death is slippery indeed, and your early intervention may have been the single greatest factor in keeping your friend from falling into the mist. Any lingering effects on his higher functions that may or may not be present when he attains consciousness once more...well, I'd do my best to see them as a welcome alternative to the complete and total loss we very nearly suffered today." He clapped a hand on Brann's shoulder, perhaps realizing he wasn't the best at offering comforting words, his face somewhat contorted with regret. "You did a good job, I suppose is what I mean," Emrys concluded, "Though I may meander in my usual way to get to the point. Boomer would not be alive if it weren't for you being there to aid him—his trust in you as a friend will no doubt prove rewarding to the rest of us doubters."

Emrys's eyes turned downwards, something catching his attention, and he smirked with a small chuckle of recognition. "Mercy me—I see you've been getting acquainted with another mutual friend of ours." He reached down to gently grasp Brann's wrist, raising it to bring to eye level the small green twig Brann was still clutching, examining the small flower closely. Grishka hopped sideways to reach down and snatch the twig away from the both of them, tucking it decisively beneath her wing, Brann watching it disappear with a somewhat stupefied look.

"The further out you swim to seek answers, the further away from the shore of understanding you'll be," Emrys responded, tapping a finger against his temple. "The witches we share our world with don't care much for abiding by our own pithy logics—best to simply acknowledge that whenever you feel like getting your arms around whatever trick of the mind they've played on you, rest assured, the next one they conjure will make you feel quite a bit more stupid than the last one did."

"The little totem she carries," Brann said, taking this piece of advice in stride as he stared awestruck at the raven, "Why did she show me that? When I asked her a question..."

"Ah," Emrys nodded, already knowing where this was going. "Touched on the very subject we've been discussing, I take it? No worries, I myself was puzzled by that same response the first time I met her. Though I would perjure myself to attempt to recall the name she gives it, our

Grishka's particular classification of witchcraft denies the traditional communions one must take to learn its ways. In matters of life and death, I'm afraid Grishka is no more suited to answer questions of that nature as we are, given that these nature-based beings simply do not die in the way we do." Emrys offered up his fingers once more for Grishka's beak to explore and nibble, doting on the sentient bird as if she were any other pet. "Until the day comes that our kind never again see a raven flying up above, Grishka's spirit will continue to roam the skies, adrift on a sort of...communal breeze of incarnation. She lives in each of them, unbound by the individual form she inhabits at any given time."

Brann squinted. "'We?'"

"Hm?" Emrys looked back, then nodded. "Ah, yes. You'll note I did not count myself among those immune to the affliction we call 'death,' despite my own...resistances to it." He began drifting down the hall, and once more Brann followed, though their pace was far less purposeful now. "I do not count myself among the immortals, you may be surprised to hear. I held my hands to the fires of the beyond, and they burned away my sensitivity towards them—quite literally, actually, look," Emrys said, holding his bandaged hands out in front of him for Brann to examine. "Not as much a fashion statement as a necessity of the gag reflex, as most would find it upsetting to see these hands unbound by these blessed wrappings. I once put to paper a spell of untenable purpose, and the consequences of that ill venture were my aversion to fleshly demise. Should I meet my end, it will require a tactic more suited to the damned creatures I myself have become so adept at dismissing. No offense," he added, folding his hands together apologetically as he referenced the first night he had met Brann.

Brann just shook his head. Momentarily at ease in regards to Boomer's well-being, he stared now at his own feet, becoming far more concerned with the larger question that had taken up residence in him. "I had asked Grishka what happens to us when we die," he said pointedly, cutting to the chase when Emrys would not.

"Yes, of course," Emrys sighed in response. It would appear Grishka was not the only one with a disappointing answer to that question. He pondered momentarily, an unusual beat of quiet consideration amidst his wordy ministrations. "Brann," he finally said, a questioning tone to his voice, "I'd venture that you have not seen death up close before."

"Not someone I know so well, no," Brann admitted. "Someone I...someone I'd miss, I mean."

The corners of Emrys's mouth twitched a bit. "I'm afraid it would be irresponsible of me to give an affirmation of any sort. What happens to us—you might say, where our thoughts go, where we go when we die—will remain the single unanswerable question in my scholarly pursuits."

"But you practice necromancy, I thought," Brann retorted, incredulous. "Bringing the dead back to life, killing the undead, that sort of thing. A minute ago you were just talking about a place where their souls prosper."

"I'm afraid I once again have allowed my overly articulate ways to prove my downfall." Emrys sighed, removing his wide-brimmed hat to run his palm over a sweat-shined forehead, his retreating hairline being smoothed over in the process. "I fully admit to painting a far more interesting portrait of what it means to practice the art of dying in more than just a scholarly sense, but the truth is all I can do when reaching behind the veil is to feel about in the dark. Blind, deaf, and mute. I can speak the words that will run a current through a lifeless body once more, but the impetus that animates them—it lacks..." He rubbed his fingers together, struggling to properly explain himself. "The texture, the sense of self that lends flavor to what we define as someone's soul...I can't recreate that once it has departed. Had I been forced to bring our friend Boomer back from beyond that door, I fear I'd have been pleading to an unseen and unknowable God as effectively as if my tongue had been cut from my head. A fate some would see fitting, no doubt," Emrys tried to joke. Brann didn't laugh, and Emrys fell silent.

"You mean if Boomer really had died," Brann said sullenly in an attempt to finish the thought, "You don't know if you could have brought him back...because you don't know if there's anything to bring back."

Once more, Emrys sighed, coming to a halt. He replaced his hat, then turned, putting both hands-on Brann's shoulders. "I am sorry, my young friend, truly," he said, dejected. "I'm afraid I have not felt the touch of a loved one beyond the door, nor heard the reassurance of a loving God awaiting my return home. But, before you let that fear of oblivion drag you down into the abyss," he interjected as he saw Brann's face begin to darken, "Consider this, if you will—

"—The question of life after death has given rise to an entire college of academia, in which I consider myself—all things considered—quite the novice. I could live a thousand lifetimes, from which my contribution to the book of life would amount to no more than a single page, one liable to be scratched out in corrective ink generations later." Emrys paused, then, seeing Brann examining the twig he still held a bit more closely, ended their lengthy dialogue with only this:

"Son, ask anyone I've studied under. I'm just not smart enough to answer that question."

*

"Nothing," Nes said simply.

"You didn't have to think very long about that," Brann said, surprised.

"Don't have to." Nestor sniffed, wiping grease from his cheek, succeeding only in smearing it higher up on his face. He didn't look away from his work, tooling away at a stretch of paneling, hunched low beside where Brann sat in the ship's cockpit. "You die, that's it. No reward, no great big welcoming party on the other side—no other side. You're just gone."

"Fine way to comfort the kid," Zay shot back over her shoulder, draped unprofessionally over the pilot's seat, hands off the stick this time as she uncharacteristically let Hawkshaw have complete control of the ship.

"Best way to comfort someone is to be honest with them," Nes replied. He removed what appeared to be a burnt spark plug of some kind and tossed it aside, resoldering the replaced part in its housing. "Kid's shook up over seeing his friend almost die, he's going through something we all have to go through eventually—would be cruel to try to drag it out for him by lying."

"The key point you seem to be missing," Zay said accusingly, her chair swiveling around so she could glare at Nes, "Is that it is his friend, like you said. Maybe show a little more tact."

Nestor stopped what he was doing, withdrawing from beneath the control panel to give a more direct response, saying quietly:

"Boomer is my friend too."

Zay's eyes remained narrowed, but she didn't respond, and eventually her chair spun back around.

"You don't agree with Nes?" Brann asked hopefully.

"Just because I don't like his attitude about it doesn't mean I don't agree with him," Zay returned, though she did so far less confidently. "I don't know, I don't think about it that much—never did me any favors in my previous line of work, certainly doesn't now. At least I don't try to act so certain about it, like I know better than everyone else."

"I hope you don't mean me," Hawkshaw spoke up, somewhat indignant.

"You certainly have a pattern of know-it-all-ism that is quite easily tracked," Zay grumbled.

"Well, take solace, my frumpy friend, in the knowledge that you are speaking quite a foreign language to me at present," Hawkshaw said, raising a finger demonstratively. "I am, for all intents and purposes, completely disqualified from giving any sort of opinion on this subject, given that I exist only as a simulation that mirrors your lesser fleshbags' consciousness. I don't die, I just...shut down. Couldn't give an answer if I tried, and any answer I give would be preprogrammed."

"So much for an advanced learning AI core," Zay joked, rolling her eyes.

"Hey, don't do that—don't—drag my ability to learn your primitive ways into this, hampered as they are," Hawkshaw complained, and Brann felt a wicked headache coming on as the two rival pilots began another bickering match. "You'd be surprised to know how debilitating it can be to my algorithms to spend so much time in company so lacking intelligence—

"Sweet bloody hell, you really can't shut it off, can you?" Zay's voice was raised now, and the argument was in full swing.

"We just covered that, dear. If I shut off, I literally die, by your definitions," Hawkshaw crooned. "Is that what you really want? Do you want me to die?"

"Yes! I have said this out loud, to your face, many times already!"

With that, Brann drifted out of his seat to make for the exit. He wasn't getting the answers he wanted to hear, and Nestor took notice, the engineer casting a concerned glance after him. Brann let the noise turn to mush behind the hatch above his head as he closed it, boots clicking against the ladder rungs on his descent. Reaching the bottom rung, he stepped off, turning to see with a start that Wolf was there, detached from his usual position at Red's side.

"Hard question to answer," Wolf growled, nodding upwards towards the hatch. "Not easy, seeing it happen to someone close."

Brann rubbed at his eyes, the headache only intensifying. Wolf may have had good intentions, but this was no longer of great concern to the young man at the present, beginning to feel someone nauseated. "Not like anyone cares enough to try, anyway," he said bitterly.

Wolf tilted his head. "I care."

"The fuck does that matter?" Brann snapped suddenly, his vision blurring. He didn't know why that made him so mad, but frankly, he didn't care—he'd had his fill of everyone around him being so dismissive of his feelings, and by his approximations, he was entitled to a little shitty behavior.

Wolf didn't blink, however. Brann's attitude didn't faze him, clearly. "Something's wrong."

"Yeah, no shit," Brann spat back, moving to get past the lycan. He found himself hitting a wall—Wolf's arm had stretched out to block his way, and he felt the snuffling of the werewolf's nostrils against his ear.

"No. Something's wrong," Wolf repeated. "You're different."

"Listen," Brann said, planting both hands between himself and Wolf's arm before shoving it bodily away, spinning on his heel to look the great beastman in the eye. There was an itchy fire in his spine, an unusual flaring in him, something unlike his usual conflict-averse self that was eager to get out and draw blood from someone. "You want to have another stupid fucking dialogue with me about how I've changed or grown or whatever? You can go ahead and ask 'mom' to use her magic to suck your blood out of me so I don't have to hear it—frankly, I liked you more when I didn't understand you."

Wolf seemed, impossibly, crestfallen. For the first time ever, Brann sensed a sort of reversal in who was scared of who, even if only barely. It struck him how very angry he was—it also struck him how little he cared.

"I only meant," Wolf said, avoiding direct eye contact, hunching slightly, "You smell different. Like you might be...sick."

"Graduated top of your training class, didn't you?" Brann spun once more, emboldened by his own hateful energy, coasting on it all the way down the passageway. "Stupid fucking dog."

He said it quietly enough that a person wouldn't be able to hear. He knew Wolf wasn't a normal person, and could hear quite well. Behind him, he sensed the lycan's posture drawing down, and knew the insult hit home.

Flexing his hand, Brann's aching fingers were really beginning to pain him.

*

"We've a serious problem," Lorna announced, her face grim.

The back hatch of the rover was drawn upward, somewhat resembling a clamshell yawning open—the vehicle in question, a terrain cart that could have passed for an oil tanker on first glance, looking as if it had just arrived from last century given its weathered exterior. Lorna leaned out of the hatchway, speaking to the rest of the returned party as they arrived, having just stepped off the Donnie mere moments ago—both the ship and the rover were nestled between two hills, Mercenary Row nearly a day's distance on the trail behind. They were well and truly into the Wilds now and, as Zay had mentioned only in passing to Brann, the furthest away from civilization as they were willing to travel in the sky.

"Please, keep us in suspense," Zay replied stiffly, giving an annoyed grimace as she was shuffled to the side to make way for Wolf pushing past to amble up to Lorna, the latter giving her compatriot a snout rub almost unconsciously. Wolf's tail swished about in return, signaling his glad return to his ward's side, the half day they'd spent apart likely the longest he'd been away from her in years.

The viscountess allowed the rest of the team to climb aboard before following behind, speaking to them over Brann's shoulder as he surveyed the inside of the rover: with just barely enough room to stand upright in, the cramped space definitely seemed to have everything they need in varying states of accessibility. "Perhaps someone more suited to these modern amenities can give assent," Lorna was saying as Brann sidestepped what appeared to be a dining station extending from a passenger module, the compact table cluttered with flatware and cooking utensils, "But I made several troubling discoveries when charting a course to our destination. The glowing table, the, erm, geographical display..."

"The atlas array," Zay corrected, ducking underneath an open cargo flap—Brann followed suit, catching a glimpse of white and scarlet garments spilling out.

"Yes, that," Lorna confirmed, "It allowed me to select from varying conditions of our itinerary—should we decide to travel at night, avoid any inclement weather, things of that nature—and I spent a great deal of time comparing the topography of each choice it presented me with." The four of them had come to a stop, gathered around another extended table, this one humming with electric purpose as it generated a luminescent three-dimensional map across its surface not unlike the one Nestor and Zay had referred to after their crash-landing near Lachlan.

"This is the last course I had charted, pending any other corrections the rest of you could have made once you'd arrived," Lorna continued, placing her fingertips around a dial on the broad side of the array and tweaking it slightly—the treads of the surface hissed softly, the holographic image scrolling smoothly, their overhead view of the land following the fixed perspective of a floating arrowhead. It took a moment for Brann to put together that this represented the rover, the arrow surrounded by small white and red dots that emulated a compass rose, indicating the polar directions in relation to their route—which, overall, didn't seem all that concerning to Brann. Expert though he was not, he was recalling his auxiliary training courses, the days spent learning to read a map and navigate based on geographical hazards like deep bodies of water or treacherous cliffs.

"Pretty smooth sailing," he offered, not seeing the problem so far. Lorna held up a finger, continuing to rotate the dial until the arrow came to a halt at its destination: an octagonal structure, definitely not naturally occurring, suspended beyond a manmade bridge of some sort that extended outwards from what must have been the cliffs of the Bloody Northern Coast.

"The Dakhma," Lorna noted, a slender finger pointing to the structure, "Or, at least, all of it we can see—this atlas array can't retrieve satellite data, so everything we're seeing is generated from the ground up. If it's too high a mountain or too deep a trench, it's invisible to us." She flipped a switch beside the dial, and the analog treads of the array clacked loudly as something unlocked—then, turning the dial again, the perspective of the entire display began to tilt on its axis, the holographic features of the landscape compressing and receding into the table behind the arrow as everything that lay before it began to rise up and expand. Finer details became visible, the cliffs flanking the bridge serving as a helpful point of reference to determine elevation, for example—points on the map that had seemed flat now appeared to be gentle hills, even a few tiny pinpricks representing what must have been large clusters of rocks or trees that were large enough to be detected by the array.

Impressive as the machine was, Brann couldn't help but shrug, still not seeing a problem.

"This is the same route, identical travel conditions, but mapped six hours prior." Lorna flipped the switch, and the table reset with another loud clack, their perspective flattening to the bird's eye view—then, punching in a numerical code on a panel, the hologram flickered a bit as the analog treads reset with a gentle hiss. The image was soon restored to the initial projection at the start of the route. Rotating the dial, once more the floating arrow began its journey, floating through the unassuming maze of formless obstacles.

This time, however, something new tickled at Brann's perception of the image, though he couldn't quite make sense of it—something about the way certain details had shifted or blurred, maybe? Almost like there were some sort of interference with the signal—

There, just a short distance away from the Dakhma—Brann snapped his fingers as he pointed it out. "There, what is that? Trees? Why'd they move?"

"Not trees," Lorna said, shaking her head. "Legs."

This sent a chill through Brann. "So...not trees...some giant creature, big enough to pass as part of the landscape..."

"A Goliath," Nestor muttered, shaking his head. "Well, we expected this might be the case, it doesn't change anything other than possibly what time of day we decide to move, improve our chances of avoiding it. Something that size, that slow, moving in a straight line...probably just passing through the area, not patrolling any kind of established hunting grounds or territory."

"I agree, but that's not the real problem, is it?" Zay asked, not taking her eyes off the map.

"Correct." Lorna continued scrolling past until the arrow arrived at its destination once more. "What's changed?"

The other three leaned in, attempting to discern a difference. "Can you do the—the thing—" Brann started, but Lorna was already on it, flipping the switch and tilting the elevation. One immediate difference stood out like a sore thumb: cutting through the image, leading away from the bridge—or perhaps towards it—some sort of crevice or fissure, a winding streak on the land, like someone had reached down and dragged a fingertip gently against the surface of the image...

"Kobolds," Zay announced, and Nes immediately recoiled, wiping a hand across his face with a heavy sigh.

"I thought so too, yes," Lorna agreed. "Must be hundreds of them, if they can be picked up by these weak sensors."

Brann was at a loss. "Kobold? What is that?"

"A small, obnoxious, kleptomaniac, all-around pain in the rear," Nestor said, suddenly looking very tired as he rubbed at an eye, "Like if you taught a lizard to stand on its hind legs and swear. Vicious little thieves, but largely they're just a nuisance more than anything, easy to wave off; the problem is when you get a huge mob of them together, and the things that might scare one or two away instead just make them hungry."

"And the only thing that would bring so many of them together, jealous little fucks that they are," Zay continued on Nestor's behalf, "Is a unifying leader big and mean enough to scare them all into doing its bidding."

"The Goliath?" Brann asked, but Lorna shook her head.

"Goliaths are feral creatures, largely driven by impulse, incapable of communicating with lesser forms in any meaningful way—or at least, they're not interested in doing so." Zay frowned and crossed her arms. "See them leaving the Dakhma? Probably going out hunting, looking to bring tribute back. Whatever being it is they serve, it's a sure bet it calls the

Dakhma home, so whatever it is, we'll have to get through it—and its kobold army—to find what we're after."

"Assuming the interior of the structure is still intact and the kobolds haven't completely remodeled the place." Nes nodded, looking far more pensive than usual.

All of this information, surprisingly, left Brann unmoved. "So," he began, brow furrowed as he tried to make sense of why this was so upsetting to the other three, "Instead of travelling half a day over land and trying to sneak past or outrun the giant monster we might encounter, then cutting our way through hundreds of these kobold things, then hoping we still have enough energy to do battle with their boss—which, we don't even know who or what it is, only that it's something that should worry us—why don't we just...fly for another hour or so to where we're headed," He said, pointing at the bridge. "Then we just hover up high till we see the kobolds leave, drop down real quick, run in and take the big bad boss by surprise, then get out before the little ones—or the other really big one, for that matter—come back?"

Nes looked about to scold Brann's ignorance, but Zay held out a hand, shaking her head. "He's never been into the Wilds before, relax." She gestured all about the interior of the rover. "We have to travel like this, low profile, because a small vehicle is more likely to go unnoticed to a disinterested Goliath," Zay explained to Brann with far more patience than she would have in the weeks prior. "Not to mention that even if a ship as big as the Donnie can fly over the head of a ground-walker without it swiping us out of the sky..."

"...We're just as likely to meet a flying Goliath hiding behind a cloud," Lorna chimed in helpfully. "A ship as slow as the *Myrmidon* could never outrun one of those."

"She's got a fat ass built for comfort, not speed," Nes agreed, shaking his head. "Not that I haven't done my fair share of complaining about always travelling behind schedule, but who would listen, right? I think we know which idiot we can agree for that particular design choice."

"Hey Nes?" Brann spoke up, suddenly feeling acid dripping in his belly. "Shut up."

Nes froze. "Say again?"

"Kinda tired of you always talking down to Boomer," Brann growled, nostrils flaring. "After all he's done for you, I'd be a little more grateful, and stop trying to chop him down every time you feel a little insecure about your own shitty self."

Nes, Zay, and Lorna all just stared at Brann, completely mortified by this sudden hostility. After a moment of stunned silence, Nestor replied, "Don't think the rest of us haven't noticed how pissy you've been since the fight, shipmate. I don't think I'd be out of line by saying we'd all like to take a shot at being more patient and understanding with you, given what you must be going through—"

"Please, tell me, what am I going through, exactly?" Brann's teeth were grinding together, blood boiling, hand clenching and unclenching as the knuckles burned. He scratched at his aching digits absentmindedly, staring Nes down. "What else is wrong with me that you haven't gotten a chance to pick me apart over, you and the rest of the crew? Because I can't wait to—"

Pale fingers spiderwebbed across his face, tilting his head back, then to the left, then the right. Lorna squeezed Brann's cheek firmly, then lifted his eyelid, examining the red membranes. "Were you bitten?"

Caught off guard by this sudden clinical examination, Brann felt his rage momentarily subsiding. "Bitten—what do you mean?"

"The creature in Jan-Jito," Lorna said, snatching up Brann's hand, spreading the fingers, examining his nailbeds. "Or at the fight. Or at some other time you were out of our sight. Were you bitten? Monster, person, rodent? Stung by some insect? Eaten any strange-smelling flowers? Hear someone whispering in a strange language at you from some dark alleyway?"

Brann was dumbfounded, not putting up any resistance to this alarming new level of concern for his well-being, not even as Lorna was peeling up his lip to examine his teeth. "Naw, nuffin 'ike 'at," he tried to say, tonguing at his gums somewhat self-consciously. "Wha' are yew—"

"Look, there," Lorna interrupted, tilting Brann's head so far back he thought it might twist off. "Elongated canines, inflamed lymph nodes, a wobbly dilation of the pupils—irises showing amber spots as well."

"What's wrong with him?" Nestor said, circling around the table to get a closer look. "Was he infected with something?"

"He has all the signs of early-stage haematic lycanthropy," Lorna said, visibly alarmed. "Caught early enough it isn't beyond helping, but more than far enough along we could still be burying him before the week is out—without knowing how he was infected, he's as good as lost anyway."

"What the hell?" Zay said, reaching for the knife at her belt. "Is he gonna turn into a werewolf and attack us?"

"Bury me?!" Brann stammered, growing increasingly panicked.

"Odds of survival are more the question, haematic transmissions more often than not result in fatality before victims ever change," Lorna said to Zay. "Young sir, I need you to think carefully, when in the recent past have you come into contact with any lycan; that is, any other than The Wolf?"

"I haven't, really," Brann pleaded, beginning to sweat, unsure of this new nausea was imagined or not. "He's the only one."

"That's not possible," Lorna insisted, her thumb digging firmly into his collarbone. "You're telling me you don't have the faintest idea of when you could have been exposed to werewolf blood?"

"No, I know exactly when I was," Brann asserted, wilting a bit beneath the surprising strength of Lorna's grip. "When Wolf and I did that ritual together, that was the only time it could have happened, I swear."

Lorna stiffened. "Ritual?"

"Back in the cell," Brann recalled. "When we did the—you know, so I could understand him, we did the thing with the bowl, swapping blood—?"

Immediately, he was released. Lorna's already pale face, impossibly, drained of even more of its color. "You did a transfusion ritual...with him? My Wolf?"

Brann blinked, rubbing at his shoulder. "Well, yeah, didn't he— should I...not have done that?" He stared dumbly. "Shouldn't he have already...told you?"

Nestor's hands shot up into the air. Zay giggled in terror. "You fucking idiot," she cackled. Lorna stumbled backwards, nearly losing her balance.

"You were too badly injured," Brann said, voicing his thoughts out loud as the realization was just dawning on him. "He was only concerned with you, and probably...forgot to even mention it..."

"Come with me, young man," Lorna said, and like the unforgiving vicegrip of an unholy crab, her clawlike fingers were clamped onto his earlobe, dragging Brann behind her back out of the rover. Ignoring his pained cries, Lorna dropped to the ground, forcing Brann to double over to keep his ear within reach, lest it be torn off entirely.

"You." Lorna addressed Wolf now, her free hand shooting out a finger to point accusingly at her hostage. "Did you perform a transfusion ritual with this stupid boy?"

Wolf, ears flattened, nodded. "Yes, I apologize, I should have said so sooner. I meant to as soon as you had fully recovered."

Lorna stared for a moment, then snapped back to Brann, elbow swiveling to point that angry finger at Wolf in exchange. "Did you understand what he said just now?"

"Every word of it, yeah," Brann whimpered. "He's a lot chattier than I thought he was."

Lorna finally released Brann, the young man nearly falling out of the rover, deciding instead to lower himself to sit at the edge of the hatchway instead as he rubbed tenderly at his ear. "You are utterly hopeless," she spat in disbelief. "How deranged must you be to take communion with a literal fucking werewolf?"

Brann thought this may have only been the second time he'd heard Lorna swear. "I just assumed it must have been no big deal," he reasoned. "You must have done it with him too, right? That's how you understand him, how he knew how to do it?"

Her hand reached for the sky in exasperation. "That is entirely different—I am an experienced blood mage who knew well enough to purify his blood and introduce sanctified plasmids into my body first!"

"I didn't...do any of that, so, okay, I'm sorry," Brann admitted, still rubbing at his ear. "What do we do now, then, so worst case I don't keel over and die, best case I don't turn into a werewolf like him? No offense," he added, glancing sideways at Wolf who just shrugged.

"You won't just keel over and die," she corrected, eyes narrowing. "When the infection has taken root in every white blood cell, every ounce of hemoglobin, every grain of marrow, you will quite literally spill out of your own skin. Burst open in a sludgy mess as your skeleton leaps free, snapping apart as it contorts and twists itself, reforming into the shape of the wolf—assuming you survive the first, second, or third stages of this horrific expulsion of your former self, then yes, you will transform into what you and I could call a werewolf. But not one like him," Lorna said with her head cocking to the side towards Wolf. "No, he's special. You would just become a common demon, a beast of the night, not so much mindless and unthinking—more trapped in a prison of your shattered self, forced to bear witness to every memory still left in your head warp into nightmares that drive you mad, drive you to kill and devour everyone you know in love—in this case, all of us—in hopes that your hellish consumption of our own bodies and spirits may cleanse your own of your eternal torment."

Brann squinted. "I'm guessing it won't?"

Lorna shook her head. "No, it won't."

Brann took a beat. "Well that's not very good."

"No, it isn't."

Throwing one last look of incredulous disgust his way, Lorna sidestepped Brann to stand before Wolf. "You and I will be having a conversation later that you will not enjoy. You can think about what you wish to say to me in your defense while I'm gone—you're staying behind with Emrys, in case he and the witch need help treating Boomer."

Wolf chuffed at that, arms crossing, tossing his head dejectedly. "Babysitting duty."

"Let me pour you some sympathy, believe me when I say my cup runneth over," Lorna retorted. "With luck we should be back before tomorrow—that is to say, if our young saboteur here doesn't find another way to upend things before then."

"You don't think I should stay behind too, in case my condition worsens? You made it sound like I didn't have much time," Brann worried.

Lorna drew back her coat, her fingers slipping from a pouch on her belt a long and slender needle, hollow with a notched tip. "You don't. Emrys and Grishka have an altogether different set of skills ill-suited for your particular sickness—you will be my special project for the evening."

Brann just stared, his face draining until it was as pale as Lorna's blouse.

29. The Quickening

They had left behind the smooth gravel of the more well-travelled road some time ago, and even the hardy rover was beginning to bounce and shudder on its suspension, making the tree of jars of saline clack noisily against the wall—one was pumping its clear fluid through the tubing that was piped into the gap between Brann's knuckles; another jar, the contents diluted with a deep rusty red, was draining contaminant from Brann's upper torso, the needle tucked directly behind his clavicle. While the smaller needle in his hand was practically invisible to his senses, so long as Brann didn't clench a fist, the larger one grated against his collarbone in a way he couldn't quite articulate in human language. Nevertheless, he did his best:

"This SUCKS," Brann moaned out loudly, punctuating the extended silence between himself and the other two passengers in the rover's cabin.

"You'll have to take it on faith I chose the path of lesser torment for you," Lorna replied dryly, lounging back in the seat beside Brann. "The alternative was this—" She held a finger to the needle in his torso, making him wince, "—Going straight under your tongue, into the lingual artery." She demonstrated by sliding the finger up to his throat, hooking it just behind his jawbone. "Unless you find that scenario appealing, which I'd find troublesome, given how much we're being jostled and shuffled about on this rocky path."

"I'd pay a decent sum to see that," Zay contributed, smirking from behind her workstation, a platform folded out of the wall to allow her to strip and clean her autocannon. The weapon had largely been reassembled already, the skeleton of the barrel and gas pistons exposed as Zay polished the awkward recesses of the removed dust cover.

"Is it just me," Brann continued, ignoring Zay, "Or is that third one glowing?" His gaze was fixated on the jar dangling between the other two, the liquid contents indeed giving off an almost luminescent sheen.

"It's not as simple as transfusing clean blood from another source," Lorna explained, reaching up to gently thumb at the jars' valves. "It would be physically impossible to drain every drop of tainted blood from you—miles of veins and arterial tissue, being scrubbed by hand with a brush to remove every diseased cell?" She shook her head. "No, your blood must be purified and returned to the source immediately: plasma taken from the blood of a totem deer, the creature raised in loose captivity its entire life to drink water only from blessed streams. If the jar appears to be glowing to you, it's a sign your body will be reactive to the treatment once we begin feeding its contents in."

"I can expect that will be the most painful part?"

Lorna gave a sweet smile. "Incontestably."

Brann sighed, his head thumping against the cabin wall. "Too much to ask that you brought along something to help ease things?"

Producing a small vial sealed with wax, Lorna held it before Brann's eyes, the cloudy liquid taking on the reflected color of the purple wax. "A very powerful sedative, the only kind that will work on a lycanthrope—sweetened with the juice of a Doreen Grapefruit to help it go down easier."

Brann took the vial delicately, careful not to break the fragile wax between his fingertips. "Well at least I'll have that to look forward to," he said bitterly.

"Here I was thinking all this time that the Lady Lorna was just dragging around chests full of white silk shirts and bloomers," Zay joked, snapping the dust cover back into place on her cannon before picking up the foregrip to reattach it next. "Turns out you were hauling an entire laboratory with you."

Lorna didn't reply at first, her expression souring as the noise of the rocky road quieted around them, the rover drawing to a slow stop. She stood, saber in hand, affixing the blade to her hip as she looked towards the front of the vehicle. "If it's all the same, I'd prefer everyone forget that name once more, I'm far more comfortable with 'Red'...we weren't meant to stop so soon, were we?"

Zay stood as well, looking equally stone-faced, slamming her machine cannon's foregrip into place with an intimidating clack. "No. Something's wrong."

Swinging up the clamshell hatch, both women dismounted in turn from the back of the rover, Zay holding the barrel of her autocannon aloft and Red keeping a tight grip on the hilt of her sword—rounding the corner, their boots crunched in step with each other as they drew up alongside the driver's side. Nes was already lighting up a cigarillo beside the open door, taking a long drag before resting one hand on his hip, looking pensively towards the horizon.

"I'm not one for paranoia," he was already saying before Red or Zay had the chance to ask, "So I'd rather not jump the gun here and make such unfounded claims as 'we're being watched...'" He blew a stiff cloud from the side of his mouth, lips pursed tight. "But we're being watched."

"Where?"

Nes took another drag then, cig between two fingers, lined up his hand in front of Zay's vision with the cig forming a sort of crosshairs for her. "Those rolling hills we're coming up on. From a distance, looks like this trail curves around them into the lowlands. Almost can't see it's there, but a narrow canyon cuts right through—perfect spot for someone to set up an ambush with, say, a well-placed mortar shell to close off the canyon behind us."

Red leaned forward, squinting at where the other two were pointing. "What could possibly put the idea into your head that someone is waiting to fire mortar shells at us?"

Nes slipped the cig back between his lips, jabbing a thumb over his shoulder. "On account of that skinny asshole hiding behind that boulder loading up a mortar."

"

"How marvelous! How'd you like to come work for me?"

The voice rang out from behind the rocks, harsh and ragged, and from within the rover Brann instantly recognized it as the announcer from last night's fight in Mercenary Row. Shuffling out from his hiding place, the stout little man's fur coat nearly dragged through the dirt, a gentle wake of dust following behind him, along with a steady procession of the gaudy man's goons. A greasy collection of mercs even less appealing than the sort Zay and Brann had butted heads with in the alleys, the quiet trail was suddenly alive with jangling chains and crunching steel-toed boots, and by the time the full assembly stood blocking the rover's path of retreat they measured at least a dozen strong.

"I'm fairly satisfied with my current employment benefits, thanks," Nes replied dryly, squinting behind another tight pull of his cig.

"Shame." The flamboyant leader of the gang waved a hand upwards dramatically. "Without even a chance at hearing what I have to counter with! It's a tasty little package you'd be a fool's fool to turn down, in that the main benefit offered is walking away from this dreary place alive."

Zay was already feeding a belt of ammunition from a freshly attached box mag into her autocannon, bringing her barrel up to unload fresh hell before being stopped by Nestor's cautioning hand—clearly, he had more patience for this than she did. Red stepped forward, speaking on the trio's behalf in the most diplomatic of fashions, courtesy of her aristocratic upbringing. "Surely, we've sidestepped a few lines of dialogue here—formal introductions being such a delight you would be willing to pass over? We certainly wouldn't appreciate being killed today without at least giving you our names, let alone knowing the circumstances that earned us this fate."

The fur-wrapped man bowed dutifully, his perfectly sprayed hair as unmoving as if it were carved in marble. "Trollope, my dear! Bang-up job of pointing out I almost forgot to talk at length about myself and my motivations—suffice to say, time restricting, you'll have to make do with the simple fact that my boys here—" Trollope waved his stubby arm behind himself at the assortment of mercs, "—Well, there's nothing formal about them to introduce. Some of them got a good look at your crew riding through the Row, namely that fuck who had his head collapsed in my ring last night in his showy silk sweatshirt—and when Bullet Buddy here came a-running into my office later that evening with tales of a rainbow jewel of a ship from the sky that landed in the wilderness nearby, I put two and three together."

The 'skinny asshole' Nes had spotted, a completely bald young man as pale and thin as a skeleton clutching a mortar to his chest, was grinning widely to show off his missing teeth as he waved his free hand excitedly. "Hay, I'm Bullet Buddy!"

"Hey, Bullet Buddy," Nes said cautiously. This boy was clearly a bit touched.

"You seem a man to stand on business," Red continued, "Not one forgiving of missed opportunity—if you mean to rob us or commandeer our ship which, at present, we're clearly not in possession of, why settle for what few trinkets we have on our persons when a deal could be struck that could see your men taken care of for years to come?"

Trollope snapped his fingers, the sound compounded by the loud chime of several of his rings clacking together, and his toadlike face was pulled back in an appreciative smile as he addressed his boys. "You see? This is exactly what I mean when I say choose your mark, lads—don't just eat the steak when there's a cow nearby ripe for the slaughter."

The men were all beginning to encircle the trio now, forming a semicircle around the back end of the rover, looking it over unimpressed. Bullet Buddy ducked his head beneath the clamshell top, still grinning as he waved at Brann inside.

"Hay! Bullet Buddy."

Brann nodded nervously, hand on his sword hilt. "Hey there, Bullet Buddy."

"Possibly I've not adequately explained our position," Red was saying to Trollope, similarly reaching for her saber, eyeing the bandits warily. "We've all willingness to negotiate arrangements to pay tribute, dependent on our walking away alive today, as you said—"

"As I said," Trollope interrupted, "My boys are not so formal, and try as I might, I can never seem to find a space in their heads to fit such notions as contracts and tributes. No, princess, I can spot royalty in a pool of leeches while blindfolded: you were always the tribute, one I intend to hold for obscene ransom."

"Viscountess, actually," Red corrected. Negotiations were thinning into nothingness, and even Nes was now holding a long pipe wrench he'd retrieved from its spot on the inside wall of the rover.

"Bullet Buddy, my boy," Trollope said, his eyes roaming hungrily over Red, "Would you kindly retrieve the young soldat from within and bring him out to join us?"

Bullet Buddy stepped up into the rover's hatchway, nearly falling backwards from the weight of the mortar he still had his arm wrapped around—then, a moment later, he hopped back down. "He's asleep," he said cheerfully.

"What?" Red's head spun around—Brann, sure enough, had crumpled in a heap against the wall, nearly falling out of his seat, completely unconscious as the IV's did their work in his body.

Zay was aghast. "Did this little bitch just pass out on us?"

"Anything to avoid a fight," Nes confirmed bitterly, shaking his head and brandishing the wrench in Trollope's direction. "Look, my man, we ain't got any steak for you, and your cow is now leaving—the Lady here was being nice, and you've gone and pissed that away. Get your men off our truck, we promise to leave that tragedy on your head intact."

Trollope wasn't fazed, and his men we're beginning to push at both sides of the rover, doing their best to rock it side to side on its sturdy suspension. "There's no diamonds to be mined in boredom, I'm afraid, and though I'm a shade more well-spoken than this lousy lot, I'm much like them in that I find you all to be rather fucking boring."

His thick fingers reached into his coat and pulled free a weathered old cudgel, stained visibly with old blood, his eyes widening with anticipation. "If it's all the same to you, I'll just take the diamonds."

The growing tension had reached its peak—the bandits surged forward in excitement, blades and chains at the ready—Nestor raised his wrench, Zay hefted her autocannon—

—And the sound of a gunshot split the sky and stopped everything in its place. Zay, being the first one ready to engage, looked as shocked as anyone realizing it hadn't come from her. The mercs all stumbled backwards, eyes fixed on Trollope, who himself was confused as to what had just happened...until he reached up and felt around in his hair, a finger slipping into the perfectly clean hole that had just been blasted through his solidly formed curls. Red had been visibly ready to draw her saber, but her blade remained sheathed, her long-barreled flintlock pistol having made a rare appearance in order to funnel a straight shot across Trollope's scalp instead.

"Funny you should mention feeling bored," she proclaimed loudly, no longer in a diplomatic mood.

"You are an abominable whore," Trollope moaned, his face contorted in rage as he pathetically tried to push the melting curls of hair back up into place, the entire structure falling apart.

"Spoken like my mother," was Red's rebuttal, her pistol disappearing back into her leather coat. "Put your hands on me, I turn you and your boys into red puddles of mulch. That's my final offer."

Her eyes turned skyward now, attention drawn to something above the heads of the mercs—Trollope, about to respond with appropriate hostility, caught Red's gaze and similarly turned to follow it. Above the hilly horizon, descending from the clouds above, a dark shape—like a falling meteor, except it was slowing, its trajectory curling towards their location: a ship, headed their way.

"Who the hell else did you tell about this catch, Buddy?"

Bullet Buddy shook his head indignantly, watching as the ship nearly touched down before accelerating towards them, just a few meters above ground level. "Nuh uh, nobody, n'honest! I didn't!"

"That's a Geihan transport," Nestor stated matter of factly, turning to drop the pipe wrench inside the rover before climbing inside, calling back to Red and Zay. "Get in, it's the Uhlen, we're out of this mess now. Now now now."

The mercs lurched forward in uncertainty, awaiting Trollope's permission to halt the rover's escape—they were instead met with the barrel of Zay's autocannon facing them down as she too stepped up into the open hatchway behind Red, her boots firmly planted in a wide stance to keep herself steady as the rover began to slowly rumble forward with Nes at the wheel.

"Get on down the road, little doggies," she said cheerfully, feeling right in her element. "We've got bigger problems than your mangy asses now."

Zay waited until the rover was up to speed heading into the canyon before closing the hatch, leaving the frustrated bandits in the dust that kicked up. Bullet Buddy stood next to Trollope, watching them go with sadness.

"We just gonna let them skate, boss-man?"

Trollope didn't answer, hatefully staring at the rover disappearing in the rocks before drawing a wide-mouthed flare gun from his sleeve. Raising it straight up, he clenched his fat finger around the trigger, popping off a brilliantly glowing rocket above their heads, a pillar of vivid lime-colored smoke rising skyward. Thick as mud, the green smoke was suspended in place, an incorporeal vine rising from the earth's surface—split in two by the passing ship overhead, the great dark shape wailing as it flew by, the twin engines pulling the green smoke into their intakes. Like a dragon unfurling, wings of smoke spread outwards from the sides of the spade-shaped transport ship, its nose tilted down as it closed in on its prey.

*

"Zay, we got no time, that ship is gonna be on us in seconds, I need you up top," Nes was shouting, using one hand to throttle forward while his other fiddled at the rover's control panel, as if he were looking for some kind of compartment—meanwhile, his knee kept the wheel steady, his eyes fixed on the rocky terrain fast approaching. "Red, sorry, but I need you up here with me to drive this thing, Zay's gotta man the big gun for us."

Red slid into the seat next to Nes, holding it steady with little more than a few fingers reaching across the dash, her normally cool exterior shaken by this unexpected development. "Without sounding too pampered, can I ask why you can't drive?"

"Because of this." Nes finally found purchase in the paneling, his fingers curling before pulling back sharply, exposing a frightening mess of bundled wires surrounding an intimidating block of circuit boards. "Take the wheel, I need to help Zay, that cannon of hers isn't gonna do the job on its own."

Sifting through the bundles of wire like digging through a bush, Nes tracked one along its length to make sure it wasn't powering anything important before yanking it loose, exposing an empty power socket.

"Take the driver's seat, I need to work," Nes shouted over the noise of the engine, which was only amplified by the removal of the paneling that shielded the inner workings of the rover. Doing as bidden, Red clambered as politely as she could over Nes and dropped into the seat, her heel digging into the accelerator and nearly causing her to lose control of the wheel from the sudden burst of traction—which sent the kneeling Nes tumbling backwards out of the cabin.

"Oh! Apologies!" Red cried out, mortified.

Prone on the floor of the rover, Nes had a clear view above him of Zay stepping up the ladder and punching open the roof hatch of the vehicle, which yawned open on its hydraulic pistons, the opening facing the rear of the rover—and for a brief moment sunlight flooded the cabin before being blotted out, the nose of the Uhlen's ship having locked onto them overhead.

"I'd get off the floor if I were you, old man," Zay warned as she latched a safety line onto her belt, leaving both arms free to wield her huge gun, standing on the uppermost rungs of the ladder. "Unless you wanna drown in hot shell casings."

Quickly, Nes rolled himself up onto his feet, pulling a looped bundle of power cable extensions from a nearby wall as he did before disappearing back into the driver's cabin. Zay's entire upper half emerged from the top of the rover, the open hatch at her back shielding her from the wind. The narrow sides of the canyon kept the ship from descending any further, allowing Zay a good look at it: a wingless structure, reminiscent of the head of a shovel, the lower belly distended with the hanging transport spaces no doubt filled with Uhlen waiting to disembark. Utilitarian in all ways, there was nothing elegant or pleasing about the ship—its dark chassis was visibly coated in sheets of carbonized metal that seemed to deny light from reflecting off it. Ballistic armor.

Zay would not let this deter her. Bringing her autocannon up from below, she yanked back the cocking lever and slapped down the bipod mount, using the roof of the rover to steady the cannon. There was no need to flip up the sights: at this distance, accuracy was nothing to be concerned about.

Bracing herself, Zay squeezed the trigger.

The explosive fountain of lead flew up like fireworks, the tracer rounds scattering along the underside of the Uhlen ship as if it were skipping along the surface of a lake of fire, sparks spattering against the armored paneling and filling the canyon with light and smoke. As promised, the long shell casings that didn't bounce away off the roof of the rover spiraled down into the open hatchway, mimicking the sound of rain on a tin roof, making those still conscious inside flinch. Zay maintained a steady flow of cannonfire directly into the ship's belly—it didn't matter that she wasn't piercing through the ballistic shell, as long as she could keep the lower bay from opening up to allow any boarders, or worse, for the Uhlen to return fire.

"Nestor," Red wailed, her snowy white knuckles practically glowing on the steering wheel, her elbows jerking to and fro in a panic. "I don't know what I'm doing, guidance please!"

Nes appeared in the driver's cabin, holding a metal pipe in one hand and a wickedly sharp stake in the other—with the serrated teeth emerging near its pointed end, likely it was meant for erecting a makeshift structure of some sort, though Nes had other designs for it today. "It's simple," he said, slotting the stake onto one end of the pipe, pointing ahead outside the front of the vehicle. "Keep going that way, really fast. If something gets in your way—" He twisted the makeshift spearhead hard, locking it into place with a snap. "—Turn."

Red did not find this funny. "I so very deeply hate you at this moment," she sobbed, hunching desperately over the wheel to focus on keeping the rover from smashing into a canyon wall.

With a wink, Nes crouched and set to work, stripping one end of an extension cable with a utility knife and feeding the exposed wiring into the hollow end of the pipe.

Overhead, the deafening fire of the autocannon tapered off—turning the glowing red barrel into the wind to cool it, Zay watched with healthy suspicion as the Uhlen's ship gained altitude and reduced its speed. "They're petering off," she called down, squinting through the smoke whipped up around her as it spiraled off the length of her superheated cannon.

"Keep eyes up," Nes shouted back, "Pro'ly they can see the road's about to get rough ahead of us."

Zay's eyes settled lower, and with a grimace, she swept away some of the more stubborn shell casings to readjust her weapon's aim down towards the rear of the rover. "More like behind us!"

Red's insult had not gone down smoothly—two by two, four of the ugliest battlecarts imaginable were approaching fast from behind, the canyon disappearing behind them in the wall of rising dust kicked up by their huge tires. Trollope's mercs were evenly distributed between them, two heads poking out of the armored sides of each of them, their windshields concealed by riveted metal sheets. The drivers had next to no visibility, save for the thin gaps between the metal.

The real trouble, however, was not the cheap armor Zay could easily blast through with applied fire. What had her nervously tapping the dust cover of her cannon was what each of the carts had affixed to their front ends: like bull's horns sprouting from their front axles, all four vehicles wielded giant, spiked balls clamped between rusty yokes. Big enough to act as another layer of shielding, Zay's chances of getting a clean shot in on the drivers was near zero with those forward-facing weapons blocking her view—not before they chewed through the rover...and everyone inside, anyway.

"We've got another problem," Zay yelled, checking her ammo feed and readying a fresh belt mag.

Nestor's voice was muffled, as if he were shouting from inside a cabinet. "Is this problem bulletproof?"

The bandits' engines roared, and Zay scoffed, a smile spreading across her face—it had been years since she'd actually feared for her life. It made her somewhat nostalgic.

"Doubtful."

Planting the butt of the autocannon into her shoulder, Zay's hands regained positive control of the gun, and once more she clenched down—the glowing barrel once more exploded in a rapid-fire geyser of lead. Focused like a beam on the foremost two carts, bullets streamed back and forth between the two, Zay sweeping in steady, even bursts.

There was a brief moment where their momentum faltered, but their response was quick and deliberate—as if in sync, both of the front carts revved forward, and their spiked countermeasures spun to life: motorized balls of death aligned, creating a protective wall of razor-sharp teeth, giving the drivers the confidence to accelerate and close the gap. The sound filling the canyon was like the dying shriek of a drakebat, so discomforting in its steady squeal that it made Zay wither even behind the gunfire.

There was no two ways about it, those spiked wrecking balls needed to die. With controlled precision, Zay drew a smooth line up away from the hoods of the carts, and instead focused aim on the giant spinning morningstars themselves.

The mistake almost cost her dearly. Like sawblades cutting through water's surface, glowing tracer rounds splashed in every direction as they bounced off the fast-spinning balls, Zay barely ducking out of the way in time as one screaming hot round blew through the roof hatch behind her. Clouds of red dust popped all along the canyon walls, the back end of the rover being peppered with stray shots as well—Zay might as well have tossed a belt of cluster grenades up in the air, the space between the carts and the rover becoming a sonic storm of shrapnel.

"The fuck are you DOING up there," Nestor bellowed furiously, sounding entirely unlike his usually calm self.

Her gloved hand pressed itself to her arm—streams of blood flowed over her fingers like melting wax, Zay's shoulder split wide open by the near miss; had the round made proper contact, it would have torn her arm clean off.

"Does that answer your question?!" She shouted back, her voice shaking.

Nes had finished his crafting project. Hands equipped with long rubber gloves and with four identical makeshift harpoons bundled in the crook of his arm, he stomped down to the back end of the rover, taking special care to give the unconscious Brann a good kick in the shin as he went. Smashing his fist against the release, the clamshell hatch swung upwards, daylight pooling at his feet—Nes had a clean view of Zay's bulletproof problem now, face to face with those airborne morningstars fast approaching.

Four carts, and an airship, which was currently keeping pace well behind the small convoy—it figured the Uhlen would sit back and watch with amusement as the mercs tore the rover apart.

Five targets to Nestor's four harpoons. He'd have to get creative.

One of the karts broke formation, zooming forward, aiming that spiked ball directly at the newly opened backside of the rover—at Nes. He hefted the first harpoon, the extension cable cleanly looped around his shoulder, holding his free hand out before him to guide his throw. The morningstar descended haphazardly, the bulk of it missing the open hatch and showering Nes in sparks as it sliced into the rover's back paneling—the kart peeled back, and within the breath of a second, Nes calculated his shot before launching the harpoon. Arcing up around the spinning ball, the projectile whistled a spiral tune as the trailing cable whirled around behind it, looking as if it would fly wide of its mark—until the kart's driver corrected himself. Unable to see the incoming harpoon from his seat within the mechanized coffin, the unlucky driver steered directly into its path, and the electrified javelin sunk itself directly into the kart's engine block.

A blinding flash as the engine erupted in flames, jagged blue fingers of plasma arcing between the skeletal ribs of the kart's frame, and not even the huge tires could ground the vehicle as it ruptured from within. The two bandits hanging out of the window were plastered against the sides of the kart, eyes bugging out as the full voltage of the rover's engine paralyzed them before the entire kart sprouted wings of fire and went airborne. The two rear karts fell back to give a wide berth to the newborn meteor, their compatriot disappearing within the flames, the still-spinning morningstar skipping along the canyon floor behind the fleeing rover with a comet's trail in its wake.

Zay was laughing manically, her head peeking down behind Nes. "Do it again, do it again!"

The entirety of the cable's length went taught, and quick on his feet, Nes pulled it apart at the center where the connections met with a burst of dissipating voltage—the cable still attached to the harpoon went free, slingshotted out the back of the rover, while the main extension remained connected to the front of the rover's exposed power block. Readying the next harpoon, Nes connected its cable to the main extension, snugly clicking it into place before setting the cleanly stacked coils of cable at his feet.

It seemed he may not get the chance, however. "The canyon's run out!" Red's voice from the driver's cabin rang out; sure enough, that was all the warning they got before the tight passage burst wide, nearly blinding Nes as the shadows cast by the canyon walls evaporated. They were on open plains now, a rocky wasteland split only by the long-forgotten trail they now followed, a remnant of some ancient road that had long since been swept away by the wind and weather. Nes watched in disappointment as the karts went wide, fanning out alongside one another and drifting in their lanes wide enough to avoid making easy targets of themselves, all three morningstars now spinning up to ready their attack.

If that wasn't all, Zay was pounding on the roof of the rover, prompting Nes to look skyward: sure enough, the Uhlen ship was descending once more, and this time there was no terrain cover to keep them at bay.

Seeming to read his mind, Zay let loose with the autocannon once more, aiming along the broadside of the centermost kart—her stream of bullets guided it along, lining up the strafing kart with the back of the rover once more, acting as a sort of buffer to give Nes a proper shot within his limited range. They didn't have the time to take out all three karts before the ship was on them, and Zay couldn't pull up to shoot at the Uhlen without leaving their ass wide open for the karts—either way, they would have to prepare to be boarded.

Nes was up. Harpoon two in hand, he crouched low to steady himself, wiping away debris from his eye to clear his sight—the next kart was like a sidewinder, pulling left to right to left in even pace with Zay's line of fire, her tracers almost keeping the bandits in line as if on a ghostly leash. Nes swayed to match the kart's direction and, once more using the morningstar as a target to lock onto, let his next electrified spear fly.

This driver had much better reflexes—drifting back into the harpoon's path, the kart suddenly yanked in the opposite direction, the charged spear bouncing off the hood with a colorful pop of sparks before being sucked beneath the kart's tires. Cursing, Nes quickly yanked the connecting line free, suffering a punishing slap to the cheek as the extension whipped around before vanishing into daylight.

Two harpoons left.

Emboldened, the other two karts sped forward, drawing up to flank both sides of the rover—their morningstars squealed like dying pigs, digging roughly into the rover's fat backside, and Nes could see the mercs laughing and jeering as they hung out of the third kart.

"They're going for the treads!" Zay warned, giving words to her own assignment—spinning the cannon around, she aimed at the starboard kart, funneling gunfire directly into the passenger window. At such a close range, those focused rounds punched directly through the relatively flimsy armor plating, having the desired effect of causing the kart to quickly pull off.

Zay rotated her entire torso, swinging the cannon around with her—the opposite kart had the raw end of this deal, as she had a clean shot directly at the driver's seat. Though she couldn't see his face through the narrow slits, Zay prayed it was Trollope himself at the wheel before letting the bullets fly, pouring them straight into the cabin.

Like a tomato had been burst within, the kart expelled a fine red mist that surrounded it in a cloud, the vehicle lilting to one side—the merc hanging from the opposite window had the foresight to clamber onto the kart's roof, sliding along the wet paneling before making the leap, catching himself on the railing of the rover. The other passenger was not fast enough, and Zay's gunfire cut through the exposed side of the kart like a knife, directly into him—the merc's top half fell away beneath the tires, the kart veering off into the desert before its own momentum caused it to cartwheel into a plume of dust.

With two karts still keeping a safe distance behind them, the Uhlen ship had closed the distance, its lower bay yawning open—fueled by the adrenaline of having dispatched two of the mercs, Zay ignored the one clinging to the rover's side and swung up to aim into the open bay of the ship, not even waiting to see a living target before once more opening fire.

With a fatal clang, the autocannon jammed up, and Zay shielded her eyes from the upward gush of molten steam: having been firing in sustained streams for so long with little rest between, the barrel had overheated and split down the middle, the glowing end curled upwards uselessly.

"Fuck!"

Zay slapped the popped dust cover shut, roughly dismounting and jumping off the ladder, autocannon slung under her arm. She held it forward, showing off its unfortunate state to Nes. "I'm spent. Need to swap out, and they're already on us."

Nes turned to reply, but was cut short by a pair of legs swinging around into the open hatch, kicking him square in the chest and sending him sprawling onto his back. The merc was drizzled in bloody streaks, soaked in his own comrades, his eyes wild and pierced face twisted in rage. He held aloft a compact mechanized saw, the long chainblade spinning in a blur, coming straight for the prostrate Nes.

Nes, still flat on his back, curled his leg up then kicked out powerfully, directly into the merc's knee—the entire leg collapsed sideways, making the crazed man scream out, giving Nes his opening. Wrapping one rubberized hand directly around the exposed end of the third harpoon, Nes jumped up and launched his entire body into the merc—piercing the man's chest with the harpoon in the process. The merc stumbled back, doubling over, the serrated hooks of the harpoon catching on his ribs—he stopped just short of the hatchway, mechsaw still in hand, unsteady on his feet as he prepared to attack once more. Behind him, a kart was accelerating towards the rover, looking to seize its chance once the merc had taken Nestor and Zay out.

Nes was a step ahead, however: wasting no time, he was already slapping the connections of the power cables together, connecting the impaled merc directly to the rover's power block.

"Nope!"

Illuminated from within with a juicy crackle, the merc was turned into a living lamp for a brief few seconds, his feet flying up off the ground as he was blown out the back of the rover—directly into the spinning morningstar waiting outside. Like a doll flying apart, the merc's limbs spun away in all directions, slapping a fresh coat of bright red paint across the kart's body.

Nes disconnected the cables the second the merc's body was free of the confined space, tossing the harpoon's connection aside with contempt, the disconnected plug slipping away to follow its master.

"Motherfucker made me waste it," Nes muttered bitterly, kicking aside the fourth and final harpoon as he leaned down and picked up the merc's fallen mechsaw. He held it up, squeezing the throttle and watching the chainblade spin with interest. "Oh, but this is fun, I like this. Okay, I'll trade."

Looping the handle around his belt, Nes hurried past Zay, towards the cabin. "We got one harpoon left, and it's the only thing that might bring down that ship—get your gun fixed," he ordered, not bothering to acknowledge Zay's impressed look as she sheathed her combat knife.

"Aye aye, sir," she joked.

*

Red felt Nestor's hand clapping her on the shoulder. "You're up, m'lady."

"Oh, thank heavens," she breathed, handing off the wheel as Nes took her place as driver. Stepping past him, Red emerged into the passenger space, watching as Zay laid out her cannon on the workbench to disassemble.

"Two bandits giving chase, Uhlen dropping on us overhead," Zay relayed, slapping away the still-hot barrel of the autocannon. "You okay on your own for a few minutes?"

Red had already tied back the bulk of her hair in a ponytail and was quickly pulling off her red leather coat, freeing her arms of its sleeves, her slender frame bereft of any armor now save for her long-sleeved white blouse. "A few minutes, you say?" She made a grab for the same safety hook Zay had secured herself with, clasping it around her belt at the small of her back before drawing her saber. "I'll thank you for the practice."

Zay grinned. "Attagirl."

Red barely even touched the rungs of the ladder as she sprung upwards, bringing her black stiletto heels down to plant them on either side of the open hatch, standing tall and proud atop the rover—above, the Uhlen ship was beginning its final descent, swinging wide to face its nose at an oblique angle away from the rover and to give the open bay clearance. It loomed over Red like the head of a great beast, its port windows glaring down at her like gleaming eyes, maw open to breathe flames. Instead of flames, though, something else emerged from its jaws.

A lone figure, hunching low on the ramp, limbs disproportionate to the bulky appendages affixed to their ends—it seemed near impossible to tell which end was up as the creature rolled out and off the ramp, all four limbs outstretched, metal claws splayed wide as it slammed down heavily on the rover. Like a spider, those limbs flexed and curled, the Uhlen's body contorting in strange and unpredictable directions before the head finally emerged to face Red, the torso—no, the back—parallel to the vehicle's roof as it rotated its body to straighten itself. It clasped all four clawlike appendages down, digging its artificial claws into the roof, the inhuman Uhlen staring at Red impassively through its pointed mask, devoid of any expressive features. It hunched before her, a gargoyle ready to pounce, equipped on both hands and feet with mechanical graspers designed to keep it firmly in place on top of the moving vehicle.

Not so simple as knocking the creature off, Red feared—and she wasn't as confident in her safety line as she'd liked to be. Still, the viscountess had a job to do, and she turned to stand en garde opposite the

Gargoyle.

"You've caught me at a disadvantage, I'm afraid," she called out over the loud wind, her white-blonde bangs whipping across her face. "I didn't get my stretches in beforehand."

The Gargoyle chuckled ominously through the distorted sound of its mask, and with a mechanical thunk, its hind legs released their clawed grip on the roof and raised up to turn towards Red. Those claws snapped together hungrily, held at the ready as effortlessly as if it were using its forearms, suspended aloft on either side of the Uhlen's head.

"Clearly you have." Red leveled her saber at the thing, her blouse billowing in the wind, the rest of her body rock solid on their precarious battleground of choice. "You'll forgive me if this isn't as brief as you may have hoped."

Red kicked off her back heel, and the Gargoyle, impossibly, did the same—where Red lunged forward, bringing her sword low, Gargoyle spun at the waist and leapt up, planting a foreclaw in the roof while the rest of him flowed effortlessly out of the way of Red's initial swipe—straightening up on one hand, his body pirouetted in place and bounced her back punishingly. Red's feet left the roof momentarily before she landed hard on her belly. Barely had she the time to roll out of the way before Gargoyle was on her—Red carried her roll on, one set of claws after another smashing against the metal. Foot, hand, hand, foot—those limbs seemed more like tentacles in their elasticity, the Uhlen's assault not hampered for a moment by how possible it should have been for a body to bend those ways, and by the time Red had regained her footing she was once more knocked backwards by the Gargoyle's feet rising to kick her in the chest. Her back hit the raised dome of the open hatch, nearly falling down the open hole— though there was no face to read, she knew Gargoyle was sneering at her behind that mask, his limber form retreating into itself as it once more untwisted itself into a more natural crouch position.

Red felt a draft in her blouse—those metal claws had cut through her blouse, showing off the bandages still binding her chest and shoulder.

It occurred to her only now, feeling the stiffness in her muscles, she may not have been fully recovered from her duel with the Queen. What a bother.

"I'd like to make a remark that you owe me a new shirt," Red joked, reassuming another stance, this time one that put her weight back on the defensive. "Though, truth be told, I've a whole trunk of them just like this one back in my ship's quarters."

Gargoyle jumped like a toad, all four limbs splayed, and Red narrowly sidestepped with barely her tiptoes keeping her alight on the roof—had her riposte been any quicker she may have taken off one of Gargoyle's arms, but instead her windmilling saber had to settle for carving a crescent shaped swathe along the creature's exposed side. Those metal claws all came down to catch Gargoyle on the lifted hatch, the creature hissing horribly through its electronic mouthpiece, dark blood oozing through its layers of clothing and soaking through.

Red's keen nose sniffed at her blade, instantly getting a read on the chemical composition of this thing's blood. "You used to be human," she commented, disturbed. "Though not anymore. What have you done to yourself?"

She got her answer in the form of another full-bodied attack—springboarding backwards off the hatch, the Gargoyle somersaulted through the air and bounced off the roof, once, twice—then, just as his feet kicked backwards towards Red, she successfully brought her saber up with both hands to block those hindclaws, all of her strength needed to keep them from wrenching her weapon out of her grasp. Gargoyle remained poised in a perverse handstand, windmilling his legs outwards in a gradually widening radius, forcing Red to block those spinning claws with her blade while stepping backwards out of the reach of those legs. The silvery song of her saber chimed out with each deflected blow, the shockwaves running through her trained hands powerfully, clasping fingers denying any chance of her grip failing—the Uhlen meant to overwhelm her with brute force, and she meant to deny it for as long as possible.

She reached the end of the rover, and just as those clawed feet scissored together at her head, Red leaned back, stepping out onto the clamshell hatch—and nearly decapitated herself in the process, the spinning morningstar of one of Trollope's karts leaping up to take a bite at her. Red tucked and rolled forward, beneath both the spiked ball and the Gargoyle's legs as he recovered from his pincer attack. When Red came to her feet this time, it was with pistol in hand, her face a visage of fury, her gaze searing beams of hate out towards the interceding merc kart.

"Fuck's sake," Red snapped under her breath.

Depressing the hidden switch in the weapon, a needle sprung forth and jabbed into a vein in her wrist. Like vines shooting up from the soil, arterial blood wreathed itself all down the length of the flintlock, extending the barrel to nearly double its length before she pulled the trigger. With a wet-sounding crack of thunder, boiling hot blood magic jettisoned the bullet at supersonic speed, sending a gory missile through the entire kart: the vehicle spun up into the air as the bloody sonicboom cratered the ground beneath it. Human bodies and twisted metal alike crumpled flat, the morningstar's head flying away from the wreckage into the wastes, leaving behind nothing but a scattered trail of metal debris.

"Absolutely appalling," Red groused—partly to herself, partly to her dueling partner. Quickly dismissing the summoned blood-enhancement on her pistol with a toss of her arm, her own blood dissipating into hazy vapors before she holstered the weapon and returned her attention back fully to the Gargoyle.

"Terrible form, interrupting us like that. Utterly classless. All apologies."

Gargoyle watched the wreckage for a brief moment—whether because he was impressed or because he agreed with her, he shook his head, then re-engaged with a vengeance, galloping towards Red on all fours like some wild hound.

*

Inside the rover, Zay watched in awe as the blooded bullet completely destroyed the kart, leaving only the one landlocked vehicle left in pursuit—she'd finished replacing her autocannon's barrel, slapping the locking mechanism in place and closing the dust cover once more. "Damn girl," she breathed reverently, "Leave some for the rest of us."

Barely had Zay readied her autocannon, stepping to the rear exit of the rover before the unexpected happened: at the same time the final pursuing kart suddenly squealed on its brakes, giving up nearly all the distance it had covered between itself and the rover, the Uhlen ship overhead similarly yanked up and away to fall back to higher altitudes.

"Yo, Nes," Zay shouted with no small amount of trepidation, fastening a safety line to her belt slowly. "Just out of curiosity—you uh...see any trouble coming up ahead?"

Up in the driver's seat, Nes gripped the wheel tightly, pushing as hard as he could on the throttle—that was the trouble with these electric rovers: there was never that higher gear to shift to. "You're gonna want to wake him up," was all he said in reply, referring to Brann, pulling the seat's safety harness down to click into place.

Her worst fears confirmed, Zay cursed quietly and swung the cannon around on its strap, letting it hang freely off her back as she stomped back to where Brann was still draped over the arm of his seat. "Alright, kid, time to wake up, we're at grandma's," she said humorlessly, giving a few firm slaps against his cheek as she investigated the IV connections he was hooked into. Zay didn't know the first thing about anatomy or medicine, but she knew no matter what, it was probably a bad idea to pull these needles out before the treatment was complete—still, they didn't have a choice, if the fear she'd heard in Nestor's voice was any indication, so the best deal she could cut the kid was keeping a hand towel readied to stop the inevitable bleeding.

Brann grumbled, unable to fully rouse himself—encouragement was needed. Pinching at the entrypoint where that thick surgical tubing stabbed into his collar, Zay held her breath and pulled on it, steady but swiftly—and with the tiny sound like a straw sucking in air, a small bubble of blood popping and speckling her thumb signaled the needle was free. She tossed it aside, pushing that readied towel into Brann's collarbone roughly, and within seconds his face began to wrinkle in a frown before his eyes opened and head began to raise itself unsteadily.

"Ow," was all he said, eyes looking bleary and unhappy.

"Yeah, 'ow,' get up kid," Zay dismissed, yanking out the other IV with much less resistance. "Road's about to get real rough, can't have you all full of needles when it does—"

The words didn't finish leaving her mouth before an indecipherable shout of warning from Nestor interrupted, and the entire rover lurched—Brann's mostly limp body tumbled out of his seat on top of Zay, and the wall behind him ripped itself apart around giant rocks that—

—No, not rocks, *claws*—

Zay tucked Brann into herself and let gravity send them rolling painfully out of the path of destruction, that trio of enormous talons shredding the side of the rover like paper, electrical bursts of fireworks showering down on them and the seat where Brann had sat seconds ago being pulverized.

The back half of the rover had gone airborne for a moment before slamming down hard, treads growling as they churned into the earth unevenly, making the engine whine with unbalanced effort. Red and Gargoyle were tossed from the roof mid-clash, the former meeting the end of her safety line's length before it snapped her back, her momentum carried forward into a fulcrum and slamming her hard against the side of the rover. Grunting as pain shot through the entirety of her body, Red caught her foot on one of the rover's side railings and climbed back up, stabbing the saber into the roof to steady herself—and get a good look at the newest member of the convoy giving chase.

Galloping alongside the rover, each leg as thick around as the vehicle itself, her eyes traced up the length of those four doglike appendages as they met with a broadside of flesh that rippled beneath smooth scales and a thin coating of fur alike that terminated at the great beast's shoulders—enormous ridged plates of bone rose back above its nape, the neck outstretched and visibly pumping blood through its firehose-sized veins from its powerful heart, and the head...

The unholy union of something canine and crocodilian, the Goliath's jaws were splayed wide in a terrifying predator's grin, inward-facing stalagmite fangs rising from its lower maw, which huffed in breaths of hot, dewey steam, strong enough to cut through the resistance of their headwind. Despite the length of its limbs, the rover must have been moving much faster than Red had credited it, as the giant monster's wide eyes locked onto her—it was running as fast as it could to match their pace, its knuckled claws sending up bursts of dark earth with every stride.

Red had seen something like this once, long ago in her youth: Ammitsuchus, the great Saurian Jackal of the Northern Wasteland. It had been standing guard atop the Bloody Cliffs to gaze out at the sea, watching her ship as it passed by on the tidal currents one early morning, its head rising high above the elevated coastline to nearly graze the low cloud-cover of the marine layer.

She counted their blessings—this one giving chase was much, much smaller.

A violent scampering of metal scraping into metal brought her back to reality, Red leaping up and out of the path of Gargoyle as he cut a swathe across the rover's hull, her feet finding the roof once more. She anticipated his moves now, already leaping deftly up into the air over his spiraling kick—the two combatants stood opposite once more now on the roof, keeping themselves turned to partially face the giant set of jaws panting beside them. In a moment of shared survival instincts, when the Ammit's pupil went wide like a cat preparing to pounce, both Red and Gargoyle stood their ground and lashed out at the beast's head as it swung towards them—saber and metal claws alike slashed at its tough hide, eliciting a surprised, booming yelp that made Red's bones rattle in her arms.

The Ammit pulled away, eyes fixated on her, distancing itself from the rover as the terrain began to slope—they were entering an outcropping of hills now, and for the moment, the Ammit could no longer match speed and stay within attack range.

Red needed to bring this fight with Gargoyle to its finish, and quick—Trollope's kart was fast approaching once more, the faint screech of that rusty morningstar growing louder and louder. No doubt he was a man unaccustomed to not getting his way, and even a young Goliath would not deter him from making off with some kind of profit. Shooting a quick glance skyward, the Uhlen's ship was also making a cautioned descent once more.

"Goddamn, everyone wants some," Zay was saying to herself within the rover, watching their enemies multiply through the open hatch—as well as the newly installed, ragged windows sliced lengthwise into the rover's portside, courtesy of Ammit. She'd given up trying to fully bring Brann up to speed on their situation, the young man clinging for dear life to the underside of the unfolded workbench protruding from the rover's wall.

"Please, tell me we're almost there," he was moaning, head still bouncing about as if his neck couldn't support its weight—whatever effect Red's treatment was having on his body, he was still coming out of it, and would likely need a few minutes before he was back on his feet.

"Homestretch, kid," Zay reassured the both of them, though mostly herself, her autocannon brought to bear once more as she kicked through the gashes in the wall to allow for more visibility. Her weapon remained trained on the Ammit, though she cast a sideways look at the last harpoon, still lying in wait atop its coiled cable.

A thought struck.

"Hey, kid," she said, an idea forming in real-time as she spoke, one that might just keep them alive long enough to get out of this. "Shake it off—I got a job for you."

30. The Deep

Saber clanging against claws, Red advanced on Gargoyle aggressively, her blade crisscrossing through the air in an unpredictable pattern to keep each of his limbs occupied: it was like fighting a master acrobat, a capoeiragem dance that at times twisted him into impossible positions...but Red was learning fast, the key to Gargoyle's power was his continuous spinning, much like the morningstar affixed to Trollope's kart, which was currently hugging close to the rear of the rover. Stop Gargoyle's spinning, he lost the offensive.

The hands. More often than not, his kicks flying out at Red were braced by his hands, at least one planted on the rover's roof at all times, with only brief breaks in between where he might pull off a flourishing flip or roll.

She needed more reach.

Red imagined her next moves, quickly, and knew she needed to back off—but doing so would open her up for retaliation. The only way back was forward. Two hands on her saber now, she charged in, blade held close in front of her face as she leapt directly into Gargoyle's inner circle. He responded as expected, a powerful double-kick from chest height aiming upwards, Red turning her blade to catch the impact, elbows clasped together, and let herself be tossed upwards into the air once more.

This time, though, she anticipated it, arcing backwards, end over end, legs to the sky as her arms spread apart—she didn't even feel the needle stab into her wrist, and when her boots crashed back down into the rover, her outstretched arms halted her momentum, and a brilliant scarlet arc spiraled into the sky from the edge of her blooded saber's blade. Red steadied herself on three points, her empty hand flat against the roof, and she pointed her saber forward: a declaration, challenging Gargoyle to bring about an end to this bout. Her blade, doubled in length, shone a silvery blood-red now, dripping with energy and animus that sizzled against the rover's metal roof.

They matched each other's postures now, both hunched low, and Gargoyle rumbled appreciatively. *Yes, let's end this*, he said wordlessly, swaying his hips as he readied himself.

When he pounced, he did so with one arm outstretched, straight in for her chest. Red did not lunge forward to meet him, nor did she attempt to block or parry.

She simply stood up. Straight up. Turned to one side. And, blindingly fast, with a simple twirl of her wrist, spun her saber in a full-moon moulinet.

An explosive ring of screaming blood spun out and away like the fiery trail of a rocket, surrounding the back end of the rover in a spiraling fountain of sparkling red powerful enough to slice clean through the roof they stood on.

As well as Gargoyle himself.

His severed arm clanged against the rover before slipping off to one side, flopping away into the wastes, and an unholy dissonance sprayed through his mouthpiece, the electric static sound of unimaginable pain. Gargoyle threw himself backwards, away from Red, his mechanized clawed hand unable to do much of anything to staunch the wound—a gushing stump that used to be an elbow, he was crippled for life, losing all hope of ever winning this fight in the space of a single breath.

Red took a measured step forward to solid ground as the hind end of the rover fell apart under her feet, a cleanly cut square ring of the vehicle's chassis detaching itself just behind the rear axles—taking the clamshell hatch with it. The pursuing kart sharply veered to avoid being flattened by the cross-section, but Red paid what was happening behind her no mind, simply turning her bloody saber away from her hip to show off its impressive new length and shining wetness to Gargoyle.

"Once, you were brave," she spoke aloud, proud and imperious, looking down at the pathetic, inhuman thing as she strolled confidently towards it, the creature wriggling away on its back, a futile act before the feet of his executioner. "Once, you served with meaning and distinction. Your House will fall, as you now fall—purposeless, bereft of light. Get thee gone, devil; I've no taste for you any longer."

Red cut upwards through the air before her, and the tip of the blooded saber spat boiling red acid, bursting open Gargoyle's chest and throat—he crumpled, his entire body rolling back onto his arm, the last of his strength propping himself up. His distorted breathing sounded alien, desperate, futile—a cavernous echo of life departing him, captured in the electronic soundshell of his mask for a final moment longer.

A moment too long, Red crooking her elbow and stabbing low, straight through the creature's breastplate—and when she withdrew her blade, the lifeless corpse followed, carried briefly on the saber before rolling unceremoniously off the side of the rover and disappearing into the dust. With that, the Uhlen warrior was no more.

Red dismissed the blooded length of her blade with an outward swipe, the red vapor dissipating before her, barely had she managed to sheathe the saber before she fell to one knee—blooding two weapons in a single day, a risk she'd never taken before. "Oh, I'm lightheaded now," she said to no one in particular, stifling a giggle.

This saved her life—with no warning whatsoever, Red found herself crouched between the snapping jaws of the Ammit, and only by letting herself fall completely flat did she avoid being crushed between those rows of fangs. The blood-slick roof of the rover held no purchase for her any longer, though, and with a rising scream she found herself slipping off the side, down towards the Ammit's galloping feet, where she would surely be trampled—but instead, an arm caught her at the waist, pulling her through shredded sheet-metal and insulation; when her eyes adjusted from the disappearance of the harsh sunlight, Red found herself looking up into Zay's face.

"Easy girl, I got ya," the former mercenary grinned, her gloved fist bumping against Red's chin affectionately. "We can cuddle later, but for now I need both hands, m'kay?"

Red found her footing, seeing colorful stars as she balanced herself, separating herself from Zay's embrace. "My thanks," she stammered, face flushed as the blood rushed back to her head. "Job well done, I don't mind saying!"

"Not done yet," Zay countered, slapping back on the cocking lever of her autocannon before opening up, the already destroyed wall of the rover flying apart in burning shards around the cone of her cannonfire, sending a flow of bullets straight into the broadside of the galloping Ammitsuchus. The giant beast skipped back, nearly tripping over its own giant claws as it absorbed the rounds, its impenetrable hide breaking out nonetheless in trails of stinging red welts—the Ammit's flesh was mostly bulletproof, it seemed, but that didn't stop Zay's gun from hurting like hell. Eventually, with enough sustained fire, the Ammit slowed, falling back and disappearing for a moment before its snout re-emerged, directly behind the open end of the rover.

One bad slip, anyone could fall directly into those open jaws.

Satisfied that she'd driven Ammit off for the time being, Zay turned and deftly unhooked the safety line from Red's belt. "I will be needing this, though, if you don't mind," she said, handing it off to Brann—to Red's surprise, he was standing on his own two feet, albeit propped up against the opposite wall of the rover.

"You stopped the transfusion early?" Red said, eyeing Brann with apprehension, as if he may spontaneously combust at any moment.

"No choice—unless you can repair multiple severed arteries on the fly, we needed those needles out of him when shit went sideways," Zay intoned sternly. "The rest of the treatment will need to wait til later, once we're out of this."

"I'm fine, I'm good," Brann croaked, sounding anything but as he hooked the safety line just behind the serrated teeth of the harpoon.

"As you say," Red replied, casting her eyes over the wreckage of her transfusion station, the destroyed chair littered with the wet and bloody fragments of the I.V. jars. "Afraid I don't have the materials to continue it later, so we'll just have to go on prayer from here on out."

"That's the spirit," Zay said, clapping Red on the back as she passed, taking the harpoon from Brann as she went. "You ready, soldat?"

Brann gripped the handle protruding from just behind the safety line's spool, ready to retract the line at Zay's signal. "Ready aye."

"Why hasn't it gone after them?" Red queried, pointing out past the trailing Ammit at Trollope's kart.

"We're the bigger, juicier target," Zay answered, holding the harpoon at waist level in both hands, readying her throw. "He needs some motivation to go for the lesser prey—like this!"

She charged down the truncated length of the rover and let fly, skidding to a halt just outside of the reach of the Ammit's snout, though not before the young Goliath took an expectant snap of its jaws at her—and was hooked, the harpoon's teeth digging themselves just behind one of the larger incisors. Instantly the flesh of its gums and tongue lit up with rosy pink electrical pulses, saliva foaming around its fangs, the beast roaring in pain and surprise, one forepaw raising itself high—

"Pull!" Zay bellowed, and Brann slammed himself back on the retractor switch—

—Freeing the harpoon at just the right moment as the Ammit's forelimb swiped across its face and knocked the irritating spike from its jaws. The high-pitched whine of the spooling cable sent the electrified harpoon straight back into the cabin, right into Zay's waiting hands, the broad rubber gloves making easy work of shielding her.

"Let it go," Zay commanded, and Brann flipped the switch back, disabling the spool and allowing Zay to tug on the line to give herself more slack. Before she readied her second throw, however, she stopped to watch as the Uhlen's ship was pulling in close behind, taking advantage of the fact the Ammit had its full attention locked onto the fast-moving rover. Once more, the lower bay slowly opened, and a second Uhlen stood crouched at the ready—a long, thin rifle barrel levelling itself to aim directly into the wide-open vehicle.

"Red, how smart do you think this thing is?" Zay asked, calculating her next move quickly before the Uhlen had a chance to fire.

Red paused before answering: "I mean no offense, but compared to you—"

"None taken!" It was all Zay needed to hear, and once more she charged, making as if she were going to throw the harpoon directly into the Ammit's maw once more, but stopped short just as she raised the weapon to throw.

The ploy worked. The beast clapped shut its jaws and, just as Zay had hoped, feinted to the side—the Uhlen ship had gotten greedy, had descended too low, and the tall bony shoulder blades of the galloping Goliath pounded against the underside of the ship and tore directly through the open boarding ramp. Hydraulics squealed their death cry as the ramp was torn away, the Uhlen's rifle disappearing into the plume of smoke spouting from the ship's underside, the warfighter himself barely catching himself around the jutting piston that once controlled the ramp's descent— legs dangling in the open air, he was completely helpless, at the mercy of gravity and his compatriots steering the transport ship.

Now, the Ammit was mad—as burning debris rained down on its back and neck, the beast twisted its head to the side, getting a good look at the opportunistic ship intruding on its hunt. The three passengers inside the rover watched what came next with no love lost for the Uhlen: taking several longer bounding strides forward, the Ammit dipped low into a full-bodied crouch, then, like a great jungle cat, launched itself up into the air with forelimbs outstretched...and, using all the speed and momentum built up chasing the rover, spun itself in a circle, briefly suspended in place in the air. Several thousand tons of living mass channeled all its kinetic energy into its hips, the airborne monster's long, broad tail whipping itself around and into—no, through—the Uhlen ship. The force of a small mountain slammed into the hull, and the transport ship was reduced to an oversized paperweight, the airborne wreckage spinning out aimlessly at incredible speeds, the lifeless body of the unlucky Uhlen tumbling to earth like a ragdoll.

Red gave a small cheer of delight, Zay watching with relief as the Ammit shrank away, the distance between it and its hopeful meal growing too fast for it to continue the chase, the beast hunched low as its burning eyes watched the rover disappear into the dust. Trollope must have realized that his kart now made for a potentially easier target for the frustrated Ammitsuchus and, after a moment of slowing its pace, accelerated once more as it turned sharply away—breaking off to zoom out into the wide-open wastes, off towards the direction the disabled Uhlen ship had glided. Perhaps he'd reasoned it was easier to pick at the wreckage of a crashed ship—or perhaps he just didn't want to be a meal for the Ammit. Either way, the kart was gone, and the mostly intact rover was free to continue on towards its goal, unmolested for the time being.

Zay let out a long, heavy sigh, her arms sagging as she turned to report the good news to the driver, bumping her forehead intimately against Red's shoulder as she passed her by. For Brann, she reserved a friendly punch to the chest, nodding at him in wordless appreciation for his assistance.

Nes looked as if he'd just run a marathon, his entire face and neck soaked in beads of sweat, his fingers having gripped the wheel so hard there were dents visible in the leather jacketing. He regarded Zay with wide, incredulous eyes as she stepped into the cabin.

"What in the good goddamned *hell* were you demented people *doing* back there?" He gasped, slumping forward on the wheel.

Shaky and unsteady, the fast-moving rover trundled on through the expansive wastes with ribbons of wires and thoroughly chewed-through paneling hanging limply from its destroyed hind-parts, the far-off shadow of a towering structure beginning to fade into view on the horizon.

*

The Dakhma spiked upwards from the crashing waves that

dissipated against its coppery shell, a laminate coating that surely once made the titanic lighthouse gleam beautifully when the morning sun rose from the distant skyline—and a lighthouse it was, however unexpected the party found that to be: though it was as wide at the base as the whole of Castle Jan-Jito and so tall it disappeared into the low-hanging clouds of the marine layer, its design was unmistakable. The ghostly eye of an abandoned lantern's gallery, framed by skeletal spires of arched copper that held aloft the structure's spiked dome, gazed lidlessly down at the earth and the sea below through the sifting fog above their heads; forgotten to time, no keeper to light the pyre. The looming throat of the tower widened at the middle, where it widened steeply to meet the cliffs, though it stood apart— one single entrance, a pair of battered doors that had been reduced to little more than driftwood by the damp and wind, opening up to greet the long mezzanine built around them. Leading away from the mezzanine—towards the cliffs—a wide bridge of chiseled stone, dark and slick from decades of eroding rain that had long since smoothed away any decorative craftsmanship. Like the copper exterior of the tower, time and neglect had leeched away all glory, leaving only a ruinous monument to the pride and hubris of a civilization long-dead.

Nestor had parked the beleaguered remains of the rover parallel to the edge of the cliffs, just past a loose outcropping of mangroves that surrounded the Dakhma in a wide semicircle, a misty breeze cooling their sweaty backs as the party stepped off the shredded back end of the vehicle; all save Brann, who was still nursing a headache from his crumpled seat on the floor.

"I've already radioed Hawkshaw," Nes was saying, kicking through the trailing wreckage still clinging to the rover, looking over the damage with equal parts amusement and disappointment. "No choice but to risk flying us out of here—the Uhlen airship made it damn near all the way without being taken out; at least, not from the sky. You know, I gotta say, I'm feeling fairly vindicated in my decision to spend all the coin we had on us when I picked this thing out—we wouldn't have lasted a minute out there in one of those cheaper junkheaps they were trying to push on me back on the lot."

"Yeah, the extra cupholders really saved our ass," Zay joked bitterly, holding up the flattened wad of trash that used to be one of the extending cots built into the rover's wall. "Your boss is gonna owe us some hazard pay, though, if he ever recovers."

A sharp rap on her back made Zay turn, seeing Red's admonishing glare before, realizing what she'd said, she cast her widened eyes back to the still-groggy Brann. "Oh, right. Sorry," she apologized sheepishly, letting the destroyed cot fall to the ground with a pathetic thud in the packed dirt. "I meant 'when.' Obviously."

"Nevermind that," Nes interrupted, already leading the way towards the great stone bridge. "We need to get inside before nightfall— whatever kind of fiendish delight has set up shop inside, I'd rather take my chances with it, at least when stacked against what we already know is following us. Won't stand a chance either way, though, if we stand around until those kobolds come home. Look," he said, pointing at the ground all around them, the dirt rippling in a strangely synchronous pattern: hundreds of tiny clawed feet, all moving in the same direction, forming a flowing river of pockmarked earth that led away from the mouth of the bridge.

Red was redressing herself in her leather coat as her sharp heels sunk into the dirt, following behind Nes. "I don't know about you lot, but I'm positively famished—perhaps we fish up some supper once we know we're safe?"

"You fish?" Zay asked, surprised, slinging her cannon back over her shoulder as she fell in line at the rear.

"Well—no," Red admitted, "I just thought one of you might take up the initiative..."

Zay scoffed, turning back, expecting to see Brann following close behind. "Yeah, sure thing 'Highness,' we'll just make the kid pull his weight for once. Hey, Brann—"

He was not, however, following up the rear. Instead, Brann was only just stepping off the back of the rover, digging a palm into his aching forehead, holding up the still-attached harpoon by its cable. He seemed completely in awe of it. "Did Nes make this?" He asked aloud, though no one was close enough to answer, the other three members of the party already having nearly reached the bridge.

"Hey, 'Captain Skylark,'" Nes called back, attempting to sway the dozy young man's attention, "We're heading in, move with a purpose!"

Zay knew it was too late—she heard it before she saw it, the snapping and swaying of displaced branches, the mangroves parting like water around a rapidly approaching shadow. "Oh, godammit," she breathed, already swinging up the autocannon at hip level and splitting the quiet sky apart with ripping gunfire.

Brann jolted in place, like a frightened deer, but otherwise made no attempt to flee—even as his head slowly turned, the fanged maw of the Ammitsuchus exploding out from the treeline, coming right at him.

"Brann, run!" Red screamed helplessly—she hadn't reloaded her flintlock, her hand fumbling at the pistol's rounded grip—

"Oh, shit, no!" Nes had nothing but the handsaw on him, it would barely even scratch the beast's hide—

There was no time, no time at all, and Brann was run down—the only thing he could think to do, the only reflex that activated as those jaws closed around him, was to swing his arm wide, as if attempting to knock aside the great beast's head with a whiplike lash of the harpoon-capped power cable. The rover flew apart like dried leaves, the front end tumbling away, the rest of it bursting around the Ammit's powerful body in a hail of splintered scrap. The saurian beast roared out in fury, and though they couldn't see Brann anymore, strobing arcs of static lightning lit up the side of the beast's face; the harpoon had embedded itself lengthwise just behind it's eyeridge, the power cable wrapped in chaotic fashion around its entire jawline.

The Ammit wasn't stopping—it bounded forward, erratically, hopping this way and that, claws swiping at its own head desperately—

Zay dropped into a crouch, raising the cannon to keep firing, ignoring the burning hot casings that slapped across her forehead and cheek as she focused her aim on the beast's legs, trying to bring it down before—

—The ground disappeared beneath the Ammit's feet, the writing beast stumbling out into the open air, off the side of the cliffs—

—And it was gone.

Zay tossed aside her weapon, her vision tunneling, the ringing in her ears blocking out the world around her as she sprinted as fast as she ever had in her life, not stopping until she herself had nearly carried herself right off the cliff.

Below, far, far below, the waves smashed mercilessly against the narrow beach and the rocks surrounding the base of the Dakhma. She watched, not breathing, as the distorted silhouette of the Ammit swam back towards the beach—

Seafoam leapt around the Ammit's breach, so far below that she couldn't hear its pained cries, but still Zay watched—watched as its forelimb came up, those hooked claws digging into the side of its head, then pulled, sending a small glint of metal spinning away into the sand. Shaking its great, heavy skull, the dazed beast trotted off, suffering little more than a bruised ego, leaving behind nothing in its wake, no trace of Brann at all.

None, save for a bent harpoon, standing upright in the gravelly sand, the severed end of the cable curling away towards the sea.

*

In the salt and the cold, his unseeing eyes drifted open, the black nothing wobbling into a mitosis of wobbling blue—deep, deep blue, farther down than the sun could hope to reach. The pressure on his head and chest was unbearable, his ears verging on popping yet denied the relief, and Brann was very dimly aware of a spike of bone not native to his own body that was spreading apart his ribs—the broken half of the Ammit's fang, snapped off after burying itself in him, the tip of it tickling at his lung.

Lungs which, as his sense of self and place seeped back into his body, were not currently working. His heart was not pumping. His flesh benumbed, as cold as the deep sea he drifted down into, Brann felt with certainty the fingertips of death running up his spine. The fingers of his left hand twitched, the arm curling down, bringing his hand low to feel at the protruding lump of shattered fang in his side. The water felt cloudier, warmer, and though he couldn't turn his head to see, Brann sensed the plume of blood leeching away into the dark, a smoke signal rising far above his head that beckoned the hungry ocean dwellers.

Ah. A customer. The fins trailed like warbanners behind, the blackened shell of decorative outer plating segmented around the lighter, smooth flesh—the torpedo-head of a predatory fish splitting open to reveal the ghastly smile, a thousand teeth awaiting within, those two black eyes gleaming within rings of white sclera. An ironhelm shark. Brann couldn't help but think it was sort of adorable, in a way, the ancient lord of the deep sea seeming to drift this way and that as it sniffed curiously. It smelled the blood long before it ever saw Brann, but now that they were mere meters apart, it activated, automated hunting instincts sending it into orbit around the drifting corpse that shrunk rapidly with each pass. *No point in waiting*, Brann thought dully, the survivor in him having taken the day off. *Come dig in, I'm making it easy for you today.*

The water around his ears seemed to click, like tiny sonic vibrations vibrating his inner jawbone—Brann's eyes trickled downward, between his feet. The crust of the earth descended behind him, sloping down into the even dark nothing of an oceanic canyon, and rising to meet him a shelf of rock was carpeted in spiny scales that shifted and flowed over one another. A colony of eurypterids, chattering excitedly amongst one another, their nightmarish pincers raising themselves high to welcome Brann into their embrace; what was left of him when the shark was done ripping him apart, anyway. *Everybody wants some today*, Brann dimly remembered hearing Zay say.

The ocean had other plans.

If the world itself had a pulse, Brann felt it throb powerfully, a cardiac rhythm sending minor shockwaves through his limp body—the scorpions below scattered, jetting away down into the ascending night, and the shark could only struggle to swim in place against a rising current that pushed apart the tectonic plates of the ocean floor itself—

No, Brann realized, he wasn't falling into a canyon. The far side of the earth was retreating, a continental shift that undulated in strangely organic ways, stacked coils of shining blue steel and jade—a living creature, a being so immeasurably vast it could have stretched on to touch the other side of the planet, its serpentine body slipping away into the sea with such worldly prominence that the vortex it created pulled Brann along into its influence like a leaf in a hurricane. The continental shelf disappeared behind him in an instant, and Brann was travelling faster and faster, eclipsing even the speeds of the Donnie, the gravitational well in the belly of the ocean gripping him by the ankles and pulling him across time itself.

There was a moment, a brief pause, the deepwater currents slowing stiffly, running still—Brann could no longer see the threatening shark, the fish having been pulled miles away by now into the murky sea—and once more he was drifting in place, nothing but the void of the sea as far above and below him as his failing eyes could see. Then, a shadow filled his vision, and the watery curtains parted around the head of a cosmic leviathan that so deliberately and with such deific intelligence perceived the tiny speck of Brann in the endless waters that the dying young man still felt the fear of infinity entrapping him in its expanse.

There was a hewn nobility, a shaped intention in its visage that reminded Brann distantly of the first time he'd seen the Marshal Tark, the fatherly radiance that filled the gulf of ocean between them endearing Brann to this world-serpent despite himself and his existential dread. The snout of the draconic sentinel was a mountain, one Brann could spend a day attempting to climb and still not reach the top—the eyes, twin wormholes that absorbed all light around them before they projected it back in hypnotic, phosphorescent coronas; halos that could light a city, beaming down upon the microscopic Brann across the sea.

When it spoke, it came as a rolling thunder that bashed Brann's dim consciousness across the shore, evoking life from within him that had bled away, restoring the soul within him to a wholeness and alertness that hummed with bioelectric purpose around a single syllable:

"I."

In that moment, Brann met with the living identity of the universe itself. The Godhead of the Seas knew him, inside and out, a transparent polyp of identity that stood now at the precipice of sermon, and Brann had no choice but to listen when the warm fabric of life stitched itself back together within his body as the Godhead spoke.

"STEP FORWARD, OUT BEHIND ILLUSORY CLOTH OF GRAND ILLUSION, YOUNG ONE. BE, AND BE NOT AFRAID, THAT WE MAY SHARE IN THIS GIFT."

Brann's mind and soul was tugged forward, kneeling before the invitation, sharing this space in the fringe consciousness that warmed and nurtured all life in its aura. Life itself had offered a seat at its table, and Brann was to speak, existing now only for this conversation.

"Am I dead?" The obvious question—no sound left Brann's lips, the waters silent, his lungs remaining empty.

"YOU ARE AWAKE."

It was neither answer nor dismissal—Brann sensed every word the Godhead spoke to him a choice made to communicate understanding, not information: dead, alive, it didn't matter in this moment, for he could still exist aware of himself. That would have to do, for now.

"Are you here to help me?" Stupid—Brann regretted asking immediately, entitlement licking at the back of his mind behind those words. "Us, I mean—my friends and I. What we're trying to do."

"WHAT REASSURANCES DO YOU SEEK THAT COULD

GIVE PURPOSE BEYOND THAT WHICH YOU HAVE ALREADY UNDERTAKEN FOR YOURSELF?" It wasn't an admonishment, more an expression of vexation. "WOULD YOUR LIFE BE FORFEIT, ABSENT THE COMFORT OF MY IMPRIMATUR?"

Brann supposed not. "I guess what I'm asking...do we matter? Does anything we do matter?"

The seas shifted, the distant coils of the Godhead rolling along the coast of some far-off nation, bearing the rhythm of the tides and echoes of calming waves to some sleepy village on a remote beach.

"I HAVE SHED MY SKIN AGAINST THE ICE OF EVERY GLACIER AND REEF," that inescapable voice intoned within Brann's chest, "PLANTED BUDS OF LIFE ON EVERY SHOAL. ALL WHO SHARE THIS PLANE WITH ME ON MY JOURNEY ARE COUNTED, ALL WHO HAVE BEEN FOLDED BACK INTO THE WAVES GIVEN MY THANKS. NO LIFE SPRINGS FORTH FROM ME THAT DOES NOT BEND ALL THAT THEY TOUCH AS THE WIND BENDS THE REEDS—TO LIVE AND TO DIE AT ALL IS TO MATTER."

Was there even a question that needed answering? Brann couldn't seem to shape it, couldn't wrap his arms around it—what do you ask to being that claims to have birthed all living things? What answer could even be given he would accept? Brann suspected this was the point all along.

"I don't know what to do," he offered, pathetically, a lump in his throat. "What am I supposed to do? What happens next?"

The hopeful fingers of aquamarine light stroked patterns along the Great Dragon's rainbow-blue scales, those skyscraper-sized fangs jutting from its upper jaw hiding entire schools of fish between them, forests of kelp that spanned acres sprouting along it's back.

"YOU CARRY WITHIN YOU SECRETS OF AGES, LITTLE DEMI-HUMAN," the Godhead finally said. "TENDER FLESH GIVES WAY TO KNOWLEDGE ETERNAL, THE SHAPE OF ALL THINGS TO COME MOLDED BY THE TIME YOU WILL HAVE SPENT

DOING MY WORK. NO MISSION HAVE I FOR YOU, NO DEVOTION TO MY NAME DO I SANCTION, SAVE FOR ONE TRUTH. AGELESS DEATH, STRIPPING FROM YOU ALL THAT YOU HOLD DEAR, CANNOT TAKE FROM YOU MY MOST PRECIOUS OF GIFTS TO THIS WORLD. IN THE FACE OF IT, DEATH DEFIANT, NONETHELESS, STANDS MUTE AND TOOTHLESS:

"YOU ARE LOVED, AND YOU ARE A LIVING MONUMENT TO THAT LOVE. YOU WILL DELIVER THIS SEED OF CONVICTION TO THE EMPTY MINDS AND FROZEN HEARTS OF THOSE WHO WANDER BEREFT OF HOPE. WHERE YOU WALK, THERE I WILL BE, GROWING BENEATH YOUR FEET."

The fan-like tailtip of the Godhead emerged from the shadowy depths beneath its head, the veinous membrane stretching between its spines capable of laying itself from one corner of a continent to another. It was drawing itself back, readying to send a deepwater current clear through to another hemisphere, returning Brann to the distant cliffs he'd fallen from along the way.

Brann had one last question, his thoughts encircling two truths in equal measure: first, that he'd never know the purpose of this dialogue with a Godhead, or even if it truly ever happened; second, that he was still alive, and he would go forth with a renewed sense of belonging to the world around him.

"Why me?"

The Godhead's tail paused for the briefest of moments, and though that stony face remained, as the rest of its existence, incomprehensible, Brann couldn't help but sense the faintest of smiles warming his heart.

"WHY NOT YOU?"

The tail flicked, the motion a typhoon beneath the world, and once more Brann was sent across the vast abyss in a compressed conduit that bridged the seas, everything going dark as the forces of gravity that broke around him in aquatic sonicbooms pulled him into unconsciousness.

31. The Dissident

His ears finally popped, shards of melted ice shattering all across his body as Brann breached, gasping in agony as air filled his dead and dried lungs—his hands, flailing about, smacked their palms painfully against sharp rock; he clung to them in desperation, pulling himself close to anything solid, anything he could rest against, his body slumping over hard earth in immeasurable relief. Brann sucked in one lungful after another, instinctively reaching down, his soldat reflexes taking hold and applying pressure to the wound in his side—the fang must have been pulled free from his sternum by the sheer force of the ocean currents, he couldn't feel it between his ribs anymore—

"I got him, I got him!"

The voice was muffled, dripping back out of his ears as they broke their suction, and Brann felt it before he could see or hear it—the strong grip of someone's arm around his neck, digging into his collar; like the drowning swimmer he was, Brann reached up with both arms in return, clasping hands around that muscled forearm as tight as he could, kicking up until he felt those sharp rocks beneath his boots and the pull of the water release itself about his waist.

"Easy there, killer, I got you, you're safe—"

The saltwater burned his eyes and nostrils, stringy bobs of kelp wrapped tight about his head and shoulders, Brann tugging himself free as best he could of their slimy grasp, and he looked up...at the bruised, battered, but unmistakable face of his equine friend, wrapped in an entire infirmary's worth of bloodied gauze and bandages.

"They're telling me you could have crossed a perfectly good bridge, but instead decided to take a wicked header off the cliffs like a goddamn lunatic?" Boomer was saying incredulously, and in typical fashion, his devilish grin betrayed him. "Kid, if you're waiting for permission to just do things the easy way for once, trust me, you have it—next time, just use the front door, 'kay?"

*

A sloppy looking campfire had been built at the water's edge, Brann having surfaced within the widest and lowest point of the Dakhma, in the subterranean reservoir—from their vantage point, Brann could see the rocky path turn to carved stairs that spiraled up and around the entirety of the inside of the tower, disappearing up into the tiny glint of light where the eye of the lighthouse opened up. Just below the midway point, a second pinpoint of light filtered through, the single entrance to the structure—at least, one that didn't require navigating an underwater system of hidden caves to find. For such an impressive outward appearance, there sure wasn't a lot to see inside the tower—just open air and the winding stairs.

The flapping of black wings signaled Grishka's arrival, the raven's caw echoing about the lower cavern before a smokey blur passed behind the campfire, and the avian witch of illusions sat herself down in partially human form just across from Brann. "No ting uppa, den," she said, her feathery arms shrugging off her shrinking wings as slender, clawed fingers dug unceremoniously into the fish roasting on a spit, Nestor offering her a fork silently with a look of defeat. "Only door, high door, uppa dem stairs— sealed, biggum rock, heavy heavy."

Her beak jabbed upwards, along the opposite wall, across from the main entrance—sure enough, though no light filtered through, the faint curvature of a boulder jutted out from a mirroring arched doorway, and Brann reasoned that the rocks they currently sat on must have actually been the weathered and eroded remains of the bridge that once connected both sides of the Dakhma's interior.

Around him, in the low light illuminated only by the water that cast it's reflections upwards to bathe the reservoir in a dim, green glow, Brann saw the dark shapes of the rest of his companions moving about—a sturdy, metallic grip on his shoulder, giving an encouraging shake; Hawkshaw was here, and as more faces fell into view around the fire, Brann knew the entire team was reunited once more. Red was huddled in close next to Wolf, who was resisting the overwhelming urge to lick her face with visible distress, snout turned low and eyes half-crossed as he stared at his mistress, tail beating against the blanket draped over their shoulders. Emrys was doling out forks to everyone as they sat, pulling his long coat around himself as his breath fogged—shit, it was cold, Brann realized upon seeing this, the feeling only just beginning to return to his flesh.

Zay had let her own blanket fall away, kneeling beside Brann, inspecting his exposed ribs through his torn blouse and fractured breastplate. "Kid, I'm telling you, there's nothing," she was saying in both exasperation and relief.

"That's impossible," Brann rebutted, his teeth chattering—if he could twist himself around, he would, but right now he was frozen solid. "It went straight through the ribs—"

"I'm telling you," Zay interrupted, "Other than some surface scratches and a bruise you're definitely gonna be feeling tomorrow, nothing actually punctured the skin—the armor probably deflected the worst of it, given the state it's in, but besides that you're fine."

Brann traced the fingers of his imagination around the jagged end of the split fang that had impaled him, feeling back to the sensations of having his life leak out from between his separated ribs, the hole through him undeniably fatal. For a moment, he thought to tell them of the great serpent, the conversation he'd had with an actual Godhead—then, looking to his right and seeing Boomer pout over the forked lump of steaming fish Nes passed his way, something stayed Brann from speaking up. Instead, he pulled the blanket over himself, thanking Zay quietly and turning his eyes to the fire.

"We should keep a tally," Boomer said, pulling a face over the taste of the fish, "Of all the near-death experiences we've all racked up. Brann's got one, Red's got one, pretty sure I'm in the lead with like six—ugh, seriously, we couldn't have just pulled something out of the Donnie, some frozen dinner trays or something?"

"I spent almost three hours trying to fish this up for Miss

Ladyship," Nes responded sullenly, jabbing another fork into the crispy fish. "We're not letting this hard work go to waste, especially since this fish already gave his life to fill our bellies."

"Well, maybe he shoulda thought of that before being born a fish," Boomer retorted, turning to Brann to bump shoulders with the young man.

Brann didn't find it within himself to look directly at Boomer—as if seeing him alive once more were a mirage borne out of his own brush with death, and acknowledging it directly would shatter the ghostly apparition in his mind's eye. Instead, he mulled over what he'd seen and heard, out there in the ocean deep, and asked the person he thought most qualified on the matter—

"Emrys. What's a demi-human?"

Sitting himself down to begin forking himself some handfuls of fish, Emrys blew on the shredded white meat, his gauze-wrapped hands immune to the steaming hot temperatures. "If ever I had thanks to give, I must say, what a gift it has been to travel in the company of so many willing pupils, always asking the most interesting questions and providing me opportunities to teach." Emrys tucked a wad of fish in his cheek, gasping and blowing around it in mild shock, his mouth not as resistant to the heat as his hands. "Hooah—what—-hah—what inspired this question, young Master Brann?"

"I heard the word once," Brann lied, "Just never thought to ask what it meant until now."

Emrys swallowed thoughtfully, though his sideways glance said volumes—he clearly didn't believe this answer, but chose not to press it, given Brann's recent discomforts. "Ahem—well. As with all things, there are differing schools of thoughts on the matter—"

"Any of those schools teach how to get to the point the quickest?" Zay interjected, shadows already growing beneath her eyes as Emrys spoke.

"—As I am graced with willing pupils," Emrys faltered, quickly adjusting course in navigating his own thoughts, "So too do I stand ready to learn. Yes, thank you Miss Kadzhieva, of course we have more important riddles to solve." He wiped his hands clean and shifted on his rock, leaning closer to Brann. "In more traditional circles, scholars would apply the moniker of 'demi-human' to any being perceived to be lesser, which is to say, 'less than human,' such as the beastmen—" He extended a hand towards Boomer, who waved back cheerfully, "—Or those curiosities that live beyond the reach of human contrivances." He leaned back to offer his fingers to Grishka, who pecked at them affectionately. "Where opinions diverge, however, is when it comes to exploring the curiosity that led those less transparently xenophobic minds beyond rote classification, and towards the bridging of social divides between human and 'formerly' human; those still capable of some rational thought, that is." He emphasized this last part by nodding towards Red and Wolf, the latter of whom growled low in response.

"Emrys, you're so sweet, as always," Red crooned back, stabbing her fork into the crackling flesh of the cooked fish.

"This is you getting to the point?" Zay joined in, grimacing.

Emrys held his hands up pleadingly. "There can be no half-measures in proper education, should we ever hope to pierce the ceiling of our own intelligence." Once more, he leaned towards Brann. "Though I avoid using the word myself due to its inherent stigma, I would comfortably define it as any and all beings that exist laterally to the human condition—that is to say, in a state of near humanity, though apart from it, whether due to their own design or the designs of nature."

"The Uhlen I fought," Red contributed, setting down her fork after a single forkful of fish, "His blood was cursed, infected with something— but the smell of it was unmistakably human, at least in part. Had I looked beneath the mask, I suspect I might have beheld the face of a proper devil."

"Without my own observation I couldn't say—but taking your judgment at face value, I'd caution that you fought a demi-human yourself," Emrys said, his tone taking on a less condescending edge the more Red glared back at him.

"Am I a demi-human?" Brann asked pointedly, ignoring the friction between the two of them.

Emrys paused at this, taken aback. "My friend, what could have possibly given you that idea?"

Red spoke again, choosing not to apply a barbed tongue to her words, despite her ever-present distaste for Emrys. "Our young soldat here admitted to engaging in a ritual that involved a partial transfusion with the blood of my hound, here," she said, giving a disciplinary pinch of Wolf's ear, who stared at the ground quietly. "I did what I could to purge any transformative taint, though the cleansing process could not be properly completed, and Brann had already begun to show signs of...shall we say, 'corruption.'"

Emrys's eyes went wide, taking in Brann with an entirely new perspective. "Oh, that is interesting, indeed," he breathed, already pulling his book of incantations from his coat. "Would that I could act as steward to oversee such an experiment—"

"Yeah, no, I'm afraid I must protest," Hawkshaw spoke up, "On account of you folks of living flesh and blood have the irksome tendency to assign manual labor to those of us unfortunate enough to have been born on an assembly line. By that I mean I got a radio call of some urgency? Saying we had limited time before a considerable army of kobolds returned to the nest?" He jabbed a thumb at Nes. "And I know for a fact y'all aren't gonna miss a chance to abuse your relationship with the token automaton in setting him to work reassembling an airship that's been stripped for parts by some greedy little critters."

"Bright Eyes is right," Nes agreed, standing up and kicking at Boomer's hoof. "Everyone up, on your feet, we have limited time to dig into this place, and I bet a year's salary whatever mystery we're here to solve has conveniently buried its solution behind that big-ass boulder up there."

Boomer swallowed a mouthful of fish, looking indignantly up at Nes. "Um, I'm still eating?"

Nes kicked rocks over the campfire, turning into a smoldering pit of embers. Boomer stood straight up, pointing an authoritative finger at the engineer. "You're fired."

"No, I'm not."

"Okay." Boomer let his hand fall, easily defeated as everyone else came to their feet, readying to move on. Instead, he clapped a hand against Brann's back. "C'mon kid, let's get this over with so we can get back to the Donnie, I have a feeling the both of us could use a comfy bed tonight."

Though when Brann obliged, barely had he taken a single step before Boomer's hand caught him about the collar, the towering horse crouching a bit to whisper in Brann's ear.

"Who is that?" He asked.

Brann blinked. "Who is who?"

Boomer pointed at Grishka, who paid them no mind, shaking her feathers free of any clinging bits of fish on her rocky perch.

Staring for a moment, Brann tried to process this—had Boomer's memory been affected? Was his head injury that severe? "You okay man? That's Grishka, she's came onboard along with Emrys and Hawkshaw and the rest."

Boomer's brow furrowed. "You sure?"

"Yeah, dude—she's a witch, she shapeshifts, sometimes she's all bird, sometimes all human. Woman with dark hair?"

Boomer's finger drifted, pointing questioningly at Zay.

"No, not her the other one, the one who was sitting next to Hawkshaw at your fight."

Boomer's memory was cast back, his face contorted as he visibly struggled to remember, before realization dawned on him. "They're the *same person*?"

Apparently, Grishka's illusions were more effective on Boomer than they were on everyone else. "Did you think you had a real-life bird on your payroll?"

Boomer frowned. "What, no, I just thought Hawkshaw hired a pretty call girl to come with him to the fight...you mean I paid for that?"

"She's not a call girl, she's a witch."

"But do I have to pay her, too?"

Brann was at a loss. He shrugged. "I dunno, probably, yeah?"

"I need to hire an accountant," Boomer groaned. "There are too many of you people to keep track of."

Nes overheard this as he rolled up the discarded blankets. "You had one, but you fired him when he disagreed with your suggestion that a life-size statue in your likeness would brighten up the engine room."

"There are no bad ideas," Boomer shot back, "Only those who lack the vision to bring them to life."

"Question," Red asked, raising her hand to no one in particular. She then pointed at the opposite walls overhead in turn, drawing an invisible bridge between the separate doorways. "How are we meant to enact our egress in a timely manner? Surely we're not meant to ascend those steps, then descend, then ascend once more? It took us near an hour to reach the bottom the first time."

"Good point." Zay loaded up her arms with gear, tossing her head back the way they came, towards the stairs that led to the exit. "Ladyship, you're looking even more pale around the gills than normal, so sorry, you can't be expected to stay upright in another fight—you're coming back to the ship with me. Keep watch while the old man and I assemble some kind of lightweight bridge to get the rest of you out, yeah?" She ignored Red's protests as she locked eyes with Nestor who nodded in agreement, then looked Brann and Boomer up and down, biting her lip furtively. "Honestly I'm not convinced the two of you shouldn't also come back to the ship to get some rest, but the kid looks fine despite his bellyaching and you're obviously feeling better. Besides that, I don't trust the schoolteacher and the can-opener on their own. Whatever this 'leader' thing is that's taken over the tower? If it makes an appearance, these two would probably just want to have a spirited argument with it rather than actually try to kill it."

"I'd say you're being a tad unfair in that claim—"

"Now wait just a goddamn minute—"

Both Emrys and Hawkshaw stumbled over each other's outbursts of repudiation, but fell silent as their voices blended together in an impotent garble of noise, looking sheepishly between each other as Zay nodded affirmatively. "Yeah, that's what I thought. You all find yourselves in more trouble than you can handle, send the bird back across the gap to give us word, we'll try to rush in and help, but no promises it'll be in any timely manner—either way we'll still need to find some way to bridge that gap."

Wolf padded along behind Red as she began her way up the steps, but was stopped by Nestor, who bravely stepped between them. "Not so fast—Red, we'll need your muscle here to go with them, help clear that boulder away."

Red turned, raising a hand to silence the rising growl in Wolf's throat. "No, he's right, my dear—we must remain apart for the time being, your talents are better served with the rest of the group."

Brann stepped up alongside Wolf, giving him a reassuring hand to lead him away. "C'mon, we'll get this done faster with you."

Zay nodded to herself as the party separated once more, the smaller group trailing away up behind the stairs while the rest made their way across the reservoir along the water's edge. She called down to Brann as he turned heel, though, with one final thought:

"Oi. Kid. You know what we're here for, yeah?"

Brann stopped in place, looking back over his shoulder. "This place, this tower—it's one giant gravesite, right? Supposed to be built by Geiha?"

Zay nodded. "They helped, among others, but yeah. One big monument to their past, all their biggest accomplishments."

Brann crossed his arms, looking skyward, at the tiny pinpoint of light far above where the daylight filtered in through the eye of the lighthouse. "If I know one thing about House Geiha, it's that they never miss a chance to brag about their history. If ever there was a place hiding any

528

information we could use to convince the Marshal Tark to clear our names, this would be it—though even then I'm not sure it'll be enough."

Zay was surprised. "You don't mean to fight him—you said 'convince' him. Convince him of what?"

Brann thought back to the fight with Boomer. "I never mattered to him, not really, only the last survivor of House Lachlan surrendering to House Geiha was. Whatever he wants, it's all politics—in training, they always made us call it the 'Geihan Empire', and I think Lachlan was the last House standing in Tark's way from making that a reality. I think whatever happens to the rest of the world, whatever comes next for Geiha and whoever they plan on invading next, it'll be my fault. We won't be able to stop that from happening just by challenging Tark to a fight—we'll need to expose Geiha as war criminals, show the world we aren't terrorists. We just..."

For some reason, he was reminded of Recruit Caleb, back at the Assay, the accusations leveled at him by Tark. Brann gave a small smile. "We just paid attention in history class."

The former mercenary shook her head. "I've seen a lot of shit in my time kid, and I know a bit about Geiha too, don't forget. They didn't clean up after themselves—I'm still alive. All us raiders that scrubbed Lachlan's villages? They didn't get rid of us after the job was done by killing us off quietly. They paid us. Handsomely. There are dozens of living witnesses to their crimes still out there, and I don't think any of us got the impression it was about tidying up their political reputation."

Brann looked up to Zay, studying her face. "You don't think we can stop what's coming? That what we're doing matters?"

"I think the only thing that can stop what's coming is a bullet between Tark's eyes. He's not someone you convince by dredging up the skeletons hiding in his closet. Someone with that much power, that willingness to scar the world and kill that many innocent people in the name of their chosen God, that's someone you put down. Publicly. In the town square, where everyone can watch his head roll, so there's no question about who God is really looking kindly down upon."

Brann began walking backwards, towards the direction of the rest of his companions. "Thought you didn't believe in God," he joked.

"I don't—not till I've been face to face with him. You shouldn't either," Zay cautioned loudly as Brann drew further and further away.

Brann's back was turned to Zay now, double-timing it to catch up with the group. "That's the thing," He shouted back, a newfound sense of confidence bubbling in his chest, where previously there was only doubt and dark. "I'm pretty sure I have."

*

Half-sunken into the earth, the warped hull of the Uhlen's transport ship flagged high at the back end, the yawning underside torn open beneath, like a fallen bird that had its heart ripped out by a hungry cat. Tark surveyed the damage with a bitter taste in his mouth—the crash had cost the lives of three Uhlen, not counting Gargoyle, whose remains were yet to be recovered. Likely he was already food for the scavengers of the wastes who picked at the scraps that fell from the jaws of the Goliaths—the Uhlen's numbers were dwindling fast, and Tark couldn't help but feel there was a smear of disloyalty marring their usual perfect record.

"I gave the order to stand down. I got what I needed from the deserter. What more were you hoping to glean from pursuing them into Goliath territory?"

The Speaker sidled up to Tark, arms crossed—his voice, distorted as it was through that electronic mouthpiece, nevertheless sounded entirely like that of someone dissatisfied with Tark's leadership capabilities, if his attitude weren't already making that perfectly clear. "Maybe I've been remiss in my understanding of what our House values in its troops," he said sarcastically, not even paying his superior the courtesy of standing at attention, "But I recall it being a matter of national pride to never allow open disrespect of the Geihan banner to go unchecked. You hand-picked this little fucker for open demonstration of your authority at the Assay, and he took a shot at you. Subsequent to that, your orders were unambiguous: hunt him and his cohorts down, bring them before you. Respectfully, Marshal, you're not looking at all sides of this."

"I'm expected to sanction this loss as a matter of necessary wartime expense, you mean to say," Tark responded. "You and the men were simply following my orders—I am the one who stands at odds with the best interest of House Geiha, derelict in my duties, vision clouded by uncertainty?"

"As a matter of fact, yes," The Speaker said simply. He turned oblique to face Tark, his mask impassive as ever, though his cocked hip and crossed arm was the image of dissatisfaction. "We *are* a sovereign force—all trappings and performative speeches to the lesser infantry aside, nothing moves within our sight that isn't subject to our whims. A traitor pulls a gun on the boss, we pull him apart like we're separating a fucking chicken. You want to call off the chase, well, that's all fine and dandy, Sir Marshal—but all this honorable posturing can go fuck itself. The boys and I, we're still hungry, and it seems while you were out dusting off your big shiny champion's belt, you forgot to feed us. So we went hunting."

Tark gave no response—there was a plume of dust, fast approaching. He squinted from behind his platinum mask—it was a kart, and an unsightly one at that, held together by the hopes and dreams of someone unbothered by such notions as rust or decay.

"Who's this joker, now?" The Speaker said, hand on hip, watching the traveler arrive from afar.

The oversized morningstar bounced against the resistance of the kart's suspension as it ground to a crunching halt, kicking up gravel against Tark's shins. The sheetmetal-plated driver's door squealed open, the hinges as rusty and dirtied as the rest of the vehicle, and out stepped none other than the gaudy announcer who had presided over Tark's fight.

"You told me," Trollope snarled, shifting his weight uncomfortably to more aggressively free himself from the tight doorway of the kart, tugging his furs in close about his shoulders, "I could have your so-called 'terrorists' as my prize, payment for my discretions—no self-respecting host would have ever allowed the leader of an entire House into an unsanctioned fight against said House's own duly elected Champion!"

"All apologies," Tark countered, "But I believe I said you could take them while they remained in reach, which is to say, within the borders of your little shanty town—allowing them to flee and giving chase into the deadlands? You took any and all risk of loss upon yourself."

The Speaker stood by, listening carefully to the grumblings of the sweat and dust-caked man, Trollope's once magnificent nest of sculpted hair a disgraceful mess of knots and frayed ends about his chubby face. "Do you know how much I paid out in winnings to those who, despite all accolades and prestige, bet against the Champion Fighter of not just House Geiha—but of the fucking world?" He spat like a garden hose, his words slurring together in his fury, face beet-red beneath the dust and grime. "Have you any idea what your sordid little political subterfuge has cost me and my men?!"

"If it is a matter of simple liquidity," Tark calmly beamed back, "House Geiha is always accommodating to its allies who pledge long-term service to its—"

"Fuck your House, you lizardly cocksucker," Trollope bellowed, and in his hand he suddenly brandished his favored cudgel, wagging it at Tark with murderous intent. "You'll pay me now, this instant, with whatever you—"

The spray of hot blood against Tark's clawed feet brought about silence once more, save for the wet gurgles that gave way to the deflating hiss of Trollope's lungs. The bourgeois criminal overlord was reduced to a slumped mass of lifeless blubber in the dirt, absent his own face, which had fallen away like a discarded mask beneath the upward swing of The Speaker's horrific-looking karambit. The blade glinted with dripping rubies in the evening sunlight, and the composed Uhlen coolly swiped his knife across the air in a wide arc to shake off the blood.

"Once they called you The Iron Tark," The Speaker said sardonically, sheathing the blade once more in its hidden sheath along his forearm. "The most fearsome warlord on the continent, who carved lakes of blood out of the world, their rivers draining into the sea on either coast. Once, you commanded the admiration of your men. Respectfully, sir, you've lost your touch. If it's the promise of House Geiha standing above all others you mean to fulfill, you won't move an inch towards that future if you keep letting yourself be dragged down by cowardly young orphans and..." He raised his boot, swiping away the gunky red gore that had splashed against it. "...These common backwater hicks. How can we, the Uhlen, possibly trust you're gonna have our backs again after all this?"

Tark remained silent for a moment, turning his back to The Speaker, kicking away a stray hunk of the ship's wreckage—he gazed out, through the lightly swirling cloud of smoke, across the open wastes, towards the distant coast that lay far behind the visible horizon. There was an unfortunate measure of truth in The Speaker's words—a youthful defiance, something long thought forgotten, buried beneath decades of service, was peeking through the cracks in Tark's armor. This young recruit, this single fixed point of failure Tark had identified in his grand designs, had roused within the Marshal a memory of himself. A cloudy fragment of an opaline whole, a part of him that once stood with chin held high against tyrants and men of serpentine politics. Try as he might to justify an underground cage match with a chosen figurehead representing an allegiance to their shared nation, it was unmistakably a decision he'd made in pursuit of reclaiming some personal commentary about himself. Some passage of words unspoken in the years he'd stood at the helm of House Geiha, fulfilling an agenda not his own.

More than words—a name. His name.

"The Uhlen were founded at a time House Geiha could not have needed them more," Tark finally spoke aloud, regarding The Speaker's aggrieved accusations with due penance. "When the bureaucratic notions of joined nations seeking asylum from their own bloodied pasts put to writ a narrative of fantasy—that they themselves were not creatures of war, quarreling amongst themselves for notions of land or wealth." He turned away from the horizon, facing The Speaker once more. "Our chosen House—no, *my* chosen House—had set its sights higher, on a world of unification beyond the bounds of nobless oblige—as you rightly say, beyond the posturing and the performances. I needed men of action who would not, could not, be distracted by these flights of fancy. Leaders reaching down to shake hands with the hungry and the poor and the dispossessed, the masses entirely aware their leaders were responsible for their struggle since the start, but unwilling to forego the chance at an easy and comfortable life if it meant playing along with these games of vanity and make-believe."

He stepped towards The Speaker, slowly, calmly, but with a growing aura of danger about him—Tark's black scales glinted under the sun, indigo streaks of ages past shining through the colors of his Geihan uniform, wings shifting within their harness along his back. "I needed men capable of more than what vanity asked of them. I needed men who could kill. At a word, at a thought, for no more reason than because I said so. Men who understood they were bound to a higher calling than the self-congratulating politics and the circus that kept the population happy. Men who saw the glory of a global Empire within reach, and had the claws to tear it from the grasp of the politicians."

Tark came to a halt, snout turned low, staring at the ground. He took a deep breath, and exhaled, the taste of metal and smoke on his tongue. "You have eyes to see through my hypocrisy, to see my vanity. For that, you forever have my trust as a worthy student, one I have trained to always carry our flag high, into the future. And you have my thanks."

One great, scaly hand raised itself, draping it over The Speaker's pauldron, that wide grip dwarfing the smaller human's shoulder with terrifying ownership. "But should you ever tell me to go fuck myself again, or kill in my name without my blessing, I assure you, I will have what's left of your butchered carcass fed to the rest of your 'hungry boys,' who will pull the meat from your bleeding remains as if...well, pulling apart a chicken."

Tark leaned in close, his voice barely above a whisper. "That is a personal promise made to you, clear in vision, by the one they once called The Iron Tark."

Tark stood up straight, shaking The Speaker gently by the shoulder, his face warm and serene. "Is that unambiguous enough for you, my child?"

He didn't wait for a response. He knew by the way The Speaker wilted beneath his gentle touch that his words struck true. The venerated Marshal of House Geiha, his back against the setting sun, set out towards his own personal ship, the Viola parked gracefully at the highest point of a nearby mesa. "You can find your own way back without my help," he called back, casually dismissing the last survivor of the Uhlen's transport ship, the rest of his men waiting impatiently for his return back at in Barrier City. "You got this far on your own volition. I trust your resourcefulness will see you through the return journey."

The Speaker stood silent, alone amidst the transport ship's wreckage, his shadowy silhouette fading from view amidst the coming night.

32. The Dakhma

The long walk up the steps had left Brann soaked through in sweat, his pulse racing—even after they had set to work trying to dislodge the boulder, he could still hear his heart pounding in his ears, and he reasoned that they must be fairly high above sea level at this point. Wolf's spear was wedged between the boulder and the thinnest part of the arched doorframe, where the salty ocean air had withered it the most, yet with all his might he couldn't create a gap, even as the long spear began to bend against his shoulder. Brann had joined in, shoving against the butt end of the weapon with both arms outstretched, but he had little leverage given wolf's sheer strength. Boomer sat on the higher step, nursing his still-bruised chest as he watched, shouting out orders like a foreman.

"Heave! Heave to, lads! Put your backs into it, ya slugs! Earn your keep!"

Eventually, it was too much for Hawkshaw—the visibly annoyed automaton shrugged back his long coat and drew both autopistols, his arms snapping in crisscrossing patterns through the air with machine precision as he squeezed out rapid bursts of surgically precise gunfire, sending the startled Brann and Wolf ducking for cover. Sheathing both pistols as quickly as he'd drawn them, wafting away the gunsmoke that rose from his body, Hawkshaw coolly stepped a few paces to one side as the doorframe groaned and burst outwards at its weakest points, sending the boulder rolling slowly forward—and off the edge of the narrow platform.

"I'd cover your ears," Hawkshaw warned, leaning over into open air to watch the boulder fall.

"Yeah, now he tells us," Boomer grumbled, already plastering both hands against his head.

It was a tribute to just how far up they'd climbed, the boulder freefalling for several seconds—then, like a thunderclap going off just above their heads, the enormous open chamber that formed the inside of the tower was filled wall to wall with the echoing explosion of the boulder breaking the surface of the water down below and punching a crater into the reservoir's bottom. The rattling boom sent vibrations through Brann's clenched jaw, shaking loose decades of packed dirt and detritus from within the weathered cracks in the walls, a snowfall of dust blanketing the group's heads.

Grishka, having been circling in wait far above, descended now to alight upon Brann's shoulder, the raven cawing curiously as the dust settled like a drifting pair of curtains parting around the opened doorway. Wolf stepped up to peer inside, his dilated pupils glinting green in the low light.

"Nothing's moving inside," he said to Brann, who thought to himself those words must just sound like grunting to the others.

"He says nothing's moving in there," Brann repeated, and as everyone took this as assurance it was safe to enter, everyone but Boomer lined up to do just that—he stayed, hunched in place on his chosen step, huddled in low over his knees.

"Hate to admit it," he said weakly, "But that climb took more out of me than it should have—give me a minute to catch up with y'all, would you?"

Hawkshaw looked about to argue, but Brann beat him to the punch. "Sure man," he nodded, "Take your time, we'll be just inside here. Grishka can stay out here with you, just send her in if you need anything."

Grishka cawed loudly in Brann's ear, unaccustomed to being told what to do, but nonetheless seemed to take his meaning to heart. She stepped off his shoulder roughly, gliding the short distance to Boomer, taking a perch on the stone step just above the horse's head. He looked up at her with childlike fascination.

"Now we can get to know each other, magic ladybird," he said, cooing at her as if speaking to a puppy, waggling his fingers in her direction, the raven clearly unamused. "I saw you in my dreams as I was dying, yes I did..."

Brann shot a stern glance at Hawkshaw, who shrugged passively, taking up the lead at the head of the group and stepping into the dark, followed closely by Wolf, who once more spoke up for Brann to translate:

"Smells empty, too," he said in their shared secret language. "Nothing but old damp."

Brann passed Wolf's words along. As he repeated them aloud, however, the young man was keenly aware of Emrys hovering mere inches away from the back of his neck.

"That is truly remarkable, what you're doing," the scholarly man said, audible excitement in his voice. "Real time transliteration between verbal and nonverbal languages, the ability to interpret primitive nonsense into spoken word—"

"He does speak in words," Brann deflected, "He just doesn't need to use as many as the rest of us." He paused, smiling mischievously to himself as they stepped into the dark. "You could learn a thing or two from him."

Emrys sighed, tipping his hat in defeat. "Such a polite young man you were when we met, I fear the habits of the more uncouth among our ranks have begun to seep into your impressionable young persona...oh!"

He was interrupted by the sudden moonburst of amber yellow that filled the space, a small flare dart being shot up from Hawkshaw's wrist, the tiny projectile whistling cheerfully before embedding itself in a far wall high above. Bathed in that brassy yellow glow, they could see now they stood in an antechamber lined wall to wall with bookshelves, crammed so full of very obviously decayed and rotten tomes that had soaked up years of damp it was a miracle the floor hadn't fallen through.

"Now that is just a damned shame," Emrys tittered, giving the entire chamber a thorough once over, his head shaking in disappointment. "So much knowledge, so carelessly tucked away, no caretaker to see to its preservation."

"Maybe that was the idea," Hawkshaw pointed out, twisting the joint of his wrist with a click to reload another flare, holding his arm aloft as they made for the next room. "Paying lip service to writing down all their history, documenting it all under penalty of some old treaty after the wars, then just leaving it here to rot along with anyone old enough to remember or care."

"Why build this place out here, in the wilds?" Brann asked, pressing his thumb curiously to one of the older books, the spine crumbling to wet sand under his touch. "What's the need for a lighthouse at all if there's no ships coming ashore?"

"They didn't build it in the wilds, the wilds overtook this whole region," Hawkshaw answered. "The shifting territories of the Goliath population expanded further south, taking back the more remote parts of the continent that weren't kept in check by the rest of civilized society—it's a tale as old as time, at least from what I've read in the archives installed in my head by the manufacturer. In actuality, the math suggests the Goliaths existed long before human society, and you all just took it upon yourselves to build towns and cities where you could find purchase—but in truth, the only thing separating the developed world from the wilds is where a roaming Goliath decides to dig its nest." He nodded up at the ceiling. "This lighthouse is a reminder of that—your days of conquest are numbered, folks."

Brann followed Emrys and Hawkshaw into the next chamber, and immediately without even seeing in the dark Brann could tell from the way his voice reverberated this one was much bigger. "You always sound like you don't care much for people," Brann said in a neutral tone. "What's that about?"

"I bear no illusions about my relationship with the natural-born races," Hawkshaw replied politely, taking Brann's statement in the same spirit it was offered. "I wouldn't exist without them, after all. I just like to keep a certain level of personal detachment from getting in the way of what needs to be done—hard to have much of a genuine connection with an organism that, if I may make such a comparison, only lives about as long as a hamster within the lifespan of their human owner. And even that's being generous—I start to fail or defect from my programming, I can always be repaired." He took a beat to hold his hand straight up, firing off another whistling dart, the golden flare swirling up higher and higher until it seemed to disappear altogether, were it not for the gentle starlight that suffused down upon them. "Or upgraded. Compared to you lot, I might as well be immortal."

"Well, I'll thank you for engaging with me on the topic with a little more thoughtfulness than you might show a hamster," Brann joked, and Hawkshaw gave a sarcastic curtsy. The empty space they occupied was nearly featureless, an encroaching feeling of disappointment beginning to weigh upon Brann—there was no obvious door to any 'next' room, and this one, despite its impressive size, seemed empty.

"Much as I'd love to compare definitions of personal immortality with our metal friend," Emrys said, his own eyes scanning the smooth walls with concern, "I have it on good authority it would be preferable that I show a measure of self-restraint for the time being." He elbowed Brann begrudgingly, though couldn't hide an apologetic smile. "Aside from that, I'd say we're precipitously close to a dead end in our search."

Even Wolf was sniffing about, pacing in circles on all fours around the diameter of the rounded chamber, spear slung on his back. With his heartbeat strangely still trapped in his ears, Brann looked up, far overhead—nothing but darkness beyond the reach of the flare. He looked down, at his feet, stepping across nothing but dusty tiled floor under his boots—

Brann stopped short. His boot had dragged itself through the layers of thick salt and dirt, leaving a deep scuffmark that almost seemed to catch on tiny, imperceptible cracks. He dug in his heel, scraping across the floor in a wide arc—and, sure enough, tiny gaps in the tiling seemed to reveal themselves, this one looking suspiciously like a capital letter 'G'...

"Wait," he said hesitantly. "There's carvings here, I think. On the ground." He kept kicking at the packed grime, sending muddy fragments up around more letters, spelling out a message. "Yeah, in the tile, there's something carved."

Emrys looked between Brann's feet, then up at the walls again, a dawning realization breaking across his face. "Say, dear Hawkshaw," he said, making a gesture that mimed wiping his hand across a surface. "You wouldn't happen to be in possession of any sort of 'powerwasher' among your upgrades, would you?"

"I'll improvise." Hawkshaw stepped up to the nearest wall, examining its surface carefully before setting his hands apart in a wide stance against the coating of muck. His shoulder blades clicked beneath his long coat, and a low-frequency hum filled the air around him, his arms becoming a blur—after a moment, Brann realized it wasn't his vision going off, but Hawkshaw's hands vibrating at incredible speed, the tremors beginning to ripple outwards away from him all across the wall. What started as a light dusting quickly transformed into a veritable landslide, the entire outermost layer of crusty wall falling apart in a slurry of dried mud—sure enough, the entire room was composed of polished marble tile that gleamed dully in the dim light, each tile bearing words, evenly spaced and hand-carved.

"Here, Brann," Emrys said, excited, "While he's working on that, we'll dig through this dirt here—Wolf, you can come help, put those big paws to work." He kneeled down and began clawing away clumps, his bandaged fingers sinking into the stiff muck up to the first knuckle in some places. "Dogs enjoy a good bout of digging, don't they?" He asked Brann quietly, looking for some reassurance as the surly Wolf set to work nearby.

"I don't know that I'd want to let him hear me call him a 'dog,' but, sure," Brann answered, his own fingers pulling up years of dense neglect like wads of clay.

After a few minutes of frantic scratching and scraping, separating growing heaps of chunky silt from one another, the three stepped back to survey their work on the ground—Hawkshaw, having made a near full circle around the room, clapped his steely hands together, the polymer pads of his claspers making satisfied clicks. "Have a gander at that," he drawled in undeniable admiration.

"It's not an empty chamber at all," Emrys agreed, dusting his bandaged hands off of one another with mighty claps, surrounding himself in a filthy cloud. "It's a memorial."

The dark umber of the patterned tiles shone all about them now, reflecting the golden light through the cleared layers of dirt. The walls were covered in not just words, but names—evenly spaced, stacked by the half dozen, wrapping all around them and extending far above their reach into the dark and gloom above, disappearing beneath the dirt that Hawkshaw's powerful vibrations couldn't reach. The floor, however, bore a different sort of message altogether—the centermost tile in particular, the engraving set into a plaque of enameled bronze, it read:

DEDICATED TO THOSE LOST IN TIME

BRAVE HEROES WHOSE MEMORY WE TREASURE

WHERE THE SEA MEETS HEAVEN AND EARTH

INTERRED HERE IN SPIRIT BY THE GREAT HERO
RIGEL

WE RAISE UP THE WAYWARD ONES

IN THE NAME OF THEIR NOBLE HOUSES

KAVORCKA · CHENEYE · LACHLAN · JACQUES

KLIKUSHKI · SAINTMARIE · THADDEUS · JAN-JITO

THIS MONUMENTAL ACHIEVEMENT

MADE POSSIBLE BY THE GENEROSITY

OF OUR BENEFACTOR, BURNSIDE M. GEIHA

Brann stared, dumbfounded. "That's it?" He said, feeling hollowed out inside in a way he couldn't fully understand. "That's what we came all this way for? Just a big, dusty old plaque?"

"Now that is disappointing," Hawkshaw mused, his clawlike finger scratching at his chin.

"Surely we didn't overlook anything back in the prior chamber,"

Emrys reasoned, displacing his wide-brimmed hat to wipe the sweat from his balding head. "Some volume in a protective case, or another hidden pathway..."

Brann groaned angrily, kicking at the plaque and turning in circles, his thoughts flying away from him. Hester had promised so much more, some deep secret, something they couldn't miss—Brann crouched and looked closely at the plaque, eyes scanning it rapidly, searching for some hidden message or trapdoor or anything that may prove valuable beyond just a dedication. Nothing, no switches or puzzling inscriptions, no secret symbols. A factory-pressed plaque as plain and without gilding as they come.

"Gentlemen, I'm afraid I'm at a loss," Emrys conceded, crossing his hands solemnly. "Perhaps it was the library we were meant to find, and our bookish Queen erroneously assumed there was a complete written history interred within we would have been privy to had those tomes been maintained by a lighthouse keeper..."

Wolf had trundled up dutifully next to Brann, watching the young man's crestfallen body language and offering his own powerful crouched body as a pillar for Brann to lean on. He peered down over the end of his long snout at the plaque, tracing the letterings with just the tip of his nose. Brann followed his movements, still despairing internally, his heartbeat rising to a nearly deafening tattoo within his ear canals, until—

"There's only eight Houses listed here." He pointed, counting them all. "Geiha isn't listed among them."

Emrys stepped in closer, head tilting at an awkward angle to read along. "The House name does make an appearance, though, yes?"

"The name, yes, but not as a house." Brann tapped at the bottom of the plaque. "It's a person—'our benefactor, Burnside M. Geiha,'" He read aloud. "The guy who paid for this whole tower to be built."

Hawkshaw clicked his metallic mandibles together. "Geiha was a man—the founder of the House? That's not so unusual, most of the Houses carry the name of their founders."

"As long as they have surviving family to carry that name, yes, you'd be correct," Emrys replied, his own brow furrowing as he puzzled through this. "Though near as I can tell, there hasn't ever been a 'Geiha' family name, the House was conceived after the wars as a council ruling; a sort of impartial city-state that operated under oligarchal purpose. Quite literally, the first sovereign police state," Emrys said, looking around at everyone else. "Eventually they ran out of Houses to sanction or occupy once celebrity Champions like Boomer became the proxy method to resolve international disputes, but at its core they're still a House of warfighters, not of noble blood."

"We were always expected to call it the 'Geihan Empire' in the service," Brann offered. "As in, 'emperor', who I always just assumed was Tark under a different name. Would that make this person—"

"If there were a living member under the name 'Geiha' then yes, I presume their intent was to unite the Houses under such a banner," Emrys agreed, "Though this tower was built centuries ago—while we can't dismiss outright the possibility of Burnside Geiha being something other than human, perhaps even a kuaneach himself, the chances of anyone surviving that long are next to none otherwise. Why present themselves absent of a named ruler of House nobility if he were still alive to maintain said rule? It doesn't make much sense."

Brann wiped a hand over his face, still unable to quite fit together the pieces of any of this in a way that mattered to him. "So, let's say this person, Burnside Geiha, let's say he founded the House under his name after the wars—can someone do that? Just establish themselves like that as an entire nation? I mean I guess they all had to start somewhere, but in order to do that, you'd need to—"

"Own the land upon which a nation could exist," Emrys finished. "Follow my logic, if you would. The Arbitration Wars, the longest running period of upset and border disputes in written history." He bounced his fingers off one another as he spoke, giving a visual interpretation of his thoughts as he spoke. "Eight ruling Houses, all fighting each other for whatever it was they thought threatened their sanctity—while I know their reasons were altogether separate for one another, each nation fighting for something that set them apart from one another, I wouldn't take it as a surprise if reclaiming more land for themselves were a secondary priority. If a world war is being waged, why not use it as a chance to expand your own borders if your neighbor appears weak?"

"So, these Houses are fighting between one another, and with basically no continental trade to speak of, they start to run out of resources fast," Hawkshaw joined, pacing back and forth. "You meatboys do need your food and fuel, after all—and who can afford to give up all their fancy new tech, when now you've got airships and mechs and all other sorts of weaponry with which to compliment your court wizards with? No one's gonna give up the chance to wield artificial magic, especially not in the middle of a war."

Emrys pointed to Hawkshaw in agreement. "So, what do you do? You turn to the private sector, wealthy citizens who can afford to keep your House going in the war, save face, abstain from bowing out and trading away your own land for table scraps to keep your people fed and your armies equipped. Citizens who can afford to donate lighthouses like they're park benches. Enter: one Burnside M. Geiha, a neutral party with deep pockets, who wishes to see these wars end, for the good of everyone—bring together the Houses once more, cut through the hostile negotiations, get them to see the value of renewed mutual trade."

"But that's not all he was up to," Brann finally spoke up, the fog beginning to lift. "Why not take advantage of that goodwill, buy up some land for yourself? Wouldn't the Houses be more willing to trade it away to you than to each other if it meant getting your money into their pockets?"

"Correct, because you are more than just your wealth, you are an opportunist, looking to stake a claim for yourself in the new world," Emrys grinned, appreciating the shared conclusion they all seemed to be reaching. "Eventually, when the Houses come to and decide they stand to lose more by continuing the wars than what they have to gain by re-establishing their trade relations, our friend Geiha has already bought up enough land for himself at the edge of the wilds—the cheapest parcels he can get his hands on—and here on this spot, where the Arbitration Treaty was signed, he petitions to establish House Geiha officially, promising not to operate under pursuit of personal benefit, but as a sort of safeguard the other Houses can rely on to keep them in check if they can't resolve their disputes peacefully."

"And by the time his short human lifespan is over, he can no longer be held responsible for House Geiha acting unilaterally to lay siege to or occupy territories held by the other Houses," Hawkshaw added. "No single figurehead to make those decisions—it was right there in the treaty, any actions Geiha takes is a matter of keeping peace between the Houses, there's no single person to blame anymore, save the Marshal at the head of their armies."

"Hester said she had been visited by a Geihan emissary. Talking about folding Jan-Jito into a new empire. Maybe an executor of sorts, trying to carry out Burnside Geiha's last great design. "

"Or, " Emrys countered, joining in on Brann's suppositions, "Perhaps Burnside himself, posing as a lowly emissary. I'd seldom entrust such an important diplomatic luncheon to a glorified courier. "

"Now we're just guessing, " Hawkshaw cautioned.

Brann's finger tapped the other name mentioned on the plaque. "What about this person here—'The Great Hero Rigel,' it mentions him too—could he be important to all this?"

Emrys waved this question off. "Not likely, many 'great heroes' were named in the Arbitration Wars, I couldn't imagine he mattered much to the erection of this tower beyond presiding over its christening." He spread his hands. "But an ambitious Marshal, one who has outlived his predecessors, as well as any living witnesses to the signing of the treaty? One who takes it upon himself to elevate his House, put his nation's inherited wealth to good use, form yourself an empire. Perhaps even fulfilling Burnside Geiha's dying wish to see his domain expanded from coast to coast, and knowing he's accrued enough wealth and influence to do it...except there's one little fly in the ointment, one minor House that won't play along with your designs, who doesn't want to sign over their already meager holdings to an uncertain future. So rather than try to negotiate or waste more than you're willing to spend to buy them out, you and your considerable military strength are put to better use another way—first destroying their infrastructure, then its people when they are isolated, with nowhere else to go, and no wealth of their own to buy their way back into the good graces of the other Houses who have turned a blind eye."

"Lachlan." Brann sighed and mulled over all of this for a moment, rubbing at his temples. "I feel really stupid right now," he finally admitted. "I have to be honest—I still don't get how any of this helps us at all. It's not like we can prove any of it, we're just guessing amongst ourselves. This is all just made up, as far as anyone cares."

"I'm with the kid on this," Hawkshaw said, despite himself. "I'll admit, as much as a lot of this makes sense, we have next to no solid proof of anything, save for this plaque—and all it does is suggest the possibility of House Geiha being established under false pretenses, nothing more. Hell, it doesn't even prove Geiha himself was up to no good, only that he was a nice guy who bought lighthouses."

"I'm willing to bet the financial records of the individual Houses were never shared with one another after the wars," Emrys countered. "Why rub salt in your own wounds? The matter of Geiha's specific trade deals with them wasn't a matter of any real importance once the treaty was signed. So, the only way to definitively prove what he was up to, the only single localized point where all the collaborating records would possibly still be held..."

Hawkshaw snapped his fingers. "...Would be in the heart of House Geiha itself. Barrier City's archives, in the palace."

Emrys kneeled next to Brann, running his bandaged hand over the filthy plaque. "Well, my young soldat friend, it may not be the earth-shattering revelation we hoped for, but you may have some leverage to use against your Marshal after all. By all accounts, he's one who does not perform his duties dishonestly, yes?"

Brann nodded. "He waited until I had verbally agreed to surrender Lachlan to him—even if it meant letting me escape from Barrier City to begin with. At any time when I was in the service, he could have just killed or made me prisoner, forged the documents himself. My signature was all over my enlistment papers."

Emrys stood once more, addressing Hawkshaw. "So, my manufactured friend, what do your logic processors say about that?"

Hawkshaw lifted one of his eyelid flaps, rubbing the illuminated lense with a fingertip, as if he were clearing it of debris. "That Marshal Tark would be willing to, at the very least, relinquish control of Lachlan's political power back to young Brann here if he were threatened with the possibility we might reveal to the world his House has been naughty. That's very good, Teach," he nodded sarcastically, "Blackmailing a psychotic warlord with some financial records we don't even know for sure exist. Not the single dumbest plan we've ever had, I'll give you that, I'd rank it a solid third place."

"Why wouldn't he just kill me, then?" Brann shrugged. "Scrub the evidence entirely? No risk of losing out on his plans that way if there's no one to give the power back to."

Emrys turned to Brann. "Why, I'm surprised at you, young sir. You said it yourself—the fact that you're still alive at all is proof enough he's an honorable sort. Though I'll confess, there is one matter that threatens to render all of this moot."

Hawkshaw blinked, his eyelid clicking back into place. "Which is?"

"Lachlan." Emrys put his hands on his hips. "Think on it. You're the most powerful oligarch at the head of a nation willing to wipe out an entire House by means of destabilization and genocide—why stop at leaving one single recruit in your own military alive? How does one so morally bankrupt reconcile that, if only from a position of common sense?"

Brann couldn't answer that. His head was beginning to pound, his heart never quieting itself even now after their climb. "I don't know, I can't concentrate—I think something might be wrong with me, my heart is just *pounding* right now."

Emrys rubbed at his own chest. "Curious, I was thinking the same thing."

"I'm no medbot, but even I can hear you three from here," Hawkshaw confirmed, crossing his arms. "Sounding like a war drum going off."

Brann looked sideways at Wolf, who was frozen in place, his hackles rising. "You okay?" He asked the lycan quietly.

"It's not you." Wolf gripped at his spear slowly, the fur on the back of his neck spiking up like a mohawk. "Something alive in here."

Emrys looked all about the chamber, looking fearful. "Oh dear." Carefully, his hand went into his coat, pulling free his journal and flipping open the pages. "Friends, I'm going to dispense a fairly inobtrusive life detection spell—Hawkshaw, my love, would you mind terribly cutting that plaque free so we can take it with us? I think it's time we departed this place."

"Way ahead of you." Hawkshaw was already kneeling in front of the plaque, his fingers clamping around the weathered edges of it as best they could, beginning to vibrate much like they did against the wall. "This might take a minute; it's in there pretty good..."

Finding the page he was looking for, Emrys tore it away from the journal, crumpling it between his fingers as they began to drip with glowing green embers. He stepped to the nearest wall, pressing the burning page against the stony surface, the ignited paper disintegrating—then, like a sonar pinging, a high-pitched tune whistled around them, bouncing off the walls of the chamber. Brann watched in rapt fascination as a pearlescent green shine coated the smooth marbled tiles, an almost watery sort of ripple following the sound up into the darkness above, until—

"What the hell is *that*," Brann asked with a start, grabbing for the sword on his back fearfully.

The green ripples of light faded out, and in their place, the spectral tendrils of what looked like pulsating red veins appeared, like holographic images beneath an infrared scanner, wrapping all around them. As the seconds passed, they grew brighter, more vivid, and it was clear their pulsating throbs were in sync with that quaking heartbeat Brann felt in his own chest—*the goddamned walls were alive*. Thousands of pumping veins, branching off one another like roots embedded in the stone, travelling so far above and below them that Emrys's green spell and Hawkshaw's amber flare were absorbed into the angry red light that bathed them all in an evil crimson.

"I'm afraid we've woken it up," Emrys bemoaned, already crunching another page in his hand, which burst into lime green flames. "Hawkshaw, please, do hurry, there is something very much not interested in being our friend about to show its face, if it even has one—"

"I physically cannot make this go any faster," the annoyed automaton shot back, his machine-precise digging sending streams of silt upwards in a fluid arc. The walls were beginning to tremble, the tiles shaking—a few strays even fell and shattered, prompting Brann to draw his sword defensively, Wolf similarly brandishing his spear at nothing in particular. A deep, pained rumble began rising around them, almost like some perverse whalesong with no point of origin, the entire chamber echoing the cry.

"Hawkshaw," Emrys insisted, staring at the wall—and, when Brann looked, to his horror he saw what appeared to be dark blood oozing from between the tiles.

There was a metallic ping, and Hawkshaw withdrew his hand with a start, shaking his wrist like he had been stung. "Ow! We're good, I got it," he said hurriedly, the hydraulics in his knees wheezing a bit as he lifted the heavy plaque free. He tucked the thick rectangle of bronze beneath his arm, his one free hand filling itself with an autopistol—and, just like that, the room went silent once more.

The walls stopped vibrating. The red glow dissipated, Emrys's spell wearing off, and once more they were squinting in the low light of the dying flare. All was calm.

"No time for skylarking," Emrys insisted, still clenching his fist around a green fireball. "Let's be off, now, now, now."

Brann had turned towards the doorway, but found their exit blocked: like silent vines sprouting from the jungle floor, shining red tubes of organic flesh had filled the doorframe, pulling themselves taut, looking like veinous musculature stretching itself across the gap. Testing their elasticity, Brann hesitantly prodded the squared tip of his sword between those corded veins—they tightened visibly, squeezing his blade back out, leaving it smeared with sticky mucus.

"Too late for that," he announced, holding the glistening blade away from himself, turning in circles to look about—they were surrounded in the most literal sense.

All at once, their attention was drawn sharply to one spot—their various weapons pointing at the newly exposed patch of grout and dirt, where the plaque had been dismounted. The soil shifted, displaced in a rising pillar, a hill forming in the dirt that quickly and quietly reached knee-height—before, like a volcano erupting, pulsing tentacles of ribboned flesh burst up high into the air before draping themselves across the surrounding floor tiles, their moist tips curling in to grip, pulling something free from their roots in the ground.

"Oh dear," Emrys breathed, "I know what this is."

At first, it almost seemed humanoid—like a hunched figure, rising from the ground, its rounded head curling up from its shoulders. The illusion quickly dissipated, though, as that head spread itself around a turgid tube, peeling back its outer layer of flesh to reveal a flowering maw of hook-shaped teeth. Like a leech seeking a meal, that mouth made small, wet popping noises, its inner throat gulping at the air—the neck of the toothy tube snaking out towards them slowly, the four of them backing away from the eyeless creature.

"Looks hungry—I think that means I'm safe," Hawkshaw joked, but kept his pistol raised nonetheless, his aim locked onto that suction cup mouth.

"A Capillarian," Emrys whispered, cancelling his equipped spell by holding his burning hand up at face level and blowing out the flame, green ash scattering all about. "I'm afraid I haven't written any incantation strong enough to kill it—these are beings of pure animus. Take care not to attack it directly—its grown so deep into these walls, one clench of its body could bring the entire tower down around us."

Brann stood side to side with Wolf, the two of them drifting away from Emrys and Hawkshaw, their weapons held in front of them defensively—the long, tube-like head of the Capillarian had extended far enough to split the group in half, still blindly clamping its jaws at the air as it hunted. "So, what do we do?" Brann hissed quietly, unsure if Emrys was whispering because it could detect sound or not.

"We need to paralyze it," Emrys responded, directing them all with his hands. "Spread out, everyone, confuse it, give it warm bodies to chase— but keep your distance, and keep quiet. We need it to expose itself further."

Following his lead, the four of them began to drift apart, hunching slightly, the space between them growing until they formed a circle around the center of the room. The Capillarian wobbled slightly, its visibly throbbing 'neck' dripping with tar-like saliva, those ice-white fangs capped with sharp, blood-red points, which themselves seemed to dribble dark fluid down their length. The nervous flesh of the primeval creature twitched in the open air, the extended mouth drawing itself out further and further, its languid movements following the circling men with predatory intent. It couldn't see them, but every so often, that veinous tube would fold in on itself and whip the head back in another direction, towards where it detected someone's footsteps. By the time it seemed to reach the extent of its reach, Brann found his back against the wall tiles—with the leech-mouth of the unholy beast snaking through the air in his direction.

"Out of room," he said, hushed, trying not to sound panicked—he couldn't trust himself not to take a swing at that mouth, and as it honed in on him, those foul teeth waggling in unison, Brann felt himself drawing that sword high to strike. He locked eyes with Emrys, who was shaking his head, mouthing a single word: *Don't.*

To Brann's left, Wolf stood from his crouch, spear reaching forward to point—they all saw it, a whitish knob of what could have been tendon or cartilage, forming at the base of the creature's outstretched neck. It rolled itself out, over the spread veins that thrummed against the ground, a sort of soft joint upon which the entire creature's exposed body rotated. Emrys pointed to that white knob knowingly, beckoning Wolf to close in on it. That was their target, and their window was closing fast, the dripping teeth mere inches away from Brann's face now—

The whitish knob tensed up, and leaping nearly vertically upwards into the air, Wolf spun in a full circle to generate enough kinetic energy to bring his spear down with a crushing force that split that joint nearly in two—like steam bursting from a pipe, red mist sprayed upwards in a geyser, and once more the entire chamber was filled with the deafening screech of some hideous vocalization that seemed to radiate off the Capillarian's entire veinous body. As fast as he had struck, Wolf's speed was no match for how quickly the phallic neck of the Capillarian rolled in on itself, lancing that leechmaw forward blindingly fast to embed its teeth directly into his shoulder. Yelping out, Wolf's pained snarl became one of fury as he responded in kind, sinking his own fangs into the leech's neck—his main arm went limp, those fangs pumping some sort of numbing venom into him, and eventually his spear clattered against the tiles uselessly.

"Get it off him!" Emrys wailed, tearing a fresh spell from his journal—he raised his arm high, ghostly green flame surging around him, and an enormous skeletal hand emerged from the floor, those bony fingers clenching around the neck of the Capilliarian and tugging, hard—even the giant hand wasn't strong enough to fully remove the suctioned mouth from Wolf's arm, though it kept that injured white joint exposed. Hawkshaw, unable to get a clean shot from his corner of the room, instead turned himself and set to another task: unloading his weapon upon the sealed doorway, peppering the tightly stretched cords of flesh with small-arms fire. The ungodly screech of the creature modulated in pitch as a result, and while the walls began to shake in a terrifying omen, they held firm—unfortunately, just as Hawkshaw seemed to make some progress in shooting his way through that arterial gateway, his pistol ran dry, and fresh veins burst from between the stones to replenish the beast's hold.

"I can't get through fast enough," he called loudly, "You need to put this thing down, now!"

Ducking beneath the extended throat of the creature, Brann scurried across the ground, nearly on all fours as the coiling veins that continued to sprout from their hole were coated in a sticky patina of thinned, bloody mucus that threatened to trip him up and send him sprawling. Eventually, he found himself face to face with the cartilaginous bulb, the fractured bulk of it still spewing pink foam, and with a powerful swing Brann let his sword fly across its rounded body. The blade sunk itself in partway, meeting with the visible gouge Wolf had left in it, and it took all of Brann's might to detach himself.

"Fuck!" He shouted above the noise, wiping red moisture from his face. "I barely left a scratch!"

"Keep going!" Was all he got in reply, a second skeletal hand joining the first—like an enormous game of spectral tug of war, those conjured hands were awash in green smoke that pooled around their legs, Emrys bringing himself to his knees and pulling at the air tightly—the skeletal hands matched his movements, all of his ability focused in on trying to remove the Capillarian's leech mouth from Wolf's body, the lycan beginning to sag and stumble on unsteady feet. He was losing blood, fast, a bright red ring of it dripping down his torso from around the teeth embedded in his shoulder.

With wild abandon, Brann smashed his sword down again and again against the knobbed joint, hacking at it like a frenzied lumberjack, the hard tissue crackling around his strikes—meanwhile, Hawkshaw had abandoned his first idea, holstering his pistol and instead taking the heavy bronze plaque up in both arms, gripping it tight and bashing it against the fleshy door like a battering ram. Though ineffective at first, the wider impact zone of the plaque seemed to gain headway, the flesh bruising and wilting beneath the attacks—with nothing to regrow, the weakened flesh began to sag.

"I'm almost out!" Hawkshaw shouted, and all at once, it happened: Brann's final swing split the knob down the middle, finishing Wolf's initial cut through the cartilage, and Emrys fell backwards, sent prostrate as the skeletal hands successfully ripped the Capilliarian free from Wolf. The beastman crumpled, barely catching himself on one knee, his fur almost white as his drained body attempted to right itself, paw scrabbling about blindly on the ground to grab for his spear. Sheathing his own blade, Brann made a dash for Wolf, wrapping an arm around his uninjured shoulder and using his own weight to heft him up, the two of them stumbling together towards the exit.

Emrys reached out, swiping his journal up off the ground, and froze momentarily—the walls were beginning to shake, the rest of the Capilliarian's extensive veins and muscles coming alive around them, tiles beginning to rain down all around them within the chamber. A nightmarish display of writhing flesh, seeping blood and mucus, and horrific flashes of bioluminescent bulbs within the crimson veins burst open their watery membranes around yellowish eyes that gazed down at them with hate. The irises were cloudy with squiggly red flagella, their sclera bloodshot, and behind those dark pupils there seemed to be more leech-like mouths wriggling beneath the surface. Galvanized, the sight of such unknowable dread sent Emrys back up onto his feet and sprinting for the exit, just as the ropey pipes burst beneath the savagery of the plaque.

Emrys collided with Brann and Wolf, who themselves dove headfirst against the wall, taking Hawkshaw with them—all four men sprawled in a heap on the other side of the fleshy portal, which spat hot, thick blood all around them, soaking into the rotten books that crushed and flattened wetly beneath their boots as they came to their feet. The flare had died, the four of them hobbling towards the bright light of the exit, not daring to look back at the unknowable legions of leechmaws that stretched out through the darkness in an effort to snare them and drag them back into the Capilliarian's belly.

"Boomer!" Brann bellowed, Wolf's weight dragging him down, the lycan barely clinging to consciousness at this point. "We're out! Let's go!"

"Why are you yelling at me—oh *fuck*!" Boomer's head peeked in from behind the doorframe, then quickly withdrew itself as he saw the writhing mass of flesh surging out behind them. Brann and Wolf exited first, rolling off to one side on the stone platform, and Hawkshaw followed, still clutching the heavy plaque to his chest. Emrys, trailing behind, had a spell ready in his hand, tucking the journal away in one smooth motion as he spun in the doorframe, arm outstretched—

The hungry, yawning maw of a leech swallowed Emrys's arm, nearly up to the shoulder, and in that same instant was illuminated from within by a green light, one that raced down its throat like a bolt of lightning—and, like a disgusting display of flowers sprouting along a tree branch, ghastly skeletal torsos pulled themselves free of the leech's neck, rising from their fleshy grave and reaching out to nowhere. The blood-rich neck of the Capillarian leech withered and died, drying out in seconds, the emergent skeletal souls that grew along its length vanishing in a flash of ectoplasmic energy.

"The bridge!" Boomer shouted, and sure enough, when Brann uncoupled himself from Wolf's weakened form, he could see the silhouettes of Zay and Nes waving at them from across the gap in the dying evening light. The gap itself had been connected by the flimsiest, most terrifying facsimile of a bridge Brann could have imagined—it looked like a treadmill had been unspooled, laid out end to end, across an assembly of cross-hatched girders held together by little more than gravity. On the opposite end, Nes stood at the ready, holding what appeared to be a hand trigger at the ready, connected by a cable to the treadmill. He was shouting something back at them, the words lost in a jumble of echoes, but Brann took his meaning.

"Everyone get on!" He ordered, half-dragging Wolf along, shoving the werewolf forward roughly towards the bridge behind Boomer and

Hawkshaw. Emrys, however, was still attempting to pull himself free, the deadened flesh of the leech suctioned around his arm not letting him go so easily, the teeth still waggling uselessly—though the deadened mouth couldn't take him as its prize, it was only a matter of time before those other leeches approaching closed the gap, the sound of bookshelves collapsing beneath boiling flesh escaping the antechamber.

"Get it off me!" Emrys pleaded, and Brann quickly wrapped his arms around the older man's waist, pulling hard—to no avail, the grip of the Capilliarian's mouth too strong even in death. Brann felt a pair of powerful arms around him—the weakened Wolf, doing his best to help, biting into Brann's blouse to gain as much traction as possible. Then, another pair of arms, and another—Boomer and Hawkshaw, hugging each other close in an awkward group hug, all pulling together, inching backwards towards the bridge—until, finally, Brann felt pliant rubber beneath his feet—

"Now!" Someone yelled out, and the entire world lurched backwards, the entire group sprawling in an ungainly heap across the treadmill, which shot them backwards into open space towards the lighthouse exit faster than Brann had thought possible. He craned his neck up, arms still wrapped around Emrys's shoulders, watching the upside-down silhouettes of their companions at the exit racing towards them.

The treadmill was moving too fast, and Brann saw Hawkshaw's grip on the heavy plaque beginning to slip—

And there was a metallic clang, and a flash of sparks that splashed against Brann's face and made him flinch, and when he opened his eyes again, he saw the plaque falling away far below—

Then, looking back down, at his feet, past Emrys—the collapsing doorframe of the antechamber filled with a dozen rampaging leeches, hissing and spraying bloody saliva across the stone platform, unable to grow outwards any further. The Capillarian had embedded itself too deeply, grown too much, filling the farthest wall of the lighthouse tour, unable to pull itself free without crushing itself beneath the entire crumbling structure.

The treadmill disappeared beneath Brann, and suddenly the entire group was sent rolling across smooth stone, his arms instinctively tucking themselves in to shield his head as he was sent skidding across the broken bridge. The warmth of the late day's sunlight kissed at his face, and hoping the world would stop spinning soon, Brann pulled his hands from his eyes—they were outside, free once more, far beyond the monster's reach.

Seconds later, he was pulled upright, Zay running her gloved hand over Brann's head to check him for injuries. "You're alright, kid," she assured, pulling him along with her back towards the lighthouse entrance, "Though I can't say the same for rest of you guys."

Wolf, looking ready to heave up his guts, was kneeling shakily on all-fours, crawling towards the dirt—Red was on him in seconds, her motherly embrace bringing him in close, staining her pure white blouse against his bleeding shoulder. Boomer, looking dazed, was laughing to himself, spread out on his back. Hawkshaw, the only one besides Brann who had already come to his feet, was dealing with his arm being broken, the limb bent back around his shoulder at an awkward angle.

"Sorry kid," he apologized, "I tried to hold onto it."

The worst of all of them, however, was Emrys: pale-faced and wide-eyed, the clergy man was curled on his side in a fetal position, hugging his arm close to himself—and Brann could see even from a distance the limb had been shredded by the leech. Nearly completely degloved at the elbow, his bandages long gone, Brann could see the exposed skin of his hand for the first time—and though it came as no surprise, it was still disquieting to see the decayed flesh clinging to Emrys's bony fingers, as if the rest of him had stayed the same age while his forearm had begun to decompose in its grave. The mummified arm wasn't bleeding much, the inner workings of his hands long dead, but that didn't stop those teeth from turning the papery skin into a shredded mess.

"Dearie me," Emrys gasped, a nervous chuckle escaping him as he surveyed the damage. "I've really let myself go, it seems."

33. The Stowaway

Upon the makeshift table set up on a crate, Emrys had laid out his supplies—fresh gauze, embalming fluid, a mulehair brush, stiff twine, and a handful of tiny iron runic charms that Brann had no hope of recognizing. He'd taken it upon himself to help the clergyman rewrap his arm, and was kneeling beside the cross-legged Emrys, following his instructions quietly and carefully.

"No need to be gentle, tie it off tightly," Emrys was assuring him, Brann having bound the damaged, corpselike arm in a dual helix pattern using the twine, the warped radial bone mostly twisting itself back into place. "Gauze next, but don't just go leaping headfirst into it, there's a particular order the runes must be layered in with it. You may begin here just below the elbow. I'll hand you the correct rune when it comes time to add it."

Brann looked about briefly at the rest of the team, seeing them make final preparations for takeoff. Red and Grishka had seen Wolf back on board already, taking him to get his wounds attended to, leaving Zay, Boomer, and Nes to scavenge the destroyed rover for any surviving supplies—Hawkshaw wasn't much use with a broken arm, and instead stood sentry near the Donnie's nose, good hand on the grip of one of his pistols.

"We haven't had the best of luck lately, have we?" Brann asked, surveying everyone in turn, using one hand to hold the gauze in place while wrapping it in steady, even measure up Emrys's arm. "We came all this way for nothing—without the plaque, we have no proof of anything."

Emrys gestured for Brann to pause, then plucked from the tabletop one of the runes, handing it to the younger man and pointing at the bare space where it should be set in the gauze. "Just place it there and wrap another layer around it, tight as you can—just make sure the iron doesn't touch bare skin." He waited, watching Brann secure the rune in place, tucked snugly within the gauze. "Perfect. Do all of them just as you did that one." He looked away, scratching his chin thoughtfully. "On the contrary,

I'd say our luck is holding fine—in fact, this may be our most fortuitous venture yet. We've potentially unearthed a long-buried secret behind the genesis of the House who forcefully adopted you into its service, and all it cost us was a roll of medical gauze from your pouch and a hunk of old metal that may or may not have proved useful to piecing together a much larger puzzle. No casualties, save for one woozy lycanthrope, who will be well on his way to recovery after a nice, bloody steak. All told, that's a new record for our woeful little troupe, if you ask me."

"You don't think this was a tremendous waste of time?" Brann couldn't keep the bitterness from his voice, continuing up Emrys's arm, wrapping one rune after another in place as Emrys handed them off in turn.

"I think we're allowed a little hopeful speculation," Emrys replied cheerfully, pointing back at the dark shape of the lighthouse in the dusk. "This structure, long abandoned, may have very well held the single remaining physical piece of evidence recounting the existence of a very rich man who, despite all his supposed favorable reputations among the Houses, went to very great lengths to excuse himself from being mentioned in the history books. Now, whatever his reasons for doing so, it would seem a great oversight to leave this plaque naming him intact—perhaps it was a simple lapse in judgment, perhaps the territory had been taken back by Goliaths and he simply assumed the tower would never be rediscovered. Either way, he got sloppy. Sloppy men don't build nations in their name. Agh!"

He jolted, as if stung by an ant—Brann had let one of the runes slip, the iron sizzling against the desiccated flesh of Emrys's arm. "Sorry," Brann apologized, quickly straightening the rune in the center of the gauze. "I just—I guess I still don't see how this helps us at all with Tark," he confessed, the young man failing to grasp the bigger picture.

Emrys held the next rune aloft, rolling it between his fingers. "When I became a student of the necromantic," He ruminated aloud, "I was a very sad, scared person. Originally, I had sought to study the school of persuasive mysticism, learn what it is that compelled human behavior by learning the magics that could turn their own free will sideways. My distaste for the detached way my peers manipulated their subjects, so easily and freely disregarding the sanctity of the soul, dug a deep pit of sorrow inside me—seeing how easily one could dispatch a person's sense of self, I began to fear there was no such thing at all. That we were all just puppets of...flesh, of circumstance, coincidence, with no real soul at all." He tugged open his coat ruefully, rubbing his hand against his own chest. "If we are soulless, then there is no reason to live as human, to be curious or to seek freedom, happiness, or love. It all disappears into the pit, into nothingness, when this flesh expires—so, in my perverse logic borne of this sadness and fear, I instead turned to necromancy. I felt that if I could find a way to extend the lifespan of this flesh, then my soul would remain bound to this world, and I'd never have reason for fear or sorrow again."

He laughed a bit, pushing his hat off his head, holding it to fan himself with the brim. "Dearie me, talk about the best-laid plans. My reward for my selfishness, you see plain here—I reached beyond the door, through the veil that separates this plane and the void, and I held the void in my hands, and it burned something fierce—my own fears made manifest, as now I carry with me always the unliving reminder of what awaits the rest of me when my time comes." Emrys replaced his hat, turning to Brann, watching the young man fasten the last rune in place just beneath his knuckles. "Apologies if this seems I've wandered too far afield from addressing your concerns—allow me to come to the point.

"I was so afraid of my own mortality, of the fear of the Great Beyond, that in the pursuit of saving my own soul, I gave a part of it away, like that." He snapped. "As freely as a breath of air from my lungs. I live now on borrowed time, every minute I continue to draw that same breath stolen from another life, unearned, undeserved. If they say the man who fears suffers twice, then a thousand sufferings will be tallied beneath my name when my time finally comes. The fear of death is the most potent, intoxicating motivator. It will turn men into beasts, it will turn love into hate. I don't know any more than you do who this Burnside Geiha was, nor do I believe he was immune from this fear—if he lived as I suspect he did, surrounded by wealth and luxury and all the power in the world disposable to him, then he may not have been so willing to part with it when the time finally came for him to face his own end. His designs on a lasting legacy, be they an empire or something else, could have stripped him of his careful nature, his fear of the Beyond far outweighing his fear of mortal recompense for his sins."

Emrys held his freshly bound hand aloft, flexing the fingers, tipping his hat thankfully to Brann as he found the work satisfactory. "What else would one accrue such vast riches for, if not the unconscious pursuit of immortality? The unspoken self-delusion that one could simply buy more life?"

Brann shook his head—he didn't feel Emrys was getting to the point at all. "It doesn't sound like someone willing to sign his legacy over to someone like Tark."

"No, my bright young friend, no, it does not." Emrys clapped Brann on the shoulder, standing to his feet and pulling down his sleeve. "It does, however, sound like someone who may explore other schools of thought— say, that perhaps the solution to defying death lies beyond our reach, but within reach of those who already exist in defiance of it."

Brann's brow furrowed—then, his eyes went wide, finally taking Emrys's meaning. "You mean the exdead. You think he was experimenting with them, trying to take on their abilities for himself? The ones we've discovered in the other provinces are just...mistakes he was trying to bury?"

"As I said, hopeful speculation." Emrys bowed once more in thanks, stepping back up the Donnie's cargo ramp. "Take me not for a prophet— merely someone whose curiosity persists beyond his own reach. Though I believe this particular curiosity to be very much worth exploring further. Yes, my dear, has the time come we departed?"

Zay had jogged up to the pair of them, looking as irritable as Brann had ever seen her. "We've got a problem."

*

Brann and Emrys had followed Zay at a brisk pace up the length of the Donnie, towards the bow, where the nose dipped away from the cockpit. Nes was standing beside Boomer, holding an arm out in front of the horseman, as if keeping him at bay, while Hawkshaw had drawn a pistol with his still-functional arm—and it wasn't until Brann drew up beside them he could see why. A skinny, pale man, trussed up in filthy leather garb, holding a mortar tightly to his chest with the barrel aimed up directly beneath the Donnie's cockpit.

"It's not our fault you were left behind," Nes was saying, his tone sounding more impatient than fearful. "Your boss has a shitty valuation of his men, is all—"

"Ain't nothin' you can say gonna wave me off!" Bullet Buddy was wailing, his hand clasped around the trigger of the weapon near its base, the hollow clanking sound as the visibly distraught merc shook the barrel about telling Brann there was a shell loaded and ready to fire. "I'm takin' youse all as my hostages, you gonna get me paid, that's that! So get yer asses in the cargo hold, or I blow the ship's head off!"

"Think about it, kid," Nes responded, "Who is gonna pay our ransom? There's no one for miles—the ship needs a pilot to get you back to civilization, we can't exactly get you there if we're all tied up." He waved silently at Brann as he arrived, less a greeting, more a way of nonverbally saying he had things under control.

"Hey Bullet Buddy," Brann said, attempting to sound calm to keep things from escalating.

"Hay." Bullet Buddy waved back politely before gripping the mortar even tighter, staring wide-eyed at Nes. "Lotta fancy talk for a hostage, tryna trick me! You don't think I ken fly this hunk outta here, think I ain't smart enough to be a pilot!"

Zay snorted. Nes ignored her, shaking his head. "I think you're plenty smart, Buddy—"

"Bullet Buddy!" The skinny young man gripped the mortar's trigger even tighter in warning. "Gotsta say the whole thing, else it ain't count!"

"...Bullet Buddy," Nes corrected, his face contorting somewhat as he suppressed his laughter. "Okay then. I'm Nestor, this is my ship—"

"My ship," Boomer, Zay and Hawkshaw all said at once in an indignant chorus.

Nes sighed. "Our ship," he corrected again. "We can't just let you tie us all up, else we won't be able to fly you back and get you paid. You can't fly the ship yourself, especially not if you're holding onto that big cannon there the whole time—"

"It's real big!" Bullet Buddy exclaimed proudly.

Nes nodded, somewhat taken aback, but nonetheless agreeing. "It's *real* big indeed, Bullet Buddy. So, why not put the real big mortar down, we all get on board—"

"Nes, if you let this little twerp step one foot on my ship, I'm breaking him in half," Zay said contemptuously, gripping the hilt of her combat knife.

Bullet Buddy's mouth gaped wide as he pointed at Zay, then at Nes, wagging his finger accusingly—Nes spun on his heel, hissing at Zay. "Really not helping to defuse the situation, girl!"

Nes spun back, holding up his hands. "Don't mind her, you're just making us nervous, is all," he offered, looking to the others in turn and nodding. "It's been a minute since any of us have gone up against someone so big and scary, y'know?"

"Yeh, and y'all SHOULD be scared," Bullet Buddy insisted, chin held high. "I ken blow us all to the moon!"

"Not the best strategy in securing financial independence, but I respect the verve," Nes said, struggling not to make it sound like a joke. "Okay, Bullet Buddy, we're all plenty scared, and we all want to fly out of here and get you paid, so it all sounds like we're on the same page here, right?"

Bullet Buddy spun in place suddenly, startled by a noise behind him.

"Whazzat? Who be there? Youse got more friends hidin' to ambush me? Tricks!"

"No, no tricks, no ambush," Nes replied, genuinely looking concerned as he waved at everyone to start backing off while Bullet Buddy's back was turned. "Could just be a wildcat, or a bird, y'know..."

The barrel of Bullet Buddy's mortar swung about wildly, aimed at the treeline, and sure enough Brann could hear something moving about beyond the fringe of the mangroves. "Come outta there, or I'll shootcha!" Bullet Buddy cried out, his voice cracking unconvincingly. There was no response, at least not directly—but the sounds of twigs breaking and metal clinking began to fill the clearing, along with a rising symphony of hoots and chirps, like dozens of owls had just awoken for their night of hunting.

"Kobolds," Nes said quietly, cautioning everyone to get back to the cargo ramp. "Bullet Buddy, you coming, or—?"

Like a strangled cat, Bullet Buddy's earsplitting screech rang out into the dark, his only warning before he fired his mortar directly into the treeline—the shell launched with a wet *thunk* before whistling off between the mangroves, and a split second later a massive fireball blossomed up and out above the branches. Instantly, there was a cacophony of hissing screams, and low to the ground, Brann could make out an army of dark little figures scurrying out of the path of destruction, silhouetted by the dissipating flash of fire behind them.

"Time to go," Nes said casually, ushering everyone along now that they had the opportunity to break rank—Bullet Buddy would need to reload, and there wasn't enough time before the kobolds would be on them. Hawkshaw and Zay were shoulder to shoulder as they sprinted ahead, trying to outpace each other—not out of fear, Brann noted as they argued with one another, but competing to see who would get to the pilot's chair first. Clearing the ramp, they climbed the cargo ladder in turn, Brann at the rear of the procession—taking a last look about, part of him wishing Bullet Buddy had gotten wise and was following along behind, Brann hesitated before slapping the cargo ramp's switch. Poor guy was on his own, now.

Brann must have been well-familiarized with the ship, now, considering how quickly he found himself ascending into the cockpit behind the others, save Boomer who had returned to his quarters to pass out. Hawkshaw and Zay were already bickering in usual fashion at their respective stations, Nes stepping between them to key in the launching procedures for the ship, not bothering to intervene otherwise—there would never be a time Hawkshaw and Zay got along when it came to who got to fly the Donnie. Brann stepped up behind them, watching over Zay's shoulder at the scene that unfolded just outside.

Bullet Buddy stood, head and shoulders well above what must have been a hundred little critters—stubby little horns, short tails waggling excitedly, lizardlike claws grasping at their short spears. They had encircled the lone merc, visibly agitated, though surprisingly not making any obvious efforts to engage him—rather, they seemed fascinated by him, their huge round eyes gazing up at him behind their short, boxy little snouts.

"Why aren't they tearing him apart?" Zay asked, throttling up the Donnie's engines, the hull beginning to hum and rattle slightly.

"Imagine that, they're even more civilized than you," Hawkshaw retorted, his working hand firmly wrapped around the control stick.

Zay had taken note of her rival's injury and kicked across the space between them, attempting to displace Hawkshaw from his seat roughly. "You don't even have both arms you dickhead, get outta here, you're gonna crash us into a mountain—"

"Quiet, both of you," Nes finally snapped, pointing two fingers out the windshield. "Look."

Brann leaned in closer, watching as Bullet Buddy's shaky arms stretched out, offering the mortar to the kobolds. A half dozen short little arms extended, clawed hands taking the offered mortar as if it were some kind of holy sacrament, gifted to them by a superior being. The gods had granted them fire, at long last, several of them dropping their spears to run their little clawed hands over the barrel of the mortar, maws agape with wonder at the machine that could clear forests with a single blast.

"Look at that, they've got themselves a new toy," Hawkshaw mused.

Zay pulled back on the controls, and the ship began to rise off the ground, startling some of the kobolds who threw their spears uselessly against the metallic nose of the great mechanical beast. The last Brann saw of Bullet Buddy before they were fully airborne was the skinny young man being hoisted up on the kobolds shoulders, the congregation of little beasties crowdsurfing him along towards the lighthouse tower, his fearful eyes staring up at the Donnie before it disappeared behind the trees.

*

Several hours had passed, night fully falling beyond the horizon, and though it had only been a couple days, Brann was deeply relieved to feel the Donnie's engines at full power beneath his feet. In these past few weeks, it seemed as long as they were in flight, the Donnie was the safest place in the world for Brann and his friends, capable of flying them far beyond the reach of Tark or his Uhlen or any other monster that might have a go at them. This time, however, he was aware of an unfamiliar new sensation—one of purposeful determination, the ship flying eastward for the first time since he'd boarded that fateful day of the Assay. Back towards Geiha.

"I don't mind saying I'm already starved," Emrys was saying, standing up from his seat in the rear of the cockpit. "Nestor, Brann, let's take a peek in the galley, see what we can whip up—we'll bring some back for Zaydat, if she doesn't mind flying solo for a while. Hawkshaw?"

The android spun his seat around, the yellow beams of his eyes narrowed at Emrys. "Are you suggesting I abandon my post?"

Emrys almost looked as if he were going to speak to the contrary, but thought better of it, opting for brevity and honesty instead. "Yes. Yes I am."

Hawkshaw's mechanical mandibles clicked together to process this momentarily. "Alright, then." He shrugged and stood, his broken arm hanging limp at his side, twisted hand facing away awkwardly. "I like to watch you freaks eat anyway, gives me a chance to get this arm fixed. Zay, keep that engine a'purrin' for me, would you, my dear.

"Blow me," she responded, re-centering herself at the control console.

Hawkshaw clenched his fist, looking almost disappointed that Zay wasn't fully matching his energy. "Heard that one before," he muttered to himself sadly, following the other three men as they descended the cockpit ladder.

"Truthfully, I'd like to take the opportunity to share with you two this theory of mine I've already informed Brann of," Emrys admitted, the four of them making quick work of navigating their way towards the ship's kitchens. "If we've not decided on our next destination, I believe I can offer a suggestion that may bring this messy little voyage of ours to a close."

"Aw, and say goodbye to all your pretty faces?" Hawkshaw joked, already pulling open the hatch to the stairs that led down into the galley and common area. Brann felt a pang at this—Hawkshaw may have been joking, but it struck a nerve in him. He hadn't yet considered that there may soon come a time he'd be parting ways with everyone.

The thought did not sit well with him.

"Did Boomer come through on his way to bed? He left the main lights on again," Nes grumbled, and sure enough the brightly illuminated tiles of the cafeteria beneath them reflected the overhead lamps.

"Emrys thinks we should go back to Barrier City," Brann spoke up, holding the railing as they descended the metal steps.

"More accurately," Emrys said, "The palace, on a sort of infiltration mission into their archives—I believe we could find in them the leverage we need to call Tark and his hounds off the hunt for our pelts."

"You mean to go into the capital city of everyone who hates us the most?" Hawkshaw replied incredulously, rounding the stairs and calling back to Emrys loudly, his voice echoing off the tiles. "You really think Tark isn't just gonna—"

He stopped. Literally. Brann collided with the automaton from behind, Hawkshaw rooted in place—when the young man stepped around to complain, he understood: Grishka, fully human, was sitting at the galley's bar, leaning back on her shoulders, laughing flirtatiously with an uninvited guest. A guest who, despite having his back turned to them, was undoubtedly a kuaneach—tall, broad, thickly muscled, a longsword hanging from his belt and a shield strapped across his back. When Grishka locked eyes with her newly arrived companions, she went wide-eyed, and shimmered out of focus before flying away from the bar in her panicked raven form. Barely had the kuaneach turned to see the cause of the disruption when Hawkshaw had already drawn down on him, a deafening burst of pistolfire ripping through the galley.

"Get down!" Brann barely heard Nes shout over the gunfire, the older man sprawling across his back and pulling them both to the ground, ricochets pinging off the metal bar and ceiling—a bright tracer lanced across Brann's shoulder, ripping a hole clean through his blouse, missing his flesh by a hair's breadth. The kuaneach had turned fully, not even drawing his own sword and shield as Hawkshaw's bullets bounced off his scales, the imposing dragon simply holding his arms up high and shouting—

"I surrender! You win!"

"Hawkshaw, stop shooting!" Nes kicked at Hawkshaw's shin, and the automaton obliged—Brann's ears were left ringing in the subsequent calm, gunsmoke wreathing all about them, along with a dozen streaks of carbon decorating the tiled floors and walls. From behind the metal stairs, Emrys poked his head out cautiously, a smoking hole blown cleanly through the brim of his hat.

The kuaneach let his arms drop to his sides—though he didn't appear outwardly hostile, he was nothing if not intimidating, a compliment to his species in terms of sheer athleticism. Taut arm muscles flexed as they crossed in front of his chest, his body mostly naked, save for the black leather halter top and loose-fitted cream-colored pants he wore. His scales, snowy white, gleamed almost blindingly bright beneath the overhead lights, dazzling gold trim accenting his horned features—in fact, it looked as if he'd once stood beneath a rain shower of molten gold, ribbony rivulets racing across his hide. Draped across his bare shoulders, Brann thought the kuaneach was wearing a shawl made of white birdfeathers. Looking closer, however, it was no garment at all, but rather a mane that sprouted from between those shoulder blades, running up the back of the dragon's neck and cresting just above the nape, some of the feathers standing straight up from his crown like a bird's crest. Everything about him seemed regal, almost angelic, in a draconian sort of way.

"All apologies, I suppose I should have paid my fare up front!" The kuaneach rumbled, his voice as calm and unbothered as any, though his narrowed eyes and raised eyebrow belied his true feelings. He looked down at himself, arms unfolding, and reached between his abdominal muscles—a bullet had split itself there, embedding itself between his bellyscales. As if brushing off lint, the kuaneach swiped a hand across his front a few times, the mushroomed bullet clattering loudly to the tile, leaving not even a bruise behind.

"I couldn't help but overhear," the stranger continued, stepping forward from the bar, hands going to his hips as he cocked his head. A small smile tickled the corners of his fanged maw, his expression almost mischievous.

"You have some business with my brother, yeah?"

ACT IV

THIS SIDE OF FATE

34. The Roost

The morning light streamed in through the shutters of the common area, which usually remained shut during flight—though, since Zay had already cleared dangerous airspace, the ship was currently set to autopilot out of the reach of any flying Goliaths. The nine crewmates of the Donnie were joined now, circled on the couches around the tenth passenger, the somewhat smug kuaneach positively radiant in the sunlight that reflected off his whitegold scales—if Brann stared too long, he feared he'd be hypnotized, the dragon having an absolutely undeniable aura of trustworthiness about him.

That is, undeniable by all but Hawkshaw, who was still apologizing for his earlier attack. "Look, some big armed beastman finds his way onboard in the middle of the most dangerous territory imaginable, of course my defensive programming is gonna kick in," he was attempting to explain to Boomer, who couldn't stop looking over the damage done to his ship's galley.

"Awful, just awful," Boomer was saying, barely even acknowledging Hawkshaw. His attention was split between the scattered bullet holes and the new guest he was playing host to, looking over the radiant kuaneach's golden visage almost enviously. "So, I've already got a small army on my payroll," he said apologetically, playing with a bandage that had started to come loose against his snout. "I'll have to confer with my financial advisor, when I find one worth hiring, but—"

The kuaneach held a clawed hand up, shaking his head warmly. "No, please, you misunderstand. I'm the one who wishes to pay you, for an expedient trip back to my homeland—I can commence with a down payment, this should help cover the damage I inadvertently brought to your ship." He pulled an oversized charger from his pants pocket, bigger than any human wallet Brann had seen, and thumbed the release—with several smooth clicks, a pile of scalenes slid into his open palm, the gems set in them the most vivid opaline colors imaginable. Brann couldn't figure the value of those scales off the top of his head, but they were worth far more than any he'd ever seen, that much was certain.

Boomer reached forward to scoop up those scales, not paying the galley a second glance after he did—apparently, he was not so unused to seeing such a huge amount of money in such a small pile. "Well, damn, alright then, welcome aboard, Mister...uh..."

The kuaneach bowed slightly, tapping his forehead in a mock salute. "Gideon. Though I find it crass, in some circles they call me Gideon the Golden; I don't need to elaborate further, I'm sure."

"I've seen you before," Brann said, pointing to Zay in her seat across the circle. "We did, I mean. Back in Mercenary Row, just a couple days ago."

Gideon snapped his fingers at Brann, waving his hand in confirmation. "I was there, yes, though not for you—at least, not initially. In truth, I had meant to intercept my brother before his next fight—have a sort of heart-to-heart, if you will, on matters of no concern to your party. When I heard tell he'd be going up against none other than the Champion of his own House, however, well..." He shrugged, almost sheepishly, looking rueful. "Perhaps I'm feeling I owe you all recompense for not intervening sooner, as I hadn't expected him to behave with such...brutality."

"So, Gideon," Nes said, sounding slightly less enamored with this new shipmate than Boomer. "You say you're Tark's brother, and we've crossed paths before on what you say was a matter 'unrelated' to us—why then, if I may ask, did you see the need to sneak aboard our ship, out in the middle of the wilds, no less? I find it hard to believe you were just taking a stroll through Goliath territory on a lark."

Gideon bowed once more. "Hence, why I made the point of saying I was not there 'initially' for you. Being fully honest, after I saw this young one leaving the fight with a half-dead Champion on his back—" He nodded at Brann indicatively, "I set to tracking that loathsome gangster, following them in pursuit of their next quarry."

"Trollope," Zay said sourly.

"Correct. You see..." Gideon paused, choosing his next words carefully, a roguish smile dancing behind his eyes. "I pride myself on being something of a...well." He cleared his throat. "A wandering hero—a lone traveler, righting the wrongs of evildoers."

"Oh godammit, here we go," Hawkshaw grimaced.

"By my approximation, there was going to be another chance for me to make a grab at a small measure of glory," Gideon continued, undeterred, "Though I underestimated the capable warriors the Champion of Geiha had in his employ! With the exception of perhaps myself and my brother, I haven't seen such a crew of able-bodied fighters in many a moon."

"Let's get back to that bit about your brother, actually," Nes said, redirecting the conversation before it went too far afield into self-congratulating. "The Marshal Tark. What assurances do we have you don't plan on turning us over to him, assuming you haven't alerted him to our exact location, already?"

Gideon shot a sideways glance at Boomer. "Capable as they are, they certainly are a paranoid bunch," he joked, though he dutifully cleared his throat and addressed Nes honestly. "I don't care much for my brother, I never have—you'd probably find this hard to swallow, but he's always been something of a—ahem, a weakling, in the parlance of my kind."

Brann couldn't help but laugh nervously. "You serious?"

"Oh, trust me, the surprise is mutual," Gideon agreed, turning to Brann. "I had heard he was in the area, and planned on reuniting with him in the old ways of our tribe, possibly by bashing a large rock over his head."

"How sweet," Red snarked.

"You have seen it yourselves, firsthand—he's...changed. Humorless, unreceptive to much of anything besides rote violence." Gideon shook his head. "I would not have found a warm welcome in my brother's arms if I had confronted him, I would have found an enemy. In our homeland, we don't suffer fools lightly, and even the closest of family can be subject to mortal combat with one another if our agendas are found conflicting with one another."

"Where is that?" Brann asked. "Your homeland, I mean?"

Gideon's arms spread. "The Roost," he said simply. "The one and only birthplace of all kuaneachs. Though we are trained and sold off at a tender young age to any and all willing nations who seek to employ our allegiances, there has only ever been one village we spawn from—and there will only ever be the one, as long as wayward souls like Tark remember where they come from."

"When you say 'sold off,' do you mean..."

Emrys answered Brann's question on Gideon's behalf. "Oh yes, you heard him right," he said, "Forgive me if I'm overstepping my bounds, Sir Gideon, but I've been told those of your race selected for warfighting are in fact auctioned off by your own parents to the highest bidder?"

"That is generalizing a bit, but, yes," Gideon half-shrugged. "We do not as a point of pride fight our own wars, we are sold into service, priced for our abilities and hardiness—I don't mind saying I went for a princely sum." He seemed proud of this, unbothered entirely by the dark implications of such a trade.

"Who paid?" Asked Hawkshaw. "I mean, who do you work for? You said you were a lone wanderer of sorts, so I imagine..."

"Currently, I am on the market, and have been for some time." Gideon folded his hands together. "I have not led a House nor acted its champion in many years, and admit I do enjoy the accolades and prestige that comes from being a hero to any and all in their time of need, irrespective of their allegiances. My first term of service was paid for by a now defunct House, one I'd imagine none of you have heard of at this point—the former House Lachlan."

The air itself seemed to freeze, all eyes turning to Brann. He didn't make eye contact with anyone, save for Gideon himself, ignoring the attention—instead, impassively, he simply asked:

"Why'd you leave?"

The shift in the room's energy was not lost on Gideon, who looked around the circle curiously, though he kept his musings to himself. "I was released from my service, quite erroneously, if I may say so," he answered. "I led what was barely more than a handful of loose townships to what I would consider great victory many times in the later years of what has since come to be known as the Arbitration Wars—they thanked me for my deeds with a discharge and a lifetime of riches I couldn't hope to spend on my lonesome, courtesy of an anonymous benefactor who had chosen to back the House during the war. I'm afraid their generosity was, at least in part, misplaced, as not long after House Lachlan fell beneath the wheels of time, absent a proper Champion or military leader in their court."

There was an unspoken understanding between Brann and Emrys at this last statement, the latter of whom leaned forward earnestly in his seat. "Please, cast your mind back, if you would—can you recall anything at all about this benefactor? Did they ever pay a visit to court in person; a name that escapes you printed on some ledger or in some passing communique, perhaps?"

Gideon shook his head. "I'm sorry, apart from simply so much time having gone by, I was never privy to such matters—nor was I ever very interested. I had always assumed I would lead my appointed House to death or glory, and never should the two be denied to a kuaneach who serves honorably, save in the rarest of instances." He gestured to himself. "Such as myself. I'd be the first kuaneach to have their conscription bought out among my family—I suppose in part that's why my brother and I have never seen eye to eye on much."

Brann had found himself, at some point, wandering out of his seat as Gideon spoke—Emrys, knowing all too well why, similarly left his couch and stood with Brann, a friendly arm draped across his shoulder as he continued his interrogation of Gideon. "Did you ever meet a man, then, one who bore House Geiha's name before its formation? Burnside M. Geiha, specifically? Did he ever meet with Tark in private before his conscription into their service? Surely Tark was present when House Geiha was first christened?"

Again, Gideon just shook his head. "I don't mean to be rude, but these are questions for the historians and yeomen—I never concerned myself with anything more than the next battle." He crossed his arms once more. "If it helps your cause, after I left The Roost, I never crossed arms with my brother Tark, nor did we so much as share war stories in the years following—my proximity to him in Mercenary Row was just the most recent example of our relationship in its purest form: as two ships passing in the night, silent and dark."

He watched Brann's body language with a sort of detached interest, and though the family resemblance was nigh undetectable, Brann could feel the same sort of all-knowing and penetrative gaze on him he'd felt at the Assay, when Tark had looked down upon him.

"I may not have the answers you'd hoped for to whatever ails you," Gideon continued, "But I'd nevertheless call this a fortuitous meeting—I see now that while I had meant to court your party as a potential savior, I'd be satisfied with simply being a broker of sorts, instead." He stepped back, coolly taking a seat on one of the couches in the circle, his long and heavy tail draped across the furniture beside him. "I can connect you with the most valuable font of information you could possibly hope for, if your aim is to take up arms against Tark. And I'd do it for no steeper a price than simply ferrying me to our shared destination, as money is of no concern to me."

Brann stopped his thoughtless wandering, staring Gideon full in the face now. "Who?"

Gideon gave a small smile, that same air of mischief about him as when he first introduced himself, then chuckled, breaking out into a full, toothy grin, those draconic fangs glinting against his equally white scales. "Well, my mother, of course." He cocked his head. "Tark's mother, where you're concerned. Provided, of course, you promise to behave yourselves; it's been many a moon since I brought even one friend home to stay the night, let alone an entourage."

"Now why in the good goddamned hell," Zay guffawed impatiently, clapping the sofa cushions on either side of herself as she pulled herself to her feet, "Would Tark's own birth mother let us in on some insider information on how we could face him, in combat or otherwise? What possible reason would she have to help us if it meant possibly killing him?"

Gideon raised an eyebrow. "The same birth mother who sold him to a lance of religious zealots mere days after he aged out of warfighter training?" He sniffed, paying no heed to Zay's disbelief. "We are not a sentimental sort, us dragonfolk. My own family even less so. While my mother may have some softness about her unbecoming of the typical broodmother, she has never been one to shirk her duty when the time comes to send her offspring packing. You might even say she'd find it a matter of personal responsibility to answer for Tark's behavior, should you convince her he's been..." He paused, tasting his next word, savoring it. "...Misbehaving."

"So, he wasn't sold directly to Burnside Geiha, then," Nes interjected, "Assuming that he ever met the man. What happened to these religious zealots, the ones he was first sold to, as you said?"

Gideon didn't skip a beat. "He killed them. All of them. In single combat, one by one."

The room fell silent for a spell, and Emrys leaned in close to Brann, the scholarly man shaking with anticipation. "My young friend, I do believe we'll stand to benefit greatly from a short side venture to this 'Roost,'" he said in hushed tones.

Brann nodded.

*

After the circle broke, Gideon following Zay back to the cockpit to plug in their destination's coordinates, Brann felt a hand on his back—Nes stood beside him, the engineer rapping a knuckle against his breastplate.

"You're out of uniform there, soldat," Nes joked, noting the damage Brann's armor had received, in particular the jagged hole over his ribs where the Ammit's fang had pierced. "Looking more than a little worse for wear. Thought about maybe dropping the doe-eyed Geihan recruit look, getting something a little more personalized, now that you're pretty much outta the club for good?"

Brann looked himself over—in truth, he couldn't help it, still dressing dutifully in his old uniform every morning. It had become second nature, the idea of dressing down for a more casual look something he hadn't considered since before his conscription. "I don't really know what else to wear," he admitted, face a little red.

Nes sized him up, nodding to himself. "I got some side projects waiting in the wings, I'll see what I can do. In the meantime, take that shit off, you look like a goober." He slapped Brann's stomach with an open palm, following the crowd out of the common area.

"You know how to make armor?" Brann asked after him, turning in place.

Nes spread his arms, smirking as he went. "Brother, I designed your whole fit."

Brann felt gobsmacked; he looked around aimlessly, stunned at this new information about Nestor. He wanted to give chase, interrogate the older man further, but was stopped at the bottom of the stairs by another hand in the queue bidding for his attention.

Red pulled Brann aside quietly out of earshot of everyone else. She stood with him by the stairs, watching the rest of their crewmates disappear up into the space above before speaking—her arms were crossed, her energy nervous. She stared at Brann's face, silently, scanning it for a moment that stretched on and on, until:

"How are you feeling?" She finally asked awkwardly, unused to such face value chat.

Brann's eyebrows raised somewhat, expecting a bit more than that. "Uh. Doing fine. Is that what you wanted to talk about?"

Red fidgeted, making a show of examining the fingernails of one hand before abandoning that pretense hurriedly, looking somewhat annoyed at herself. "Gives me no pleasure to have to ask, considering how stupid you've behaved." She seemed to want to redirect that annoyance at him, rather than confront it—Brann definitely got the feeling Red did not spend a lot of time doing this sort of thing with the common folk.

He made it easier on her. "Well, that's what happens when you let a soldat walk about on his own, not giving him any orders. We're sort of a stupid species—like lemmings. Gotta corral us to keep us from walking off a cliff."

Brann hadn't even realized the joke he'd just made until Red's face cracked, unable to resist a small giggle—she shoved playfully at him, cradling her elbows, looking far more relaxed as a result. "You asked Emrys back at the tower what a 'demi-human' was—where did you come across this term?" She asked, beginning to hone in on her line of inquiry.

Brann lied. "Just heard it in passing. Can't remember where."

Red's reaction mirrored Emrys's, her expression one of dubious scrutiny. Brann couldn't explain exactly why he was so apprehensive to bring up his experience in the ocean—maybe he was afraid it would be dismissed as a vision conjured by his dying brain, the last hallucinations of a dying man.

Whatever his reasons for keeping the Godhead's words to himself were, Red didn't seem interested in pressing. "It's interesting timing you should happen to conjure such a phrase," she continued. "I don't care much for the waffling explanation the professor gave—in my own schoolings, we were always ascribing the label in very specific situations, easily understood by all. My consort, The Wolf—he is, in the parlance of my people, a textbook demi-human."

"But not Boomer?" Brann asked. "It's not just a term you use to describe any beastman or other race?"

"No." Red traced a fingertip through the air in front of her, and Brann realized she was following an imaginary route of his own circulatory system. "Your veins now pump inhuman blood—though I tentatively see your partial transfusion as mostly a success, I cannot guarantee there won't be complications in the future. You'd do well to see a physician of Jan-Jito in due time."

Brann gave a thumbs up. "I'll make an appointment. Honestly, I feel fine, you said yourself we'd know by now if I was about to grow fangs and go mental."

"That is not my concern." Red uncrossed her arms, breaking eye contact. "I have a request of you—The Wolf is slow to recover, I believe there to be some toxicity at work in his blood, keeping it thinned. I'd ask you, if you are indeed feeling up to the task, to donate a measure of your own to bring him back to full function. I ask this with all due sensitivity and respect for your own agency, of course."

Brann shrugged. "Red, of course I'll donate some blood. Honestly, you're really worrying too much about me, I feel great. I'm in perfect health."

"It's not your health I regard with sympathy." She tilted her tricorne hat back, her face apologetic in a way her words couldn't quite manage. "It's the implications that such an act would carry."

"Implications of what?"

Red locked eyes once more. "That you are no longer fully human."

That struck a chord. Brann withered a bit—that notion would take more than a little time to try and reconcile. Now was not the time. "I'll meet you in the medbay," he said flatly, hoping he sounded unaffected by this revelation as he climbed the steps.

Even without looking back, he could feel Red watching him go, a wisp of dread tickling at the back of his neck.

*

"Before we make landfall, there are a few things I'd like to make clear," Gideon declared imperiously—he stood, once more the center of attention in the cargo bay with everyone but Zay assembled before him, tightening his sword and shield more securely across his body. "While The

Roost does not feel the need to so jealously protect ourselves as to attack outlanders on sight, your presence is allowed only with unspoken understandings of the due respect you pay to the ground you tread—venturing so armed beyond the line of sight of those who choose to be your host, myself included, may be seen as an act of aggression met with a grievous response. If you find yourself in someone's home or private domain without invitation, you are already dead—simply put, stay with the group. I'll keep you safe, my children." Gideon winked at Brann, addressing them all in turn as he ran down his instructions, his clawed feet clicking against the metal floor in a way that made Brann wince—it sounded just like Tark walking amongst them.

"Man's kinda full of himself, ah?" Boomer whispered in Brann's ear. Brann resisted the urge to point out the irony of this statement.

"Next, you may be called upon to perform certain tasks by complete strangers," Gideon continued. "It may be a request as simple as holding a clothesline, it may be as demanding as being called to spar against a warrior in training." Gideon shook his head. "Do not, under any circumstances, decline. You are guests, treated with as much hospitality as any resident kuaneach—this too comes with it unspoken understandings of respect. If our mothers and brothers seek your contribution to their daily chores, it is a sign of hostility to turn them down, and this too may be met with a grievous response. Simply thank them for the request, agree to give aide, and ask to be reunited with your companions once it is done. We are, for the most part, excellent judges of character and physical ability; we would not ask you to perform any task you would be unfit for."

The engines roared in their ears, growing louder and broader in a rising wall of noise—the ship was landing. The floor beneath them shook a bit, before settling, the landing struts making contact with solid earth. Gideon turned to face the ramp, awaiting its descent. "Beyond that, there is only one thing you need remember: be honest, at all times, in all ways. We dragons have no taste for dishonesty; there is nothing so foul on the tongue as sharing words with a liar."

The overhead speakers fuzzed a bit, Zay's distorted voice coming through. "Anchors dropped. Be down in a second." The speakers clicked off, and Nestor hit the ramp switch, the hydraulics groaning as daylight burst in.

The first and most striking thing Brann noticed was a complete lack of green vegetation. The soil seemed black, loose as gravel, but smooth and uniform. The cargo ramp touched down, and nary a waft of dust was disturbed—it was like the ground was composed of solidified oil, a sort of soft sheen reflecting the muted sunlight filtering through the dense gray clouds above. Zay arrived as promised a moment later, and nine pairs of feet fell in line walking down the ramp (Grishka, in raven form, remained comfortably perched on Emrys's shoulder)—when Brann's boots stepped off, indeed it felt like he was standing on soft pearls of silica.

The second thing he saw as he stepped out from beneath the canopy of the Donnie's hull was the topography—an almost frightening sight, one he needed time to process, the earth itself seeming to challenge Brann's understanding of physics. Rising from the black, pearlescent sand, dozens of spires of porous stone rose all around them—but as Brann's eyes traced up their length, they actually seemed to widen the higher up they went, until at their highest points they flared outwards, forming spirals of spiked growths, evenly arranged around the rims like sawblades.

"Helixtrees," Gideon said, catching Brann's eye. "Look like they're made of stone, don't they?"

"They're not?" Brann asked, looking curiously to the closest helixtree. The rough surface seemed rocky enough.

Gideon just smirked, not answering. "Come on then. A short hike we'll make of it."

The earth beneath their feet was absent the expected crunch of dirt; the more Brann walked, the more uncomfortable he felt, in that he'd almost expected the softness beneath him to yield to gravity and swallow him up. It didn't help matters that he felt about twenty pounds lighter, having taken Nestor's suggestion and stripping off his armor. He felt a few sideways looks, heard a few giggles—instead, he wore the same dressy outfit he'd worn to Boomer's tournament fight, his loose-fitted blouse blowing in the wind. Brann wished inwardly he could be less self-conscious, especially in present company—with as long as he'd been travelling with everyone, surely he'd be used to their sensibilities by now.

"Pay these chuckleheads no nevermind," Boomer proclaimed loudly, breaking the silence as they walked, matching Brann's stride. "Their jealousy is unbecoming. Us eligible bachelors, we gotta look good, nah?"

"Nah," Zay retorted from the rear, dressed in little more than the same white tanktop and utility pants she sported on the daily. Boomer looked her up and down quickly before holding up a hand, shielding Zay from his view, rolling his eyes at Brann.

"Like I was saying," he said, shaking his head—it went a long way to put Brann at ease, prompting a smile from the young man.

Looking up, the dark clouds seemed to fluidly roll past, threatening rain but never quite delivering—Brann wondered just how high up they were, the elevation bringing them so close that the clouds seemed more like fog rolling by, barely cresting the tops of the helixtrees. The land itself was so alien, but part of him connected with it, the lifelessness of it all betraying a sense of coziness. There were no busy city skylines on the horizon, no great lumbering predators—it was peaceful, despite its eeriness.

After a few minutes of walking, Gideon's prediction proved accurate, and the ground sloped upwards—an easy climb, the hill drew away from them, a circular formation around a steep descent. If Brann didn't know any better, he'd think this was the massive crater formed by a falling meteor—

His train of thought was derailed by Gideon standing at the crest of the hill, leaning forward to support his weight on one knee as he gestured down below. "There it is. The only true home fit for my kind."

The crater ran deep, at its center a shattered portal in the glassy earth, like a dark pupil at the center of a great eye. The party gathered around to peer down at it, visibly confused, as there were no visible structures to speak of. No one spoke for a few moments, until Boomer broke rank in proper droll fashion.

"Love what you've done with the place."

Gideon beckoned for them to follow, descending down the steep side of the crater on impossibly steady feet. "I confess, I'm a bit more sentimental than I expected, it has been near a century since I last saw home. Come along."

*

Descending into the pupil of the eye down a hewn ramp carved from the inner earth beneath the crater, the ten travelers were taken on a long roundabout that circled the distant bedrock below—and the veritable township that had been built out of the stone arches and bridges sprouting from the floor. There were a few standing structures here and there, mostly hut-like stacks of sheet rock, but for the most part it appeared a system of interconnected caves and open portals dug through the aeolian stone formations. The lower they trekked and the more of the town they circled, the more The Roost unfolded to them, overlapping arches acting as stone curtains to smaller mesas and inselbergs, the bigger of which were cut open at their base to allow passage beneath, colorful banners and tapestries acting as visual guides. No ship could ever hope to pass through the eye, limiting all traffic to this single rampway; though they needn't worry about stepping aside for anyone on the narrow path as none of the tiny figures moving far below were making their way up towards the surface at present. Brann got the impression as he drew close enough to begin making out features of individual kuaneach that there wasn't much reason for them to leave—not much above to speak of worth leaving for.

"We call these the Warrens," Gideon was informing them, gesturing out into open space at the formed systems of arches and caves below, the porous foundation of the crater gradually forming a dome over their heads. "Most of the population lives in these caves—the rest of them who haven't left home can usually be found at the Temple, further below, though we won't be seeing it. None besides those in training for service or their instructors step foot below the Warrens."

"What are all those funny lookin' holes everywhere?" Boomer drew his outstretched fingers between several in question—the bedrock floor did indeed seem to yawn open, gaping pits smoothly descending into the darkness puncturing the ground the kuaneachs walked on every few hundred yards or so.

"Rain sinuses—when the crater above fills with water, it all falls into the Warrens, cascading off the arches in every direction—hence why all the caves are dug facing away from the Eye," Gideon answered. "It all drains into those sinuses, into the temple below—the only source of water afforded to the acolytes in training. They drink and bathe only when the rains come."

"Ugh," Red scoffed, and Brann couldn't tell if she was more disgusted at the cruelty of it or the idea of such infrequent showers.

"Try to understand," Gideon reasoned, sensing the group's trepidation. "We are, in many ways, a kind people. We have a grand capacity for compassion far beyond most humans—but there is great strength to be found in us as well, one that proves the envy of any who would fancy themselves a warlord or a tyrant. To court humans is to be the death of them." Gideon came to a halt for a moment. "Those of us who leave The Roost do so for no purpose beyond the destruction of others. We learn at a young age to take responsibility for our teeth, our claws, our blades—when to use them, and more importantly, when not to use them."

He looked directly at Brann now, and for a moment, Brann saw Tark in Gideon's eyes.

"My brother understood this lesson better than most. At the cost of a much greater suffering than his peers. The greater the suffering, the wiser the warrior. That's how we are raised, and how we face the world."

Nestor cocked his head at this. "How you rule it, you mean?"

Gideon shook his head. "My kind don't value political power. But we do respect those who have it—insofar as we cannot reclaim it for those more deserving."

"Or those who can bid higher for you at auction," Zay retorted bitterly.

Brann could see by Gideon's posture he knew he wasn't making any allies by trying to apologize for Tark. The whitegold kuaneach went quiet for a moment, then tossed his head back down the ramp. "We're almost there."

There was a tension in the air about them, despite the outward friendliness the kuaneach showed in passing as the group finally set foot into the Warrens. Brann didn't sense any fear from these people—most barely gave more than a slight smile or a nod, their scaled arms hauling baskets of produce or yokes of powders and dyes—but he knew even the eldest and least adept of them could easily kill him where he stood if he drew sword against them. Their soft, loose-fitted clothes belied their bestial nature, cotton robes and skirted tunics flowing over iron scales and wicked talons, even the most androgynous of them sporting the naturalborn armaments of a dragon.

The more Brann studied of them beyond that, however, the more Brann began to see the diversity present in the kuaneach physiology. He'd already noticed Gideon's lack of wings, despite being Tark's brother, but that seemed less a curiosity the deeper into the Warrens they hiked—almost no two kuaneachs looked alike. Rocky scales of almost mineral-like quality gave way to smoother, serpentine bodies. Some kuaneachs whipped their tails about like lizards, others crouched beneath the weight of their shellbacks like tortoises—to say nothing of the dazzling array of colors. One elder female reached down to play with her grandchildren, their bright red and orange dewlaps flapping in excitement—yet in the cave just next door, Brann could see two sisters arguing over a recipe as they prepared a meal together, one of them a solid pearly green while the other threatened to disappear into the shadows beneath her charcoal hide.

Brann was about to speak up, voicing his fascination with the kuaneachs, then caught sight of Emrys—the scholarly man, visibly awed as well, kept his lips tightly pursed. It then dawned on Brann, somewhat embarrassed at himself, that it wouldn't be terribly polite to make commentary as if they were visiting a zoo.

Boomer lacked such inhibitions. "Look at all of them, they're so *pretty*," he said in awe.

The horse grunted, turning to frown at Zay, who had smacked the back of his head with an open palm. She gave him a wide-eyed stare, apologizing on his behalf to Gideon. "Don't mind our boss, he didn't mean anything by it, he's just an idiot."

"It's alright, we're creatures to be admired," Gideon replied, not seeming to mind one bit. "Else why would we be born with such a variety of gifts to show off? This is it."

He brought the party to a halt, forming a half-circle around one of the caves at ground level, unassuming and undecorated save for the single glowing crystalline torch embedded in a standing sconce. Gideon motioned for them to stay put as he cleared his throat, hesitating before ducking inside. The way his horns barely cleared the overhead awning even as he hunched over, Brann suspected Gideon had grown significantly since he had left home.

A few moments passed, the silence growing more than a little awkward, then once more he emerged—if Brann didn't know any better, he almost thought he saw relief on Gideon's face.

"Huh. Not home." Gideon shrugged. "She must be at Temple."

"Thought you said only instructors were allowed inside," Hawkshaw said.

Gideon flashed a look of understanding. "Yes, I did."

"Wait, back on the ship you called her a—what was it—" Zay asked, snapping her fingers.

"Broodmother. She was, for a time." Gideon crossed his arms, leaning back against the stone wall. "While most kuaneach typically settle into an occupation for life, my mother is anything but typical, even among my kind. She never was one to—"

In an instant, Gideon went rigid, standing at attention. The rest of the group turned in unison, Brann peeking out from behind Boomer's broad back.

She had appeared behind them, quiet as snow, not a word spoken in greeting. Tightly wrapped lengths of cloth adorned her limbs, an equally tight-fitting tunic her only other article of clothing, the kuaneach female dressed as if for athletic pursuit. Brann felt his stomach turn at the sight of her: no more fitting an introduction as Tark's mother could be stated as eloquently as seeing her doused head-to-toe in streaks of blood. Her clothes were soaked through, her smooth, blue scales dripping, looking as if she'd just stepped out from beneath a gory downpour.

"Marm," Gideon said stiffly, nodding in a slight bow. He opened his arms, signaling his guests. "This is my mother, Ula. The Temple's Master-at-Arms."

Ula stepped between the parted bodies, barely paying them a second glance, moving swiftly and quietly. Her bare feet barely even left clawmarks in the packed dirt, the slight kuaneach as light as a feather, a far cry from her hulking sons. With the slightest twitch of her fingers, Ula wordlessly beckoned Gideon to follow her inside her cave, disappearing out of sight as quickly as she'd come.

Gideon bowed, looking as uncertain as the rest of them. "All apologies—wait one. I'll explain things to her. She's—you—well, you saw, it's—"

The normally composed kuaneach went silent and gave another small bow, carefully stripping himself of his arms, setting the sword and shield against the inner wall of the cave before following his mother.

Red, rolling her eyes, was none-too-impressed. She scratched beneath Wolf's chin. "My sympathies," she said dryly, once Gideon was out of earshot.

35. The Warning

The inner dome of the Warrens was alight with more of those same crystalline torches, the sunlight streaming down from the Eye above fading away some time ago. The nine companions lounged about, awaiting Gideon's return, exchanging grumbles and desires for a meal soon. Wolf had curled himself in a heap, Zay and Red leaning back against him, playing a game of marbles in the dirt, while Grishka's nimble beak assisted in reattaching some of the harder to reach wirings in Hawkshaw's mostly re-affixed arm. Emrys had taken it upon himself to replenish the pages of his journal. Boomer, Nes and Brann all sat cross-legged, the horse dealing them each a new hand of cards.

"Kid, you sure you've played this before?" Nes was saying, splashing the pot with scalenes, the little pyramids clinking against one another. "We can always change rulesets—"

"Yes, I'm telling you, it was our only game back in training," Brann was saying, laughing defensively. "I can't help it if I'm having some bad luck lately."

"Luck!" Boomer scoffed, matching Nestor's bet. "No such thing. Passion! Fire! The will to win! That's what you're missing, guy."

"I'll remember that next time you blame bad luck for my paycheck being late," Nes snickered, blowing cigarillo smoke out the side of his mouth.

"Blame not the wind for the way the bush—" Boomer paused, stumbling over his own idiom. "Wait. No, it's—the bush doesn't grow, unless the wind blows, so you shouldn't blame—or, no, fuck. If the wind is blowing through your bush, don't blame—"

"Shut up and play," Nes said, tapping the deck impatiently.

They wouldn't get the chance for another hand, however—once more, Ula appeared in the doorway, having cleaned herself up significantly. Her scales steamed a bit, freshly scrubbed, and her athletic gear had been swapped out for a comfortable looking kimono. She stepped out of her cave, looking about sternly, and when she spoke it was with as little patience as someone of her station was afforded.

"Which one of you lot pledged themselves to my son?" She asked, looking about imperiously, eyes narrowing as they looked down her slim snout. "Who among you challenged Tark?"

Brann, feeling as though he'd been plunged into ice, stood slowly, raising a hand. "That would be me, Marm."

Ula looked Brann up and down quickly, registering a quizzical look—Brann was only as tall as she was. She strode past the rest of the group, coming to stand directly before him—then, before Brann could even hope to react, Ula lashed out with an open palm directly into his chest, sending the young man cartwheeling backwards through the air.

"Oy!" Boomer shouted, his deck of cards sent flying.

The party was on their feet without hesitation, ready to step to Brann's defense, but Gideon's quick appearance kept them at bay, the kuaneach ushering them back—this was Brann's problem to deal with.

Brann leapt upright, one hand clutching at his chest, his breathing ragged and painful—his other hand unsheathed his sword, swinging the blade wide, holding it aloft and at the ready. The young soldat tensed at the knees, crouching low, ready to fight.

"Well, let's get this over with," he growled angrily, waving Ula in with the squared tip of his sword. "C'mon then, 'Marm,' pick a weapon, let's go!"

Ula stepped in close once more, though this time, her steps were slower, her posture relaxed—she tilted her head, staring at Brann, examining him thoroughly.

"I don't see a coward," she said loudly, addressing Gideon behind her. "An idiot, perhaps, young and foolish—but not a coward."

Boomer, fists unclenching, held his arms aloft. "He's cured!"

Brann was taken aback. His sword faltered, arm going limp at his side. "You don't wanna kill me, then?"

"I don't know about that," Ula joked, walking a circle around Brann. "You may be the first person to take up arms against one of my sons and live."

Zay looked to Gideon, who held up his hands with mock humility.

"That in itself is a matter worth exploring further. I'll make up my mind about killing you later." Ula flared her sleeves, tightening her kimono. "Come, young soldat. We visit my library. The rest of you, my kitchen is open to you—clean up after yourselves, or my son will be cleaning you up."

Brann couldn't help but feel a swell of pride, everyone watching him go as he tagged along behind Ula dutifully—the way he'd stood up for himself, the way everyone else had stood up for him. Only a few weeks ago, he'd probably only get a laugh from his teammates by being sent sprawling.

They had come to care for him.

*

Ula didn't waste any time, moving at a brisk pace everywhere she went, leading Brann on a deliberate path straight to the furthest edges of the Warrens. The ground yielded before them to another wide ramp, one that led directly down into the earth in a smooth slope, a cavern adorned with black banners on either side of it awaiting them.

"Inside," she commanded, Brann taking the lead at her assurance. Ula may not have spoken as much as Tark was prone to, but that didn't make her any less intimidating, nor did her shorter stature. Despite being a vision of kuaneach femininity, she barked like a seasoned drill commander, Brann falling in just as if he were back in training. This was a woman who had no time for fools, and even less reason to suffer them.

The cave opened up after a brief passageway to a wide, layered space, several overlapping floors all connected with more stone ramps—on every floor, there sat a collection of shelves, all tightly packed with any number of cloth scrolls and books. A library of sorts, though Brann didn't get the impression this place had many visitors from the public, the quiet and somber atmosphere broken only by the crackling sounds of those crystal torches and their sparkling embers trickling upwards.

"The Temple Archives," Ula said, directing Brann to a large desk, kicking out a chair for him to take. "Sit."

Brann obeyed, hands on his knees, feeling like a student awaiting a lesson from an irritable professor.

"This is as far into the Temple as you will be permitted, for the time being," said Ula, her tone impassive, speaking with a militant cadence. "Let me perfectly clear: I am not interested in your business with the greater will of House Geiha or its officials. My only concern is what has transpired between you and the Marshal. His onus is not to cater to defiant young men, it is to quash them—what makes you worth more than the rest of the recruits you served alongside?"

Brann shook his head. "Nothing, Marm."

"Now is not the time to play humble. 'Nothing' is no answer, I expect information."

Exhaling, Brann nodded, rubbing his palms against his knees. "I was—am—the last surviving member of House Lachlan. Tark—er, the Marshal, sorry—he wanted me to willingly surrender my House to Geiha, to him. I don't fully know why yet, but my friends and I, we suspect he's intending on using the cumulative power of several Houses to unite them under an empire. In fact, they're already calling Geiha an empire back in Barrier City, it was sort of..." He licked his lips bitterly. "...In the rules."

"Kuaneachs do not seek power for themselves." Ula paced back and forth somewhat as she interrogated Brann. "We'll come back to that. Why did Tark leave you alive after, I presume, you surrendered?"

"I did, yes." Brann cleared his throat. "I don't know. That's not—I don't mean to hide anything, I honestly don't know. He almost killed my best friend, so it's not like he had any great moral quandaries about it."

Ula snapped her clawed fingers. "Speak not on the morals of our kind, your opinion is irrelevant." She paused, choosing her next question carefully. "What are you and your friends after? What is your purpose?"

"Marshal Tark branded us terrorists, plastered our faces all over the continent, I imagine my friends would like their names and reputations cleared. That means confronting Tark, one way or another."

Her pacing stopped. "You said 'your friends' would like that. Not you?"

Brann shrugged.

Ula looked sideways at him. "You don't care about ever stepping foot in the capital cities again?"

"I was never really welcome in them to begin with," Brann replied unflinchingly. "I don't really give a shit what anyone thinks about me."

"Yet you still seek to face my son." Ula drew herself up. "Why? What could you stand to gain from what would certainly spell your doom?"

"After what I've seen? What I've been through?" Brann shook his head. "To be honest, I think I just want to answer for what he did to Boomer. I don't care who he is, what he's planning, he needs to be put in check. If I can't do that alone, maybe the rest of my crew can. They don't deserve to have their lives ruined just for falling in with me. They're good people."

"And what have you seen that has made you so..." Ula waved a hand. "Emboldened?"

Thinking back, Gideon had told them to always be honest, no matter what, and if anyone were to believe him, it would be a member of Tark's family. Brann decided it was time to come clean.

"I almost died, just the other day. Maybe I did. I fell beneath the ocean, drowning. I saw something—I could have imagined it. I don't think so. It was real to me." He tried to put into words the sights, the words that had been spoken to him, but Brann found himself strangely unable to, overcome by a swell of emotion. "Something, someone—a great dragon. Like a snake, one that could wrap around the whole world if it wanted. It knew me as if it had always known me. It told me—" Brann swallowed down a lump in his throat. "It gave me a reason not to die down there. It sent me on my way. No—more like it set my way forward for me. It put me on a path. One that leads back home. Back to Tark."

Ula stared at Brann full in the face, arms crossed. Brann met her gaze—not with defiance, but with honesty, feeling more vulnerable than he could remember feeling.

"You communed with a Godhead." She didn't accuse, she didn't ask. It was a statement. Ula accepted Brann's story without question. "You've been made a missionary to its cause. What cause that may be is for you to discover, and you alone. No friends to bear you along, no aid may you request."

"Are you suggesting I leave everyone behind, go out on my own?" Brann shook his head. "No Marm. I'm not gonna do that. I won't leave my friends. They're all I care about now. No one can make me do that."

Ula twitched—she seemed to know something Brann didn't on the matter. "It wouldn't be your decision to make, if indeed a Godhead set you on the path it chose for you."

On a nearby shelf, a neatly arranged row of thin cloth bundles was stacked together—Ula plucked free one of these bundles, holding it up and appraising the runic emblems decorating its flat surface. Satisfied she'd made the right choice, she raised a hand, beckoning Brann with her fingers, the same way she had Gideon. "Come with me. Let me show you why I brought you here."

Deep in the archives, Ula presented Brann with another chamber. Spires of stone encircled them, stalagmites that nearly reached the ceiling, surrounding a lone pedestal of sorts. It almost looked like a turntable, the kind Brann would see the wealthier citizens of Barrier City use to play recorded music, back when he was a young street urchin spying on them through their apartment windows.

How far away that all seemed, now.

"This is a room of reflection," Ula explained. "When acolytes have finished their training and seek purpose that cannot be read from a contract, or when a kuaneach has lost their way in the world, they come here. Not as significant as a conversation with a Godhead," Ula admitted, "Though no one leaves here without a greater sense of self. You may stand to benefit from its use moreso than anyone."

"Why's that?" Brann asked, cautious, appraising the stone pedestal with some suspicion.

Ula didn't blink. "Because you have the most to lose, whether you realize it or not."

She stretched out an arm, bidding Brann towards another, smaller chamber, one hidden behind a gap in the stone pillars by a veil of beads. "Inside, take a seat. Lay down if you like." Ula unwrapped the cloth bundle, and from inside, another layer of folded rice paper similarly unwrapped itself, revealing a translucent disc of emerald sheen. "This record will play a single song—there will be no lyrics to discern, no hidden message. Just simple instrumentation, an arrangement that is carefully composed to touch something within the listener. When the music begins, close your eyes, and let it take you where it will."

Ula set the disc in place on the turntable, and it gently slid down the length of the center spindle, disappearing beneath the rim of the plinth. As if activated by the weight of the disc, four identical clawlike arms arose from hidden slits within the pedestal, arranged symmetrically around the rim of the plinth, their sharp needles pointing inwards. Ula once more held out her hand, bidding Brann to enter the subchamber beyond.

Again, heeding Gideon's words, Brann knew better than to argue against what was being asked of him. He turned to face the curtain of beads stepping inside—and immediately felt the same calming effect fall over him as when he'd entered Grishka's home in the woods. The beads held the same pacifying enchantment as those naturally grown tendrils in her burrow, that seemed to be the only explanation—regardless, if indeed this was a place meant for self-reflection, then it only stood to reason Brann should be as comfortable as possible.

Especially considering the furniture. It was a stone bed that awaited him, a decorative rug draped over it, though decoration was its only purpose—laying back on the stone surface, Brann had little cushioning between his back and the hard stone. It was cold, almost uncomfortably so, and within moments he felt the circulation in his flesh slow.

"I guess I'm not supposed to actually fall asleep in here?" He asked, calling out through the curtain of beads.

Ula did not respond. Instead, the stone walls seemed to vibrate, and sure enough, the room around Brann began to fill with a low frequency thrum—and, though he couldn't place exactly what kind, he began to sense the sound of curling fingers against the strings of some spectral instrument. There was a calm in it, a center of peaceful introspection the chords all seemed to wreathe themselves around, even if Brann didn't fully understand the progression of it.

Close your eyes, Ula had said. "Alright then," Brann said aloud, and did just that, adjusting his back against the stone bed.

The sounds of the foreign instrumental began to rise, not so much around him, but within—the steady beating against those strings, the somber wail of a wood flute hollowing its way through his chest, and soon enough the ascending thumping of bassy drums that cleared away the dirt and fractured colors behind his eyelids.

*

The surface of the earth had become a vast ocean of dried mud, absent all life and color, a rusted facsimile of a desert—sheets of dried mud, cracked and craggy, blanketed these dead lands like the scales on a dragon's back. The sky was a murky, terracotta brown, the clouds as burned and leeched of water as the earth below, only a black smear of ashen foreboding separating them on the horizon. In the middle of these deadlands, apart from all the noise and color and hope of the world, He was there.

A tall skeleton, leaf of gold wrapping between His bones, shedding the dust of His former self in a cape of shadow dragging behind Him as He levitated off the surface of the desert. Arms wide open, outstretched to heaven, head hanging low, ribcage split open as if burst by the inward stab of some great, blunt weapon. The skeleton's shadow lengthened behind Him, spreading across the land, reaching beyond the horizon and clinging to those smokey clouds—and as the sky above began to churn and grow stormy, darkened funnels reaching towards earth as if the fingers of God had broken through the clouds, He raised His head.

The eyeless skull blazed with terrestrial fire, burning deep in His cavities, the inside of His head sparking with the furious remnants of a severed soul. His empty eyes turned skyward, bony jaw hanging open in a silent scream, rejoicing at the appearance of his promised halo: a hole in the sky, an impossible circle in the clouds that framed the sun's reddened eye, positioned behind the skeleton's head as an unholy corona. The gold leaf spread, wrapping itself in multiplying layers of splendor, the gold beginning to stream off the skeleton's joints in ribbons of glimmering viscera.

The dead earth cracked open, fissures splitting between tectonic plates, and from the deep below arose even more skeletons—torsos without legs, their spines dragging behind them like reptilian tails, every skull transfixed in a silent scream to mimic their Maker. Giant skeletal hands clawed into the dirt, dragging those enormous corpses across a plain as dead as they were, marching forward into destruction behind their golden messiah. Black tornadoes tore into the desiccated wastes, following the path carved in the dust by the march of the torsos, all of what remained of creation disappearing into the clay and the rising wall of the approaching storm. There was no rain in that rolling blanket of clouds, only lightning and whirlwinds of glass.

The light of the sun burned, melting the gold right of the bones of the skeletal idol, his crossed legs flowing with the robes of streaming, molten metal—and just as those eye sockets grew enraged, flames spouting like tears that blackened the skull's cheekbones, his outstretched arms drew forward and clasped their hands together briefly. When they opened, in his withered, clawlike fingers, which themselves were dripping with golden rings, a pair of dice were revealed—simple, unremarkable, and carved from polished stone.

The skeleton's hand tilted forward, and those dice fell, hurtling towards the earth—and where they impacted, the dust cratered, turning to mud once more, and from those craters sprung forth twin fountains of clear, icy water, gushing from the desert as if it had been fatally wounded—

Brann snapped awake, feeling the weight of existential dread in his belly, the images in his head clinging to his brain matter even as he tried to shake them off. The music was just winding down, the hum of those strings fading out, and Brann wiped the dew of sweat from his forehead. He rolled off the stone bed, parting the curtain of beads with a hand and stepping into the turntable chamber, where Ula stood waiting with another bundle in her hands.

"What did I just see?" Brann asked, voice shaking, his hands soon beginning to follow—he felt the sweat continue to run off his brow, down the sides of his neck.

"I could never know," was Ula's blunt reply. "Nor would I have a hope of divining its meaning were you to tell me. Your reflections are your own, their meaning yours to interpret." She opened the second bundle, the disc streaked with sapphire. "Shall we continue?"

"Why are you doing this?" Brann wiped his face, blinking hard, as if that might finally rid him of what he'd seen. "How many more of these 'reflections' do you expect me to sit through?"

Ula was already replacing the first record with the second, gently pressing the sapphire disc into place on the spindle. "You've not asked the question you've come to ask, nor would I expect you to. No mother, even a kuaneach, could sanction the death of her own child." She folded the emerald disc back into its wrappings, turning her back on Brann, heading back to the archives—presumably to return the first disc to its shelf and find a third.

"This is the price for my blessing," Ula called back before she disappeared. "Reflect on your visions, and when you've seen enough, you may yet be ready to face Tark."

Brann was left alone once more. The stone pillars were beginning to hum, the music swelling within the reflection chamber. Hesitantly, he stepped back behind the curtain, blinking away the torpor of his last trance before submitting himself to another—he hoped this next vision would be less horrific. The drums of this next song were deeper, more insistent, the strings being scraped with a frustration that compelled the submission of the listener towards its call to action. Brann laid himself back, heart thumping in his chest to the rhythm of the war drums, and closed his eyes.

*

The red sun shone more, except now it hung low in a cloudless sky, over an earth that had not yet fully decayed. The trees were in full bloom, the late spring beginning to yield to the coming summer, swirls of locusts blowing across fields of flowers in search of the summer's first crops. On the horizon, a convoy was moving, coming this way: not machine, but a living parade, a procession of great, leathery beasts. A family of elephants, young and old, traipsing across the flowered fields from a land afar. They'd come to this place, these strange new lands, in search of a promised peace. The eldest among them tossed their scarred trunks, batted their torn ears, shielding their youth from the afternoon sun with their towering bodies—their children did not yet know strife, and would not, if their parents could find them a home.

The flower petals swirled all about the herd in the cooling wind of oncoming eventide, and the herd came to a halt at long last, standing before a high palisade wall of great wooden stakes. The wall had been carved from the grandest of trees, reaching high above the heads of even the tallest elephants, shielding them all from the setting sun. The mud beneath them splashed and bubbled as the herd stamped their feet in unison, an expectant call ringing out from their trunks, their young ones joining in to sound their relief. Beyond the wall lie safety, lie shelter, and a season of harvest to feed them all—more than they could have ever hoped for, and less than they deserved, after so much struggle along their journey.

After a time, the herd went silent. Their feet stilled, their joy quieting.

Were they forgotten? Had they not come to the right place?

In the shadow of that palisade wall, it began to rain. Not the promised rain of late spring, but the agonizing sizzle of boiling tar, the shower on their heads causing an uproar among the herd. Bodies fell back, crashing into one another, the elders rolling themselves over to shield their young, chaos and pain reigning among the peace-seeking giants. A stampede broke out, the herd retreating back, their flesh scarred and steaming, leaving behind those too weak and too heavily burned to escape the tar. Those unfortunate few sunk into the mud, sorrowful eyes closing, staring up at that cruel oaken wall that had denied them.

The sun fell behind the world, and night sky reigned above. The stars whirled by overhead, time dilating as the song seemed to hang on a single, penetrative note—then, the morning sun rose once more, only to quickly disappear beneath the horizon, and it was night again—and rapidly, night became day, and soon the entire summer was flashing by, the flowers shrinking into green growth, the first edges of gold beginning to show on the fringes of those fields.

Then the red sun appeared once more, and time slowed, and again it was late afternoon. The horizon darkened, shifting and undulating beneath another parading convoy—the elephants had returned.

But now there were no young children among their ranks, nor beleaguered elders. All that remained were their most stout, their hardiest warriors, their tusks wrapped in barbed wire and their skulls gleaming with bony helms. The march of the great beasts flattened the fields where once vibrant flowers bloomed, the locusts washing away in a tidal wave against the evening sky, the drying trees falling to splinters beneath the unstoppable herd. In their trunks, the angry beasts held aloft the cherry red flames of wrathful torches, great planks of wood soaked in fat that burned at both ends. The late sky above grew dark, the only stars visible those cast up by those torches.

As if sensing their approach, the palisade wall once more was shrouded in its dark shadow, the drizzle of tar making the mud below start to bubble and pop. The scorned herd would not be denied this time—with a great

602

war cry, their trunks raised skyward in unison, trumpeting their singular purpose. Gaining speed, the herd charged forward, stamping through the swampy mud and crushing the bones of their own dearly departed. Like the sea breaking on a levy, the herd smashed against and across and through those palisades, ignoring the avalanche of wooden debris that collapsed all around them, a righteous fury destroying the wall that mocked and betrayed them. Under a savage sun, the once peaceful giants had brought down their enemy, and the oily tar of the swamp began to spark and burn. The last of the elephants was alight in a vortex of fire, their destructive momentum carrying with them a sweeping tide of flames that burned flesh and earth alike.

While they pressed on, towards an uncertain future, the herd left behind them a reminder to the rest of the world of their terrible vengeance—the burning fields and trampled wall, ivory tusks of their long-dead comrades still curling up out of the flames towards the night sky. And far beyond, back towards the horizon, silhouetted by the setting sun just as it made its final descent, a lone figure stood watch: a jackal, its jaws clamped around a torch of her own. The jackal that had given the herd the gift of its vengeful fire.

The song ended just as Brann's eyes opened, this time without the pressing dread of the last vision weighing on his chest. His fists were clenched, the nails digging into his palms—he unclenched them slowly, letting the anger dissipate from within him, the stone bed cooling his heated blood. There was little he could discern from the two visions he'd seen so far, and he remained unmoved by Ula's opaque intentions for showing them to him. Still, he rose from the stone bed, passing through the beads to find the third disc waiting for him in Ula's hands—this one was a deep ruby red, barely translucent at all, though he could still see the vague shadow of Ula's fingers behind it as she held it above the spindle.

"The final song," she was saying, settling the disc into place. "Are you ready to begin?"

"I didn't ask for permission to kill Tark, you're right," Brann proclaimed boldly—perhaps he'd been more stirred by that last vision than he thought. "Because that isn't what I'm after. I want to face him, yes, to intercede in...whatever it is he's got planned. Hundreds of recruits my own age, young men just like me, were forced into serving under his name. They'll be forced to die in his name. If the other Houses don't fall in line with his new empire, then who knows how many more will die along with them—all for nothing, except the pride of a House that hasn't even existed long enough to matter to the history books. You don't have to give me permission to kill him—I don't even know that I can. But you can't see what we've seen and know what we know and not feel like he has to be stopped."

For a moment, Ula's hands froze in place, the ruby record inches from the turntable. She locked eyes with Brann, and he saw his words had little effect.

"Last vision," she repeated insistently. "Then we talk."

*

Snow had fallen on these dead plains, had been falling for weeks, months—and in that endless snow, fires burned, down to their root, to the marrow of the earth itself even, leaving scorched craters where once funeral pyres had stood. No living creature walked among the dead, no hand outstretched from the miles and miles of decayed armor. This battlefield had fallen silent and still, save for those towering plumes of smoke that continues to rise in place of the trees long since cut down to their trunks. Fractured spears, splintered rifles, crushed helms and shattered shields—one could step across from one body to the next, each nearly completely submerged in the snow, and never touch solid ground again. These plains stretched the world entire, at least, as far as could be seen by his eyes.

A lone survivor: a small, fluffy sparrow, no claws of iron, no beak of steel. A tiny creature, beating its wings in steady measure, tucking them in close to glide through the air between beats, its journey long and aimless. The dead plains below held no purchase for it, no growth to feed from, no insects eating from the corpses—all was frozen metal and ash beneath the snow, and all would be so forever, the life having gone from this forgotten world, the light of the fading sun soon to follow. The sparrow pursued nothing, saw nothing, found nothing—and yet, still it beat its little wings, against the cold and the coming night, which would finally snuff out the single candle still illuminating this forgotten sorrow.

There.

It was small, smaller even than the tiny sparrow. There was a flash of it, and then it was gone—the sparrow circled, high above the fields, above the black dead and white snow. Again, he saw it.

The sparrow tucked in his wings, holding them close, falling towards the earth like a miniscule meteor, and just before disaster it beat against the rushing wind and caught itself just above the surface of the snow.

The single, green stem of a wilting flower. A fruiting bud, maybe, one that would grow into something more, a mighty tree, or a meager berry bush—something living, something pliant, something green. It didn't matter to the sparrow. It was alive. Weak, and without much hope, but alive, growing between the metal fingers of a skeleton trapped within its armored husk.

The sparrow hopped in close, fluffing his feathers against the piercing cold, and plucked the flower free from the dirt. The thin, dried roots came up with the stem—it could still yet live. If the sparrow could fly far enough, fast enough, find a home for it, the flower could yet grow, give food, give life back to the plains.

But the night was coming, and coming fast. The wind was picking up, the cold prickling beneath the sparrow's downy plumage. The little bird took to the sky once more, clutching the flower's stem tight to his underbelly, wrapping his little claws around it. Higher he climbed, and harder the wind blew, threatening to pull the sparrow back to earth, smash him against the snow and metal and burning earth.

His little wings spread, wide as they could, catching a headwind— like the great eagles that once soared, the tiny sparrow was made master of these plains beneath him, inheriting all that he could see stretching on and on past the horizon. On he flew, forever forward into that horizon, passing over those endless plains, that endless death. The clouds above were stained black with soot, the snow below erasing everything in a white blanket of nothingness. Still, the sparrow flew on, diligently, searching for warm soil that may take the dying flower in its embrace, pursuing a happiness that may never come.

The light was fading. The smoke was closing in. All was growing dark, even the white snow beginning to fall away into nothing.

And still, the sparrow flew on.

The song died. Brann's eyes stared at the stone ceiling, his whole body feeling as cold as the surface he lied upon.

He took a moment to collect himself before standing—there was no anger, no fear. His mind was made clear, and a creeping sadness took their place, an illusion of who and what he was beginning to shimmer, threatening to break entirely. A small part of him didn't even want to leave the reflection chamber.

Brann passed through the beaded curtains, coming face to face with Ula once more. He didn't speak, his face telling all—and Ula saw.

"Your arrogance could bring your own end, but your violent self-importance will bring the end of all," she said, confirming his unspoken thoughts. "You are young. You have been wronged, yes. And you're right—my son deserves to die."

She tucked the wrapped disc back under her arm, stepping forward and touching Brann on the elbow, showing for the first time the tenderness of a mother. "But I fear you've misunderstood your role in things. For all your pantomime of a hero, you simply lack the teeth of one. You were trained as a soldat—but you are no warrior. Not like Tark. You haven't experienced what is needed to rise above yourself and make a change in the world that will be remembered."

Brann grimaced. "You mean I haven't won any real battles?"

Ula shook her head sympathetically. "You haven't lost any."

She let this hang in the air between them, then, turning to leave, left Brann with a final parting wisdom. "Tark's armored hide is immune to any weapon you could bring to bear against him. His scales are a mother's pride, and the pride of his race entire. But I hope you remember well, when the time comes, these words I impart: it is that very pride that will be is undoing."

Ula departed, leaving Brann to find his own way back. "I have nothing more to say on the matter. Be well on your journey."

36. The Promise

Nes was waiting for Brann upon his return, the cave behind him lit by candlelight within, as well as the vibrant sounds of dinner and conversation. He held up his holoscreen, a message illuminating his face in the dim light of the Warrens, sunlight no longer streaming down upon them from the Eye.

"We've just been invited back to the city," he said, sounding less than enthused.

"What?" Brann took the screen from him, scanning the message. It was an official communique from the Director of Entertainment, on behalf of House Geiha. He held the holoscreen up in disbelief. "It's an invitation for Boomer to fight."

"Not just any fight," Nes corrected, taking the holoscreen back. "A challenge for his seat as House Champion. They've lined up his replacement—they're making it official, cutting ties with him. I suppose their story on his being taken hostage by the rest of us terrorists finally ran out, and now they're cutting ties. If he refuses the fight, he forfeits the title by default—if he loses the fight, he loses the title."

"And if he wins the fight?"

Nes puffed on his cig. "You've seen him. The shape he's in. That ain't gonna happen."

Brann didn't let this slide. "You know, for someone who claims to be his oldest friend, you sure give him a lot of shit. I've only known him a few weeks and even I can see how much he loves you—believes in you. Maybe you'd feel less need to smoke so much if you returned the favor once in a while."

Nes drew deep on the cig, the cherry burning up towards his fingers—and held it, his lungs full of smoke. He mused on Brann's words for a second, then:

"You know what, kid?" He blew the smoke out, a long stream of it, sending a farewell cloud up towards the Eye above. Then he let the cigarillo fall, scattering its ashes across the dirt, before crunching it beneath his boot. "You're absolutely right. Nasty habit—think I'll quit."

Brann blinked. "Yeah?"

"Yeah." Nes rubbed his boot into the dirt a bit longer than he needed to, the cig already well doused. "I ain't gonna lie, my life didn't turn out all that great—I never got to retire off the pension that was coming to me, back when I thought Geiha would take care of me, after all the shit I did for them. I never got to see the world for more than a few minutes at a time, beyond the Donnie's peepholes, between stops in cities Boomer insisted we visit for a few more kisses from the fans. I was never a rich man, and though I lied to myself a good long time about it, never an important one either."

Brann saw a softness in Nes he wasn't used to seeing, in this moment—the wrinkles in the engineer's face seemed to smooth themselves out, and he almost threatened a smile. "I fell in with some wacky folks, I ain't gonna lie—but however this all shakes out, you've all made it worthwhile. Boomer most of all. That moron never let a day go by he didn't brew me a cup of his shitty coffee first thing in the morning."

He turned inward, and Brann let Nes collect his thoughts quietly.

"I owe him for that." Nes elbowed Brann. "Thanks for setting me straight, kid. C'mon, food's been ready for a minute."

*

Sliced, roasted meat of pink sheen heaped upon a serving plate passed before Brann; the tender prime rib of some enormous breed of livestock, its fatty juices pooling on the plate beneath. He scarcely had time to fork a slice away from the stack for himself before another serving tray appeared. Glistening, buttery rolls, steaming hot from the oven, speckled with flakes of salt—then, when they too were passed down the table, a bowl of green stalk vegetables, julienne-cut and crispy from being cooked in animal fat, seasoned so liberally Brann could taste their peppery profile just from a whiff. His plate was quickly becoming overcrowded, but not quick enough: next came a heaping dollop of riced appleroot, whipped with cream and chives, melty white cheese blanketing their golden peaks. The precious little space left on his dish would find itself packed with yet another few accoutrements: a pan-fried strip of bright red fish, garnished with a slice of venom-purple citrus fruit; a vibrant orange scoop of crumbly sausage hash, colored by the sweet onions and peppers; marrow-black sauteed mushrooms, soaked through with their savory gravy that spilled out onto the tablecloth.

"You can thank our resident witch for the spread," Zay said with a nudge, directing Brann's attention down the table—the avian was darting back and forth between the kitchen and the cozy little dining space the party occupied, each time returning with a new entree.

"She doesn't talk much, does she?" Gideon asked as politely as he could around a mouthful of meat. "Haven't heard a word since I met you folks."

"Our Grishka is less of the social type, more the caustic element that keeps things lively when we're at risk of getting too comfortable with one another," Emrys replied, taking another heaping tray of crispy veggies from Grishka thankfully. "She finds her own ways of communicating with us in turn, usually through one of her favored pranks."

"Is that why my favorite shampoo went missing from my quarters?" Red asked, looking offended.

"Yes and no," Zay answered, sipping from a tall glass of liquor. "That was me, actually, but only because my shampoo was being replaced for a week straight with empty bottles. Thought I was losing my mind. When I finally got fed up and snuck into your room to steal some, I came back to find my shower stacked to the ceiling with brand new bottles of the stuff."

"What the—" Red started.

"You're welcome to as much as you can carry," Zay guffawed, setting down her glass after tipping it in Grishka's direction. Red's face disappeared behind her hands, concealing her own embarrassed laughter.

"Sounds like you've been host to a Tengu spirit," Gideon nodded.

Emrys perked up at this, excited to learn a new word. "Is that right? A 'Tengu'..."

Brann was confused. "I thought she was a—what'd you call her? A 'wacky-wacky'?"

"'Omahkaiikíí'," Emrys nodded, frowning. "It took me weeks to learn how to pronounce it correctly... Grishka, did you just make that word up to make me think I'd discovered a previously undocumented tribe of witch the day we met?"

Grishka gave an innocent whistle.

"Hell's bells, I've been had," Emrys grumbled, hand going to his temple as if stricken by a sudden migraine.

"Typical tengu mischief. Woodland spirits that take the form of birds," Gideon explained, dragging his knife through another buttery slice of roast. "Often live on the fringes of society, never too close, never too far. They enjoy the company of others insofar as they can steal from or fool about with them."

"That's our Grishka to the letter," Hawkshaw chuckled from his private table, polishing his pistols while everyone ate. "Long as I've been at the Outpost, she's stopped in once a full moon or so just to poke up some mischief with the locals. Singlehandedly kept me from committing murder when one troublesome fella was picking a fight with the barkeep—a whiff of some of that pixie dust she keeps in her pouch, the dude couldn't see through all the mushrooms growing out of his face."

"Holy shit," Zay breathed.

"Oh, he was fine," Hawkshaw said, waving away the fearful looks his story prompted. "Granted, he spent all of the next day getting his face plucked by the local porter, poor bastard. After that, though, he was nothing short of a model customer."

"Serves me right for thinking I'd already divined everything there was to know about our mysterious matron," Emrys said, grinning sheepishly. Grishka set another plate in front of him, her beak digging affectionately into his collar.

Brann chuckled to himself, and Zay took notice.

"What?"

Brann tapped at his chest. "I had a little pin," he said, "My corpsman pin. Supposed to identify me on the field. Went missing the first day we met her. Still haven't been able to find it."

"You know what, I bet she's the reason why I haven't been able to find a bag of those oatsnacks I like back on the ship for a hot minute," Boomer reasoned, wagging his fork in Grishka's direction from his seat next to Zay.

Zay shook her head. "No, that was also me."

"What? Why?"

She took another sip, her expression blank. "Because I don't like you."

The table quieted a moment before breaking into laughter, Boomer looping an arm around Zay's neck, pretending to strangle her. After the noise lulled, Brann took an opportunity to redirect, turning to Gideon. "Are you joining us when we fly back to Barrier City?"

Gideon swallowed, setting down his knife and fork, his smile fading. "I've a reckoning of my own to bring to bear with my brother, but no. Respectfully, this is not my fight, and I believe I'd be more hindrance than help when the time for you to face him comes."

"You don't think we can win?"

"I think it's less a matter of winning," Gideon said, not making eye contact, "More a matter of understanding."

Brann set down his own utensils. "Ula said the same thing to me." He leaned back, arms crossed. "What is it we don't understand about Tark? I feel like I've gotten a pretty good read on him, all things considered."

Gideon was once more in the unfortunate position of having to defend his brother. "He has left you alive more than once. My brother has never been shy about bloodshed. I believe, in his own way, he's extended you and your friends a kind of mercy—why, I cannot say. But, for the time being anyway, it seems he stands to benefit little from your death."

"Yeah, he'd rather have an angry mob do the work for him," Hawkshaw interjected bitterly, slapping his pistol's slide back into place.

"Perhaps I'm being unclear. Let me try this from another angle." Gideon shifted in his seat, claws tapping on the table. "Have you considered the possibility, however remote it may be, that your goals and his may not be so at odds with one another as you might think?"

"Not if his goal is to kill himself," Brann said sarcastically.

"Is it a matter of killing him?" Gideon tilted his head. "Or a matter of removing him from power?"

"Why would he want to resign as Geiha's Marshal?" Brann frowned. "With as much power as he controls? Doesn't make sense."

"You're right, it doesn't. Because we kuaneach cannot, as a matter of principle, ever abandon our post."

Nestor, who had been quietly nursing a humble lowball glass, swirled the amber liquid under his nose. "Only death or the highest authority in their chain of command can release them from service."

"But Tark is the Marshal," Brann said. "He is the highest authority in Geiha."

Gideon's brow raised.

Brann was beginning to see the full picture. "So. No one to release him from his service, he's stuck at the head of his House, even if he no longer wants to be..."

"As Marshal, he cannot act or vote to act directly against his own House, and as a kuaneach, he would not even if it were morally correct to do so. We serve at all costs, to any end. The only exception," Gideon added, almost as an afterthought, "Is when we are in a position where we are asked to take up arms against our forebears."

Nes tipped back his whiskey, scoffing into the glass. "You wanna ask dear old mom if she wants to hitch a ride with us in your place?"

"She would not obey. Besides—she may not have to."

Nes paused, mid-sip. "Meaning?"

Gideon folded his clawed hands together. "As far back as I can remember, Tark has always been fascinated with the stories about our grandfather. A great kuaneach, one of the most revered in our history. Even before the Arbitration Wars, he led countless campaigns not just in the name of the Houses, but on behalf of all manner of tribes and peoples who lived under tyranny. A great hero, he was—Rigel, the Diamant."

"Rigel?" Brann and Emrys exchanged looks. "That was the name on the plaque—"

"—The plaque I nearly lost an arm to, yes, glad we all made the connection." Hawkshaw was putting away his tools now, both pistols practically glistening in the candlelight. "Apparently the only other name worth mentioning in the dedication besides Geiha and the other Houses themselves."

"He disappeared shortly after the wars ended," Gideon nodded. "This was a matter of great concern to Tark—he had always hoped to meet our predecessor. All the Roost held firm to the belief that Rigel would be the latest kuaneach to walk the Ascendent's Path."

"What does that mean?" Brann asked.

But Gideon had already set to finishing his plate. "Another time, perhaps, as this will not help you in your cause. Suffice to say, Tark has only ever had one clear vision for himself: living up to Rigel's legacy. I never considered myself so vain."

"Clearly not," Red said, regarding the polished white-gold scales of their host with a sideways glance as she passed Wolf a huge slice of meat from her plate, the lycan snapping it up in a nanosecond.

"Oh, you're admiring them?" Gideon winked at Red, flexing his arm—the gold tips of his scales glimmered in the candlelight. "Speaking of vain, we were two peas in a pod, once upon a time—Tark's scales were as brilliant as my own, in his own way. When we became acolytes together, I'd find him smearing ash and ink on himself to mute the brighter colors, make himself less of a target to the endless cruelty. One less taunt the other trainees could attack him with, I suppose. Not me, however—I always polished my scales with pride."

"You mean we coulda been eating like this the whole time back on the ship?" Boomer said incredulously, ignoring Gideon's reminiscing entirely and spooning himself another heaping pile of hash. "What do I pay you people for, anyway?"

"You don't pay us," Zay clapped back. "Haven't heard a whisper on a regular paycheck, let alone all that backpay you owe me for my last ship."

Boomer was mortified, hunching low, his mouth already crammed full as he mumbled. "Ah'll 'et around to it, o'ay..?"

"If you don't mind, Gideon, I'm gonna set light to that firepit I saw out front," Nes declared as he stood from his seat, clean plate and whiskey in hand. "Anyone who would like to join me to work out the details of our next flight, be my guest."

"There's usually some beer in the icebox, help yourselves—I never cared for it, kuaneachs make for lousy brewmasters." Gideon stood as well, bowing to the table. "I'll leave you all to it. I'm owed a proper thrashing back at Temple before bed—I did not leave on the best of terms after my last visit, it's time I took my licks for that."

"Oh, Red here knows a thing or two about not getting on with mom," Zay joked, elbowing Red, who rolled her eyes in return.

*

Brann had chosen to accompany Nes outside, helping to pass him blocks of firewood from the nearby stack as the older engineer set to sparking the embers. "Gideon may be onto something," he said, handing off one last split log before dusting off his hands. "About Tark, I mean."

"And how's that?" Nes asked, gently coaxing the flames to life, still tasting at the rim of his lowball glass.

"After his fight with Boomer, he pulled back. Said he was done chasing us for the time being. But the Uhlen kept coming, they were on us the very next day with that dropship."

"Your point?" Nes wasn't impressed.

"Well." Brann sat back on a rock, leaning forward to watch Nes work. "Maybe they're not on the same page as Tark. They could have disagreed about letting us go, came after us on their own, without his saying so. Maybe they aren't as loyal to him as they seem."

"Dissent among the ranks. You're thinking Tark's losing his grip on the wheel." Nes shook his head, sitting back as well, the flames beginning to climb higher on their own now. "Doubt it. Not saying you're wrong, in fact I'd like to think you're right, kid—but in all my years, since I first met him, the Marshal has never been anything but in total control of things. I'd have a hard time imagining what kind of authority would be needed to turn his own men against him."

Brann pondered this for a moment. "Didn't take much for me," he offered.

Nes didn't reply, just giving a half-shrug—everyone else had begun filtering out of the cave, cutting their conversation short.

"Drink, and be merry!" Boomer was saying in an affected accent, handing out corked beers, arms full of clinking bottles. "For tomorrow we ride to victory!"

"The fight is in three days," Nes corrected.

"Okay, in three days, we ride to victory!"

Red took two bottles, handing them both to Wolf. "Actually, from here, it'll take approximately that long to reach Barrier City, we'll still have to leave early tomorrow to make it in time."

Boomer exhaled long and loud in resignation, sitting himself on a rock. "Alright, fine, tomorrow we start riding for roughly three days to victory, happy?"

"Hey, can I have one?" Hawkshaw asked, reaching towards Boomer for a beer.

"Sure," Zay answered, flicking her cork at Hawkshaw in reply, bouncing it off his face. She and Red fell together, cackling at the automaton's blank expression.

"When you fall asleep tonight, I'm gonna taser you and leave you behind when we fly off," Hawkshaw grumbled, wiping flecks of beer foam from his faceplates.

"Yeah, it'll be the only way you ever fly my ship without me," Zay said between laughs, trying to catch her breath. "Take your shot."

"The Donnie is still my ship, thanks very much," Nes said quietly, taking a swig of beer.

"Catch!" Boomer lashed out an arm, and Brann had a split second to grab the bottle out of the air. "Can I say something without you all making fun of me?" He said, eyeing the bottle apprehensively.

"You've never had beer." Boomer shook his head. "Unacceptable. I'm withdrawing my support for House Geiha, they have no respect for their troops."

"Now, now, folks, let's not be so quick to mock the boy, he's barely old enough to have had a chance to try the stuff, anyway," Emrys scolded, wagging his fingers at the group. He kneeled down next to Brann, taking the bottle from him gently. "Now, son, pay close attention—what you're gonna want to do is take the cork out first..."

Brann shoved the professor bodily, another wave of laughter erupting around them. "I hate all of you."

Emrys caught himself on the backhand, tilting his hat back into place before it fell off. "See, because that's what keeps the liquid in the bottle—"

"Well now look at this!" Hawkshaw spoke up, head turned back to look at the cave. Brann followed suit, and the circle was a symphony of whistles and catcalls: Grishka had stepped out, still in hybrid form, wearing a bright lavender sundress that practically glowed against her dark feathers. The avian woman spun about, showing off the frills, giving a small curtsy— a self-conscious smile tickled at the corners of her beak, and Brann realized this may have been the first time she'd ever felt comfortable enough to try wearing anything else besides her usual alchemist's garb.

"Looking sharp, girl!" Zay clapped, nudging Red. "And you said she could never pull off people's clothes.

"How dare you!" Red said indignantly, mouth agape, though she clapped as well. "I never said..."

"Whose dress is this, Grishka?" Hawkshaw asked, taking a beer from Boomer to offer it to the witch.

"Ula." Grishka sat cross-legged on a rock, nearly splitting the skirt in the process, apparently unfamiliar with how such clothing was meant to be worn. "She give, biggum gift, no more wear. I accept."

Red frowned. "But how did Ula give you permission to take it if she's still back at the Temple—"

"We've already established she can be in two places at once, us and our shampoo are living proof of that," Zay said in a hushed voice so as not to embarrass Red, who nonetheless dropped the question immediately, realizing the obvious.

"Wear into city. Look allem pretty for fight." Grishka nodded in self-satisfaction, not bothering to uncork the bottle, instead holding it between her talons as she clacked her beak loudly around the glass neck.

"Speaking of." Nes stood, one hand on his hip, assuming an authoritative stance over the conversation. "We've already given our reply that Boomer will accept the challenge—he'll be going up against an unknown, someone named 'Krieger' who apparently has proven a worthy successor in the eyes of House Geiha's council members. This guy must be worth his salt if they opted for an up-and-comer rather than poach an established fighter from one of the other Houses' circuits."

"Nes, please," Boomer said, holding up a hand. "Undefeated champion, eh? Give me some credit, here, I got this."

Brann could see his words having their desired effect on Nes, who wisely chose not to bring up Boomer's recent bout with Tark. "Be that as it may, we can't all just rent box seats and show up to watch in a stadium full of spectators again—didn't really work out too well last time. They'll be on the lookout for us before we even step foot in the city."

"Boomer has to go to the fight, that much is obvious." Hawkshaw gestured to himself and Zay. "The harlot and I will take the Donnie, park it outside the city, find another way in—question is," He continued, ignoring the punches raining down against his shoulder as he fended off Zay, "Who goes with Boomer and who goes with us? We'll be splitting up, no way around that."

"We'll divide into threes; Team A goes to the fight with Boomer to get him out if things go sideways, Team B finds their way into the archives, Team C stays with the ship and facilitates our escape from the city—"

"I'm Team B," Boomer held up a hand. "B for 'Boomer!'"

"You can't be Team B," Nes argued, "You're the one fighting, idiot."

"B for 'Boomer,'" Boomer repeated, chugging on his beer.

"Alright, fine, Team A goes to the archives—"

Boomer snapped his fingers, jaw dropping. "A for 'Archives!'"

"—And Team B goes to the fight," Nes spoke over Boomer, ignoring him. "Team C clears our exit. If memory serves, Grishka was human at the last fight—so they'll be expecting her in human form." Nes pointed between her and Boomer. "She goes with him, looking just like she does right now. Team B."

"I'll wager that save Emrys, none of you have much experience navigating a library catalogue, let alone an entire city's historical archives," Red offered. "The two of us will be Team A. My love, I'm afraid there's no disguise that would keep you from drawing unwanted attention even if you hadn't had your face plastered all over the holonet." She turned to Wolf, stroking beneath his chin to placate him, his ears drooping. "You'll go with Team C, stay outside the city walls."

"That's not fair..."

Only Brann and Red understood these words as Wolf whined in protest, and Nes continued. "So, Team C is a lock. Neither Her Ladyship nor Emrys knows the palace as well as I do, and I doubt they've done any serious remodeling since I was there, so I'll be with them in case there's any stubborn electronic security needs disabling."

"Which just leaves me," Brann said. "Team B, of course. Tark will be at the fight, that's my chance to get to him."

Everyone went silent. Brann looked around the circle, everyone refusing eye contact. "What?"

Nes sighed. "Kid, we know you mean well, but...you just aren't ready to take him on alone. Hell, I wouldn't even put us all against him as a group. Besides that, the only way we're gonna have a chance at clearing our names is finding what we can in those archives that'll help us expose his and Geiha's crimes, and getting out of the city before we're caught."

Brann shook his head. "So, we wait until we have what we need, then confront Tark with it while he's still in the city with us. I don't understand the problem with that."

"Who's to say he won't just burn the records once we put them in front of his face?" Nes shook his head. "We can't trust him, not even to blackmail him. No, we get out of Barrier City, take the evidence to the other Houses, show the world, plaster it all over the holonet. No negotiating, no confrontation. We do it behind his back so he has no way to suppress it."

"We still have to stop him though, right?" Brann was beginning to unravel, feeling his sense of pride and purpose slip through his fingers as his companions all wilted at his words. "We stop Tark. Okay, fine, we do what we have to do to expose Geiha, then we go back for him after we've cleared our names. It's Tark, it's always been about Tark, hasn't it? He's gotta go down."

"Kid." Nes was the only one maintaining eye contact, not blinking as he shook his head. "It was never about Tark. You and him, that...that's personal. I know it seems—"

"Of course it's personal." Brann was beginning to tremble, feeling a rising frustration strangle his words, causing him to stammer. "Me and him, that's—it's personal, but it's still—it can be both, Nes, it's me and it's Lachlan, and it's everyone else he's—"

But Nes just kept shaking his head. "No. We gotta do this the right way. Charging headlong into battle with that? We lose before we even get a shot at showing the world who he is. What they've done. The only way Tark goes down, I mean *really* goes down, is if we get out without getting caught."

"You said it yourself, Nes," Brann persisted, on his feet now. "Only thing stops a kuaneach is death. He won't stop—he puts himself up for auction, another House takes him in, he just goes on putting more young recruits to death, brainwashing them and making them die for his bullshit cause—"

"That's just...the way the world works." Nes took a seat on the rock next to Brann's, gesturing for the young man to sit back down. "C'mon, kid, this is life. There's always someone in charge, someone who doesn't deserve to be, deciding when youth go off and die on their say-so. That's not gonna change with you and Tark."

"Bullshit." Brann crossed his arms, refusing to sit. He looked around at everyone in disbelief. "Bullshit. Bullshit! I don't wanna hear that, that's no excuse. House Geiha needs to be taken apart, they can't be allowed to get away with what they've done, and neither can Tark. It all goes away."

"Then what?" Zay stood as well, meeting Brann at eye level. "We go after the other Houses, too? You don't think they've all got skeletons in the closet? You think Geiha is the only House who paid me under the table to do their dirty work? Listen to what Nes is saying, we want the same thing as you—"

"No, you don't want the same thing," Brann interrupted, beginning to pace back and forth. "You don't want the same thing at all. You didn't see what he was like back in Barrier City. You didn't see what he did to Boomer in that ring. He deserves everything bad that he's ever done, every terrible thing he's ever allowed to happen with his blessing, to get shoved right back into his face. Fuck him. Fuck anyone who says otherwise."

"Brann," Boomer spoke up, unusually serious. "If it's about getting your life back, I've got money. Man, I've got all the money in the world, I'll set you up somewhere—"

Brann's shoulder cracked from how hard he lobbed his beer, shattering the unopened bottle across the logs, flames shooting up violently into the night. "I don't want your FUCKING money," he bellowed, feeling his vocal cords tear. "I want TARK! I want his neck on my FUCKING sword."

Wolf was the next on his feet, striding past the campfire, hackles raised—but, despite Brann's expectations, he didn't growl or threaten or snap at him. The werewolf instead buried his great head against Brann's chest, nearly bowling him over—Wolf was trying to comfort Brann, calm him down, sensing the young man holding back tears before Brann even realized he was doing it.

"That can't happen," Hawkshaw said, as sympathetically as he could. "It's just not possible. Not if you want any of us to survive past the next few days."

"We get what we came for, we get out," Red agreed, her eyes wet. "Simple as. There's no time to right every wrong in the world, Brann. There's not enough of *us* for that."

Wolf finally won Brann over, pushing him back down onto his rock. Brann was stunned, his face stinging. He tasted blood in his throat.

"All this time," he whispered. "All the shit you people gave me. Calling me a coward. And in the end, you're all the ones who want to run away."

Nes kneeled beside Brann. "You can hate us, man. You've earned the right. God knows we ain't been kind to you, not always. But believe it or not, we wanna see you do some good in this world." He bumped his fist against Brann's arm. "We wanna see you *live* to do that. Get past Tark. In a few days' time, he'll be history, anyway. He'll be in shackles, on his way to some House Tribunal. We'll still be alive. We'll be here for you, man. Always. And you know what, maybe when time has passed, and you're older, and you're done hating us. Maybe we make it up to you. We all get together, we make a promise to travel the world, help everyone we find needs it. Find a real cause we can affect the outcome of. Be the ones in charge for once in our lives. We be our own House, outside of all the noise, all the bullshit."

"We travel in privileged company, my young friend," Emrys added, taking off his hat. "What we've accomplished, even now, just trying to survive to the next day? Everything we've proven capable of? Nothing short of miracles, in a world that doesn't believe in them, no less. You can take us with you into a better future, find a world for us and everyone like us without the Uhlen and the Tark's and the Burnside Geiha's."

"We can pull every string, ask every favor," said Red. "I squeeze my mother; she relinquishes the throne. We've got time to heal, to make things right—one day, we find the next Tark, stop him on the way up, bring a fleet of corsairs to his doorstep the day of his inauguration."

"I win this fight, which I will," Boomer said cheerfully, "I'm never at risk of being challenged for the title ever again—I'll be immortal! All the money I've got now, can you imagine how much I can put myself up for? What the other Houses will be willing to pay to have me as their Champion? I could ask for anything, and they'd pay it!"

"Anywhere you want to go, the can-opener and I, we'll take you there." Zay punched Hawkshaw once more. "You ever been to another continent? I haven't. We'll fly across the ocean if you want, somewhere they've never heard of Geiha or Tark. Shit, I hear they don't even have the Great Houses across the sea."

Hawkshaw flipped Zay the bird. "Pretty sure she's full of shit, but, she's right about one thing. I could be persuaded to be your pilot, assuming you actually let me fly the goddamn ship by myself."

"I see the world," Grishka nodded excitedly, still holding her corked beer. "You give dresses? Snacks? I go allem places, yes yes."

Nes placed a hand on Brann's knee, shaking it. "All of that? That's painting a picture of a pretty bright future, kid. We live a long time, we carry the truth, walking together until we can't walk anymore. Let us give that to you. Let that be us."

Wolf spoke now, directly into Brann's ear. The only one who could hear and understand it. "Is Tark worth more to you than us?"

Brann didn't answer. Not with his words, anyway. Wiping his face of tears, he stood, tightening his swordbelt. Checking the weapon was straight on his back, he turned his back on the circle, leaving the fire behind him as he walked off into the Warrens, back towards the Eye. Towards the ship.

He walked alone tonight. He could find his way back to the Donnie. Tonight, Brann didn't need comfort. He needed to be right.

Tark needed to die.

37. The Rain

At some point between stepping out of the Eye and boarding the Donnie, Brann experienced an interruption of service in his eyesight.

Within the breath of a second later, he found himself blinking away venomous spots of color, the world fading back into existence around him. A kaleidoscope folded in on itself across his eyes until the black creases began to vanish, revealing a wood plank ceiling. He was spread-eagled, on his back, with no memory of how he'd gotten here—wherever here was—and he tasted gunpowder. There was a lantern on the wall, casting its flickering orange glow across the wood, and the muted sound of rain falling on the roof outside.

"Finally awake, eh? On your feet, then, soldat," a voice slurred from beyond his peripheral vision.

Brann willed himself to sit up, the effort taking enormous strength of mind—tiny shocks lanced through his limbs, and the gunpowder taste worsened. He recognized the symptoms from his training: someone had electrocuted him, knocked him out. His forearms dragged on old, damp wood—a cabin, of sorts, the walls covered in raggedy pelts of small wildlife. The oil lantern burned above an unlit fireplace, which dripped black tar from within, the rain from above soaking its soot-covered bricks.

The voice mumbled something else Brann couldn't understand— he turned, a dozy hand slapping itself across his face, fingers tingling. The voice came from a sorry looking man, unkempt and bedraggled, wearing furs that could have been pulled from the very walls of the cabin. "Up and attem, boy," the man was saying around a gooseneck bottle he tipped against his lips, soaking his beard with wine.

"Give it back," Brann groaned, head pulsing with the flittering vestiges of electrocution—the man held a stun baton in one hand, Brann's sword in the other.

The wino chuckled, shaking his head and gulping down more of that bottle. "Nah. Got a job for you. Get up, c'mon ya daisyhead."

A scream—a woman, her voice splitting the air in the distance, snapping Brann back to reality. He looked to the door, feeling a chill, and the scream stopped suddenly.

"What was that?"

The bottle clunked against a rickety table, the man sitting on a stool, the soft wood squeaking and threatening to fall apart any moment. "That," the drunk man said, supping at his lips to collect the saliva pooling there, "Is your problem now."

Another scream, this one cut short much sooner, then another—the sound of a host of people, villagers all crying out in fear and pain, the sound mixing with the stormy atmosphere. "You can call me 'Mayor,' even though—well, technically we don't have a mayor," Mayor said thoughtfully, ignoring the building sounds of terror outside the cabin. "If we did, I'd be it. So, that's what you can call me. And you are trespassing, which means I get to take you prisoner. And around here—" He lifted the bottle once more, barely even making it into his mouth, a healthy splash of wine staining his furs. "—Prisoners get put to work. So, get to work."

"Work how?" The screams were closer now. Brann stood shakily to his feet, praying his knees wouldn't buckle, legs feeling as if they'd been asleep for days. "Doing what? What is that out there, where am I? You can't just kidnap people man, I'm no trespasser."

Mayor sucked his tongue, his bleary eyes staring at Brann from within red, puffy sockets. He reached into his furs, pulling out an antique holoscreen, cracked and worn. He thumbed it on and tossed it onto the table with a clatter—and through the spiderwebbed polyglass, Brann saw his own face staring back at him, his recruit photograph. An electronic wanted poster, pulled from Geiha's netbanks.

"You're a runaway, and a criminal. You step foot anywhere outside Barrier City, you're trespassing. Decent bounty, too—just posted today. Lucky me, I was out having a walk beneath the clouds, taking a piss, and there you were—wandering like a lost lamb."

"I wasn't lost, I'm with people, my friends," Brann argued, stepping towards Mayor, reaching towards his sword. "Give that back and let me go, I don't have time for whatever this shit is—"

The stun baton crackled to life, pointing itself in Brann's direction. Mayor may have been totally shitfaced drunk, but that didn't seem to hamper his reflexes much. "Step back. Slowly."

Brann lowered his arm, narrowing his eyes defiantly, taking a half-step back. "That's my sword." The screams were drawing ever closer, the sound of glass shattering, wood crashing. "And from the sound of things, you don't need a prisoner—you need help. Some kind of local wildlife? You need someone combat worthy? Yeah, okay, I'll help, if it means letting me go. Just give me back my sword."

Mayor laughed, a wheezing, wet noise—he was drinking himself into an early grave, by the look and sound of him. He dumped the baton on the table, filling his hand with the wine bottle in its place. "That thing," he said, pointing at the door behind him, "Has been coming after us. Day after day. For weeks. Came up from the south—and every night, it takes. Started with one. One at a time, yeah? Little old lady at the well, one evening, just—" Mayor snapped his fingers. "Gone, just like that. Then, two, then four. Now, these past few nights, it just..."

He shook his head, averting his eyes from Brann, sucking at his teeth. Mayor seemed perpetually on the verge of tears, though they never came. "These are good, decent folks. Come up to the fringe of the wilds, looking for solace. Peace from the hustle and bustle of city life, back where the Houses take all our money, have all the power, all the say. What we eat. Tell us what to wear, how to act, what medicine to take." He looked back to Brann, shaking his head. "No man knows better than the man who knows himself. All we wanted was to be left alone. Then, all the holonews is saying hey, Geiha's Champion, he's gone rogue—and there's terrorists roaming free, and then days later there's monsters taking our babies, our mothers, and our whole world is ending. Not enough of us left to stop what's out there, now, and it knows it."

Brann held up his arms passively. "Okay. I'm sure you're fine people, whatever—but if you let me go, I can bring back my friends, we can help you. There's nothing out there we can't handle, you just gotta show some trust, yeah? I'm not a criminal. I'm just someone like you, someone who knew best for himself. We all did. We all just want to help where we can."

There was a loud pop, then another—gunshots, and a horrible wailing noise, something inhuman and primal. It was closer than ever, now, just outside the door. Mayor leaned back on his stool, not bothering to even turn around, his back to that door as if he couldn't be bothered by what was coming.

"You know how you coulda saved this place?" Mayor was nodding, breaths coming short and labored now, the drunken man stricken with fatal dread. He'd accepted his fate well before Brann had ever woken up. "You showed up just a couple days ago, even—I claim your bounty, I pay to take all these people away, far away from here. Doesn't matter now. You're too late to help, too late to be worth anything to bargain with. Only thing you're good for now is..." He trailed off, the words dying on his lips. There was a shadow at the window, and Brann smelled a familiar, sickly sweetness, bile and perfume.

"Let us help," Brann repeated urgently, eyes darting between the Mayor and the door behind him. "Give me the sword. Take me back to my ship, my friends will be waiting for me there. There's still time, if you just cut the shit and stop crying."

Mayor seemed slightly taken back by this. He looked to the sword in one hand, the bottle in the other, the stun baton on the table. Outside, everything had gone quiet, save for the gentle patter of rain on the wooden roof.

"How about that," he chuckled, an abysmal, strangled sound. "Kid's got some spit after all."

Mayor stood, wobbly, uncertainly, regarding Brann with fresh eyes—

The cabin exploded inwards in a wall of flesh and shattered logs, a horrible scream catching in Mayor's chest as a giant hand snatched him up like a doll, bursting his ripe flesh in a deluge of steaming blood that splashed across everything, including Brann. Then, he was gone, the hand drawn back into the night, the opposite wall of the cabin having been disintegrated, leaving a great, yawning hole for the rain to pour in.

The black curtains of hair appeared first, the long, sticky locks dragging through the pooling blood and debris. A ghoulish visage within, an evil, drawn smile around black gums and blunted teeth, the tapering skull of the creature gored and flayed open with rot. Sugary ammonia filled Brann's nostrils. Spindly arms, bent at all the wrong angles, impossibly jointed, creaked and rolled forward, tugging the massive corpse into the cabin. Brann didn't even realize he was stepping away from it until his back hit the wall, the only exit being filled by the creature's head and shoulders.

It had found him.

The Beast of Lachlan craned its neck against the natural curve of its spine, the head suspended only a few feet above ground level, meeting Brann's height. Lidless, rotten eyes, streaked with blood and rainwater, fixed themselves with a manic joy on the young Lachlanite—the last of its coveted flesh, alone at last. It wanted to take its time, savor this moment, relish the scent of fear in the air as it snorted and huffed like some hound at the hunt.

Brann turned away, avoiding direct eye contact—no more than a few feet away, his sword lay, a few disembodied fingers still curling at its hilt. The Beast of Lachlan dragged itself forward, its massive hand bringing itself down with unholy irony, directly on top of the sword.

He was back in the mines, that exdead Corpse pursuing him, daring him to break, to sob, or run, or rage. Brann's upper lip twitched in disgust— he didn't dare give this thing the satisfaction. If he showed fear, he was dead, if he tried to fight, he was dead—his only hope of surviving a few seconds longer was to deny the Beast. Neglect its desires. Keep his head, his heart, in check.

Brann didn't make eye contact again, even as that head drifted closer, his vision filling with the unfocused impression of those glaring eyes, wide and crazed. He let his arms slowly go to his sides, relaxing them, and let himself slide down the wall—slowly, carefully, but deliberately, as if he were just having himself a nice sit. No trouble, no cause for alarm. Brann sat against that wall, head tilted away from the freakish chimera, not paying it any mind. It didn't deserve his respect, or his fear.

The Beast hissed, the rising screech in its throat a mutant amalgamation of the dying gasps of hundreds of humans, all melded into its decaying mass. It demanded submission. A hand slammed against the wall above Brann's head, sending a shower of wooden splinters down on him. Brann barely batted an eye.

"You," He said quietly, just above a whisper, keeping his voice measured and unbothered. "You are just...so fucking boring."

Brann refused to die scared. The Beast refused to take him without tasting his fear. Decades of frustrated desires, its purpose held at bay, the screeching became unbearably loud now, its fleshy fingers scratching at the floor until it carved great, bleeding grooves in them. All of Lachlan had yielded to its rot, and now this one, this single, defiant little scab, would not surrender.

The fingers of Brann's left hand tickled at something cold, metallic. He carefully clasped his hand around it—the stun baton, tossed from the table, coming to rest beside him.

There was a flutter of wings beyond the collapsed wall, a dark blur streaking past in a quiet flash of lightning, the thunder distant and delayed. A raven's feather drifted past the doorway, buoyed on the breeze.

"I'm done with you."

Brann snarled, two-handing the baton, driving its crackling tip directly into that skull's exposed nasal cavity—the blue light of plasma flashed behind its cloudy sclera, and the Beast wailed, snapping back and away from Brann, clawing at its own face.

The sword was in Brann's hands in a second—the massive corpse thrashed about, demolishing the entire cabin around him in moments, and the young man scarcely rolled out of the way of its death throes before being crushed—he was outside, in the rain and night, coming up onto his feet amidst a row of pulverized homes just like the one he'd escaped. One cabin still stood, and on its roof, a lone figure stood, raising her autocannon and opening fire on the Beast, a searing beam of tracer rounds whizzing over Brann's head. Zay held the weapon close to her chest, under her arm, legs stanced wide to steady herself, teeth gritted behind the wet spikes of hair plastered against her face.

The Beast rolled itself over, onto its belly, attempting to draw itself up to height—but Zay hadn't come alone. A flash of silver, a revving of a handsaw, and both the Beast's achilles tendons were sliced open before it could fully stand, prompting another furious scream. Red and Nes darted back into the rain, disappearing into the shadows, and in their place, Wolf charged forth, leaping up to bring his spear down through the Beast's pallid torso. Before it had a chance to plant its hands and shake Wolf off its back, he'd already dislodged himself, taking care to twist the spear as he went—black muck oozed forth, spluttering disgustingly in a heap beneath the corpse.

Brann raised his own blade, ready to charge in—but a hand kept him back. Boomer strode past, leaving Brann a carefree wink as he tossed his soaked mane out of his eyes—bruised, but not beaten, the horseman sprinted forward faster than Brann had ever seen him move. Boomer body-slammed the wrong side of the Beast's elbow, kicking his legs out for extra power as he went. The joint snapped sickeningly, the arm caving in, and the Beast was left with one good limb to hold itself aloft. It lashed out, its good arm swinging wide, hand reaching out to snatch up Boomer—

—And connected with air, Boomer easily sidestepping it, leaving behind a shadow of himself. Through the rain, Brann could see sparkling dust showering down upon the Beast, and every time it tried to make a grab for Boomer, another illusory copy of him appeared elsewhere. Soon, a dozen identical copies of him surrounded the writhing corpse—and overhead, again, Brann saw Grishka's wings silhouetted against another flash of lightning. The Boomer copies all moved as one, bouncing on their hooves playfully, their thumbs swiping across their snouts to taunt the Beast. Then, once more, they sprinted forward, converging all on one spot where they merged—and a single Boomer, the real one, was airborne in a spinning jump-kick. His broad hoof connected with center-mass, driving that embedded stun baton even deeper into the skull, and with another flash of arcing electricity inside its head the corpse's eyes began to weep black blood.

Again, it rose up, breaking its own spine in wrathful agony, the Beast of Lachlan reaching skyward—then brought its hand down, against and into its own face, peeling away at the remaining rotten flesh that still clung to bone like some tattered mask. The black tendrils of its veins, creeping out across white bone, withered and snaked backwards, retreating beneath its flesh—the baton could not be removed now, it was too deep. For a moment, the Beast tossed its head back and forth, the hair whipping about in the rain—and it swallowed.

The baton crackled beneath its flesh, the weapon sparking within its neck, its throat, slipping down into its belly. The Beast of Lachlan shuddered, static building within, before it erupted in a shower of sparking lightning that etched into its flesh, a blinding display of power—the lightning came from within now, echoing the flashes across the sky above, a raging fulguration made flesh. It breathed in ozone, appearing as if it were about to exhale pure electric destruction—then found itself silenced by the rippling pistolfire tearing across its neck. Soft fleshy decay yielded to Hawkshaw's autopistols, his surgically precise aim puncturing the Beast's throat, its earsplitting cries becoming impotent gurgles. Clutching at its own throat, it regarded the automaton with abject fury, teeth gnashing.

Before the Beast could lash out once more, the ground beneath it began to shimmer, as if liquified, before becoming illuminated in green flames—and from the flames, skeletal hands as big as the Beast's own burst upwards, grasping at those pale limbs, locking them in place tightly.

Stepping into view, Emrys held both fists below his waist, the ectoplasmic fire flowing from his hands into the earth, bridging his body and the realm of the dead beyond—and when his arms raised, so too did more ghostly arms, wrapping themselves all around the pale expanse of the corpse's mass. The white-blue flashes of fulmination were quieted beneath the green fervor of the truly dead, binding the Beast of Lachlan to the earth.

This was their opportunity.

Appearing from the shadows and rain once more, they all marched forward, shoulder to shoulder—Nes, Red, Wolf, and Boomer, weapons and fists at the ready. Red's saber raised, lengthening itself in glorious, bloody sheen. Nestor's handsaw sparked in the rain.

The Beast roared, black wet ooze spewing over its thin, tight lips, those permanently wide eyes darting back and forth between each of its tormentors in turn. They broke off, surrounding the corpse—Zay followed suit, reloading a fresh box mag, her glowing barrel sizzling in the downpour. Grishka perched on Emrys's shoulder, her caws sounding like the gleeful cackles of a hag. Hawkshaw had also reloaded, whistling a cheerful tune as he spun his pistols with pure showmanship. The last to join in was Brann, gripping his own sword, facing the corpse head-on. Surrounding the Beast of Lachlan, all nine members of the *Myrmidon* formed an inverse summoning circle of sorts, intending on sending this soulless aberration back to its grave.

Steel and silver and magic fire grew hot, reflecting the lightning back into the Beast's gaping eyes. The nine companions all chose their cut of meat, and set to carving.

Blooded saber shredded foul breast to ribbons. Lycan spear buried itself deep, over and over, into coiled, dead intestine. Pistol rounds wrote their initials across the Beast's back while high caliber rounds pounded through it, turning the internal skeleton to pulp. Ghostly flame of summoned skeletons twisted limbs, and earth-shaking kicks crushed bone and burst joints. Tendons and cables of muscle flew apart beneath the cursive speech of a handsaw casually dragging itself through thick flesh. A raven took flight, streamers of congealed arteries trailing behind it into the night sky, raining down around the ruined corpse like confetti.

Brann came face to face with the exdead giant, regarding it with the same defiance and disgust as he had back in the cabin. The blackened, hemorrhaged eyes stared back at him, still hungry for their prize: his body and soul.

The former soldat let his sword rest across his shoulder, tapping thoughtfully, as if weighing his options. Brann of Lachlan stared back at the fetid Beast of Lachlan, and laughed softly, making his decision. The corpse's chest was laid bare, its diseased heart spilling out into the mud, spiny flagella of corruption whipping all about in distress.

The parasitic heart, the source of its evil. Brann remembered Emrys's words, that no human weapon could unmake an exdead organism. Truth be told, this dissuaded him little—it wasn't a weapon that would deliver the killing stroke. It was the Beast of Lachlan's very own failure, manifest in human form, taking back the lost dignity of his homeland, of a forgotten people the world had let die.

The Sparrow had returned, holding the blade of his homeland aloft. He brought it down, hard. Again. And again. And again, he stabbed, and stabbed, and twisted, and stabbed. The rotten, fruited flesh ruptured all across its surface, and as it oozed its putrid discharge into the mud, the entire corpse grew still, then silent.

The rain kept falling. Brann pulled his sword free from that false heart, the root of unlife twitching, severed from its host.

Footsteps approached—Brann didn't need to look up to see he'd been joined on either side by his friends, all regarding this enormous wreckage of flesh with mutual distaste. No words were spoken—none need be spoken.

The blurry shapes of the few surviving villagers stepped forward, from beyond the trees, clambering out of ditches. Their faces, smeared with mud and the blood of their dead, regarded this troupe of heroes with a newfound hope. They didn't have anything to give in return—they had nothing left, nothing but their meager lives. So, they wept, silently, thankfully, falling to their knees amidst the wreckage of their village.

There was no celebrating to be had—this apparition didn't deserve the dignity of having its remains danced upon. Brann sheathed his sword, and turned, and walked away. One at a time, his companions followed, falling in line behind their youngest crewmate. Their faces looked to the sky, blinking through the downpour, and they were baptized in the sky's grateful acknowledgment of what they had achieved here tonight. The souls of an entire nation were allowed to rest at long last, silently diminished, seeping into the earth.

And the rain kept falling.

38. The Disguise

The next three days were simultaneously the shortest and longest days of Brann's life.

The Donnie flew, course unaltered, directly across the continent towards Barrier City—no stops, no interruptions, with most of Brann's time spent in his room. Despite their victory over the Beast of Lachlan, there was still a gulf between him and the other members of the crew—and besides that, Brann remained unconvinced he was not right about Tark deserving their attention. Time better served in solitude while mentally preparing for the monumental task at hand, he became intimately acquainted with his ceiling, staring at it while playing imagined conversations in his head wherein the others could finally see his point of view. Naturally, his own internal dialogues became tiresome, and by the evening of the final day Brann was feeling the need for social reconnect.

Stepping barefoot from his bed, wearing only his sleeper tee and bottoms, Brann's hand went to the door latch—then, to his face. He rubbed at his chin and throat. He hadn't shaved recently, or gotten a haircut since he'd left the service, beginning to look nothing short of scruffy. He looked to the mirror on the wall opposite: he couldn't be sure, but it seemed he might have been a few inches taller than when he first boarded the Donnie. A growth phase, perhaps. He didn't feel that much older, but his appearance told a different story. Especially the eyes. There was a storminess to them now—an absence of his usual anxieties, replaced with a bruised sort of determination. The eyes of someone who was forced to grow up quickly in a very short amount of time.

He wasn't sure he liked what he saw in the mirror.

Brann opened his door, and recoiled in surprise, mirroring his visitor's shock. Boomer had been waiting just behind the door, standing silently, presumably about to knock. Too late.

"Jeez, you mind not scaring me like that?" Boomer complained, dusting his perfectly clean blouse off.

"You're the one playing scarecrow in my doorway," Brann countered.

"Well, my doorway, but, yeah, I guess I see how you might..." Boomer coughed, reorienting himself. "We're having a little roundtable in the common area, sort of a final refresher before tomorrow. No one is saying it out loud, but they're all wondering where you're at, so I figured I'd be the brave one and come find you."

Brann saluted. "Thanks for being so courageous. I was heading down for some food anyway."

"Cool." Boomer nodded thoughtfully, shifting his weight about in place.

Brann waited. "All good?"

"Oh, yeah, sure, let's go, I'll walk down with you, obviously." Boomer snapped himself out of it, falling into step with Brann down the passageway. The young human eyed his equine friend the entire time, watching his body language carefully.

"Everything okay? You nervous about the fight tomorrow, maybe?"

"Nervous? Hell no." Boomer snorted, tossing his head. "About a fight, never. I don't get nervous. Never been nervous in my life. Don't know the meaning of the word. If you ever asked me what nervous meant, I don't even think I could—"

"I get it." Brann cut him off. Boomer was definitely nervous. This would be his first time back in the ring since Tark—and there was no way his injuries hadn't left him rattled. Boomer wouldn't say it, but Brann wouldn't push the subject, either. No sense in aggravating things. Brann bumped his elbow against Boomer. "You're gonna kill it tomorrow, champ."

Boomer's response was less than encouraging. "Yeah, I know." No smirk or arrogant comment. His face was expressionless.

That scared Brann more than anything.

*

There was not a circle of their friends awaiting their arrival, unfortunately; it seemed whatever meeting had taken place, it was wrapped up moments ago, with only Nes and Grishka remaining in the galley. Nes was behind the bar, working on a brew of coffee, while Grishka sat in hybrid form on her preferred stool in the corner. Nes set a glass in place, the orange, frothy liquid beginning to fill the glass as he set to clearing away the dirty plates lining the bar, pausing at Brann and Boomer's appearance at the foot of the stairs.

"Ah. Evening gents." He wiped away the spot he'd just cleared with a hand towel, tossing it back over his shoulder. "Just put away a tray of roasted kettlebird, should still be warm if you want some."

"Thanks, but I already had some Nes." Boomer sat at the bar, giving a confused look.

"Clearly, you were the one I was talking to." Nes turned to head back past the kitchen doors, halting to await Brann's answer. "So?"

"Yeah, I'll have a plate." Brann sat beside Boomer, looking down the bar at Grishka. A thought occurred to him. "Can she eat poultry? Would that be like...cannibalism or something?"

Nes looked at Grishka. Then back to Brann. The engineer shook his head, clearly the wrong man to answer such lofty questions, stepping through the doors into the kitchen with his stack of plates.

"Guess I took too long to knock on your door," Boomer said ruefully, looking around at the empty galley.

"You didn't knock at my door."

"Yeah, that's my point." Boomer reached over the bar, taking the steaming glass of coffee off the brewing station just as it finished filling. "He can make himself another," he whispered to Brann with a wink.

"You ever heard of this new guy they're putting you up against?" Brann tried to recall the name. "What was it...Krueger? Krieger?"

Boomer sipped at the drink stiffly. "Nah. Never."

"Can you look him up? His record, I mean, get an idea of what to expect?" Brann reached over the bar, scooping up Nestor's holoscreen, typing in the name to run a search. "Maybe see if you can prepare yourself against whatever style of fighting he uses, or—"

"Hey you mind dropping it?" Boomer slapped the glass down, hard. The steaming contents splashed out, running down his hand. He didn't even flinch at the heat. "Quit giving me shit, I've got it handled. Maybe you all forgot, but I am the best fighter in the world."

Brann clicked off the screen, setting it aside. Clearly, he wasn't the first one to bring up the subject tonight.

Nes appeared a moment later, pushing past the doors with a fresh plate of food in hand. "Oh, sure, help yourself. Dick." He set the plate before Brann, using his hand towel to wipe up Boomer's spill, starting on another glass for himself. "You didn't miss much at our meeting, kid. Mostly just rehashing what we already knew. Though there is one wrinkle we still need to iron out in the plan."

"What's that?" Brann forked at the white meat impassively, trying not to look too wounded by Boomer's attitude.

"You." Nes set the new glass in place, cranking the lever to start the brew. "Three staying behind, three sneaking into the palace without being seen, three going to the fight. Of those three, you're the only one who will be taken into custody on sight, assuming this isn't all a huge trap laid for Boomer—which, given how much face Geiha would stand to lose if it weren't a legitimate fight to replace him, I seriously doubt. So, we need to come up with a convincing enough disguise for you that you won't set off every alarm the moment you step foot in that stadium."

"Not to sound entitled, but, how's that new armor coming along?" Brann took a small bite, realizing only then he had never tasted kettlebird before. "If you've got a new visor for me, I can always just wear that..."

"Nope. They'll be doing ID checks at the security checkpoints, they'll make you lift it. Can't just put a paper bag over it and call it a day, sadly, we need to think a little more creatively than that. Unfortunately—

and this should answer your first question—while I can put together a pretty classy new set of armor in no time at all, I'm a little bit shit at making someone's face look not like their face. Not much tech on board with us right now that could pull something like that off."

Brann pushed the meat around on his plate. "Service entrance? Maintenance passage? I could go in uniform, bluff my way in through some back way."

"Also no." Nes lifted his new cup to Boomer, toasting the horse sarcastically for not stealing this one. "Even if your uniform weren't torn to shit, Geiha has the most sophisticated facial recognition software in the world working for them—if the free cameras flying around the stadium don't catch you, a patrolling security automaton will. Only need one to spot you to bring the whole Nightwatch down on your location in minutes."

A lightning quick flutter of wings was their only warning before Grishka butted her way into the conversation with a single word: "Change!"

"Fuck me," Boomer jolted, spilling his glass again. "Freaky witch stealth moves—"

"We already said that wouldn't work, Grishka," Brann said with a shake of his head. "Not a matter of clothing, it's my face—it's been all over the Geihan news feeds since before I even met any of you, I'm sure."

"Yes. Change." Grishka repeated the word, scooting herself closer on the stool next to Brann. "'Member talk-talk? You me? Allem time, change youself?"

Nes leaned against the bar, eyebrow raised. "This her being all philosophical again, or..?"

"No, I'm pretty sure she means it very literally." Brann pushed aside his plate. "What do you mean, Grishka, like—change my face? How do you expect me to do that?"

"Not face. Alla. Alla you." Grishka wobbled her head, drawing an imaginary outline around his profile with her beak. "Change. No human, no 'night-wash.'"

"It's 'Nightwatch,'" Nes corrected, "And he *is* human, there's not a lot we can do about that. We aren't all shapeshifters like you."

Brann furrowed his brow, tapping on the bar. "Actually, Nes, according to Red, that might not be the case."

"What? Which part?"

Brann leaned in close to Grishka, whispering quietly to her so the other two couldn't hear. Grishka nodded alongside him, giving a squawk of agreement.

"You wanna clue us in on what you're scheming over there, kids?" Boomer craned his neck over, Brann's shoulder, as if he might be able to better see what they were talking about that way.

They broke apart, Grishka dipping under her wing to peruse the pouches on her belt, Brann addressing Nes. "Is Red asleep? We need to bring her in on this."

*

Red stared at Brann, thoroughly perplexed. Her arms were crossed, fingers tapping against her elbow as she tried to process what she'd just been presented with, the five of them standing in the passageway outside her quarters.

"I suppose it's *possible*," she finally admitted, sounding reluctant to do so. "Though such a thing would be beyond my abilities; in fact, it could be considered a recusant act of dark magic among my kind—"

"We're not asking if you can do it, only if it were possible," Brann assured her, pointing a thumb to Grishka beside him. "She'll be the one mixing up a solution; that is, as long as you don't believe using my blood for that sort of thing would have any negative side effects—"

"I didn't say that," Red cautioned.

"I dunno about any of this," Nes said, the practical-minded man shaking his head. "With all you've been through? Treating your body that way, with that kind of experimental magic? I'm starting to like that bag-on-the-head idea a lot more now—"

"I'm still not even fully sure you aren't at risk of keeling over on us," Red continued, "Let alone what might happen should we attempt to exacerbate your condition. Lycanthropy is an exceptionally rare outcome on the other side of a dangerous curse, introducing other witchcrafts into the mix to deliberately provoke an as-of-yet unproven kind of reaction—"

"I think it's a great idea, let's go for it," Boomer said confidently, resting his arm on Brann's shoulder. "Favor the bold, says I, let fortune take care of the rest."

Nes shot Boomer a disapproving look, quietly muttering how incorrect that phrasing was, while Brann spoke up on his own behalf. "Whatever the worst that could happen to me is, I'm pretty sure I've already come through to the other side of it. I'm not afraid of what 'could' go wrong if we try this, I'm afraid of what 'will' go wrong if we don't. So, it's my decision—if this is something we can do, then let's do it. That's final."

Nes and Red exchanged doubtful looks, neither of them fully on board. Still, the engineer sighed, pointing down the passageway. "Worker's barracks are this way—let's use their showers. In case this makes a mess."

Grishka bobbed her head in excitement, the heavy pouch in her beak jostling about.

*

"How long is it gonna last?" Nes called back over his shoulder, his voice echoing about the tiled walls, back turned to the open shower stalls.

"She says until I 'take it off,' whatever that means," Brann called back, having occupied one such stall, his clothes draping themselves over the top of the divider as he stripped. "Think it's a mental thing, or maybe there's an antidote she'll give me or something, I don't know."

"Oh, that's reassuring." Nes and Red stared at one another, the latter looking a nervous wreck, biting at her knuckles. "Just so you know, if you spontaneously combust all over the place, you're cleaning your own damn self up."

"Deal." Brann's hand reached out from the shower stall, palm spread open, awaiting Grishka's offering. The witch had measured together a small sample of Brann's blood and several of her innominate powders in a slender vial, dropping the mixture into Brann's outstretched hand unceremoniously, perched on the shower rod overhead in raven form.

"Hey, careful," Brann said nervously, worried he might drop the vial. He leaned out partways, uncorking the solution and tipping it towards his companions. "To your health," he joked.

"How about we drink to yours, instead." Nes wrung his hands together, exhaling towards the ceiling. "Such a *dumb* idea."

But Brann had already downed the whole thing, giving a shudder at the taste. "Waugh. Gnarly." He disappeared back into his shower stall, drawing the curtain closed, and the wait began.

Boomer inched his way across the tiles, held back by a cautioning hand from Red. Nes gave it a few moments, the sound of labored breathing and pained grunts coming from the stall. "You okay in there?" He eventually asked. "Need anything? Water? An exorcist?"

"Fine," was Brann's curt reply, though the sound of flesh crackling and joints popping were growing louder, more disgusting—Red held a hand in front of her mouth, fighting down the urge to retch. Boomer just stared, slack-jawed, mildly entertained by all of this.

"Ow. OW, shit!" One mighty crack, then another, cartilage and tendons snapping into a new configuration—Nes kept his eye on Grishka, staring down into Brann's stall from her perch with great interest. If she wasn't sounding the alarm, then he wouldn't either. "That sounded comfortable," Nes joked, loud enough for Brann to hear.

"Yeah, those were the two big ones. Ow. Okay—I think I'm done." A pause, the shuffling of a body moving about within the stall; a hollow sort of clacking sound. "Yeah, all done." Brann's clothes were tugged off the divider as he set to redressing himself. Then, a stretch of silence—

presumably, he was staring at himself in the mirror. "God, this is so goddamn *freaky*," he breathed loudly.

"You gonna show the class, or should we come in and rescue you?"

"No, just—give me a second." More silence, the seconds ticking by. Whatever had happened to Brann, it needed time for him to come to terms with it.

"Don't laugh," he eventually declared after a long sigh, sounding calm but deathly serious.

"No promises," Nes shot back, Red taking a deep breath to prepare herself.

The shower curtain was pulled back, and Brann stepped into full view, presenting himself for appraisal. "Verdict?" He asked.

The three onlookers stood, slack-jawed, and Nes couldn't help but snort before clapping a hand over his mouth. Red was mystified, leaning forward and squinting, as if trying to bring Brann into better focus. Boomer, eyes as big as dinner plates, raised an accusing finger.

"Who *are* you?! What have you done with Brann?!"

39. The Ingress

From his vantage point in the lifeboat, staring out the porthole window, Brann got his first good look at Barrier City for the first time in his life from above. Growing up within its walls, he always imagined them to be so high—now, the walls encircling the city seemed anything but tall, barely meeting the heights of the single-story buildings. He mentally traced his footsteps back from the airfield to the south back around the curve of the river, towards the palace, which was unsurprisingly the most impressive landmark: bronzed rooftops, all domes and pillars, nestled at the highest elevation within the city behind its own surrounding walls. While Brann could see the city stretch on towards the horizon, the morning sun glinting off the windows of the taller apartment buildings, trying to spot other familiar points of interest just became a jumbled mess in his mind—from up here, descending from the cloud layer, it all just looked like a big sprawl of chaos.

"Huh."

Sitting across from him, Grishka and Boomer held hands as if they were a couple attending a gala, dressed in matching outfits—she in her gifted sundress, he in an open-necked silk shirt, challenging Grishka's lavender getup for sheer vibrancy.

"What's up? Happy to be home?" Boomer asked.

Brann shook his head. "No. Just—never seen the city like this before. Looks like it happened by accident. I always imagined it would be more..."

"Impressive?" Boomer looked out the window as well. "Most cities all look the same, unless you're Mongillo or something. You humans aren't really the best urban planners."

The lifeboat circled the city on its descent, and for a brief moment, Brann could spot the Donnie, its shiny hull reflecting the sun in a tiny pinprick of light—the ship was making its own descent, towards the vastness of the red clay plains to the north of the city. He couldn't see it land before the lifeboat turned away once more, but he caught a glimpse of Taree

Mountain: the only geography visible outside of Geiha from within its walls, its smooth slopes ramping up away from the plains to rise up and greet the low cloud cover.

The whole world seemed so much smaller to Brann now.

They were descending towards the stadium now, the only building in the entire city visibly larger than the palace itself. Built like an ovular coliseum, a creamy white shell of canvas draped over the bowl in lieu of a solid roof, secured in place by powerful cables looped through enormous metal bollards. Brann had never seen inside it, let alone been this close. Their trajectory took them behind the south-facing wall, private landing pads clustered in the stadium's shadow—with a start, Brann could see a pair of missile catapults tracking their lifeboat, rectangular stacks rotating on their turrets. Nes had assured him no air defenses would engage such a tiny craft, even if the Nightwatch had been given orders to shoot down the Donnie itself, but that didn't stop Brann from feeling his stomach turn with unease. They were in the belly of the beast, now.

The shaky craft began to vibrate intensely, landing boosters firing now, slowing the lifeboat. Hydraulics engaged with a shuddering clunk, the lifeboat landed on its outstretched feet, and the autopilot and engines powered down simultaneously. Touchdown.

"Alrighty, here we go," Boomer said, unbuckling his harness, barely able to stand in the enclosed space. "I'll take the lead, you two just—" He looked between Grishka and Brann, hunched over in place. "Just. Don't talk, mkay? I'll take the lead."

Unlatching the door locks, the side of the lifeboat slid open on its runners smoothly, allowing Boomer to step off and bring himself to full height in the open air with a stretch. "Morning, gents," he cheered, waving at the Nightwatch standing in formation on the catwalk ahead.

"Hey, good to see you, sir." Gripping at his armored vest, elbows relaxed, one of the Nightwatch stepped forward. "I'm hoping you'll understand when we tell you we're gonna need to profile your escorts here, make sure you haven't been accompanied by any known troublemakers—orders from upstairs and all."

"Oh, sure, sure, I get it," Boomer nodded, waving Grishka and Brann off the boat, the latter of whom pulled along Boomer's luggage trunk behind him. "You need passports, or...?"

"Nah, we're not going through customs on this." Pushing back the shades on the bridge of his nose, the Nightwatchman tugged a holoscreen free from his vest, his shoulder radio buzzing with chatter. He tapped a few inputs into the screen, gesturing at Grishka and Brann authoritatively. "Folks, mind stepping forward for me, answering a few questions, we'll have you on your way in no time." He stood before Grishka, addressing her first as he typed on the screen, and in his peripherals, Brann could see the faces of the Donnie's crew arranged in a stacked grid through the translucent glass. "Name?"

Without hesitation: "Grishka."

Brann and Boomer whipped their heads around in shock.

"And your relationship?" The Nightwatchman pointed between Grishka and Boomer, unfazed. Quickly, the realization settled in—they had the facial snapshot of a human woman from Boomer's fight in Mongillo, but they'd have no way of knowing Grishka's name, regardless of what form she took. She was a witch from the wilds, living off the record. Brann exhaled with relief, disguising it as a cough.

Grishka looked at Boomer, and Brann saw that familiar mischievous glint in her eyes. "Fiancé."

Rotating on his heel, the stone-faced Nightwatchman looked at Boomer, who shrugged meekly. "Well, congratulations sir, guess I haven't been paying as much attention to the news as I should be." He swiped away a pop-up window on his screen, apparently satisfied. "Okay, no more questions, you're good."

Tensing, Brann held his breath, the Nightwatchman stepped sideways, standing before him now. A new window opened, and once more, Brann saw through the lightly-opaque glass the mirrored snapshot of his own face in the corner of the screen.

"Name?"

Brann cleared his throat, but before he could speak, Boomer piped up on his behalf. "This is my valet—uh, François. He doesn't speak much."

"Okay, valet..." More typing, and Brann suppressed another sigh as he saw his face disappear from the corner of the screen—no facial recognition was sophisticated enough to match to his current appearance. "Any employee records we can pull from to verify?"

"Uh, no, he's sort of a self-hire," Boomer lied. "On account of all my former employees turning out to be—well, terrorists, and all that. Picked this guy up out on a publicity tour in Meerschaw, before all that nasty business."

"Wait one." The security officer swiped through some logs, going backwards until he settled on one date in particular. "Yeah, got that scheduled stop here, okay. Just make sure you finalize that paperwork, get it to the Entertainment offices as soon as you're able, yeah? All due respect, you're still technically an employee as well, sir, you gotta get everyone in your charge on file with the offices before we can let you leave the city after today's fight."

Boomer saluted. "Will do, absolutely."

"In the meantime—I hate to be that guy, but..." The Nightwatch all stepped forward, pulling down their sleeves in unison, showing off the patches on their shoulders. "You mind doing some signatures for us before you go in?"

"Of course—in fact, here—" Boomer bid Brann to set down his trunk, unlatching the lid and throwing it open—his boxing trunks and robe were folded up and stacked neatly next to a haphazard pile of signed headshots and posters. Boomer scooped out an armful of signed canvas paper and began distributing it among the waiting Nightwatch, the stoic men all drifting in close to collect the spoils of their assigned post. "Don't be shy, take a few, give 'em to the kids at home!"

*

Once Boomer had finished signing and thanking the Nightwatch, they headed in, passing through the cavernous back passageways of the Stadium that seemed to stretch on for miles. All at once, their earpieces crackled to life, Zay speaking to them through the Donnie's private channel.

"You hear that, 'bossman'? Even the cops are cracking down on fair pay for employees. Better get our paperwork started."

"Yeah, yeah," Boomer dismissed, his little finger reseating the tiny radio in his ear. "Just get your hours to Nes or whatever, he'll handle the rest."

"Actually, you never officially promoted me to be your manager after firing the last one," piped up Nes, "So you'll still need to do all that yourself. Or hire another accountant."

"Ugh." Boomer pulled a face, nodding and waving at the box office staff as they passed. "Would I have to pay them, too?"

"One usually follows the other, yes."

"That's it, I'm retiring." Boomer led Grishka and Brann up a flight of stairs, towards the stadium offices. "Or, not really, just—I gotta find a way to get people to work for me for free. Keeping track of how much money I owe everyone is too complicated."

"You poor thing. How did it go at the first checkpoint?"

Brann spoke up now, the trunk he steered beside himself clunking its way up the stairs on its unsteady wheels. "Fine. No trouble at all. They never recognized me."

"No one could recognize you—-I must commend your ingenuity, young sir." Emrys was speaking now to congratulate Brann. "Never would I ever have thought of such a thing, you must promise to let me conduct a private study on you, should we ever manage to get out of the city alive."

"For once, I agree with the transient," Red admitted. "I'll need to inform my own House of this unseen use of blood magic. Never has there been on record a demi-human who survived a botched transfusion."

"You're all gonna have to get used to disappointment," Brann argued, patting the vial in his pocket. "As soon as we're back on board I'm dropping the look."

"Alright, let's stay focused, folks." Nes keyed back in, ignoring Emrys's protests. "Lady Red, Emrys and I are just coming up on a bend now, this maintenance tunnel is gonna take us right up beneath the palace. Was this the route you took to the airfield, Brann?"

"No, I took the high road, along the river. Didn't even know there was a tunnel."

"Really? Huh. Brave of you, hoofing it in broad daylight like that." A pause. "Hawkshaw, how's it going on our exit?"

*

"You're gonna love this," Hawkshaw said, speaking into his built-in comms, looking out over the river from his vantage point beneath the city wall. From here, he had clear line of sight to both the palace and stadium, as well as the river that ran between them both. "You know the river that cuts through the city? It's manmade. Partially, anyway. I'm tapped into Geiha's infrastructure network, there's a series of drainage outlets all along the channel they dug to keep from flooding the lower elevations when it rains. Guess where the outlets all lead."

Zay spoke. "Back out into the river outside the city, headed downstream to where I parked."

"Where 'we' parked, my dear, don't be a glory-grubber." Hawkshaw walked along the concrete embankment, following the wall back towards where he came from. Security was light at this hour in the morning, but that wouldn't be the case once the fight was underway, and those passages would be sealed for a full week according to the logs he was mentally scanning. "Worst case, I hope you meatboys packed some snacks, if we get stuck underground we won't be going anywhere for a while—they're not

650

gonna take any chances, maintenance manholes will lock all over the city until at least next week."

"Then we better hope we can find a boat. Any suggestions?" Nes asked.

"One sec." The records whizzed by behind Hawkshaw's ocular sensors as he rapidly scanned their contents. "Looks like there's a boathouse connected to the southern gatehouse of the palace—oh, and look at that: the gatehouse is only a few meters from the entrance to the archives. That's got group A covered, easy day."

"And group B, in case they can't fly out the way they came?"

Hawkshaw scanned once more, turning to face the stadium. "Mm, no boathouses to speak of, but you know what? There's some sightseeing ferries that disembark upriver to let people off at the stadium. If Boomer wears a big hat and keeps his mouth shut, he might be able to slip through the crowd and get on board one, then group B can rendezvous with A at your chosen stop along the river."

"Should we have reason to think we won't just be able to fly out?" Brann asked, sounding worried.

"Not unless someone in group A does something extraordinarily stupid to get themselves noticed at the palace," Hawkshaw answered, still hiking along the inside of the wall. The hatch he'd used was coming up just around the next corner. "That, or you remove your disguise early and get flagged by facial recognition."

Turning the corner, Hawkshaw expected to find an empty alcove, instead running headlong into someone, their back turned to him. "Oh, all apologies," Hawkshaw offered, quickly straightening up and mentally preparing his processors to bluff his way through this encounter.

The figure turned, and Hawkshaw found himself looking in the mirror—an identical model, the automaton's metallic faceplates were trimmed with green and platinum paint, Geiha's colors. "No, my mistake," the other android apologized, holding up his own clawed hand. "Was there a mix-up in assignment again? Up on the board they had me down for hatch patrol..."

"No, you know what," Hawkshaw quickly said, snapping his fingers. "It was my fault, I didn't check the board last night, I just looked at the holonet schedule. In fact—" Working as fast as he could, Hawkshaw internally edited an old copy of a duty log he pulled from the net, syncing it to today's date on Geiha's server. An unencrypted file that small, he could only hope the intrusion wouldn't go noticed by the server's automated protection. "Yeah, see that there? They just uploaded an old schedule."

"Let me check." The amber irises in the other automaton's eye lenses flickered as it connected. "Oh yeah, how about that. Wonder what dumbass organic did that. I'll head back and get it fixed with the duty officer."

"No, no need I'll go on and take care of that, this was the last stop on my patrol anyway." Hawkshaw backed away, arms up apologetically. "That'll teach me to expect 'human error' not to screw up my daily routine."

"I hear that." The other automaton turned back towards the hatch, tapping the numerical pad next to it. The electronic locks thunked into place loudly. "Have a better one, pal."

"Yeah, you too." Hawkshaw turned, walking briskly back along the wall, towards the palace. He keyed his radio back on. "Uh, yeah, so, things just got a little more complicated."

Nes spoke. "Meaning?"

"They're using SICA models for auxiliary security throughout the city today. I guess they didn't trust the Nightwatch not to let someone slip through the cracks."

"That's your model. Is this good or bad?"

"Could be good." Hawkshaw paused. "Could be bad. Most likely bad. In fact, let's call it all bad. They're already working on locking maintenance hatches, so our only way out of the city now is the river. That, and the other thing."

"What other thing?"

"Me." Hawkshaw sighed. "If an alarm does get tripped, the first thing the Nightwatch is gonna do is activate the latent emergency transponders embedded in every automaton they've got roaming the city. Which means when they go down the list and get to the frequency bands set in every SICA model by our manufacturer..."

"Then literally *every* SICA model in the city goes into search and destroy mode," Zay finished. "Meaning you. Boy, so much for being the superior form of life, huh, tinman?"

"Thanks, darling, I can always count on you to be understanding." Hawkshaw adjusted course, heading for the stadium. "So, we best not alert security, otherwise you guys will have to leave me behind. Being that I've already got all sorts of intimate details on all of you stored away in my memory banks, it's a lose-lose if that happens. I'll head for the ferries, since I'm stuck behind the wall now—help clear the crowd for Team B's river exit."

"If you go psycho-bot on us," Zay crooned, "Do I have your permission to finally disable your ass? As you say, it's a matter of safety for all of us..."

"If I go psycho-bot, you have permission to blow me to bits." Hawkshaw mused on this thought a bit. "Though I'd really, really prefer not to be blown to bits today, so let's do this right, yeah?"

*

"You hear that, boy?" Zay rotated in her pilot's chair, autocannon draped loosely across her body. "I might finally get to shut the can-opener up for good."

Wolf didn't take the bait. The lycan sat back on his haunches, resting his snout on his forelimb, spear held tight against his shoulder. He whined quietly to himself, ignoring Zay entirely.

There was ill-omen hanging over them all. Zay sensed it too. She sighed, turning her chair back, putting both feet up on the control console.

Across the clay plains, she could make out the tiny specks of ships beginning their descent into the city below. The out-of-towners were arriving, and in a couple hours, the stadium would be filled to the rafters with fans waiting to see the definitive fight of Geiha's entire history. Between automated security, the Nightwatch, and the inevitable appearance that Tark and his Uhlen would be making, the odds were stacked against them.

Zay looked to her left, at the empty navigator seat beside her. She clutched her autocannon tighter.

*

"Watch your step." Nes held Red's hand, assisting her up the ladder, Emrys following close behind. The underground passage let out only a few hundred yards from the palace wall—they found themselves in a small park, cordoned off from the rest of the city by the river. Up the hill, another small portal through the wall was visible—likely a passage for sentries to entire and exit the palace grounds while on patrol. If they were quick, they would likely be able to avoid any such patrol, especially considering all the manpower needed to keep watch on the stadium. The underground hike had taken a considerable amount of time, the overhead sun already at its peak—the fight would be starting soon, which left them little time to linger about.

"Hawkshaw, I'm dropping you some coordinates, let me know when you've received," Nes said, tapping something into his holoscreen.

"Wait one." Pause. "Yep, just got 'em. Mind telling me what this is?"

"A present. Hey, kid, you listening?" Nes was addressing Brann now. "I've left you a little something, in case things go sideways—there's a cache along the riverbank, back where we first met. If you find yourself in a tight spot on your way out of the city, be sure to make a grab for it. Remember the spot?"

"Yeah, I remember."

"Check in with Hawkshaw just in case you get lost, he's got the location saved now. We're just reaching the palace," he said, making his way up the grassy hill alongside Red and Emrys. "Everyone else where they're supposed to be? Any questions or doubts, the door's shutting behind us, now's the time to speak your piece."

*

"No going back now, we're in it," Boomer answered for everyone. "Besides, I'm already in my trunks."

Boomer was reclined back in his dressing room chair, facing the mirror and combing his mane back away from his eyes. Indeed, he'd already ditched his travel wear, the shimmering fabric of his boxing trunks and matching robe flowing over him loosely. "I sent Brann and Grishka ahead to my box, get a bird's eye view of the stadium—heh, get it." He set down the comb, spinning in his chair. "Not much time left before my walkout, everyone, I think this is where I leave you. Soon as I win this, I'll try to make a quick exit—hopefully there won't be too many desperate mothers throwing their babies up in the air for me to sign. Boomer out."

With that, he twisted the earpiece out and plopped it onto the dresser behind him—it wouldn't do him or anyone else any good to keep it in during the fight, the rest was up to his team. Standing up, Boomer bounced on his hooves, shadowboxing the air and performing his breathing exercises. Beside his dresser, his trunk sat, lid open—the hilt of Brann's sword visible in the space once occupied by Boomer's clothes.

*

The bowl of the stadium below was beginning to fill up quickly, thousands of tiny figures filing through the rows of seats as the doors opened for general audiences. Arms crossed, Tark stood imperiously at the highest point of the stadium, in Boomer's private box overlooking all. He'd been monitoring Boomer's arrival remotely from his own holoscreen, and had no reason to suspect the two strangers accompanying the horse—

unfortunately, too much bureaucratic red tape disallowed the sharing of private citizens' information between Houses, so he had no real dossier to speak of on them. Still, if Recruit Brann had any cause to return to the city, he would have been flagged by any of the hundreds of cameras monitoring all the ports—likely the young man had stayed behind on Boomer's ship, parked in the clay plains just outside the reach of the city's surveillance, along with the rest of his companions. Likely, Tark would never see the former soldat again.

Still, Tark was restless, and there had been a brief moment where motion sensors had signaled unusual movement in the maintenance tunnels leading towards the palace this morning. Deciding his energies were better spent investigating that anomaly, Tark regarded the silhouette of the bird flying overhead thoughtfully for a moment, then turned away from the railing. He pushed open the doors to the box—

—And nearly knocked down the young donkey standing just behind the doors in the process, sending the startled beastman reeling.

"All apologies, my fault entirely," Tark admitted, taking a step to one side as the anxious looking fellow collected himself, bowing to Tark wordlessly. He was undoubtedly one of Boomer's personal servants, judging by the expensive clothes he wore; that and the fact that he had access to the fighter's private box at all. The donkey avoided eye contact as he sidestepped the Marshal on his way into the box.

"Hold fast a moment," Tark said, a thought striking him.

The young donkey froze, back turned to him.

Tark reached into the vest of his brigandine, pulling free an ashen colored envelope. He reached out towards the donkey, letting the quiet crinkle of the paper prompt the servant to turn back towards him. "What's your name, servant?"

Bowing once more, the donkey still refused eye contact—he must have been properly intimidated by the Marshal's presence. "François," the valet said, voice just above a whisper.

"You are in the employ of Geiha's Champion fighter, yes? That puts you in my employ as well. I have a task for you." Tark waved the offered letter, encouraging François to accept it. He did. "This message comes direct from my desk, and is meant for your Master's eyes only. Deliver it in my stead, see that he gets it. No delays now; off you go."

The donkey's hand was shaking as he tucked the envelope into his own blouse, bowing once more to Tark, then quickly exiting the box. Tark watched the young valet go, then closed the doors behind himself, following his memory's pathways back towards the closest underground maintenance hatch. Once more, his thoughts turned to Recruit Brann.

Yes, the more he ruminated on it, the more Tark decided their paths would never cross again.

40. The Letter

The door to Boomer's dressing room was flung open, then slammed shut just as quickly—Brann wiped the sweat from his broad forehead, the transformed soldat tugging at his long ears angrily. "How do you keep these things from doing whatever the hell they want," he groaned, interrupting Boomer's exercises. "It's like having two bigass radar dishes growing out of my brain, I can't *stand* it."

Boomer stood up straight, regarding the reluctant donkey with amusement. "I think they look good—makes you seem more relatable, ya know? Better than those shriveled little hunks of bacon you humans have clinging to your heads."

Brann keyed his mic, ignoring Boomer. "I just ran into Tark upstairs—he's here, he knows we're here, he could be coming your way. This is a bad idea; we need to bail—"

"Whoa there, easy kid," Nes reassured him. "How do you know he knows anything? Where was he exactly, what was he doing?"

"He's—he was—in Boomer's private box, looked like he was leaving—I watched him head downstairs. Wherever he's going, it's obviously more important to him right now, and the only place that could be is the palace. Did you guys see any cameras, were you spotted underground at all—?"

"No one saw us, you are being paranoid," Red interrupted. "Calm down. We'd have the sense not to let that happen, trust."

"You wanna bet your lives on it?" Brann argued. "We either take him out, here and now, or risk having him come down on us just when we think it's safe. There's no reason it should have been this easy to get Boomer into the stadium."

"We've been over this, Brann, Tark can't stand in the way of letting Geiha's Champion fight in an official title match. This is how they mean to replace Boomer—they need him to fight, and to lose." Brann could hear in Nestor's voice the older man was not taking his concerns seriously. "Take a breath, relax, everything is going just as planned. The only thing you need to worry about on your end is Boomer winning that fight—he might not be fully recovered from that last bout, despite what he says to the contrary."

Brann watched Boomer, the horse resuming his shadowboxing. "You want me to pass those concerns along to him?"

Nes didn't answer the question. "We're at the entrance to the archives now. Going quiet. Keep calm and keep focused, we'll be back on the Donnie in no time." Click.

Brann took his hand away from his ear. "Nes says you got this," he lied.

"Doesn't sound like him," Boomer responded, not taking his eyes off the wall opposite him. His fists were a blur, vascular arms already coated in a sheen of sweat. Brann studied his movements carefully, watching the pugilist's body language, listening to the frustrated snorts between breaths.

"Do you? Got this?" Brann cautioned.

Finishing off a combo of swipes, Boomer exhaled, letting his arms go slack. He rolled his shoulders, not even paying Brann the courtesy of facing him when he answered: "You people worry too much. If you can't trust me to win a fight, why'd you even come along with me at all?"

There wasn't an outright hostility in his words—but just enough of a sourness that Brann relented nonetheless. He'd been at Boomer's side every chance he'd gotten since the horse had regained consciousness after Tark's brutal victory over him—and yet, the groundwaters were polluted, their friendship seeming to lose potency every time they spoke. Brann decided to leave the subject alone—no one knew Boomer better than Boomer, after all.

"I'm gonna head back to the box. Watch the fight from there."

Boomer didn't miss a beat, arms punching at the air once more. "Yeah, you do that."

He waited until he heard the door close behind him, leaving Boomer alone in the dressing room once more. Sighing heavily, the horse let his arms fall to his sides once more, hands going to his hips as he caught his breath. He rubbed at his forehead, cursing himself mentally—this was not him. There was something wrong, something missing, and he had to find the way back to shore. Fast. His friendship with Brann counted on it.

Boomer turned, looking to the door. Then, frowning, he stepped around his dresser, peering into the open trunk beside it.

Brann's sword was gone.

*

Perched high above the stadium, the wail of the crowd and electric guitars of Boomer's walkout music rose up to buffet beneath Grishka's wings, as powerful as any headwind. In this hybrid form, she had no ears to speak of. Instead, she held the little device up between the pollexes of her wings, just beside her beak as she spoke into it. "No Brann. Missing."

Zay replied, "What do you mean, 'no Brann?' Where'd he go?"

Grishka may have been looking down at the stadium from above, but her corporeal form was seated in Boomer's box, just as planned. Her projected self surveyed the entire stadium bowl, searching carefully—unless Brann had gotten himself lost on the way, he was not attending the fight. "Not here. No Brann. Tark here, before. Maybe follow."

"Brann, are you still there? Can you hear us?"

Nothing, radio silence. "Godammit," Zay hissed. "We're gonna have to change things up. Hawkshaw, is there a way into the city via the river? I'm gonna take Wolf in and go save this idiot, before he wrecks this whole operation for us all."

*

"Wait one." Standing outside a bustling cafe, watching the opening ceremonies of the fight on the cafe's holoscreens through the ceiling-height glass windows, Hawkshaw scanned the city planning documents in his head.

"You're not getting this far into the city without getting spotted, that's a foregone conclusion, all the underground hatches have already been sealed. There's a blindspot where the cameras can't quite see the outflow of the river from the east bank, so if you come up from the southeast you should be okay to at least get inside the walls. Beyond that, I wouldn't risk going any further in than the edge of the airfields, there's too much security watching."

"We can do better than that," Zay argued. "What if you meet us at the airfield, pretend we're your prisoners, and you're taking us in for processing? That should at least get us as far as the stadium."

Hawkshaw shook his head, continuing to watch as Boomer appeared on the holoscreens, waving to the crowds and cameras. "Boomer's coming out on stage right now, by the time the fight's over you'll only have just made it past the wall. Besides, I can't make that bluff work, the automaton security protocols would have already triggered the second any SICA units had your faces in sight—programming is shoot to kill, only the Nightwatch has the discretion to make arrests. Nah, the kid's on his own for now. All we can do is pray he doesn't find Tark before we're clear of the archives."

The cafe sat just across the street from the ferry piers—turning his back on the screens, Hawkshaw marched down the pier, striding past the passengers waiting to board. He maintained the outward appearance of a sentry bot on duty, keeping his line of sight above eye level, pretending as if he were scanning the crowd for troublemakers—then, the moment the next ferry arrived, he stepped onboard. If he rode the ferry upstream, towards the stadium pier, he hoped to get a better look at the security along the banks of the river not afforded to him by the city plans.

Hawkshaw stood at the far end of the ferry, at parade rest, while the rest of the passengers clambered on. Up at the bow, another SICA unit stood watch as well, coldly scanning the crowd just as Hawkshaw did.

Automatons on every ferry, it seemed.

*

Following the stairwell back down towards the stadium offices made for slow going, Brann still stumbling over his new hooves—this awkward form was all limbs and unbalanced weight, everything that made walking upright thrown into disarray. More times than he could count, he found himself bending forward as he walked, the ropey tail behind him trying to correct his posture. Navigating these manmade halls and mezzanines as a beastman was not easy; he wondered to himself how Boomer and Wolf managed it without going mental.

The envelope in his hand was tickling at his fingertips, baiting his curiosity.

Ducking away from an oncoming procession of porters, lined up with their mobile service stations as they headed towards the upper bowl, Brann stepped into a nearby office that had been left open. The lights were out; he leaned against the propped door, turning the letter over in his hands. It was sealed with dark green wax, stamped with an insignia Brann knew immediately to be Tark's—a stenciled silhouette of the kuaneach's mask.

He slipped a finger under the lip, tearing through it. Tucked inside, a carefully folded note of stationary, bearing the letterhead of the Geihan military with a single line of printed text. Brann took a breath, steadying himself, then read:

Fight harder next time.
-Tark

The flashbang in Brann's mind blinded him to the world for a moment, his ears searing with boiling blood. He crushed the envelope in his shaking hands, stuffing it into his trousers —and in the same motion, withdrew the second vial Grishka had given him—the transformation reversal—uncorking it as he stormed out of the office.

Just down this passageway, he saw a windowless exit, the words "MAINTENANCE TUNNELS" painted across it with an arrow pointing forward. Brann marched towards this exit, tossing back the vial and downing its contents. His sword was slung across his back, the scabbard's leather belt tightening itself across his chest—and with a mighty kick, Brann burst through the unlocked maintenance exit, drawing his blade as he stepped into the dark

*

The next electronic lock dinged open, and the doors slid open, Nes beckoning his teammates to enter the next room. "We're going as quick as we can, we're into the secure records now—the only room more heavily secure than this one is the Undervault, which is Marshal access only. I don't know if I could crack that open even if I tried, so we'll have to hope what we're looking for is in here."

Emrys and Red broke apart, following opposite paths around the circular room, a massive rotunda stacked high with towering shelves. Every shelf was so tightly packed and neatly catalogued with books and holotapes behind their glass barriers, it would have been impossible to search them all one by one. "What exactly are we looking for, Nestor," Emrys asked nervously, hands running over the glass barriers aimlessly. "There's too many decimal and symbol markers on all these shelves to make any sense of!"

Nes crossed the rotunda towards the single standalone terminal in the center, just beside the domed entrance to the Undervault. "We need financial records for every deal made between Geiha and the other Houses during and immediately after the Arbitration Wars," he answered, booting up the terminal to access the library's catalogue system. "That narrows it down to a very specific span of time, in a very specific section—and I can narrow it down even more." He typed as fast as he could, the results populating just as quickly on the holoscreen, highlighting specific marked sections on a three-dimensional map. "We're only interested in transactions that were signed by hand, with Burnside Geiha's name on them, which means we need to search..."

The screen flashed a highlighted wall on the map, yellow indicators marking all the records that mentioned the keywords 'BURNSIDE', 'TARIFF', or 'CESSION'.

Nes snapped his fingers, pointing at the shelves in question. "...That wall." He punched in a few more commands, the glass barriers sliding open around the chosen shelves. "You two stick to raw documents, I'll look through the holoscreens, see if I can find anything you missed. I'm willing to bet any remaining evidence of these land sales would be signed in ink, any electronic transcriptions being severely limited. Let's get to work."

The three of them moved in, Red and Emrys sliding their own ladders around the rotunda to stack up against the shelves, most of the paper documents being held at the higher elevations. "I recognize we stand to benefit little from naysaying," Red said cautiously, climbing her ladder, "But—"

"Any well-kept House is going to keep records of all their legitimate dealings, no matter how dubious or ill-mannered they may seem in retrospect," Emrys interrupted, suppressing Red's doubt. "We won't need to find any documents that read 'We, House Geiha, are war criminals and here's our written proof'—we simply need to locate enough documented land trades or sideways dealings with the Houses that paint a portrait of an opportunistic tycoon speaking out of both sides of his mouth to convince a Tribunal of Geiha's war-profiteering."

"Goodness gracious me, could you possibly have made that sentence run on any longer?" Red groaned. "Please, professor, learn to condense your thoughts."

"Take it on good faith," Emrys half-shouted from his higher spot on his ladder, already flipping rapidly through a yellowed tome, "That I simply enjoy speaking to you and the others so much that I find fulfillment in making these moments last as long as possible."

Red similarly was scanning through a scroll, not looking up as she called back: "I assure you, there's no need to feel so burdened by your social obligations—you can shut the fuck up anytime."

*

The entire world had turned out to see his victory today. Boomer shook his wrapped hands high, waving at every tiny face smiling and cheering for him today, shouting his own raucous joy back at them. The lights flashed from their stacked fixtures; the free cameras whirled about in a cyclone overhead. His triumphant ballad, his signature walkout music, blared on every speaker, filled every heart. This was his temple, his church: Boomer was here to deliver a sermon, a communion of fists.

The music trickled off, replaced by the thumping, deferential anthem of today's challenger. There wasn't much showmanship to his opponent's entrance—hands on hips, standing in the center of the ring, Boomer scoffed to himself. The man entered, breaking from his corner, tossing his hooded robe aside with little care for the audience. He didn't even look up or wave at them. The man called Krieger simply approached Boomer—hands wrapped, head shaved, trunks a simple black. There was nothing remarkable or shows about him. Nothing outwardly threatening.

Yet when he stared into Boomer's eyes, his expressionless face left the horse's mouth feeling dry. There was a vacancy to Krieger, a lack of vision—he was here, on command, nothing more. He gave a simple nod, a simple bow.

There was something very wrong with him. No fighter, none seeking glory in the ring, would face down the world champion with only a nod to greet him. There were no taunts or smiles, no snarls or jeers. Only a detachment from everything, leaving Boomer alone in this ring with himself.

This man was simply here to fight. To kill.

Boomer looked to Krieger's collarbone—just below it, a small tattoo, across his pectoral.

The Geihan Infantry's emblem, branded into Krieger's flesh.

The bell sounded.

*

The point where the river and the maintenance tunnel intersected was joined by a large cistern, pulling the excess water from the river overhead to keep its levels stable—Tark came to the edge of the underground lake, the shallow waters undulating calmly. This was where the motion sensors had detected movement—every now and then, large fish determined enough to fight the current found their way up into the drainage outlets. Ordinarily, Tark wouldn't have bothered, but on this day in particular, this close to the palace...

There was no fish he could see, the crystal clear waters illuminated from below. The entire lake was still, empty. And yet, his holoscreen held aloft, Tark could see plain as day the blinking point of light signaling a motion alert—it had returned, moments ago, just before he'd entered the cistern. There was definitely something, or someone, down here with him.

He opted for the direct approach to this conundrum.

"You've the pleasure of being host to Marshal Tark today," he announced loudly, his smooth voice bouncing off the cistern's low ceiling, echoing around the support pillars rising from the water. "I might have suggested a more personable venue, if consulted. If you've any business at the palace today, perhaps I can save you the trip; speak with you directly, here."

There was something in the water, floating towards him from upstream. Tark kneeled beside the lake, reaching towards it as it bobbed closer—a small, misshapen object. Crumpled paper. He plucked it from the water, tilting it to let the water run off and to let the light from below brighten it.

An opened, ash gray envelope, crushed by someone's hand, the wax seal broken. His own stamp.

Tark examined it a moment, then let the envelope fall once more, splashing delicately. "How curious," he said, standing, turning to face upstream. "I believe I said your Master's eyes only. This won't do."

From the opposite embankment, the shadows parted around a familiar face. Brann, reverted to his original form, staring Tark down—for the first time since the two had met, he didn't avert Tark's gaze. Rather, he locked eyes, unblinking, unbroken, face grim and determined. There was a purpose about him today. An omen.

"This won't do at all." Tark sized Brann up. He chuckled humorlessly, removing the weathered mask from his snout. "Oh, you've got the eyes of a destroyer today, young one. I can taste the smoke rising from your rageful ghost." He let the mask fall, the platinum adornment splashing in the waters of the cistern.

Brann turned slightly, showing off the sword he held, resting across his shoulder. He wasn't challenging Tark, not just yet—he was welcoming him.

"Tell me." Tark wiped the water on his hand across his brow, rubbing it into his scales. "What storm rides behind you, today? What measured destiny to you hope to pry from my lifeless corpse?"

Brann answered, plain and true. "I'm rescinding my surrender. House Lachlan no longer recognizes your claim."

Tark stepped forward, hands clasped behind his back. "You'll forgive me, but. 'House Lachlan', 'its people'? I'm afraid we may live a world apart from one another." His talons clicked against the moist stone floor, heavy footfalls slow and deliberate. "In my world—this world—House Lachlan no longer exists. Its people do not exist. According to all natural and manmade laws, I have subsumed your entitlements to say otherwise." He stopped; a duelist's length left between them.

"You are no longer Recruit Brann of House Lachlan. In this new world, you are simply..." Tark shrugged. "A nameless orphan. An urchin from the streets."

Then, Brann did the unthinkable. He laughed.

"Man," he said, shaking his head, sword tapping impatiently. "I just *do not* care."

Tark felt a smile creeping across his muzzle. His clawtips tickled at the hilt of his axe, strapped across his back. "You'd submit yourself to the mercy of the Assay, then?"

Brann shook his head once more. He assumed the stance of a soldat, sword leveled, squared tip pointed at Tark's chest. "Oh, you're at my mercy today, Marshal."

Tark drew his axe proudly. He inhaled deep, breathing in lungful of static, relishing this moment; for the first time in years, he faced the barbarians at the gates. A sovereign force, unbound by pomp and circumstance, challenging him for neither ceremony, nor glory—but for his life.

A proper, mortal enemy.

"At last," Tark smiled.

41. The Mistake

"Nothing," Red bemoaned, tossing down yet another useless scroll, a scattered pile of documents and holoscreens building up beneath their ladders. "We were fools to believe they would have retained anything so damning; this was a wasted effort. We shouldn't have come here."

"I'm gonna side with Emrys here," Nes argued, having reinstated himself at the terminal, searching more possible keywords. "There's no possible way they could pass a House Council audit if they didn't have something worthwhile, and Geiha has always had an immaculate history with the Council."

He had one more idea. "Emrys, what was the other name on that plaque? The one from the Dakhma? It mentioned Burnside Geiha himself, and..."

"And 'The Great Hero Rigel', the same Rigel spoken of at dinner. Tark and Gideon's grandfather." Emrys discarded his own scroll, wiping the sweat from his forehead beneath his wide-brimmed hat. "And may I say, I find it exceptionally disconcerting that despite his supposed contributions to the war efforts, he has not been mentioned once in any of these records. A great war hero, simply disappeared from history. Inconceivable."

Nes searched for the name, the catalogue processing his request. This search took far longer than the others. Finally, after a full minute, the map blinked once more; though none of the shelves were highlighted this time. Nes peered closer, rereading the search results thoroughly. The only location of any records containing that name were—

"In there." He pointed to the entrance to the Undervault before him, a sense of foreboding surrounding the humble domed structure.

"So that's it, then?" Red clambered down her ladder, heels clicking against the wide steps. "There's no getting in, you said."

"I said I didn't know if I could get in, there's a difference." Returning to the terminal's main screen, the option to access the vault door locks was guarded by a frighteningly long passcode entry box. Nes opted for the manual option, opening the side panel of the terminal instead. "Required passkey is a seventeen-digit code that only the Marshal would have, one that resets every 2 hours by the looks of it—so even if we'd stolen it right off his desk this morning, it would have been useless by the time we got this far."

The bundled wires were all marked with colored bands and symbols as baffling to the average person as the library's catalogue system—though Nes was not the average person. He recognized this as the very same alphabet used by privately contracted engineers that were shared between the houses; the vault itself may have been Geihan, but this terminal was built by his own people. Nes set to work sorting through the masses of cables, tracking each individual strand as quickly as he could to where they sat soldered into the transistor paneling.

"What are we looking for, if you don't mind me asking?" Emrys was hovering over Nestor's shoulder, utterly bewildered by the apparent chaos of identical bundles of cables.

"Anything that doesn't belong." Nes emphasized this with a tap of his finger alongside one of the bundles. "These connectors aren't joined to any external source. A closed circuit, which leads..."

He followed the cables up the inside of the terminal, his fingertips meeting a smooth, metallic block. It was well-concealed, embedded deep behind the circuit boards, almost completely camouflaged—save for the grooved marks melding the box's corners to the paneling.

"Thank God for lazy welders," Nes cackled, pulling the handsaw from his belt. Positioning it right along the rough seam of the box, he turned his head away, ducking out of the way of the sparks that leapt out at him when he activated the saw.

Seconds later, the hand tool cut through soft cables, then a snap of ozone spat curls of smoke out from within the terminal—and the vault door slid open, the rotating wall of the dome revealing the waiting glass elevator within.

"Ladies first," Emrys said with a bow, stepping out of Red's way.

"Quite." The viscountess stepped into the elevator, looking all about the transparent box. "How far down are we going?"

Nes stepped inside behind the two of them, tapping the single button on the wall. "All the way."

The dome rotated closed once more, rising up above their heads, the glass box disappearing into the deep shaft.

*

Brann compressed his stance a millimeter at a time, knees straining with how slowly he lowered himself, spreading his feet. Infantry training prompted the soldat to always go on the offensive when possible, but he remembered all too well the mistakes of Recruit Caleb—there was no psychological advantage to be had against Tark. This was to be a fight of patience, of careful plotting, looking for weakness in—

The wide swing of Tark's axe would have split Brann in half at the waist, had it not been so broadly telegraphed. Brann stumbled back a few steps, the massive axe burying itself with a deafening smash into the stone wall, an explosion of dust forming a smokescreen between them. Barely did Brann have time to correct his posture before Tark emerged in the dust, striding forward confidently—and, with an open palm, the towering kuaneach slapped away Brann's sword as easily as if it were a toy. The blade whistled as it cartwheeled through the air, splashing in the water, and Tark's claws were at Brann's collar—lifting the young soldat, Tark held him aloft with one hand, threatening to throttle him with nothing but his clenched fingers.

"Top marks for infiltration," Tark said loudly over Brann's pained grunts, "Though it seems we have a ways to go yet on your close combat skills."

Winding up his elbow, Tark heaved Brann to one side, punching into the stone wall with the smaller human's body. Feeling an agonizing crunch in his shoulder and back, Brann cried out, the crumbling wall dusting his face with gravelly debris. As Brann was held there against the wall, Tark cocked his head to one side and reached forward, plucking out Brann's earpiece between his claws. Giving the tiny device a thoughtful examination, Tark hummed curiously. Then, he crushed the earpiece between his fingers, watching Brann's face drain of hope as he did.

"Deep breath now."

Tark pulled back, tossing Brann like a ragdoll through the air, the glowing surface of the lake rising to meet him—he crashed through the water, falling into cold silence, buffeted by a churning cloud of bubbles. Disoriented for a moment, Brann kicked outwards until he felt rock beneath his boot—the floor of the lake. Steadying, he planted both feet, standing straight up; the water broke over his head, and he was breathing air once more, the shallow waters splashing around him at about waist-height.

"You should be thanking me," Tark called out to him from the embankment, yanking his axe free from the wall. "It's a rarity to receive my teachings directly, let alone twice in a lifetime. The other recruits may get jealous—they'll say I've chosen you as my favorite."

"I don't want your teachings," Brann spat, pushing his soaked bangs out of his eyes and splashing the water as he looked for his sword. "I don't want anything from you—if I could cut your shitty indoctrinations out of me like a tumor, I wouldn't hesitate."

There, at his feet—he kicked up with one boot, hand lashing out into the water to snatch up the sword as it rose to the surface. Brann swiped at the air to shake off moisture before planting the blade against his shoulder once more, holding it away from him and raising his empty fist towards Tark.

"Ah, the retreating high-stance—afraid you'll have to cut deeper than that to get me out of your head." Tark stepped off the embankment, the water rolling away from him, barely reaching above his knees. "Every move you make comes directly from my own playbook, soldat."

"Just stop fucking talking, already," Brann growled, rolling his torso forward and lashing out with his sword arm—the downward stroke cleaved through the water's surface cleanly, Tark stepping to one side, watching the blow pass him by.

"That's my boy. *Very* clean." He responded with another slap, this time sending Brann stumbling backwards, face stinging—had he struck any harder, Brann's nose would have been broken. "Faster, now."

"Hargh!" Brann snarled, nose bloodied as he leapt up, stabbing the squared tip of his sword at Tark's neck—his wrist was caught, mid-stroke, by Tark's free hand, the Marshall still neglecting any real use of his axe.

"I said *faster*!"

Tark's clenched fist barreled into Brann's chest, knocking the air from his lungs and sending the young man hurtling backwards against the lake's surface. Brann bobbed there like a cork, drifting downstream as he gasped for air, loosing an inhuman growl—he righted himself awkwardly, feet finding purchase once more against the lakebed. In this water, he was rooted in place every time he hoped to get enough leverage to strike out at Tark—keeping him firmly on the defensive. Abysmal conditions turning already hopeless odds even more against him.

Business as usual, then.

Tark crossed the gap quickly, trudging forward, unbothered by the waters—Brann stood firm, waiting for another chance to strike, having assumed the same defensive stance. Rather than attacking first this time, though, Brann waited for another swipe of Tark's claws before feinting out of their way—and, like a coiled snake striking, lashed out with his sword arm once more. The blade connected with scales, the length of his sword skipping along Tark's arm ineffectually, sending sparks up into the air as if he'd struck stone.

"At long last." Tark halted his advance, twisting his arm, showing off the crystalline growth of his scales—the surface of his sturdy flesh had turned mineral in an instant, deflecting any chance of Brann's sword finding purchase. "You've struck a blow. My, my."

He rolled his shoulder, flexing his clawed fingers, the crystalline flesh receding back into smooth, black scales. The kuaneach gave a mock salute with one finger, acknowledging Brann's achievement—before raising his battleaxe before him in both hands, assuming his own offensive stance.

"Now, we can begin."

Lightning fast, the pole of his axe lanced outwards, cracking itself against Brann's skull, knocking him unconscious.

*

The second round kicked off with Boomer already stumbling back on the defensive, Krieger's iron palms beating a mean tattoo into Boomer's body—anytime he found himself curling in to shield his torso, a punishing elbow or flying knee would sweep in from either side, leaving streaked abrasions across the width of his snout. Before the first round had ended, Boomer was already sporting a bloodied nose—now, it was a matter of finding the time between blows to wipe the blood from his eyes. This opponent was no sports fighter, every series of attacks he brought down on Boomer meant to blind or deafen or cripple. This wasn't a fight to win—it was a fight to survive.

The ropes repelled Boomer, trapping him down on one knee, unable to move from the spot as Krieger set to pummeling at his head with stabbing elbows. Boomer tanked the worst of the blows across his wide neck, protecting his head at the cost of his shoulders—just so he could get low, low enough to force Krieger in closer.

There, he saw it—Krieger's ankle would twist up on every right-elbow strike, his weight shifting between feet. Boomer timed his roll carefully, letting himself fall to the canvas, kicking forward towards Krieger's leg. The maneuver was narrowly dodged, Krieger half-skipping back to avoid it, but it was enough interruption to give Boomer a chance to bounce back onto his hooves and bring his fists with him. Two meaty left hooks bent Krieger to one side, exposing his head, and Boomer's right fist was already coming down hard on the man's skull—a crack across his face, and Krieger was sent reeling, having no choice but to disengage entirely as his eyes went wide and unseeing.

The crowd erupted, stirred by Boomer's resurgence into the second round—teeth slick with wet rust, Boomer grinned back at them, waving in the applause. A beaten face meant nothing to him, this was an average bout of friendly sparring where he came from. Still, he didn't keep his eyes off Krieger for long, dreading a reprisal. The bruises left by Tark were beginning to ache beneath his skin, welcoming dread.

For once in his life, Boomer feared defeat.

He countered this fear by going on the offensive, rushing forward to barrel straight into Krieger—Boomer was no grappler, but based on Krieger's reliance on elbows and knees, neither was he—the two of them slammed into the canvas, bouncing heavily, with Boomer quickly rolling himself on top. Planting his knees on either side of Krieger, left arm hooking under Krieger's armpit and across his neck, Boomer dug into his opponent's exposed belly and side with a series of machine-gun jabs. He needed to knock the air out of the man's lungs, drain his stamina; Boomer couldn't afford to spend the next round purely on the defensive, his upper body already battered and worn.

He'd anticipated this—Krieger's legs were curling up, wrapping around Boomer's waist—he tightened his abdomen, preparing to roll out and break the grapple before Krieger could flip him—but those strong legs never clenched. Instead, Krieger's feet travelled further up, beneath Boomer's ribcage, and dug their heels in—Boomer's lungs seized, and with a pained wheeze, he was rolled forward, end over end. His back slammed into the canvas, knees drawing up instinctively between himself and Krieger, keeping his enemy from being able to put him in a hold.

This was also a mistake—Krieger unfolded one of Boomer's legs, wrapping his entire weight around it, and kicked forward, bending

Boomer's knee the entirely wrong way. It went taut with a disgusting pop—
Boomer bellowed out in pain, responding with an unconscious swing of his
arm, fist plowing directly into Krieger's ear. The blow lifted Krieger off him,
and was definitely painful, but nowhere near as bad as the damage done to
Boomer's leg. He stood, his weight all on his good leg now, and the crowd
groaned at the sight: looking down at himself, his leg bent sideways at the
knee, the cartilage collapsed at the joint. The limb was useless, unable to
support his weight, dragging along behind him.

The world quieted now, Boomer's ears burning, blotting out the
murmurs of the audience—he slapped away the blood from his eyes
ineffectually, trying to clear the blurred silhouette of Krieger from his ailing
vision. He looked up, frantically searching, until he found it—his box, high
above the heads of the crowd. The seats were empty. Brann wasn't there.
Nobody was watching.

Boomer was all alone.

There was no being rid of him; Krieger bolted forward, sending
another flying knee up, and Boomer had no choice but to plant himself and
deflect with his arms—the maneuver proved to be a feint, and Krieger
brought his weight downwards, driving his fist into and through Boomer's
head. In a flash of light, Boomer was back in the ring with Tark, his brain
shaken about inside his skull—Krieger's elbows were on him once more,
bashing into Boomer's face as his arms went limp and the bell sounded—

*

The elevator shaft opened up on a massive underground chamber,
a slender catwalk rising up to meet them—there was little of interest to draw
the eye, save for the far wall, a complex series of enormous steel bars layered
across and atop one another. The entire far side of the vault appeared to be
one enormous tessellation of locks, entirely obscuring what they protected
behind an impenetrable wall of iron. As the elevator settled itself in place
before the catwalk, the glass box sliding open around them, the three

companions found themselves looking about for anything that might actually be worth hiding down here.

"Testing, testing, can anyone hear us?" Silence from his earpiece—Nes nodded. "Yeah, what I figured, no signal down here. No one's gonna know what we find down here until we're topside again, so let's be quick about it."

"Not much of a vault, is it?" Emrys asked, peering over the rails of the catwalk as they crossed—beneath them, a dark abyss, stretching unknowably deep into the earth below.

"Perhaps it was left unfinished," Red wondered aloud, her heels echoing off the metal catwalk. "Just a pit to throw their secrets into, so the entire world may forget about them."

"Or they're keeping those secrets behind that wall," Nes mused, pointing ahead. The long catwalk terminated at a sort of suspended platform, another terminal overlooking the abyss, a few meters away from the iron bars of the secured wall.

"If that's the case, they certainly weren't taking any chances." They stopped short of the suspended platform, necks craned upward, taking in the expansive sight of the overly complicated locks. Emrys tilted his hat back, rubbing at his forehead. "Can't imagine anything as simple as financial documents warranted all of this, no matter how damning they may be."

Nes was already tapping away at the terminal, frowning as he tabbed through the various windows—one in particular made him pause, and he input his selection hesitantly. The side of the terminal extended with a hydraulic hiss, a strange device somewhat resembling a medical pressure cuff appearing from a hidden compartment—and a second later, a massive needle stabbed outwards into the air from the cuff, making him jump backwards in alarm.

"That's because they're not hiding documents in there," Nes said, looking to Red. The viscountess stepped forward, visibly disturbed by the needle—she ran her fingers down it, recognizing it immediately.

"No," she agreed. "This isn't a records vault—it's not a vault at all.

It's an Animus Chamber."

"You don't mean..."

Emrys and Nes winced in unison as Red deliberately pricked a fingertip on the needle, letting the blood form in a tiny dewdrop before pressing her finger into a waiting slot in the terminal. A moment later, the terminal screen flashed green, beeping cheerfully, and the wall before them began unwinding—layers of locks unsealing, the steel bars receding back into their hidden slots, a deafening cascade of mechanisms whirring and pistons thumping. The wall before them parted like a great fissure in the side of a mountain, a dense cloud of steam venting itself, drifting down into the darkness below. In the shadowy fissure, a tremendous shape loomed, glinting metal and stone.

No, not stone—scales.

The hydraulics continued to hiss, and in another puff of steam, the shape drifted forward, towards the platform. Inch by inch, it emerged from shadow, the profile of the great sentinel revealing itself in the dim light of the Undervault—its snowy white head, the size of a small ship on its own, atop a powerful neck bound by thick manacles. Enormous, saurian, its eyes hidden beneath a domed visor that acted as both blinders and restrain. The Goliath's maw was drawn back in a frozen, wicked grin, exposed teeth tightly clenched—a single fang in its head was the size of a person, and as gravity uncoiled the chain binding its neck from within the vault, those fangs came to rest inches from the platform the three humans stood on.

"We should not have come down here," Nes murmured quietly.

"What unholy deeds have we unearthed?" Red breathed, the domed visor atop the Goliath's head beginning to glow from within, its snout dipping forward to bring the glass of the dome level with their platform. "What evil has been at work here?"

"Unless I'm fatally mistaken," Emrys said, stepping forward cautiously, "I believe we have discovered the resting place of Rigel, the Diamant Ascended. This is no feral Goliath—it's a kuaneach."

The giant beast, its pallid scales drawn taut around bone, as if dehydrated, did not move consciously. Its weight and structure were being manipulated by the chains binding it to the inside of the vault, and as its head continued to lower, dozens of pipes were made visible, connected to the back of its skull and visor and leading back upwards, disappearing far above their heads. The light within the glass dome was bright enough now to similarly reveal its contents.

There was a man inside.

"Are you two seeing this shit?" Nes asked, rubbing his eyes. "There's someone *inside* this thing's head."

Rigel's desiccated carcass, vast and lifeless, was host to a unique parasite. The red glass of the dome, so thick it was almost opaque, was shielding the ancient-looking man inside—fragile, pale, as lifeless as Rigel himself, draped in pure white robes like an interred corpse. The elderly man was bathed in the light of a panel of instruments surrounding him, as if he were seated in the cockpit of some ship.

Then, slowly, the man stirred.

"He's still alive," Emrys said, reaching out towards the dome—his bandaged hand curled, knuckles rapping gently against the red glass. "Hello, sir? Can you hear us?"

The infinite wrinkles of the old man's face folded back around eyelids that barely opened, the unseeing eyes searching for the source of the noise.

"We should leave," Red cautioned, hand going to her saber. "This is not natural—this is terrible magic here, something meant to be forgotten..."

The old man's eyes looked straight at her—he saw them now. The veil of sleep had dissipated from his hazy eyes, and he looked between the three visitors in turn. Wordlessly, he unfolded his arms, one shaky hand raising itself—with a tremendous effort, that bony hand extended a withered finger.

"What's he pointing at?" Nes asked, following the old man's finger.

Red, once more, stood before the giant needle protruding from the terminal. "This. He wants us to activate the Animus."

"What is an 'Animus', exactly?" This was beyond Nes, the practical-minded man standing in disturbed awe in such a presence.

"This chamber is of Jan-Jito design—blood magic, stilling the heart of this Goliath, ensuring it slumbers forever. That is, until its awoken once more."

"By what?"

Red raised her hand, looking to the tiny pinprick on her finger. "Blood. Namely, a blood mage's transfusion."

"So," Nes stepped towards her, examining the terminal, "If either I or Emrys had tried to activate the needle..."

"Your blood would not have been sufficient. Only a Jan-Jito blood mage can activate an Animus. One drop from me was enough to awaken this man, whoever he is."

"I believe we can declare that mystery solved, actually." Emrys maintained eye contact with the man behind the glass. "If this Goliath is the Ascendent Rigel, then this must be none other than the presumed dead Burnside Geiha."

"No fuckin' way." Nes watched, the wrinkled finger of the old man still pointing emphatically at the needle. "Two hundred-something year old Geiha?"

"In the flesh. And he wants our Lady Red to continue the rite of awakening, apparently." Emrys looked to Red. "You say one drop was enough to stir him awake—if you were to attempt to awaken Rigel, the Animus would need..."

She nodded. "All of it. A slumbering creature this size? I would surely lose my life in trying."

"This is all too fucked up for me," Nes chuckled, shaking his head. "What is happening? Why—what even—"

"Don't you see, old friend? This is the sin we've been looking to uncover all along." Emrys narrowed his eyes, regarding Burnside with equal parts contempt and fascination. "A would-be emperor, reducing himself to chrysalis form, using the body of a transcendent war hero to sustain himself for the long slumber—eventually, to be reawakened, reassume their shared former glory." He shook his head. "What torturous madness would resign oneself to such a fate, I could never..."

Burnside's eyes were looking panicked now, realizing they understood him perfectly—they just weren't going along with what he was asking of them. He jabbed his curled finger, commanding them silently, his mouth slack.

"Oh, he needs it bad." Nes waved back at Burnside, shaking his head. "Sorry, old chap—no can do. We need our Red alive, no breakfast in bed for you today. C'mon, let's go—we got what we came for."

But Red didn't move. Her hand, fingers curling reflexively, hovered above the needle, as if contemplating it.

"Red?" Nes abandoned pretense of nobility, addressing the hesitant woman as a friend now. "What are you doing, girl? You look like you've got something dangerous on your mind..."

Red looked to him, then to Emrys, frowning. "It can't be coincidence, can it?" The question was more for herself than for either of them. "Why here, why this place—why me? No one else could ever..."

"Uhh, no, you said yourself," Nes argued, reaching out to grab for Red's arm gently. "Any blood mage could activate an Animus chamber, I'm positive coincidence is exactly what this is—Emrys, you mind...?"

But Emrys was hesitating as well. He stroked his chin thoughtfully. "Was Lady Red in particular meant to find this place? Doubtful; I'm sure Burnside intended to have Jan-Jito folded into his new empire by the time he was to be awoken—likely he believes us to be here to offer Lady Red to his designs. But, consider—why would a great hero who served House Geiha be reduced to such a state?" He turned back, appraising the great beast. "May we consider, for a moment, that while Burnside Geiha performed this ritual for his own benefit…Rigel was put into this foul hibernation against his will?" Emrys pointed at the manacles, the great shackles clasped around the Goliath's neck. "He sleeps in bondage. This is not the tomb of a great war hero—this is his prison, and Geiha his imprisoner."

Nes stood at odds between his two friends. "You aren't. You can't be seriously considering—"

Red faced Nes now, and to his horror, spoke the unthinkable: "You remember Gideon's words: only Tark's forebears can put an end to him. We believed ourselves unable to stop him, to help Brann—but perhaps this is how we do it."

Emrys exhaled solemnly. "We put an end to Geiha's crimes, and bring its rulers to justice…by reawakening Rigel."

The spectral giant loomed over them, its toothy grin an ill omen.

*

Brann burst up out of the water, gasping for breath—he'd blacked out for only a moment, his sword threatening to roll out of his slack fingers—and it took all the strength in him to inhale, tighten his grip, and swing his sword arm across his body to knock away Tark's downward axe strike. Tark had shown him mercy, letting gravity take the axe, rather than swing directly into Brann's limp body, giving him just enough time to recover and parry. Brann winked an eye, shocks of pain blurring his sight, a knot forming just above his brow where Tark's handle had struck him—

The distraction almost cost Brann dearly, Tark having pirouetted on the spot and swinging his axe in a wide circle around himself—Brann dove to one side, submerging himself just as the stone pillar beside him exploded, disintegrating easily around the massive battleaxe. But no matter how agile he was, Brann simply wasn't tall enough: the water dragged him down by the waist, preventing him from moving more than one slow step at a time. And Tark was tall, very tall, the water parting easily around his knees with each stride. No reprieve was afforded to Brann—within the same breath upon resurfacing, he once more was knocked aside, barely blocking the broadside of Tark's axe.

"I tire of this," Tark growled, spreading his arms wide, Brann scrambling to pull himself up to full height above the water's surface. "Is this all the fury you boast? Have I truly mistaken your impotence for baneful scorn?" He slapped Brann once more across the face, his claws raking—blood sprinkled into the frothy water, Brann clutching at his head.

"Give me your rage, boy!" Tark brandished his axe, crouching in the water, bringing his head to Brann's height as he roared. "Give me storied pain! Give me *everything*!"

Screaming in Tark's face, Brann's eyes wide and frenzied, he hacked and slashed with wild fervor—sparks bounced off Tark's neck and head, those scales hardening into organic stone in seconds, deflecting Brann's most powerful blows. Not a mark was left on Tark, no matter how hard or hateful Brann's sword bit at him. Thunder cracked, sparks spat, and when Brann's arms were exhausted and his chest heaved, Tark hadn't so much as blinked.

The Marshal drew himself back up, slowly, looking down his long snout—for a moment, Brann almost thought he saw regret. It was quickly replaced with disgust.

"I send you out into the world, trammeled with poisoned purpose," Tark rumbled bitterly, "And you return, purposeless and neutered. You play-act the warrior—but your heart is resigned to failure."

He let his axe fall, the massive head splashing the water, coming to rest against the lakebed.

"You don't deserve the mercy of my blade."

Brann stared, face dripping with water and blood—the pole of the axe stood upright out of the lake. Tark's arms were at his sides. The air between them chilled.

The sword in his hand once more raised, and Brann heaved forward, one last defiant swipe aimed at Tark's neck—the kuaneach's huge hand easily snatched Brann's wrist in the air, gripping tight, the sword wobbling in Brann's loosened hand.

Tark stepped forward—once. Twice. He slowly, almost casually, wrapped his other huge hand around Brann's neck and torso. His fingers tightened. Brann seized, his breath cutting off, lungs squeezed—the young man stared up at Tark, the solemn-faced Marshal walking Brann backwards, slowly choking the life out of him as he brought him to the lake's edge.

"A quiet failure," Tark nodded, tightening his grip—Brann felt his windpipe closing itself off, the air whistling through his flaring nostrils. "That's what you are. My quiet, little failure."

The edges of Brann's vision darkened, colored spots whirling about—his knees buckled, and he realized Tark was gently pushing him under, the water rising to his chest, then his shoulders—then it overtook him, and his boots scraped as they kicked out, his body going horizontal. Brann's teeth were clenched so hard he feared they may burst. His hand slapped at Tark's, begging wordlessly for air, for mercy.

He sank lower, into the lake. Tark's snout breached the surface of the water above him—those draconic eyes stared at him, unblinking, watching Brann suffocate. Watching him drown.

This was how Brann died.

In his head, he saw those visions, Ula's words recycled in a useless garble of meaningless portent—the warnings, all ignored, blurring together in a slurry of fading consciousness. Brann saw the faces of the other recruits, resigned to their fates, pulling down their visors to march towards their Assay. He saw the faces of his friends, disappointed—the disdain he'd endured, the neglect, long before he'd been worthy of their company. He felt shame as he was diminished—he'd leave this world having been nothing but a burden to the crew of the Donnie. He was dying just as he lived.

The words in his ears bubbled up towards the surface of the water, disconnected, conversations replaying automatically.

"Make what you don't like better." Grishka.

"You got pulled into one of life's big lies, just like we all do." Nes.

"You wanna guarantee a win? You gotta look the part, always." Boomer.

Tark's snout was close to Brann's face, now. The water around his scales was murky, oily. Clouded by something dark.

"His scales are a mother's pride." Ula.

Brann let his sword fall away. He reached up, hand greeting Tark's face. His fingers rubbed gently over Tark's snout, thumb wiping something away—ink. Across the bridge of Tark's snout. The ink was washed away by Brann's tender touch, and beneath it, a vivid streak of bright blue scales.

"You don't have to pretend anymore." Zay.

The contempt in Tark's face retreated. The Marshal softened his gaze, eyes widening slightly, sorrow and shame creeping in. Brann recognized himself in those eyes, his thoughts cast far back, back to his younger years. On the streets of Geiha, at the mercy of its predators, those willing to exploit a pretty young orphan. The sorrow and shame he swallowed every day, burying it deep, hiding his pain.

Tark's grip loosened on Brann's throat, just for a moment.

That was enough.

Brann rolled aside, out of Tark's grasp, unseeing eyes looking for his sword—his hand made contact, wrapping around the handle. His boots found the ground. He kicked upwards, breaching the surface, leaping up to plant his boots on Tark's hips—and, with a primal roar, Brann emptied his crushed lungs, driving the sword down into Tark's chest with both hands.

The air rushed back into his nostrils, and he gasped, sucking life back into himself. His vision was still blurry—Brann wiped the water away from his brow, blinking away dark fog, coughing painfully. He opened both eyes fully, looking down.

His sword was buried deep in crystalline growths, Tark's scales sprouting an impenetrable shield of gemstone to protect his heart. Nonetheless, the Marshal was still, making no moves to dislodge the sword, to protect himself. He simply stood there, looking down sorrowfully at the blade.

"That's a killing blow," he admitted ruefully. One hand raised itself, claws stroking the bright blue scales across his snout. Brann was witness to something he was never meant to see—and though his sword found no purchase, the young soldat had landed another blow, one far more devastating and destructive.

Brann stepped backwards, off of Tark, back onto the embankment behind him. He gripped his sword tightly, and tugged it free of Tark's stony scales.

The kuaneach drifted back into the lake, still shielding his face with one hand, averting Brann's eyes. After a moment, Brann spoke.

"I've disarmed you," He declared, his voice hoarse—he pointed with his sword, out towards the lake, at the hilt of Tark's axe still jutting up from the water. "I've landed a killing blow in single combat. I've passed your Assay."

He paused. Emboldened by Tark's retreat, Brann sucked in more air, puffing out his chest proudly.

"I am all that remains of Lachlan. I'm taking back control of my House from you."

Tark didn't respond, still shrinking back, away from Brann.

"And I'm taking control of House Geiha. You are dismissed, Marshal."

Tark stopped. He looked through his fingers at Brann, still trying to conceal his exposed shame.

It was no use. He was defeated, and he knew it.

His hand slipped free of his snout, his face bearing that bright blue streak, unable to hide Tark's true face anymore.

"Lachlan is yours. I concede defeat. But, still remains, my duty to Geiha—what claim do you have on her borders? This duel was witnessed by no council, no House Tribunal. You need more than my word."

Brann sheathed his sword across his back. "As we speak, Boomer is fighting to retain his status as Geiha's Champion—when he wins, we'll take what we've found in Geiha's archives to the other Houses, show them how Burnside Geiha was buying up land from the other Houses, helping them fund their Arbitration Wars. Playing all sides against each other. He was a war profiteer—this whole House was built on sand. We're tearing it down. And you with it, if you stand in our way."

"Archives." Tark's brow furrowed. He stepped towards Brann, cautiously. He seemed oddly concerned. "What do you mean by that?"

Brann pointed across the lake, towards the far passageway that led towards the palace. "My friends have already infiltrated Geiha's archives— they'll find whatever records you've been hiding. It may not be enough to immediately dissolve House Geiha, but it's a step in the right direction. When we can prove what Geiha did to Lachlan—"

"Do they mean to enter the Undervault?"

Brann didn't expect this question. Tark was beginning to make him uneasy with these questions. "If the records are there, yes. Nestor—you remember him? He's with them now, he can get through any security. Whatever you're hiding, he can find it."

Then, Brann saw something he'd never seen before in Tark. Something he'd never thought possible.

Fear.

"They must be stopped. Immediately." Tark trudged through the sloshing water, retrieving his axe, beckoning Brann to follow. His entire demeanor had changed, his voice nervous. "Come—we've wasted too much time as it is."

"Wait, wait," Brann held up his hands, not understanding. "What's down there? What are you hiding that they aren't supposed to find?"

Tark's response was simple:

"Calamity."

42. The Coup

"We're leaving, and that's final. Red, do *not* touch that needle. This is not why we came here." Nes was storming off, back towards the elevator, motioning for the other two to follow. "We make for Cheneye, or for Saintmarie, or for any House willing to listen, and we get them to send an envoy straight to this palace and down here to see this shit. Whatever deals Geiha cut with the old heads of state, I'm willing to bet using their money to conduct freak experiments on a war hero wasn't one of them, they'll have more than enough to take it from here—"

"This is not a state matter, Nestor, this is a quantifiable evil at work," Emrys reasoned, motioning towards the petrified Goliath protruding from the wall. "We can't expect a council of politicians or lawmakers to intervene on something they can't understand, let alone something *we* barely understand—"

"I'm not signing off on the death of one of our own to resurrect some forgotten relic, one who may not even remember—no, one who may not even be able to *think* for himself anymore," Nes argued. "What do we really know about the kuaneach, what happens to them when they 'transcend'? They're fanatics; we could set loose a monster on the world, and that would be on us, not Geiha!"

"Respectfully." Red spoke up now, addressing Nes. "My blood, my body, is my own; how I choose to give my life is not a matter for committee."

"Neither is this. We're leaving." Nes turned again, crossing the catwalk towards the elevator. "Come on."

A noise stopped him—a heavy, metallic thunk. Something was released, somewhere. The three of them turned back, looking to the platform.

Inside the red dome, Burnside was pressing his gnarled finger against several switches in turn—steam hissed out from beneath his glass chrysalis, cascading down over Rigel's face. The old man was glaring at Red now, trembling with anger—he knew they intended to leave him here. This was not according to his designs.

He raised a clenched fist at the three, finger hovering momentarily over another switch. He pressed it.

Another loud clunk, and the dome slid up, backwards, away from Rigel's head—the glass chrysalis, unseated, hovered in the air a moment on the end of a mechanical crane arm. Then, the arm curled up and away, back into the vault, taking Burnside Geiha with it.

"Oh dear," said Emrys.

"There's no way that can mean anything good for us, which means we're out, now." Nes reached out, grabbing Red by the arm.

The whistle of silvered steel kissed coldly at his neck, and Nes froze in place. Red tilted her saber beneath his chin enough to tilt Nestor's head back, the blade scraping audibly against his stubble.

"You forget yourself, friend. Familiar trappings aside, a member of House nobility I remain."

Nes swallowed quietly, but stared back at Red, defiantly pushing his throat forward on the sword. "Respectfully, your Ladyship: fuck off with that nonsense. Nobility means nothing to me—I'm a contractor."

For a moment, Red's stony gaze faltered, the corners of her lips twitching.

Emrys stepped between the two, dutifully separating Red's saber from Nestor's throat with a bandaged finger. "Let's make a deal, shall we? Nestor, old boy, clearly the Viscountess needs to come to a self-realization on her own terms, at which time I fully trust she will see the wisdom in your words. My Lady, this is a good man clearly acting out of a selfless concern for your well-being; I'd wager that grants him leniency for his breach of decorum, aye?"

Red glared at Emrys.

"Good! So," Emrys continued, guiding Nes away, "You and I will head topside by ourselves—only momentarily, while we give the Lady a moment to herself," he said, speaking over Nes before he could interrupt.

"Then, when we've contacted the others, inform them of what we've found down here and we've all come to a decision on how to best proceed, we return for Lady Red and pass along the verdict—perhaps outside perspective will bring her around."

Nes hesitated, visibly fighting the urge to dig in his heels and continue arguing. Eventually, Emrys's words got through, and he nodded, pointing a finger at Red. "We'll be back in ten minutes—and you're coming with us, even if I have to tie you up and carry you out on my shoulder."

Red sheathed her saber. "Then I'll see you soon, friends."

But as Nes turned towards the elevator, he missed the silent exchange of resolute nods Red and Emrys shared with one another.

*

Wolf was pacing back and forth in the cockpit, keeping Zay on edge, the former merc biting her nails as she waited for someone—anyone—to report back in. It had been over an hour since any updates came through, surely the fight must be over by now—

The radio crackled to life, and Zay jerked forward in her seat, kicking her boots off the control panel, keying the mic. "Yeah, hello? Who is it, what's happening?"

"It's Hawkshaw." Some static. "Yeah, I made it to the outer wall of the palace. The broadcast is saying—yeah, it's...it's not good. Boomer's flagging, hard, looks like we're losing this one."

Wolf's head popped into Zay's view over her shoulder, spinning her chair slightly with his bulk, his ears alert as he stared intently at the speakerbox. He was waiting for Hawkshaw to mention something about Red. Zay leaned in close, keying the mic again. "Okay, so, what does that mean for us? What about Team A, have they checked in yet?"

"Nothing yet, but with Brann gone rogue and the fight winding down before they've cleared the city, I think we can assume this whole operation's been shot to shit. Only silver lining is I'm still talking to you, which means no one's triggered security yet."

"Do you see the boathouse yet?" Zay asked.

"I'm heading in now, but if they're not out in ten minutes, I'm going into the archives after them. They've taken too long as it is, something's—"

Hawkshaw went quiet. Zay waited, holding her breath. "Yeah?"

"Getting some chatter on another channel. The Uhlen just got tipped off, something's happening at the palace. They've been made."

"Pump your brakes, we don't know that yet—hey!" Zay lurched back in her seat, Wolf bounding out of the cockpit as if his tail had caught fire. "Godammit, you freaked the dog—hang on, we're coming your way, I guess!" Zay released the mic and leapt to her feet, autocannon strapped to her back, following Wolf outside.

"What, no? That's stupid? What are you—hey, are you there?" Hawkshaw stammered, speaking to an empty cockpit now.

Boots pounding metal and carpeted passageways, Zay raced after Wolf, following the echoing noise left in his wake out into the cargo bay of the ship. Sliding down the ladder, Zay untangled herself from a mess of mesh netting Wolf had knocked aside—she looked out across the plains, the lycan galloping on all fours towards the city, a dark blur against the red clay.

"Goddamn idiot," Zay hissed, taking a moment to activate her own earpiece and slip it in, setting off after Wolf at a brisk pace. "Hey Team A, if you can hear me, we should have put a leash on Wolf, he's headed your way—and so are the Uhlen, so you better be ready to go, fast!"

*

Another spinning kick sent Boomer reeling—his hooves slipped on the slick canvas, the entire ring sprinkled with freckles of bright blood, both his and Krieger's. Mostly his. The equine fighter was barely in the fight anymore, all of his living will summoned to keep himself upright on his one good leg, though even that was beginning to fail him. Krieger advanced on him endlessly, pushing Boomer back, making laps around the ring. Fists, elbows and kicks alike stripped away Boomer's defenses anytime he tried to raise his arms—he was beaten in every way, save the one that mattered most: he refused to fall, no matter what.

The belabored Krieger halted, his chest heaving, the man spitting pink saliva—he needed to catch his own breath, working himself to the point of exhaustion just to keep Boomer on the run. He stood over the horseman, flexing his bloodied hands, attempting to restore circulation to his pulpy fingers—so many blows had been delivered to Boomer's solid head and midsection that Krieger's wrapped hands were peeling and blackened around the knuckles. It was like fighting a brick wall.

Boomer wobbled on his good knee, propping himself up on it—unbalanced, his head swayed, too heavy for his shoulders. Eyes swollen and purple, he tilted his head, staring up at Krieger.

And grinned through his split lips.

The crowd, left hoarse and exhausted themselves from this endurance test of a fight, once more cheered Boomer on—and for the first time since the opening bell, Boomer saw the frustrated Krieger's face twitch. This fight should have been over hours ago.

Krieger responded to Boomer's defiance with a downwards hook, knocking the horse's grinning face for a loop. Then another, for good measure. No words were exchanged, the mute fighter reticent as ever, but the message was clear.

Take the hint. Go down. You've lost.

But Boomer was a sore loser. His fists clenched against the canvas, and his moment had arrived.

The core of Boomer's very being engaged, and in the split second before Krieger struck a third time, Boomer stood up.

The uppercut rocketed upwards, directly into Krieger's head, catching the man mid-swing. The entire accumulated energy of Boomer's body was delivered through kinetic energy into the man's brainpan, his jaw crunching—and in his last moments alive, Krieger's look of surprise faded into nothing as his eyes rolled back.

The two bodies fell together—Boomer, fully spent, and Krieger's lifeless corpse—they landed parallel to one another, face to face, the canvas welcoming Boomer like the softest of mattresses in its cozy embrace.

The roar of the crowd was a distant ocean, waves crashing on a beach somewhere far from Boomer. As his eyes closed in a dreamy smile, he was deaf to the sound of the loudspeaker, the declaration of the judges that his body had hit the ground first, and therefore rendered Krieger the winner. As the world faded to dark, Boomer didn't mind that it was because of a black bag that was pulled over his head, or that he was being dragged out of the ring by his legs, or that several members of security were denying the medic from checking Krieger's pulse.

He didn't mind that the crowd was booing over the decision that he had lost. In Boomer's mind, he'd made the kid proud—that earned him a good sleep for a while.

Boomer remained a champion in his head, undefeated. He was the best there ever was, and ever would be. And that's all there was to it.

*

The overwhelming tidal wave of the crowd's fury had proven too much for Grishka—retreating from the stands, she ducked into the passage leading back to Boomer's dressing room, shielding her head from the noise with both wings. Personal discomfort aside, she needed to inform the others of the result of Boomer's fight, and there was no way she would be heard over the din of the stadium.

Walking at any pace with her avian legs was awkward, her hybrid form ill-suited for proper flight and proper strides alike. Nonetheless, she knew better than to draw attention to herself, and even with the gift of illusion at her beck and call, the odds were well-stacked against her in a stadium so crammed full of people. So, like a flightless bird would, Grishka walked down the hall, awkwardly bobbing her upper body to balance her weight properly.

The dressing room door was mercifully close to Boomer's box. She ducked inside, closing the door behind her—even then, the crowd was so loud, Grishka doubted she would be able to adequately communicate with the team. No choice but to wait it out or leave the stadium altogether, and the latter sounded just fine to her.

But a moment's hesitation came. Something caught her eye, pulling Grishka's attention towards the opposite wall. A flash of lavender—her own dress, reflected back at her from Boomer's dressing room mirror. The sundress hung off her shoulders unevenly, her wings hunched back to keep the straps of the garment from slipping off. Grishka blinked, looking herself up and down properly for the first time in many, many decades. Sure, there had been mirrors aplenty aboard the *Myrmidon*, but none presenting her own visage back to herself with such glamorous composition. The lights surrounding the vanity made her feathers shine almost blue, midnight sky glistening wetly across her wings.

There were unbidden feelings of turmoil bubbling up from within herself, the tengu spirit finding herself aware and present in the moment that creatures of her ability and longevity rarely fathomed. She craned her neck, delicately tugging her shoulder strap back into place. The dress righted itself on that side, but sagged more on the other—it simply wasn't designed for her frame.

With an inward sigh, Grishka stood tall, her reflection becoming a shimmering blur. Before her now, her human self stared back, the dress fitting properly now. It hugged her modest curves, the bright fabric melding seamlessly against her radiant skin, the black-painted nails of her fingers dragging themselves up her front. She reached up even higher, running her fingers through her dark, feathered hair, tugging the locks down until they dragged across her face, her piercing eyes staring back at herself through the distressed bangs.

There was never a doubt in her mind that she was attractive—as a raven, the tengu witch was a model avatar of nature, of omens and futures to come. Between forms, her hybrid self often met with courtship from the beastmen and wildlings of the woods, extolling her mischievous personality with a scruffy kindness.

But in all her life, since before she could remember her life before her days as a witch, she'd never imagined herself as being so conventionally...

Grishka kissed at her fingertip, feeling the softness of her lip.

... Human.

A melancholy tugged at her heart. An expectation—no, more than that, an understanding of what was to come, the twilight breaching the horizon of her mind's eye. There was a finality to the way she allowed herself to admire her own reflection now, as if this might be the only chance she would have to look so beautiful.

She almost didn't want to leave this room. But her newfound friends depended on it, even if they didn't know it. The quiet witch thanked herself for this moment, this silent gift of the self, and blew a farewell kiss to the mirror. This body was taken for granted for so long, she'd almost forgotten what a joy it could be to simply...be.

These silly humans had no idea how lucky they had it; to be so beautifully fragile. So delicately mortal.

Grishka would put this gift to good use. She owed it to herself.

*

To say Brann was uncomfortable at Tark's side was an understatement, to say the least. Putting aside the fact he practically had to jog just to match the kuaneach's long strides, Brann had to fight not to stare at Tark, nearly being caught more than once shooting up nervous glances at the Marshal. The passage stretched on for what seemed like miles, and they'd been travelling for what seemed like miles.

Brann unconsciously felt his vision creeping up once more, and this time, found Tark staring back at him—the two quickly broke eye contact.

Apparently, the discomfort was mutual.

Tark decided to break the silence first. "The company we keep, eh?"

Was that a joke?

Brann scoffed, the sound strangled in his throat. "No shit."

Tark chuckled quietly.

It *was* a joke.

What the *fuck* was happening.

Brann couldn't believe the words coming out of his mouth: "Your mom says hi. Your brother, too."

This caused a notable change in Tark's stride. "Oh?"

Brann decided not to relay Ula's words about Tark deserving to die. He wasn't exactly sure their relationship had reached that level of trust yet. "He—Gideon—came to see you, at the..." Brann steered his thoughts away from the fight with Boomer. "At Mercenary Row. We flew him back to your home village. I spoke with Ula, she took me into the Temple."

Even without looking directly at him, Brann could sense Tark's surprise at this. "Now that is interesting," the kuaneach admitted. "To what end?"

Brann chewed his lip. "No offense, Marshal, but—you're gonna have to cut me some slack here, this is a really weird conversation coming off the back of a really weird turn of events. I'm sort of freaking out internally right now."

Tark looked down at Brann. And laughed.

Not rudely, not haughtily. He genuinely found it funny. Brann had never heard the stoic Marshal make such a sound—it was oddly warm.

"I suppose so." Tark scratched his chin a bit. "To the business at hand, then. Afterwards, perhaps if we should cross paths again, then..."

He trailed off. There was something oddly terrifying about that notion.

Up ahead, in the dark, an overhead lamp was shining on a far wall—beneath it, an exit.

"This leads to the surface," Tark said, nodding at the door. Coming up on the right, the wall of the passage concaved around a culvert, leading off in the opposite direction from the exit hatch. "That leads to the boathouse—I assume your planned point of egress?" Tark pointed towards the culvert, into the darkness beyond.

"Sharp as ever, Marshal," Brann nodded.

"Under no circumstances should you allow your companions to enter the Undervault. What awaits them is nothing short of their extinction, and possibly that of us all." Tark ushered Brann towards the culvert. "There will be time enough to decide on a course for our own futures after you've intercepted them. Trust that I would not ask this of you unless it were the most grievous of plagues they may unleash."

Tark halted, stopping Brann short with an extended arm. "All things considered," he said, almost as an afterthought, "You need not refer to me as your 'Marshal' anymore... Brann."

He sounded like he might have a conniption, the way he sheepishly spoke the name aloud, minus any condescension in his voice or attached rank alongside Brann's name. Tark was coming to terms with his surrender, it seemed, and Brann did his part not to make things too painful for the kuaneach.

"What should I call you instead, then?" Brann asked. "Any other titles you like to go by...'Tark'?"

The part of him that had graduated basic training still feared reprisal at addressing his former commanding officer on a first name basis. Tark considered this for a moment. "Actually, there is one..."

He didn't get the chance to tell Brann—the exit hatch before them opened.

The Uhlen had found them.

"Ah, there you are, Marshal." The Speaker came to a stop beneath the overhead lamp, a dozen of his comrades filing in behind him, forming a wall of bodies before the exit. They were all armed and ready, fanning out on The Speaker's wordless command, directing them to move in alongside him towards Tark and Brann. "I see you've finally made good on your promises—excellent. We'll take the traitor up top and have ourselves a nice homecoming for him, how's that sound?"

Tark looked to Brann, nodding at the Culvert behind them. "Go."

Brann already had a hand on his sword. "You sure? You've seen me fight, I can help—"

"You've already earned your freedom today, boy," Tark interrupted, "As well as my respect. Don't go losing it by dying pointlessly."

Brann walked backwards, retreating towards the culvert, followed by The Speaker's watchful gaze. He shot up his middle finger at the Uhlen, disappearing behind the corner, trotting off into the darkness towards the boathouse.

The Speaker swung his gaze back towards Tark dramatically, hand on his hip. "Now, Marshal, what'd you go and do a fool thing like that for?" He didn't sound surprised at all—on the contrary, he seemed to find this quite amusing. "Letting a confirmed terrorist and outspoken enemy of Geiha live—that's verging on treason."

Tark reached behind his hip, taking hold of his axe. "All apologies. It was not my intention to merely verge."

The assembled Uhlen all laughed among one another, sharing nudges and excited nods. The Speaker pointed an accusing finger at Tark. "We all know you won't come quietly, Boss—in fact, we're hoping you don't. You and I both know this has been a long time coming. All those years babysitting these gormless citizens—you went soft. There's no room in our new Empire for soft."

Tark shook his head. "There was never going to be an 'Empire'— you've prostituted yourselves to a sick old man who would sacrifice his entire House before ever facing his own death with dignity."

"That's *his* decision to make," The Speaker shouted, "*Not* yours! The Marshal was only ever steward to the true leader of our House. Our allegiance is to Geiha—where's yours? To that coward? That fucking *traitor?*"

Tark inhaled deeply. He closed his eyes, neck craning back, face turned to the ceiling. He reached back, his claws finding the leather harness bound between his shoulder blades—and unclasped the fasteners. The leather belts jingled as the harness came undone, falling to the stone floor behind him. Tark rolled his shoulders, the joints in his wings cracking as he unfurled them, flexing the appendages, relishing in the feeling of being so satisfyingly unbound.

The Uhlen, even in their numbered strength, all took a step backwards—the weapons they held, guns and swords and hammers, were all sheathed now. They knew from experience there was no defeating Tark in a straight fight. Instead, they all filled their hands with identical batons, capped with a smooth steel sphere at their ends—the Uhlen flexed their wrists, and the spheres crackled to life, spitting arcs of electricity intermittently. They couldn't pierce Tark's hide, but they could surely attempt to render him unconscious.

If they lived long enough to try.

"Comrades, today your Marshal has been relieved of his command," Tark declared, holding his axe lengthwise in front of himself. "All that remains now..."

He snapped his arm back, and with a sharp clang, the lug cylinder at the weapon's throat split down the middle—the axe unfolded itself, doubling its length in an instant, axeheads at each end of its shaft. The twinbladed poleaxe twirled itself around Tark's hand, its fearsome length nearly reaching floor to ceiling now. The sovereign kuaneach crouched slightly, giving a slight nod: a warrior's sign of respect towards the blood about to be spilled.

"... Is Iron."

The Uhlen lunged forward, fast as lightning.

Tark was faster.

The first of them had tried to be clever, feinting and coming in low at Tark's side—but the upward swing of Tark's poleaxe was merely to gain momentum for his backwards stab. The far end of his weapon came swinging in from behind the Uhlen, cleaving him in two. A pair of legs wobbled for a moment, deprived of their motivation. The torso splattered beside them, head twitching, arms reaching towards those legs uselessly.

The legs toppled over, a geyser of blood spraying across Tark's face. He didn't even blink, his snout dripping.

The other Uhlen hesitated, but reengaged, keeping shoulder to shoulder now. Tark's weapon spun in a whirlwind before him, denying anyone else from getting close enough to strike. The Speaker roared back at Tark to rally the others, and once more their electric batons spat blue plasma, the stun weapons jabbing forward into Tark's path—though they were knocked aside, jolts of electricity shot up Tark's arm as a result, making the kuaneach stumble.

An opening. The Uhlen stepped in close, stabbing their batons in at Tark's arm. Electric sparks bounced off his scales, and Tark grunted as he fell to one knee, nearly losing hold of his axe. Nearly. Swinging in wide, his powerful fist plowed into the chest of an Uhlen, the force of the blow bouncing the smaller man off the wall, leaving a crater in the bricks. The space he left was quickly filled by another Uhlen, who raised his baton high, aiming it directly at Tark's face.

Too slow. Tark stepped back, lifting off his knee, and swung his paralyzed arm upwards. The arm was numbed, but his grip held true, and the head of his axe severed the Uhlen's leg at the thigh—ignoring the screams, Tark let the Uhlen fall over, catching his axe with the other hand just in time to deflect another pair of eager batons. The two soldat had foolishly put themselves between Tark and the wall behind them. Tark informed them of this tactical error by whipping his massive tail around, into their bellies—two limp bodies crumpled against the wall, their visors clacking together as they fell into a heap.

A stabbing pain in his side—Tark bellowed, his wing shooting out behind him, alight with electricity. The three batons digging into his kidney were quickly sapping his strength, the enormous kuaneach lilting to one side as his muscles seized. He fell to his knee once more, and with a fourth baton joining the others, he inevitably lost his grip. The poleaxe fell, clattering to the ground, his clawed fingers spasming uncontrollably.

The Speaker stood before Tark now, at face height. The expressionless visor nonetheless held utter contempt for his former commander-in-chief, the man savoring this moment of victory. He leaned in close, the head of his baton spitting along Tark's neck, crackling spittle making the flesh there tingle.

"Seems you've trained us a little too well, Marshal," The Speaker taunted.

And he was right. Tark had held nothing back, instructing every Uhlen that had passed under his command with a personal level of care and supervision. Every lesson, every tool of war, gifted to each soldat in turn, until every man was as profoundly adept at killing as the next.

There was one tool, however, he could not give to them. One quirk of biology that humans had not yet come to wield.

Tark's jaws snapped forward, clamping down hard, at the sweet spot between the gullet and the shoulder. Fangs sunk in deep, blood filling his maw. As the Speaker writhed in agony, screaming so loud his vocal processor shorted out and went silent, Tark raised his good arm to cup the man's head from behind, embracing him.

Then, he bit down, hard, and wrenched his hand to the side.

The Speaker didn't split in two even halves—moreso, as his spinal column went one way, the rest of his torso went the other, taking the vital organs with it. As the Uhlen's body was reduced to a collapsed heap of meat and entrails, Tark spat out the crushed remains of an esophagus, holding aloft the severed trophy of manskull. An arm, as well as a tail of vertebrae, dangled from the Speaker's severed head—the visor, intact, obscured the face from view. Tark could only imagine the look of surprise permanently transfixed on the smug Uhlen's stupid face before another stun baton stabbed into his temple, and the kuaneach fell into black sleep.

43. The Fall

The elevator dome swiveled open, Nes and Emrys stepping out into the archives once more. The moment they cleared the box, their earpieces crackled to life, and Nes spoke to anyone who might be listening.

"Team A here, we found what we came for, but it's—" He looked at Emrys, searching for the word. "—Complicated. Suffice to say, it won't be as easy as walking out with an armful of documents."

A hiss of static. Then: "About time, old man, we've been trying to get through," Zay barked back, sounding out of breath. "Wolf split, he's making for the city, we're almost at the wall—Hawkshaw, what's the word on the boathouse?"

"I've got a dinghy secured, ready to go," Hawkshaw replied. "Just waiting on you slow bodies."

"Does anyone have any updates on Boomer or the kid?" Zay asked.

"All bad, very bad," Grishka spoke up, breaking her long silence. "Boomer gone. Fight over."

"'Gone?'" Nes repeated. "What do you mean, 'gone?'"

"Wait one, I'll check," Hawkshaw interjected, going quiet for a moment as he did so. Then, when he spoke again, he sounded somber and defeated. "She's right. They're saying Boomer lost the fight on a technicality and has been taken into Nightwatch custody."

Zay groaned. "So that's it, then? We're fucked?"

"Not just yet. Hawkshaw, what are they saying about the other fighter, Krieger?"

"Funny you should ask," Hawkshaw said in response to Nes. "They're keeping mum on him—most peculiar, they declared Boomer a loser without naming Krieger the winner."

Nestor smiled to himself. "That's my boy, Boomer."

"You think Krieger lost after all?" Emrys asked quietly, interpreting Nestor's reaction.

"I think Krieger is no longer with us, and House Geiha is absent a Champion for the time being." Nes spoke back into the mic. "Nothing we can do for Boomer now. We'll have to trust he'll be kept alive long enough for us to plan a rescue down the line, we need to focus on finding Brann and making our exit. About what we've found in the archives—"

"Whatever it is, that'll have to wait as well," Zay interrupted, "Hawkshaw says the Uhlen have already been tipped off and are on your way. Grab what you can and get out, this whole operation has run aground."

Nes frowned. "How much time do we have?"

"Considering how long you spent out of earshot? None." Hawkshaw's voice was urgent once more. "If they're not already standing in front of you, they'll be knocking on the door any second, so listen to Zay and make for the exit, now."

"But we—" Nes turned, cutting himself off as he saw Emrys. The professor had already crumpled up a page in his burning hand, holding his journal open with the other. He gave Nes an apologetic shake of his head.

"All apologies, my dear. I hope in time you'll come to forgive us for this."

Emrys let loose the page with an underhanded toss, the green fireball splashing at Nestor's feet.

Instantly, the engineer was bound in place, arms pinned at his side by the spectral arms wrapping themselves around his body—it was useless to struggle, the wide-eyed Nes unable to even speak, a bony hand clasping itself over his mouth. Emrys seemed to drift backwards, away from him— but in actuality, it was Nes being pulled away, the ghostly shroud of limbs carrying him towards the archives exit at an increasing pace. The further away he flew from Emrys, the closer to the ground the arms pulled him, until eventually he sank into the floor beyond the doorway and disappeared into the flames altogether.

"For once, I find myself in complete agreement with the Lady," Emrys muttered sadly to the empty room before him. "I must defer to her judgment on this matter."

No sooner had the ghostly embers dissipated before a steady procession of boots crossed the threshold of the archives, the ashes of Nestor's departure wafting away in their wake. More than a half dozen Uhlen stormed into the room, looking all the worse for wear—clearly, these soldat had encountered someone else before Emrys. Someone who had put up quite a fight, judging by their cracked visors and bloodied armor.

"Afternoon, gentlemen," Emrys announced cheerfully as he held aloft his journal. "And at risk of sounding derisive, may I say, you look as if you've all had a brush with Death himself today. Unprepared for such a meeting, were we?"

The Uhlen didn't respond to the taunt, at least not verbally—their weapons spoke on their behalf, the sounds of blades being drawn and machine guns racking filling the chamber.

"Indeed." Emrys nodded, as if finding the response quite illuminating. "Then perhaps I could do you the courtesy of arranging a more formal introduction?"

*

Brann burst through the door, finding himself face to face with the twin barrels of a pair of boxy autopistols—Hawkshaw awaited him on the other side, ready for battle, and for a moment Brann felt a chill. Had the security protocols been tripped in the automaton?

But those fears dissipated once Hawkshaw recognized his human companion, the bot holstering his pistols apologetically. "Damn good to see you, kid, where you been?" He looked Brann up and down, the servos in his eyebrow clicking as it shot up. "You look like you lost a fight with a brick wall."

"Not too far off the mark," Brann admitted, cradling his shoulder as he stepped around—Hawkshaw stood beside a small pier, a dinghy moored alongside it. "This how we're getting out? Where are the others?"

"Not even gonna lie, if you run off again after I tell you this, I might just kneecap you," Hawkshaw warned, raising his hands. "It's not good news, and I know you're prone to reacting... shall we say, boldly?"

Brann's chest rose and fell visibly, still catching his breath after running through the tunnels, trying his best to keep his composure. "Boomer lost the fight."

Hawkshaw let his hands fall, nodding solemnly. "He's alive, in custody. Look, kid, we'll come back for him, but right now we gotta go, this whole place is about to go up in arms. Geiha won't risk the fallout from the other Houses they stand to take if they assassinate their own Champion, loss or not. We retreat now, we live to get him out another d—."

Hawkshaw froze, then tapped the side of his head, and suddenly he was broadcasting the audio from his internal radio for Brann to hear, a mess of gunshots and screams and what sounded like—

"—Wolf's gone mental—anyone can hear—, get out NOW—"

Zay's voice was barely audible in the crackling pops between gunshots. Hawkshaw and Brann held eye contact as they listened in, knowing what it meant: Wolf had reached the city and had set upon the Nightwatch. The alarm would sound any moment—

—And in that moment, the opposite doors of the boathouse swung open, and Nes barged in, his eyes dark and stormy. After Hawkshaw once more lowered his raised pistols at the latest intruder, Nes wordlessly climbed aboard the dinghy, setting to untying it from the short pier.

"Nes, where is everyone?"

"Gone." Nes brushed Brann off, eyes in a dead stare as he worked.

"What do you mean, 'gone'?"

Nes pushed past roughly, the dinghy's mooring line bundled in his arms. "They're staying put. Goddamn idiots wanna play hero?" He was talking to himself more than to Brann, grumbling between breaths. "Fine by me. Less dead weight on the ship dragging us down."

"We can't let them awaken Rigel," Brann argued, "Tark—"

The bundled line scattered across the pier as Nes threw it down bodily, spinning on his heel and shouting in Brann's face. "Goddammit, Brann, enough about Tark—can you learn to mind your own shit for once?! They made their choice, it's time to move on!"

Hawkshaw was at Nestor's side in an instant, gripping the man's arm tightly. "Hey friend," he said calmly, despite his narrowed eye apertures, "Mind backing off the kid a bit?"

Nes stared Hawkshaw down, unmoved. "I could pull that fake brain in your head apart in seconds," he growled in warning. "Turn what makes you 'you' into a pocketwatch."

"Well, at least then I'd never be late for anything," Hawkshaw quipped without skipping a beat and without loosing his grip. "But in the meantime, I'm gonna need you to step outside yourself and be a team player with us again, yeah?"

Nes kept his lips pursed tight, seeming to come to his senses as he looked to Brann again. Taking Hawkshaw's meaning, he nodded slightly, and the automaton's clawed hand released his arm.

"If we stay, we're dead too," he reinforced, albeit a degree more calmly now. "Get on the boat, kid, c'mon."

Hawkshaw interrupted Brann before he had a chance to protest again. "He is right—they made their choice, the right thing for us to do is to respect their wishes and get ourselves out of the city." He turned to the young soldat now, knuckling affectionately at Brann's chin. "They're grown-ups. They can take care of themselves. If they make it out, we'll be waiting for them on the other side."

It was two against one, and Brann was beginning to see nothing was going the way he wanted today. He shook his head, but remained silent.

"Outstanding. All aboard, we're getting out of here." Hawkshaw followed Nes off the pier and onto the dinghy, taking the helm and beckoning Brann to follow. "Just a little trip down the river, and we'll be home free."

*

The bullets ripped through Emrys as he advanced on the Uhlen, flipping casually through the pages of his journal and whistling a tune, not even minding his coat being peppered with frayed holes or the flesh of his cheek being torn open.

"I believe I had a page for just such an occasion, somewhere here..." He mused jokingly, somewhat relishing the rising panic in his enemies, the masked soldaten breaking formation to form a semicircle around him. "Ah! Found it." Emrys grinned, his exposed jaw muscles hanging in tatters from his chin as he pretended not to notice. "Ready to begin whenever you are, gents."

The Uhlen's guns ran dry, the tinkle of shell casings reverberating around the chamber. Those without guns held their blades at the ready, though they refused to advance, still sizing up this seemingly invincible foe.

"No?" Emrys shook his head, still smiling. "Damn shame. Well, *I'm* ready."

He tore the selected page from his journal and crushed it, casting it from his palm as if he were rolling dice. The embers bounced haphazardly across the ground, and the Uhlen scattered out of the way, putting their backs to the surrounding walls.

Their mistake. The embers leeched into the floor, green flames carving spiraling swathes around Emrys, and every book and scroll lining the chambers exploded outwards—clusters of skeletal arms, reaching forth as if trying to escape their own graves, clawing and snatching aimlessly at the air. The Uhlen who had strayed too close to the shelves found themselves snagged in the bramble of the ghostly arms, screaming and flailing—the arms passed them up and around the walls, tearing into and through them as they went. The thrashing bodies were plucked apart like insects, until the phantasmal arms were passing nothing but severed limbs between one another, surrounding the remaining Uhlen in a whirlpool of their own comrades' detritus.

Emrys held the source flame in his palm, concentrating on the spell as he carefully plucked several more pages from his journal between his fingertips, passing them into his free hand before tucking the journal away. He pressed the corners of the pages into the exposed bullet wounds on his chest, pinning the pages to his torso for easy access, bearing them proudly as if they were award ribbons.

"By my count, there's still six of you left," he proclaimed, raising a page between his fingers. "One hand should be sufficient for the task, I think."

The first Uhlen that charged forward met no resistance as he buried his shortsword in Emrys, twisting the blade with a bold war cry. Barely flinching, Emrys locked eyes with the Uhlen through the visor, lowering the page into the Uhlen's field of view before crumpling it. He pressed the green flames of his fingertips to the Uhlen's temple, and a ghosthand burst from the Uhlen's face, tearing apart the man's skull from within—Emrys stepped backwards, allowing the soldat to fall to the ground, not even bothering to remove the shortsword jutting from his side.

"Perdoa, esquexe..." Emrys began reciting an ancient passage from memory as if he were a priest praying for his congregation, the Uhlen all lunging forward at once now to hack their pound of flesh from him. "Perus noe renonci ao teus deberus di espallur i conecementis aos ignorantus," he continued, voice raised above the din of his own body being savaged, pulling pages from himself and delivering spells onto the Uhlen's heads. "Paru qui noe atipen a verdadi nis falsides..."

Swords and hatchets thudded against bone and flesh uselessly, Emrys cooly disbursing death to the Uhlen one at a time—one found his armor burned away by ghostly flames, leaving nothing but his own skeleton beneath, before the bones crumpled to a useless heap. Another was sent skyward by a giant arm, the bony apparition gripping the Uhlen like a doll before yanking itself back into the ground, leaving a splattered smear in its wake. They were waging war on death itself, and defeat was all but assured.

Until one Uhlen, circling around cautiously, saw through the mysticism—keeping outside of Emrys's peripherals, he stepped in close, taking aim at the source of the magics: the holyman's bandaged arms. With two swift strokes, his sword sliced up, then down, quelling the ghostly flames filling the room in an instant.

Emrys stumbled back in shock, eyes popping wide—iron runes clinked against the ground as they slipped free of their wrappings, the bandages unravelling silently. He raised his arms before him, sleeves slipping back behind his elbows, revealing the stumps of his withered forearms. Emrys's link to the other side had been severed, and the faintest wisps of necromagic dripped like plasma from his dead flesh.

He chuckled, trembling, knowing his end at long last. "Me and my big mouth, yeah? Suppose I should have heeded their advice after all."

The victorious Uhlen stepped forward, reaching into Emrys's coat and pulling out the journal. He gripped the pages forcefully in his fist, ripping the little leather book apart in one confident swipe of his arm, tossing them up into the air.

The shredded pages drifted down around Emrys as he sunk to his knees, his flesh beginning to shrink away from his bones. He'd reached the limits of his borrowed time, and it was being reclaimed now, the centuries catching up to him and rotting him away where he stood. His wide hat sunk low over the hollowed-out sockets of his eyes, the skeleton that was once Emrys bowing, keeping his final prayer to himself, whispering quietly to himself between his chattering teeth. In moments, the corpse was still, and Emrys drifted away on his final rattling breath between those barren ribs.

The three surviving Uhlen brushed past the kneeling skeleton, towards the elevator. As an afterthought, Emrys's killer paused, turning to deliver one final insult: he planted his foot on the back of Emrys's coat, shoving forward. The kick sent the skeleton toppling over, dusty bone fragments crashing across the hard tiles. The wide-brimmed hat was buffeted upwards, the skeleton turning to sand and whispers, borne away on an enigmatic wind that flew Emrys far away from this place.

*

The elevator was moving behind her. Lady Red stood before the terminal, gazing up at the hideous grin stretching across Rigel's frozen skull, considering everything that had brought her to this moment. Her mind wandered over her past journeys; her rebellious youth, her many fights with Queen Hester. Her nights abroad, spent gazing up at the stars in Wolf's embrace, consoling the wounded soul of a man trapped within the beast's form. If not for her, Wolf would have been slaughtered long ago; executed at the whims of her own mother, no less.

"Oh Wolfie," she said quietly, hand hovering above the shining silver needle, "I hope you can forgive me for leaving you like this. Perhaps now, Mother will see in you what I did."

Her mother. Red looked back over her shoulder as the elevator arrived at the far end, the Uhlen stepping out, already reloading their guns. She wondered if her mother would approve of what she was about to do. It was funny, in a way—Red had spent her entire life denying her mother's wishes, living out of spite for her parentage. Now, in this last act, she found herself caring more about what Hester thought of her than she ever had before. She chuckled, turning back to the needle, recalling one of Queen Hester's favorite phrases at court:

"We must pay no mind to the rabble," Red said to herself, the Uhlen assembled behind her. "We must pay no mind at all."

The gunshots echoed all about the Animus chamber, and Red felt herself crumple, catching herself on one knee—she barely felt the needle stab upwards into her arm as she fell, piercing her artery.

Gasping for air, she hefted herself up, draping herself across the terminal—with all the ceremony of swatting away an irksome fly, an annoyed Red drew her saber and activated its needle, slicing haphazardly behind her with an arc of boiling blood. The head and shoulders of the Uhlen closest to her lifted away from the rest of his body, falling away from the catwalk, his detached arms toppling alongside the rest of his body on the catwalk.

"As I was saying." Red looked upwards, watching Rigel's features carefully. The Dampyr blood was draining from her rapidly, being pumped into the Goliath before her. Red began to drift off, clutching the needle weakly, a faint smile tickling at the corners of her mouth. In her last moments, she thought of the problematic young upstart that had set all this into motion—the young man who had saved her life and restored her Mother's sanity.

"You'd better be right about this, Brann," she said faintly, drifting away as the tremendous beast before her began to shudder. "Or I'll haunt you forever."

The entire chamber rumbled. The platform wobbled, the Uhlen catching themselves on the railing of the catwalk—everything was bathed in an eerie white light as Rigel's mask illuminated, his muscles beginning to twitch all along his neck and jawline. His heart thudded loudly, ominously: the ritual was complete, and Rigel was awake.

The Goliath's wide jaws snapped even wider, his neck snapping free of its imprisoning shackles. The devil cracked a smile, its entire body beginning to pull away from the wall. The earth quaked as iron stung and snapped, chains and locks bursting in a shower of sparks that rained down on the Uhlen. They barely had time to turn heel and flee for the elevator before the catwalk gave way in the tremors, sending them tumbling into the abyss below.

Lady Lorna slumbered on in quiet bliss, enjoying the warmth of the white light that washed over her, dreaming of a morning in the gardens— Hester at one side, Wolf at the other. The gravel and sparks splashing across her face were the gentle kiss of drifting flower petals in her dream, and Rigel's deafening roar was only a wave breaking on Jan-Jito's shores.

Red slept on, not minding the rush of wind on her ears as she fell. An eternal lullaby in a garden of promise, where she dreamed her Mother was proud of her now.

What a dream she dreamed.

44. The Severing

The dinghy wove in between passing ferries, the boats honking their displeasure in response—though the SICA units aboard the crafts looked on curiously, they didn't raise an alarm or open fire, which put Brann's mind at ease. The whole city wasn't yet on alert, and there may yet still be time to reach the outer wall of the city and stop Wolf from ruining their escape plans. The sun was beginning to set behind the city wall, casting amber sparkles across the river's surface, the dinghy plowing through the reflections as it sped on. Emrys and Red would return on their own terms, he assured himself—they were more than capable. If he could survive his encounter with Tark, as inexperienced as he was, then surely the two of them could handle a few Uhlen stragglers.

"There's our stop," Hawkshaw called over the motor—they'd reached the city wall, a huge mesh grate allowing the river to continue flowing out while barring any water crafts from exiting this way. Not far from the outlet, Brann could see an alcove in the wall, a maintenance hatch visible—likely the same point of entry the others had used.

"It's sealed good and proper now," Hawkshaw said, seeming to read Brann's thoughts. "I don't have access to the door codes, and trying to break through will trigger the alarm. Our best bet is cutting through that grate—Nes?"

"On it." Nestor unhooked the handsaw from his belt, squeezing the trigger to throttle it up. "Getting all sorts of problems solved with this thing," he remarked, stepping up off the dinghy and onto the embankment, ducking under the arched ceiling of the outlet's passage.

"Ah shit—stay low, kid." Hawkshaw motioned for Brann to get down as he stepped off the dinghy as well, and peeking over the embankment, Brann saw why—an approaching SICA sentry, dressed as if he were a Nightwatchman. The sentry waved down Hawkshaw, and the two fell in step together, making for the alcove door.

"Perimeter sensors tripped," Brann could hear the sentry say.

"Something or someone made their way into this tunnel—same one we sealed earlier, weird right?"

"Yeah, definitely weird," Hawkshaw agreed, standing beside the door and scratching his chin thoughtfully. "You think we should unlock it and take a peek inside, make sure no one's trying to breach?"

"Can't hurt." The sentry rapidly tapped his metal fingers on the numpad, and the door chimed open.

"Hey, thanks bud." Hawkshaw patted the sentry on the shoulder before nonchalantly snatching his claws at the sentry's spine, ripping an important looking component out of his twin's lower back. The sentry unit wobbled briefly before collapsing in a heap, his motor functions completely disabled.

Hawkshaw dusted his hands together with a few metallic clicks, waving Brann over. "Brann, Nes, change of plans—we're good, door's unlocked." He kicked at the crumpled SICA unit. "He can't raise an alarm without his neural link intact, but all these units are on monitored patrols— staying in one place for too long will definitely raise suspicion, so let's get out, fast."

The door swung open behind him as he was speaking—turning on his heel, Hawkshaw was now face to face with Zay, who was breathing heavily and soaked in sweat.

"Wolf," she gasped, clutching at her cannon. "Is he—?"

"Talk about good timing," Hawkshaw said, nonplussed. "No, we haven't seen him, and had you tried opening that door ten seconds sooner you'd've been shot."

"Fuck!" Zay kicked the door wide open furiously. "I lost sight of him just outside the wall."

"This whole plan's gone off the rails. Join the party," Hawkshaw replied, gingerly propping the door open with the prone sentry's leg. "You can stay here and look for him, or come with us back to the ship—today seems to be an exercise in free will, so either way works for us."

Zay adjusted the autocannon in her arms, waving Brann and Nes in, looking utterly defeated. "Let's get the fuck out of here, that idiot should've stayed put on the ship."

"My thoughts exactly." Hawkshaw stepped aside to allow Nes into the tunnel, Brann following closely behind. Before either Hawkshaw or Zay could enter, however, there was a hiss of radio feedback coming from somewhere nearby—everyone froze in place, searching for the source.

"...Repeat, there's heavy activity in your sector. You have any sort of visual, Thirteen?"

It was the SICA unit. Zay rolled the limp android over with her boot, revealing a hand radio strapped to his belt. An apparent failsafe, in case his neural link failed—a human touch Hawkshaw had overlooked. Zay glared at Hawkshaw, who deflated visibly, cursing quietly to himself.

"Overwatch, no response from Unit Thirteen."

A second voice on the line.

"Copy good, go to stations."

In the distance, a siren began to wail.

Zay began to raise her autocannon. Hawkshaw's shoulders sagged, his expression pained.

"Run," he said.

An electronic pulse emanated from the sentry's temple, urgent and shrill. Then, a second later, the same sound came from Hawkshaw, who snapped his head back to attention.

His hands were filled in an instant, raising his pistols towards Zay. She was already taking aim as well. Both fired simultaneously; both fell backwards in the same moment, their shots meeting in a single moment of deafening climax. Then, they were silent, and still.

Seconds oozed past. Raising from his crouched position in the doorway, Brann pulled his hands from his ears, heart thudding as he stepped towards the two where they lay. Gunsmoke and dust whirled about his legs, his boots crunching softly in the dirt.

Zay was propping herself up on an elbow, a shaky hand sliding across her belly to staunch the heavy flow of red pouring from the wounds beneath her breast. "Oh," she said, staring down at the damage. "Yeah, you got me."

Hawkshaw was faring about as well—though he couldn't bleed, the automaton pushed himself up on the stumps of his former hands, frayed wires sparking and sizzling against the ground. He looked down to survey his legless body, Zay's higher caliber rounds having torn him in half at the waist. "Yeah, I think you might have grazed me, too," he replied. His vocal processors sounded strained, smoke pouring from within the gaping bullet hole in his chest. "We'll call it even, yeah?"

Nes kneeled at Zay's side, aiding in putting pressure on the wounds with his hand on hers. He looked to Brann solemnly. "You don't have your medpak on you, do you?"

Brann felt sick. He shook his head.

"Hey tin-man," Zay called out, gritting her teeth. "You calmed down now?"

Hawkshaw let himself slump back in the dirt, raising one of his maimed arms to wave it in acknowledgment. "Yeah, I'm good now. My bad everyone."

Zay nodded at Brann. "Go pick him up," she said, raising herself to her feet with a pained effort. "We're getting out of here."

"Zay," Nes warned, trying to push her back.

She smacked his hand away, using her still-smoking cannon as a crutch to support her weight. "I said we're leaving," she barked, coughing wetly. Blood flecked on her lower lip. "There's supplies back on the ship to fix us up. Shaw, stop lying about."

Hawkshaw giggled as Brann reached down to him. "Hey, good one! That was clever." He craned his neck, watching his severed spine twitch with hydraulic whirrs. "Look what I can make it do," he joked to Brann, the young man lifting Hawkshaw up over his shoulders.

"Can automatons go into shock?" Brann asked. "I think that's what's happening to you right now."

"Oh, I can't feel a thing," Hawkshaw replied cheerfully. "Don't worry about that, my pain receptors automatically shut down in the event of catastrophic system damage. Yeah, that means I'm proper fucked, now. No saving this body, it's a full neural transfer for me. Zay, was this your plan all along; get me out of the picture so you can finally have the pilot seat all for yourself?"

"Oh, absolutely," Zay said, not missing a beat, leaning on Nes for support as they walked into the tunnel. "And you fell for the trap. Finally, I got to shoot your dumb ass."

*

The maintenance tunnel passed under and through both inner and outer layers of the city wall—as a consequence, it passed under the river at one point, water dripping on the heads of the four intruders as they traversed the dimly lit passage. The rumbling of water overhead created a strange, uncomfortable aura around them in the tunnel, the sound a deep echo in the dark.

"Once the water goes quiet," Hawkshaw was saying, his vocal processors still sounding somewhat fried, "That means we're on the other side of the river, close to one of the main gates of the city—the hatch exits before that, so keep an eye out for the latch, its old and hard to spot."

"I remember where it is," Zay answered back from ahead. Her voice was lower, huskier.

Brann felt the hairs on the back of his neck stand up—for a moment, he was back in the mines under Jan-Jito. There was a raspy breathing behind him, drawing closer.

He spun around suddenly.

Nothing behind them but dark.

"Uhh, kid?" Hawkshaw asked quizzically. "What's up? You forget something?"

The pale apparition he expected to see disappeared from his mind's eye, the fearborne hallucination vanishing. Brann took a deep breath. He felt he was losing his grip, being pulled back into a deep dark hole he thought he'd finally climbed out of.

"No," he said, turning back, picking up the pace. "Remembered something, actually."

"Uh huh." Hawkshaw shifted on Brann's shoulder. "Maybe you can tell me about it later, when we aren't running for our lives. Hey, speaking of running—"

"Found it," Nes interrupted, stopping Hawkshaw from cracking wise again. The latch was rusted and warped, bent awkwardly out from the wall, the door itself crusted over with sediment and hardened clay. "The Donnie is a straight shot out across the plains from here, so get ready to—"

The moment he began opening the door, several small bullet holes appeared in the craggy surface, sending dirt and debris showering over their heads. All at once they ducked down, out of view from the ajar door, the sound of a man's voice yelling at them from just outside.

"Throw out your weapons and come out, hands up!"

"Godammit, of course they'd have covered this exit already," Zay hissed, scooping up a handful of red dirt to scrub her blood-slicked hands dry with. "Good going, Zay, tripping the perimeter sensors, chasing after that stupid dog—"

"Nightwatch," said Hawkshaw. "Hang on, let me try something." He cleared his throat with a mechanical sounding buzz, then called back out: "Why don't *you* throw us *your* weapons, eh? Assholes?"

"Nes," Zay growled, "Give me my gun, I'm gonna shoot him again."

Nes obliged, swinging her autocannon off his shoulder and passing it over. "They'll have sealed the other door behind us by now. There's no going back, so it's do or die: let's get creative, people."

"I shot my load already," Hawkshaw scoffed. "Y'all have any better ideas, be my guest."

"I got one." Brann rolled the crippled automaton off his shoulder, setting him against the wall.

"Uh, Brann?" Zay said apprehensively. "What are you doing?"

Brann relieved himself of his sword, slipping the scabbard off his back. Holding it by the strap, he tossed it out the door, the weapon thudding into the clay outside. "I'm coming out," he called loudly. "Don't shoot me."

"Brann, you step foot out that door, I'm gonna blow your legs off next," Zay snarled.

Brann's head was spinning. He'd skipped the entire fear and apprehension stage of this production and went straight to self-sacrifice—*how unlike me*, he thought. "It's my decision, and I've lost enough friends today," he argued. "You're all getting out of here."

He slipped his hands out of the doorway, then the rest of him followed slowly—Brann half expected a bullet to tear the top of his skull off the moment he appeared. The five officers waiting outside opted not to fire, much to his relief—they stood in a semi-circle before him, rifles all aimed at his chest, trussed up in tac gear befitting outer wall sentries.

"Holy shit, is that him?" One of the officers gasped.

"Hell yeah it is, brother." Their leader, a lieutenant, stepped forward, lowering his gun slightly. "We've had your pictograph on our 'most valuable fugitives' board for weeks, kid," he said, grinning. "Good day for us—bad day for you."

There was movement behind the officers—Brann tilted his head, catching a flash of color. Lavender.

The lieutenant reached behind his waist, producing a set of shackles. "Cross your arms together for me," he ordered, stepping towards Brann. "I'm taking you in. Maybe you can share an overnight cell with the horse before you're executed, if you don't fuck with me."

She was there suddenly, beside one of the officers. A very human Grishka traced her hand up the man's arm. Brann watched the officer turn slowly, confused, caught entirely off guard by the attractive woman cradling his cheek. She raised her other hand, a colorful powder heaped in her palm. She blew on the powder, as if blowing the man a kiss, sending it wafting across his face.

The lieutenant froze in place as his subordinate began screaming behind him. He turned just in time to see the younger Nightwatchmen clutching at his head—centipedes were boring out of every orifice, even chewing their way through some new ones, his face bursting outwards around the fiery orange arthropods.

"What the fuck!" Another officer stumbled back in terror, aiming his rifle at Grishka and firing off a volley.

But she wasn't there—she'd casually appeared beside him next in another cloud of powder, whispering something in his ear, something Brann couldn't hear over the gunfire. His rifle went silent, and the officer stood straight, his jaw going slack. As Brann watched, that jaw continued to droop, stretching far past the human body's natural elasticity, and his entire face appeared as if it were melting—soon, his gooey eyes rolled back into his sagging head, his flesh dripping off his skeleton in mossy clumps as his final breath was accompanied with the exhalation of several slick vines.

Grishka winked at Brann, her eyes flashing a raven's black mischief. She nodded upwards, at something above his head—Brann turned to see what it was, just in time to duck out of the way of the dark meteor hurtling to the earth. A familiar spear drove itself down into the lieutenant, rooting him to the spot. Wolf crouched beside him, his chest and shoulders heaving in a trembling rage, eyes full of sorrow.

"She's gone," he said, for Brann's ears only. "The witch told me."

Brann didn't answer at first. He kneeled to pick up his sword, re-equipping it across his back. He reached out tentatively, clutching at Wolf's shoulder.

"Get us out of here," he finally said, "And you'll be carrying out her last wishes."

Wolf grunted, reaching his arm out to grip his spear. He yanked it free of the earth, and the impaled lieutenant slid down its length like a ragdoll—Wolf rattled the weapon to shake the man's body loose in a splash of gore. Whipping it around, he leapt for the next officer, taking advantage of the man's horror at what had become of his fellow Nightwatchmen and catching him off guard. He fell quickly, without a sound, other than that of Wolf's spear finding his heart.

The last officer was caught in a frenzy, screaming and firing at random—everywhere he looked, Grishka was there; every time he fired, she was gone, drawing closer with each shot. He whipped his rifle around, firing in rapid bursts, hoping to catch her everywhere she wasn't—

—Until Brann found himself staring the officer in the eyes, the gun pointed in his direction, and the officer pulled the trigger before he realized someone was in his line of fire—

—And Brann heard a hail of bullets as they thudded into flesh—

—And he opened his eyes, and saw a lavender dress filling his vision, fresh red roses blossoming across the fabric.

Brann had no time to avoid the officer's crazed fire, and Grishka had teleported herself in front of him instead. A round had pierced all the way through; Brann's hand went to his shoulder, feeling the bullet lodged there. He didn't even register the pain as he stared, Grishka turning slightly to meet his gaze, smiling faintly.

For the first time since they'd met, Brann's vision held—there was no air of illusory magic about her, no strange alterations to his perception. She was simply in this one place, at this moment in time, just for him. Smiling that same mischievous smile, as if she was savoring a personal joke no one else would ever hear the punchline to.

And then Brann felt the pain in his shoulder, and in that same instant, Grishka raised her arms, and the ravens appeared.

Like embers rising from flames, she dissolved. Dozens, hundreds, thousands of ravens, spiraling up from within her, each cell of her being birthed in a flurry of black wings. A maelstrom of birds, cawing and shrieking, spiriting away the witch from head to toe. Brann and the others cowered beneath the rising wall of the avian storm, watching in equal measures of awe and terror as the lavender dress vanished, and the entire sky was blotted out. The Nightwatchman let his rifle clatter to the ground, turning to run—but his sin was not to be forgiven by the tengu spirits, and suddenly he found himself lifted off the ground, carried away towards the horizon amidst the ravenous flock. Brann could scarcely see the flashes of white and pink flesh as the officer was set upon, the ravens a black cloud of fury and scorn—and then there was nothing but the ravens themselves, the man simply vanishing without a trace.

Grishka had taken to the skies, a host of dark seraphim unto herself, the cacophony of ravens that had sprung from her temporarily mortal body set free upon the land. Like a cloud of distilled omen, they circled far above their heads; above the city entire, even, creating a smokey haze in the red evening sky.

And as quickly and quietly as she'd come into his life, she now was gone, leaving Brann staring up at her hundreds of thousands of children that rose up to meet the coming night.

A tiny object far above his head glinted in the setting sun, and then Brann heard a clink as something fell into the clay at his feet. He reached down, wrapping his shaky fingers around it, holding it up to see.

His corpsman pin, missing ever since Grishka had first come aboard the Donnie. As shiny and polished as the day he'd lost it.

Brann couldn't help but laugh, the sound more like a sob in his ears.

Maybe he was starting to get the joke after all.

Zay shoved her way out of the door, finding herself up close and personal with the Nightwatchman whose head was disintegrating into centipedes. Disgusted, she unloaded on him, cannonfire ripping through his body until it went still; with a final pop, hundreds of the leggy critters burst from their makeshift hive, scurrying for cover.

"We won't make it to the Donnie before reinforcements come if we keep hanging back here," she said hoarsely. "And it won't be more Nightwatch they send our way next."

Nes followed her out, dragging Hawkshaw along with him—Wolf intervened, hefting up the automaton effortlessly, cradling the torso under his arm. From this position, Hawkshaw was stuck staring up at the sky, watching the hurricane of ravens far above.

"Ah hell," he said ruefully, "I didn't even get to see her off. Bye bye, Grishka—take care, girl."

"Zay's right," Nes said, nodding on ahead—across the plains, the Donnie was waiting, its colorful profile a mere dot against the backdrop of Mount Taree rising behind it. "Won't do us any good lollygagging—if we're all that's left, then there's nothing for it, and we gotta go, now."

Sucking down the pain in his shoulder, Brann set off behind the others on the long run across the plains. In their wake, a black feather drifted to the earth, settling amidst the footprints in the clay.

*

You should have kept running.

You've made your choice, and now it's time.

This is all your fault.

These prickly burrs lodged themselves in Brann's thoughts as they half ran, half dragged each other across the red clay plains. The closer the Donnie drew, the stronger the feeling grew that he was fooling himself about ever stepping foot on it again. It was too great a reward to hope for, that he might escape today; that any of them might yet survive. Everything had fallen apart, and the reality of their monumental defeat was only teasing at the back of Brann's mind—where did it all go wrong? Which wrong move did they make; what wrong turn did they take?

He couldn't think and breathe at the same time while running. So, his breaths puffed as he ran, and his thoughts gave chase, waiting for the moment he stumbled and fell, that they might descend on him like a hungry predator.

They were nearly there, the descended ramp of the ship in sight. Step one foot aboard, and safety was all but guaranteed.

The sound of mosquitos, whizzing by his head; an irritant buzz of high-pitched whistles. The clay all around him began to bubble and pop.

"Get down!" Someone shouted, and he heard rain clattering against the Donnie's hull under a cloudless sky. Only when wolf bodily tackled him to the soft earth did Brann understand they were being fired upon, bullets streaming down and splashing all around them. Only then did he hear the firecracker report of distant autocannons, their wet ripples echoing across the plains at the muted speed of sound. Digging himself out from under Wolf's arm, Brann looked back towards the city.

Their pursuers were approaching fast, low-slung ground vehicles, the dark profiles of mounted guns at their rear—even at this distance, the glint of emerald and chromed platinum was unmistakable; Geihan infantry assault karts. Light ordnance to allow for maximum speed, it stood to reason they wouldn't have sent anything larger if the intent was to intercept their quarry on the open plains.

Brann saw a silver lining in this almost immediately.

"Zay," he called out cautiously.

"Yeah?"

"If we're in range, so are they."

A pause. Then: "Good point!"

He heard her dragging herself across the soft clay, then the click of her autocannon's bipod extending. With the GIAK's accelerating towards them, firing from this distance while moving, they couldn't get a perfect lock on a target that was flush against the ground. Zay had the advantage of stability, of being able to take her time and line up her shots against much larger targets.

Brann heard Zay's breathing slow to almost nothing. Then she inhaled sharply.

Her autocannon issued its response to the approaching challengers, its roar coming in short, measured bursts. Brann kept his head low as he watched, the GIAK's beginning to swerve in a delayed reaction to the bullet rain finding their own heads now. Then, a few volleys in, Zay hit something vital: one of the GIAK's sent up a wall of red clay as it veered suddenly, then leapt up into a vicious barrel roll.

"Got one," Zay said flatly, as if she were in a casual session of target practice. "Keep low and make for the Donnie, I'll have the rest taken out by the time you get aboard."

Obliging, Brann stood along with Wolf, and from his back Brann heard Hawkshaw answer Zay: "You sure you can't twist my arm into staying and helping out? I can't really hold a gun at the moment, but I can give you moral support—"

"Good idea, leave the gimp," Zay said between trigger pulls, "I can find out if he's got a self-destruct button somewhere and use him as a landmine."

"Well, it was nice knowing you, skin-sister, don't get run over now!" Hawkshaw tapped his stubby arm against Wolf's shoulder. "Onward, stallion."

They barely made it several yards further before something halted them—a sudden quake; a deep lurching sensation in their bellies, as if the ground they stood upon had sunken into itself. Catching themselves on a stumble, they all turned back towards the city once more.

Brann knew that whatever it was, the seismic event must have been significant if it meant the GIAK's had all come to a sudden stop. Their guns were silent, the vehicles turning profile, away from the pursuit of their prey. The infantrymen in those vehicles were watching along with Brann, he could tell—it was impossible not to at the sight. Within the walls of the city, the earth had split open.

And something was crawling out.

The clouds of ravens above the city began to undulate in hypnotic, coordinated swirls. They were no longer flying in distant, erratic formations; they were circling now, an ominous stormhead brewing amidst their gathering numbers. Beneath that black storm, a white mountain peak stretched towards the sky, drawing up and into itself—then, stretching out and away. The gleaming sheen of metal struts unfolding, extending—the artificial wings of a biomechanical being of tremendous size. Beneath the skeletal frame of those flightless wings, great and powerful shoulders, capped with ghostly white bone, the flesh having long since been rotted away.

"Red did it," Nes declared for all to hear. "Rigel's been revived."

Behind him, Brann could hear Wolf's sorrowful whine.

"Something's wrong," Brann said, not taking his eyes off the terrible sight. "Why does he look like that?"

Bony shoulders rotated to give way to bony spines; the truth of Rigel's existence was settling in all too slow for Brann. He knew the answer before it was said aloud, as that long neck with its exposed vertebrae craned upwards; and the great head of the deathly beast rose up from behind the walls of the city, and Brann could see the cold glow of terrestrial fire from within a vacant skull.

"He's not Rigel anymore," Nes finally answered, and in his voice, Brann heard defeat. "He's an exdead."

Tark's ancestor raised his jaws to the sky, to the ravens circling all about his mountainous form of snowy white, and from him came the disembodied scream of a hundred thousand dead souls crying out to the indifferent God that had bound them to this forsaken Goliath. The iron crown that obscured his eyeless sockets illuminated, much like the infantry visors of Geiha that Brann was all-too familiar with, and those silvery steel bones sprouting from Rigel's shoulders flexed once more. Black ghostflame ignited from within their frames, and Rigel's avernal wings blinded all who bore witness to his rebirth, their abyssal heat searing across the red evening sky.

"Tark tried to warn me," Brann groaned, feeling his fingers digging into his hair. "I should have listened. Why didn't I *listen?*"

There was a rush of air all around them, and then it went still, and quiet. Static crackled against Brann's skin. Rigel was drawing himself up, bony claws contorting as they clenched, his neck arching high above his shoulders—all around him, the light of the evening sky seemed to dim, being pulled into an unseen gravity field. Then, Brann saw it—what could have been a newborn star, a tiny pinprick of white light veiled by shadow, hovering within Rigel's exposed ribcage. It grew larger and brighter by the second, a flickering spark that gained life and heat, pulling more light and energy into its condensing singularity—

You were wrong.

You were so wrong.

Rigel's jaws snapped wider, the young star in his chest vanishing into smoke.

Brann's heart sank.

And from those jaws, a concentrated beam of pulsar fire erupted, searing across the skyline of the city and boring into the earth. Blinding hot death carved a swathe through everything and everyone—Brann heard the screams in his head before they ever reached his ears. Buildings were cut down like reeds beneath the laserlike blast, steel and concrete and flesh and spirit melting into nothingness, fiery explosions blossoming all around the city. An indiscriminate and precise flood of antimatter disintegrating everything that lay before it; Rigel's neck drifted to and fro, his jaws aiming the ray of death with purposeful intent. A paintbrush of erasure, wiping the canvas of Barrier City clean of all life and creation, branding the surface of the earth with scorch and scorn.

He should never have run; he should never have stopped running; everyone and everything was dead because of him—

Brann turned away from the horror just as Rigel's jaws snapped shut, stifling his ray of judgment for the time being; Nes was already marching towards the Donnie, resolved in purpose and stride.

"Nes!" Brann jogged, then ran to catch up, feeling the heat of the dying city burning his back. "Nes, stop!"

He reached out, and grabbed for Nestor's arm; the old man yanked it away, turning to face Brann with a clenched jaw and wide eyes.

"We did this," he growled, leveling an accusatory finger at Brann's eye level. "And we're stopping it. *I'm* stopping it. Let me go."

"But how? What can we—"

Brann looked past Nes. The Donnie.

The reactor.

"Don't you fucking dare," Brann whispered.

Nestor's eyes softened, and he blinked, as if stunned by the weight of his own resolve. What he'd planned on doing only just now registered as Brann protested, and for a moment, he almost seemed to falter.

Almost.

Nes reached out both hands, taking hold of Brann's shoulders.

"When I first met you kid," he said, his eyes wet, "I was a tired old man convinced the earth was solid. That I could reach out, touch it, and understand it all. I'd seen everything, lived through everything—maybe lived too much."

He bowed his head for a moment. "I can't think about what comes next. I can't let myself see past now, the need to do something in this moment. I can't think about crossing over into...nothing."

Nes raised his head once more. "So right now, I need you to do something for me. I need you to believe. Believe harder than you ever believed in anything. For me, and for the both of us—believe that I'm not flying into nothing. Believe that I'm flying through it and into something more, beyond all this. Don't say it's over, and don't say goodbye. Tell me the earth isn't solid, here in this moment—believe it, and I'll believe you."

Brann sucked in a sharp breath, the lump in his throat threatening to choke him. He bit his lower lip until it bled. He stared back at Nes, determined in his gaze, a single hope of beautiful possibility held in his mind's eye as he imagined seeing his friend again, years from now, on some distant plane.

Brann didn't speak. He nodded, unblinking. Nes saw in his eyes that assurance of tomorrow, and nodded back.

"Thanks for flying with me, kid." Nes let his hands drop to his sides. "Those dumbasses back there—they liked to talk up a big game, but the truth is there was only ever one captain. And she was always *my* ship."

*

Fastened in the pilot's seat, quickly flipping the switches that began the ship's startup sequence, Nestor's jaw was firmly set to the point his breathing made his nostrils flare. Clenching a fist to keep his hand from shaking, he let the rising sound of the engines overwhelm him, stifling the sound of his rapid heartbeat in his ears. The Donnie's heartbeat took over instead, the sound of its reactor thrumming its monotonous tune to him like a golden harp, soothing him somewhat. He was in the ship's care now— all he had to do was steer for a few seconds, and she'd do the rest.

He pulled back on the stick, and with a prolonged lurch as the landing gear clung to the clay below, Nes was airborne—hovering above the rusty red plains, he gently coaxed the Donnie into a smooth yaw. The horizon lilted ever so lightly, and then he saw the city slide into view—and with it, Rigel, his blackfire wings making Nes squint somewhat, even moreso than the setting sun beyond. With the great beast now in sight, he held firm, bringing the ship's rotation to a stop—and Rigel was dead ahead now, in his mental crosshairs. Holding in place for a moment, Nes let go of the controls, reaching into his vest. He removed his lighter, along with the crumpled stem of a stale cigarillo, one of the last ones he'd ever rolled.

"Sorry Brann," he said as he lit up, "Promise I'll quit for real after this one."

Taking the longest drag of his life, eyes lidded, Nes watched through the blue smoke as his vision tunneled around the exdead Goliath he would be introducing himself to shortly. Still clutching the cig between his fingers, his other hand gripped the stick once more, and he exhaled slowly, savoring the taste of his old life on his tongue.

"Fire in one hand, steel in the other."

*

Brann and the others watched the Donnie ascend slowly, hovering just above their heads as it rotated, then remained in place for a few moments. The great ship was a spectacular display of reflected rainbow colors in the evening light as it stared into the sun, and its nose dipped forward slightly—almost as if Nestor was nodding goodbye to them.

Then the engines flexed their nozzles and fired up, spouting blue fountains from their widening apertures, and the engines began to tilt on their axes and lift the ship up and over Nestor's companions below. Brann shielded his eyes against the buffeting cushion of air as the *Myrmidon* lifted off for its final flight, and when the engines were fully aligned, she was off— gaining speed and altitude in equal measure, heading straight for the city. For Rigel.

The Donnie shrank away from the earth, reaching for heaven— even without its old aquatic landing floats, she still cut a gorgeous profile in the red sky, and Brann held onto every second he could as he burned the image of her into his mind. If this was the last time he was to see her, then he—

The screaming green lance of laserlight cut through the dark silhouette of the Donnie, and a second later, a burst of flaming light made Brann wince—an explosion sent the ship off course, black smoke trailing behind it. The city's automated air defenses were still active. The EMAC round had severed one of the Donnie's engines from her tail end, and the fiery comet hurtled straight down towards the city—in the opposite direction of the wide arc the falling Donnie was now making.

Brann felt his knees buckle. Nestor's plan had failed, and in a few moments, he would crash into the earth—all for nothing.

For Nes, Brann began to pray.

*

The earsplitting alarms all around him might as well have been gnats buzzing about for all the attention Nes paid them, his teeth gritted around the stub of his ashen cig, knuckles turning white as he gripped the control stick with both hands. The engines were screaming in protest as they attempted to make up for the sudden lack of thrust, and he knew he couldn't recover altitude fast enough to make another pass above the city— there was no time, the engines would stall or burn out before he righted the craft; he'd have slammed into the surface well before he got the chance—

Sucking in air, Nes slowed time for himself, letting the last nub of his cigarillo calm his mind and direct his next moves. He reached up, watching the horizon curve carefully for a few extended seconds, mentally calculating the ship's trajectory.

Then, he shut off the remaining portside engine, applied full throttle to both starboard engines, and yanked the flight stick hard to the left, opening all flaps as he did.

The Donnie's hull squealed as its entire weight was suddenly thrown skyward, inverse to the force of gravity pulling upon it, and for a split second it seemed as if it may stall outright and fall straight down—then the engines reached full power, and Nes felt his stomach turn as the horizon inverted along with the ship, and he began to spin. Slowly at first, the surface of the earth crossing over the nose of the Donnie—the city walls were coming into view as he descended—then, faster and faster, its trajectory realigning itself to Nestor's original flight path as it locked into a fatal barrel roll.

And, though the world seemed to spin out of control, Nes could see the telltale white of Rigel's massive form growing closer and closer, dead center in his sights once more.

"Mind the afterburn, motherfucker."

And Nestor squeezed down on the throttle switch, and did exactly that—engaging the ship's afterburners, firing the spinning craft forward towards its target at mach speed.

*

Brann watched it unfold in horrible clarity, witnessing the catastrophe as both a helpless bystander and guilty party, knowing everything he saw in those moments happened because of him and his mistakes.

The Donnie was in a tailspin, losing altitude even as its nose remained pointed skyward, careening back towards the city on the full strength of only half its engines. Then, the blue flames flickered on its rear, and a moment later a sonicboom made Brann's ears pop—and the Donnie became a bullet in the dark red sky, firing itself directly at the woeful beast standing amidst the wreckage of Barrier City.

Rigel took no notice of the comparatively tiny craft, his ribcage already glowing that same deathly starlight glow as he charged up another beam—the evening sky turned to night in seconds as his white form once more drew in all light around him, preparing to fire—

—And in the second his jaws cracked wide once more, Rigel turned his great head suddenly, his eyeless visor still registering unmistakable surprise as the *Myrmidon* let fly and passed through his skull like a bullet.

There was a half second where the world seemed to freeze, and then light returned to the sky, and Rigel's head turned supernova. The fiery projectile that once was called the Donnie dissipated behind the white-hot explosion like arterial spray from a shotgun blast, and a radioactive shockwave buffeted the ravens circling the city backwards in a growing sphere of displaced energy. The shockwave raced across the clay plains in an approaching wall of liquified earth that nearly toppled Brann over, the young man barely having the presence of mind to clamp his hands over his ears in time to save himself from being permanently deafened by the world-rending blast. Rigel's head was no more, his entire upper torso being crushed beneath the force of the blast, his ghostfire wings flickering out and the steel bones curling inwards like the legs of a dead spider. The blinding airburst above Barrier City spread outwards, blue and black fire against a deep red sky—and as Brann shielded his eyes against the epicenter of the blast with a hand, he could see the skeletal form of Rigel disintegrate in seconds before it fully fell to the ground. The city disappeared in a sickly gray cloud that mushroomed out from within that fireball, then consumed it fully—the earth quaked all around, then the light of the explosion faded into a dying star above the city; and the roar of the shockwave dissipated, and the clay plains were silent once more.

Rigel was gone. The Donnie was gone. And Nestor was gone.

And in that terrible, soul-numbing moment of acceptance, Brann new the day's suffering was not yet done with him.

The GIAK's were on the move again, slowly at first, their occupants seemingly unsure of what to do next—but they were human as well, and emotionally driven, and they'd just seen their home destroyed. And though they seemed to turn away at first, their engines roared, and the vehicles spun back around, accelerating for Brann and his friends once more.

Stranded without a ship now, without wings to ferry them to safety, they had no choice but to run. Zay shouldered her autocannon, wiping her eyes as she grabbed at Brann's collar forcefully. He barely moved, wobbling on his feet, eyes staring into nothing as the GIAK's approached.

"We make a run for Taree Mountain," Zay ordered, pointing past Brann. "It's our only chance. We stay here, we're dead, we run—" She swallowed hard, faltering. "We run," she said simply, not daring to finish the thought.

Then she looked up, and let go of Brann, stepping backwards. Hawkshaw's eyes were drawn back as well, and Brann felt something—someone—brush by him. Then Wolf was at his side, not paying any heed to Zay's wishes. Instead, he was walking out to greet the incoming foes, his spear trailing alongside him in the dirt.

"I said we're running for it," Zay repeated, knowing it was futile. "That's an order, Wolf."

Wolf would not obey. He turned, briefly, grunting softly. Only Brann heard his final words in that bestial farewell:

"She's waiting."

Lady Red's faithful protector took off running, hunched low, spear raising itself to point towards his targets. They were his prey now—not the other way around.

The GIAK's were only a hundred yards or so away when they opened fire once more, and Brann could see the low profile of their gunners now, heads peeking out behind their mounted turrets—Wolf didn't even flinch when the searing hot bullets passed through him, the lycan sprinting through the red mist, his haunches tensing before he leapt straight up into the air. His spear rose high above his head, and his momentum carried him forward, a dark lupine shadow silhouetted against the dying starburst in the sky beyond—

And like a missile he hurtled towards the earth once more, his spear whistling in his arcing descent before slamming itself directly into the shielded roof above where the driver sat in the GIAK below. As effortlessly as if he were piercing soft flesh instead of vehicular armor, Wolf crouched on the kart's roof and withdrew his spear, the weapon glistening wetly before he plunged it into the passenger's seat next. With one hand, he snatched outwards, gripping the barrel of the mounted gun before its user could swing it around fully towards him—muscles bulging, face contorted in hellish fury, Wolf roared at the terrified gunner who let loose a volley aimlessly in a vain effort to shoot the predator down. The GIAK veered off, away from the direction of the mountain—and, much to Brann's shame and relief, the other two karts followed, determined to give aide to their comrades in immediate danger.

"Go! Take Hawkshaw—don't stop running!"

Brann did as he was told, sucking in the deepest, coldest breath of his life as he lifted the severed automaton onto his shoulders once more and set off, breaking his gaze painfully—the last he saw of Wolf, the bleeding lycanthrope had let go of his spear and was reaching for the helpless gunner's head with outstretched claws. The GIAK's seemed to forget all about Brann and the other two for the time being, driven by pure reactionary emotion, abandoning all pretense of duty to protect their city.

The city was all but gone now. The sky turned dark, and gray, and lifeless. And as Brann found himself running away from his home city once more, the gray sky began to weep, dark ash and snow falling from the clouds overheard. The ravens continued to whirl about for a while before withdrawing into the night, their distant calls growing quieter and quieter as Brann and Zay approached the foothills, Hawkshaw clutching tightly at Brann's back.

The day belonged to the ravens now, and the night would be illuminated by a single, dim star; a sorrowful lantern burning out into nothing as it slowly vanished, taking with it all hope of a brighter tomorrow.

45. The Peak

Nothing could survive on this mountaintop.

The trees, frozen and dead, hadn't seen growth since the last age. The snow had frozen and re-frozen into a sheen of white crystal capping every stone and branch, the ground barely even acknowledging Brann's footsteps with quiet crunches, even with Hawkshaw on his back. The automaton, without hands or legs to speak of, had looped his inverted elbows over Brann's shoulders and beneath the young man's arms. Brann tried not to complain, but Hawkshaw's inorganic shell had turned freezing cold the higher they climbed, stinging Brann's skin through his blouse, no doubt leaving icy abrasions beneath the clothing. Hawkshaw had been reduced to a semi-living backpack of sorts now, and despite his cold flesh his torso proved far lighter than Brann had expected, given his metal exo-frame.

Or perhaps, in Brann's dulled grief, he simply didn't notice the weight. The cold mountain certainly didn't notice, regarding the three survivors with indifference befitting that of the ancient elements of nature—white, motionless quietude. Snow and stone and still air beneath a sky as grey as the dead.

Zay's breathing was the only sound apart from Brann's own—and a frightening sound it was, to the point a part of him wished he could block it out. The more his concern for her health grew, the more that part of him grew—he'd already tried mentioning it to her, offering to slow or stop several times along the trail, but each time Zay refused, each time with increasing threats against him. Eventually, she faltered—though she still would not take Brann's help, she begrudgingly accepted Hawkshaw's long coat when Brann draped it over her shoulders. Without a word of thanks, she continued on, bidding Brann to follow.

Brann didn't take it personally. He knew Zay well enough now to know she didn't mean it. She was a soldat, like him, and pressed on through the pain—as long as their mission lay before them, she would see it through. Their mission was to get to the top of this mountain. After that, perhaps back to the bottom. After that, perhaps it was as simple as surviving.

Zay was a survivor. Brann reassured himself she would see it through. She was the strongest person he'd ever met. Not even this mountain, in its confident agelessness, could stop her.

Zay was a few meters ahead, when she stumbled, falling to one knee—fast as he could manage, Brann was at her side. He looked to Zay's wound, then to her grim face, daring him to say something.

He said nothing. Instead, he shifted Hawkshaw's weight to one shoulder, and leaned down, taking her arm around his back. Brann stood, his back and legs straining from the added weight—Zay gritted her teeth, hissing a quiet obscenity at him, but he didn't care. They were near the top now, and he would see them all there. Zay would just have to sulk to herself.

After another hour or so, the trail leveled out, finally. It had been a full day since they'd set off up the mountain—a full day to reach the sight that now lay before them: there, ahead, between the skeletons of the snow-shorn trees. A humble cabin. The lone fortress at the peak of Taree Mountain—Redfield's Rest. Unattended in what must have been decades, reclaimed by the wilds—Barrier City acted as the outermost fringe of civilization on the continent, guarding against the encroaching Deadlands.

Or, it used to, Brann realized with a start as they reached the cabin's front porch—Barrier City was likely to disappear entirely now, after all that had happened, having fallen to ruin.

Did they do this? Were they responsible for destroying all those lives?

"Inside." Zay spoke through a shaky gasp, her throat congealed with rising damp. Her hand clutched her blackened side so tightly it might as well have been frozen there, the blood sticking in the cold—an icy cauterization, courtesy of Mount Taree.

Brann hefted Hawkshaw up on his back as he stepped out from under Zay, allowing her to come to both feet on her own. She seemed shaky, but nonetheless stood up straight, giving Brann the slightest of nods. It was all he was going to get.

Brann turned to try the doorknob. For a moment, he feared the last occupants had locked it—but, with a forceful shove, the door unstuck, ice chips clattering to the wooden floor. Beyond the threshold, the cabin was dark, empty—even dust couldn't survive in its cold desolation, the air tangy with rust. Brann stepped inside, immediately setting to locating a source of fire. Pulling open the pantry doors, there was nothing, save for an antique clothes iron. The drawers in the small kitchen—no flint, no steel, no matches. Brann searched around the stone fireplace next. Though he could find no lighters, the fuel sat at the ready, a forgotten stack of logs and kindling neatly assembled in the grate. Perhaps the last visitor here had forgotten to light it—or perhaps they'd simply perished before getting the chance, lacking the tools to light it themselves.

"Here, get me close." Hawkshaw spoke quietly over Brann's shoulder, next to his ear—Brann tried to ignore the distortion in the automaton's voice, leaning in close to the fireplace. Unhooking one arm, Hawkshaw reached out, the frayed wiring where his hand used to be beginning to sizzle. With a snap of ozone, the wires sparked, and the kindling caught light—in moments, the orange of newly birthed embers warmed away the gray, and in that moment, Brann was made acutely aware just how bitterly cold he was. Grunting with primal need, he fell to all fours, cradling the spreading glow of the fire with both hands, rubbing them together frantically—he pressed his hot palms to his face, his chest; anywhere he thought might carry the heat through his bloodstream quickly.

"Brann."

Hawkshaw spoke again, interrupting Brann's efforts to warm himself. He realized—he and Hawkshaw were alone. Zay had not entered the cabin.

Prying himself away from the comfort of the flames, Brann stood to his feet, looking to the empty doorway. He waited a few moments. Still, Zay did not enter.

Brann crossed the threshold once more, peeking his head around the corner. Zay stood, chest heaving, resting her weight against the wall of the cabin. She gripped the barrel of her autocannon tightly for additional support, the butt of the weapon digging into the soft wood of the porch. Her eyes had glazed over, unfocused, a string of drool dangling from her lip like a tiny icicle.

"Zay," Hawkshaw said quietly, his exposed servos whirring as he pulled himself up Brann's back. "Come inside and warm up. You'll feel better."

Zay seemed to need a minute to process this. She swiveled her head around, facing in their general direction without making eye contact. Her reflexes were slowing to a crawl, her body weak. And yet:

"I'll feel better when we're through this. Someone has to stand watch."

She was slurring her words. Brann made his attempt:

"How about you let one of us stand watch first? You can come inside, get warm by the fire, and when you're feeling better—"

Zay just laughed him off. It was a pained, hollow sound. A precursor to a death rattle. "You..? Him..?" She shook her head slowly. "Nah. I take first watch."

"But—"

"Okay, Zay," Hawkshaw said, nudging Brann, a silent acknowledgment of Zay's wishes. "We'll be just inside, taking a load off. Maybe you can pop off a few rounds at some birds, if that'll improve your mood. Then when you're done sulking, come in for a hand of cards or something."

Zay's face softened, an almost dreamy smile appearing. "Yeah, right," she drawled, chuckling quietly. "A 'hand'. Good one, dumbass."

Hawkshaw nudged Brann again. As Brann turned to head back inside, a hand snatched at his collar—Zay held him in place, leaning in close to speak. Her smile was gone now, in its place something Brann was unused to seeing on her face: fear. When she spoke next, it was with a tremendous effort, not just because of her wounds—Brann sensed she was struggling to put into words exactly what it was she wanted to say to him. Even so close to the end, Zay kept her pride.

"If anyone asks," she stammered, "I c-carried you. Up..."

Brann hesitated, but nodded. He offered a small smile of his own as consolation. "Yeah, of course you did. You carried both of us."

Zay nodded, her smile partially returning. She released Brann's collar, patting it smooth, satisfied. She took hold of her cannon once more, gripping the barrel with both hands, using it as a cane as she stumbled forward. One; two unsteady steps, off the porch. Then, to a nearby rock, its flat surface blanketed in frost. Zay grunted as she leaned down, sweeping the snow off, clearing a patch. She turned, and sat, autocannon planted between both feet. She drew Hawkshaw's coat around herself, settling in for her watch. The dead forest and grey sky were all there was to see, but that didn't matter: she was getting the job done.

*

"Brann. Brann, wake up."

He was curled against the wood, a shaggy wool blanket drawn over him. Brann forced his eyes open, his joints creaking, both from the exertion of the day's travel and the cold that had leeched into his bones. He looked to Hawkshaw, who was hovering above him, the automaton propping his torso up on his elbows—the trail of snow behind him indicated he'd dragged himself out the door and back. Brann didn't know how long he'd been asleep, but it must have been at least several hours, judging by what Hawkshaw said next.

"I ran a sweep of the area—down the mountain, on the far side. There's an old settlement, only a few structures—not a real town to speak of, most likely abandoned, but there may be supplies you can take. Something to keep you going for a while. There's no food or water up here and you haven't had either in at least a day; you won't survive at this altitude for much longer. You stand a better chance if we leave now, before nightfall."

It wasn't lost on Brann, Hawkshaw's choice of words. "You mean 'we' stand a better chance," he corrected.

Hawkshaw didn't respond, his amber eyes casting their solemn glow across Brann's face.

With every fragmented part of him protesting, Brann pulled himself to his feet, the cold instantly biting into him as the blanket lifted from the ground. He kept it drawn around himself, the only protection he had against the elements. He stretched, grunting as his spine popped. Then, exhaling, he nodded, crouching to extend Hawkshaw a helping hand.

"Okay then. Point the way."

Hawkshaw hooked his elbow around Brann's arm and, with some struggle, climbed aboard. Retaking his place on Brann's back, he pressed in close, centering their gravity together—Brann was thankful to feel the automaton's metal plating warming his back. Hawkshaw must have spent a good deal of time absorbing heat from the fireplace before waking him.

"I'll just tell Zay we're on the move," Brann said, stepping out of the cabin.

"Brann—"

"Hey, Zay," Brann called out.

Zay's back remained turned to them, fixed upon her rock, unmoved. She didn't respond.

Curious. "Zay? We're leaving now, Hawkshaw says…"

In his peripheral, Brann could see Hawkshaw shaking his head.

Zay was intent on ignoring him. Snow had settled on her shoulders, the long trenchcoat fluttering in the meek breeze. Even her knuckles seemed to have accrued a light dusting of frost, trimming her black gloves with white.

Brann didn't budge. He was at the cliff's edge, refusing to look over the precipice. If he didn't acknowledge it, maybe…

"Zay. Come on. Time to go."

Nothing.

"Zay."

No.

"Brann," Hawkshaw whispered. "It'll be dark soon. She'll catch up."

The trees seemed to agree on Zay's behalf, the wind rattling their branches a bit; a crackling chorus of frozen bark.

Brann didn't want to think it, didn't want to speak it. He saw a way through this latest revelation in Hawkshaw's false promise, and he took it. Nodding, he stepped off the porch, setting off into the woods once more.

He took the long way around, giving Zay a wide berth. He didn't want to see her face, didn't want to break the illusion. She'd catch up to them when she was ready—though she'd have to hurry, as Hawkshaw was right, and it would be nighttime soon. After all:

Nothing could survive on this mountaintop.

46. The Gutter

It was scarcely a few minutes on before Brann came to a halt once more, the peak of the mountain looming behind him. The blanket flapped at his knees in the wind, and he drew it tighter around himself, rooted to the spot.

"Brann?" Hawkshaw leaned over his shoulder. "You should keep moving. This isn't—"

"Just." Brann held up a hand from beneath the blanket, quieting Hawkshaw, shaking his head. "Just, give me a minute."

He was considering their destination. An abandoned township at the foot of the mountain, where maybe he could find some food to get him through another day or two. Then what? Retreat into the Deadlands beyond? Try to make it on foot all the way back to civilization, around Geiha's borders? Even if he managed all that, what came next? What was the point—surviving?

Why care about that anymore?

And even then, there was something he felt he'd forgotten. Something tickling at the back of his mind, buried beneath the settled avalanche of the past day's events. There was something he was meant to recall, something Nes had passed on, before—

"The cache," Brann finally said. "The one Nes left. Back in the city. Do you know what's in it?"

Hawkshaw shook his head. "He didn't clue me in on that, no. All I know is what he told you, that you should make a grab for it if you found yourself in a jam. But, listen kid, that's not worth—"

Brann wasn't listening, already turning heel. Rather than make his way back towards the peak, he was close enough to the top of the mountain he could circle around the precipice and reach the southwestern slope with little time wasted. He was bound for Geiha once more, his pace quickening as his feet found newfound purpose. "You said yourself they took Boomer into custody, right? He survived the fight—that means he's still there, waiting for us to come for him."

"You saw what Rigel did to the city," Hawkshaw protested. "I know he's your friend, but think rationally about this for a second—"

"Thinking rationally is what put me on this mountain." Brann's breaths came in sharp, determined puffs, his upper lip sweating from the condensation forming. "We tried things your way. I survived this long by doing exactly what I was told not to do by people who thought rationally. I'm not leaving my friend behind to die while I run away again."

"Brann—"

"You wanna stop me?" Brann challenged. "All you gotta do is start walking the opposite direction."

"Point taken. Still—you know you're the one person they'll be looking for, if they're even looking for anyone anymore. Not just the Uhlen, or the Nightwatch, but *everyone*—they'll have blamed us for Rigel, they'll have your name and face plastered on every holoscreen, 'Public Enemy One', the man responsible for unleashing the end of the world on the city. You won't have a disguise to get you back in."

"Only if we wait. If we wait, they'll have time enough to rebuild, to start asking 'why' and to point fingers. If we go in now, there may still be enough chaos and unrest to provide cover. No one will be looking for us as long as there's still fires to put out."

Hawkshaw faltered, and Brann could hear his words getting through to the automaton, even if he didn't want to admit it. "The way things sounded, Boomer went down hard during the fight. Just because he was alive then doesn't mean he is now—even if he wasn't killed in Rigel's attack, he would have needed immediate medical attention, which—"

"He's alive. He survived Tark. He can survive anything."

Brann knew Hawkshaw knew better than to argue with the logic of human hope. The crippled bot sighed ruefully, but when his arms tightened around Brann's shoulders, the young soldat knew he was back on board with the plan. "You're gonna want to follow the same trail back down,"

Hawkshaw grumbled. "It'll be easier going downhill."

"It's always easier going back the way you came," said Brann, arms swinging as he trudged on.

*

The cloud cover from the mountain followed Brann all the way down to the clay plains, conjoining with the clouds that had formed over the city—the red sky had cooled, replaced with endless gray. Though the cold faded behind Brann, the snow persisted—even as he discarded the blanket somewhere on the plains, the gray continued to fall from the sky. He reached a hand skyward as he hiked on, catching some across his fingers. There was as much ash in the clouds as there was moisture, the flakes crumbling beneath his fingertips in smears of wet carbon.

"Don't breathe it in," Hawkshaw cautioned. "Use your scarf."

Brann obliged, pulling up the garment and tightening it around his face, covering his nose and mouth. An imperfect disguise to be sure, but an unexpected boon nonetheless—doubtless he'd enter the city to find the rest of the population masking in much the same way. No one would find him suspicious as long as he kept to the alleys and the backstreets.

"Now that is just..." Hawkshaw shook his head. "I don't even know what you'd call that."

They'd reached the outer wall of the city. Hawkshaw was looking ahead, at the point where the wall had caved in on itself—as a result of an object that had fallen from the sky, smashing a hole through the wall like a meteorite. The object in question became apparent as Brann drew closer, and he recognized it immediately, despite the damage it had suffered: still smoking, the engine that had detached from the Donnie looked like a crumpled tin can in its crater.

"I'd call that really good luck," answered Brann simply, not wasting any time climbing over the rubble of the wall, not paying the engine a second glance. There were many complicated emotions that arose from the sight, and none of them were worth his time to entangle himself in right now. Hawkshaw understood, turning his own head away from the crater as they pressed on, changing the subject for both their benefits.

"Whatever happens, you need to start thinking about what comes next," he said. "Whether or not—I mean, if we find him—"

"We're getting Boomer out, there's no 'if' about it."

Hawkshaw adjusted. "What I mean to say is, after that. You need a destination, somewhere to land. We'll be at the airfield soon, and there's bound to be some working ships somewhere. Find one, and make for Cheneye. Do you remember where we met?"

"The outpost. I can find it."

"Find it. Find Mother Superior—she may run a brothel, but don't let that fool you, she has more resources than anyone. Not just money, but connections. She'll get you somewhere safe. Find her, ask for her help, and tell her I sent you. You're gonna make it."

Brann didn't like the way Hawkshaw was talking. The way he said 'you'—not 'us'.

"I know we're gonna make it," Brann replied, furrowing his brow. "You worry too much, man. I know you lost your balls when you lost your lower half, but, even still…"

This got a chuckle from Hawkshaw, though Brann didn't believe it. It was hollow, mirthless—just like Zay's.

"You're gonna make it, kid," Hawkshaw repeated, and left it at that.

They were crossing the airfields now, though they were nigh unrecognizable—scattered wreckage from destroyed ships, ashen snow piling up overnight in swathes of serpentine dunes. Brann couldn't remember a time when there weren't freighters or charter ships constantly taking off and landing at the strips. There was a silence now, not unlike the silence atop Taree Mountain—a lifelessness, everything drained of color and noise.

"We're coming to the river now," Brann said, nodding ahead. "Where Nes and I first met—the Donnie was moored there, at the end of the moat. The cache should be…"

His sentence trailing off, Brann's pace slowed somewhat. There was no water lapping at the edges of the moat that he could see, the concrete dock buried beneath the towering, smoldering carcass of a cargo ship that had crashed into the earth. The river seemed to have evaporated entirely—and, as Brann stood at the edge of the moat, he saw the cause for it plainly: Rigel's superheated beams had disintegrated the concrete channels running beneath the river, draining the water into the soft earth. The moat was no longer a moat, but rather a canyon, stretching deep into the earth—pitiful little waterfalls trickled into the depths all along the concrete embankment, scattered remnants of various ships peeking out from within the fissure.

"These airfields were built atop the plains," Hawkshaw explained, sounding defeated. "Looks like Rigel blasted through the artificial river—take that away, and it's just…nothing but soft clay underneath, all the way to the bedrock. Who knows how deep this goes."

"There," Brann said, pointing. The concrete embankment was gone, but the far side of the moat was cut away at a sloping angle—about midway up the slope, cradled by the curled fingers of twisted rebar jutting from the shattered concrete, there rested a black seabag. Someone had packed it full, the way it bulged.

"That must be the cache. This is where the Donnie was moored when Nes and I first met."

"How do you plan on reaching it?" Hawkshaw queried, trying to keep the doubt from his voice. "Rigel cut a swathe all around the rim of the city, this canyon could stretch on for a mile or more. Even if we leave the cache here, we'll still have to find our way across somehow eventually."

Brann looked to the fallen ship strewn across the dock. "I could climb across that," he offered, tracing an imaginary route with a finger. "It looks sturdy enough. If I shimmy across that exposed—"

The universe had other plans, revealing its sense of humor as an explosion rocked the entire shell of the cargo ship from somewhere deep within, causing Brann to stumble back. The nearest side of the hull sagged further into the canyon, supporting girders that kept it intact falling into the abyss below. The broken ship was slowly but surely losing all structural integrity, collapsing under its own massive weight as the electrical fires burned it from the inside out.

"Okay," Hawkshaw nodded, pretending to sound enthusiastic. "Okay. Yeah. I think I got it. It's not that far across, if you were to get a running start—"

"*What?*"

Hawkshaw reassured Brann as he spoke, keeping his voice calm. "Just, trust me on this, I've done the calculations already. It may look like a long gap, but if you get a running start, you can jump across to the other side and catch yourself on the far slope. The clay is soft enough that you won't slide off. You'll make it, trust me."

"You're putting too much faith in my legs," Brann argued, craning his neck over the edge of the moat. "There's no way I could make that—"

"Brann." Hawkshaw was firm now, dropping the false optimism. "I know what I'm talking about. I have a supercomputer in my head. The math checks out. You're *gonna make it.*"

Again, Brann felt disquieted by the way Hawkshaw said that last part. *You're* gonna make it.

Hawkshaw seemed to read his thoughts, not giving Brann time to process his words. "Don't freeze up now," he barked. "Step back. Several paces. There you go."

As Brann obliged, stepping back from the edge, he felt his heart-rate rising—there would be no second attempt if he missed. He tried not to imagine the sensation of falling, of counting the seconds that passed, freefalling through nothing—

"You ready?" Hawkshaw tightened his arms around Brann's back, cutting off the circulation to his arms. "No thinking about it. Just a full sprint, fast as you can. Jump with both feet, tuck in, reach out. I got you. You're gonna make it, promise."

"More promises," Brann said bitterly, taking a deep breath, counting down. "Three...two..."

He kicked off his back foot, charging forward, knees popping from the effort. His arms were a blur at his sides, his knees nearly reaching his chest with his stride, Brann sprinting like an absolute lunatic straight for his demise. He made the cliff, and without looking down, coiled his spine like a spring, then released—his feet cleared the ground, launching him skyward, making him the envy of jackrabbits the world over.

And yet, in that split second, Brann knew deep down it wasn't enough, his heart plummeting as he saw the far bank rushing past. He had been tricked; he hadn't run fast enough, hadn't jumped hard enough, he was falling into the earth—

There was a moment of relief that doused his fears, his body carrying itself forward in a sudden jolt, his legs instinctively kicking out beneath him once more to stretch himself out and into a lengthening arc. Brann felt this moment wash over him before he even felt his body slam into soft clay, before his brain had registered the feeling of Hawkshaw's arms releasing themselves; the feeling of a full-bodied shove against his back as the weight on his shoulders uncoupled.

Brann slid a few feet, but the moist clay had absorbed most of the impact, and his boots sank into the dirt—he had made the far side. Quickly, he rolled himself over, letting loose a frustrated scream as reality caught up with him.

Hawkshaw hadn't lied. Brann made the jump. The legless automaton had given him a parting gift of a midair boost, using his own body as a springboard to shove Brann forward. As a consequence, Brann was denied his goodbyes as he caught a final glimpse of the automaton's torso tumbling straight down, arms outstretched, Hawkshaw winking back at him slyly as he disappeared into the gutter below.

47. The Broken

His family was gone.

Brann stood in the city square, turning this way and that, aimlessly searching the faces of the crowd—their mouths cloaked in scarves to protect from the ashen snow, their eyes sorrowful and unseeing, unknowing of Brann's own personal little world of pain he ruled over. A shrinking universe trapping him amidst an entire city of other universes, each with their own rulers, each live seeking shelter and food and solace in the embrace of their missing family and friends, lost beneath the rubble and ash.

Yet Brann could feel nothing, except the throbbing absence of his own family.

Did anyone even care?

Where were they going? What were they trying to accomplish? *He* was alone. *His* family was gone.

Why did no one care?

Had he been here a minute? An hour? A day? He didn't know where to go, what to do—he knew Boomer was here, somewhere, the last connection he had to the salted earth he'd hoped to build a future upon. There was no home left for him to go to, except Boomer, and Brann didn't even know if his friend was still alive after everything that had happened. Was it worth it to look for him? Was it worth it to hope? What was left for him, even if he did find Boomer? What was left for them to return to, with the rest of their companions gone, with the Donnie gone?

The cloaked bodies continued to brush by, knocking him this way and that in their pursuit of trinkets, their rhetorical pleas to him if Brann had seen 'this person' or 'their child' falling mute upon his ears. He couldn't hear anything but the silent snow.

The pathway opened up between the bodies, almost as if by providence. A passage between the buildings, an alleyway he faintly recognized from his younger days, prowling these very streets. He felt called to it, compelled into that tight passage, between those passing bodies. The way to Boomer was through these alleys, the map embedded in his long-buried memories—if only Brann could find the will to read it once more.

He didn't even feel his feet as he drifted into the alley, into the shadows, the nervous crowds disappearing behind him. Brann might as well be levitating, his boots barely leaving imprints in the snow behind him. The alleys of his youth welcomed him, back into their uncertain maze, back into the enigmatic solitude he once wondered if he'd ever escape.

Once again, he was a child of the streets, and once again no one cared.

Perhaps he was never meant to leave here at all, and he was a fool to have ever tried.

Brann had to find Boomer, and soon—before this maze claimed him for its own forever.

*

A full day had passed. Brann had fallen all too easily into his old ways, slipping into familiar cracks and alcoves to avoid the Nightwatch, mapping out a zigzagging route through the city, away from the population centers. Boomer would be too easily spotted in a crowd—if he was still in the city (Brann tried not to think the words 'still alive'), he would be doing the same.

At least, so Brann thought. Hoped, anyway. It all hinged on hope, now—it was all he had left.

It was well into the night now, the yellow starbursts of portable lamps affixed to generators the only light by which Brann could navigate—though it ill benefited him to draw too close to those lamps, as he could make out the telltale uniforms of the Nightwatch milling about beneath them, directing the citizens back to their homes. Keeping to the shadows, Brann watched with a growing unease as the displaced civilians were turned away time and time again—the Nightwatch wasn't interested in giving aid, it seemed, but rather only had restoring order and quiet. People were shrugged off as they pleaded for help, their homes burning; rifles were brandished and slammed butt-first into the faces of those attempting to dig through dumpsters for scraps of food. At one point, Brann ducked for cover as a rapid succession of small arms fire rang out; a band of looters had broken into a cafe across the street, grabbing up armfuls of pastries, and were swiftly gunned down by an awaiting Nightwatch patrol the moment they stepped outside. The beauty and sheen of the city had been peeled away from the city's bones, and beneath it, an ugly darkness was oozing up from within.

There was shouting beyond the next alleyway. Brann sidestepped a collapsed wall, hugging the building until he came to its corner, peeking his head out around the corner. Where the alleys intersected, he could see several blocks down, the parallel alleys painted yellow by the streetlamps still operating. There were shadows moving about two blocks down, shuffling about—Brann lurched back when one spun suddenly, keeping out of sight. Confident he hadn't been spotted, he leaned back out once more after a moment.

They weren't Nightwatch. A gaggle of civilians, shushing one another as they tugged along a trunk, trying in vain to keep it quiet—as heavy as it was, it was scraping along the concrete and dragging through the stray rubble and glass. Brann watched as they all froze in place, hugging the shadows just as he did, the shouting drawing nearer. Several gunshots rang out from behind the buildings, and then there was silence. The Nightwatch hadn't been after them—they all relaxed, confident the patrol had moved on, gathering around the trunk once more.

A much bigger shape, a taller man, shrouded in thick wrappings— he emerged from the peripheral alley, effortlessly hefting the heavy trunk up in his arms. The way he tossed his big head to motion everyone to follow him was instantly familiar to Brann, and as the tall man turned, Brann saw a flash of blonde horsetail.

Boomer.

Brann tripped over his own feet as he detached from the wall, nearly faceplanting into glass—he caught himself on his hands instead, the glass powder sticking to his palms and tearing pockmarks into his skin. Brushing the glass away, he ignored the blood trickling down his wrists as he raced down the alley in the same direction the group of scavengers had gone. Building after building flew by as he ran, slowing only to look down each alley in turn—the scavengers had moved quickly with Boomer carrying their trunk for them. Brann skidded to a halt as he came to what he believed to be the intersection he'd seen them crossing. They had already cleared the block. Following the scrapings left by the trunk, Brann reoriented himself down the same alley the group had disappeared into and set off once more. He was practically sprinting on his toes, trying to keep as quiet as possible while still moving quickly. His breathing became ragged, excited—he could scarcely believe he'd found Boomer, trying not to let his tears streak his vision as he ran.

The alley terminated on a dark street, and Brann quickly checked both ways—no patrols. No scavengers either. He let his eyes adjust somewhat, seeing the light footprints in the snow, dead ahead. They had crossed the road here, which meant so would he. If memory served him right, there was a small copse of trees just beyond, separating the roads in a wide median. Perfect place for someone to remain hidden as they crossed.

Keeping light on his feet, Brann crossed quickly, trying to look hurried but not in a hurry—there was a key difference when it came to arousing suspicion, and he couldn't count on it being impossible that a patrol was hiding in the darkness, beyond the reach of the streetlamps.

Across the road, there was a snowbank, rising higher than Brann's head—the middle of it had sunken in, as if several bodies had clambered over it, and indeed there were clumps of snow still tumbling down the gentle slope from the recent disturbance. Brann followed suit, dragging himself up and over—

Lights flashed before his eyes, and Brann ducked down quickly, cursing himself. Beyond the snowbank, the Nightwatch had set a trap, the generators powering their portable lamps roaring to life. Keeping himself flush along the embankment, Brann remained still. Teeth gritted, he counted the seconds, listening carefully to the shouting beyond—the Nightwatch were issuing orders to the scavengers, but it didn't seem Brann had been spotted. He didn't have time to wait for this patrol to move on, however, especially not if Boomer was waiting for him down below. So Brann gritted his teeth, rolling over carefully and pulling himself back up, cheek to the snow as he peered with one eye over the crest of the snowbank at the scene.

There were about six of them, facing away from Brann with their backs to a ditch they'd just climbed out of. The scavengers were all wrapped up in scarves and blankets, arms raised—and at the center of them, the unmistakable silhouette of Brann's best friend. Boomer was wrapped in the same ragged clothing and scarves as the rest of them, foregoing his usual vibrant wardrobe in favor of survivor's solidarity. The horse didn't have his arms raised, still holding the trunk at waist height, even as the Nightwatch officers closed in with their pistols raised. They were ordering him to drop the trunk, and Brann felt a sting of dread; Boomer was not one to do as he was told.

Most days, at least. Relieved, Brann sighed as Boomer let the trunk fall, the impact causing the lid to pop open on its own. One of the officers kicked the lid back, revealing its contents: glass bottles of water and tea; sacks of nuts and other unidentifiable edibles; a stack of warm clothes, folded in tight bundles.

"Now this doesn't belong to you, does it?" An officer sneered, his gloved hand tossing the contents of the trunk, and Brann recognized him as well—the same security officer who had asked for Boomer's autograph outside the stadium. He was wearing an all-weather parka now, a sergeant's emblem velcroed to the shoulder. Seems even the lowly security officers had been promoted to the task of stopping the looters in the city—and as always, Boomer's allegiance remained with the citizens; his fans. Using his own trunk to collect and hand out supplies and coats instead of signed photos and tee shirts.

Brann would hug Boomer the first chance he got.

The Sergeant was twirling his finger now, motioning for the captured group to turn around, ordering them to keep their hands raised. A lamp was sweeping around the perimeter of the trees, coming for Brann—he ducked low once more, the beam of light passing overhead. Waiting until he was well clear, he raised his head once more.

The scavengers' hands were being tied behind their backs, even more officers entering the clearing from beyond the lamps—there were easily twice as many of them as there were captives, all leveling their pistols at the backs of the civilians. Boomer's eyes were turned upwards, back towards Brann.

They locked eyes. Brann remained frozen in place, heart thudding in his ears.

Boomer slowly, silently, tugged the scarf away from his snout, revealing his grin. Arms still raised, he clenched one hand into a fist. The other curled, outstretching a finger, which he crooked in Brann's direction.

Oh no.

Boomer spoke now, prompting the officers to break rank and draw closer to him. Brann couldn't make out everything he was saying, the horse speaking quietly—but he did catch part of it, borne up to Brann's ears on the night breeze:

"...Ever wondered why they call me 'Boomer'?"

One of the officers reached up, grasping at Boomer's wrists. Boomer, still staring up at Brann, winked.

The horse pirouetted on one hoof, his fist coming down like a hammer, straight into the officer's face with a sickening crack. The concaved head of the Nightwatchman bobbed awkwardly atop his shoulders, the officer stumbling backwards before falling. The other officers were shouting again, taking aim, but the Sargeant stopped them:

"Orders are to take him alive! Do not fire!"

The scavengers all used this opportunity to make good their own escape—as Boomer descended on another officer, the civilians split, running for the trees. The Sargeant did not show them the same courtesy of restraint, however, and the officers opened fire freely, gunning all five survivors down in seconds. Their bodies fell, twitching in the snow, hands still tied behind their back. To the Nightwatch, their lives weren't worth the supplies they had been trying to smuggle across town.

A second officer fell, Boomer crushing his head with a powerful stomp. The others turned their weapons on him once more, some of them pulling their stun batons, warning him to stop—Brann gripped at the sword on his back, knuckles popping from the sheer force of it.

If he stayed put, Boomer was dead.

If he joined the fight, they were both dead.

"Stop," he whispered, praying Boomer would hear his words. "Stop, now."

Boomer whipped around, disarming one of the officers with a scorpion kick—the stun baton disappeared into the snow, and drawing that same leg back, Boomer carried his momentum forward into a high kick into the Nightwatchman's chest. The man's body tumbled backwards, his bullet resistant vest doing little to stop his ribs from being broken.

Brann could see the moment it happened, and was powerless to stop it. The Sargeant reconsidered his orders, his mind being made up for him by Boomer's defiance. The former security officer strolled forward, unbothered by the sight of his comrades being beaten down, drawing his own sidearm smoothly.

The moment Boomer turned, already slinging his arm forward in a mean right hook, the Sergeant raised his pistol and fired directly into Boomer's forehead.

Brann didn't even hear the gunshot. His senses failed him, the world ending for him in that single moment.

Boomer swayed in the breeze, knees wobbling, eyes unfocused. His arm hung slack, though he still clenched his fists—his big, lumbering body hadn't caught up with the death of his brain just yet, and the horse stepped forward, past the Sargeant. Then, his nervous system shut down, and he suddenly fell in a lifeless heap, sending up a burst of snow all around him.

The Sargeant stood over him, holstering his sidearm. "What a waste," he sighed, sounding utterly without remorse. Placing his boot on Boomer's shoulders, he shoved forward, rolling the horse's heavy body into the ditch unceremoniously.

"Circle back the way they came," he called to the other officers, holding his handtorch aloft. "There may be stragglers."

Brann's skull was splitting, his heart about to burst from his chest. With all his might, he clenched his eyes shut, trying to clear away the image of Boomer's limp corpse in the ditch—then, drawing a deep breath, he shoved back off the embankment. He had no choice now but to do the one thing he swore he'd never do again.

He ran.

The officers crested the embankment, stumbling in the slippery snow, the beams of light from their torches sweeping across the road. They followed the tracks leading back, into the alleyway, and shone forward.

There was no trace of anyone else. The alley was empty, filled only by the quiet whistle of the night wind.

If anyone had come this way, they were gone now.

Long gone.

ACT V

INVISIBLE

48. The Reaping

One season of winter had turned, begetting another, and another. The sky above Barrier City was evergray, the clouds never breaking to let the sun in, not even during the typically fierce summer months. The snow had stopped, though the dark ash left its stain permanently upon the earth, leaving the buildings and the streets of the capitol city blanketed in streaked shadows. It never rained on the clay plains anymore, the red earth cracking and drying out, leaving only rusty swathes of ceramic stretching away from the city for miles. None of the trees in the parks regrew their leaves, their branches withering to white and brittle.

The world had stilled here, in this place, evacuating even the seasons. The winter had receded, leaving only a permanent fifth season: the dead season, an unending time of listless decay and quiet.

Few bodies remained outdoors for long in the eerie ghost city, the citizens keeping their ventures from their homes brief and quiet—the Nightwatch had cordoned off most of the streets, keeping all the survivors centralized as much as possible, not far from the palace. The agricultural and industrial sectors had all died, and the only labor was randomly enforced by the Nightwatch, who would sometimes burst into a home and drag out its occupants. They were set to work, clearing the persisting ruins and debris of the destroyed city—but without equipment, training, or professional oversight, little progress had been made these past few years. A hollowed-out building might collapse just as the rubble from one was cleared, and the street was rendered impassable yet again. Time would not allow Barrier City to rebuild, and the dead sky would not allow it to regrow.

And the ravens had returned.

Every year they came, appearing quietly, only a few at first. Then, more. Soon, they lined every building, every powerline, looking down from their perches at the city's denizens in silent judgment. They arrived right on schedule, their numbers peaking in the late afternoon, on the anniversary of the day the city died. The day of the dead Goliath's rampage, which had taken from the citizens their livelihoods and sense of freedom.

The day that had come to be known colloquially as Raven's Day. For every year, on this day, the ravens returned. And watched. And waited. And, just as the sun fell, disappeared once more into the night, until next year—when the gray summer gave way to gray autumn, and the early days of gray winter began.

This Raven's Day afternoon, they had amassed in numbers never before seen—as the Nightwatch patrolled the roads, their gazes remained fixed on the skyline. The black birds had clustered together so tightly, shoulder to shoulder, that they could blanket the city in an early nightfall if they all spread their wings at once. The roof of every home, every abandoned apartment building, every restaurant and shop corner—all of it belonged to the ravens now, their dark little eyes blinking impassively, watching every move that every solitary Nightwatch officer made.

Not a word was spoken by anyone walking the streets. The black omen that had descended on Barrier City wouldn't be denied its respect this Raven's Day.

Until the radios of the Nightwatch patrols all crackled to life, and the order was given—all available units in the area were to return to the palace. An emergency signal had been tripped within its walls, and with the infantry disbanded and Uhlen dissolved, there was no one to protect the newly christened Emperor.

He had laid claim to Geiha's territories not long after Rigel's emergence—the long-lost namesake of his late progenitor, Burnside Geiha II. Though he was a sickly old man, he had all the evidence he needed to prove his heritage, and with no Marshal to act as steward, the city had fallen under his rule. Or, rather, under the rule of the Nightwatch—little was seen or heard of the so-called Emperor since his arrival. Nothing had changed for the citizens of the city since their promised emancipation from the previous oligarchy.

Nothing, save for the arrival of the ravens.

In the palace grounds now, the bulk of the Nightwatch's remaining forces stood assembled—they numbered less than fifty, standing in rank and file in the palace courtyard, where once the infantry held their Assay ceremonies. There were so few left because there were so few citizens, now: those who hadn't died from unknown illnesses, descending upon them in the ashen wake of the first Ravensday, had slipped quietly from the city in the night. When the Nightwatch couldn't coerce them into staying put through curfews and constant patrols, the cordons began, and the city shrank into itself. At the center of it, the palace; at the center of the palace, this courtyard; within this courtyard, the sum total of the city's so-called lawful protectors.

And the ravens.

They had followed the officers to the palace, quietly flitting from rooftop to rooftop. The largest unkindness ever assembled now loomed over the palace walls and rooftops, nearly concealing the gray sky overhead. Not even the most rigid and dutiful of officer could help but stare back up at the silent watchers.

The ravens hadn't descended upon the city today. The ravens had descended on *them*.

There was a new superstition growing now in the hearts of the Nightwatch. They all stood at the ready, awaiting the results of the palace sweep—so far, no obvious intrusions had been detected, no trespassers.

It was as if the call had come from the ravens themselves, beckoning them to return here. To stand trial, awaiting judgment.

It was late afternoon now. Almost nightfall.

One of the ravens cawed sharply, suddenly, as if announcing something.

It was time.

*

The abrupt sound rang through the courtyard, causing the assembled officers to startle. Then a second, repeating the first bird's call. Then they all began to shift, and caw, and flap their wings, until a rolling storm of deafening cries broke upon the Nightwatch's heads. The nervous officers among them even drew their sidearms, flinching as black feathers began raining down upon them like a gentle black snowfall.

A younger officer, sweaty and frightened, jerked his pistol back and forth between the ravens. He had broken rank, stepping back, attempting to retreat beneath a nearby balcony—where one of the raven's flew from its perch, screeching in his face.

He fell, firing his pistol skyward, shielding his face with an arm.

The ravens did not like this.

A black cloud descended on the officer, the birds swirling around the cowardly man until he was invisible to the rest of his comrades, screaming for help—they all began firing into the maelstrom of birds. A foolhardy attempt to save him. As the ravens disbursed to avoid the gunfire, they left behind only the bullet-ridden corpse of the young officer, his eyes and tongue having disappeared from his head.

"Hold your fire!" An officer shouted above the din, his voice cracking. "There's too many of us, we're all in the crossfire!"

Another deafening noise split the air—this one inorganic. Electronic. Feedback from the loudspeakers arranged around the courtyard, addressing the assembly of officers now. A voice, flat and cold and sardonic, issued forth.

"Officers of the Nightwatch," it said, "Your attention goes now to your former Marshal and myself. Conduct yourselves accordingly—your Assay is now in full effect."

The speakers wrenched loudly as they clicked off. The officers, confused, looked about—the ravens were still cawing, though they sounded less threatening. More...excited, now. Elated, even.

It came like a silent sawblade spinning inversely to its own arc, the massive weight of the colossal object suspending it briefly in the air before losing all forward momentum and slicing smoothly into the center of the crowd. A hapless lieutenant was split down the middle, the resulting thunderclap of the earthbound axe making the entire assembly of officers flinch.

The castanet clicking of talons broke the shocked silence, the heavy footfalls of the approaching former Marshal echoing out from within the darkened palace foyer.

"I'm afraid you've all been found wanting," The Iron Tark proclaimed, strolling forward confidently into the gray light of day. "We've no room for cowards and murderers in this city any longer. You will all be removed from the palace grounds—with no small amount of satisfaction."

The wall of gunfire that broke upon Tark did nothing to slow his pace as he coolly yanked his axe free of the cratered concrete where once stood a lieutenant, a shimmering arc of blood soaring skyward behind the blade of the weapon before it came down upon the Nightwatchmen. Tark's hide sizzled, crystalline scales sprouting beneath every bullet that streaked across him. The axe fell, again and again, limbs and bodies sent airborne with each swing.

Behind the frantic wave of bodies attempting to flee the courtyard, stumbling and trampling one another as they fell back, another figure appeared. A shadow of grievous portent; silently rising amidst the carnage, appraising the scene impassively. The man wore a flexible suit of armor, lightweight and slim-fitted, all carbon steel and burgundy mesh polymer. His visor was not unlike the old Geihan infantry helms, save for a crucial modification: Tark's former mask, weathered and streaked with scoremarks, had been affixed to the crown. Upon the crest of this craftwork visor, where it rested on the man's forehead, a symbol had been painted. A bloody red corona, dripping down the bridge of the visor's snout—an artistic impression of a gunshot wound.

Reaching back between his shoulders, the armored man drew his sword. With all eyes on Tark's rampage, none of the frantic men seemed to notice as their retreat took them directly into the path of this newcomer.

Resting his square-tipped weapon against his shoulder, The Sparrow advanced into the courtyard.

Quietly, discretely, he carved his path through the crowd. While Tark swung with wild abandon, felling several men at a time, The Sparrow was precise and deliberate. A wide-eyed officer raised his pistol, and The Sparrow swiftly took his arm. When a furious sergeant attempted to tackle him to the ground, The Sparrow deftly tossed the sergeant over his shoulder, his silent sword leaving the man disemboweled upon the ground behind him.

A baton crackled, bashing itself against the back of The Sparrow's head in a shower of sparks. Recoiling from the blow, the silent reaper of Lachlan turned slowly, head cocked at an angle curiously. When the officer raised the baton once more, The Sparrow kicked off his back foot, a powerful headbutt plowing through the next strike—blinded by his own attack, sparks burning his corneas, the officer couldn't react to defend himself against the square-tipped blade rapidly jabbing itself into his torso over and over. The blind man fell, and The Sparrow turned once more, proceeding on towards the dark entrance to the palace.

He stepped carefully over the fallen bodies and severed limbs in the snow, not paying any mind as he brushed past Tark. The Sparrow had greater purpose here today, waiting for him inside the sheltered darkness of the palace. Up the short steps he climbed, wiping his sword clean between his folded arm. He crossed the threshold, heading inside.

Another shot rang out, and The Sparrow stumbled—he braced against the wall, looking down at himself. The bullet had torn through his side, just above his hip. The wound bled freely; The Sparrow turned, looking back out over the courtyard.

The offending officer was aiming at The Sparrow's chest now. He didn't get the chance to fire a second time—Tark was upon him, wrapping the man in a crushing bear hug. Silently, The Sparrow nodded to Tark, and Tark nodded back. Together they ignored the man's screams as Tark wrenched his arms apart. The Sparrow didn't even bother to watch as parts of the officer flew in different directions, simply continuing on into the silent palace, leaving the bloodied snows of the courtyard behind him.

Just ahead, past the foyer, the main hall gave way to a flight of ornate marble stairs, leading up to the audience chamber. The tall doors were sealed shut, and two Nightwatch officers stood guard, already raising their rifles to fire upon the intruder. The Sparrow paid no heed to the high caliber rounds splashing against him, the bulk of the fire clustered on his head and face. Tark's impenetrable mask deflected each ill-advised shot, sending hot tracers spinning away as The Sparrow lightly ascended the stairs, barely reacting to the ricochets and stray shots that tore through the burgundy mesh between his armor plates. At the top, the officers shouted for him to stand down—instead, The Sparrow took their legs and weapons away, his sword whistling between their bodies like the searing cry of a predatory shrike. Wresting the rifle away from one of the fallen Nightwatchman, The Sparrow silenced the man's spitting and cursing with a quick stab, and raised the rifle in his other hand towards the locked doors before him.

The high-powered rounds blasted a halo around the door's handles, and The Sparrow kicked his way through the broken lock, the doors swinging open slowly. The rifle clattered to the ground, his boots clicking wetly against the polished marble floor, the only sound filling the chamber apart from the mechanized whirrs that emanated from Burnside Geiha's chrysalis.

Gray sunlight from an overhead window filtered through the red glass dome, and inside, The Sparrow could see the old man peeking back at him, shrouded in white linens. Without Rigel's body to feed nutrients into the chrysalis, the detached pod had been attached to several life support machines, each independently working the quasi-immortal's body functioning. As The Sparrow drew nearer, Geiha withdrew from view inside his dome, the linens shifting as he vainly attempted to hide from the approaching reaper.

As The Sparrow closed the gap between them, he reached out and lifted an ornate chair, carrying it with him before setting it down in front of the chrysalis. Grunting quietly, still bleeding from the gunshots that had grazed him, he hefted himself up onto the chair and used it to climb atop the chrysalis, boots clicking against the thick red glass. Below him, Burnside Geiha stared up in a mixture of fear and defiance, the wrinkles in his old face nearly swallowing his beady yellow eyes entirely.

His breathing was growing a little shallower, sounding labored through his electronic mouthpiece—The Sparrow reached up, unclasping his visor, lifting the entire helmet away. The draconic mask removed now, Brann could properly meet Geiha's gaze now. His face was scarred, a new crease having formed for each year past since he'd last stepped foot into this palace—but he knew it made no difference. Burnside wouldn't have recognized him anyway, the two having never been face to face before now. They were perfect strangers to one another.

And yet.

"This introduction has been long overdue," Brann said, tapping his sword against his shoulder, visor cradled under his other arm. "Burnside Geiha, I take it? 'Emperor' Geiha himself? You can call me Brann, though I suspect our conversation won't last long enough for you to make much use of my name."

The withered old man pushed aside the linens obscuring his face, sneering back up at his uninvited guest. "No, I suspect not," he rasped. He sounded decayed already, like speaking would break something vital inside his chest that kept him breathing. "Though I'm likely the one to be talking to a ghost soon, if those are any indication," Geiha said, nodding at Brann's gunshot wounds.

Brann shifted a little, wiping a trickle of blood from his breastplate nonchalantly. "I wouldn't worry too much about that," he replied. "I'd be more worried about yourself—namely, how much of you will still be attached by the time we're done speaking."

49. The Adjudication

The squared edge of Brann's sword chipped into the dome of Geiha's chrysalis, flakes of glass turning to powder beneath the sharp bite of the blade. Brann tapped the sword there slowly, thoughtfully, as he listened quietly to Burnside's speech.

"This is all your fault, you know," the old relic rasped, hacking coughs into his fist as its accusing finger wagged up at Brann. "You left the city in the state it's in now—because of you lot, Rigel was set free. Because of you, my citizens are starving, left in the cold."

"You would have set him free eventually anyway," Brann replied stiffly, emphasizing his point with another tap of his sword. "And we wouldn't have been there to stop him. You'd have used him as a weapon against the whole world. Against your own people, even, if they didn't fall in line."

"And who kept them in line to begin with?" Geiha's voice seemed to crack as his pitch raised, like his vocal cords had gone unused for a century, unable to fully produce the tone of voice he meant to take. "Who kept them fed and homed? Gave them the luxury of comfortable living? They wanted for nothing—they worked happily, they were rewarded, giving up nothing but their time and energy and receiving everything in return."

"Time and energy are all we have in life. Your rewards were playthings for children. They were never free to live their own lives the way they wanted—they were trapped here, behind these walls, with the promises of soft cushions and big screens to occupy their attentions, as they worked their lives away to grow your already endless fortunes."

"Give a man the choice," Geiha retorted, "Between absolute freedom and easy comforts, and he'll take the latter every time. People don't want freedom, they don't want to decide the course of their futures—they don't even want to be rich. They wouldn't know what to do with wealth if they had it. No, they want to live without fear, without hunger, knowing exactly how they'll spend their days, knowing there won't be any change.

No great disruptions to the easy lives provided to them. You take that away from them, you think they'll care that you 'returned their freedom' to them?" He smiled wickedly, shaking his head. "No, child. No. No, no, no. You become a pariah. You become the anchor weighing them down, the enemy they must unite against. Reason, truth, individuality—these things fly away from them the moment they stand to lose comfort. That's what I gave to them, what I promised, what I delivered: comfort. What can you give them?"

"You're asking the wrong question," Brann answered, raising his arms slightly—the tip of his sword hovered above the glass dome. "What can you give *me*?"

Burnside scoffed. "What do you want? Money? Your homeland, returned? What?"

Brann stabbed down, hard. The sword pierced the dome in a puff of powdered glass, the blade burying itself into Geiha's chest. The old corpse gurgled in shock, his face contorting horrendously—it was the first real thing he'd felt in decades. Pain.

"Boomer." *Thunk.* "Nestor." *Thunk.* "Zaydat." *Thunk.* With each name, Brann withdrew his sword, stabbing downward again. Eight names. Eight strokes of his sword piercing into Geiha's ribs, chips of glass scattering everywhere. "Lorna. Wolf. Grishka." *Thunk. Thunk. Thunk.*

"Emrys. Hawkshaw."

Thunk. Thunk.

"*That* is what I want. My family. I want them back."

"You won't kill me," Burnside panted, gritting his yellowed teeth. "I am the dead among the living, the living among the dead—you cannot truly harm me. I have endured lifetimes of agony, and I will endure you."

"That depends on your definition of 'harm'."

Thunk.

Burnside gave a pitiful wet whimper as the punishment began anew, his bloodless flesh parting like gelatin beneath the sword, the rubbery flesh attempting to heal itself between each stab. "What do you *want*?" He pleaded, utterly helpless and confused.

"Boomer." *Thunk.* "Nes." *Thunk.* "Zay." *Thunk.* "Red." *Thunk.* "Wolf." *Thunk.* "Grishka." *Thunk.* "Emrys." *Thunk.* "Hawkshaw—am I being unclear? Have I gotten through to you yet?"

The old man spat up at his glass canopy. "Stupid. Selfish. Unable to see past your own self-pity. You have me at your mercy, you could have anything you wanted, and you waste your breath on this childish tantrum."

"Oh, make no mistake," Brann nodded, "I'll have your money, too. Every last scale you possess will be taken from you, and returned to the people you claim to serve—their years of service and subjugation to your whims won't go unrewarded. You'll die here, alone, in the dark, as all the world learns of your greed and heresy. And those unholy little science projects of yours? They'll follow you to the grave, you have my word on that."

Burnside glared up at Brann, then cackled without smiling, his eyes narrowed to slits. "Now who's not getting through? I've told you, boy. I can't die. You believe I created this? The Exdeath? It has existed long before me—I simply perfected it. I stripped it of its malignancies, and from its ageless curse, I found the secret to everlasting life. I have—no, I *am* the answer to death. The greatest fear of all who live, brought to heel beneath my will. Would that you boasted such grand designs—instead, you stand here, crying and mewling over a few hapless idiots who got what they deserved."

Brann ignored this jab, redirecting instead. "You had a meeting once, in Jan-Jito, with Queen Hester's predecessor. Do you remember?"

Burnside sneered. "I've dined with hundreds of kings and queens, all hoping to taste of my wealth. You seriously expect me to remember one afternoon among so many?"

"Actually, yes." Brann tapped the sword against the glass. "This one was special. This was the first time since the wars that you did not get the answer you wanted—you offered to bring Jan-Jito under your wing, and they declined. I bet that must have bruised your ego a fair bit."

Burnside soured at this, grumbling as he shifted about in his linens. "A minor setback. They'll come around, eventually—diplomacy is a long game, and I have eternity to play it."

"Ahh, but you're not so patient as you say," Brann corrected. "You were very offended by this meeting. To the point you let loose one of your experiments beneath the Queen's castle—hoping one day she'd wander below and find herself face to face with the consequences of her scorn. No one turns down the wealthiest man alive, right? You couldn't suffer that indignity."

"Speculation and drivel," Geiha dismissed, snorting. "Get to the point."

"As I said," Brann repeated, "You aren't so patient. The fabled Geihan Empire you dreamed of, spent your whole life piecing together, parcel by parcel—all that land you bought up, and yet when the time came to execute your vision, you hit a snag. After the wars, you found money wasn't enough to buy the loyalty of the Houses that weren't interested in whoring themselves out to you. You couldn't buy Jan-Jito, just like you couldn't buy Lachlan—so you tried to have them removed instead." He paused, raising his sword into view—the stained silk kerchief still wrapped around its hilt from long ago, ever since Jan-Jito's queen had gifted it to him. "One more successfully so than the other. But you didn't count on Queen Hester, or her daughter running away from home. And you certainly didn't count on me."

"I don't need to be patient," Burnside spat, "Not when I wield the Exdeath. If you won't give yourself to reason and riches, then you will be made to yield before its influence. If you doubt me, then look to your homeland, boy, and just remember the fate their defiance earned them."

Brann raised his sword to strike once more, then hesitated. He mulled over Geiha's words for a moment. "Tell me more. You say you didn't create it—then what is it?"

"Like all evil in this world," Geiha explained impatiently, "It begins with a root. Perhaps you've seen it. A wicked heart, living outside the body of its progenitor, black and molded—it doesn't require nourishment, nor air, nor purpose. It simply is. And, eventually, whether by chance or by intent, it will find a living body, and attach itself. When that happens, a monster is born—tireless, uncaring, unfeeling, save for perhaps what one could only describe as a sexual urge to cause unlife. To kill, at the cusp of fear, and to satisfy its lusts on the fears of its victims. Then, in an unholy union, to join with them, expanding its reach and its desires. A seed of anti-life, forever germinating, spreading its essence. It is the slow death of our world—and believe me, boy, it is patient. It may take centuries, millennia even—but it will win out in the end. The only cure for it is to harness it before it gets the chance."

"A black heart," Brann puzzled. "A root. Like a tumor; one that can be cut out. I've done it before. What's to stop me from cutting it out of you?"

"Cut away," Geiha dismissed. "Peel and slice and chop to your heart's content. I was not so crass as to simply join with it physically—I melded with it, showed it the respect it deserved with an offering of a titan. Rigel's body shielded me from the evil it bore, and through the proxy of his flesh delivered unto me nothing but the bliss of eternity. It is not in me—it *is* me."

Brann silenced Geiha with another quick stab, tilting his head at the sound of the man's cry. "Yes, I can really sense the bliss just pouring out of you," he said dryly.

"Stop, stop this at once, please," Geiha gasped, growling, foam at his lips. "You have nothing left to gain from me, I've answered your questions—your quarrel is with Tark, not me!"

"On the contrary. I've settled up with the good Marshal—well, former Marshal, that is." Brann twisted the sword, listening to the glass and flesh crunch around it, ignoring Geiha's groans. "Once upon a time, I did see him as the enemy. The source of my suffering. For a while, I even blamed myself—questioned my decisions, my path in life. Wondered if I loved enough, gave enough. If having my friends taken from me was because I didn't fight hard enough, or for the right reasons. Now, standing here, I see it plain: it was always you. The man in the coffin, buying his next breath of air with the lives of others. Hoarding eternity for himself, leeching off the good and decent people of the world."

The glass had been shaved away, creating a hole big enough for a fist to fit through. As he continued to pay the dead old man's disgusting sounds no heed, Brann had been cutting into him purposefully, searching—and he saw it now, through the glass: the whipping tendrils of some foreign organism, squirming about between Geiha's exposed ribs, clinging to the membranes of his desiccated soft tissues.

"There you are, little guy," Brann crooned. "Afraid this is where our conversation comes to a close. I'll be taking that everlasting life from you now—see how long you can live in bliss without that black little tumor in you."

"Wait," Geiha pleaded once more, beginning to sound genuinely fearful now. "Wait. Just, think about what you're doing—I've told you, the root will persist. Cut it from me, turn it into mincemeat, it won't matter— one day, eventually, it will find another host. A single cell can survive infinity. Take it from me, you'll be dooming another to become an unliving monster someday. Can you live with that guilt? The knowledge that you'll have unleashed yet more monsters on the world?"

Brann hesitated. In that moment, his mind wandered back, into the years past, when he once breathed the ocean waters of his own death—the message given to him by a Godhead. The purpose he was meant for: to spread love, to nurture the hearts of others.

"You know what?" Brann said, the corners of his mouth twitching. "For once, you and I are in complete agreement. I couldn't bear to live with that sin."

Geiha relaxed somewhat, relieved, even with the sword still spreading his ribcage. To his horror, however, Brann reached through the glass nonetheless, his arm slipping into that hole and into Geiha's body.

"So, I'll be your sin eater, and keep it to myself," Brann continued, gripping that slippery tentacle tightly—Geiha's loudest screams yet came now as Brann pulled mightily, tearing the living root of Exdeath from his body. Brann held the black heart aloft in his hand, watching it writhe in his grip, unclasping his breastplate with the other hand. "If this thing can survive eternity, as you say, then I'll consider it a debt paid to those I've lost by keeping it—and you—from hurting anyone else ever again. I'm glad we could come to a civil arrangement, old man."

"B-but..." Burnside wheezed, his entire body trembling. "No...human...host...can survive..."

"Luckily for the both of us," Brann retorted, "I'm only partially human now."

But Geiha couldn't hear him anymore. The old corpse was breathings its last, the saggy flesh collapsing in on itself as unseeing eyes stared up remorsefully at Brann, the weight of all the world crushing the last of Geiha into himself. Brann tucked the black root under his breastplate, feeling about, until the tendrils found bare flesh. It was painful, yes—feeling the parasitic heart rip him open and burrow inside—but Brann didn't care. He closed his eyes, gritting his teeth, picturing the faces of his friends in his mind as he let eternity enter him.

"Sorry guys," he said quietly. "It's gonna be a little longer before I can see you all again."

*

The city square slowly began to fill with the scant remains of Geiha's citizens, the bedraggled people gathering around the defunct fountain at its center, trickling in from the nearby alleys. The call had gone out: the Nightwatch was gone. The Emperor was gone. They were to meet their new leader now, their latest liberator. Surely, he would have the answers, and would carry them away from this dead season. Surely, he would restore the sun to the gray skies.

On the low wall surrounding the fountain pool, Brann stood tall, visor cradled beneath his arm. His sword, still streaked with the blood of the Nightwatch—as well as the dark ichor of Geiha's body—dangled limply from his hand. He appraised the citizens that surrounded him, just as they appraised him—when he felt he had sufficient audience, looking out at a crowd of several hundred, he spoke.

"House Geiha is dead," he bellowed, sounding neither proud nor fearsome. "I have killed it. Along with its false Emperor."

He gave a moment for this to sink in. No one seemed to react much, save for a few quiet murmurs. Brann took a deep breath, choosing his next words carefully. He raised his visor aloft, holding it as if it were a severed head.

"You've all been here before. Promised a brighter future, and a better tomorrow—if only we all pull together, and put in the work." He let the visor fall dramatically, the headpiece clattering to the ground. "I can't make those kinds of promises. I won't even try. All I can tell you instead is this—the city is yours. The land is yours. I don't want it, and I won't keep it."

He pointed behind him, back towards the palace. "Geiha's vaults are open to you. Its riches are yours—do with them what you want. Be your own leaders. Form your own Houses. Buy your own nobility—no one will stop you. I've made sure of that."

Brann let his arm fall, raising his sword to silence the rising cross-chatter of the crowd. "But before you do, I have a task for each citizen of this city who stands before me today. Your freedom and your futures come at a small price."

He let the sword fall. "You must hear my story, and judge me accordingly. If I am to be your prisoner, if I am to be executed, or if I am to go from this place, as free as the rest of you—that is your decision to make."

Brann waited for the crowd to fall silent once more. He sensed an unease about them, and rightly so, as he was about to confess what could prove to be an unforgivable sin.

"My name is Brann. I was not born here, in the city," He continued, "I am not a native citizen of House Geiha. My heritage comes from House Lachlan. The same House that was undermined and dissolved. A genocide wrought by the designs of House Geiha, who sought to bring the other Houses together under the banner of a new Empire." He waved his sword demonstratively, raising an eyebrow. "Probably you wondered why you had someone calling yourselves 'Emperor' to begin with, well. There's your answer. It was all shadowy plots and subterfuge—they didn't want you to know their plans, or the damage they caused to the rest of the world as a result.

"Anyway. I grew up here, in this city, among you, but not one of you. I was an orphan on the streets. I lived off your trash, and in your gutters. I stole from you." He swallowed the lump in his throat. "I sold myself to you. I gave away my dignity, for a few nights rest in a warm bed. I saw no value in myself, and no future. Until I was conscripted into the Geihan infantry."

He paused, scanning the faces of the crowd. Brann sighed once more. He'd promised himself: warts and all. "But I didn't serve honorably. I never deployed to protect our borders; I never did anything to keep a single one of you safe. Instead, I ran. I was scared, and I was selfish, and I deserted before I even stepped foot outside the palace walls. When I did, I shot someone, another member of the infantry, out on his morning patrol. He's probably long dead by now." Another pause. "I fell in with...some people. You all heard of the terrorists who abducted your Champion some years back, well." Brann spread his arms, shrugging. "Here I am. All that's left of them.

"We travelled the continent, looking for something that could prove Geiha's crimes. Trying to find a way to clear our names, restore our honor. Instead, we caused all of this." He waved his sword skyward. "We made a mistake. *I* made a mistake. A terrible one. And as a result, we awakened Rigel and caused the destruction of this city. For all the lies the

Nightwatch told you, that much is true—we were wrong. We were so wrong."

He waited a moment, letting the citizens grumble amongst themselves—the tension was building among their ranks, and Brann could see the whites of some of their eyes, an anger beginning to surface. It was time to conclude his speech, he knew.

"I won't tell you I did all this for the right reasons," he said, voice straining. "I won't tell you that you have to see things from my point of view. All I can say in my defense is I've paid a steep price for my sins." He inhaled; a deep, shuddering breath. "I've paid a lot. Maybe not enough, maybe too much—that's why I've brought you all here today. For you to decide. I'm not your savior, I'm not your Emperor, and I'm certainly not your terrorist. I was a scared kid who ran away from his duties for entirely selfish reasons."

He raised his arms out towards the crowd. "And I've brought you all down into the pit with me. What happens to me next, I leave entirely up to you—my life is in your hands. Do with it what you will. I won't fight— and I won't run. Not anymore."

The crowd was mostly silent as they processed all of this. He waited. And waited. No one wanted to be the first to speak, it seemed.

Save for one. The crowd began to part, and a single figure stepped forth. He was unsteady, bearing his weight on an old cane, though he seemed fairly young—barely older than Brann. He stood before Brann, turning to the crowd to speak his piece.

"I can back up his story," the stranger said, coughing as he spoke. "Excuse me. At least, in part—he mentioned shooting a passerby on his patrol when he fled the palace. Well, that infantryman didn't die. He got pretty fucked up, sure—but he's alive today, standing here to tell you his side of things."

A few members of the crowd gasped. Brann stared down at the stranger, frozen in shock. The infantryman looked back up at Brann, his eyes frowning, even as his mouth smiled. He nodded and addressed the crowd once more.

"My name is Pinely," he said, suppressing his coughs as best he could. "Formerly a ship's technician—like Brann here, I never amounted to much in the service." He chuckled. "I always cursed my luck that day—I had switched duty days with a buddy of mine so he could take leave. He wanted to go back home to Mongillo, and I owed him a favor. I took a bullet for him, the bastard, and I've never let him live it down."

Pinely's smile faded, and he cleared his throat. "Brann deserted his post, and he shot me as he ran. All that is true. What he didn't tell you, and what I suspect he wanted to keep to himself, is how he also saved my life."

He looked back at Brann, tears shining in his eyes. "I hated you man. I really did. I had to take my walking papers—medical ejection from the service. I'll never breathe or walk right again, thanks to you."

Pinely shook his head, incredulous. "But you stopped. You could have left me there to bleed out and die. Most guys would have. Hell, anyone else going AWOL would have, definitely. But you stopped for me, and you saved me from bleeding out."

Addressing the crowd a final time, Pinely raised his voice: "I'm still here today for the same reason he is: he wants to make things right. I say we let him. Fuck it."

Pinely limped back into the crowd. "That's all. Defense rests."

The square was silent for a time, and in the peoples' eyes Brann could see every emotion fighting each other for control. His judge and jury were the same, and they operated on instinct and raw nerves, lacking objectivity. This court would deliver a verdict borne purely of emotion and gut feelings.

Brann stepped off the fountain wall, standing level with the crowd now. "Do with me as you will," he said. "I've said all I came here to say."

The bodies began to shift. Feet scraped cement. One by one, they began to disperse—perhaps it was greed, or indifference, or a general sense of self-preservation. Perhaps he'd reached them on a personal level, and they had found forgiveness afforded to him. Whatever the case, the crowd began surging forward past him, around the fountain, towards the palace.

One older woman stopped before Brann. Her eyes were dark, shrouded in a fog of grief. Wordlessly, she damned him with a slap across the face. Brann winced, but matched her stare, his own grief plain to see.

This was sufficient for her. The old mother moved on with the crowd.

Another slap. Then, after a moment's reprieve, another. Several citizens lined up to deliver their own personal stamp to the court's verdict, and it didn't take long before Brann's face was left tender and bruised. They had all lost something because of him, and though they were amenable to the rest of the population's decision, that didn't mean they had to like it.

Eventually, the city square was empty once more. Only Brann remained. The judgment rendered, he tasted the blood in his mouth bitterly before spitting it, wiping his nose and sniffing. He looked about for his helmet, kneeling to scoop it off the ashen ground and dusting it clean.

A caw sounded overhead. Brann looked up and about for the source, spotting a solitary raven overlooking the square. Perched on the roof of a nearby bar, it ruffled its feathers, tilting its head towards him expectantly.

"Yeah, I know," Brann replied sullenly. "I'm taller now. Still growing, looks like."

Tucking the visor under his arm, Brann crossed the square, entering the bar.

50. The Sparrow

Naturally, there was no bartender on duty—this business had long stopped running, probably since the day Rigel had first emerged. Brann had helped himself, finding a coffee brewing machine beneath stacks of dusty rags—with a cursory rinse, it was ready to use, and he sat now with a freshly brewed glass of the hot, orange-brown liquid. He didn't drink, however. Sitting at the center of the bar, he looked to his left. Then to his right. On either side of him, lines of empty stools. A conversation failed to spark, the empty gray space remaining quiet, only the dust joining him for a seat.

The door swung open behind him. Brann didn't even bother looking up—he knew the sound of those heavy footfalls, those castanet claws. The kuaneach crossed the wooden floor, the planks creaking beneath his weight. The stool next to Brann scraped the floor as it was drawn back, and Tark sat himself down next to the much smaller man, sighing softly— he'd had a hard day of labor, and was ready for a drink. Tark reached over the bar, plucking a bottle of ale from the open icebox. He uncorked it with his teeth, nodding to the invisible bartender as he tossed it back. His maw wrapped around the neck of the bottle, and Brann turned his head slowly, watching with something between fascination and disgust as the contents of the bottle were drained in seconds.

Unwrapping his tongue from around the glass neck, Tark exhaled with satisfaction, sliding the empty bottle away as he reached for another. He uncorked this one a tad more delicately now, the cork between his clawtips as he nodded towards Brann's glass.

"Not gonna drink?" He asked.

Brann tipped the glass back towards himself, staring into the dark liquid. "Not my favorite drink," he answered quietly.

Tark blinked. "Then why go to the trouble of making it?"

Brann shrugged.

Hesitating, Tark looked at his own bottle before setting it down in front of Brann and reaching for another. "Drink with me," he said. It wasn't an order, as per his usual cadence of speaking. It was a request.

Brann took the bottle between his lips, taking a swig along with Tark.

He swallowed, lips pursed in a frown. "Tastes like old oatmeal."

Tark snorted, nodding in reluctant agreement. The two of them took another swig together, miming each other's movements.

Minutes ticked past. Brann had set his visor on the bar next to himself—Tark reached over, tilting it under his palm to survey what Brann had done with his old mask. Brann smiled to himself a little, remembering back to their first meeting, and couldn't help but chuckle.

"What?"

Brann took another sip. "'For all intents and purposes, I am your new father,'" he said, quoting Tark's old speech from the Assay.

Tark snorted, his own face cracking into a sheepish smile. "Hey, listen, that line worked on every other recruit I ever tried it on."

Brann's eyebrows waggled. "Maybe in the moment, but you know they were all joking about it with each other immediately after the Assay ended, right?"

Tark nodded, giving a half shrug. "You're probably right about that, yes."

Brann set the bottle down, rotating it on the smooth surface of the bar between his fingertips. "You ever break something," he began, his question sounding more rhetorical to his ears than he intended, "And when you try to put it back together, you just keep breaking more and more pieces of it off—until eventually there's nothing to put back together, because it's all just... pieces?"

Tark mulled over this question, swiping a claw over the blue streak across his snout as he did. "Yes, I have."

Brann didn't look up from his bottle. "How do you put a person back together?"

Tark's answer was simple: "One piece at a time."

They sat in silence together for a few moments, taking turns at their respective bottles.

Tark watched Brann drink. He seemed to be reaching back, into his past, searching for something more he could offer. Some deeper wisdom that might help heal Brann's heart.

But the silence was deafening, and his bottle was nearly empty.

The gray and cold filled the space between them, threatening to suffocate them both.

Tark set his bottle down, unfinished. He stood up, pushing off the bar, making the wood creak in protest. He stared at the bottle, wondering if he should drain it, or take it with him.

He did neither. Instead, he turned to leave, speaking back over his shoulder as he went—his last goodbye to Brann.

"We never break," he said. "Not really. The entire world will put its most cruel and heartless of agents upon us, doing everything they can to put us to the grind; mold us to their hateful designs. But eventually, when we've reached the limits of what we are made to endure, we are compelled to give some back. Pit a single soul against the world, demanding everything from them—and you may find it surprising who breaks first."

With that, Tark was gone, exiting the bar and leaving Brann in solitary silence once more.

Brann set aside the bottle of ale, pulling the glass of coffee towards himself again. He looked to his left. Then to his right.

Empty stools, absent of conversation. Only dust and gray.

He raised the glass, taking a sip.

As bitter a drink as it ever was.

Epilogue

The tale reached its end, and Oded slumped forward. The burden of this sorrowful tale weighed heavy on his already weak body. He felt the sympathetic pull in his chest of a kindred spirit, reaching out to him across the years—perhaps a century, perhaps a millennium. The Exdead root in his own chest recoiled, digging its hooks into his aching heart. This young man from another age, his story—though Oded could not fully grasp why or how, he knew he was meant to bear Brann's burden forward into the future.

"This young soldier—this 'Sparrow'—he suffers as I suffer to this day, doesn't he?" Oded lifted his head, the Godhead across the desert seas nodding solemnly.

"THOUGH YOUR PATHS WILL NEVER CROSS, YOU WALK IN HIS FOOTSTEPS EVEN NOW. HIS WINGS BEAT ON, CEASELESSLY, AGAINST MORTALITY'S DESIGNS. BARELY A FLEDGLING, HE HAS FACED IMMEASURABLE LOSS, AND WILL CONTINUE TO LOSE ALL HE HOLDS DEAR, UNTIL THE BLACK HEARTS YOU SHARE BEAT NO MORE."

Oded nodded. "It was not without reason I was meant to receive this story, then—I will refresh myself with its lessons, ruminate on its—"

"NO."

Oded faltered, confused.

"THE STORY DOES NOT END HERE, AND YOU ARE NO MERE AUDIENCE TO IT. YOUR LIFE, YOUR JOURNEY, WILL CONTINUE TO SHAPE AND MOLD IT INTO A NEW AGE. BY TASKING YOU AS I HAVE, I WILL SEND YOU FORTH AS MY BROTHER ONCE DID THE YOUNG SPARROW, AND THROUGH YOU, EXECUTE THE WILL OF THE GODHEADS. I HAVE ALREADY PROMISED YOU SALVATION AND SATISFACTION—THESE BEAR THE COST OF YOUR SERVICE. A SERVICE TO A STORY, UNTOLD, UNENDING, YOUR BODY THE

PAGES UPON WHICH MY KIND WRITE IT. EVEN NOW, YOU BEAR ITS WORDS."

Oded touched his face, the tattooed scripture tingling lightly.

"Will I be allowed to die someday?"

"YES."

That wasn't quite the question he meant to ask. Oded rephrased.

"Will I live to see the end of the world?"

The sand at his feet began to shift, swirling, sinking into a shallow pit—and at its center, a slender stone column emerged. As Oded kneeled, it seemed he was meant to reach for it, given the way it tilted towards him.

He reached down, and gripped the stone tightly, and he knew in that moment it was the handle of a weapon. Oded pulled upwards, unsheathing it from its sandy forge. Beneath his hand rose a massive pillar of shapely quartz, hewn into the diamond edges of an enormous greatsword, one that surely weighed more than his entire sickly body. Nevertheless, he held the gleaming stone blade above the sands as best he could, feeling rejuvenated by its purposeful weight. Oded felt his strength returning to him as he raised it higher, watching the burning red light of the sun refract against its white-blue facets.

When the Godhead spoke one final time, Oded received an answer he wished he hadn't asked for, but to which he knew his entire existence was now owed:

"YOU WILL LIVE TO SEE THE END OF YOUR WORLD. AND THIS MALIGNANCY YOU BEAR WILL BE ITS DESTROYER."

Oded took a breath, and looked to the horizon. The Godhead was gone. He remained alone in the desert now, amidst these carvings of the forgotten dead.

He looked once more to the empty plinth. Oded cast his thoughts back to the story he'd just heard, and to its unsung hero.

And suddenly, crossing the endless desert seemed such a short journey to make, indeed.